TALES FROM THE KLONDIKE

A Treasury of Jack London's Best Short Stories

JACK LONDON

CONTENTS

THE WHITE SILENCE

'CARMEN WON'T LAST MORE than a couple of days.' Mason spat out a chunk of ice and surveyed the poor animal ruefully, then put her foot in his mouth and proceeded to bite out the ice which clustered cruelly between the toes.

'I never saw a dog with a highfalutin' name that ever was worth a rap,' he said, as he concluded his task and shoved her aside. 'They just fade away and die under the responsibility. Did ye ever see one go wrong with a sensible name like Cassiar, Siwash, or Husky? No, sir! Take a look at Shookum here, he's—' Snap! The lean brute flashed up, the white teeth just missing Mason's throat.

'Ye will, will ye?' A shrewd clout behind the ear with the butt of the dog whip stretched the animal in the snow, quivering softly, a yellow slaver dripping from its fangs.

'As I was saying, just look at Shookum here—he's got the spirit. Bet ye he eats Carmen before the week's out.' 'I'll bank another proposition against that,' replied Malemute Kid, reversing the frozen bread placed before the fire to thaw. 'We'll eat Shookum before the trip is over. What d'ye say, Ruth?' The Indian woman settled the coffee with a piece of ice, glanced from Malemute Kid to her husband, then at the dogs, but vouchsafed no reply. It was such a palpable truism that none was necessary. Two hundred miles of unbroken trail in prospect, with a scant six days' grub for themselves and none for the dogs, could admit no other alternative. The two men and the woman grouped about the fire and began their meager meal. The dogs lay in their harnesses for it was a midday halt, and watched each mouthful enviously.

'No more lunches after today,' said Malemute Kid. 'And we've got to keep a close eye on the dogs—they're getting vicious. They'd just as soon pull a fellow down as not, if they get a chance.' 'And I was president of an Epworth once, and taught in the Sunday school.' Having irrelevantly delivered himself of this, Mason fell into a dreamy contemplation of his steaming moccasins, but was aroused by Ruth filling his cup.

'Thank God, we've got slathers of tea! I've seen it growing, down in Tennessee. What wouldn't I give for a hot corn pone just now! Never mind, Ruth; you won't starve much longer, nor wear moccasins either.' The woman threw off her gloom at this, and in her eyes

I

welled up a great love for her white lord—the first white man she had ever seen—the first man whom she had known to treat a woman as something better than a mere animal or beast of burden.

'Yes, Ruth,' continued her husband, having recourse to the macaronic jargon in which it was alone possible for them to understand each other; 'wait till we clean up and pull for the Outside. We'll take the White Man's canoe and go to the Salt Water. Yes, bad water, rough water—great mountains dance up and down all the time. And so big, so far, so far away—you travel ten sleep, twenty sleep, forty sleep'—he graphically enumerated the days on his fingers—'all the time water, bad water. Then you come to great village, plenty people, just the same mosquitoes next summer. Wigwams oh, so high—ten, twenty pines.

'Hi-yu skookum!' He paused impotently, cast an appealing glance at Malemute Kid, then laboriously placed the twenty pines, end on end, by sign language. Malemute Kid smiled with cheery cynicism; but Ruth's eyes were wide with wonder, and with pleasure; for she half believed he was joking, and such condescension pleased her poor woman's heart.

'And then you step into a—a box, and pouf! up you go.' He tossed his empty cup in the air by way of illustration and, as he deftly caught it, cried: 'And biff! down you come. Oh, great medicine men! You go Fort Yukon. I go Arctic City—twenty-five sleep—big string, all the time—I catch him string—I say, "Hello, Ruth! How are ye?"—and you say, "Is that my good husband?"—and I say, "Yes"—and you say, "No can bake good bread, no more soda"—then I say, "Look in cache, under flour; good-by." You look and catch plenty soda. All the time you Fort Yukon, me Arctic City. Hi-yu medicine man!' Ruth smiled so ingenuously at the fairy story that both men burst into laughter. A row among the dogs cut short the wonders of the Outside, and by the time the snarling combatants were separated, she had lashed the sleds and all was ready for the trail.—'Mush! Baldy! Hi! Mush on!' Mason worked his whip smartly and, as the dogs whined low in the traces, broke out the sled with the gee pole. Ruth followed with the second team, leaving Malemute Kid, who had helped her start, to bring up the rear. Strong man, brute that he was, capable of felling an ox at a blow, he could not bear to beat the poor animals, but humored them as a dog driver rarely does—nay, almost wept with them in their misery.

'Come, mush on there, you poor sore-footed brutes!' he murmured, after several ineffectual attempts to start the load. But his patience was at last rewarded, and though whimpering with pain, they hastened to join their fellows.

No more conversation; the toil of the trail will not permit such extravagance.

And of all deadening labors, that of the Northland trail is the worst. Happy is the man who can weather a day's travel at the price of silence, and that on a beaten track. And of all heartbreaking labors, that of breaking trail is the worst. At every step the great webbed shoe sinks till the snow is level with the knee. Then up, straight up, the deviation of a fraction of an inch being a certain precursor of disaster, the snowshoe must be lifted till the surface is cleared; then forward, down, and the other foot is raised perpendicularly for the matter of half a yard. He who tries this for the first time, if haply he avoids bringing his shoes in dangerous propinquity and measures not his length on the treacherous footing, will give up exhausted at the end of a hundred yards; he who can keep out of the way of the dogs for a whole day may well crawl into his sleeping bag with a clear conscience and a pride which passeth all understanding; and he who travels twenty sleeps on the Long Trail is a man whom the gods may envy.

The afternoon wore on, and with the awe, born of the White Silence, the voiceless travelers bent to their work. Nature has many tricks wherewith she convinces man of his finity—the ceaseless flow of the tides, the fury of the storm, the shock of the earthquake, the long roll of heaven's artillery—but the most tremendous, the most stupefying of all, is the passive phase of the White Silence. All movement ceases, the sky clears, the heavens are as brass; the slightest whisper seems sacrilege, and man becomes timid, affrighted at the sound of his own voice. Sole speck of life journeying across the ghostly wastes of a dead world, he trembles at his audacity, realizes that his is a maggot's life, nothing more.

Strange thoughts arise unsummoned, and the mystery of all things strives for utterance.

And the fear of death, of God, of the universe, comes over him—the hope of the Resurrection and the Life, the yearning for immortality, the vain striving of the imprisoned essence—it is then, if ever, man walks alone with God.

So wore the day away. The river took a great bend, and Mason headed his team for the cutoff across the narrow neck of land. But the dogs balked at the high bank. Again and again, though Ruth and Malemute Kid were shoving on the sled, they slipped back. Then came the concerted effort. The miserable creatures, weak from hunger, exerted their last strength. Up—up—the sled poised on the top of the bank; but the leader swung the string of dogs behind him to the right, fouling Mason's snowshoes. The result was grievous.

Mason was whipped off his feet; one of the dogs fell in the traces; and the sled toppled back, dragging everything to the bottom again.

Slash! the whip fell among the dogs savagely, especially upon the one which had fallen.

'Don't,—Mason,' entreated Malemute Kid; 'the poor devil's on its last legs. Wait and we'll put my team on.' Mason deliberately withheld the whip till the last word had fallen, then out flashed the long lash, completely curling about the offending creature's body.

Carmen—for it was Carmen—cowered in the snow, cried piteously, then rolled over on her side.

It was a tragic moment, a pitiful incident of the trail—a dying dog, two comrades in anger.

Ruth glanced solicitously from man to man. But Malemute Kid restrained himself, though there was a world of reproach in his eyes, and, bending over the dog, cut the traces. No word was spoken. The teams were doublespanned and the difficulty overcome; the sleds were under way again, the dying dog dragging herself along in the rear. As long as an animal can travel, it is not shot, and this last chance is accorded it—the crawling into camp, if it can, in the hope of a moose being killed.

Already penitent for his angry action, but too stubborn to make amends, Mason toiled on at the head of the cavalcade, little dreaming that danger hovered in the air. The timber clustered thick in the sheltered bottom, and through this they threaded their way. Fifty feet or more from the trail towered a lofty pine. For generations it had stood there, and for generations destiny had had this one end in view—perhaps the same had been decreed of Mason.

He stooped to fasten the loosened thong of his moccasin. The sleds came to a halt, and the dogs lay down in the snow without a whimper. The stillness was weird; not a breath rustled the frost-encrusted forest; the cold and silence of outer space had chilled the heart and smote the trembling lips of nature. A sigh pulsed through the air—they did not seem to actually hear it, but rather felt it, like the premonition of movement in a motionless void. Then the great tree, burdened with its weight of years and snow, played its last part in the tragedy of life. He heard the warning crash and attempted to spring up but, almost erect, caught the blow squarely on the shoulder.

The sudden danger, the quick death—how often had Malemute Kid faced it! The pine needles were still quivering as he gave his commands and sprang into action. Nor did the Indian girl faint or raise her voice in idle wailing, as might many of her white sisters. At his order, she threw her weight on the end of a quickly extemporized handspike, easing the pres-

3

sure and listening to her husband's groans, while Malemute Kid attacked the tree with his ax. The steel rang merrily as it bit into the frozen trunk, each stroke being accompanied by a forced, audible respiration, the 'Huh!' 'Huh!' of the woodsman.

At last the Kid laid the pitiable thing that was once a man in the snow. But worse than his comrade's pain was the dumb anguish in the woman's face, the blended look of hopeful, hopeless query. Little was said; those of the Northland are early taught the futility of words and the inestimable value of deeds. With the temperature at sixty-five below zero, a man cannot lie many minutes in the snow and live. So the sled lashings were cut, and the sufferer, rolled in furs, laid on a couch of boughs. Before him roared a fire, built of the very wood which wrought the mishap. Behind and partially over him was stretched the primitive fly—a piece of canvas, which caught the radiating heat and threw it back and down upon him—a trick which men may know who study physics at the fount.

And men who have shared their bed with death know when the call is sounded. Mason was terribly crushed. The most cursory examination revealed it.

His right arm, leg, and back were broken; his limbs were paralyzed from the hips; and the likelihood of internal injuries was large. An occasional moan was his only sign of life.

No hope; nothing to be done. The pitiless night crept slowly by—Ruth's portion, the despairing stoicism of her race, and Malemute Kid adding new lines to his face of bronze.

In fact, Mason suffered least of all, for he spent his time in eastern Tennessee, in the Great Smoky Mountains, living over the scenes of his childhood. And most pathetic was the melody of his long-forgotten Southern vernacular, as he raved of swimming holes and coon hunts and watermelon raids. It was as Greek to Ruth, but the Kid understood and felt—felt as only one can feel who has been shut out for years from all that civilization means.

Morning brought consciousness to the stricken man, and Malemute Kid bent closer to catch his whispers.

'You remember when we foregathered on the Tanana, four years come next ice run? I didn't care so much for her then. It was more like she was pretty, and there was a smack of excitement about it, I think. But d'ye know, I've come to think a heap of her. She's been a good wife to me, always at my shoulder in the pinch. And when it comes to trading, you know there isn't her equal. D'ye recollect the time she shot the Moosehorn Rapids to pull you and me off that rock, the bullets whipping the water like hailstones?—and the time of the famine at Nuklukyeto?—when she raced the ice run to bring the news?

'Yes, she's been a good wife to me, better'n that other one. Didn't know I'd been there?

'Never told you, eh? Well, I tried it once, down in the States. That's why I'm here. Been raised together, too. I came away to give her a chance for divorce. She got it.

'But that's got nothing to do with Ruth. I had thought of cleaning up and pulling for the Outside next year—her and I—but it's too late. Don't send her back to her people, Kid. It's beastly hard for a woman to go back. Think of it!—nearly four years on our bacon and beans and flour and dried fruit, and then to go back to her fish and caribou. It's not good for her to have tried our ways, to come to know they're better'n her people's, and then return to them. Take care of her, Kid, why don't you—but no, you always fought shy of them—and you never told me why you came to this country. Be kind to her, and send her back to the States as soon as you can. But fix it so she can come back—liable to get homesick, you know.

'And the youngster—it's drawn us closer, Kid. I only hope it is a boy. Think of it!—flesh of my flesh, Kid. He mustn't stop in this country. And if it's a girl, why, she can't. Sell my furs; they'll fetch at least five thousand, and I've got as much more with the company. And handle my interests with yours. I think that bench claim will show up. See that he gets a good schooling; and Kid, above all, don't let him come back. This country was not made for white men.

'I'm a gone man, Kid. Three or four sleeps at the best. You've got to go on. You must go on! Remember, it's my wife, it's my boy—O God! I hope it's a boy! You can't stay by me— and I charge you, a dying man, to pull on.'

'Give me three days,' pleaded Malemute Kid. 'You may change for the better; something may turn up.'

'No.'

'Just three days.'

'You must pull on.'

'Two days.'

'It's my wife and my boy, Kid. You would not ask it.'

'One day.'

'No, no! I charge—'

'Only one day. We can shave it through on the grub, and I might knock over a moose.'

'No—all right; one day, but not a minute more. And, Kid, don't—don't leave me to face it alone. Just a shot, one pull on the trigger. You understand. Think of it! Think of it! Flesh of my flesh, and I'll never live to see him!

'Send Ruth here. I want to say good-by and tell her that she must think of the boy and not wait till I'm dead. She might refuse to go with you if I didn't. Goodby, old man; good-by.

'Kid! I say—a—sink a hole above the pup, next to the slide. I panned out forty cents on my shovel there.

'And, Kid!' He stooped lower to catch the last faint words, the dying man's surrender of his pride. 'I'm sorry—for—you know—Carmen.' Leaving the girl crying softly over her man, Malemute Kid slipped into his parka and snowshoes, tucked his rifle under his arm, and crept away into the forest. He was no tyro in the stern sorrows of the Northland, but never had he faced so stiff a problem as this. In the abstract, it was a plain, mathematical proposition—three possible lives as against one doomed one. But now he hesitated. For five years, shoulder to shoulder, on the rivers and trails, in the camps and mines, facing death by field and flood and famine, had they knitted the bonds of their comradeship. So close was the tie that he had often been conscious of a vague jealousy of Ruth, from the first time she had come between. And now it must be severed by his own hand.

Though he prayed for a moose, just one moose, all game seemed to have deserted the land, and nightfall found the exhausted man crawling into camp, lighthanded, heavyhearted. An uproar from the dogs and shrill cries from Ruth hastened him.

Bursting into the camp, he saw the girl in the midst of the snarling pack, laying about her with an ax. The dogs had broken the iron rule of their masters and were rushing the grub.

He joined the issue with his rifle reversed, and the hoary game of natural selection was played out with all the ruthlessness of its primeval environment. Rifle and ax went up and down, hit or missed with monotonous regularity; lithe bodies flashed, with wild eyes and dripping fangs; and man and beast fought for supremacy to the bitterest conclusion. Then the beaten brutes crept to the edge of the firelight, licking their wounds, voicing their misery to the stars.

The whole stock of dried salmon had been devoured, and perhaps five pounds of flour remained to tide them over two hundred miles of wilderness. Ruth returned to her husband, while Malemute Kid cut up the warm body of one of the dogs, the skull of which had been crushed by the ax. Every portion was carefully put away, save the hide and offal, which were cast to his fellows of the moment before.

Morning brought fresh trouble. The animals were turning on each other. Carmen, who still clung to her slender thread of life, was downed by the pack. The lash fell among them unheeded. They cringed and cried under the blows, but refused to scatter till the last wretched bit had disappeared—bones, hide, hair, everything.

Malemute Kid went about his work, listening to Mason, who was back in Tennessee, delivering tangled discourses and wild exhortations to his brethren of other days.

Taking advantage of neighboring pines, he worked rapidly, and Ruth watched him make a cache similar to those sometimes used by hunters to preserve their meat from the wolverines and dogs. One after the other, he bent the tops of two small pines toward each other and nearly to the ground, making them fast with thongs of moosehide. Then he beat the dogs into submission and harnessed them to two of the sleds, loading the same with everything but the furs which enveloped Mason. These he wrapped and lashed tightly about him, fastening either end of the robes to the bent pines. A single stroke of his hunting knife would release them and send the body high in the air.

Ruth had received her husband's last wishes and made no struggle. Poor girl, she had learned the lesson of obedience well. From a child, she had bowed, and seen all women bow, to the lords of creation, and it did not seem in the nature of things for woman to resist. The Kid permitted her one outburst of grief, as she kissed her husband—her own people had no such custom—then led her to the foremost sled and helped her into her snowshoes. Blindly, instinctively, she took the gee pole and whip, and 'mushed' the dogs out on the trail. Then he returned to Mason, who had fallen into a coma, and long after she was out of sight crouched by the fire, waiting, hoping, praying for his comrade to die.

It is not pleasant to be alone with painful thoughts in the White Silence. The silence of gloom is merciful, shrouding one as with protection and breathing a thousand intangible sympathies; but the bright White Silence, clear and cold, under steely skies, is pitiless.

An hour passed—two hours—but the man would not die. At high noon the sun, without raising its rim above the southern horizon, threw a suggestion of fire athwart the heavens, then quickly drew it back. Malemute Kid roused and dragged himself to his comrade's side. He cast one glance about him. The White Silence seemed to sneer, and a great fear came upon him. There was a sharp report; Mason swung into his aerial sepulcher, and Malemute Kid lashed the dogs into a wild gallop as he fled across the snow.

THE SON OF THE WOLF

MAN RARELY PLACES a proper valuation upon his womankind, at least not until deprived of them. He has no conception of the subtle atmosphere exhaled by the sex feminine, so long as he bathes in it; but let it be withdrawn, and an ever-growing void begins to manifest itself in his existence, and he becomes hungry, in a vague sort of way, for a something so indefinite that he cannot characterize it. If his comrades have no more experience than himself, they will shake their heads dubiously and dose him with strong physic. But the hunger will continue and become stronger; he will lose interest in the things of his everyday life and wax morbid; and one day, when the emptiness has become unbearable, a revelation will dawn upon him.

In the Yukon country, when this comes to pass, the man usually provisions a poling boat, if it is summer, and if winter, harnesses his dogs, and heads for the Southland. A few months later, supposing him to be possessed of a faith in the country, he returns with a wife to share with him in that faith, and incidentally in his hardships. This but serves to show the innate selfishness of man. It also brings us to the trouble of 'Scruff' Mackenzie, which occurred in the old days, before the country was stampeded and staked by a tidal-wave of the che-cha-quas, and when the Klondike's only claim to notice was its salmon fisheries.

'Scruff' Mackenzie bore the earmarks of a frontier birth and a frontier life.

His face was stamped with twenty-five years of incessant struggle with Nature in her wildest moods,—the last two, the wildest and hardest of all, having been spent in groping for the gold which lies in the shadow of the Arctic Circle. When the yearning sickness came upon him, he was not surprised, for he was a practical man and had seen other men thus stricken. But he showed no sign of his malady, save that he worked harder. All summer he fought mosquitoes and washed the sure-thing bars of the Stuart River for a double grub-stake. Then he floated a raft of houselogs down the Yukon to Forty Mile, and put together as comfortable a cabin as any the camp could boast of. In fact, it showed such cozy promise that many men elected to be his partner and to come and live with him. But he crushed their aspirations with rough speech, peculiar for its strength and brevity, and bought a double supply of grub from the trading-post.

As has been noted, 'Scruff' Mackenzie was a practical man. If he wanted a thing he usually got it, but in doing so, went no farther out of his way than was necessary. Though a son of toil and hardship, he was averse to a journey of six hundred miles on the ice, a second of two thousand miles on the ocean, and still a third thousand miles or so to his last stamping-grounds,—all in the mere quest of a wife. Life was too short. So he rounded up his dogs, lashed a curious freight to his sled, and faced across the divide whose westward slopes were drained by the head-reaches of the Tanana.

He was a sturdy traveler, and his wolf-dogs could work harder and travel farther on less grub than any other team in the Yukon. Three weeks later he strode into a hunting-camp of the Upper Tanana Sticks. They marveled at his temerity; for they had a bad name and had been known to kill white men for as trifling a thing as a sharp ax or a broken rifle.

But he went among them single-handed, his bearing being a delicious composite of humility, familiarity, sang-froid, and insolence. It required a deft hand and deep knowledge of the barbaric mind effectually to handle such diverse weapons; but he was a past-master in the art, knowing when to conciliate and when to threaten with Jove-like wrath.

He first made obeisance to the Chief Thling-Tinneh, presenting him with a couple of pounds of black tea and tobacco, and thereby winning his most cordial regard. Then he mingled with the men and maidens, and that night gave a potlach.

The snow was beaten down in the form of an oblong, perhaps a hundred feet in length and quarter as many across. Down the center a long fire was built, while either side was carpeted with spruce boughs. The lodges were forsaken, and the fivescore or so members of the tribe gave tongue to their folk-chants in honor of their guest.

'Scruff' Mackenzie's two years had taught him the not many hundred words of their vocabulary, and he had likewise conquered their deep gutturals, their Japanese idioms, constructions, and honorific and agglutinative particles. So he made oration after their manner, satisfying their instinctive poetry love with crude flights of eloquence and metaphorical contortions. After Thling-Tinneh and the Shaman had responded in kind, he made trifling presents to the menfolk, joined in their singing, and proved an expert in their fifty-two-stick gambling game.

And they smoked his tobacco and were pleased. But among the younger men there was a defiant attitude, a spirit of braggadocio, easily understood by the raw insinuations of the toothless squaws and the giggling of the maidens. They had known few white men, 'Sons of the Wolf,' but from those few they had learned strange lessons.

Nor had 'Scruff' Mackenzie, for all his seeming carelessness, failed to note these phenomena. In truth, rolled in his sleeping-furs, he thought it all over, thought seriously, and emptied many pipes in mapping out a campaign. One maiden only had caught his fancy,—none other than Zarinska, daughter to the chief. In features, form, and poise, answering more nearly to the white man's type of beauty, she was almost an anomaly among her tribal sisters. He would possess her, make her his wife, and name her—ah, he would name her Gertrude! Having thus decided, he rolled over on his side and dropped off to sleep, a true son of his all-conquering race, a Samson among the Philistines.

It was slow work and a stiff game; but 'Scruff' Mackenzie maneuvered cunningly, with an unconcern which served to puzzle the Sticks. He took great care to impress the men that he was a sure shot and a mighty hunter, and the camp rang with his plaudits when he brought down a moose at six hundred yards. Of a night he visited in Chief Thling-Tinneh's lodge of moose and cariboo skins, talking big and dispensing tobacco with a lavish hand. Nor did he fail to likewise honor the Shaman; for he realized the medicine-man's influence with his people, and was anxious to make of him an ally. But that worthy was high and

8

mighty, refused to be propitiated, and was unerringly marked down as a prospective enemy.

Though no opening presented for an interview with Zarinska, Mackenzie stole many a glance to her, giving fair warning of his intent. And well she knew, yet coquettishly surrounded herself with a ring of women whenever the men were away and he had a chance. But he was in no hurry; besides, he knew she could not help but think of him, and a few days of such thought would only better his suit.

At last, one night, when he deemed the time to be ripe, he abruptly left the chief's smoky dwelling and hastened to a neighboring lodge. As usual, she sat with squaws and maidens about her, all engaged in sewing moccasins and beadwork. They laughed at his entrance, and badinage, which linked Zarinska to him, ran high. But one after the other they were unceremoniously bundled into the outer snow, whence they hurried to spread the tale through all the camp.

His cause was well pleaded, in her tongue, for she did not know his, and at the end of two hours he rose to go.

'So Zarinska will come to the White Man's lodge? Good! I go now to have talk with thy father, for he may not be so minded. And I will give him many tokens; but he must not ask too much. If he say no? Good! Zarinska shall yet come to the White Man's lodge.'

He had already lifted the skin flap to depart, when a low exclamation brought him back to the girl's side. She brought herself to her knees on the bearskin mat, her face aglow with true Eve-light, and shyly unbuckled his heavy belt. He looked down, perplexed, suspicious, his ears alert for the slightest sound without.

But her next move disarmed his doubt, and he smiled with pleasure. She took from her sewing bag a moosehide sheath, brave with bright beadwork, fantastically designed. She drew his great hunting-knife, gazed reverently along the keen edge, half tempted to try it with her thumb, and shot it into place in its new home. Then she slipped the sheath along the belt to its customary resting-place, just above the hip. For all the world, it was like a scene of olden time,—a lady and her knight.

Mackenzie drew her up full height and swept her red lips with his moustache, the, to her, foreign caress of the Wolf. It was a meeting of the stone age and the steel; but she was none the less a woman, as her crimson cheeks and the luminous softness of her eyes attested.

There was a thrill of excitement in the air as 'Scruff' Mackenzie, a bulky bundle under his arm, threw open the flap of Thling-Tinneh's tent. Children were running about in the open, dragging dry wood to the scene of the potlach, a babble of women's voices was growing in intensity, the young men were consulting in sullen groups, while from the Shaman's lodge rose the eerie sounds of an incantation.

The chief was alone with his blear-eyed wife, but a glance sufficed to tell Mackenzie that the news was already told. So he plunged at once into the business, shifting the beaded sheath prominently to the fore as advertisement of the betrothal.

'O Thling-Tinneh, mighty chief of the Sticks And the land of the Tanana, ruler of the salmon and the bear, the moose and the cariboo! The White Man is before thee with a great purpose. Many moons has his lodge been empty, and he is lonely. And his heart has eaten itself in silence, and grown hungry for a woman to sit beside him in his lodge, to meet him from the hunt with warm fire and good food. He has heard strange things, the patter of baby moccasins and the sound of children's voices. And one night a vision came upon him, and he beheld the Raven, who is thy father, the great Raven, who is the father of all the Sticks. And the Raven spake to the lonely White Man, saying: "Bind thou thy moccasins upon thee, and gird thy snow-shoes on, and lash thy sled with food for many sleeps and fine tokens for the Chief Thling-Tinneh. For thou shalt turn thy face to where the mid-spring sun is wont to sink below the land and journey to this great chief's hunting-grounds. There thou shalt make big presents, and Thling-Tinneh, who is my son, shall become to thee as a father. In his lodge there is a maiden into whom I breathed the breath of life for thee. This maiden shalt thou take to wife." 'O Chief, thus spake the great Raven; thus do I lay many presents at thy feet; thus am I come to take thy daughter!' The old man drew his furs about him with crude consciousness of royalty, but delayed reply while a youngster crept in, delivered a quick message to appear before the council, and was gone.

'O White Man, whom we have named Moose-Killer, also known as the Wolf, and the Son of the Wolf! We know thou comest of a mighty race; we are proud to have thee our potlach-guest; but the king-salmon does not mate with the dogsalmon, nor the Raven with the Wolf.' 'Not so!' cried Mackenzie. 'The daughters of the Raven have I met in the camps of the Wolf, —the squaw of Mortimer, the squaw of Tregidgo, the squaw of Barnaby, who came two ice-runs back, and I have heard of other squaws, though my eyes beheld them not.' 'Son, your words are true; but it were evil mating, like the water with the sand, like the snow-flake with the sun. But met you one Mason and his squaw' No?

He came ten ice-runs ago,—the first of all the Wolves. And with him there was a mighty man, straight as a willow-shoot, and tall; strong as the bald-faced grizzly, with a heart like the full summer moon; his-' 'Oh!' interrupted Mackenzie, recognizing the well-known North-land figure, 'Malemute Kid!' 'The same,—a mighty man. But saw you aught of the squaw? She was full sister to Zarinska.' 'Nay, Chief; but I have heard. Mason—far, far to the north, a spruce-tree, heavy with years, crushed out his life beneath. But his love was great, and he had much gold. With this, and her boy, she journeyed countless sleeps toward the winter's noonday sun, and there she yet lives,—no biting frost, no snow, no summer's midnight sun, no winter's noonday night.'

A second messenger interrupted with imperative summons from the council.

As Mackenzie threw him into the snow, he caught a glimpse of the swaying forms before the council-fire, heard the deep basses of the men in rhythmic chant, and knew the Shaman was fanning the anger of his people. Time pressed. He turned upon the chief.

'Come! I wish thy child. And now, see! Here are tobacco, tea, many cups of sugar, warm blankets, handkerchiefs, both good and large; and here, a true rifle, with many bullets and much powder.' 'Nay,' replied the old man, struggling against the great wealth spread before him. 'Even now are my people come together. They will not have this marriage.'

'But thou art chief.' 'Yet do my young men rage because the Wolves have taken their maidens so that they may not marry.' 'Listen, O Thling-Tinneh! Ere the night has passed into the day, the Wolf shall face his dogs to the Mountains of the East and fare forth to the Country of the Yukon. And Zarinska shall break trail for his dogs.' 'And ere the night has gained its middle, my young men may fling to the dogs the flesh of the Wolf, and his bones be scattered in the snow till the springtime lay them bare.' It was threat and counter-threat. Mackenzie's bronzed face flushed darkly. He raised his voice. The old squaw, who till now had sat an impassive spectator, made to creep by him for the door.

The song of the men broke suddenly and there was a hubbub of many voices as he whirled the old woman roughly to her couch of skins.

'Again I cry—listen, O Thling-Tinneh! The Wolf dies with teeth fast-locked, and with him there shall sleep ten of thy strongest men,—men who are needed, for the hunting is not begun, and the fishing is not many moons away. And again, of what profit should I die? I know the custom of thy people; thy share of my wealth shall be very small. Grant me thy child, and it shall all be thine. And yet again, my brothers will come, and they are many, and their maws are never filled; and the daughters of the Raven shall bear children in the lodges of the Wolf. My people are greater than thy people. It is destiny. Grant, and all this wealth is thine.' Moccasins were crunching the snow without. Mackenzie threw his rifle to cock, and loosened the twin Colts in his belt.

'Grant, O Chief!' 'And yet will my people say no.' 'Grant, and the wealth is thine. Then shall I deal with thy people after.' 'The Wolf will have it so. I will take his tokens,—but I would warn him.' Mackenzie passed over the goods, taking care to clog the rifle's ejector, and capping the bargain with a kaleidoscopic silk kerchief. The Shaman and half a dozen young braves entered, but he shouldered boldly among them and passed out.

'Pack!' was his laconic greeting to Zarinska as he passed her lodge and hurried to harness his dogs. A few minutes later he swept into the council at the head of the team, the woman by his side. He took his place at the upper end of the oblong, by the side of the chief. To his left, a step to the rear, he stationed Zarinska, her proper place. Besides, the time was ripe for mischief, and there was need to guard his back.

On either side, the men crouched to the fire, their voices lifted in a folk-chant out of the forgotten past. Full of strange, halting cadences and haunting recurrences, it was not beautiful. 'Fearful' may inadequately express it. At the lower end, under the eye of the Shaman, danced half a score of women. Stern were his reproofs of those who did not wholly abandon themselves to the ecstasy of the rite. Half hidden in their heavy masses of raven hair, all disheveled and falling to their waists, they slowly swayed to and fro, their forms rippling to an ever-changing rhythm.

It was a weird scene; an anachronism. To the south, the nineteenth century was reeling off the few years of its last decade; here flourished man primeval, a shade removed from the prehistoric cave-dweller, forgotten fragment of the Elder World. The tawny wolf-dogs sat between their skin-clad masters or fought for room, the firelight cast backward from their red eyes and dripping fangs. The woods, in ghostly shroud, slept on unheeding.

The White Silence, for the moment driven to the rimming forest, seemed ever crushing inward; the stars danced with great leaps, as is their wont in the time of the Great Cold; while the Spirits of the Pole trailed their robes of glory athwart the heavens.

'Scruff' Mackenzie dimly realized the wild grandeur of the setting as his eyes ranged down the fur-fringed sides in quest of missing faces. They rested for a moment on a newborn babe, suckling at its mother's naked breast. It was forty below,—seven and odd degrees of frost. He thought of the tender women of his own race and smiled grimly. Yet from the loins of some such tender woman had he sprung with a kingly inheritance,—an inheritance which gave to him and his dominance over the land and sea, over the animals and the peoples of all the zones. Single-handed against fivescore, girt by the Arctic winter, far from his own, he felt the prompting of his heritage, the desire to possess, the wild danger—love, the thrill of battle, the power to conquer or to die.

The singing and the dancing ceased, and the Shaman flared up in rude eloquence.

Through the sinuosities of their vast mythology, he worked cunningly upon the credulity of his people. The case was strong. Opposing the creative principles as embodied in the Crow and the Raven, he stigmatized Mackenzie as the Wolf, the fighting and the destructive principle. Not only was the combat of these forces spiritual, but men fought, each to his totem. They were the children of Jelchs, the Raven, the Promethean fire-bringer; Mackenzie was the child of the Wolf, or in other words, the Devil. For them to bring a truce to this perpetual warfare, to marry their daughters to the arch-enemy, were treason and blasphemy of the highest order. No phrase was harsh nor figure vile enough in branding Mackenzie as a sneaking interloper and emissary of Satan. There was a subdued, savage roar in the deep chests of his listeners as he took the swing of his peroration.

'Aye, my brothers, Jelchs is all-powerful! Did he not bring heaven-borne fire that we might be warm? Did he not draw the sun, moon, and stars, from their holes that we might see? Did he not teach us that we might fight the Spirits of Famine and of Frost? But now Jelchs is angry with his children, and they are grown to a handful, and he will not help.

'For they have forgotten him, and done evil things, and trod bad trails, and taken his enemies into their lodges to sit by their fires. And the Raven is sorrowful at the wickedness of his children; but when they shall rise up and show they have come back, he will come out of the darkness to aid them. O brothers! the Fire-Bringer has whispered messages to thy Shaman; the same shall ye hear. Let the young men take the young women to their lodges; let them fly at the throat of the Wolf; let them be undying in their enmity! Then shall their women become fruitful and they shall multiply into a mighty people! And the Raven shall lead great tribes of their fathers and their fathers' fathers from out of the North; and they shall beat back the Wolves till they are as last year's campfires; and they shall again come to rule over all the land! 'Tis the message of Jelchs, the Raven.' This foreshadowing of the Messiah's coming brought a hoarse howl from the Sticks as they leaped to their feet. Mackenzie slipped the thumbs of his mittens and waited. There was a clamor for the 'Fox,' not to be stilled till one of the young men stepped forward to speak.

'Brothers! The Shaman has spoken wisely. The Wolves have taken our women, and our men are childless. We are grown to a handful. The Wolves have taken our warm furs and given for them evil spirits which dwell in bottles, and clothes which come not from the beaver or the lynx, but are made from the grass.

And they are not warm, and our men die of strange sicknesses. I, the Fox, have taken no woman to wife; and why? Twice have the maidens which pleased me gone to the camps of the Wolf. Even now have I laid by skins of the beaver, of the moose, of the caribou, that I might win favor in the eyes of Thling-Tinneh, that I might marry Zarinska, his daughter. Even now are her snow-shoes bound to her feet, ready to break trail for the dogs of the Wolf. Nor do I speak for myself alone.

As I have done, so has the Bear. He, too, had fain been the father of her children, and many skins has he cured thereto. I speak for all the young men who know not wives. The Wolves are ever hungry. Always do they take the choice meat at the killing. To the Ravens are left the leavings.

'There is Gugkla,' he cried, brutally pointing out one of the women, who was a cripple.

'Her legs are bent like the ribs of a birch canoe. She cannot gather wood nor carry the meat of the hunters. Did the Wolves choose her?' 'Ai! ai!' vociferated his tribesmen.

'There is Moyri, whose eyes are crossed by the Evil Spirit. Even the babes are affrighted when they gaze upon her, and it is said the bald-face gives her the trail.

'Was she chosen?' Again the cruel applause rang out.

'And there sits Pischet. She does not hearken to my words. Never has she heard the cry of the chit-chat, the voice of her husband, the babble of her child.

'She lives in the White Silence. Cared the Wolves aught for her? No! Theirs is the choice of the kill; ours is the leavings.

'Brothers, it shall not be! No more shall the Wolves slink among our campfires. The time is come.' A great streamer of fire, the aurora borealis, purple, green, and yellow, shot across the zenith, bridging horizon to horizon. With head thrown back and arms extended, he swayed to his climax.

'Behold! The spirits of our fathers have arisen and great deeds are afoot this night!' He stepped back, and another young man somewhat diffidently came forward, pushed on by his comrades. He towered a full head above them, his broad chest defiantly bared to the frost. He swung tentatively from one foot to the other.

Words halted upon his tongue, and he was ill at ease. His face was horrible to look upon, for it had at one time been half torn away by some terrific blow. At last he struck his breast with his clenched fist, drawing sound as from a drum, and his voice rumbled forth as does the surf from an ocean cavern.

'I am the Bear,—the Silver-Tip and the Son of the Silver-Tip! When my voice was yet as a girl's, I slew the lynx, the moose, and the cariboo; when it whistled like the wolverines from under a cache, I crossed the Mountains of the South and slew three of the White Rivers; when it became as the roar of the Chinook, I met the bald-faced grizzly, but gave no trail.' At this he paused, his hand significantly sweeping across his hideous scars.

'I am not as the Fox. My tongue is frozen like the river. I cannot make great talk. My words are few. The Fox says great deeds are afoot this night. Good! Talk flows from his tongue like the freshets of the spring, but he is chary of deeds.

'This night shall I do battle with the Wolf. I shall slay him, and Zarinska shall sit by my fire. The Bear has spoken.' Though pandemonium raged about him, 'Scruff' Mackenzie held his ground.

Aware how useless was the rifle at close quarters, he slipped both holsters to the fore, ready for action, and drew his mittens till his hands were barely shielded by the elbow gauntlets. He knew there was no hope in attack en masse, but true to his boast, was prepared to die with teeth fast-locked. But the Bear restrained his comrades, beating back the more impetuous with his terrible fist. As the tumult began to die away, Mackenzie shot a glance in the direction of Zarinska. It was a superb picture. She was leaning forward on her snow-shoes, lips apart and nostrils quivering, like a tigress about to spring. Her great black eyes were fixed upon her tribesmen, in fear and defiance. So extreme the tension, she had forgotten to breathe. With one hand pressed spasmodically against her breast and the other as tightly gripped about the dog-whip, she was as turned to stone. Even as he looked, relief came to her. Her muscles loosened; with a heavy sigh she settled back, giving him a look of more than love—of worship.

Thling-Tinneh was trying to speak, but his people drowned his voice. Then Mackenzie strode forward. The Fox opened his mouth to a piercing yell, but so savagely did Mackenzie whirl upon him that he shrank back, his larynx all agurgle with suppressed sound. His discomfiture was greeted with roars of laughter, and served to soothe his fellows to a listening mood.

'Brothers! The White Man, whom ye have chosen to call the Wolf, came among you with fair words. He was not like the Innuit; he spoke not lies. He came as a friend, as one who would be a brother. But your men have had their say, and the time for soft words is past.

'First, I will tell you that the Shaman has an evil tongue and is a false prophet, that the messages he spake are not those of the Fire-Bringer. His ears are locked to the voice of the Raven, and out of his own head he weaves cunning fancies, and he has made fools of you. He has no power.

'When the dogs were killed and eaten, and your stomachs were heavy with untanned hide and strips of moccasins; when the old men died, and the old women died, and the babes at the dry dugs of the mothers died; when the land was dark, and ye perished as do the salmon in the fall; aye, when the famine was upon you, did the Shaman bring reward to your hunters? did the Shaman put meat in your bellies? Again I say, the Shaman is without power. Thus I spit upon his face!' Though taken aback by the sacrilege, there was no uproar. Some of the women were even frightened, but among the men there was an uplifting, as though in preparation or anticipation of the miracle. All eyes were turned upon the two central figures. The priest realized the crucial moment, felt his power tottering, opened his mouth in denunciation, but fled backward before the truculent advance, upraised fist, and flashing eyes, of Mackenzie. He sneered and resumed.

'Was I stricken dead? Did the lightning burn me? Did the stars fall from the sky and crush me? Pish! I have done with the dog. Now will I tell you of my people, who are the mightiest of all the peoples, who rule in all the lands. At first we hunt as I hunt, alone.

'After that we hunt in packs; and at last, like the cariboo-run, we sweep across all the land.

'Those whom we take into our lodges live; those who will not come die. Zarinska is a comely maiden, full and strong, fit to become the mother of Wolves. Though I die, such shall she become; for my brothers are many, and they will follow the scent of my dogs.

'Listen to the Law of the Wolf: Whoso taketh the life of one Wolf, the forfeit shall ten of his people pay. In many lands has the price been paid; in many lands shall it yet be paid.

'Now will I deal with the Fox and the Bear. It seems they have cast eyes upon the maiden. So? Behold, I have bought her! Thling-Tinneh leans upon the rifle; the goods of purchase are by his fire. Yet will I be fair to the young men. To the Fox, whose tongue is dry with many words, will I give of tobacco five long plugs.

'Thus will his mouth be wetted that he may make much noise in the council. But to the Bear, of whom I am well proud, will I give of blankets two; of flour, twenty cups; of tobacco, double that of the Fox; and if he fare with me over the Mountains of the East, then will I give him a rifle, mate to Thling Tinneh's. If not? Good! The Wolf is weary of speech. Yet once again will he say the Law: Whoso taketh the life of one Wolf, the forfeit shall ten of his people pay.'

Mackenzie smiled as he stepped back to his old position, but at heart he was full of trouble. The night was yet dark. The girl came to his side, and he listened closely as she told of the Bear's battle-tricks with the knife.

The decision was for war. In a trice, scores of moccasins were widening the space of beaten snow by the fire. There was much chatter about the seeming defeat of the Shaman; some averred he had but withheld his power, while others conned past events and agreed with the Wolf. The Bear came to the center of the battle-ground, a long naked hunting-knife of Russian make in his hand. The Fox called attention to Mackenzie's revolvers; so he stripped his belt, buckling it about Zarinska, into whose hands he also entrusted his rifle. She shook her head that she could not shoot,—small chance had a woman to handle such precious things.

'Then, if danger come by my back, cry aloud, "My husband!" No; thus, "My husband!"'

He laughed as she repeated it, pinched her cheek, and reentered the circle. Not only in reach and stature had the Bear the advantage of him, but his blade was longer by a good two inches. 'Scruff' Mackenzie had looked into the eyes of men before, and he knew it was a man who stood against him; yet he quickened to the glint of light on the steel, to the dominant pulse of his race.

Time and again he was forced to the edge of the fire or the deep snow, and time and again, with the foot tactics of the pugilist, he worked back to the center. Not a voice was lifted in encouragement, while his antagonist was heartened with applause, suggestions, and warnings. But his teeth only shut the tighter as the knives clashed together, and he thrust or eluded with a coolness born of conscious strength. At first he felt compassion for his enemy; but this fled before the primal instinct of life, which in turn gave way to the lust of slaughter.

The ten thousand years of culture fell from him, and he was a cave-dweller, doing battle for his female.

Twice he pricked the Bear, getting away unscathed; but the third time caught, and to save himself, free hands closed on fighting hands, and they came together.

Then did he realize the tremendous strength of his opponent. His muscles were knotted in painful lumps, and cords and tendons threatened to snap with the strain; yet nearer and nearer came the Russian steel. He tried to break away, but only weakened himself. The fur-clad circle closed in, certain of and anxious to see the final stroke. But with wrestler's trick, swinging partly to the side, he struck at his adversary with his head. Involuntarily the Bear leaned back, disturbing his center of gravity. Simultaneous with this, Mackenzie tripped properly and threw his whole weight forward, hurling him clear through the circle into the deep snow. The Bear floundered out and came back full tilt.

'O my husband!' Zarinska's voice rang out, vibrant with danger.

To the twang of a bow-string, Mackenzie swept low to the ground, and a bonebarbed arrow passed over him into the breast of the Bear, whose momentum carried him over his crouching foe. The next instant Mackenzie was up and about. The bear lay motionless, but across the fire was the Shaman, drawing a second arrow. Mackenzie's knife leaped short in the air. He caught the heavy blade by the point. There was a flash of light as it spanned the fire. Then the Shaman, the hilt alone appearing without his throat, swayed and pitched forward into the glowing embers.

Click! Click!—the Fox had possessed himself of Thling-Tinneh's rifle and was vainly trying to throw a shell into place. But he dropped it at the sound of Mackenzie's laughter.

'So the Fox has not learned the way of the plaything? He is yet a woman.

'Come! Bring it, that I may show thee!' The Fox hesitated.

'Come, I say!' He slouched forward like a beaten cur.

'Thus, and thus; so the thing is done.' A shell flew into place and the trigger was at cock as Mackenzie brought it to shoulder.

'The Fox has said great deeds were afoot this night, and he spoke true. There have been great deeds, yet least among them were those of the Fox. Is he still intent to take Zarinska to his lodge? Is he minded to tread the trail already broken by the Shaman and the Bear?

'No? Good!'

Mackenzie turned contemptuously and drew his knife from the priest's throat.

'Are any of the young men so minded? If so, the Wolf will take them by two and three till none are left. No? Good! Thling-Tinneh, I now give thee this rifle a second time. If, in the days to come, thou shouldst journey to the Country of the Yukon, know thou that there shall always be a place and much food by the fire of the Wolf. The night is now passing into the day. I go, but I may come again. And for the last time, remember the Law of the Wolf!' He was supernatural in their sight as he rejoined Zarinska. She took her place at the head of the team, and the dogs swung into motion. A few moments later they were swallowed up by the ghostly forest. Till now Mackenzie had waited; he slipped into his snow-shoes to follow.

'Has the Wolf forgotten the five long plugs?' Mackenzie turned upon the Fox angrily; then the humor of it struck him.

'I will give thee one short plug.' 'As the Wolf sees fit,' meekly responded the Fox, stretching out his hand.

THE MEN OF FORTY MILE

WHEN BIG JIM BELDEN ventured the apparently innocuous proposition that mush-ice was 'rather pecooliar,' he little dreamed of what it would lead to.

Neither did Lon McFane, when he affirmed that anchor ice was even more so; nor did Bettles, as he instantly disagreed, declaring the very existence of such a form to be a bugaboo.

'An' ye'd be tellin' me this,' cried Lon, 'after the years ye've spint in the land! An' we atin' out the same pot this many's the day!' 'But the thing's agin reason,' insisted Bettles.

'Look you, water's warmer than ice—' 'An' little the difference, once ye break through.'

'Still it's warmer, because it ain't froze. An' you say it freezes on the bottom?' 'Only the anchor-ice, David, only the anchor-ice. An' have ye niver drifted along, the water clear as glass, whin suddin, belike a cloud over the sun, the mushy-ice comes bubblin' up an' up till from bank to bank an' bind to bind it's drapin' the river like a first snowfall?' 'Unh, hunh! more'n once when I took a doze at the steering-oar. But it allus come out the nighest side-channel, an' not bubblin' up an' up.' 'But with niver a wink at the helm?'

'No; nor you. It's agin reason. I'll leave it to any man!' Bettles appealed to the circle about the stove, but the fight was on between himself and Lon McFane.

'Reason or no reason, it's the truth I'm tellin' ye. Last fall, a year gone, 'twas Sitka Charley and meself saw the sight, droppin' down the riffle ye'll remember below Fort Reliance. An' regular fall weather it was—the glint o' the sun on the golden larch an' the quakin' aspens; an' the glister of light on ivery ripple; an' beyand, the winter an' the blue haze of the North comin' down hand in hand. It's well ye know the same, with a fringe to the river an' the ice formin' thick in the eddies—an' a snap an' sparkle to the air, an' ye a-feelin' it through all yer blood, a-takin' new lease of life with ivery suck of it. 'Tis then, me boy, the world grows small an' the wandtherlust lays ye by the heels.

'But it's meself as wandthers. As I was sayin', we a-paddlin', with niver a sign of ice, barrin' that by the eddies, when the Injun lifts his paddle an' sings out, "Lon McFane! Look ye below!" So have I heard, but niver thought to see! As ye know, Sitka Charley, like meself, niver drew first breath in the land; so the sight was new. Then we drifted, with a head over ayther side, peerin' down through the sparkly water. For the world like the days I spint with the pearlers, watchin' the coral banks a-growin' the same as so many gardens under the sea. There it was, the anchor-ice, clingin' an' clusterin' to ivery rock, after the manner of the white coral.

'But the best of the sight was to come. Just after clearin' the tail of the riffle, the water turns quick the color of milk, an' the top of it in wee circles, as when the graylin' rise in the spring, or there's a splatter of wet from the sky. 'Twas the anchor-ice comin' up. To the right, to the lift, as far as iver a man cud see, the water was covered with the same.

An' like so much porridge it was, slickin' along the bark of the canoe, stickin' like glue to the paddles. It's many's the time I shot the self-same riffle before, and it's many's the time after, but niver a wink of the same have I seen. 'Twas the sight of a lifetime.' 'Do tell!' dryly commented Bettles. 'D'ye think I'd b'lieve such a yarn? I'd ruther say the glister of light'd gone to your eyes, and the snap of the air to your tongue.' ''Twas me own eyes that beheld it, an' if Sitka Charley was here, he'd be the lad to back me.' 'But facts is facts, an' they ain't no gettin' round 'em. It ain't in the nature of things for the water furtherest away from the air to freeze first.' 'But me own eyes-' 'Don't git het up over it,' admonished Bettles, as the quick Celtic anger began to mount.

'Then yer not after belavin' me?' 'Sence you're so blamed forehanded about it, no; I'd b'lieve nature first, and facts.'

'Is it the lie ye'd be givin' me?' threatened Lon. 'Ye'd better be askin' that Siwash wife of yours. I'll lave it to her, for the truth I spake.' Bettles flared up in sudden wrath. The Irishman had unwittingly wounded him; for his wife was the half-breed daughter of a Russian fur-trader, married to him in the Greek Mission of Nulato, a thousand miles or so down the Yukon, thus being of much higher caste than the common Siwash, or native, wife. It was a mere Northland nuance, which none but the Northland adventurer may understand.

'I reckon you kin take it that way,' was his deliberate affirmation.

The next instant Lon McFane had stretched him on the floor, the circle was broken up, and half a dozen men had stepped between.

Bettles came to his feet, wiping the blood from his mouth. 'It hain't new, this takin' and payin' of blows, and don't you never think but that this will be squared.' 'An' niver in me life did I take the lie from mortal man,' was the retort courteous. 'An' it's an avil day I'll not be to hand, waitin' an' willin' to help ye lift yer debts, barrin' no manner of way.'

'Still got that 38-55?' Lon nodded.

'But you'd better git a more likely caliber. Mine'll rip holes through you the size of walnuts.'

'Niver fear; it's me own slugs smell their way with soft noses, an' they'll spread like flap-jacks against the coming out beyand. An' when'll I have the pleasure of waitin' on ye? The waterhole's a strikin' locality.' ''Tain't bad. Jest be there in an hour, and you won't set long on my coming.' Both men mittened and left the Post, their ears closed to the remonstrances of their comrades. It was such a little thing; yet with such men, little things, nourished by quick tempers and stubborn natures, soon blossomed into big things.

Besides, the art of burning to bedrock still lay in the womb of the future, and the men of Forty-Mile, shut in by the long Arctic winter, grew high-stomached with overeating and enforced idleness, and became as irritable as do the bees in the fall of the year when the hives are overstocked with honey.

There was no law in the land. The mounted police was also a thing of the future. Each man measured an offense, and meted out the punishment inasmuch as it affected himself.

Rarely had combined action been necessary, and never in all the dreary history of the camp had the eighth article of the Decalogue been violated.

Big Jim Belden called an impromptu meeting. Scruff Mackenzie was placed as temporary chairman, and a messenger dispatched to solicit Father Roubeau's good offices. Their position was paradoxical, and they knew it. By the right of might could they interfere to prevent the duel; yet such action, while in direct line with their wishes, went counter to their opinions. While their rough-hewn, obsolete ethics recognized the individual prerogative of wiping out blow with blow, they could not bear to think of two good comrades, such as Bettles and McFane, meeting in deadly battle. Deeming the man who would not fight on provocation a dastard, when brought to the test it seemed wrong that he should fight.

But a scurry of moccasins and loud cries, rounded off with a pistol-shot, interrupted the discussion. Then the storm-doors opened and Malemute Kid entered, a smoking Colt's in his hand, and a merry light in his eye.

'I got him.' He replaced the empty shell, and added, 'Your dog, Scruff.' 'Yellow Fang?' Mackenzie asked.

'No; the lop-eared one.' 'The devil! Nothing the matter with him.' 'Come out and take a look.' 'That's all right after all. Buess he's got 'em, too. Yellow Fang came back this morning and took a chunk out of him, and came near to making a widower of me. Made a rush for Zarinska, but she whisked her skirts in his face and escaped with the loss of the same and a good roll in the snow. Then he took to the woods again. Hope he don't come back. Lost any yourself?' 'One—the best one of the pack—Shookum. Started amuck this morning, but didn't get very far. Ran foul of Sitka Charley's team, and they scattered him all over the street. And now two of them are loose, and raging mad; so you see he got his work in. The dog census will be small in the spring if we don't do something.'

'And the man census, too.' 'How's that? Who's in trouble now?' 'Oh, Bettles and Lon McFane had an argument, and they'll be down by the waterhole in a few minutes to settle it.' The incident was repeated for his benefit, and Malemute Kid, accustomed to an obedience which his fellow men never failed to render, took charge of the affair. His quickly formulated plan was explained, and they promised to follow his lead implicitly.

'So you see,' he concluded, 'we do not actually take away their privilege of fighting; and yet I don't believe they'll fight when they see the beauty of the scheme. Life's a game and men the gamblers. They'll stake their whole pile on the one chance in a thousand.'

'Take away that one chance, and—they won't play.' He turned to the man in charge of the Post. 'Storekeeper, weight out three fathoms of your best half-inch manila.'

'We'll establish a precedent which will last the men of Forty-Mile to the end of time,' he prophesied. Then he coiled the rope about his arm and led his followers out of doors, just in time to meet the principals.

'What danged right'd he to fetch my wife in?' thundered Bettles to the soothing overtures of a friend. "Twa'n't called for,' he concluded decisively. "Twa'n't called for,' he reiterated again and again, pacing up and down and waiting for Lon McFane.

And Lon McFane—his face was hot and tongue rapid as he flaunted insurrection in the face of the Church. 'Then, father,' he cried, 'it's with an aisy heart I'll roll in me flamy blankets, the broad of me back on a bed of coals. Niver shall it be said that Lon McFane took a lie 'twixt the teeth without iver liftin' a hand! An' I'll not ask a blessin'. The years have been wild, but it's the heart was in the right place.' 'But it's not the heart, Lon,' interposed Father Roubeau; 'It's pride that bids you forth to slay your fellow man.' 'Yer Frinch,' Lon replied. And then, turning to leave him, 'An' will ye say a mass if the luck is against me?' But the priest smiled, thrust his moccasined feet to the fore, and went out upon the white breast of the silent river. A packed trail, the width of a sixteen-inch sled, led out to the waterhole. On either side lay the deep, soft snow. The men trod in single file, without conversation; and the black-stoled priest in their midst gave to the function the solemn aspect of a funeral. It was a warm winter's day for Forty-Mile—a day in which the sky, filled with heaviness, drew closer to the earth, and the mercury sought the unwonted level of twenty below. But there was no cheer in the warmth. There was little air in the upper strata, and the clouds hung motionless, giving sullen promise of an early snowfall. And the earth, unresponsive, made no preparation, content in its hibernation.

When the waterhole was reached, Bettles, having evidently reviewed the quarrel during the silent walk, burst out in a final "Twa'n't called for,' while Lon McFane kept grim silence. Indignation so choked him that he could not speak.

Yet deep down, whenever their own wrongs were not uppermost, both men wondered at their comrades. They had expected opposition, and this tacit acquiescence hurt them. It seemed more was due them from the men they had been so close with, and they felt a vague sense of wrong, rebelling at the thought of so many of their brothers coming out, as on a gala occasion, without one word of protest, to see them shoot each other down. It appeared their worth had diminished in the eyes of the community. The proceedings puzzled them.

'Back to back, David. An' will it be fifty paces to the man, or double the quantity?'

'Fifty,' was the sanguinary reply, grunted out, yet sharply cut.

But the new manila, not prominently displayed, but casually coiled about Malemute Kid's arm, caught the quick eye of the Irishman, and thrilled him with a suspicious fear.

'An' what are ye doin' with the rope?' 'Hurry up!' Malemute Kid glanced at his watch.

'I've a batch of bread in the cabin, and I don't want it to fall. Besides, my feet are getting cold.' The rest of the men manifested their impatience in various suggestive ways.

'But the rope, Kid' It's bran' new, an' sure yer bread's not that heavy it needs raisin' with the like of that?' Bettles by this time had faced around. Father Roubeau, the humor of the situation just dawning on him, hid a smile behind his mittened hand.

'No, Lon; this rope was made for a man.' Malemute Kid could be very impressive on occasion.

'What man?' Bettles was becoming aware of a personal interest.

'The other man.' 'An' which is the one ye'd mane by that?' 'Listen, Lon—and you, too, Bettles! We've been talking this little trouble of yours over, and we've come to one conclusion. We know we have no right to stop your fighting-' 'True for ye, me lad!' 'And we're not going to. But this much we can do, and shall do—make this the only duel in the history of Forty-Mile, set an example for every che-cha-qua that comes up or down the Yukon. The man who escapes killing shall be hanged to the nearest tree. Now, go ahead!'

Lon smiled dubiously, then his face lighted up. 'Pace her off, David—fifty paces, wheel, an' niver a cease firin' till a lad's down for good. 'Tis their hearts'll niver let them do the deed, an' it's well ye should know it for a true Yankee bluff.'

He started off with a pleased grin on his face, but Malemute Kid halted him.

'Lon! It's a long while since you first knew me?' 'Many's the day.' 'And you, Bettles?'

'Five year next June high water.' 'And have you once, in all that time, known me to break my word' Or heard of me breaking it?' Both men shook their heads, striving to fathom what lay beyond.

'Well, then, what do you think of a promise made by me?' 'As good as your bond,' from Bettles.

'The thing to safely sling yer hopes of heaven by,' promptly endorsed Lon McFane.

'Listen! I, Malemute Kid, give you my word—and you know what that means that the man who is not shot stretches rope within ten minutes after the shooting.' He stepped back as Pilate might have done after washing his hands.

A pause and a silence came over the men of Forty-Mile. The sky drew still closer, sending down a crystal flight of frost—little geometric designs, perfect, evanescent as a breath, yet destined to exist till the returning sun had covered half its northern journey.

Both men had led forlorn hopes in their time—led with a curse or a jest on their tongues, and in their souls an unswerving faith in the God of Chance. But that merciful deity had been shut out from the present deal. They studied the face of Malemute Kid, but they studied as one might the Sphinx. As the quiet minutes passed, a feeling that speech was incumbent on them began to grow. At last the howl of a wolf-dog cracked the silence from the direction of Forty-Mile. The weird sound swelled with all the pathos of a breaking heart, then died away in a long-drawn sob.

'Well I be danged!' Bettles turned up the collar of his mackinaw jacket and stared about him helplessly.

'It's a gloryus game yer runnin', Kid,' cried Lon McFane. 'All the percentage of the house an' niver a bit to the man that's buckin'. The Devil himself'd niver tackle such a cinch—and damned if I do.' There were chuckles, throttled in gurgling throats, and winks brushed away with the frost which rimed the eyelashes, as the men climbed the ice-notched bank and started across the street to the Post. But the long howl had drawn nearer, invested with a new note of menace. A woman screamed round the corner. There was a cry of, 'Here he comes!' Then an Indian boy, at the head of half a dozen frightened dogs, racing with death, dashed into the crowd. And behind came Yellow Fang, a bristle of hair and a flash of gray. Everybody but the Yankee fled.

The Indian boy had tripped and fallen. Bettles stopped long enough to grip him by the slack of his furs, then headed for a pile of cordwood already occupied by a number of his comrades. Yellow Fang, doubling after one of the dogs, came leaping back. The fleeing animal, free of the rabies, but crazed with fright, whipped Bettles off his feet and flashed on up the street. Malemute Kid took a flying shot at Yellow Fang. The mad dog whirled a half airspring, came down on his back, then, with a single leap, covered half the distance between himself and Bettles.

But the fatal spring was intercepted. Lon McFane leaped from the woodpile, countering him in midair. Over they rolled, Lon holding him by the throat at arm's length, blinking under the fetid slaver which sprayed his face. Then Bettles, revolver in hand and coolly waiting a chance, settled the combat.

"Twas a square game, Kid,' Lon remarked, rising to his feet and shaking the snow from out his sleeves; 'with a fair percentage to meself that bucked it.' That night, while Lon McFane sought the forgiving arms of the Church in the direction of Father Roubeau's cabin, Malemute Kid talked long to little purpose.

'But would you,' persisted Mackenzie, 'supposing they had fought?' 'Have I ever broken my word?' 'No; but that isn't the point. Answer the question. Would you?' Malemute Kid straightened up. 'Scruff, I've been asking myself that question ever since, and—'

'Well?'

'Well, as yet, I haven't found the answer.'

IN A FAR COUNTRY

WHEN A MAN JOURNEYS into a far country, he must be prepared to forget many of the things he has learned, and to acquire such customs as are inherent with existence in the new land; he must abandon the old ideals and the old gods, and oftentimes he must reverse the very codes by which his conduct has hitherto been shaped. To those who have the protean faculty of adaptability, the novelty of such change may even be a source of pleasure; but to those who happen to be hardened to the ruts in which they were created, the pressure of the altered environment is unbearable, and they chafe in body and in spirit under the new restrictions which they do not understand. This chafing is bound to act and react, producing divers evils and leading to various misfortunes. It were better for the man who cannot fit himself to the new groove to return to his own country; if he delay too long, he will surely die.

The man who turns his back upon the comforts of an elder civilization, to face the savage youth, the primordial simplicity of the North, may estimate success at an inverse ratio to the quantity and quality of his hopelessly fixed habits. He will soon discover, if he be a fit candidate, that the material habits are the less important. The exchange of such things as a dainty menu for rough fare, of the stiff leather shoe for the soft, shapeless moccasin, of the feather bed for a couch in the snow, is after all a very easy matter. But his pinch will come in learning properly to shape his mind's attitude toward all things, and especially toward his fellow man. For the courtesies of ordinary life, he must substitute unselfishness, forbearance, and tolerance. Thus, and thus only, can he gain that pearl of great price—true comradeship. He must not say 'thank you'; he must mean it without opening his mouth, and prove it by responding in kind. In short, he must substitute the deed for the word, the spirit for the letter.

When the world rang with the tale of Arctic gold, and the lure of the North gripped the heartstrings of men, Carter Weatherbee threw up his snug clerkship, turned the half of his savings over to his wife, and with the remainder bought an outfit. There was no romance in his nature—the bondage of commerce had crushed all that; he was simply tired of the ceaseless grind, and wished to risk great hazards in view of corresponding returns. Like many

21

another fool, disdaining the old trails used by the Northland pioneers for a score of years, he hurried to Edmonton in the spring of the year; and there, unluckily for his soul's welfare, he allied himself with a party of men.

There was nothing unusual about this party, except its plans. Even its goal, like that of all the other parties, was the Klondike. But the route it had mapped out to attain that goal took away the breath of the hardiest native, born and bred to the vicissitudes of the Northwest. Even Jacques Baptiste, born of a Chippewa woman and a renegade voyageur (having raised his first whimpers in a deerskin lodge north of the sixty-fifth parallel, and had the same hushed by blissful sucks of raw tallow), was surprised. Though he sold his services to them and agreed to travel even to the never-opening ice, he shook his head ominously whenever his advice was asked.

Percy Cuthfert's evil star must have been in the ascendant, for he, too, joined this company of argonauts. He was an ordinary man, with a bank account as deep as his culture, which is saying a good deal. He had no reason to embark on such a venture—no reason in the world save that he suffered from an abnormal development of sentimentality. He mistook this for the true spirit of romance and adventure. Many another man has done the like, and made as fatal a mistake.

The first break-up of spring found the party following the ice-run of Elk River. It was an imposing fleet, for the outfit was large, and they were accompanied by a disreputable contingent of half-breed voyageurs with their women and children. Day in and day out, they labored with the bateaux and canoes, fought mosquitoes and other kindred pests, or sweated and swore at the portages. Severe toil like this lays a man naked to the very roots of his soul, and ere Lake Athabasca was lost in the south, each member of the party had hoisted his true colors.

The two shirks and chronic grumblers were Carter Weatherbee and Percy Cuthfert. The whole party complained less of its aches and pains than did either of them. Not once did they volunteer for the thousand and one petty duties of the camp. A bucket of water to be brought, an extra armful of wood to be chopped, the dishes to be washed and wiped, a search to be made through the outfit for some suddenly indispensable article—and these two effete scions of civilization discovered sprains or blisters requiring instant attention. They were the first to turn in at night, with score of tasks yet undone; the last to turn out in the morning, when the start should be in readiness before the breakfast was begun.

They were the first to fall to at mealtime, the last to have a hand in the cooking; the first to dive for a slim delicacy, the last to discover they had added to their own another man's share. If they toiled at the oars, they slyly cut the water at each stroke and allowed the boat's momentum to float up the blade. They thought nobody noticed; but their comrades swore under their breaths and grew to hate them, while Jacques Baptiste sneered openly and damned them from morning till night. But Jacques Baptiste was no gentleman.

At the Great Slave, Hudson Bay dogs were purchased, and the fleet sank to the guards with its added burden of dried fish and pemican. Then canoe and bateau answered to the swift current of the Mackenzie, and they plunged into the Great Barren Ground. Every likely-looking 'feeder' was prospected, but the elusive 'pay-dirt' danced ever to the north. At the Great Bear, overcome by the common dread of the Unknown Lands, their voyageurs began to desert, and Fort of Good Hope saw the last and bravest bending to the towlines as they bucked the current down which they had so treacherously glided.

Jacques Baptiste alone remained. Had he not sworn to travel even to the never-opening ice? The lying charts, compiled in main from hearsay, were now constantly consulted.

And they felt the need of hurry, for the sun had already passed its northern solstice and was leading the winter south again. Skirting the shores of the bay, where the Mackenzie disembogues into the Arctic Ocean, they entered the mouth of the Little Peel River. Then began the arduous up-stream toil, and the two Incapables fared worse than ever. Towline and pole, paddle and tumpline, rapids and portages—such tortures served to give the one a deep disgust for great hazards, and printed for the other a fiery text on the true romance of adventure. One day they waxed mutinous, and being vilely cursed by Jacques Baptiste, turned, as worms sometimes will. But the half-breed thrashed the twain, and sent them, bruised and bleeding, about their work. It was the first time either had been manhandled.

Abandoning their river craft at the headwaters of the Little Peel, they consumed the rest of the summer in the great portage over the Mackenzie watershed to the West Rat. This little stream fed the Porcupine, which in turn joined the Yukon where that mighty highway of the North countermarches on the Arctic Circle.

But they had lost in the race with winter, and one day they tied their rafts to the thick eddy-ice and hurried their goods ashore. That night the river jammed and broke several times; the following morning it had fallen asleep for good. 'We can't be more'n four hundred miles from the Yukon,' concluded Sloper, multiplying his thumb nails by the scale of the map. The council, in which the two Incapables had whined to excellent disadvantage, was drawing to a close.

'Hudson Bay Post, long time ago. No use um now.' Jacques Baptiste's father had made the trip for the Fur Company in the old days, incidentally marking the trail with a couple of frozen toes.

Sufferin' cracky!' cried another of the party. 'No whites?' 'Nary white,' Sloper sententiously affirmed; 'but it's only five hundred more up the Yukon to Dawson. Call it a rough thousand from here.' Weatherbee and Cuthfert groaned in chorus.

'How long'll that take, Baptiste?' The half-breed figured for a moment. 'Workum like hell, no man play out, ten—twenty—forty—fifty days. Um babies come' (designating the Incapables), 'no can tell. Mebbe when hell freeze over; mebbe not then.' The manufacture of snowshoes and moccasins ceased. Somebody called the name of an absent member, who came out of an ancient cabin at the edge of the campfire and joined them. The cabin was one of the many mysteries which lurk in the vast recesses of the North. Built when and by whom, no man could tell.

Two graves in the open, piled high with stones, perhaps contained the secret of those early wanderers. But whose hand had piled the stones? The moment had come. Jacques Baptiste paused in the fitting of a harness and pinned the struggling dog in the snow. The cook made mute protest for delay, threw a handful of bacon into a noisy pot of beans, then came to attention. Sloper rose to his feet. His body was a ludicrous contrast to the healthy physiques of the Incapables. Yellow and weak, fleeing from a South American fever-hole, he had not broken his flight across the zones, and was still able to toil with men. His weight was probably ninety pounds, with the heavy hunting knife thrown in, and his grizzled hair told of a prime which had ceased to be. The fresh young muscles of either Weatherbee or Cuthfert were equal to ten times the endeavor of his; yet he could walk them into the earth in a day's journey. And all this day he had whipped his stronger comrades into venturing a thousand miles of the stiffest hardship man can conceive. He was the incarnation of the unrest of his race, and the old Teutonic stubbornness, dashed with the quick grasp and action of the Yankee, held the flesh in the bondage of the spirit.

'All those in favor of going on with the dogs as soon as the ice sets, say ay.' 'Ay!' rang out eight voices—voices destined to string a trail of oaths along many a hundred miles of pain.

'Contrary minded?' 'No!' For the first time the Incapables were united without some compromise of personal interests.

'And what are you going to do about it?' Weatherbee added belligerently.

'Majority rule! Majority rule!' clamored the rest of the party.

'I know the expedition is liable to fall through if you don't come,' Sloper replied sweetly; 'but I guess, if we try real hard, we can manage to do without you.

What do you say, boys?' The sentiment was cheered to the echo.

'But I say, you know,' Cuthfert ventured apprehensively; 'what's a chap like me to do?'

'Ain't you coming with us.' 'No—o.' 'Then do as you damn well please. We won't have nothing to say.' 'Kind o' calkilate yuh might settle it with that canoodlin' pardner of yourn,' suggested a heavy-going Westerner from the Dakotas, at the same time pointing out Weatherbee. 'He'll be shore to ask yuh what yur a-goin' to do when it comes to cookin' an' gatherin' the wood.' 'Then we'll consider it all arranged,' concluded Sloper.

'We'll pull out tomorrow, if we camp within five miles—just to get everything in running order and remember if we've forgotten anything.' The sleds groaned by on their steel-shod runners, and the dogs strained low in the harnesses in which they were born to die.

Jacques Baptiste paused by the side of Sloper to get a last glimpse of the cabin. The smoke curled up pathetically from the Yukon stovepipe. The two Incapables were watching them from the doorway.

Sloper laid his hand on the other's shoulder.

'Jacques Baptiste, did you ever hear of the Kilkenny cats?' The half-breed shook his head.

'Well, my friend and good comrade, the Kilkenny cats fought till neither hide, nor hair, nor yowl, was left. You understand?—till nothing was left. Very good.

Now, these two men don't like work. They'll be all alone in that cabin all winter—a mighty long, dark winter. Kilkenny cats—well?' The Frenchman in Baptiste shrugged his shoulders, but the Indian in him was silent. Nevertheless, it was an eloquent shrug, pregnant with prophecy. Things prospered in the little cabin at first. The rough badinage of their comrades had made Weatherbee and Cuthfert conscious of the mutual responsibility which had devolved upon them; besides, there was not so much work after all for two healthy men. And the removal of the cruel whiphand, or in other words the bulldozing half-breed, had brought with it a joyous reaction. At first, each strove to outdo the other, and they performed petty tasks with an unction which would have opened the eyes of their comrades who were now wearing out bodies and souls on the Long Trail.

All care was banished. The forest, which shouldered in upon them from three sides, was an inexhaustible woodyard. A few yards from their door slept the Porcupine, and a hole through its winter robe formed a bubbling spring of water, crystal clear and painfully cold. But they soon grew to find fault with even that. The hole would persist in freezing up, and thus gave them many a miserable hour of ice-chopping. The unknown builders of the cabin had extended the sidelogs so as to support a cache at the rear. In this was stored the bulk of the party's provisions.

Food there was, without stint, for three times the men who were fated to live upon it. But the most of it was the kind which built up brawn and sinew, but did not tickle the palate.

True, there was sugar in plenty for two ordinary men; but these two were little else than children. They early discovered the virtues of hot water judiciously saturated with sugar, and they prodigally swam their flapjacks and soaked their crusts in the rich, white syrup.

Then coffee and tea, and especially the dried fruits, made disastrous inroads upon it. The first words they had were over the sugar question. And it is a really serious thing when two men, wholly dependent upon each other for company, begin to quarrel.

Weatherbee loved to discourse blatantly on politics, while Cuthfert, who had been prone to clip his coupons and let the commonwealth jog on as best it might, either ignored the subject or delivered himself of startling epigrams. But the clerk was too obtuse to appreciate the clever shaping of thought, and this waste of ammunition irritated Cuthfert.

He had been used to blinding people by his brilliancy, and it worked him quite a hardship, this loss of an audience. He felt personally aggrieved and unconsciously held his muttonhead companion responsible for it.

Save existence, they had nothing in common—came in touch on no single point.

Weatherbee was a clerk who had known naught but clerking all his life; Cuthfert was a master of arts, a dabbler in oils, and had written not a little. The one was a lower-class man who considered himself a gentleman, and the other was a gentleman who knew himself to be such. From this it may be remarked that a man can be a gentleman without possessing the first instinct of true comradeship. The clerk was as sensuous as the other was aesthetic, and his love adventures, told at great length and chiefly coined from his imagination, affected the supersensitive master of arts in the same way as so many whiffs of sewer gas. He deemed the clerk a filthy, uncultured brute, whose place was in the muck with the swine, and told him so; and he was reciprocally informed that he was a milk-and-water sissy and a cad. Weatherbee could not have defined 'cad' for his life; but it satisfied its purpose, which after all seems the main point in life.

Weatherbee flatted every third note and sang such songs as 'The Boston Burglar' and 'the Handsome Cabin Boy,' for hours at a time, while Cuthfert wept with rage, till he could stand it no longer and fled into the outer cold. But there was no escape. The intense frost could not be endured for long at a time, and the little cabin crowded them—beds, stove, table, and all—into a space of ten by twelve. The very presence of either became a personal affront to the other, and they lapsed into sullen silences which increased in length and strength as the days went by. Occasionally, the flash of an eye or the curl of a lip got the better of them, though they strove to wholly ignore each other during these mute periods.

And a great wonder sprang up in the breast of each, as to how God had ever come to create the other.

With little to do, time became an intolerable burden to them. This naturally made them still lazier. They sank into a physical lethargy which there was no escaping, and which made them rebel at the performance of the smallest chore. One morning when it was his turn to cook the common breakfast, Weatherbee rolled out of his blankets, and to the snoring of his companion, lighted first the slush lamp and then the fire. The kettles were frozen hard, and there was no water in the cabin with which to wash. But he did not mind that. Waiting for it to thaw, he sliced the bacon and plunged into the hateful task of bread-making. Cuthfert had been slyly watching through his half-closed lids.

Consequently there was a scene, in which they fervently blessed each other, and agreed, henceforth, that each do his own cooking. A week later, Cuthfert neglected his morning ablutions, but none the less complacently ate the meal which he had cooked. Weatherbee grinned. After that the foolish custom of washing passed out of their lives.

As the sugar-pile and other little luxuries dwindled, they began to be afraid they were not getting their proper shares, and in order that they might not be robbed, they fell to gorging themselves. The luxuries suffered in this gluttonous contest, as did also the men.

In the absence of fresh vegetables and exercise, their blood became impoverished, and a loathsome, purplish rash crept over their bodies. Yet they refused to heed the warning.

Next, their muscles and joints began to swell, the flesh turning black, while their mouths, gums, and lips took on the color of rich cream. Instead of being drawn together by their misery, each gloated over the other's symptoms as the scurvy took its course.

They lost all regard for personal appearance, and for that matter, common decency. The cabin became a pigpen, and never once were the beds made or fresh pine boughs laid underneath. Yet they could not keep to their blankets, as they would have wished; for the frost was inexorable, and the fire box consumed much fuel. The hair of their heads and faces grew long and shaggy, while their garments would have disgusted a ragpicker. But they did not care. They were sick, and there was no one to see; besides, it was very painful to move about.

To all this was added a new trouble—the Fear of the North. This Fear was the joint child of the Great Cold and the Great Silence, and was born in the darkness of December, when the sun dipped below the horizon for good. It affected them according to their natures.

Weatherbee fell prey to the grosser superstitions, and did his best to resurrect the spirits which slept in the forgotten graves. It was a fascinating thing, and in his dreams they came to him from out of the cold, and snuggled into his blankets, and told him of their toils and troubles ere they died. He shrank away from the clammy contact as they drew closer and twined their frozen limbs about him, and when they whispered in his ear of things to come, the cabin rang with his frightened shrieks. Cuthfert did not understand —for they no longer spoke—and when thus awakened he invariably grabbed for his revolver. Then he would sit up in bed, shivering nervously, with the weapon trained on the unconscious dreamer. Cuthfert deemed the man going mad, and so came to fear for his life.

His own malady assumed a less concrete form. The mysterious artisan who had laid the cabin, log by log, had pegged a wind-vane to the ridgepole. Cuthfert noticed it always pointed south, and one day, irritated by its steadfastness of purpose, he turned it toward the east. He watched eagerly, but never a breath came by to disturb it. Then he turned the vane to the north, swearing never again to touch it till the wind did blow. But the air frightened him with its unearthly calm, and he often rose in the middle of the night to see if the vane had veered—ten degrees would have satisfied him. But no, it poised above him as unchangeable as fate.

His imagination ran riot, till it became to him a fetish. Sometimes he followed the path it pointed across the dismal dominions, and allowed his soul to become saturated with the Fear. He dwelt upon the unseen and the unknown till the burden of eternity appeared to be crushing him. Everything in the Northland had that crushing effect—the absence of life and motion; the darkness; the infinite peace of the brooding land; the ghastly silence, which made the echo of each heartbeat a sacrilege; the solemn forest which seemed to guard an awful, inexpressible something, which neither word nor thought could compass.

The world he had so recently left, with its busy nations and great enterprises, seemed very far away. Recollections occasionally obtruded—recollections of marts and galleries and crowded thoroughfares, of evening dress and social functions, of good men and dear women he had known—but they were dim memories of a life he had lived long centuries agone, on some other planet. This phantasm was the Reality. Standing beneath the wind-vane, his eyes fixed on the polar skies, he could not bring himself to realize that the Southland really existed, that at that very moment it was a-roar with life and action.

There was no Southland, no men being born of women, no giving and taking in marriage.

Beyond his bleak skyline there stretched vast solitudes, and beyond these still vaster solitudes.

There were no lands of sunshine, heavy with the perfume of flowers. Such things were only old dreams of paradise. The sunlands of the West and the spicelands of the East, the smiling Arcadias and blissful Islands of the Blest—ha! ha! His laughter split the void and shocked him with its unwonted sound. There was no sun.

This was the Universe, dead and cold and dark, and he its only citizen. Weatherbee? At such moments Weatherbee did not count. He was a Caliban, a monstrous phantom, fettered to him for untold ages, the penalty of some forgotten crime.

He lived with Death among the dead, emasculated by the sense of his own insignificance, crushed by the passive mastery of the slumbering ages. The magnitude of all things appalled him. Everything partook of the superlative save himself—the perfect cessation of wind and motion, the immensity of the snow-covered wildness, the height of the sky and the depth of the silence. That wind-vane—if it would only move. If a thunderbolt would fall, or the forest flare up in flame.

The rolling up of the heavens as a scroll, the crash of Doom—anything, anything! But no, nothing moved; the Silence crowded in, and the Fear of the North laid icy fingers on his heart.

Once, like another Crusoe, by the edge of the river he came upon a track—the faint tracery of a snowshoe rabbit on the delicate snow-crust. It was a revelation.

There was life in the Northland. He would follow it, look upon it, gloat over it.

He forgot his swollen muscles, plunging through the deep snow in an ecstasy of anticipation. The forest swallowed him up, and the brief midday twilight vanished; but he pursued his quest till exhausted nature asserted itself and laid him helpless in the snow.

There he groaned and cursed his folly, and knew the track to be the fancy of his brain; and late that night he dragged himself into the cabin on hands and knees, his cheeks frozen and a strange numbness about his feet. Weatherbee grinned malevolently, but made no offer to help him. He thrust needles into his toes and thawed them out by the stove. A week later mortification set in.

But the clerk had his own troubles. The dead men came out of their graves more frequently now, and rarely left him, waking or sleeping. He grew to wait and dread their coming, never passing the twin cairns without a shudder. One night they came to him in his sleep and led him forth to an appointed task. Frightened into inarticulate horror, he awoke between the heaps of stones and fled wildly to the cabin. But he had lain there for some time, for his feet and cheeks were also frozen.

Sometimes he became frantic at their insistent presence, and danced about the cabin, cutting the empty air with an axe, and smashing everything within reach.

During these ghostly encounters, Cuthfert huddled into his blankets and followed the madman about with a cocked revolver, ready to shoot him if he came too near.

But, recovering from one of these spells, the clerk noticed the weapon trained upon him.

His suspicions were aroused, and thenceforth he, too, lived in fear of his life. They watched each other closely after that, and faced about in startled fright whenever either passed behind the other's back. The apprehensiveness became a mania which controlled them even in their sleep. Through mutual fear they tacitly let the slush-lamp burn all night, and saw to a plentiful supply of bacon-grease before retiring. The slightest movement on the part of one was sufficient to arouse the other, and many a still watch their gazes countered as they shook beneath their blankets with fingers on the trigger-guards.

What with the Fear of the North, the mental strain, and the ravages of the disease, they lost all semblance of humanity, taking on the appearance of wild beasts, hunted and desperate. Their cheeks and noses, as an aftermath of the freezing, had turned black.

Their frozen toes had begun to drop away at the first and second joints. Every movement brought pain, but the fire box was insatiable, wringing a ransom of torture from their miserable bodies. Day in, day out, it demanded its food—a veritable pound of flesh—and they dragged themselves into the forest to chop wood on their knees. Once, crawling thus in search of dry sticks, unknown to each other they entered a thicket from opposite sides.

Suddenly, without warning, two peering death's-heads confronted each other. Suffering had so transformed them that recognition was impossible. They sprang to their feet, shrieking with terror, and dashed away on their mangled stumps; and falling at the cabin's door, they clawed and scratched like demons till they discovered their mistake.

Occasionally they lapsed normal, and during one of these sane intervals, the chief bone of contention, the sugar, had been divided equally between them. They guarded their separate sacks, stored up in the cache, with jealous eyes; for there were but a few cupfuls left, and they were totally devoid of faith in each other.

But one day Cuthfert made a mistake. Hardly able to move, sick with pain, with his head swimming and eyes blinded, he crept into the cache, sugar canister in hand, and mistook Weatherbee's sack for his own.

January had been born but a few days when this occurred. The sun had some time since passed its lowest southern declination, and at meridian now threw flaunting streaks of yellow light upon the northern sky. On the day following his mistake with the sugar-bag, Cuthfert found himself feeling better, both in body and in spirit. As noontime drew near and the day brightened, he dragged himself outside to feast on the evanescent glow, which was to him an earnest of the sun's future intentions. Weatherbee was also feeling somewhat better, and crawled out beside him. They propped themselves in the snow beneath the moveless wind-vane, and waited.

The stillness of death was about them. In other climes, when nature falls into such moods, there is a subdued air of expectancy, a waiting for some small voice to take up the broken strain. Not so in the North. The two men had lived seeming eons in this ghostly peace.

They could remember no song of the past; they could conjure no song of the future. This unearthly calm had always been—the tranquil silence of eternity.

Their eyes were fixed upon the north. Unseen, behind their backs, behind the towering mountains to the south, the sun swept toward the zenith of another sky than theirs. Sole spectators of the mighty canvas, they watched the false dawn slowly grow. A faint flame began to glow and smoulder. It deepened in intensity, ringing the changes of reddish-yellow, purple, and saffron. So bright did it become that Cuthfert thought the sun must surely be behind it—a miracle, the sun rising in the north! Suddenly, without warning and without fading, the canvas was swept clean. There was no color in the sky. The light had gone out of the day.

They caught their breaths in half-sobs. But lo! the air was aglint with particles of scintillating frost, and there, to the north, the wind-vane lay in vague outline of the snow.

A shadow! A shadow! It was exactly midday. They jerked their heads hurriedly to the south. A golden rim peeped over the mountain's snowy shoulder, smiled upon them an instant, then dipped from sight again.

There were tears in their eyes as they sought each other. A strange softening came over them. They felt irresistibly drawn toward each other. The sun was coming back again. It would be with them tomorrow, and the next day, and the next.

And it would stay longer every visit, and a time would come when it would ride their heaven day and night, never once dropping below the skyline. There would be no night.

The ice-locked winter would be broken; the winds would blow and the forests answer; the land would bathe in the blessed sunshine, and life renew.

Hand in hand, they would quit this horrid dream and journey back to the Southland.

They lurched blindly forward, and their hands met—their poor maimed hands, swollen and distorted beneath their mittens.

But the promise was destined to remain unfulfilled. The Northland is the Northland, and men work out their souls by strange rules, which other men, who have not journeyed into far countries, cannot come to understand.

An hour later, Cuthfert put a pan of bread into the oven, and fell to speculating on what the surgeons could do with his feet when he got back. Home did not seem so very far away now. Weatherbee was rummaging in the cache. Of a sudden, he raised a whirlwind of blasphemy, which in turn ceased with startling abruptness. The other man had robbed his sugar-sack. Still, things might have happened differently, had not the two dead men come out from under the stones and hushed the hot words in his throat. They led him quite gently from the cache, which he forgot to close. That consummation was reached; that something they had whispered to him in his dreams was about to happen. They guided him gently, very gently, to the woodpile, where they put the axe in his hands.

Then they helped him shove open the cabin door, and he felt sure they shut it after him—at least he heard it slam and the latch fall sharply into place. And he knew they were waiting just without, waiting for him to do his task.

'Carter! I say, Carter!' Percy Cuthfert was frightened at the look on the clerk's face, and he made haste to put the table between them.

Carter Weatherbee followed, without haste and without enthusiasm. There was neither pity nor passion in his face, but rather the patient, stolid look of one who has certain work to do and goes about it methodically.

'I say, what's the matter?'

The clerk dodged back, cutting off his retreat to the door, but never opening his mouth.

'I say, Carter, I say; let's talk. There's a good chap.' The master of arts was thinking rapidly, now, shaping a skillful flank movement on the bed where his Smith & Wesson lay. Keeping his eyes on the madman, he rolled backward on the bunk, at the same time clutching the pistol.

'Carter!' The powder flashed full in Weatherbee's face, but he swung his weapon and leaped forward. The axe bit deeply at the base of the spine, and Percy Cuthfert felt all consciousness of his lower limbs leave him. Then the clerk fell heavily upon him, clutching him by the throat with feeble fingers. The sharp bite of the axe had caused Cuthfert to drop the pistol, and as his lungs panted for release, he fumbled aimlessly for it among the blankets. Then he remembered. He slid a hand up the clerk's belt to the sheath-knife; and they drew very close to each other in that last clinch.

Percy Cuthfert felt his strength leave him. The lower portion of his body was useless, The inert weight of Weatherbee crushed him—crushed him and pinned him there like a bear under a trap. The cabin became filled with a familiar odor, and he knew the bread to be burning. Yet what did it matter? He would never need it. And there were all of six cupfuls of sugar in the cache—if he had foreseen this he would not have been so saving the last several days. Would the wind-vane ever move? Why not' Had he not seen the sun today? He would go and see. No; it was impossible to move. He had not thought the clerk so heavy a man.

How quickly the cabin cooled! The fire must be out. The cold was forcing in.

It must be below zero already, and the ice creeping up the inside of the door. He could not see it, but his past experience enabled him to gauge its progress by the cabin's temperature. The lower hinge must be white ere now. Would the tale of this ever reach the world? How would his friends take it? They would read it over their coffee, most likely, and talk it over at the clubs. He could see them very clearly, 'Poor Old Cuthfert,' they murmured; 'not such a bad sort of a chap, after all.' He smiled at their eulogies, and passed on in search of a Turkish bath. It was the same old crowd upon the streets.

Strange, they did not notice his moosehide moccasins and tattered German socks! He would take a cab. And after the bath a shave would not be bad. No; he would eat first.

Steak, and potatoes, and green things how fresh it all was! And what was that? Squares of honey, streaming liquid amber! But why did they bring so much? Ha! ha! he could never eat it all.

Shine! Why certainly. He put his foot on the box. The bootblack looked curiously up at him, and he remembered his moosehide moccasins and went away hastily.

Hark! The wind-vane must be surely spinning. No; a mere singing in his ears.

That was all—a mere singing. The ice must have passed the latch by now. More likely the upper hinge was covered. Between the moss-chinked roof-poles, little points of frost began to appear. How slowly they grew! No; not so slowly. There was a new one, and there another. Two—three—four; they were coming too fast to count. There were two growing together. And there, a third had joined them.

Why, there were no more spots. They had run together and formed a sheet.

Well, he would have company. If Gabriel ever broke the silence of the North, they would stand together, hand in hand, before the great White Throne. And God would judge them, God would judge them!

Then Percy Cuthfert closed his eyes and dropped off to sleep.

TO THE MAN ON THE TRAIL

'DUMP IT IN!.' 'But I say, Kid, isn't that going it a little too strong? Whisky and alcohol's bad enough; but when it comes to brandy and pepper sauce and-' 'Dump it in. Who's making this punch, anyway?' And Malemute Kid smiled benignantly through the clouds of steam. 'By the time you've been in this country as long as I have, my son, and lived on rabbit tracks and salmon belly, you'll learn that Christmas comes only once per annum. And a Christmas without punch is sinking a hole to bedrock with nary a pay streak.'

'Stack up on that fer a high cyard,' approved Big Jim Belden, who had come down from his claim on Mazy May to spend Christmas, and who, as everyone knew, had been living the two months past on straight moose meat. 'Hain't fergot the hooch we-uns made on the Tanana, hey yeh?' 'Well, I guess yes. Boys, it would have done your hearts good to see that whole tribe fighting drunk—and all because of a glorious ferment of sugar and sour dough. That was before your time,' Malemute Kid said as he turned to Stanley Prince, a young mining expert who had been in two years. 'No white women in the country then, and Mason wanted to get married. Ruth's father was chief of the Tananas, and objected, like the rest of the tribe. Stiff? Why, I used my last pound of sugar; finest work in that line I ever did in my life. You should have seen the chase, down the river and across the portage.' 'But the squaw?' asked Louis Savoy, the tall French Canadian, becoming interested; for he had heard of this wild deed when at Forty Mile the preceding winter.

Then Malemute Kid, who was a born raconteur, told the unvarnished tale of the Northland Lochinvar. More than one rough adventurer of the North felt his heartstrings draw closer and experienced vague yearnings for the sunnier pastures of the Southland, where life promised something more than a barren struggle with cold and death.

'We struck the Yukon just behind the first ice run,' he concluded, 'and the tribe only a quarter of an hour behind. But that saved us; for the second run broke the jam above and shut them out. When they finally got into Nuklukyeto, the whole post was ready for them.

'And as to the forgathering, ask Father Roubeau here: he performed the ceremony.' The Jesuit took the pipe from his lips but could only express his gratification with patriarchal smiles, while Protestant and Catholic vigorously applauded.

'By gar!' ejaculated Louis Savoy, who seemed overcome by the romance of it. 'La petite squaw: mon Mason brav. By gar!' Then, as the first tin cups of punch went round, Bettles the Unquenchable sprang to his feet and struck up his favorite drinking song: 'There's Henry Ward Beecher And Sunday-school teachers, All drink of the sassafras root; But you bet all the same, If it had its right name, It's the juice of the forbidden fruit.'

'Oh, the juice of the forbidden fruit,' roared out the bacchanalian chorus, 'Oh, the juice of the forbidden fruit; But you bet all the same, If it had its right name, It's the juice of the forbidden fruit.'

Malemute Kid's frightful concoction did its work; the men of the camps and trails unbent in its genial glow, and jest and song and tales of past adventure went round the board.

Aliens from a dozen lands, they toasted each and all. It was the Englishman, Prince, who pledged 'Uncle Sam, the precocious infant of the New World'; the Yankee, Bettles, who drank to 'The Queen, God bless her'; and together, Savoy and Meyers, the German trader, clanged their cups to Alsace and Lorraine.

Then Malemute Kid arose, cup in hand, and glanced at the greased-paper window, where the frost stood full three inches thick. 'A health to the man on trail this night; may his grub hold out; may his dogs keep their legs; may his matches never miss fire.' Crack!

Crack! heard the familiar music of the dog whip, the whining howl of the Malemutes, and the crunch of a sled as it drew up to the cabin. Conversation languished while they waited the issue.

'An old-timer; cares for his dogs and then himself,' whispered Malemute Kid to Prince as they listened to the snapping jaws and the wolfish snarls and yelps of pain which proclaimed to their practiced ears that the stranger was beating back their dogs while he fed his own.

Then came the expected knock, sharp and confident, and the stranger entered.

Dazzled by the light, he hesitated a moment at the door, giving to all a chance for scrutiny. He was a striking personage, and a most picturesque one, in his Arctic dress of wool and fur. Standing six foot two or three, with proportionate breadth of shoulders and depth of chest, his smooth-shaven face nipped by the cold to a gleaming pink, his long lashes and eyebrows white with ice, and the ear and neck flaps of his great wolfskin cap loosely raised, he seemed, of a verity, the Frost King, just stepped in out of the night.

Clasped outside his Mackinaw jacket, a beaded belt held two large Colt's revolvers and a hunting knife, while he carried, in addition to the inevitable dog whip, a smokeless rifle of the largest bore and latest pattern. As he came forward, for all his step was firm and elastic, they could see that fatigue bore heavily upon him.

An awkward silence had fallen, but his hearty 'What cheer, my lads?' put them quickly at ease, and the next instant Malemute Kid and he had gripped hands. Though they had never met, each had heard of the other, and the recognition was mutual. A sweeping introduction and a mug of punch were forced upon him before he could explain his errand.

How long since that basket sled, with three men and eight dogs, passed?' he asked.

'An even two days ahead. Are you after them?' 'Yes; my team. Run them off under my very nose, the cusses. I've gained two days on them already—pick them up on the next run.' 'Reckon they'll show spunk?' asked Belden, in order to keep up the conversation, for Malemute Kid already had the coffeepot on and was busily frying bacon and moose meat.

The stranger significantly tapped his revolvers.

'When'd yeh leave Dawson?' 'Twelve o'clock.' 'Last night?'—as a matter of course.

'Today.' A murmur of surprise passed round the circle. And well it might; for it was just midnight, and seventy-five miles of rough river trail was not to be sneered at for a twelve hours' run.

The talk soon became impersonal, however, harking back to the trails of childhood. As the young stranger ate of the rude fare Malemute Kid attentively studied his face. Nor was he long in deciding that it was fair, honest, and open, and that he liked it. Still youthful, the lines had been firmly traced by toil and hardship.

Though genial in conversation, and mild when at rest, the blue eyes gave promise of the hard steel-glitter which comes when called into action, especially against odds. The heavy jaw and square-cut chin demonstrated rugged pertinacity and indomitability. Nor, though the attributes of the lion were there, was there wanting the certain softness, the hint of womanliness, which bespoke the emotional nature.

'So thet's how me an' the ol' woman got spliced,' said Belden, concluding the exciting tale of his courtship. '"Here we be, Dad," sez she. "An' may yeh be damned," sez he to her, an' then to me, "Jim, yeh—yeh git outen them good duds o' yourn; I want a right peart slice o' thet forty acre plowed 'fore dinner." An' then he sort o' sniffled an' kissed her. An' I was thet happy—but he seen me an' roars out, "Yeh, Jim!" An' yeh bet I dusted fer the barn.' 'Any kids waiting for you back in the States?' asked the stranger.

'Nope; Sal died 'fore any come. Thet's why I'm here.' Belden abstractedly began to light his pipe, which had failed to go out, and then brightened up with, 'How 'bout yerself, stranger—married man?' For reply, he opened his watch, slipped it from the thong which served for a chain, and passed it over. Belden picked up the slush lamp, surveyed the inside of the case critically, and, swearing admiringly to himself, handed it over to Louis Savoy. With numerous 'By gars!' he finally surrendered it to Prince, and they noticed that his hands trembled and his eyes took on a peculiar softness. And so it passed from horny hand to horny hand—the pasted photograph of a woman, the clinging kind that such men fancy, with a babe at the breast. Those who had not yet seen the wonder were keen with curiosity; those who had became silent and retrospective. They could face the pinch of famine, the grip of scurvy, or the quick death by field or flood; but the pictured semblance of a stranger woman and child made women and children of them all.

'Never have seen the youngster yet—he's a boy, she says, and two years old,' said the stranger as he received the treasure back. A lingering moment he gazed upon it, then snapped the case and turned away, but not quick enough to hide the restrained rush of tears. Malemute Kid led him to a bunk and bade him turn in.

'Call me at four sharp. Don't fail me,' were his last words, and a moment later he was breathing in the heaviness of exhausted sleep.

'By Jove! He's a plucky chap,' commented Prince. 'Three hours' sleep after seventy-five miles with the dogs, and then the trail again. Who is he, Kid?' 'Jack Westondale. Been in going on three years, with nothing but the name of working like a horse, and any amount of bad luck to his credit. I never knew him, but Sitka Charley told me about him.' 'It seems hard that a man with a sweet young wife like his should be putting in his years in this Godforsaken hole, where every year counts two on the outside.' 'The trouble with him is clean grit and stubbornness. He's cleaned up twice with a stake, but lost it both times.' Here the conversation was broken off by an uproar from Bettles, for the effect had begun to wear away. And soon the bleak years of monotonous grub and deadening toil were being forgotten in rough merriment. Malemute Kid alone seemed unable to lose himself, and cast many an anxious look at his watch. Once he put on his mittens and beaver-skin cap, and, leaving the cabin, fell to rummaging about in the cache.

Nor could he wait the hour designated; for he was fifteen minutes ahead of time in rousing his guest. The young giant had stiffened badly, and brisk rubbing was necessary to bring him to his feet. He tottered painfully out of the cabin, to find his dogs harnessed and everything ready for the start. The company wished him good luck and a short chase, while Father Roubeau, hurriedly blessing him, led the stampede for the cabin; and small wonder, for it is not good to face seventy-four degrees below zero with naked ears and hands.

Malemute Kid saw him to the main trail, and there, gripping his hand heartily, gave him advice.

'You'll find a hundred pounds of salmon eggs on the sled,' he said. 'The dogs will go as far on that as with one hundred and fifty of fish, and you can't get dog food at Pelly, as you probably expected.' The stranger started, and his eyes flashed, but he did not interrupt. 'You can't get an ounce of food for dog or man till you reach Five Fingers, and that's a stiff two hundred miles. Watch out for open water on the Thirty Mile River, and be sure you take the big cutoff above Le Barge.' 'How did you know it? Surely the news can't be ahead of me already?' 'I don't know it; and what's more, I don't want to know it. But you never owned that team you're chasing. Sitka Charley sold it to them last spring. But he sized you up to me as square once, and I believe him. I've seen your face; I like it. And I've seen—why, damn you, hit the high places for salt water and that wife of yours, and—' Here the Kid unmittened and jerked out his sack.

'No; I don't need it,' and the tears froze on his cheeks as he convulsively gripped Malemute Kid's hand.

'Then don't spare the dogs; cut them out of the traces as fast as they drop; buy them, and think they're cheap at ten dollars a pound. You can get them at Five Fingers, Little Salmon, and Hootalinqua. And watch out for wet feet,' was his parting advice. 'Keep a-traveling up to twenty-five, but if it gets below that, build a fire and change your socks.'

Fifteen minutes had barely elapsed when the jingle of bells announced new arrivals. The door opened, and a mounted policeman of the Northwest Territory entered, followed by two half-breed dog drivers. Like Westondale, they were heavily armed and showed signs of fatigue. The half-breeds had been born to the trail and bore it easily; but the young policeman was badly exhausted. Still, the dogged obstinacy of his race held him to the pace he had set, and would hold him till he dropped in his tracks.

'When did Westondale pull out?' he asked. 'He stopped here, didn't he?' This was supererogatory, for the tracks told their own tale too well.

Malemute Kid had caught Belden's eye, and he, scenting the wind, replied evasively, 'A right peart while back.' 'Come, my man; speak up,' the policeman admonished.

'Yeh seem to want him right smart. Hez he ben gittin' cantankerous down Dawson way?'

'Held up Harry McFarland's for forty thousand; exchanged it at the P.C. store for a check on Seattle; and who's to stop the cashing of it if we don't overtake him? When did he pull out?'

Every eye suppressed its excitement, for Malemute Kid had given the cue, and the young officer encountered wooden faces on every hand.

Striding over to Prince, he put the question to him. Though it hurt him, gazing into the frank, earnest face of his fellow countryman, he replied inconsequentially on the state of the trail.

Then he espied Father Roubeau, who could not lie. 'A quarter of an hour ago,' the priest answered; 'but he had four hours' rest for himself and dogs.' 'Fifteen minutes' start, and he's fresh! My God!' The poor fellow staggered back, half fainting from exhaustion and disappointment, murmuring something about the run from Dawson in ten hours and the dogs being played out.

Malemute Kid forced a mug of punch upon him; then he turned for the door, ordering the dog drivers to follow. But the warmth and promise of rest were too tempting, and they objected strenuously. The Kid was conversant with their French patois, and followed it anxiously.

They swore that the dogs were gone up; that Siwash and Babette would have to be shot before the first mile was covered; that the rest were almost as bad; and that it would be better for all hands to rest up.

'Lend me five dogs?' he asked, turning to Malemute Kid.

But the Kid shook his head.

'I'll sign a check on Captain Constantine for five thousand—here's my papers—I'm authorized to draw at my own discretion.'

Again the silent refusal.

'Then I'll requisition them in the name of the Queen.' Smiling incredulously, the Kid glanced at his well-stocked arsenal, and the Englishman, realizing his impotency, turned for the door. But the dog drivers still objecting, he whirled upon them fiercely, calling them women and curs. The swart face of the older half-breed flushed angrily as he drew himself up and promised in good, round terms that he would travel his leader off his legs, and would then be delighted to plant him in the snow.

The young officer—and it required his whole will—walked steadily to the door, exhibiting a freshness he did not possess. But they all knew and appreciated his proud effort; nor could he veil the twinges of agony that shot across his face. Covered with frost, the dogs were curled up in the snow, and it was almost impossible to get them to their feet. The poor brutes whined under the stinging lash, for the dog drivers were angry and cruel; nor till Babette, the leader, was cut from the traces, could they break out the sled and get under way.

'A dirty scoundrel and a liar!' 'By gar! Him no good!' 'A thief!' 'Worse than an Indian!'

It was evident that they were angry—first at the way they had been deceived; and second at the outraged ethics of the Northland, where honesty, above all, was man's prime jewel.

'An' we gave the cuss a hand, after knowin' what he'd did.' All eyes turned accusingly upon Malemute Kid, who rose from the corner where he had been making Babette comfortable, and silently emptied the bowl for a final round of punch.

'It's a cold night, boys—a bitter cold night,' was the irrelevant commencement of his defense. 'You've all traveled trail, and know what that stands for. Don't jump a dog when he's down. You've only heard one side. A whiter man than Jack Westondale never ate from the same pot nor stretched blanket with you or me.

'Last fall he gave his whole clean-up, forty thousand, to Joe Castrell, to buy in on Dominion. Today he'd be a millionaire. But, while he stayed behind at Circle City, taking care of his partner with the scurvy, what does Castell do? Goes into McFarland's, jumps the limit, and drops the whole sack. Found him dead in the snow the next day. And poor Jack laying his plans to go out this winter to his wife and the boy he's never seen. You'll notice he took exactly what his partner lost—forty thousand. Well, he's gone out; and what are you going to do about it?' The Kid glanced round the circle of his judges, noted the softening of their faces, then raised his mug aloft. 'So a health to the man on trail this night; may his grub hold out; may his dogs keep their legs; may his matches never miss fire.

'God prosper him; good luck go with him; and—' 'Confusion to the Mounted Police!' cried Bettles, to the crash of the empty cups.

THE PRIESTLY PREROGATIVE

THIS IS the story of a man who did not appreciate his wife; also, of a woman who did him too great an honor when she gave herself to him. Incidentally, it concerns a Jesuit priest who had never been known to lie. He was an appurtenance, and a very necessary one, to the Yukon country; but the presence of the other two was merely accidental. They were specimens of the many strange waifs which ride the breast of a gold rush or come tailing along behind.

Edwin Bentham and Grace Bentham were waifs; they were also tailing along behind, for the Klondike rush of '97 had long since swept down the great river and subsided into the famine-stricken city of Dawson. When the Yukon shut up shop and went to sleep under a three-foot ice-sheet, this peripatetic couple found themselves at the Five Finger Rapids, with the City of Gold still a journey of many sleeps to the north.

Many cattle had been butchered at this place in the fall of the year, and the offal made a goodly heap. The three fellow-voyagers of Edwin Bentham and wife gazed upon this deposit, did a little mental arithmetic, caught a certain glimpse of a bonanza, and decided to remain. And all winter they sold sacks of bones and frozen hides to the famished dog-teams. It was a modest price they asked, a dollar a pound, just as it came. Six months later, when the sun came back and the Yukon awoke, they buckled on their heavy moneybelts and journeyed back to the Southland, where they yet live and lie mightily about the Klondike they never saw.

But Edwin Bentham—he was an indolent fellow, and had he not been possessed of a wife, would have gladly joined issued in the dog-meat speculation. As it was, she played upon his vanity, told him how great and strong he was, how a man such as he certainly was could overcome all obstacles and of a surety obtain the Golden Fleece. So he squared his jaw, sold his share in the bones and hides for a sled and one dog, and turned his snowshoes to the north. Needless to state, Grace Bentham's snowshoes never allowed his tracks to grow cold. Nay, ere their tribulations had seen three days, it was the man who followed in the rear, and the woman who broke trail in advance. Of course, if anybody hove in sight, the position was instantly reversed. Thus did his manhood remain virgin to the travelers who passed like ghosts on the silent trail. There are such men in this world.

How such a man and such a woman came to take each other for better and for worse is unimportant to this narrative. These things are familiar to us all, and those people who do them, or even question them too closely, are apt to lose a beautiful faith which is known as Eternal Fitness.

Edwin Bentham was a boy, thrust by mischance into a man's body,—a boy who could complacently pluck a butterfly, wing from wing, or cower in abject terror before a lean, nervy fellow, not half his size. He was a selfish cry-baby, hidden behind a man's mustache and stature, and glossed over with a skin-deep veneer of culture and conventionality. Yes; he was a clubman and a society man, the sort that grace social functions and utter inanities with a charm and unction which is indescribable; the sort that talk big, and cry over a toothache; the sort that put more hell into a woman's life by marrying her than can the most graceless liber-tine that ever browsed in forbidden pastures. We meet these men every day, but we rarely know them for what they are. Second to marrying them, the best way to get this knowledge is to eat out of the same pot and crawl under the same blanket with them for—well, say a week; no greater margin is necessary.

To see Grace Bentham, was to see a slender, girlish creature; to know her, was to know a soul which dwarfed your own, yet retained all the elements of the eternal feminine. This was the woman who urged and encouraged her husband in his Northland quest, who broke trail for him when no one was looking, and cried in secret over her weakling woman's body.

So journeyed this strangely assorted couple down to old Fort Selkirk, then through fivescore miles of dismal wilderness to Stuart River. And when the short day left them, and the man lay down in the snow and blubbered, it was the woman who lashed him to the sled, bit her lips with the pain of her aching limbs, and helped the dog haul him to Malemute Kid's cabin. Malemute Kid was not at home, but Meyers, the German trader, cooked great moose-steaks and shook up a bed of fresh pine boughs. Lake, Langham, and Parker, were excited, and not unduly so when the cause was taken into account.

'Oh, Sandy! Say, can you tell a porterhouse from a round? Come out and lend us a hand, anyway!' This appeal emanated from the cache, where Langham was vainly struggling with divers quarters of frozen moose.

'Don't you budge from those dishes!' commanded Parker.

'I say, Sandy; there's a good fellow—just run down to the Missouri Camp and borrow some cinnamon,' begged Lake.

'Oh! oh! hurry up! Why don't—' But the crash of meat and boxes, in the cache, abruptly quenched this peremptory summons.

'Come now, Sandy; it won't take a minute to go down to the Missouri—'

'You leave him alone,' interrupted Parker. 'How am I to mix the biscuits if the table isn't cleared off?'

Sandy paused in indecision, till suddenly the fact that he was Langham's 'man' dawned upon him. Then he apologetically threw down the greasy dishcloth, and went to his master's rescue.

These promising scions of wealthy progenitors had come to the Northland in search of laurels, with much money to burn, and a 'man' apiece. Luckily for their souls, the other two men were up the White River in search of a mythical quartz-ledge; so Sandy had to grin under the responsibility of three healthy masters, each of whom was possessed of peculiar cookery ideas. Twice that morning had a disruption of the whole camp been imminent, only averted by immense concessions from one or the other of these knights of the chafing-dish. But at last their mutual creation, a really dainty dinner, was completed.

Then they sat down to a three-cornered game of 'cut-throat,'—a proceeding which did away with all casus belli for future hostilities, and permitted the victor to depart on a most important mission.

This fortune fell to Parker, who parted his hair in the middle, put on his mittens and bearskin cap, and stepped over to Malemute Kid's cabin. And when he returned, it was in the company of Grace Bentham and Malemute Kid,—the former very sorry her husband could not share with her their hospitality, for he had gone up to look at the Henderson Creek mines, and the latter still a trifle stiff from breaking trail down the Stuart River.

Meyers had been asked, but had declined, being deeply engrossed in an experiment of raising bread from hops.

Well, they could do without the husband; but a woman—why they had not seen one all winter, and the presence of this one promised a new era in their lives.

They were college men and gentlemen, these three young fellows, yearning for the flesh-pots they had been so long denied. Probably Grace Bentham suffered from a similar hunger; at least, it meant much to her, the first bright hour in many weeks of darkness.

But that wonderful first course, which claimed the versatile Lake for its parent, had no sooner been served than there came a loud knock at the door.

'Oh! Ah! Won't you come in, Mr. Bentham?' said Parker, who had stepped to see who the newcomer might be.

'Is my wife here?' gruffly responded that worthy.

'Why, yes. We left word with Mr. Meyers.' Parker was exerting his most dulcet tones, inwardly wondering what the deuce it all meant. 'Won't you come in? Expecting you at any moment, we reserved a place. And just in time for the first course, too.' 'Come in, Edwin, dear,' chirped Grace Bentham from her seat at the table.

Parker naturally stood aside.

'I want my wife,' reiterated Bentham hoarsely, the intonation savoring disagreeably of ownership.

Parker gasped, was within an ace of driving his fist into the face of his boorish visitor, but held himself awkwardly in check. Everybody rose. Lake lost his head and caught himself on the verge of saying, 'Must you go?' Then began the farrago of leave-taking. 'So nice of you—' 'I am awfully sorry' 'By Jove! how things did brighten—' 'Really now, you—' 'Thank you ever so much—' 'Nice trip to Dawson—' etc., etc.

In this wise the lamb was helped into her jacket and led to the slaughter. Then the door slammed, and they gazed woefully upon the deserted table.

'Damn!' Langham had suffered disadvantages in his early training, and his oaths were weak and monotonous. 'Damn!' he repeated, vaguely conscious of the incompleteness and vainly struggling for a more virile term. It is a clever woman who can fill out the many weak places in an inefficient man, by her own indomitability, re-enforce his vacillating nature, infuse her ambitious soul into his, and spur him on to great achievements. And it is indeed a very clever and tactful woman who can do all this, and do it so subtly that the man receives all the credit and believes in his inmost heart that everything is due to him and him alone.

This is what Grace Bentham proceeded to do. Arriving in Dawson with a few pounds of flour and several letters of introduction, she at once applied herself to the task of pushing her big baby to the fore. It was she who melted the stony heart and wrung credit from the rude barbarian who presided over the destiny of the P. C. Company; yet it was Edwin Bentham to whom the concession was ostensibly granted. It was she who dragged her baby up and down creeks, over benches and divides, and on a dozen wild stampedes; yet everybody remarked what an energetic fellow that Bentham was. It was she who studied maps, and catechised miners, and hammered geography and locations into his hollow head, till everybody marveled at his broad grasp of the country and knowledge of its conditions. Of course, they said the wife was a brick, and only a few wise ones appreciated and pitied the brave little woman.

She did the work; he got the credit and reward. In the Northwest Territory a married woman cannot stake or record a creek, bench, or quartz claim; so Edwin Bentham went down to the Gold Commissioner and filed on Bench Claim 23, second tier, of French Hill. And when April came they were washing out a thousand dollars a day, with many, many such days in prospect.

At the base of French Hill lay Eldorado Creek, and on a creek claim stood the cabin of Clyde Wharton. At present he was not washing out a diurnal thousand dollars; but his dumps grew, shift by shift, and there would come a time when those dumps would pass through his sluice-boxes, depositing in the riffles, in the course of half a dozen days, several hundred thousand dollars. He often sat in that cabin, smoked his pipe, and dreamed beautiful little dreams,—dreams in which neither the dumps nor the half-ton of dust in the P. C. Company's big safe, played a part.

And Grace Bentham, as she washed tin dishes in her hillside cabin, often glanced down into Eldorado Creek, and dreamed,—not of dumps nor dust, however. They met frequently, as the trail to the one claim crossed the other, and there is much to talk about in the North-land spring; but never once, by the light of an eye nor the slip of a tongue, did they speak their hearts.

This is as it was at first. But one day Edwin Bentham was brutal. All boys are thus; besides, being a French Hill king now, he began to think a great deal of himself and to forget all he owed to his wife. On this day, Wharton heard of it, and waylaid Grace Bentham, and talked wildly. This made her very happy, though she would not listen, and made him promise to not say such things again. Her hour had not come.

But the sun swept back on its northern journey, the black of midnight changed to the steely color of dawn, the snow slipped away, the water dashed again over the glacial drift, and the wash-up began. Day and night the yellow clay and scraped bedrock hurried through the swift sluices, yielding up its ransom to the strong men from the Southland.

And in that time of tumult came Grace Bentham's hour.

To all of us such hours at some time come,—that is, to us who are not too phlegmatic. Some people are good, not from inherent love of virtue, but from sheer laziness. But those of us who know weak moments may understand.

Edwin Bentham was weighing dust over the bar of the saloon at the Forks—altogether too much of his dust went over that pine board—when his wife came down the hill and slipped into Clyde Wharton's cabin. Wharton was not expecting her, but that did not alter the case. And much subsequent misery and idle waiting might have been avoided, had not Father Roubeau seen this and turned aside from the main creek trail. 'My child,—' 'Hold on, Father Roubeau! Though I'm not of your faith, I respect you; but you can't come in between this woman and me!' 'You know what you are doing?' 'Know! Were you God Almighty, ready to fling me into eternal fire, I'd bank my will against yours in this matter.' Wharton had placed Grace on a stool and stood belligerently before her.

'You sit down on that chair and keep quiet,' he continued, addressing the Jesuit. 'I'll take my innings now. You can have yours after.'

Father Roubeau bowed courteously and obeyed. He was an easy-going man and had learned to bide his time. Wharton pulled a stool alongside the woman's, smothering her hand in his.

'Then you do care for me, and will take me away?' Her face seemed to reflect the peace of this man, against whom she might draw close for shelter.

'Dear, don't you remember what I said before? Of course I-' 'But how can you?—the wash-up?' 'Do you think that worries? Anyway, I'll give the job to Father Roubeau, here. 'I can trust him to safely bank the dust with the company.' 'To think of it!—I'll never see him again.' 'A blessing!' 'And to go—O, Clyde, I can't! I can't!' 'There, there; of course you can, just let me plan it.—You see, as soon as we get a few traps together, we'll start, and-' 'Suppose he comes back?' 'I'll break every-' 'No, no! No fighting, Clyde! Promise me that.' 'All right! I'll just tell the men to throw him off the claim. They've seen how he's treated you, and haven't much love for him.'

'You mustn't do that. You mustn't hurt him.' 'What then? Let him come right in here and take you away before my eyes?' 'No-o,' she half whispered, stroking his hand softly.

'Then let me run it, and don't worry. I'll see he doesn't get hurt. Precious lot he cared whether you got hurt or not! We won't go back to Dawson. I'll send word down for a couple of the boys to outfit and pole a boat up the Yukon. We'll cross the divide and raft down the Indian River to meet them. Then—' 'And then?' Her head was on his shoulder.

Their voices sank to softer cadences, each word a caress. The Jesuit fidgeted nervously.

'And then?' she repeated.

'Why we'll pole up, and up, and up, and portage the White Horse Rapids and the Box Canon.' 'Yes?' 'And the Sixty-Mile River; then the lakes, Chilcoot, Dyea, and Salt Water.' 'But, dear, I can't pole a boat.' 'You little goose! I'll get Sitka Charley; he knows all the good water and best camps, and he is the best traveler I ever met, if he is an Indian. All you'll have to do, is to sit in the middle of the boat, and sing songs, and play Cleopatra, and fight—no, we're in luck; too early for mosquitoes.'

'And then, O my Antony?' 'And then a steamer, San Francisco, and the world! Never to come back to this cursed hole again. Think of it! The world, and ours to choose from! I'll roll out. Why, we're rich! The Waldworth Syndicate will give me half a million for what's left in the ground, and I've got twice as much in the dumps and with the P. C. Company. We'll go to the Fair in Paris in 1900. We'll go to Jerusalem, if you say so.

'We'll buy an Italian palace, and you can play Cleopatra to your heart's content. No, you shall be Lucretia, Acte, or anybody your little heart sees fit to become. But you mustn't, you really mustn't-' 'The wife of Caesar shall be above reproach.' 'Of course, but—' 'But I won't be your wife, will I, dear?' 'I didn't mean that.' 'But you'll love me just as much, and never even think—oh! I know you'll be like other men; you'll grow tired, and—and-'

'How can you? I—' 'Promise me.' 'Yes, yes; I do promise.' 'You say it so easily, dear; but how do you know?—or I know? I have so little to give, yet it is so much, and all I have. O, Clyde! promise me you won't?'

'There, there! You mustn't begin to doubt already. Till death do us part, you know.'

'Think! I once said that to—to him, and now?' 'And now, little sweetheart, you're not to bother about such things any more.

Of course, I never, never will, and—' And for the first time, lips trembled against lips.

Father Roubeau had been watching the main trail through the window, but could stand the strain no longer.

He cleared his throat and turned around.

'Your turn now, Father!' Wharton's face was flushed with the fire of his first embrace.

There was an exultant ring to his voice as he abdicated in the other's favor. He had no doubt as to the result. Neither had Grace, for a smile played about her mouth as she faced the priest.

'My child,' he began, 'my heart bleeds for you. It is a pretty dream, but it cannot be.'

'And why, Father? I have said yes.' 'You knew not what you did. You did not think of the oath you took, before your God, to that man who is your husband. It remains for me to make you realize the sanctity of such a pledge.' 'And if I do realize, and yet refuse?'

'Then God'

'Which God? My husband has a God which I care not to worship. There must be many such.' 'Child! unsay those words! Ah! you do not mean them. I understand. I, too, have had such moments.' For an instant he was back in his native France, and a wistful, sad-eyed face came as a mist between him and the woman before him.

'Then, Father, has my God forsaken me? I am not wicked above women. My misery with him has been great. Why should it be greater? Why shall I not grasp at happiness? I cannot, will not, go back to him!' 'Rather is your God forsaken. Return. Throw your burden upon Him, and the darkness shall be lifted. O my child,—' 'No; it is useless; I have made my bed and so shall I lie. I will go on. And if God punishes me, I shall bear it somehow. You do not understand. You are not a woman.' 'My mother was a woman.'

'But—' 'And Christ was born of a woman.' She did not answer. A silence fell. Wharton pulled his mustache impatiently and kept an eye on the trail. Grace leaned her elbow on the table, her face set with resolve. The smile had died away. Father Roubeau shifted his ground.

'You have children?'

'At one time I wished—but now—no. And I am thankful.' 'And a mother?' 'Yes.' 'She loves you?' 'Yes.' Her replies were whispers.

'And a brother?—no matter, he is a man. But a sister?' Her head drooped a quavering 'Yes.' 'Younger? Very much?' 'Seven years.' 'And you have thought well about this matter? About them? About your mother? And your sister? She stands on the threshold of her woman's life, and this wildness of yours may mean much to her. Could you go before her, look upon her fresh young face, hold her hand in yours, or touch your cheek to hers?'

To his words, her brain formed vivid images, till she cried out, 'Don't! don't!' and shrank away as do the wolf-dogs from the lash.

'But you must face all this; and better it is to do it now.' In his eyes, which she could not see, there was a great compassion, but his face, tense and quivering, showed no relenting.

She raised her head from the table, forced back the tears, struggled for control.

'I shall go away. They will never see me, and come to forget me. I shall be to them as dead. And—and I will go with Clyde—today.' It seemed final. Wharton stepped forward, but the priest waved him back.

'You have wished for children?' A silent 'Yes.' 'And prayed for them?' 'Often.' 'And have you thought, if you should have children?' Father Roubeau's eyes rested for a moment on the man by the window.

A quick light shot across her face. Then the full import dawned upon her. She raised her hand appealingly, but he went on.

'Can you picture an innocent babe in your arms? A boy? The world is not so hard upon a girl. Why, your very breast would turn to gall! And you could be proud and happy of your boy, as you looked on other children?—' 'O, have pity! Hush!' 'A scapegoat—'

'Don't! don't! I will go back!' She was at his feet.

'A child to grow up with no thought of evil, and one day the world to fling a tender name in his face. A child to look back and curse you from whose loins he sprang!'

'O my God! my God!' She groveled on the floor. The priest sighed and raised her to her feet.

Wharton pressed forward, but she motioned him away.

'Don't come near me, Clyde! I am going back!' The tears were coursing pitifully down her face, but she made no effort to wipe them away.

'After all this? You cannot! I will not let you!' 'Don't touch me!' She shivered and drew back.

'I will! You are mine! Do you hear? You are mine!' Then he whirled upon the priest. 'O what a fool I was to ever let you wag your silly tongue! Thank your God you are not a common man, for I'd—but the priestly prerogative must be exercised, eh? Well, you have exercised it. Now get out of my house, or I'll forget who and what you are!' Father Roubeau bowed, took her hand, and started for the door. But Wharton cut them off.

'Grace! You said you loved me?' 'I did.' 'And you do now?' 'I do.' 'Say it again.'

'I do love you, Clyde; I do.' 'There, you priest!' he cried. 'You have heard it, and with those words on her lips you would send her back to live a lie and a hell with that man?'

But Father Roubeau whisked the woman into the inner room and closed the door. 'No words!' he whispered to Wharton, as he struck a casual posture on a stool. 'Remember, for her sake,' he added.

The room echoed to a rough knock at the door; the latch raised and Edwin Bentham stepped in.

'Seen anything of my wife?' he asked as soon as salutations had been exchanged.

Two heads nodded negatively.

'I saw her tracks down from the cabin,' he continued tentatively, 'and they broke off, just opposite here, on the main trail.' His listeners looked bored.

'And I—I thought—'

'She was here!' thundered Wharton.

The priest silenced him with a look. 'Did you see her tracks leading up to this cabin, my son?' Wily Father Roubeau—he had taken good care to obliterate them as he came up the same path an hour before.

'I didn't stop to look, I—' His eyes rested suspiciously on the door to the other room, then interrogated the priest. The latter shook his head; but the doubt seemed to linger.

Father Roubeau breathed a swift, silent prayer, and rose to his feet. 'If you doubt me, why —' He made as though to open the door.

A priest could not lie. Edwin Bentham had heard this often, and believed it.

'Of course not, Father,' he interposed hurriedly. 'I was only wondering where my wife had gone, and thought maybe—I guess she's up at Mrs. Stanton's on French Gulch. Nice weather, isn't it? Heard the news? Flour's gone down to forty dollars a hundred, and they say the che-cha-quas are flocking down the river in droves.

'But I must be going; so good-by.' The door slammed, and from the window they watched him take his guest up French Gulch. A few weeks later, just after the June high-water, two men shot a canoe into mid-stream and made fast to a derelict pine. This tightened the painter and jerked the frail craft along as would a tow-boat. Father Roubeau had been directed to leave the Upper Country and return to his swarthy children at Minook. The white men had come among them, and they were devoting too little time to fishing, and too much to a certain deity whose transient habitat was in countless black bottles.

Malemute Kid also had business in the Lower Country, so they journeyed together.

But one, in all the Northland, knew the man Paul Roubeau, and that man was Malemute Kid. Before him alone did the priest cast off the sacerdotal garb and stand naked. And why not? These two men knew each other. Had they not shared the last morsel of fish, the last pinch of tobacco, the last and inmost thought, on the barren stretches of Bering Sea, in the heartbreaking mazes of the Great Delta, on the terrible winter journey from Point Barrow to the Porcupine? Father Roubeau puffed heavily at his trail-worn pipe, and gazed on the reddisked sun, poised somberly on the edge of the northern horizon.

Malemute Kid wound up his watch. It was midnight.

'Cheer up, old man!' The Kid was evidently gathering up a broken thread.

'God surely will forgive such a lie. Let me give you the word of a man who strikes a true note: If She have spoken a word, remember thy lips are sealed, And the brand of the Dog is upon him by whom is the secret revealed.

If there be trouble to Herward, and a lie of the blackest can clear, Lie, while thy lips can move or a man is alive to hear.'

Father Roubeau removed his pipe and reflected. 'The man speaks true, but my soul is not vexed with that. The lie and the penance stand with God; but—but—'

'What then? Your hands are clean.' 'Not so. Kid, I have thought much, and yet the thing remains. I knew, and made her go back.' The clear note of a robin rang out from the wooden bank, a partridge drummed the call in the distance, a moose lunged noisily in the eddy; but the twain smoked on in silence.

THE WISDOM OF THE TRAIL

SITKA CHARLEY HAD ACHIEVED the impossible. Other Indians might have known as much of the wisdom of the trail as he did; but he alone knew the white man's wisdom, the honor of the trail, and the law. But these things had not come to him in a day. The aboriginal mind is slow to generalize, and many facts, repeated often, are required to compass an understanding. Sitka Charley, from boyhood, had been thrown continually with white men, and as a man he had elected to cast his fortunes with them, expatriating himself, once and for all, from his own people. Even then, respecting, almost venerating their power, and pondering over it, he had yet to divine its secret essence—the honor and the law. And it was only by the cumulative evidence of years that he had finally come to understand. Being an alien, when he did know, he knew it better than the white man himself; being an Indian, he had achieved the impossible.

And of these things had been bred a certain contempt for his own people—a contempt which he had made it a custom to conceal, but which now burst forth in a polyglot whirlwind of curses upon the heads of Kah-Chucte and Gowhee. They cringed before him like a brace of snarling wolf dogs, too cowardly to spring, too wolfish to cover their fangs. They were not handsome creatures. Neither was Sitka Charley. All three were frightful-looking. There was no flesh to their faces; their cheekbones were massed with hideous scabs which had cracked and frozen alternately under the intense frost; while their eyes burned luridly with the light which is born of desperation and hunger. Men so situated, beyond the pale of the honor and the law, are not to be trusted. Sitka Charley knew this; and this was why he had forced them to abandon their rifles with the rest of the camp outfit ten days before. His rifle and Captain Eppingwell's were the only ones that remained.

'Come, get a fire started,' he commanded, drawing out the precious matchbox with its attendant strips of dry birchbark.

The two Indians fell sullenly to the task of gathering dead branches and underwood. They were weak and paused often, catching themselves, in the act of stooping, with giddy motions, or staggering to the center of operations with their knees shaking like castanets.

After each trip they rested for a moment, as though sick and deadly weary. At times their

44

eyes took on the patient stoicism of dumb suffering; and again the ego seemed almost burst forth with its wild cry, 'I, I, I want to exist!'—the dominant note of the whole living universe.

A light breath of air blew from the south, nipping the exposed portions of their bodies and driving the frost, in needles of fire, through fur and flesh to the bones. So, when the fire had grown lusty and thawed a damp circle in the snow about it, Sitka Charley forced his reluctant comrades to lend a hand in pitching a fly. It was a primitive affair, merely a blanket stretched parallel with the fire and to windward of it, at an angle of perhaps forty-five degrees. This shut out the chill wind and threw the heat backward and down upon those who were to huddle in its shelter. Then a layer of green spruce boughs were spread, that their bodies might not come in contact with the snow. When this task was completed, Kah-Chucte and Gowhee proceeded to take care of their feet. Their icebound moccasins were sadly worn by much travel, and the sharp ice of the river jams had cut them to rags.

Their Siwash socks were similarly conditioned, and when these had been thawed and removed, the dead-white tips of the toes, in the various stages of mortification, told their simple tale of the trail.

Leaving the two to the drying of their footgear, Sitka Charley turned back over the course he had come. He, too, had a mighty longing to sit by the fire and tend his complaining flesh, but the honor and the law forbade. He toiled painfully over the frozen field, each step a protest, every muscle in revolt. Several times, where the open water between the jams had recently crusted, he was forced to miserably accelerate his movements as the fragile footing swayed and threatened beneath him. In such places death was quick and easy; but it was not his desire to endure no more.

His deepening anxiety vanished as two Indians dragged into view round a bend in the river. They staggered and panted like men under heavy burdens; yet the packs on their backs were a matter of but a few pounds. He questioned them eagerly, and their replies seemed to relieve him. He hurried on. Next came two white men, supporting between them a woman. They also behaved as though drunken, and their limbs shook with weakness. But the woman leaned lightly upon them, choosing to carry herself forward with her own strength. At the sight of her a flash of joy cast its fleeting light across Sitka Charley's face. He cherished a very great regard for Mrs. Eppingwell. He had seen many white women, but this was the first to travel the trail with him. When Captain Eppingwell proposed the hazardous undertaking and made him an offer for his services, he had shaken his head gravely; for it was an unknown journey through the dismal vastnesses of the Northland, and he knew it to be of the kind that try to the uttermost the souls of men.

But when he learned that the captain's wife was to accompany them, he had refused flatly to have anything further to do with it. Had it been a woman of his own race he would have harbored no objections; but these women of the Southland—no, no, they were too soft, too tender, for such enterprises.

Sitka Charley did not know this kind of woman. Five minutes before, he did not even dream of taking charge of the expedition; but when she came to him with her wonderful smile and her straight clean English, and talked to the point, without pleading or persuading, he had incontinently yielded. Had there been a softness and appeal to mercy in the eyes, a tremble to the voice, a taking advantage of sex, he would have stiffened to steel; instead her clear-searching eyes and clear-ringing voice, her utter frankness and tacit assumption of equality, had robbed him of his reason. He felt, then, that this was a new breed of woman; and ere they had been trail mates for many days he knew why the sons of such women mastered the land and the sea, and why the sons of his own womankind could not prevail against them. Tender and soft! Day after day he watched her, muscle-weary, exhausted, indomitable, and the words beat in upon him in a perennial refrain. Tender and soft! He knew her feet had been born to easy paths and sunny lands, strangers to the moccasined pain of the North, unkissed by the chill lips of the frost, and he watched and marveled at them twinkling ever through the weary day.

She had always a smile and a word of cheer, from which not even the meanest packer was excluded. As the way grew darker she seemed to stiffen and gather greater strength, and when Kah-Chucte and Gowhee, who had bragged that they knew every landmark of the way as a child did the skin bails of the tepee, acknowledged that they knew not where they were, it was she who raised a forgiving voice amid the curses of the men. She had sung to them that night till they felt the weariness fall from them and were ready to face the future with fresh hope. And when the food failed and each scant stint was measured jealously, she it was who rebelled against the machinations of her husband and Sitka Charley, and demanded and received a share neither greater nor less than that of the others.

Sitka Charley was proud to know this woman. A new richness, a greater breadth, had come into his life with her presence. Hitherto he had been his own mentor, had turned to right or left at no man's beck; he had moulded himself according to his own dictates, nourished his manhood regardless of all save his own opinion. For the first time he had felt a call from without for the best that was in him, just a glance of appreciation from the clear-searching eyes, a word of thanks from the clear-ringing voice, just a slight wreathing of the lips in the wonderful smile, and he walked with the gods for hours to come. It was a new stimulant to his manhood; for the first time he thrilled with a conscious pride in his wisdom of the trail; and between the twain they ever lifted the sinking hearts of their comrades. The faces of the two men and the woman brightened as they saw him, for after all he was the staff they leaned upon. But Sitka Charley, rigid as was his wont, concealing pain and pleasure impartially beneath an iron exterior, asked them the welfare of the rest, told the distance to the fire, and continued on the back-trip.

Next he met a single Indian, unburdened, limping, lips compressed, and eyes set with the pain of a foot in which the quick fought a losing battle with the dead. All possible care had been taken of him, but in the last extremity the weak and unfortunate must perish, and Sitka Charley deemed his days to be few. The man could not keep up for long, so he gave him rough cheering words. After that came two more Indians, to whom he had allotted the task of helping along Joe, the third white man of the party. They had deserted him. Sitka Charley saw at a glance the lurking spring in their bodies, and knew they had at last cast off his mastery. So he was not taken unawares when he ordered them back in quest of their abandoned charge, and saw the gleam of the hunting knives that they drew from the sheaths. A pitiful spectacle, three weak men lifting their puny strength in the face of the mighty vastness; but the two recoiled under the fierce rifle blows of the one and returned like beaten dogs to the leash. Two hours later, with Joe reeling between them and Sitka Charley bringing up the rear, they came to the fire, where the remainder of the expedition crouched in the shelter of the fly.

'A few words, my comrades, before we sleep,' Sitka Charley said after they had devoured their slim rations of unleavened bread. He was speaking to the Indians in their own tongue, having already given the import to the whites. 'A few words, my comrades, for your own good, that ye may yet perchance live. I shall give you the law; on his own head by the death of him that breaks it. We have passed the Hills of Silence, and we now travel the head reaches of the Stuart. It may be one sleep, it may be several, it may be many sleeps, but in time we shall come among the men of the Yukon, who have much grub. It were well that we look to the law. Today Kah-Chucte and Gowhee, whom I commanded to break trail, forgot they were men, and like frightened children ran away.

'True, they forgot; so let us forget. But hereafter, let them remember. If it should happen they do not...' He touched his rifle carelessly, grimly. 'Tomorrow they shall carry the flour and see that the white man Joe lies not down by the trail. The cups of flour are counted; should so much as an ounce be wanting at nightfall... Do ye understand? Today there were others that forgot. Moose Head and Three Salmon left the white man Joe to lie in the snow. Let them forget no more. With the light of day shall they go forth and break trail. Ye have heard the law. Look well, lest ye break it.' Sitka Charley found it beyond him to keep the line close up. From Moose Head and Three Salmon, who broke trail in advance, to Kah-Chucte, Gowhee, and Joe, it straggled out over a mile. Each staggered, fell or rested as he saw fit.

The line of march was a progression through a chain of irregular halts. Each drew upon the last remnant of his strength and stumbled onward till it was expended, but in some miraculous way there was always another last remnant. Each time a man fell it was with the firm belief that he would rise no more; yet he did rise, and again and again. The flesh yielded, the will conquered; but each triumph was a tragedy. The Indian with the frozen foot, no longer erect, crawled forward on hand and knee. He rarely rested, for he knew the penalty exacted by the frost.

Even Mrs. Eppingwell's lips were at last set in a stony smile, and her eyes, seeing, saw not. Often she stopped, pressing a mittened hand to her heart, gasping and dizzy.

Joe, the white man, had passed beyond the stage of suffering. He no longer begged to be let alone, prayed to die; but was soothed and content under the anodyne of delirium. Kah-Chucte and Gowhee dragged him on roughly, venting upon him many a savage glance or blow. To them it was the acme of injustice.

Their hearts were bitter with hate, heavy with fear. Why should they cumber their strength with his weakness? To do so meant death; not to do so—and they remembered the law of Sitka Charley, and the rifle.

Joe fell with greater frequency as the daylight waned, and so hard was he to raise that they dropped farther and farther behind. Sometimes all three pitched into the snow, so weak had the Indians become. Yet on their backs was life, and strength, and warmth.

Within the flour sacks were all the potentialities of existence. They could not but think of this, and it was not strange, that which came to pass. They had fallen by the side of a great timber jam where a thousand cords of firewood waited the match. Near by was an air hole through the ice. Kah-Chucte looked on the wood and the water, as did Gowhee; then they looked at each other.

Never a word was spoken. Gowhee struck a fire; Kah-Chucte filled a tin cup with water and heated it; Joe babbled of things in another land, in a tongue they did not understand.

They mixed flour with the warm water till it was a thin paste, and of this they drank many cups. They did not offer any to Joe; but he did not mind. He did not mind anything, not even his moccasins, which scorched and smoked among the coals.

A crystal mist of snow fell about them, softly, caressingly, wrapping them in clinging robes of white. And their feet would have yet trod many trails had not destiny brushed the clouds aside and cleared the air. Nay, ten minutes' delay would have been salvation.

Sitka Charley, looking back, saw the pillared smoke of their fire, and guessed. And he looked ahead at those who were faithful, and at Mrs. Eppingwell. 'So, my good comrades, ye have again forgotten that you were men? Good! Very good. There will be fewer bellies to feed.' Sitka Charley retied the flour as he spoke, strapping the pack to the one on his own back. He kicked Joe till the pain broke through the poor devil's bliss and brought him

47

doddering to his feet. Then he shoved him out upon the trail and started him on his way. The two Indians attempted to slip off.

'Hold, Gowhee! And thou, too, Kah-Chucte! Hath the flour given such strength to thy legs that they may outrun the swift-winged lead? Think not to cheat the law. Be men for the last time, and be content that ye die full-stomached.

Come, step up, back to the timber, shoulder to shoulder. Come!' The two men obeyed, quietly, without fear; for it is the future which pressed upon the man, not the present.

'Thou, Gowhee, hast a wife and children and a deerskin lodge in the Chipewyan. What is thy will in the matter?' 'Give thou her of the goods which are mine by the word of the captain—the blankets, the beads, the tobacco, the box which makes strange sounds after the manner of the white men. Say that I did die on the trail, but say not how.' 'And thou, Kah-Chucte, who hast nor wife nor child?' 'Mine is a sister, the wife of the factor at Koshim. He beats her, and she is not happy. Give thou her the goods which are mine by the contract, and tell her it were well she go back to her own people. Shouldst thou meet the man, and be so minded, it were a good deed that he should die. He beats her, and she is afraid.' 'Are ye content to die by the law?' 'We are.' 'Then good-bye, my good comrades. May ye sit by the well-filled pot, in warm lodges, ere the day is done.' As he spoke he raised his rifle, and many echoes broke the silence. Hardly had they died away when other rifles spoke in the distance. Sitka Charley started.

There had been more than one shot, yet there was but one other rifle in the party.

He gave a fleeting glance at the men who lay so quietly, smiled viciously at the wisdom of the trail, and hurried on to meet the men of the Yukon.

THE WIFE OF A KING

I.

ONCE WHEN THE northland was very young, the social and civic virtues were remarkably alike for their paucity and their simplicity. When the burden of domestic duties grew grievous, and the fireside mood expanded to a constant protest against its bleak loneliness, the adventurers from the Southland, in lieu of better, paid the stipulated prices and took unto themselves native wives. It was a foretaste of Paradise to the women, for it must be confessed that the white rovers gave far better care and treatment of them than did their Indian copartners. Of course, the white men themselves were satisfied with such deals, as were also the Indian men for that matter. Having sold their daughters and sisters for cotton blankets and obsolete rifles and traded their warm furs for flimsy calico and bad whisky, the sons of the soil promptly and cheerfully succumbed to quick consumption and other swift diseases correlated with the blessings of a superior civilization.

It was in these days of Arcadian simplicity that Cal Galbraith journeyed through the land and fell sick on the Lower River. It was a refreshing advent in the lives of the good Sisters of the Holy Cross, who gave him shelter and medicine; though they little dreamed of the hot elixir infused into his veins by the touch of their soft hands and their gentle ministrations. Cal Galbraith, became troubled with strange thoughts which clamored for attention till he laid eyes on the Mission girl, Madeline. Yet he gave no sign, biding his time patiently. He strengthened with the coming spring, and when the sun rode the heavens in a golden circle, and the joy and throb of life was in all the land, he gathered his still weak body together and departed.

Now, Madeline, the Mission girl, was an orphan. Her white father had failed to give a bald-faced grizzly the trail one day, and had died quickly. Then her Indian mother, having no man to fill the winter cache, had tried the hazardous experiment of waiting till the salmon-run on fifty pounds of flour and half as many of bacon. After that, the baby, Chook-ra, went to live with the good Sisters, and to be thenceforth known by another name.

But Madeline still had kinsfolk, the nearest being a dissolute uncle who outraged his vitals with inordinate quantities of the white man's whisky. He strove daily to walk with the gods, and incidentally, his feet sought shorter trails to the grave. When sober he suffered exquisite torture. He had no conscience. To this ancient vagabond Cal Galbraith duly presented himself, and they consumed many words and much tobacco in the conversation that followed. Promises were also made; and in the end the old heathen took a few pounds of dried salmon and his birch-bark canoe, and paddled away to the Mission of the Holy Cross.

It is not given the world to know what promises he made and what lies he told—the Sisters never gossip; but when he returned, upon his swarthy chest there was a brass crucifix, and in his canoe his niece Madeline. That night there was a grand wedding and a potlach; so that for two days to follow there was no fishing done by the village. But in the morning Madeline shook the dust of the Lower River from her moccasins, and with her husband, in a poling-boat, went to live on the Upper River in a place known as the Lower Country. And in the years which followed she was a good wife, sharing her husband's hardships and cooking his food. And she kept him in straight trails, till he learned to save his dust and to work mightily. In the end, he struck it rich and built a cabin in Circle City; and his happiness was such that men who came to visit him in his home-circle became restless at the sight of it and envied him greatly.

But the Northland began to mature and social amenities to make their appearance.

Hitherto, the Southland had sent forth its sons; but it now belched forth a new exodus—this time of its daughters. Sisters and wives they were not; but they did not fail to put new ideas in the heads of the men, and to elevate the tone of things in ways peculiarly their own. No more did the squaws gather at the dances, go roaring down the center in the good, old Virginia reels, or make merry with jolly 'Dan Tucker' They fell back on their natural stoicism and uncomplainingly watched the rule of their white sisters from their cabins.

Then another exodus came over the mountains from the prolific Southland.

This time it was of women that became mighty in the land Their word was law; their law was steel. They frowned upon the Indian wives, while the other women became mild and walked humbly. There were cowards who became ashamed of their ancient covenants with the daughters of the soil, who looked with a new distaste upon their dark-skinned children; but there were also others—men—who remained true and proud of their aboriginal vows. When it became the fashion to divorce the native wives. Cal Galbraith retained his manhood, and in so doing felt the heavy hand of the women who had come last, knew least, but who ruled the land.

One day, the Upper Country, which lies far above Circle City, was pronounced rich. Dog-teams carried the news to Salt Water; golden argosies freighted the lure across the North Pacific; wires and cables sang with the tidings; and the world heard for the first time of the Klondike River and the Yukon Country. Cal Galbraith had lived the years quietly. He had been a good husband to Madeline, and she had blessed him. But somehow discontent fell upon him; he felt vague yearnings for his own kind, for the life he had been shut out from—a general sort of desire, which men sometimes feel, to break out and taste the prime of living. Besides, there drifted down the river wild rumors of the wonderful El Dorado, glowing descriptions of the city of logs and tents, and ludicrous accounts of the che-cha-quas who had rushed in and were stampeding the whole country.

Circle City was dead. The world had moved on up river and become a new and most marvelous world.

Cal Galbraith grew restless on the edge of things, and wished to see with his own eyes.

So, after the wash-up, he weighed in a couple of hundred pounds of dust on the Company's big scales, and took a draft for the same on Dawson. Then he put Tom Dixon in charge of his mines, kissed Madeline good-by, promised to be back before the first mush-ice ran, and took passage on an up-river steamer.

Madeline waited, waited through all the three months of daylight. She fed the dogs, gave much of her time to Young Cal, watched the short summer fade away and the sun begin its long journey to the south. And she prayed much in the manner of the Sisters of the Holy Cross. The fall came, and with it there was mush-ice on the Yukon, and Circle City kings returning to the winter's work at their mines, but no Cal Galbraith. Tom Dixon received a letter, however, for his men sledded up her winter's supply of dry pine. The Company received a letter for its dogteams filled her cache with their best provisions, and she was told that her credit was limitless.

Through all the ages man has been held the chief instigator of the woes of woman; but in this case the men held their tongues and swore harshly at one of their number who was away, while the women failed utterly to emulate them. So, without needless delay, Madeline heard strange tales of Cal Galbraith's doings; also, of a certain Greek dancer who played with men as children did with bubbles. Now Madeline was an Indian woman, and further, she had no woman friend to whom to go for wise counsel. She prayed and planned by turns, and that night, being quick of resolve and action, she harnessed the dogs, and with Young Cal securely lashed to the sled, stole away.

Though the Yukon still ran free, the eddy-ice was growing, and each day saw the river dwindling to a slushy thread. Save him who has done the like, no man may know what she endured in traveling a hundred miles on the rim-ice; nor may they understand the toil and hardship of breaking the two hundred miles of packed ice which remained after the river froze for good. But Madeline was an Indian woman, so she did these things, and one night there came a knock at Malemute Kid's door. Thereat he fed a team of starving dogs, put a healthy youngster to bed, and turned his attention to an exhausted woman. He removed her icebound moccasins while he listened to her tale, and stuck the point of his knife into her feet that he might see how far they were frozen.

Despite his tremendous virility, Malemute Kid was possessed of a softer, womanly element, which could win the confidence of a snarling wolf-dog or draw confessions from the most wintry heart. Nor did he seek them. Hearts opened to him as spontaneously as flowers to the sun. Even the priest, Father Roubeau, had been known to confess to him, while the men and women of the Northland were ever knocking at his door—a door from which the latch-string hung always out. To Madeline, he could do no wrong, make no mistake. She had known him from the time she first cast her lot among the people of her father's race; and to her half-barbaric mind it seemed that in him was centered the wisdom of the ages, that between his vision and the future there could be no intervening veil.

There were false ideals in the land. The social strictures of Dawson were not synonymous with those of the previous era, and the swift maturity of the Northland involved much wrong. Malemute Kid was aware of this, and he had Cal Galbraith's measure accurately.

He knew a hasty word was the father of much evil; besides, he was minded to teach a great lesson and bring shame upon the man. So Stanley Prince, the young mining expert, was called into the conference the following night as was also Lucky Jack Harrington and his violin. That same night, Bettles, who owed a great debt to Malemute Kid, harnessed up Cal Galbraith's dogs, lashed Cal Galbraith, Junior, to the sled, and slipped away in the dark for Stuart River.

II.

'So; one—two—three, one—two—three. Now reverse! No, no! Start up again, Jack. See—this way.' Prince executed the movement as one should who has led the cotillion.

51

'Now; one—two—three, one—two—three. Reverse! Ah! that's better. Try it again. I say, you know, you mustn't look at your feet. One—two—three, one—two—three. Shorter steps! You are not hanging to the gee-pole just now. Try it over.

'There! that's the way. One—two—three, one—two—three.' Round and round went Prince and Madeline in an interminable waltz. The table and stools had been shoved over against the wall to increase the room. Malemute Kid sat on the bunk, chin to knees, greatly interested. Jack Harrington sat beside him, scraping away on his violin and following the dancers.

It was a unique situation, the undertaking of these three men with the woman.

The most pathetic part, perhaps, was the businesslike way in which they went about it.

No athlete was ever trained more rigidly for a coming contest, nor wolf-dog for the harness, than was she. But they had good material, for Madeline, unlike most women of her race, in her childhood had escaped the carrying of heavy burdens and the toil of the trail. Besides, she was a clean-limbed, willowy creature, possessed of much grace which had not hitherto been realized. It was this grace which the men strove to bring out and knock into shape.

'Trouble with her she learned to dance all wrong,' Prince remarked to the bunk after having deposited his breathless pupil on the table. 'She's quick at picking up; yet I could do better had she never danced a step. But say, Kid, I can't understand this.' Prince imitated a peculiar movement of the shoulders and head—a weakness Madeline suffered from in walking.

'Lucky for her she was raised in the Mission,' Malemute Kid answered. 'Packing, you know,—the head-strap. Other Indian women have it bad, but she didn't do any packing till after she married, and then only at first. Saw hard lines with that husband of hers. They went through the Forty-Mile famine together.' 'But can we break it?' 'Don't know.

'Perhaps long walks with her trainers will make the riffle. Anyway, they'll take it out some, won't they, Madeline?' The girl nodded assent. If Malemute Kid, who knew all things, said so, why it was so. That was all there was about it.

She had come over to them, anxious to begin again. Harrington surveyed her in quest of her points much in the same manner men usually do horses. It certainly was not disappointing, for he asked with sudden interest, 'What did that beggarly uncle of yours get anyway?' 'One rifle, one blanket, twenty bottles of hooch. Rifle broke.' She said this last scornfully, as though disgusted at how low her maiden-value had been rated.

She spoke fair English, with many peculiarities of her husband's speech, but there was still perceptible the Indian accent, the traditional groping after strange gutturals. Even this her instructors had taken in hand, and with no small success, too.

At the next intermission, Prince discovered a new predicament.

'I say, Kid,' he said, 'we're wrong, all wrong. She can't learn in moccasins.

'Put her feet into slippers, and then onto that waxed floor—phew!' Madeline raised a foot and regarded her shapeless house-moccasins dubiously. In previous winters, both at Circle City and Forty-Mile, she had danced many a night away with similar footgear, and there had been nothing the matter.

But now—well, if there was anything wrong it was for Malemute Kid to know, not her.

But Malemute Kid did know, and he had a good eye for measures; so he put on his cap and mittens and went down the hill to pay Mrs. Eppingwell a call. Her husband, Clove Eppingwell, was prominent in the community as one of the great Government officials.

The Kid had noted her slender little foot one night, at the Governor's Ball. And as he also knew her to be as sensible as she was pretty, it was no task to ask of her a certain small favor.

On his return, Madeline withdrew for a moment to the inner room. When she reappeared Prince was startled.

'By Jove!' he gasped. 'Who'd a' thought it! The little witch! Why my sister—' 'Is an English girl,' interrupted Malemute Kid, 'with an English foot. This girl comes of a small-footed race. Moccasins just broadened her feet healthily, while she did not misshape them by running with the dogs in her childhood.' But this explanation failed utterly to allay Prince's admiration. Harrington's commercial instinct was touched, and as he looked upon the exquisitely turned foot and ankle, there ran through his mind the sordid list—'One rifle, one blanket, twenty bottles of hooch.' Madeline was the wife of a king, a king whose yellow treasure could buy outright a score of fashion's puppets; yet in all her life her feet had known no gear save red-tanned moosehide. At first she had looked in awe at the tiny white-satin slippers; but she had quickly understood the admiration which shone, manlike, in the eyes of the men. Her face flushed with pride. For the moment she was drunken with her woman's loveliness; then she murmured, with increased scorn, 'And one rifle, broke!' So the training went on. Every day Malemute Kid led the girl out on long walks devoted to the correction of her carriage and the shortening of her stride.

There was little likelihood of her identity being discovered, for Cal Galbraith and the rest of the Old-Timers were like lost children among the many strangers who had rushed into the land. Besides, the frost of the North has a bitter tongue, and the tender women of the South, to shield their cheeks from its biting caresses, were prone to the use of canvas masks. With faces obscured and bodies lost in squirrel-skin parkas, a mother and daughter, meeting on trail, would pass as strangers.

The coaching progressed rapidly. At first it had been slow, but later a sudden acceleration had manifested itself. This began from the moment Madeline tried on the white-satin slippers, and in so doing found herself. The pride of her renegade father, apart from any natural self-esteem she might possess, at that instant received its birth. Hitherto, she had deemed herself a woman of an alien breed, of inferior stock, purchased by her lord's favor. Her husband had seemed to her a god, who had lifted her, through no essential virtues on her part, to his own godlike level. But she had never forgotten, even when Young Cal was born, that she was not of his people. As he had been a god, so had his womenkind been goddesses. She might have contrasted herself with them, but she had never compared.

It might have been that familiarity bred contempt; however, be that as it may, she had ultimately come to understand these roving white men, and to weigh them.

True, her mind was dark to deliberate analysis, but she yet possessed her woman's clarity of vision in such matters. On the night of the slippers she had measured the bold, open admiration of her three man-friends; and for the first time comparison had suggested itself. It was only a foot and an ankle, but—but comparison could not, in the nature of things, cease at that point. She judged herself by their standards till the divinity of her white sisters was shattered. After all, they were only women, and why should she not exalt herself to their midst? In doing these things she learned where she lacked and with the knowledge of her weakness came her strength. And so mightily did she strive that her three trainers often marveled late into the night over the eternal mystery of woman.

In this way Thanksgiving Night drew near. At irregular intervals Bettles sent word down from Stuart River regarding the welfare of Young Cal. The time of their return was approaching. More than once a casual caller, hearing dance-music and the rhythmic pulse of feet, entered, only to find Harrington scraping away and the other two beating time or arguing noisily over a mooted step. Madeline was never in evidence, having precipitately fled to the inner room.

On one of these nights Cal Galbraith dropped in. Encouraging news had just come down from Stuart River, and Madeline had surpassed herself—not in walk alone, and carriage and grace, but in womanly roguishness. They had indulged in sharp repartee and she had defended herself brilliantly; and then, yielding to the intoxication of the moment, and of her own power, she had bullied, and mastered, and wheedled, and patronized them with most astonishing success. And instinctively, involuntarily, they had bowed, not to her beauty, her wisdom, her wit, but to that indefinable something in woman to which man yields yet cannot name.

The room was dizzy with sheer delight as she and Prince whirled through the last dance of the evening. Harrington was throwing in inconceivable flourishes, while Malemute Kid, utterly abandoned, had seized the broom and was executing mad gyrations on his own account.

At this instant the door shook with a heavy rap-rap, and their quick glances noted the lifting of the latch. But they had survived similar situations before. Harrington never broke a note. Madeline shot through the waiting door to the inner room. The broom went hurtling under the bunk, and by the time Cal Galbraith and Louis Savoy got their heads in, Malemute Kid and Prince were in each other's arms, wildly schottisching down the room.

As a rule, Indian women do not make a practice of fainting on provocation, but Madeline came as near to it as she ever had in her life. For an hour she crouched on the floor, listening to the heavy voices of the men rumbling up and down in mimic thunder. Like familiar chords of childhood melodies, every intonation, every trick of her husband's voice swept in upon her, fluttering her heart and weakening her knees till she lay half-fainting against the door. It was well she could neither see nor hear when he took his departure.

'When do you expect to go back to Circle City?' Malemute Kid asked simply.

'Haven't thought much about it,' he replied. 'Don't think till after the ice breaks.' 'And Madeline?'

He flushed at the question, and there was a quick droop to his eyes. Malemute Kid could have despised him for that, had he known men less. As it was, his gorge rose against the wives and daughters who had come into the land, and not satisfied with usurping the place of the native women, had put unclean thoughts in the heads of the men and made them ashamed.

'I guess she's all right,' the Circle City King answered hastily, and in an apologetic manner. 'Tom Dixon's got charge of my interests, you know, and he sees to it that she has everything she wants.' Malemute Kid laid hand upon his arm and hushed him suddenly. They had stepped without. Overhead, the aurora, a gorgeous wanton, flaunted miracles of color; beneath lay the sleeping town. Far below, a solitary dog gave tongue.

The King again began to speak, but the Kid pressed his hand for silence. The sound multiplied. Dog after dog took up the strain till the full-throated chorus swayed the night.

To him who hears for the first time this weird song, is told the first and greatest secret of the Northland; to him who has heard it often, it is the solemn knell of lost endeavor. It is the plaint of tortured souls, for in it is invested the heritage of the North, the suffering of countless generations—the warning and the requiem to the world's estrays.

Cal Galbraith shivered slightly as it died away in half-caught sobs. The Kid read his thoughts openly, and wandered back with him through all the weary days of famine and disease; and with him was also the patient Madeline, sharing his pains and perils, never doubting, never complaining. His mind's retina vibrated to a score of pictures, stern, clear-cut, and the hand of the past drew back with heavy fingers on his heart. It was the psychological moment. Malemute Kid was half-tempted to play his reserve card and win the game;

but the lesson was too mild as yet, and he let it pass. The next instant they had gripped hands, and the King's beaded moccasins were drawing protests from the outraged snow as he crunched down the hill.

Madeline in collapse was another woman to the mischievous creature of an hour before, whose laughter had been so infectious and whose heightened color and flashing eyes had made her teachers for the while forget. Weak and nerveless, she sat in the chair just as she had been dropped there by Prince and Harrington.

Malemute Kid frowned. This would never do. When the time of meeting her husband came to hand, she must carry things off with high-handed imperiousness. It was very necessary she should do it after the manner of white women, else the victory would be no victory at all. So he talked to her, sternly, without mincing of words, and initiated her into the weaknesses of his own sex, till she came to understand what simpletons men were after all, and why the word of their women was law.

A few days before Thanksgiving Night, Malemute Kid made another call on Mrs. Eppingwell. She promptly overhauled her feminine fripperies, paid a protracted visit to the drygoods department of the P. C. Company, and returned with the Kid to make Madeline's acquaintance. After that came a period such as the cabin had never seen before, and what with cutting, and fitting, and basting, and stitching, and numerous other wonderful and unknowable things, the male conspirators were more often banished the premises than not. At such times the Opera House opened its double storm-doors to them.

So often did they put their heads together, and so deeply did they drink to curious toasts, that the loungers scented unknown creeks of incalculable richness, and it is known that several checha-quas and at least one Old-Timer kept their stampeding packs stored behind the bar, ready to hit the trail at a moment's notice.

Mrs. Eppingwell was a woman of capacity; so, when she turned Madeline over to her trainers on Thanksgiving Night she was so transformed that they were almost afraid of her. Prince wrapped a Hudson Bay blanket about her with a mock reverence more real than feigned, while Malemute Kid, whose arm she had taken, found it a severe trial to resume his wonted mentorship. Harrington, with the list of purchases still running through his head, dragged along in the rear, nor opened his mouth once all the way down into the town. When they came to the back door of the Opera House they took the blanket from Madeline's shoulders and spread it on the snow. Slipping out of Prince's moccasins, she stepped upon it in new satin slippers. The masquerade was at its height. She hesitated, but they jerked open the door and shoved her in. Then they ran around to come in by the front entrance.

III.

'Where is Freda?' the Old-Timers questioned, while the che-cha-quas were equally energetic in asking who Freda was. The ballroom buzzed with her name.

It was on everybody's lips. Grizzled 'sour-dough boys,' day-laborers at the mines but proud of their degree, either patronized the spruce-looking tenderfeet and lied eloquently— the 'sour-dough boys' being specially created to toy with truth—or gave them savage looks of indignation because of their ignorance. Perhaps forty kings of the Upper and Lower Countries were on the floor, each deeming himself hot on the trail and sturdily backing his judgment with the yellow dust of the realm. An assistant was sent to the man at the scales, upon whom had fallen the burden of weighing up the sacks, while several of the gamblers, with the rules of chance at their finger-ends, made up alluring books on the field and favorites.

Which was Freda? Time and again the 'Greek Dancer' was thought to have been discovered, but each discovery brought panic to the betting ring and a frantic registering of new wagers by those who wished to hedge. Malemute Kid took an interest in the hunt, his advent being hailed uproariously by the revelers, who knew him to a man. The Kid had a good eye for the trick of a step, and ear for the lilt of a voice, and his private choice was a marvelous creature who scintillated as the 'Aurora Borealis.' But the Greek dancer was too subtle for even his penetration. The majority of the gold-hunters seemed to have centered their verdict on the 'Russian Princess,' who was the most graceful in the room, and hence could be no other than Freda Moloof.

During a quadrille a roar of satisfaction went up. She was discovered. At previous balls, in the figure, 'all hands round,' Freda had displayed an inimitable step and variation peculiarly her own. As the figure was called, the 'Russian Princess' gave the unique rhythm to limb and body. A chorus of I-told-you-so's shook the squared roof-beams, when lo! it was noticed that 'Aurora Borealis' and another masque, the 'Spirit of the Pole,' were performing the same trick equally well. And when two twin 'Sun-Dogs' and a 'Frost Queen' followed suit, a second assistant was dispatched to the aid of the man at the scales.

Bettles came off trail in the midst of the excitement, descending upon them in a hurricane of frost. His rimed brows turned to cataracts as he whirled about; his mustache, still frozen, seemed gemmed with diamonds and turned the light in varicolored rays; while the flying feet slipped on the chunks of ice which rattled from his moccasins and German socks. A Northland dance is quite an informal affair, the men of the creeks and trails having lost whatever fastidiousness they might have at one time possessed; and only in the high official circles are conventions at all observed. Here, caste carried no significance. Millionaires and paupers, dog-drivers and mounted policemen joined hands with 'ladies in the center,' and swept around the circle performing most remarkable capers. Primitive in their pleasure, boisterous and rough, they displayed no rudeness, but rather a crude chivalry more genuine than the most polished courtesy.

In his quest for the 'Greek Dancer,' Cal Galbraith managed to get into the same set with the 'Russian Princess,' toward whom popular suspicion had turned.

But by the time he had guided her through one dance, he was willing not only to stake his millions that she was not Freda, but that he had had his arm about her waist before. When or where he could not tell, but the puzzling sense of familiarity so wrought upon him that he turned his attention to the discovery of her identity. Malemute Kid might have aided him instead of occasionally taking the Princess for a few turns and talking earnestly to her in low tones. But it was Jack Harrington who paid the 'Russian Princess' the most assiduous court. Once he drew Cal Galbraith aside and hazarded wild guesses as to who she was, and explained to him that he was going in to win. That rankled the Circle City King, for man is not by nature monogamic, and he forgot both Madeline and Freda in the new quest.

It was soon noised about that the 'Russian Princess' was not Freda Moloof. Interest deepened. Here was a fresh enigma. They knew Freda though they could not find her, but here was somebody they had found and did not know. Even the women could not place her, and they knew every good dancer in the camp. Many took her for one of the official clique, indulging in a silly escapade. Not a few asserted she would disappear before the unmasking. Others were equally positive that she was the woman-reporter of the Kansas City Star, come to write them up at ninety dollars per column. And the men at the scales worked busily.

At one o'clock every couple took to the floor. The unmasking began amid laughter and delight, like that of carefree children. There was no end of Oh's and Ah's as mask after mask was lifted. The scintillating 'Aurora Borealis' became the brawny negress whose income from washing the community's clothes ran at about five hundred a month. The twin 'Sun-Dogs' discovered mustaches on their upper lips, and were recognized as brother Fraction-Kings of El Dorado. In one of the most prominent sets, and the slowest in uncovering, was Cal Galbraith with the 'Spirit of the Pole.' Opposite him was Jack Harrington and the 'Russian Princess.' The rest had discovered themselves, yet the 'Greek Dancer' was still missing. All eyes were upon the group. Cal Galbraith, in response to their cries, lifted his partner's mask. Freda's wonderful face and brilliant eyes flashed out upon them. A roar went up, to be squelched suddenly in the new and absorbing mystery of the 'Russian Princess.' Her face was still hidden, and Jack Harrington was struggling with her. The dancers tittered on the tiptoes of expectancy. He crushed her dainty costume roughly, and then—and then the revelers exploded. The joke was on them. They had danced all night with a tabooed native woman.

But those that knew, and they were many, ceased abruptly, and a hush fell upon the room.

Cal Galbraith crossed over with great strides, angrily, and spoke to Madeline in polyglot Chinook. But she retained her composure, apparently oblivious to the fact that she was the cynosure of all eyes, and answered him in English. She showed neither fright nor anger, and Malemute Kid chuckled at her well-bred equanimity. The King felt baffled, defeated; his common Siwash wife had passed beyond him.

'Come!' he said finally. 'Come on home.' 'I beg pardon,' she replied; 'I have agreed to go to supper with Mr. Harrington. Besides, there's no end of dances promised.'

Harrington extended his arm to lead her away. He evinced not the slightest disinclination toward showing his back, but Malemute Kid had by this time edged in closer. The Circle City King was stunned. Twice his hand dropped to his belt, and twice the Kid gathered himself to spring; but the retreating couple passed through the supper-room door where canned oysters were spread at five dollars the plate.

The crowd sighed audibly, broke up into couples, and followed them. Freda pouted and went in with Cal Galbraith; but she had a good heart and a sure tongue, and she spoiled his oysters for him. What she said is of no importance, but his face went red and white at intervals, and he swore repeatedly and savagely at himself.

The supper-room was filled with a pandemonium of voices, which ceased suddenly as Cal Galbraith stepped over to his wife's table. Since the unmasking considerable weights of dust had been placed as to the outcome. Everybody watched with breathless interest.

Harrington's blue eyes were steady, but under the overhanging tablecloth a Smith & Wesson balanced on his knee. Madeline looked up, casually, with little interest.

'May—may I have the next round dance with you?' the King stuttered.

The wife of the King glanced at her card and inclined her head.

AN ODYSSEY OF THE NORTH

I.

THE SLEDS WERE SINGING their eternal lament to the creaking of the harness and the tinkling bells of the leaders; but the men and dogs were tired and made no sound. The trail was heavy with new-fallen snow, and they had come far, and the runners, burdened with flint-like quarters of frozen moose, clung tenaciously to the unpacked surface and held back with a stubbornness almost human.

Darkness was coming on, but there was no camp to pitch that night. The snow fell gently through the pulseless air, not in flakes, but in tiny frost crystals of delicate design. It was very warm—barely ten below zero—and the men did not mind. Meyers and Bettles had raised their ear flaps, while Malemute Kid had even taken off his mittens.

The dogs had been fagged out early in the afternoon, but they now began to show new vigor. Among the more astute there was a certain restlessness—an impatience at the restraint of the traces, an indecisive quickness of movement, a sniffing of snouts and pricking of ears. These became incensed at their more phlegmatic brothers, urging them on with numerous sly nips on their hinder quarters. Those, thus chidden, also contracted and helped spread the contagion. At last the leader of the foremost sled uttered a sharp whine of satisfaction, crouching lower in the snow and throwing himself against the collar. The rest followed suit.

There was an ingathering of back hands, a tightening of traces; the sleds leaped forward, and the men clung to the gee poles, violently accelerating the uplift of their feet that they might escape going under the runners. The weariness of the day fell from them, and they whooped encouragement to the dogs. The animals responded with joyous yelps. They were swinging through the gathering darkness at a rattling gallop.

'Gee! Gee!' the men cried, each in turn, as their sleds abruptly left the main trail, heeling over on single runners like luggers on the wind.

Then came a hundred yards' dash to the lighted parchment window, which told its own story of the home cabin, the roaring Yukon stove, and the steaming pots of tea. But the home cabin had been invaded. Threescore huskies chorused defiance, and as many furry forms precipitated themselves upon the dogs which drew the first sled. The door was flung open, and a man, clad in the scarlet tunic of the Northwest Police, waded knee-deep among the furious brutes, calmly and impartially dispensing soothing justice with the butt end of a dog whip. After that the men shook hands; and in this wise was Malemute Kid welcomed to his own cabin by a stranger.

Stanley Prince, who should have welcomed him, and who was responsible for the Yukon stove and hot tea aforementioned, was busy with his guests. There were a dozen or so of them, as nondescript a crowd as ever served the Queen in the enforcement of her laws or the delivery of her mails. They were of many breeds, but their common life had formed of them a certain type—a lean and wiry type, with trail-hardened muscles, and sun-browned faces, and untroubled souls which gazed frankly forth, clear-eyed and steady.

They drove the dogs of the Queen, wrought fear in the hearts of her enemies, ate of her meager fare, and were happy. They had seen life, and done deeds, and lived romances; but they did not know it.

And they were very much at home. Two of them were sprawled upon Malemute Kid's bunk, singing chansons which their French forebears sang in the days when first they entered the Northwest land and mated with its Indian women. Bettles' bunk had suffered a similar invasion, and three or four lusty voyageurs worked their toes among its blankets as they listened to the tale of one who had served on the boat brigade with Wolseley when he fought his way to Khartoum.

And when he tired, a cowboy told of courts and kings and lords and ladies he had seen when Buffalo Bill toured the capitals of Europe. In a corner two half-breeds, ancient comrades in a lost campaign, mended harnesses and talked of the days when the Northwest flamed with insurrection and Louis Riel was king.

Rough jests and rougher jokes went up and down, and great hazards by trail and river were spoken of in the light of commonplaces, only to be recalled by virtue of some grain of humor or ludicrous happening. Prince was led away by these uncrowned heroes who had seen history made, who regarded the great and the romantic as but the ordinary and the incidental in the routine of life. He passed his precious tobacco among them with lavish disregard, and rusty chains of reminiscence were loosened, and forgotten odysseys resurrected for his especial benefit.

When conversation dropped and the travelers filled the last pipes and lashed their tight-rolled sleeping furs. Prince fell back upon his comrade for further information.

'Well, you know what the cowboy is,' Malemute Kid answered, beginning to unlace his moccasins; 'and it's not hard to guess the British blood in his bed partner. As for the rest, they're all children of the coureurs du bois, mingled with God knows how many other bloods. The two turning in by the door are the regulation 'breeds' or Boisbrules. That lad with the worsted breech scarf—notice his eyebrows and the turn of his jaw—shows a Scotchman wept in his mother's smoky tepee. And that handsome looking fellow putting the capote under his head is a French half-breed—you heard him talking; he doesn't like the two Indians turning in next to him. You see, when the 'breeds' rose under the Riel the full-bloods kept the peace, and they've not lost much love for one another since.' 'But I say, what's that glum-looking fellow by the stove? I'll swear he can't talk English. He hasn't opened his mouth all night.' 'You're wrong. He knows English well enough. Did you follow his eyes when he listened? I did. But he's neither kith nor kin to the others. When they talked their own patois you could see he didn't understand. I've been wondering myself what he is. Let's find out.' 'Fire a couple of sticks into the stove!'

Malemute Kid commanded, raising his voice and looking squarely at the man in question.

He obeyed at once.

'Had discipline knocked into him somewhere.' Prince commented in a low tone.

Malemute Kid nodded, took off his socks, and picked his way among recumbent men to the stove. There he hung his damp footgear among a score or so of mates.

'When do you expect to get to Dawson?' he asked tentatively.

The man studied him a moment before replying. 'They say seventy-five mile. So? Maybe two days.' The very slightest accent was perceptible, while there was no awkward hesitancy or groping for words.

'Been in the country before?' 'No.' 'Northwest Territory?' 'Yes.' 'Born there?' 'No.'

'Well, where the devil were you born? You're none of these.' Malemute Kid swept his hand over the dog drivers, even including the two policemen who had turned into Prince's bunk. 'Where did you come from? I've seen faces like yours before, though I can't remember just where.' 'I know you,' he irrelevantly replied, at once turning the drift of Malemute Kid's questions.

'Where? Ever see me?' 'No; your partner, him priest, Pastilik, long time ago. Him ask me if I see you, Malemute Kid. Him give me grub. I no stop long. You hear him speak 'bout me?' 'Oh! you're the fellow that traded the otter skins for the dogs?' The man nodded, knocked out his pipe, and signified his disinclination for conversation by rolling up in his furs. Malemute Kid blew out the slush lamp and crawled under the blankets with Prince.

'Well, what is he?' 'Don't know—turned me off, somehow, and then shut up like a clam. 'But he's a fellow to whet your curiosity. I've heard of him. All the coast wondered about him eight years ago. Sort of mysterious, you know. He came down out of the North in the dead of winter, many a thousand miles from here, skirting Bering Sea and traveling as though the devil were after him. No one ever learned where he came from, but he must have come far. He was badly travel-worn when he got food from the Swedish missionary on Golovin Bay and asked the way south. We heard of all this afterward. Then he abandoned the shore line, heading right across Norton Sound. Terrible weather, snowstorms and high winds, but he pulled through where a thousand other men would have died, missing St. Michaels and making the land at Pastilik. He'd lost all but two dogs, and was nearly gone with starvation.

'He was so anxious to go on that Father Roubeau fitted him out with grub; but he couldn't let him have any dogs, for he was only waiting my arrival, to go on a trip himself. Mr. Ulysses knew too much to start on without animals, and fretted around for several days. He had on his sled a bunch of beautifully cured otter skins, sea otters, you know, worth their weight in gold. There was also at Pastilik an old Shylock of a Russian trader, who had dogs to kill. Well, they didn't dicker very long, but when the Strange One headed south again, it was in the rear of a spanking dog team. Mr. Shylock, by the way, had the otter skins. I saw them, and they were magnificent. We figured it up and found the dogs brought him at least five hundred apiece. And it wasn't as if the Strange One didn't know the value of sea otter; he was an Indian of some sort, and what little he talked showed he'd been among white men.

'After the ice passed out of the sea, word came up from Nunivak Island that he'd gone in there for grub. Then he dropped from sight, and this is the first heard of him in eight years. Now where did he come from? and what was he doing there? and why did he come from there? He's Indian, he's been nobody knows where, and he's had discipline, which is unusual for an Indian. Another mystery of the North for you to solve, Prince.' 'Thanks awfully, but I've got too many on hand as it is,' he replied.

Malemute Kid was already breathing heavily; but the young mining engineer gazed straight up through the thick darkness, waiting for the strange orgasm which stirred his blood to die away. And when he did sleep, his brain worked on, and for the nonce he, too, wandered through the white unknown, struggled with the dogs on endless trails, and saw men live, and toil, and die like men. The next morning, hours before daylight, the dog drivers and policemen pulled out for Dawson. But the powers that saw to Her Majesty's interests and ruled the destinies of her lesser creatures gave the mailmen little rest, for a week later they appeared at Stuart River, heavily burdened with letters for Salt Water.

However, their dogs had been replaced by fresh ones; but, then, they were dogs.

The men had expected some sort of a layover in which to rest up; besides, this Klondike was a new section of the Northland, and they had wished to see a little something of the Golden City where dust flowed like water and dance halls rang with never-ending revelry. But they dried their socks and smoked their evening pipes with much the same gusto as on their former visit, though one or two bold spirits speculated on desertion and the possibility of crossing the unexplored Rockies to the east, and thence, by the Mackenzie Valley, of gaining their old stamping grounds in the Chippewyan country.

Two or three even decided to return to their homes by that route when their terms of service had expired, and they began to lay plans forthwith, looking forward to the hazardous undertaking in much the same way a city-bred man would to a day's holiday in the woods.

He of the Otter Skins seemed very restless, though he took little interest in the discussion, and at last he drew Malemute Kid to one side and talked for some time in low tones.

Prince cast curious eyes in their direction, and the mystery deepened when they put on caps and mittens and went outside. When they returned, Malemute Kid placed his gold scales on the table, weighed out the matter of sixty ounces, and transferred them to the Strange One's sack. Then the chief of the dog drivers joined the conclave, and certain business was transacted with him.

The next day the gang went on upriver, but He of the Otter Skins took several pounds of grub and turned his steps back toward Dawson.

'Didn't know what to make of it,' said Malemute Kid in response to Prince's queries; 'but the poor beggar wanted to be quit of the service for some reason or other—at least it seemed a most important one to him, though he wouldn't let on what. You see, it's just like the army: he signed for two years, and the only way to get free was to buy himself out. He couldn't desert and then stay here, and he was just wild to remain in the country.

'Made up his mind when he got to Dawson, he said; but no one knew him, hadn't a cent, and I was the only one he'd spoken two words with. So he talked it over with the lieutenant-governor, and made arrangements in case he could get the money from me—loan, you know. Said he'd pay back in the year, and, if I wanted, would put me onto something rich. Never'd seen it, but he knew it was rich.

'And talk! why, when he got me outside he was ready to weep. Begged and pleaded; got down in the snow to me till I hauled him out of it. Palavered around like a crazy man.

'Swore he's worked to this very end for years and years, and couldn't bear to be disappointed now. Asked him what end, but he wouldn't say.

'Said they might keep him on the other half of the trail and he wouldn't get to Dawson in two years, and then it would be too late. Never saw a man take on so in my life. And when I said I'd let him have it, had to yank him out of the snow again. Told him to consider it in the light of a grubstake. Think he'd have it? No sir! Swore he'd give me all he found, make me rich beyond the dreams of avarice, and all such stuff. Now a man who puts his life and time against a grubstake ordinarily finds it hard enough to turn over half of what he finds. Something behind all this, Prince; just you make a note of it. We'll hear of him if he stays in the country—' 'And if he doesn't?' 'Then my good nature gets a shock, and I'm sixty some odd ounces out.' The cold weather had come on with the long nights, and the sun had begun to play his ancient game of peekaboo along the southern snow line ere aught was heard of Malemute Kid's grubstake. And then, one bleak morning in early January, a heavily laden dog train pulled into his cabin below Stuart River. He of the Otter Skins was there, and with him walked a man such as the gods have almost forgotten how to fashion. Men never talked of luck and pluck and five-hundred-dollar dirt without bringing in the name of Axel Gunderson; nor could tales of nerve or strength or daring pass up and down the campfire without the summoning of his presence. And when the conversation flagged, it blazed anew at mention of the woman who shared his fortunes.

As has been noted, in the making of Axel Gunderson the gods had remembered their old-time cunning and cast him after the manner of men who were born when the world was young. Full seven feet he towered in his picturesque costume which marked a king of Eldorado. His chest, neck, and limbs were those of a giant. To bear his three hundred pounds of bone and muscle, his snowshoes were greater by a generous yard than those of other men. Rough-hewn, with rugged brow and massive jaw and unflinching eyes of palest blue, his face told the tale of one who knew but the law of might. Of the yellow of ripe corn silk, his frost-incrusted hair swept like day across the night and fell far down his coat of bearskin.

A vague tradition of the sea seemed to cling about him as he swung down the narrow trail in advance of the dogs; and he brought the butt of his dog whip against Malemute Kid's door as a Norse sea rover, on southern foray, might thunder for admittance at the castle gate.

Prince bared his womanly arms and kneaded sour-dough bread, casting, as he did so, many a glance at the three guests—three guests the like of which might never come under a man's roof in a lifetime. The Strange One, whom Malemute Kid had surnamed Ulysses, still fascinated him; but his interest chiefly gravitated between Axel Gunderson and Axel Gunderson's wife. She felt the day's journey, for she had softened in comfortable cabins during the many days since her husband mastered the wealth of frozen pay streaks, and she was tired. She rested against his great breast like a slender flower against a wall, replying lazily to Malemute Kid's good-natured banter, and stirring Prince's blood strangely with an occasional sweep of her deep, dark eyes. For Prince was a man, and healthy, and had seen few women in many months. And she was older than he, and an Indian besides. But she was different from all native wives he had met: she had traveled—had been in his country among others, he gathered from the conversation; and she knew most of the things the women of his own race knew, and much more that it was not in the nature of things for them to know. She could make a meal of sun-dried fish or a bed in the snow; yet she teased them with tantalizing details of many-course dinners, and caused strange internal dissensions to arise at the mention of various quondam dishes which they had well-nigh forgotten. She knew the ways of the moose, the bear, and the little blue fox, and of the wild amphibians of the Northern seas; she was skilled in the lore of the woods, and the streams, and the tale writ by man and bird and beast upon the delicate snow crust was to her an open book; yet Prince caught the appreciative twinkle in her eye as she read the Rules of the Camp. These rules had been fathered by the Unquenchable Bettles at a time when his blood ran high, and were remarkable for the terse simplicity of their humor.

Prince always turned them to the wall before the arrival of ladies; but who could suspect that this native wife—Well, it was too late now.

This, then, was the wife of Axel Gunderson, a woman whose name and fame had traveled with her husband's, hand in hand, through all the Northland. At table, Malemute Kid baited her with the assurance of an old friend, and Prince shook off the shyness of first acquaintance and joined in. But she held her own in the unequal contest, while her husband, slower in wit, ventured naught but applause. And he was very proud of her; his every look and action revealed the magnitude of the place she occupied in his life. He of the Otter Skins ate in silence, forgotten in the merry battle; and long ere the others were done he pushed back from the table and went out among the dogs. Yet all too soon his fellow travelers drew on their mittens and parkas and followed him.

There had been no snow for many days, and the sleds slipped along the hardpacked Yukon trail as easily as if it had been glare ice. Ulysses led the first sled; with the second came Prince and Axel Gunderson's wife; while Malemute Kid and the yellow-haired giant brought up the third.

'It's only a hunch, Kid,' he said, 'but I think it's straight. He's never been there, but he tells a good story, and shows a map I heard of when I was in the Kootenay country years ago. I'd like to have you go along; but he's a strange one, and swore point-blank to throw it up if anyone was brought in. But when I come back you'll get first tip, and I'll stake you next to me, and give you a half share in the town site besides.' 'No! no!' he cried, as the other strove to interrupt. 'I'm running this, and before I'm done it'll need two heads.

'If it's all right, why, it'll be a second Cripple Creek, man; do you hear?—a second Cripple Creek! It's quartz, you know, not placer; and if we work it right we'll corral the whole thing —millions upon millions. I've heard of the place before, and so have you. We'll build a town —thousands of workmen—good waterways—steamship lines—big carrying trade—light-draught steamers for head reaches—survey a railroad, perhaps—sawmills—electric-light plant—do our own banking—commercial company—syndicate—Say! Just you hold your hush till I get back!' The sleds came to a halt where the trail crossed the mouth of Stuart River. An unbroken sea of frost, its wide expanse stretched away into the unknown east.

The snowshoes were withdrawn from the lashings of the sleds. Axel Gunderson shook hands and stepped to the fore, his great webbed shoes sinking a fair half yard into the feathery surface and packing the snow so the dogs should not wallow. His wife fell in behind the last sled, betraying long practice in the art of handling the awkward footgear. The stillness was broken with cheery farewells; the dogs whined; and He of the Otter Skins talked with his whip to a recalcitrant wheeler.

An hour later the train had taken on the likeness of a black pencil crawling in a long, straight line across a mighty sheet of foolscap.

II.

One night, many weeks later, Malemute Kid and Prince fell to solving chess problems from the torn page of an ancient magazine. The Kid had just returned from his Bonanza properties and was resting up preparatory to a long moose hunt.

Prince, too, had been on creek and trail nearly all winter, and had grown hungry for a blissful week of cabin life.

'Interpose the black knight, and force the king. No, that won't do. See, the next move-'

'Why advance the pawn two squares? Bound to take it in transit, and with the bishop out of the way-' 'But hold on! That leaves a hole, and-' 'No; it's protected. Go ahead! You'll see it works.' It was very interesting. Somebody knocked at the door a second time before Malemute Kid said, 'Come in.' The door swung open. Something staggered in.

Prince caught one square look and sprang to his feet. The horror in his eyes caused Malemute Kid to whirl about; and he, too, was startled, though he had seen bad things before. The thing tottered blindly toward them. Prince edged away till he reached the nail from which hung his Smith & Wesson.

'My God! what is it?' he whispered to Malemute Kid.

'Don't know. Looks like a case of freezing and no grub,' replied the Kid, sliding away in the opposite direction. 'Watch out! It may be mad,' he warned, coming back from closing the door.

The thing advanced to the table. The bright flame of the slush lamp caught its eye. It was amused, and gave voice to eldritch cackles which betokened mirth.

Then, suddenly, he—for it was a man—swayed back, with a hitch to his skin trousers, and began to sing a chantey, such as men lift when they swing around the capstan circle and the sea snorts in their ears: Yan-kee ship come down de ri-ib-er, Pull! my bully boys! Pull! D'yeh want—to know de captain ru-uns her? Pull! my bully boys! Pull! Jon-a-than Jones ob South Caho-li-in-a, Pull! my bully. He broke off abruptly, tottered with a wolfish snarl to the meat shelf, and before they could intercept was tearing with his teeth at a chunk of raw bacon. The struggle was fierce between him and Malemute Kid; but his mad strength left him as suddenly as it had come, and he weakly surrendered the spoil. Between them they got him upon a stool, where he sprawled with half his body across the table.

A small dose of whiskey strengthened him, so that he could dip a spoon into the sugar caddy which Malemute Kid placed before him. After his appetite had been somewhat cloyed, Prince, shuddering as he did so, passed him a mug of weak beef tea.

The creature's eyes were alight with a somber frenzy, which blazed and waned with every mouthful. There was very little skin to the face. The face, for that matter, sunken and emaciated, bore little likeness to human countenance.

Frost after frost had bitten deeply, each depositing its stratum of scab upon the half-healed scar that went before. This dry, hard surface was of a bloody-black color, serrated by grievous cracks wherein the raw red flesh peeped forth. His skin garments were dirty and in tatters, and the fur of one side was singed and burned away, showing where he had lain upon his fire.

Malemute Kid pointed to where the sun-tanned hide had been cut away, strip by strip—the grim signature of famine.

'Who—are—you?' slowly and distinctly enunciated the Kid.

The man paid no heed.

'Where do you come from?' 'Yan-kee ship come down de ri-ib-er,' was the quavering response.

'Don't doubt the beggar came down the river,' the Kid said, shaking him in an endeavor to start a more lucid flow of talk.

But the man shrieked at the contact, clapping a hand to his side in evident pain. He rose slowly to his feet, half leaning on the table.

'She laughed at me—so—with the hate in her eye; and she—would—not—come.' His voice died away, and he was sinking back when Malemute Kid gripped him by the wrist and shouted, 'Who? Who would not come?' 'She, Unga. She laughed, and struck at me, so, and so. And then-' 'Yes?'

'And then—' 'And then what?' 'And then he lay very still in the snow a long time. He is-still in—the—snow.' The two men looked at each other helplessly.

'Who is in the snow?' 'She, Unga. She looked at me with the hate in her eye, and then—'

'Yes, yes.' 'And then she took the knife, so; and once, twice—she was weak. I traveled very slow. And there is much gold in that place, very much gold.' 'Where is Unga?' For all Malemute Kid knew, she might be dying a mile away. He shook the man savagely, repeating again and again, 'Where is Unga? Who is Unga?' 'She—is—in—the—snow.' 'Go on!' The Kid was pressing his wrist cruelly.

'So—I—would—be—in—the snow—but—I—had—a—debt—to—pay. It—was—heavy— I—had—a-debt—to—pay—a—debt—to—pay I—had-' The faltering monosyllables ceased as he fumbled in his pouch and drew forth a buckskin sack. 'A—debt—to—pay—five—pounds —of—gold-grub— stake—Mal—e—mute—Kid—I—y—' The exhausted head dropped upon the table; nor could Malemute Kid rouse it again.

'It's Ulysses,' he said quietly, tossing the bag of dust on the table. 'Guess it's all day with Axel Gunderson and the woman. Come on, let's get him between the blankets. He's Indian; he'll pull through and tell a tale besides.' As they cut his garments from him, near his right breast could be seen two unhealed, hard-lipped knife thrusts.

III.

'I will talk of the things which were in my own way; but you will understand. I will begin at the beginning, and tell of myself and the woman, and, after that, of the man.' He of the Otter Skins drew over to the stove as do men who have been deprived of fire and are afraid the Promethean gift may vanish at any moment. Malemute Kid picked up the slush lamp and placed it so its light might fall upon the face of the narrator. Prince slid his body over the edge of the bunk and joined them.

'I am Naass, a chief, and the son of a chief, born between a sunset and a rising, on the dark seas, in my father's oomiak. All of a night the men toiled at the paddles, and the women cast out the waves which threw in upon us, and we fought with the storm. The salt spray froze upon my mother's breast till her breath passed with the passing of the tide. But I—I raised my voice with the wind and the storm, and lived.

'We dwelt in Akatan—' 'Where?' asked Malemute Kid.

'Akatan, which is in the Aleutians; Akatan, beyond Chignik, beyond Kardalak, beyond Unimak. As I say, we dwelt in Akatan, which lies in the midst of the sea on the edge of the world. We farmed the salt seas for the fish, the seal, and the otter; and our homes shouldered about one another on the rocky strip between the rim of the forest and the yellow beach where our kayaks lay. We were not many, and the world was very small. There were strange lands to the east—islands like Akatan; so we thought all the world was islands and did not mind.

'I was different from my people. In the sands of the beach were the crooked timbers and wave-warped planks of a boat such as my people never built; and I remember on the point of the island which overlooked the ocean three ways there stood a pine tree which never grew there, smooth and straight and tall. It is said the two men came to that spot, turnabout, through many days, and watched with the passing of the light. These two men came from out of the sea in the boat which lay in pieces on the beach. And they were white like you, and weak as the little children when the seal have gone away and the hunters come home empty. I know of these things from the old men and the old women, who got them from their fathers and mothers before them. These strange white men did not take kindly to our ways at first, but they grew strong, what of the fish and the oil, and fierce. And they built them each his own house, and took the pick of our women, and in time children came. Thus he was born who was to become the father of my father's father.

'As I said, I was different from my people, for I carried the strong, strange blood of this white man who came out of the sea. It is said we had other laws in the days before these men; but they were fierce and quarrelsome, and fought with our men till there were no more left who dared to fight. Then they made themselves chiefs, and took away our old laws, and gave us new ones, insomuch that the man was the son of his father, and not his mother, as our way had been. They also ruled that the son, first-born, should have all things which were his father's before him, and that the brothers and sisters should shift for themselves. And they gave us other laws. They showed us new ways in the catching of fish and the killing of bear which were thick in the woods; and they taught us to lay by bigger stores for the time of famine. And these things were good.

'But when they had become chiefs, and there were no more men to face their anger, they fought, these strange white men, each with the other. And the one whose blood I carry drove his seal spear the length of an arm through the other's body. Their children took up the fight, and their children's children; and there was great hatred between them, and black doings, even to my time, so that in each family but one lived to pass down the blood of them that went before. Of my blood I was alone; of the other man's there was but a girl. Unga, who lived with her mother. Her father and my father did not come back from the fishing one night; but afterward they washed up to the beach on the big tides, and they held very close to each other.

'The people wondered, because of the hatred between the houses, and the old men shook their heads and said the fight would go on when children were born to her and children to me. They told me this as a boy, till I came to believe, and to look upon Unga as a foe, who was to be the mother of children which were to fight with mine. I thought of these things day by day, and when I grew to a stripling I came to ask why this should be so.

'And they answered, "We do not know, but that in such way your fathers did." And I marveled that those which were to come should fight the battles of those that were gone, and in it I could see no right. But the people said it must be, and I was only a stripling.

'And they said I must hurry, that my blood might be the older and grow strong before hers. This was easy, for I was head man, and the people looked up to me because of the deeds and the laws of my fathers, and the wealth which was mine. Any maiden would come to me, but I found none to my liking. And the old men and the mothers of maidens told me to hurry, for even then were the hunters bidding high to the mother of Unga; and should her children grow strong before mine, mine would surely die.

'Nor did I find a maiden till one night coming back from the fishing. The sunlight was lying, so, low and full in the eyes, the wind free, and the kayacks racing with the white seas. Of a sudden the kayak of Unga came driving past me, and she looked upon me, so, with her black hair flying like a cloud of night and the spray wet on her cheek. As I say, the sunlight was full in the eyes, and I was a stripling; but somehow it was all clear, and I knew it to be the call of kind to kind.

'As she whipped ahead she looked back within the space of two strokes—looked as only the woman Unga could look—and again I knew it as the call of kind. The people shouted as we ripped past the lazy oomiaks and left them far behind. But she was quick at the paddle, and my heart was like the belly of a sail, and I did not gain. The wind freshened, the sea whitened, and, leaping like the seals on the windward breech, we roared down the golden pathway of the sun.' Naass was crouched half out of his stool, in the attitude of one driving a paddle, as he ran the race anew. Somewhere across the stove he beheld the tossing kayak and the flying hair of Unga. The voice of the wind was in his ears, and its salt beat fresh upon his nostrils.

'But she made the shore, and ran up the sand, laughing, to the house of her mother. And a great thought came to me that night—a thought worthy of him that was chief over all the people of Akatan. So, when the moon was up, I went down to the house of her mother, and looked upon the goods of Yash-Noosh, which were piled by the door—the goods of Yash-Noosh, a strong hunter who had it in mind to be the father of the children of Unga. Other young men had piled their goods there and taken them away again; and each young man had made a pile greater than the one before.

'And I laughed to the moon and the stars, and went to my own house where my wealth was stored. And many trips I made, till my pile was greater by the fingers of one hand than the pile of Yash-Noosh. There were fish, dried in the sun and smoked; and forty hides of the hair seal, and half as many of the fur, and each hide was tied at the mouth and big bellied with oil; and ten skins of bear which I killed in the woods when they came out in the spring. And there were beads and blankets and scarlet cloths, such as I got in trade from the people who lived to the east, and who got them in trade from the people who lived still beyond in the east.

'And I looked upon the pile of Yash-Noosh and laughed, for I was head man in Akatan, and my wealth was greater than the wealth of all my young men, and my fathers had done deeds, and given laws, and put their names for all time in the mouths of the people.

'So, when the morning came, I went down to the beach, casting out of the corner of my eye at the house of the mother of Unga. My offer yet stood untouched.

'And the women smiled, and said sly things one to the other. I wondered, for never had such a price been offered; and that night I added more to the pile, and put beside it a kayak of well-tanned skins which never yet had swam in the sea. But in the day it was yet there, open to the laughter of all men. The mother of Unga was crafty, and I grew angry at the shame in which I stood before my people. So that night I added till it became a great pile, and I hauled up my oomiak, which was of the value of twenty kayaks. And in the morning there was no pile.

'Then made I preparation for the wedding, and the people that lived even to the east came for the food of the feast and the potlatch token. Unga was older than I by the age of four suns in the way we reckoned the years. I was only a stripling; but then I was a chief, and the son of a chief, and it did not matter.

'But a ship shoved her sails above the floor of the ocean, and grew larger with the breath of the wind. From her scuppers she ran clear water, and the men were in haste and worked hard at the pumps. On the bow stood a mighty man, watching the depth of the water and giving commands with a voice of thunder. His eyes were of the pale blue of the deep waters, and his head was maned like that of a sea lion. And his hair was yellow, like the straw of a southern harvest or the manila rope yarns which sailormen plait.

'Of late years we had seen ships from afar, but this was the first to come to the beach of Akatan. The feast was broken, and the women and children fled to the houses, while we men strung our bows and waited with spears in hand. But when the ship's forefoot smelled the beach the strange men took no notice of us, being busy with their own work. With the falling of the tide they careened the schooner and patched a great hole in her bottom. So the women crept back, and the feast went on.

'When the tide rose, the sea wanderers kedged the schooner to deep water and then came among us. They bore presents and were friendly; so I made room for them, and out of the largeness of my heart gave them tokens such as I gave all the guests, for it was my wedding day, and I was head man in Akatan. And he with the mane of the sea lion was there, so tall and strong that one looked to see the earth shake with the fall of his feet. He looked much and straight at Unga, with his arms folded, so, and stayed till the sun went away and the stars came out. Then he went down to his ship. After that I took Unga by the hand and led her to my own house. And there was singing and great laughter, and the women said sly things, after the manner of women at such times. But we did not care. Then the people left us alone and went home.

'The last noise had not died away when the chief of the sea wanderers came in by the door. And he had with him black bottles, from which we drank and made merry. You see, I was only a stripling, and had lived all my days on the edge of the world. So my blood became as fire, and my heart as light as the froth that flies from the surf to the cliff. Unga sat silent among the skins in the corner, her eyes wide, for she seemed to fear. And he with the mane of the sea lion looked upon her straight and long. Then his men came in with bundles of goods, and he piled before me wealth such as was not in all Akatan. There were guns, both large and small, and powder and shot and shell, and bright axes and knives of steel, and cunning tools, and strange things the like of which I had never seen. When he showed me by sign that it was all mine, I thought him a great man to be so free; but he showed me also that Unga was to go away with him in his ship.

'Do you understand?—that Unga was to go away with him in his ship. The blood of my fathers flamed hot on the sudden, and I made to drive him through with my spear. But the spirit of the bottles had stolen the life from my arm, and he took me by the neck, so, and knocked my head against the wall of the house. And I was made weak like a newborn child, and my legs would no more stand under me.

'Unga screamed, and she laid hold of the things of the house with her hands, till they fell all about us as he dragged her to the door. Then he took her in his great arms, and when she tore at his yellow hair laughed with a sound like that of the big bull seal in the rut.

'I crawled to the beach and called upon my people, but they were afraid. Only Yash-Noosh was a man, and they struck him on the head with an oar, till he lay with his face in the sand and did not move. And they raised the sails to the sound of their songs, and the ship went away on the wind.

'The people said it was good, for there would be no more war of the bloods in Akatan; but I said never a word, waiting till the time of the full moon, when I put fish and oil in my kayak and went away to the east. I saw many islands and many people, and I, who had lived on the edge, saw that the world was very large. I talked by signs; but they had not seen a schooner nor a man with the mane of a sea lion, and they pointed always to the east. And I slept in queer places, and ate odd things, and met strange faces. Many laughed, for they thought me light of head; but sometimes old men turned my face to the light and blessed me, and the eyes of the young women grew soft as they asked me of the strange ship, and Unga, and the men of the sea.

'And in this manner, through rough seas and great storms, I came to Unalaska. There were two schooners there, but neither was the one I sought. So I passed on to the east, with the world growing ever larger, and in the island of Unamok there was no word of the ship, nor in Kadiak, nor in Atognak. And so I came one day to a rocky land, where men dug great holes in the mountain. And there was a schooner, but not my schooner, and men loaded upon it the rocks which they dug. This I thought childish, for all the world was made of rocks; but they gave me food and set me to work. When the schooner was deep in the water, the captain gave me money and told me to go; but I asked which way he went, and he pointed south. I made signs that I would go with him, and he laughed at first, but then, being short of men, took me to help work the ship. So I came to talk after their manner, and to heave on ropes, and to reef the stiff sails in sudden squalls, and to take my turn at the wheel. But it was not strange, for the blood of my fathers was the blood of the men of the sea.

'I had thought it an easy task to find him I sought, once I got among his own people; and when we raised the land one day, and passed between a gateway of the sea to a port, I looked for perhaps as many schooners as there were fingers to my hands. But the ships lay against the wharves for miles, packed like so many little fish; and when I went among them to ask for a man with the mane of a sea lion, they laughed, and answered me in the tongues of many peoples. And I found that they hailed from the uttermost parts of the earth.

'And I went into the city to look upon the face of every man. But they were like the cod when they run thick on the banks, and I could not count them. And the noise smote upon me till I could not hear, and my head was dizzy with much movement. So I went on and on, through the lands which sang in the warm sunshine; where the harvests lay rich on the plains; and where great cities were fat with men that lived like women, with false words in their mouths and their hearts black with the lust of gold. And all the while my people of Akatan hunted and fished, and were happy in the thought that the world was small.

'But the look in the eyes of Unga coming home from the fishing was with me always, and I knew I would find her when the time was met. She walked down quiet lanes in the dusk of the evening, or led me chases across the thick fields wet with the morning dew, and there was a promise in her eyes such as only the woman Unga could give.

'So I wandered through a thousand cities. Some were gentle and gave me food, and others laughed, and still others cursed; but I kept my tongue between my teeth, and went strange ways and saw strange sights. Sometimes I, who was a chief and the son of a chief, toiled for men—men rough of speech and hard as iron, who wrung gold from the sweat and sorrow of their fellow men. Yet no word did I get of my quest till I came back to the sea like a homing seal to the rookeries.

'But this was at another port, in another country which lay to the north. And there I heard dim tales of the yellow-haired sea wanderer, and I learned that he was a hunter of seals, and that even then he was abroad on the ocean.

'So I shipped on a seal schooner with the lazy Siwashes, and followed his trackless trail to the north where the hunt was then warm. And we were away weary months, and spoke many of the fleet, and heard much of the wild doings of him I sought; but never once did we raise him above the sea. We went north, even to the Pribilofs, and killed the seals in herds on the beach, and brought their warm bodies aboard till our scuppers ran grease and blood and no man could stand upon the deck. Then were we chased by a ship of slow steam, which fired upon us with great guns. But we put sail till the sea was over our decks and washed them clean, and lost ourselves in a fog.

'It is said, at this time, while we fled with fear at our hearts, that the yellow-haired sea wanderer put in to the Pribilofs, right to the factory, and while the part of his men held the servants of the company, the rest loaded ten thousand green skins from the salt houses. I say it is said, but I believe; for in the voyages I made on the coast with never a meeting the northern seas rang with his wildness and daring, till the three nations which have lands there sought him with their ships.

'And I heard of Unga, for the captains sang loud in her praise, and she was always with him. She had learned the ways of his people, they said, and was happy. But I knew better—knew that her heart harked back to her own people by the yellow beach of Akatan.

'So, after a long time, I went back to the port which is by a gateway of the sea, and there I learned that he had gone across the girth of the great ocean to hunt for the seal to the east of the warm land which runs south from the Russian seas.

'And I, who was become a sailorman, shipped with men of his own race, and went after him in the hunt of the seal. And there were few ships off that new land; but we hung on the flank of the seal pack and harried it north through all the spring of the year. And when the cows were heavy with pup and crossed the Russian line, our men grumbled and were afraid.

For there was much fog, and every day men were lost in the boats. They would not work, so the captain turned the ship back toward the way it came. But I knew the yellow-haired sea wanderer was unafraid, and would hang by the pack, even to the Russian Isles, where few men go. So I took a boat, in the black of night, when the lookout dozed on the fo'c'slehead, and went alone to the warm, long land. And I journeyed south to meet the men by Yeddo Bay, who are wild and unafraid. And the Yoshiwara girls were small, and bright like steel, and good to look upon; but I could not stop, for I knew that Unga rolled on the tossing floor by the rookeries of the north.

'The men by Yeddo Bay had met from the ends of the earth, and had neither gods nor homes, sailing under the flag of the Japanese. And with them I went to the rich beaches of Copper Island, where our salt piles became high with skins.

'And in that silent sea we saw no man till we were ready to come away. Then one day the fog lifted on the edge of a heavy wind, and there jammed down upon us a schooner, with close in her wake the cloudy funnels of a Russian man-of-war. We fled away on the beam of the wind, with the schooner jamming still closer and plunging ahead three feet to our two. And upon her poop was the man with the mane of the sea lion, pressing the rails under with the canvas and laughing in his strength of life. And Unga was there—I knew her on the moment—but he sent her below when the cannons began to talk across the sea.

As I say, with three feet to our two, till we saw the rudder lift green at every jump—and I swinging on to the wheel and cursing, with my back to the Russian shot. For we knew he had it in mind to run before us, that he might get away while we were caught. And they knocked our masts out of us till we dragged into the wind like a wounded gull; but he went on over the edge of the sky line—he and Unga.

'What could we? The fresh hides spoke for themselves. So they took us to a Russian port, and after that to a lone country, where they set us to work in the mines to dig salt. And some died, and—and some did not die.' Naass swept the blanket from his shoulders, disclosing the gnarled and twisted flesh, marked with the unmistakable striations of the knout. Prince hastily covered him, for it was not nice to look upon.

'We were there a weary time and sometimes men got away to the south, but they always came back. So, when we who hailed from Yeddo Bay rose in the night and took the guns from the guards, we went to the north. And the land was very large, with plains, soggy with water, and great forests. And the cold came, with much snow on the ground, and no man knew the way. Weary months we journeyed through the endless forest—I do not remember, now, for there was little food and often we lay down to die. But at last we came to the cold sea, and but three were left to look upon it. One had shipped from Yeddo as captain, and he knew in his head the lay of the great lands, and of the place where men may cross from one to the other on the ice. And he led us—I do not know, it was so long—till there were but two. When we came to that place we found five of the strange people which live in that country, and they had dogs and skins, and we were very poor. We fought in the snow till they died, and the captain died, and the dogs and skins were mine. Then I crossed on the ice, which was broken, and once I drifted till a gale from the west put me upon the shore. And after that, Golovin Bay, Pastilik, and the priest. Then south, south, to the warm sunlands where first I wandered.

'But the sea was no longer fruitful, and those who went upon it after the seal went to little profit and great risk. The fleets scattered, and the captains and the men had no word of those I sought. So I turned away from the ocean which never rests, and went among the lands, where the trees, the houses, and the mountains sit always in one place and do not move. I journeyed far, and came to learn many things, even to the way of reading and writing from books. It was well I should do this, for it came upon me that Unga must know these things, and that someday, when the time was met—we—you understand, when the time was met.

'So I drifted, like those little fish which raise a sail to the wind but cannot steer. But my eyes and my ears were open always, and I went among men who traveled much, for I knew they had but to see those I sought to remember. At last there came a man, fresh from the mountains, with pieces of rock in which the free gold stood to the size of peas, and he had heard, he had met, he knew them. They were rich, he said, and lived in the place where they drew the gold from the ground.

'It was in a wild country, and very far away; but in time I came to the camp, hidden between the mountains, where men worked night and day, out of the sight of the sun. Yet the time was not come. I listened to the talk of the people. He had gone away—they had gone away—to England, it was said, in the matter of bringing men with much money together to form companies. I saw the house they had lived in; more like a palace, such as one sees in the old countries. In the nighttime I crept in through a window that I might see in what manner he treated her. I went from room to room, and in such way thought kings and queens must live, it was all so very good. And they all said he treated her like a queen, and many marveled as to what breed of woman she was for there was other blood in her veins, and she was different from the women of Akatan, and no one knew her for what she was. Aye, she was a queen; but I was a chief, and the son of a chief, and I had paid for her an untold price of skin and boat and bead.

'But why so many words? I was a sailorman, and knew the way of the ships on the seas. I followed to England, and then to other countries. Sometimes I heard of them by word of mouth, sometimes I read of them in the papers; yet never once could I come by them, for they had much money, and traveled fast, while I was a poor man. Then came trouble upon them, and their wealth slipped away one day like a curl of smoke. The papers were full of it at the time; but after that nothing was said, and I knew they had gone back where more gold could be got from the ground.

'They had dropped out of the world, being now poor, and so I wandered from camp to camp, even north to the Kootenay country, where I picked up the cold scent. They had come and gone, some said this way, and some that, and still others that they had gone to the country of the Yukon. And I went this way, and I went that, ever journeying from place to place, till it seemed I must grow weary of the world which was so large. But in the Kootenay I traveled a bad trail, and a long trail, with a breed of the Northwest, who saw fit to die when the famine pinched. He had been to the Yukon by an unknown way over the mountains, and when he knew his time was near gave me the map and the secret of a place where he swore by his gods there was much gold.

'After that all the world began to flock into the north. I was a poor man; I sold myself to be a driver of dogs. The rest you know. I met him and her in Dawson.

'She did not know me, for I was only a stripling, and her life had been large, so she had no time to remember the one who had paid for her an untold price.

'So? You bought me from my term of service. I went back to bring things about in my own way, for I had waited long, and now that I had my hand upon him was in no hurry.

'As I say, I had it in mind to do my own way, for I read back in my life, through all I had seen and suffered, and remembered the cold and hunger of the endless forest by the Russian seas. As you know, I led him into the east—him and Unga—into the east where many have gone and few returned. I led them to the spot where the bones and the curses of men lie with the gold which they may not have.

'The way was long and the trail unpacked. Our dogs were many and ate much; nor could our sleds carry till the break of spring. We must come back before the river ran free. So here and there we cached grub, that our sleds might be lightened and there be no chance of famine on the back trip. At the McQuestion there were three men, and near them we built a cache, as also did we at the Mayo, where was a hunting camp of a dozen Pellys which had crossed the divide from the south.

'After that, as we went on into the east, we saw no men; only the sleeping river, the moveless forest, and the White Silence of the North. As I say, the way was long and the trail unpacked. Sometimes, in a day's toil, we made no more than eight miles, or ten, and at night we slept like dead men. And never once did they dream that I was Naass, head man of Akatan, the righter of wrongs.

'We now made smaller caches, and in the nighttime it was a small matter to go back on the trail we had broken and change them in such way that one might deem the wolverines the thieves. Again there be places where there is a fall to the river, and the water is unruly, and the ice makes above and is eaten away beneath.

'In such a spot the sled I drove broke through, and the dogs; and to him and Unga it was ill luck, but no more. And there was much grub on that sled, and the dogs the strongest.

'But he laughed, for he was strong of life, and gave the dogs that were left little grub till we cut them from the harnesses one by one and fed them to their mates. We would go home light, he said, traveling and eating from cache to cache, with neither dogs nor sleds; which was true, for our grub was very short, and the last dog died in the traces the night we came to the gold and the bones and the curses of men.

'To reach that place—and the map spoke true—in the heart of the great mountains, we cut ice steps against the wall of a divide. One looked for a valley beyond, but there was no valley; the snow spread away, level as the great harvest plains, and here and there about us mighty mountains shoved their white heads among the stars. And midway on that strange plain which should have been a valley the earth and the snow fell away, straight down toward the heart of the world.

'Had we not been sailormen our heads would have swung round with the sight, but we stood on the dizzy edge that we might see a way to get down. And on one side, and one side only, the wall had fallen away till it was like the slope of the decks in a topsail breeze. I do not know why this thing should be so, but it was so. "It is the mouth of hell," he said; "let us go down." And we went down.

'And on the bottom there was a cabin, built by some man, of logs which he had cast down from above. It was a very old cabin, for men had died there alone at different times, and on pieces of birch bark which were there we read their last words and their curses.

'One had died of scurvy; another's partner had robbed him of his last grub and powder and stolen away; a third had been mauled by a baldface grizzly; a fourth had hunted for game and starved—and so it went, and they had been loath to leave the gold, and had died by the side of it in one way or another. And the worthless gold they had gathered yellowed the floor of the cabin like in a dream.

'But his soul was steady, and his head clear, this man I had led thus far. "We have nothing to eat," he said, "and we will only look upon this gold, and see whence it comes and how much there be. Then we will go away quick, before it gets into our eyes and steals away our judgment. And in this way we may return in the end, with more grub, and possess it all." So we looked upon the great vein, which cut the wall of the pit as a true vein should, and we measured it, and traced it from above and below, and drove the stakes of the claims and blazed the trees in token of our rights. Then, our knees shaking with lack of food, and a sickness in our bellies, and our hearts chugging close to our mouths, we climbed the mighty wall for the last time and turned our faces to the back trip.

'The last stretch we dragged Unga between us, and we fell often, but in the end we made the cache. And lo, there was no grub. It was well done, for he thought it the wolverines, and damned them and his gods in one breath. But Unga was brave, and smiled, and put her hand in his, till I turned away that I might hold myself. "We will rest by the fire," she said, "till morning, and we will gather strength from our moccasins." So we cut the tops of our moccasins in strips, and boiled them half of the night, that we might chew them and swallow them. And in the morning we talked of our chance. The next cache was five days' journey; we could not make it. We must find game.

'"We will go forth and hunt," he said.

'"Yes," said I, "we will go forth and hunt." 'And he ruled that Unga stay by the fire and save her strength. And we went forth, he in quest of the moose and I to the cache I had changed. But I ate little, so they might not see in me much strength. And in the night he fell many times as he drew into camp. And I, too, made to suffer great weakness, stumbling over my snowshoes as though each step might be my last. And we gathered strength from our moccasins.

'He was a great man. His soul lifted his body to the last; nor did he cry aloud, save for the sake of Unga. On the second day I followed him, that I might not miss the end. And he lay down to rest often. That night he was near gone; but in the morning he swore weakly and went forth again. He was like a drunken man, and I looked many times for him to give up, but his was the strength of the strong, and his soul the soul of a giant, for he lifted his body through all the weary day. And he shot two ptarmigan, but would not eat them. He needed no fire; they meant life; but his thought was for Unga, and he turned toward camp.

'He no longer walked, but crawled on hand and knee through the snow. I came to him, and read death in his eyes. Even then it was not too late to eat of the ptarmigan. He cast away his rifle and carried the birds in his mouth like a dog. I walked by his side, upright. And he looked at me during the moments he rested, and wondered that I was so strong. I could see it, though he no longer spoke; and when his lips moved, they moved without sound.

'As I say, he was a great man, and my heart spoke for softness; but I read back in my life, and remembered the cold and hunger of the endless forest by the Russian seas. Besides, Unga was mine, and I had paid for her an untold price of skin and boat and bead.

'And in this manner we came through the white forest, with the silence heavy upon us like a damp sea mist. And the ghosts of the past were in the air and all about us; and I saw the yellow beach of Akatan, and the kayaks racing home from the fishing, and the houses on the rim of the forest. And the men who had made themselves chiefs were there, the lawgivers whose blood I bore and whose blood I had wedded in Unga. Aye, and Yash-Noosh walked with me, the wet sand in his hair, and his war spear, broken as he fell upon it, still in his hand. And I knew the time was meet, and saw in the eyes of Unga the promise.

'As I say, we came thus through the forest, till the smell of the camp smoke was in our nostrils. And I bent above him, and tore the ptarmigan from his teeth.

'He turned on his side and rested, the wonder mounting in his eyes, and the hand which was under slipping slow toward the knife at his hip. But I took it from him, smiling close in his face. Even then he did not understand. So I made to drink from black bottles, and to build high upon the snow a pile—of goods, and to live again the things which had happened on the night of my marriage. I spoke no word, but he understood. Yet was he unafraid. There was a sneer to his lips, and cold anger, and he gathered new strength with the knowledge. It was not far, but the snow was deep, and he dragged himself very slow.

'Once he lay so long I turned him over and gazed into his eyes. And sometimes he looked forth, and sometimes death. And when I loosed him he struggled on again. In this way we came to the fire. Unga was at his side on the instant. His lips moved without sound; then he pointed at me, that Unga might understand. And after that he lay in the snow, very still, for a long while. Even now is he there in the snow.

'I said no word till I had cooked the ptarmigan. Then I spoke to her, in her own tongue, which she had not heard in many years. She straightened herself, so, and her eyes were wonder-wide, and she asked who I was, and where I had learned that speech.

'"I am Naass," I said.

'"You?" she said. "You?" And she crept close that she might look upon me.

'"Yes," I answered; "I am Naass, head man of Akatan, the last of the blood, as you are the last of the blood." 'And she laughed. By all the things I have seen and the deeds I have done may I never hear such a laugh again. It put the chill to my soul, sitting there in the White Silence, alone with death and this woman who laughed.

'"Come!" I said, for I thought she wandered. "Eat of the food and let us be gone. It is a far fetch from here to Akatan." 'But she shoved her face in his yellow mane, and laughed till it seemed the heavens must fall about our ears. I had thought she would be overjoyed at the sight of me, and eager to go back to the memory of old times, but this seemed a strange form to take.

'"Come!" I cried, taking her strong by the hand. "The way is long and dark. Let us hurry!" "Where?" she asked, sitting up, and ceasing from her strange mirth.

'"To Akatan," I answered, intent on the light to grow on her face at the thought. But it became like his, with a sneer to the lips, and cold anger.

'"Yes," she said; "we will go, hand in hand, to Akatan, you and I. And we will live in the dirty huts, and eat of the fish and oil, and bring forth a spawn—a spawn to be proud of all the days of our life. We will forget the world and be happy, very happy. It is good, most good. Come! Let us hurry. Let us go back to Akatan." And she ran her hand through his yellow hair, and smiled in a way which was not good. And there was no promise in her eyes.

'I sat silent, and marveled at the strangeness of woman. I went back to the night when he dragged her from me and she screamed and tore at his hair—at his hair which now she played with and would not leave. Then I remembered the price and the long years of waiting; and I gripped her close, and dragged her away as he had done. And she held back, even as on that night, and fought like a she-cat for its whelp. And when the fire was between us and the man. I loosed her, and she sat and listened. And I told her of all that lay between, of all that had happened to me on strange seas, of all that I had done in strange lands; of my weary quest, and the hungry years, and the promise which had been mine from the first. Aye, I told all, even to what had passed that day between the man and me, and in the days yet young. And as I spoke I saw the promise grow in her eyes, full and large like the break of dawn. And I read pity there, the tenderness of woman, the love, the heart and the soul of Unga. And I was a stripling again, for the look was the look of Unga as she ran up the beach, laughing, to the home of her mother. The stern unrest was gone, and the hunger, and the weary waiting.

'The time was met. I felt the call of her breast, and it seemed there I must pillow my head and forget. She opened her arms to me, and I came against her. Then, sudden, the hate flamed in her eye, her hand was at my hip. And once, twice, she passed the knife.

'"Dog!" she sneered, as she flung me into the snow. "Swine!" And then she laughed till the silence cracked, and went back to her dead.

'As I say, once she passed the knife, and twice; but she was weak with hunger, and it was not meant that I should die. Yet was I minded to stay in that place, and to close my eyes in the last long sleep with those whose lives had crossed with mine and led my feet on unknown trails. But there lay a debt upon me which would not let me rest.

'And the way was long, the cold bitter, and there was little grub. The Pellys had found no moose, and had robbed my cache. And so had the three white men, but they lay thin and dead in their cabins as I passed. After that I do not remember, till I came here, and found food and fire—much fire.' As he finished, he crouched closely, even jealously, over the stove. For a long while the slush-lamp shadows played tragedies upon the wall.

'But Unga!' cried Prince, the vision still strong upon him.

'Unga? She would not eat of the ptarmigan. She lay with her arms about his neck, her face deep in his yellow hair. I drew the fire close, that she might not feel the frost, but she crept to the other side. And I built a fire there; yet it was little good, for she would not eat. And in this manner they still lie up there in the snow.'

'And you?' asked Malemute Kid.

'I do not know; but Akatan is small, and I have little wish to go back and live on the edge of the world. Yet is there small use in life. I can go to Constantine, and he will put irons upon me, and one day they will tie a piece of rope, so, and I will sleep good. Yet—no; I do not know.' 'But, Kid,' protested Prince, 'this is murder!' 'Hush!' commanded Malemute Kid. 'There be things greater than our wisdom, beyond our justice. The right and the wrong of this we cannot say, and it is not for us to judge.' Naass drew yet closer to the fire. There was a great silence, and in each man's eyes many pictures came and went.

THE GOD OF HIS FATHERS

I.

ON EVERY HAND stretched the forest primeval,—the home of noisy comedy and silent tragedy. Here the struggle for survival continued to wage with all its ancient brutality. Briton and Russian were still to overlap in the Land of the Rainbow's End—and this was the very heart of it—nor had Yankee gold yet purchased its vast domain. The wolf pack still clung to the flank of the cariboo-herd, singling out the weak and the big with calf, and pulling them down as remorselessly as were it a thousand, thousand generations into the past. The sparse aborigines still acknowledged the rule of their chiefs and medicine men, drove out bad spirits, burned their witches, fought their neighbors, and ate their enemies with a relish which spoke well of their bellies. But it was at the moment when the stone age was drawing to a close. Already, over unknown trails and chartless wildernesses, were the harbingers of the steel arriving,—fair-faced, blue-eyed, indomitable men, incarnations of the unrest of their race. By accident or design, single-handed and in twos and threes, they came from no one knew whither, and fought, or died, or passed on, no one knew whence. The priests raged against them, the chiefs called forth their fighting men, and stone clashed with steel; but to little purpose. Like water seeping from some mighty reservoir, they trickled through the dark forests and mountain passes, threading the highways in bark canoes, or with their moccasined feet breaking trail for the wolf-dogs. They came of a great breed, and their mothers were many; but the fur-clad denizens of the Northland had this yet to learn. So many an unsung wanderer fought his last and died under the cold fire of the aurora, as did his brothers in burning sands and reeking jungles, and as they shall continue to do till in the fulness of time the destiny of their race be achieved.

It was near twelve. Along the northern horizon a rosy glow, fading to the west and deepening to the east, marked the unseen dip of the midnight sun. The gloaming and the dawn were so commingled that there was no night,—simply a wedding of day with day, a scarcely perceptible blending of two circles of the sun. A kildee timidly chirped good-night; the full, rich throat of a robin proclaimed good-morrow. From an island on the breast of the Yukon a colony of wild fowl voiced its interminable wrongs, while a loon laughed mockingly back across a still stretch of river.

In the foreground, against the bank of a lazy eddy, birch-bark canoes were lined two and three deep. Ivory-bladed spears, bone-barbed arrows, buckskin-thonged bows, and simple basket-woven traps bespoke the fact that in the muddy current of the river the salmon-run was on. In the background, from the tangle of skin tents and drying frames, rose the voices of the fisher folk. Bucks skylarked with bucks or flirted with the maidens, while the older squaws, shut out from this by virtue of having fulfilled the end of their existence in reproduction, gossiped as they braided rope from the green roots of trailing vines. At their feet their naked progeny played and squabbled, or rolled in the muck with the tawny wolf-dogs.

To one side of the encampment, and conspicuously apart from it, stood a second camp of two tents. But it was a white man's camp. If nothing else, the choice of position at least bore convincing evidence of this. In case of offence, it commanded the Indian quarters a hundred yards away; of defense, a rise to the ground and the cleared intervening space; and last, of defeat, the swift slope of a score of yards to the canoes below. From one of the tents came the petulant cry of a sick child and the crooning song of a mother. In the open, over the smoldering embers of a fire, two men held talk.

"Eh? I love the church like a good son. *Bien*! So great a love that my days have been spent in fleeing away from her, and my nights in dreaming dreams of reckoning. Look you!" The half-breed's voice rose to an angry snarl. "I am Red River born. My father was white—as white as you. But you are Yankee, and he was British bred, and a gentleman's son. And my mother was the daughter of a chief, and I was a man. Ay, and one had to look the second time to see what manner of blood ran in my veins; for I lived with the whites, and was one of them, and my father's heart beat in me. It happened there was a maiden—white—who looked on me with kind eyes. Her father had much land and many horses; also he was a big man among his people, and his blood was the blood of the French. He said the girl knew not her own mind, and talked overmuch with her, and became wroth that such things should be.

"But she knew her mind, for we came quick before the priest. And quicker had come her father, with lying words, false promises, I know not what; so that the priest stiffened his neck and would not make us that we might live one with the other. As at the beginning it was the church which would not bless my birth, so now it was the church which refused me marriage and put the blood of men upon my hands. *Bien*! Thus have I cause to love the church. So I struck the priest on his woman's mouth, and we took swift horses, the girl and I, to Fort Pierre, where was a minister of good heart. But hot on our trail was her father, and brothers, and other men he had gathered to him. And we fought, our horses on the run, till I emptied three saddles and the rest drew off and went on to Fort Pierre. Then we took east, the girl and I, to the hills and forests, and we lived one with the other, and we were not married,—the work of the good church which I love like a son.

"But mark you, for this is the strangeness of woman, the way of which no man may understand. One of the saddles I emptied was that of her father's, and the hoofs of those who came behind had pounded him into the earth. This we saw, the girl and I, and this I had forgot had she not remembered. And in the quiet of the evening, after the day's hunt were done, it came between us, and in the silence of the night when we lay beneath the stars and should have been one. It was there always. She never spoke, but it sat by our fire and held us ever apart. She tried to put it aside, but at such times it would rise up till I could read it in the look of her eyes, in the very intake of her breath.

"So in the end she bore me a child, a woman-child, and died. Then I went among my mother's people, that it might nurse at a warm breast and live. But my hands were wet with the blood of men, look you, because of the church, wet with the blood of men. And the Riders of the North came for me, but my mother's brother, who was then chief in his own right, hid me and gave me horses and food. And we went away, my woman-child and I, even to the Hudson Bay Country, where white men were few and the questions they asked not many. And I worked for the company a hunter, as a guide, as a driver of dogs, till my woman-child was become a woman, tall, and slender, and fair to the eye.

"You know the winter, long and lonely, breeding evil thoughts and bad deeds. The Chief Factor was a hard man, and bold. And he was not such that a woman would delight in looking upon. But he cast eyes upon my woman-child who was become a woman. Mother of God! he sent me away on a long trip with the dogs, that he might—you understand, he was a hard man and without heart. She was most white, and her soul was white, and a good woman, and—well, she died.

"It was bitter cold the night of my return, and I had been away months, and the dogs were limping sore when I came to the fort. The Indians and breeds looked on me in silence, and I felt the fear of I knew not what, but I said nothing till the dogs were fed and I had eaten as a man with work before him should. Then I spoke up, demanding the word, and they shrank from me, afraid of my anger and what I should do; but the story came out, the pitiful story, word for word and act for act, and they marveled that I should be so quiet.

"When they had done I went to the Factor's house, calmer than now in the telling of it. He had been afraid and called upon the breeds to help him; but they were not pleased with the deed, and had left him to lie on the bed he had made. So he had fled to the house of the priest. Thither I followed. But when I was come to that place, the priest stood in my way, and spoke soft words, and said a man in anger should go neither to the right nor left, but straight to God. I asked by the right of a father's wrath that he give me past, but he said only over his body, and besought with me to pray. Look you, it was the church, always the church; for I passed over his body and sent the Factor to meet my woman-child before his god, which is a bad god, and the god of the white men.

"Then was there hue and cry, for word was sent to the station below, and I came away. Through the Land of the Great Slave, down the Valley of the Mackenzie to the never-opening ice, over the White Rockies, past the Great Curve of the Yukon, even to this place did I come. And from that day to this, yours is the first face of my father's people I have looked upon. May it be the last! These people, which are my people, are a simple folk, and I have been raised to honor among them. My word is their law, and their priests but do my bidding, else would I not suffer them. When I speak for them I speak for myself. We ask to be let alone. We do not want your kind. If we permit you to sit by our fires, after you will come your church, your priests, and your gods. And know this, for each white man who comes to my village, him will I make deny his god. You are the first, and I give you grace. So it were well you go, and go quickly."

"I am not responsible for my brothers," the second man spoke up, filling his pipe in a meditative manner. Hay Stockard was at times as thoughtful of speech as he was wanton of action; but only at times.

"But I know your breed," responded the other. "Your brothers are many, and it is you and yours who break the trail for them to follow. In time they shall come to possess the land, but not in my time. Already, have I heard, are they on the head-reaches of the Great River, and far away below are the Russians."

Hay Stockard lifted his head with a quick start. This was startling geographical information. The Hudson Bay post at Fort Yukon had other notions concerning the course of the river, believing it to flow into the Arctic.

"Then the Yukon empties into Bering Sea?" he asked.

"I do not know, but below there are Russians, many Russians. Which is neither here nor there. You may go on and see for yourself; you may go back to your brothers; but up the Koyukuk you shall not go while the priests and fighting men do my bidding. Thus do I command, I, Baptiste the Red, whose word is law and who am head man over this people."

"And should I not go down to the Russians, or back to my brothers?"

"Then shall you go swift-footed before your god, which is a bad god, and the god of the white men."

The red sun shot up above the northern sky-line, dripping and bloody. Baptiste the Red came to his feet, nodded curtly, and went back to his camp amid the crimson shadows and the singing of the robins.

Hay Stockard finished his pipe by the fire, picturing in smoke and coal the unknown upper reaches of the Koyukuk, the strange stream which ended here its arctic travels and merged its waters with the muddy Yukon flood. Somewhere up there, if the dying words of a ship-wrecked sailorman who had made the fearful overland journey were to be believed, and if the vial of golden grains in his pouch attested anything,—somewhere up there, in that home of winter, stood the Treasure House of the North. And as keeper of the gate, Baptiste the Red, English half-breed and renegade, barred the way.

"Bah!" He kicked the embers apart and rose to his full height, arms lazily outstretched, facing the flushing north with careless soul.

II.

Hay Stockard swore, harshly, in the rugged monosyllables of his mother tongue. His wife lifted her gaze from the pots and pans, and followed his in a keen scrutiny of the river. She was a woman of the Teslin Country, wise in the ways of her husband's vernacular when it grew intensive. From the slipping of a snow-shoe thong to the forefront of sudden death, she could gauge occasion by the pitch and volume of his blasphemy. So she knew the present occasion merited attention. A long canoe, with paddles flashing back the rays of the west-ering sun, was crossing the current from above and urging in for the eddy. Hay Stockard watched it intently. Three men rose and dipped, rose and dipped, in rhythmical precision; but a red bandanna, wrapped about the head of one, caught and held his eye.

"Bill!" he called. "Oh, Bill!"

A shambling, loose-jointed giant rolled out of one of the tents, yawning and rubbing the sleep from his eyes. Then he sighted the strange canoe and was wide awake on the instant.

"By the jumping Methuselah! That damned sky-pilot!"

Hay Stockard nodded his head bitterly, half-reached for his rifle, then shrugged his shoulders.

"Pot-shot him," Bill suggested, "and settle the thing out of hand. He'll spoil us sure if we don't." But the other declined this drastic measure and turned away, at the same time bidding the woman return to her work, and calling Bill back from the bank. The two Indians in the canoe moored it on the edge of the eddy, while its white occupant, conspicuous by his gorgeous head-gear, came up the bank.

"Like Paul of Tarsus, I give you greeting. Peace be unto you and grace before the Lord."

His advances were met sullenly, and without speech.

"To you, Hay Stockard, blasphemer and Philistine, greeting. In your heart is the lust of

Mammon, in your mind cunning devils, in your tent this woman whom you live with in adultery; yet of these divers sins, even here in the wilderness, I, Sturges Owen, apostle to the Lord, bid you to repent and cast from you your iniquities."

"Save your cant! Save your cant!" Hay Stockard broke in testily. "You'll need all you've got, and more, for Red Baptiste over yonder."

He waved his hand toward the Indian camp, where the half-breed was looking steadily across, striving to make out the newcomers. Sturges Owen, disseminator of light and apostle to the Lord, stepped to the edge of the steep and commanded his men to bring up the camp outfit. Stockard followed him.

"Look here," he demanded, plucking the missionary by the shoulder and twirling him about. "Do you value your hide?"

"My life is in the Lord's keeping, and I do but work in His vineyard," he replied solemnly.

"Oh, stow that! Are you looking for a job of martyrship?"

"If He so wills."

"Well, you'll find it right here, but I'm going to give you some advice first. Take it or leave it. If you stop here, you'll be cut off in the midst of your labors. And not you alone, but your men, Bill, my wife—"

"Who is a daughter of Belial and hearkeneth not to the true Gospel."

"And myself. Not only do you bring trouble upon yourself, but upon us. I was frozen in with you last winter, as you will well recollect, and I know you for a good man and a fool. If you think it your duty to strive with the heathen, well and good; but, do exercise some wit in the way you go about it. This man, Red Baptiste, is no Indian. He comes of our common stock, is as bull-necked as I ever dared be, and as wild a fanatic the one way as you are the other. When you two come together, hell'll be to pay, and I don't care to be mixed up in it. Understand? So take my advice and go away. If you go down stream, you'll fall in with the Russians. There's bound to be Greek priests among them, and they'll see you safe through to Bering Sea,—that's where the Yukon empties,—and from there it won't be hard to get back to civilization. Take my word for it and get out of here as fast as God'll let you."

"He who carries the Lord in his heart and the Gospel in his hand hath no fear of the machinations of man or devil," the missionary answered stoutly. "I will see this man and wrestle with him. One backslider returned to the fold is a greater victory than a thousand heathen. He who is strong for evil can be as mighty for good, witness Saul when he journeyed up to Damascus to bring Christian captives to Jerusalem. And the voice of the Saviour came to him, crying, 'Saul, Saul, why persecutest thou me?' And therewith Paul arrayed himself on the side of the Lord, and thereafter was most mighty in the saving of souls. And even as thou, Paul of Tarsus, even so do I work in the vineyard of the Lord, bearing trials and tribulations, scoffs and sneers, stripes and punishments, for His dear sake."

"Bring up the little bag with the tea and a kettle of water," he called the next instant to his boatmen; "not forgetting the haunch of cariboo and the mixing-pan."

When his men, converts by his own hand, had gained the bank, the trio fell to their knees, hands and backs burdened with camp equipage, and offered up thanks for their passage through the wilderness and their safe arrival. Hay Stockard looked upon the function with sneering disapproval, the romance and solemnity of it lost to his matter-of-fact soul. Baptiste the Red, still gazing across, recognized the familiar postures, and remembered the girl who had shared his star-roofed couch in the hills and forests, and the woman-child who lay somewhere by bleak Hudson's Bay.

III.

"Confound it, Baptiste, couldn't think of it. Not for a moment. Grant that this man is a fool and of small use in the nature of things, but still, you know, I can't give him up."

Hay Stockard paused, striving to put into speech the rude ethics of his heart.

"He's worried me, Baptiste, in the past and now, and caused me all manner of troubles; but can't you see, he's my own breed—white—and—and—why, I couldn't buy my life with his, not if he was a nigger."

"So be it," Baptiste the Red made answer. "I have given you grace and choice. I shall come presently, with my priests and fighting men, and either shall I kill you, or you deny your god. Give up the priest to my pleasure, and you shall depart in peace. Otherwise your trail ends here. My people are against you to the babies. Even now have the children stolen away your canoes." He pointed down to the river. Naked boys had slipped down the water from the point above, cast loose the canoes, and by then had worked them into the current. When they had drifted out of rifle-shot they clambered over the sides and paddled ashore.

"Give me the priest, and you may have them back again. Come! Speak your mind, but without haste."

Stockard shook his head. His glance dropped to the woman of the Teslin Country with his boy at her breast, and he would have wavered had he not lifted his eyes to the men before him.

"I am not afraid," Sturges Owen spoke up. "The Lord bears me in his right hand, and alone am I ready to go into the camp of the unbeliever. It is not too late. Faith may move mountains. Even in the eleventh hour may I win his soul to the true righteousness."

"Trip the beggar up and make him fast," Bill whispered hoarsely in the ear of his leader, while the missionary kept the floor and wrestled with the heathen. "Make him hostage, and bore him if they get ugly."

"No," Stockard answered. "I gave him my word that he could speak with us unmolested. Rules of warfare, Bill; rules of warfare. He's been on the square, given us warning, and all that, and—why, damn it, man, I can't break my word!"

"He'll keep his, never fear."

"Don't doubt it, but I won't let a half-breed outdo me in fair dealing. Why not do what he wants,—give him the missionary and be done with it?"

"N-no," Bill hesitated doubtfully.

"Shoe pinches, eh?"

Bill flushed a little and dropped the discussion. Baptiste the Red was still waiting the final decision. Stockard went up to him.

"It's this way, Baptiste. I came to your village minded to go up the Koyukuk. I intended no wrong. My heart was clean of evil. It is still clean. Along comes this priest, as you call him. I didn't bring him here. He'd have come whether I was here or not. But now that he is here, being of my people, I've got to stand by him. And I'm going to. Further, it will be no child's play. When you have done, your village will be silent and empty, your people wasted as after a famine. True, we will he gone; likewise the pick of your fighting men—"

"But those who remain shall be in peace, nor shall the word of strange gods and the tongues of strange priests be buzzing in their ears."

Both men shrugged their shoulder and turned away, the half-breed going back to his own camp. The missionary called his two men to him, and they fell into prayer. Stockard and Bill attacked the few standing pines with their axes, felling them into convenient breastworks. The child had fallen asleep, so the woman placed it on a heap of furs and lent a hand in fortifying the camp. Three sides were thus defended, the steep declivity at the rear precluding attack from that direction. When these arrangements had been completed, the two men stalked into the open, clearing away, here and there, the scattered underbrush. From the opposing camp came the booming of war-drums and the voices of the priests stirring the people to anger.

"Worst of it is they'll come in rushes," Bill complained as they walked back with shoul-dered axes.

"And wait till midnight, when the light gets dim for shooting."

"Can't start the ball a-rolling too early, then." Bill exchanged the axe for a rifle, and took a careful rest. One of the medicine-men, towering above his tribesmen, stood out distinctly. Bill drew a bead on him.

"All ready?" he asked.

Stockard opened the ammunition box, placed the woman where she could reload in safety, and gave the word. The medicine-man dropped. For a moment there was silence, then a wild howl went up and a flight of bone arrows fell short.

"I'd like to take a look at the beggar," Bill remarked, throwing a fresh shell into place. "I'll swear I drilled him clean between the eyes."

"Didn't work." Stockard shook his head gloomily. Baptiste had evidently quelled the more warlike of his followers, and instead of precipitating an attack in the bright light of day, the shot had caused a hasty exodus, the Indians drawing out of the village beyond the zone of fire.

In the full tide of his proselyting fervor, borne along by the hand of God, Sturges Owen would have ventured alone into the camp of the unbeliever, equally prepared for miracle or martyrdom; but in the waiting which ensued, the fever of conviction died away gradually, as the natural man asserted itself. Physical fear replaced spiritual hope; the love of life, the love of God. It was no new experience. He could feel his weakness coming on, and knew it of old time. He had struggled against it and been overcome by it before. He remembered when the other men had driven their paddles like mad in the van of a roaring ice-flood, how, at the critical moment, in a panic of worldly terror, he had dropped his paddle and besought wildly with his God for pity. And there were other times. The recollection was not pleasant. It brought shame to him that his spirit should be so weak and his flesh so strong. But the love of life! the love of life! He could not strip it from him. Because of it had his dim ancestors perpetuated their line; because of it was he destined to perpetuate his. His courage, if courage it might be called, was bred of fanaticism. The courage of Stockard and Bill was the adherence to deep-rooted ideals. Not that the love of life was less, but the love of race tradi-tion more; not that they were unafraid to die, but that they were brave enough not to live at the price of shame.

The missionary rose, for the moment swayed by the mood of sacrifice. He half crawled over the barricade to proceed to the other camp, but sank back, a trembling mass, wailing: "As the spirit moves! As the spirit moves! Who am I that I should set aside the judgments of God? Before the foundations of the world were all things written in the book of life. Worm that I am, shall I erase the page or any portion thereof? As God wills, so shall the spirit move!"

Bill reached over, plucked him to his feet, and shook him, fiercely, silently. Then he dropped the bundle of quivering nerves and turned his attention to the two converts. But they showed little fright and a cheerful alacrity in preparing for the coming passage at arms.

Stockard, who had been talking in undertones with the Teslin woman, now turned to the missionary.

"Fetch him over here," he commanded of Bill.

"Now," he ordered, when Sturges Owen had been duly deposited before him, "make us man and wife, and be lively about it." Then he added apologetically to Bill: "No telling how it's to end, so I just thought I'd get my affairs straightened up."

The woman obeyed the behest of her white lord. To her the ceremony was meaningless. By her lights she was his wife, and had been from the day they first foregathered. The converts served as witnesses. Bill stood over the missionary, prompting him when he stumbled. Stockard put the responses in the woman's mouth, and when the time came, for want of better, ringed her finger with thumb and forefinger of his own.

"Kiss the bride!" Bill thundered, and Sturges Owen was too weak to disobey.

"Now baptize the child!"

"Neat and tidy," Bill commented.

"Gathering the proper outfit for a new trail," the father explained, taking the boy from the mother's arms. "I was grub-staked, once, into the Cascades, and had everything in the kit except salt. Never shall forget it. And if the woman and the kid cross the divide to-night they might as well be prepared for pot-luck. A long shot, Bill, between ourselves, but nothing lost if it misses."

A cup of water served the purpose, and the child was laid away in a secure corner of the barricade. The men built the fire, and the evening meal was cooked.

The sun hurried round to the north, sinking closer to the horizon. The heavens in that quarter grew red and bloody. The shadows lengthened, the light dimmed, and in the sombre recesses of the forest life slowly died away. Even the wild fowl in the river softened their raucous chatter and feigned the nightly farce of going to bed. Only the tribesmen increased their clamor, war-drums booming and voices raised in savage folk songs. But as the sun dipped they ceased their tumult. The rounded hush of midnight was complete. Stockard rose to his knees and peered over the logs. Once the child wailed in pain and disconcerted him. The mother bent over it, but it slept again. The silence was interminable, profound. Then, of a sudden, the robins burst into full-throated song. The night had passed.

A flood of dark figures boiled across the open. Arrows whistled and bow-thongs sang. The shrill-tongued rifles answered back. A spear, and a mighty cast, transfixed the Teslin woman as she hovered above the child. A spent arrow, diving between the logs, lodged in the missionary's arm.

There was no stopping the rush. The middle distance was cumbered with bodies, but the rest surged on, breaking against and over the barricade like an ocean wave. Sturges Owen fled to the tent, while the men were swept from their feet, buried beneath the human tide. Hay Stockard alone regained the surface, flinging the tribesmen aside like yelping curs. He had managed to seize an axe. A dark hand grasped the child by a naked foot, and drew it from beneath its mother. At arm's length its puny body circled through the air, dashing to death against the logs. Stockard clove the man to the chin and fell to clearing space. The ring of savage faces closed in, raining upon him spear-thrusts and bone-barbed arrows. The sun shot up, and they swayed back and forth in the crimson shadows. Twice, with his axe blocked by too deep a blow, they rushed him; but each time he flung them clear. They fell underfoot and he trampled dead and dying, the way slippery with blood. And still the day brightened and the robins sang. Then they drew back from him in awe, and he leaned breathless upon his axe.

"Blood of my soul!" cried Baptiste the Red. "But thou art a man. Deny thy god, and thou shalt yet live."

Stockard swore his refusal, feebly but with grace.

"Behold! A woman!" Sturges Owen had been brought before the half-breed.

Beyond a scratch on the arm, he was uninjured, but his eyes roved about him in an ecstasy of fear. The heroic figure of the blasphemer, bristling with wounds and arrows, leaning defiantly upon his axe, indifferent, indomitable, superb, caught his wavering vision. And he felt a great envy of the man who could go down serenely to the dark gates of death. Surely Christ, and not he, Sturges Owen, had been moulded in such manner. And why not he? He felt dimly the curse of ancestry, the feebleness of spirit which had come down to him out of the past, and he felt an anger at the creative force, symbolize it as he would, which had formed him, its servant, so weakly. For even a stronger man, this anger and the stress of circumstance were sufficient to breed apostasy, and for Sturges Owen it was inevitable. In the fear of man's anger he would dare the wrath of God. He had been raised up to serve the Lord only that he might be cast down. He had been given faith without the strength of faith; he had been given spirit without the power of spirit. It was unjust.

"Where now is thy god?" the half-breed demanded.

"I do not know." He stood straight and rigid, like a child repeating a catechism.

"Hast thou then a god at all?"

"I had."

"And now?"

"No."

Hay Stockard swept the blood from his eyes and laughed. The missionary looked at him curiously, as in a dream. A feeling of infinite distance came over him, as though of a great remove. In that which had transpired, and which was to transpire, he had no part. He was a spectator—at a distance, yes, at a distance. The words of Baptiste came to him faintly:-

"Very good. See that this man go free, and that no harm befall him. Let him depart in peace. Give him a canoe and food. Set his face toward the Russians, that he may tell their priests of Baptiste the Red, in whose country there is no god."

They led him to the edge of the steep, where they paused to witness the final tragedy. The half-breed turned to Hay Stockard.

"There is no god," he prompted.

The man laughed in reply. One of the young men poised a war-spear for the cast.

"Hast thou a god?"

"Ay, the God of my fathers."

He shifted the axe for a better grip. Baptiste the Red gave the sign, and the spear hurtled full against his breast. Sturges Owen saw the ivory head stand out beyond his back, saw the man sway, laughing, and snap the shaft short as he fell upon it. Then he went down to the river, that he might carry to the Russians the message of Baptiste the Red, in whose country there was no god.

THE GREAT INTERROGATION

I.

To say the least, Mrs. Sayther's career in Dawson was meteoric. She arrived in the spring, with dog sleds and French-Canadian *voyageurs*, blazed gloriously for a brief month, and departed up the river as soon as it was free of ice. Now womanless Dawson never quite understood this hurried departure, and the local Four Hundred felt aggrieved and lonely till the Nome strike was made and old sensations gave way to new. For it had delighted in Mrs. Sayther, and received her wide-armed. She was pretty, charming, and, moreover, a widow. And because of this she at once had at heel any number of Eldorado Kings, officials, and adventuring younger sons, whose ears were yearning for the frou-frou of a woman's skirts.

The mining engineers revered the memory of her husband, the late Colonel Sayther, while the syndicate and promoter representatives spoke awesomely of his deals and manipulations; for he was known down in the States as a great mining man, and as even a greater one in London. Why his widow, of all women, should have come into the country, was the great interrogation. But they were a practical breed, the men of the Northland, with a wholesome disregard for theories and a firm grip on facts. And to not a few of them Karen Sayther was a most essential fact. That she did not regard the matter in this light, is evidenced by the neatness and celerity with which refusal and proposal tallied off during her four weeks' stay. And with her vanished the fact, and only the interrogation remained.

To the solution, Chance vouchsafed one clew. Her last victim, Jack Coughran, having fruitlessly laid at her feet both his heart and a five-hundred-foot creek claim on Bonanza, celebrated the misfortune by walking all of a night with the gods. In the midwatch of this night he happened to rub shoulders with Pierre Fontaine, none other than head man of Karen Sayther's *voyageurs*. This rubbing of shoulders led to recognition and drinks, and ultimately involved both men in a common muddle of inebriety.

"Heh?" Pierre Fontaine later on gurgled thickly. "Vot for Madame Sayther mak visitation to thees country? More better you spik wit her. I know no t'ing 'tall, only all de tam her ask one man's name. 'Pierre,' her spik wit me; 'Pierre, you moos' find thees mans, and I gif you

85

mooch—one thousand dollar you find thees mans.' Thees mans? Ah, *oui*. Thees man's name—vot you call—Daveed Payne. *Oui*, m'sieu, Daveed Payne. All de tam her spik das name. And all de tam I look rount vaire mooch, work lak hell, but no can find das dam mans, and no get one thousand dollar 'tall. By dam!

"Heh? Ah, *oui*. One tam dose mens vot come from Circle City, dose mens know thees mans. Him Birch Creek, dey spik. And madame? Her say '*Bon!*' and look happy lak anyt'ing. And her spik wit me. 'Pierre,' her spik, 'harness de dogs. We go queek. We find thees mans I gif you one thousand dollar more.' And I say, '*Oui*, queek! *Allons, madame!*'

"For sure, I t'ink, das two thousand dollar mine. Bully boy! Den more mens come from Circle City, and dey say no, das thees mans, Daveed Payne, come Dawson leel tam back. So madame and I go not 'tall.

"*Oui*, m'sieu. Thees day madame spik. 'Pierre,' her spik, and gif me five hundred dollar, 'go buy poling-boat. To-morrow we go up de river.' Ah, *oui*, to-morrow, up de river, and das dam Sitka Charley mak me pay for de poling-boat five hundred dollar. Dam!"

Thus it was, when Jack Coughran unburdened himself next day, that Dawson fell to wondering who was this David Payne, and in what way his existence bore upon Karen Sayther's. But that very day, as Pierre Fontaine had said, Mrs. Sayther and her barbaric crew of *voyageurs* towed up the east bank to Klondike City, shot across to the west bank to escape the bluffs, and disappeared amid the maze of islands to the south.

II.

"*Oui, madame, thees is de place*. One, two, t'ree island below Stuart River. Thees is t'ree island."

As he spoke, Pierre Fontaine drove his pole against the bank and held the stern of the boat against the current. This thrust the bow in, till a nimble breed climbed ashore with the painter and made fast.

"One leel tam, madame, I go look see."

A chorus of dogs marked his disappearance over the edge of the bank, but a minute later he was back again.

"*Oui, madame*, thees is de cabin. I mak investigation. No can find mans at home. But him no go vaire far, vaire long, or him no leave dogs. Him come queek, you bet!"

"Help me out, Pierre. I'm tired all over from the boat. You might have made it softer, you know."

From a nest of furs amidships, Karen Sayther rose to her full height of slender fairness. But if she looked lily-frail in her elemental environment, she was belied by the grip she put upon Pierre's hand, by the knotting of her woman's biceps as it took the weight of her body, by the splendid effort of her limbs as they held her out from the perpendicular bank while she made the ascent. Though shapely flesh clothed delicate frame, her body was a seat of strength.

Still, for all the careless ease with which she had made the landing, there was a warmer color than usual to her face, and a perceptibly extra beat to her heart. But then, also, it was with a certain reverent curiousness that she approached the cabin, while the Hush on her cheek showed a yet riper mellowness.

"Look, see!" Pierre pointed to the scattered chips by the woodpile. "Him fresh—two, t'ree day, no more."

Mrs. Sayther nodded. She tried to peer through the small window, but it was made of greased parchment which admitted light while it blocked vision. Failing this, she went round to the door, half lifted the rude latch to enter, but changed her mind and let it fall back into place. Then she suddenly dropped on one knee and kissed the rough-hewn threshold. If Pierre Fontaine saw, he gave no sign, and the memory in the time to come was never shared. But the next instant, one of the boatmen, placidly lighting his pipe, was startled by an unwonted harshness in his captain's voice.

"Hey! You! Le Goire! You mak'm soft more better," Pierre commanded. "Plenty bearskin; plenty blanket. Dam!"

But the nest was soon after disrupted, and the major portion tossed up to the crest of the shore, where Mrs. Sayther lay down to wait in comfort.

Reclining on her side, she looked out and over the wide-stretching Yukon. Above the mountains which lay beyond the further shore, the sky was murky with the smoke of unseen forest fires, and through this the afternoon sun broke feebly, throwing a vague radiance to earth, and unreal shadows. To the sky-line of the four quarters—spruce-shrouded islands, dark waters, and ice-scarred rocky ridges—stretched the immaculate wilderness. No sign of human existence broke the solitude; no sound the stillness. The land seemed bound under the unreality of the unknown, wrapped in the brooding mystery of great spaces.

Perhaps it was this which made Mrs. Sayther nervous; for she changed her position constantly, now to look up the river, now down, or to scan the gloomy shores for the half-hidden mouths of back channels. After an hour or so the boatmen were sent ashore to pitch camp for the night, but Pierre remained with his mistress to watch.

"Ah! him come thees tam," he whispered, after a long silence, his gaze bent up the river to the head of the island.

A canoe, with a paddle flashing on either side, was slipping down the current. In the stern a man's form, and in the bow a woman's, swung rhythmically to the work. Mrs. Sayther had no eyes for the woman till the canoe drove in closer and her bizarre beauty peremptorily demanded notice. A close-fitting blouse of moose-skin, fantastically beaded, outlined faithfully the well-rounded lines of her body, while a silken kerchief, gay of color and picturesquely draped, partly covered great masses of blue-black hair. But it was the face, cast belike in copper bronze, which caught and held Mrs. Sayther's fleeting glance. Eyes, piercing and black and large, with a traditional hint of obliqueness, looked forth from under clear-stenciled, clean-arching brows. Without suggesting cadaverousness, though high-boned and prominent, the cheeks fell away and met in a mouth, thin-lipped and softly strong. It was a face which advertised the dimmest trace of ancient Mongol blood, a reversion, after long centuries of wandering, to the parent stem. This effect was heightened by the delicately aquiline nose with its thin trembling nostrils, and by the general air of eagle wildness which seemed to characterize not only the face but the creature herself. She was, in fact, the Tartar type modified to idealization, and the tribe of Red Indian is lucky that breeds such a unique body once in a score of generations.

Dipping long strokes and strong, the girl, in concert with the man, suddenly whirled the tiny craft about against the current and brought it gently to the shore. Another instant and she stood at the top of the bank, heaving up by rope, hand under hand, a quarter of fresh-killed moose. Then the man followed her, and together, with a swift rush, they drew up the canoe. The dogs were in a whining mass about them, and as the girl stooped among them caressingly, the man's gaze fell upon Mrs. Sayther, who had arisen. He looked, brushed his eyes unconsciously as though his sight were deceiving him, and looked again.

"Karen," he said simply, coming forward and extending his hand, "I thought for the moment I was dreaming. I went snow-blind for a time, this spring, and since then my eyes have been playing tricks with me."

Mrs. Sayther, whose flush had deepened and whose heart was urging painfully, had been prepared for almost anything save this coolly extended hand; but she tactfully curbed herself and grasped it heartily with her own.

"You know, Dave, I threatened often to come, and I would have, too, only—only—"

"Only I didn't give the word." David Payne laughed and watched the Indian girl disappearing into the cabin.

"Oh, I understand, Dave, and had I been in your place I'd most probably have done the same. But I have come—now."

"Then come a little bit farther, into the cabin and get something to eat," he said genially, ignoring or missing the feminine suggestion of appeal in her voice. "And you must be tired too. Which way are you travelling? Up? Then you wintered in Dawson, or came in on the last ice. Your camp?" He glanced at the *voyageurs* circled about the fire in the open, and held back the door for her to enter.

"I came up on the ice from Circle City last winter," he continued, "and settled down here for a while. Am prospecting some on Henderson Creek, and if that fails, have been thinking of trying my hand this fall up the Stuart River."

"You aren't changed much, are you?" she asked irrelevantly, striving to throw the conversation upon a more personal basis.

"A little less flesh, perhaps, and a little more muscle. How did *you* mean?"

But she shrugged her shoulders and peered I through the dim light at the Indian girl, who had lighted the fire and was frying great chunks of moose meat, alternated with thin ribbons of bacon.

"Did you stop in Dawson long?" The man was whittling a stave of birchwood into a rude axe-handle, and asked the question without raising his head.

"Oh, a few days," she answered, following the girl with her eyes, and hardly hearing. "What were you saying? In Dawson? A month, in fact, and glad to get away. The arctic male is elemental, you know, and somewhat strenuous in his feelings."

"Bound to be when he gets right down to the soil. He leaves convention with the spring bed at borne. But you were wise in your choice of time for leaving. You'll be out of the country before mosquito season, which is a blessing your lack of experience will not permit you to appreciate."

"I suppose not. But tell me about yourself, about your life. What kind of neighbors have you? Or have you any?"

While she queried she watched the girl grinding coffee in the corner of a flower sack upon the hearthstone. With a steadiness and skill which predicated nerves as primitive as the method, she crushed the imprisoned berries with a heavy fragment of quartz. David Payne noted his visitor's gaze, and the shadow of a smile drifted over his lips.

"I did have some," he replied. "Missourian chaps, and a couple of Cornishmen, but they went down to Eldorado to work at wages for a grubstake."

Mrs. Sayther cast a look of speculative regard upon the girl. "But of course there are plenty of Indians about?"

"Every mother's son of them down to Dawson long ago. Not a native in the whole country, barring Winapie here, and she's a Koyokuk lass,—comes from a thousand miles or so down the river."

Mrs. Sayther felt suddenly faint; and though the smile of interest in no wise waned, the face of the man seemed to draw away to a telescopic distance, and the tiered logs of the cabin to whirl drunkenly about. But she was bidden draw up to the table, and during the meal discovered time and space in which to find herself. She talked little, and that principally about the land and weather, while the man wandered off into a long description of the difference between the shallow summer diggings of the Lower Country and the deep winter diggings of the Upper Country.

"You do not ask why I came north?" she asked. "Surely you know." They had moved back from the table, and David Payne had returned to his axe-handle. "Did you get my letter?"

"A last one? No, I don't think so. Most probably it's trailing around the Birch Creek Country or lying in some trader's shack on the Lower River. The way they run the mails in here is shameful. No order, no system, no—"

"Don't be wooden, Dave! Help me!" She spoke sharply now, with an assumption of authority which rested upon the past. "Why don't you ask me about myself? About those we knew in the old times? Have you no longer any interest in the world? Do you know that my husband is dead?"

"Indeed, I am sorry. How long—"

"David!" She was ready to cry with vexation, but the reproach she threw into her voice eased her.

"Did you get any of my letters? You must have got some of them, though you never answered."

"Well, I didn't get the last one, announcing, evidently, the death of your husband, and most likely others went astray; but I did get some. I—er—read them aloud to Winapie as a warning—that is, you know, to impress upon her the wickedness of her white sisters. And I —er—think she profited by it. Don't you?"

She disregarded the sting, and went on. "In the last letter, which you did not receive, I told, as you have guessed, of Colonel Sayther's death. That was a year ago. I also said that if you did not come out to me, I would go in to you. And as I had often promised, I came."

"I know of no promise."

"In the earlier letters?"

"Yes, you promised, but as I neither asked nor answered, it was unratified. So I do not know of any such promise. But I do know of another, which you, too, may remember. It was very long ago." He dropped the axe-handle to the floor and raised his head. "It was so very long ago, yet I remember it distinctly, the day, the time, every detail. We were in a rose garden, you and I,—your mother's rose garden. All things were budding, blossoming, and the sap of spring was in our blood. And I drew you over—it was the first—and kissed you full on the lips. Don't you remember?"

"Don't go over it, Dave, don't! I know every shameful line of it. How often have I wept! If you only knew how I have suffered—"

"You promised me then—ay, and a thousand times in the sweet days that followed. Each look of your eyes, each touch of your hand, each syllable that fell from your lips, was a promise. And then—how shall I say?—there came a man. He was old—old enough to have begotten you—and not nice to look upon, but as the world goes, clean. He had done no wrong, followed the letter of the law, was respectable. Further, and to the point, he possessed some several paltry mines,—a score; it does not matter: and he owned a few miles of lands, and engineered deals, and clipped coupons. He—"

"But there were other things," she interrupted, "I told you. Pressure—money matters— want—my people—trouble. You understood the whole sordid situation. I could not help it. It was not my will. I was sacrificed, or I sacrificed, have it as you wish. But, my God! Dave, I gave you up! You never did *me* justice. Think what I have gone through!"

"It was not your will? Pressure? Under high heaven there was no thing to will you to this man's bed or that."

"But I cared for you all the time," she pleaded.

"I was unused to your way of measuring love. I am still unused. I do not understand."

"But now! now!"

"We were speaking of this man you saw fit to marry. What manner of man was he? Wherein did he charm your soul? What potent virtues were his? True, he had a golden grip, —an almighty golden grip. He knew the odds. He was versed in cent per cent. He had a narrow wit and excellent judgment of the viler parts, whereby he transferred this man's money to his pockets, and that man's money, and the next man's. And the law smiled. In that it did not condemn, our Christian ethics approved. By social measure he was not a bad man. But by your measure, Karen, by mine, by ours of the rose garden, what was he?"

"Remember, he is dead."

"The fact is not altered thereby. What was he? A great, gross, material creature, deaf to song, blind to beauty, dead to the spirit. He was fat with laziness, and flabby-cheeked, and the round of his belly witnessed his gluttony—"

"But he is dead. It is we who are now—now! now! Don't you hear? As you say, I have been inconstant. I have sinned. Good. But should not you, too, cry *peccavi*? If I have broken promises, have not you? Your love of the rose garden was of all time, or so you said. Where is it now?"

"It is here! now!" he cried, striking his breast passionately with clenched hand. "It has always been."

"And your love was a great love; there was none greater," she continued; "or so you said in the rose garden. Yet it is not fine enough, large enough, to forgive me here, crying now at your feet?"

The man hesitated. His mouth opened; words shaped vainly on his lips. She had forced him to bare his heart and speak truths which he had hidden from himself. And she was good to look upon, standing there in a glory of passion, calling back old associations and warmer life. He turned away his head that he might not see, but she passed around and fronted him.

"Look at me, Dave! Look at me! I am the same, after all. And so are you, if you would but see. We are not changed."

Her hand rested on his shoulder, and his had half-passed, roughly, about her, when the sharp crackle of a match startled him to himself. Winapie, alien to the scene, was lighting the slow wick of the slush lamp. She appeared to start out against a background of utter black, and the flame, flaring suddenly up, lighted her bronze beauty to royal gold.

"You see, it is impossible," he groaned, thrusting the fair-haired woman gently from him. "It is impossible," he repeated. "It is impossible."

"I am not a girl, Dave, with a girl's illusions," she said softly, though not daring to come back to him. "It is as a woman that I understand. Men are men. A common custom of the country. I am not shocked. I divined it from the first. But—ah!—it is only a marriage of the country—not a real marriage?"

"We do not ask such questions in Alaska," he interposed feebly.

"I know, but—"

"Well, then, it is only a marriage of the country—nothing else."

"And there are no children?"

"No."

"Nor—"

"No, no; nothing—but it is impossible."

"But it is not." She was at his side again, her hand touching lightly, caressingly, the sunburned back of his. "I know the custom of the land too well. Men do it every day. They do not care to remain here, shut out from the world, for all their days; so they give an order on the P. C. C. Company for a year's provisions, some money in hand, and the girl is content. By the end of that time, a man—" She shrugged her shoulders. "And so with the girl here. We will give her an order upon the company, not for a year, but for life. What was she when you found her? A raw, meat-eating savage; fish in summer, moose in winter, feasting in plenty, starving in famine. But for you that is what she would have remained. For your coming she was happier; for your going, surely, with a life of comparative splendor assured, she will be happier than if you had never been."

"No, no," he protested. "It is not right."

"Come, Dave, you must see. She is not your kind. There is no race affinity. She is an aborigine, sprung from the soil, yet close to the soil, and impossible to lift from the soil. Born savage, savage she will die. But we—you and I—the dominant, evolved race—the salt of the earth and the masters thereof! We are made for each other. The supreme call is of kind, and we are of kind. Reason and feeling dictate it. Your very instinct demands it. That you cannot deny. You cannot escape the generations behind you. Yours is an ancestry which has survived for a thousand centuries, and for a hundred thousand centuries, and your line must not stop here. It cannot. Your ancestry will not permit it. Instinct is stronger than the will. The race is mightier than you. Come, Dave, let us go. We are young yet, and life is good. Come."

Winapie, passing out of the cabin to feed the dogs, caught his attention and caused him to shake his head and weakly to reiterate. But the woman's hand slipped about his neck, and her cheek pressed to his. His bleak life rose up and smote him,—the vain struggle with piti-less forces; the dreary years of frost and famine; the harsh and jarring contact with elemental life; the aching void which mere animal existence could not fill. And there, seduction by his side, whispering of brighter, warmer lands, of music, light, and joy, called the old times back again. He visioned it unconsciously. Faces rushed in upon him; glimpses of forgotten scenes, memories of merry hours; strains of song and trills of laughter—

"Come, Dave, Come. I have for both. The way is soft." She looked about her at the bare furnishings of the cabin. "I have for both. The world is at our feet, and all joy is ours. Come! come!"

She was in his arms, trembling, and he held her tightly. He rose to his feet . . . But the snarling of hungry dogs, and the shrill cries of Winapie bringing about peace between the combatants, came muffled to his ear through the heavy logs. And another scene flashed before him. A struggle in the forest,—a bald-face grizzly, broken-legged, terrible; the snarling of the dogs and the shrill cries of Winapie as she urged them to the attack; himself in the midst of the crush, breathless, panting, striving to hold off red death; broken-backed, entrail-ripped dogs howling in impotent anguish and desecrating the snow; the virgin white running scarlet with the blood of man and beast; the bear, ferocious, irresistible, crunching, crunching down to the core of his life; and Winapie, at the last, in the thick of the frightful muddle, hair flying, eyes flashing, fury incarnate, passing the long hunting knife again and again—Sweat started to his forehead. He shook off the clinging woman and staggered back to the wall. And she, knowing that the moment had come, but unable to divine what was passing within him, felt all she had gained slipping away.

"Dave! Dave!" she cried. "I will not give you up! I will not give you up! If you do not wish to come, we will stay. I will stay with you. The world is less to me than are you. I will be a Northland wife to you. I will cook your food, feed your dogs, break trail for you, lift a paddle with you. I can do it. Believe me, I am strong."

Nor did he doubt it, looking upon her and holding her off from him; but his face had grown stern and gray, and the warmth had died out of his eyes.

"I will pay off Pierre and the boatmen, and let them go. And I will stay with you, priest or no priest, minister or no minister; go with you, now, anywhere! Dave! Dave! Listen to me! You say I did you wrong in the past—and I did—let me make up for it, let me atone. If I did not rightly measure love before, let me show that I can now."

She sank to the floor and threw her arms about his knees, sobbing. "And you *do* care for me. You *do* care for me. Think! The long years I have waited, suffered! You can never know!" He stooped and raised her to her feet.

"Listen," he commanded, opening the door and lifting her bodily outside. "It cannot be. We are not alone to be considered. You must go. I wish you a safe journey. You will find it tougher work when you get up by the Sixty Mile, but you have the best boatmen in the world, and will get through all right. Will you say good-by?"

Though she already had herself in hand, she looked at him hopelessly. "If—if—if Winapie should—" She quavered and stopped.

But he grasped the unspoken thought, and answered, "Yes." Then struck with the enormity of it, "It cannot be conceived. There is no likelihood. It must not be entertained."

"Kiss me," she whispered, her face lighting. Then she turned and went away.

"Break camp, Pierre," she said to the boatman, who alone had remained awake against her return. "We must be going."

By the firelight his sharp eyes scanned the woe in her face, but he received the extraordinary command as though it were the most usual thing in the world. "*Oui, madame,*" he assented. "Which way? Dawson?"

"No," she answered, lightly enough; "up; out; Dyea."

Whereat he fell upon the sleeping *voyageurs*, kicking them, grunting, from their blankets, and buckling them down to the work, the while his voice, vibrant with action, shrilling through all the camp. In a trice Mrs. Sayther's tiny tent had been struck, pots and pans were being gathered up, blankets rolled, and the men staggering under the loads to the boat. Here, on the banks, Mrs. Sayther waited till the luggage was made ship-shape and her nest prepared.

"We line up to de head of de island," Pierre explained to her while running out the long tow rope. "Den we tak to das back channel, where de water not queek, and I t'ink we mak good tam."

A scuffling and pattering of feet in the last year's dry grass caught his quick ear, and he turned his head. The Indian girl, circled by a bristling ring of wolf dogs, was coming toward them. Mrs. Sayther noted that the girl's face, which had been apathetic throughout the scene in the cabin, had now quickened into blazing and wrathful life.

"What you do my man?" she demanded abruptly of Mrs. Sayther. "Him lay on bunk, and him look bad all the time. I say, 'What the matter, Dave? You sick?' But him no say nothing. After that him say, 'Good girl Winapie, go way. I be all right bimeby.' What you do my man, eh? I think you bad woman."

Mrs. Sayther looked curiously at the barbarian woman who shared the life of this man, while she departed alone in the darkness of night.

"I think you bad woman," Winapie repeated in the slow, methodical way of one who gropes for strange words in an alien tongue. "I think better you go way, no come no more. Eh? What you think? I have one man. I Indian girl. You 'Merican woman. You good to see. You find plenty men. Your eyes blue like the sky. Your skin so white, so soft."

Coolly she thrust out a brown forefinger and pressed the soft cheek of the other woman. And to the eternal credit of Karen Sayther, she never flinched. Pierre hesitated and half stepped forward; but she motioned him away, though her heart welled to him with secret gratitude. "It's all right, Pierre," she said. "Please go away."

He stepped back respectfully out of earshot, where he stood grumbling to himself and measuring the distance in springs.

"Um white, um soft, like baby." Winapie touched the other cheek and withdrew her hand. "Bimeby mosquito come. Skin get sore in spot; um swell, oh, so big; um hurt, oh, so much. Plenty mosquito; plenty spot. I think better you go now before mosquito come. This way," pointing down the stream, "you go St. Michael's; that way," pointing up, "you go Dyea. Better you go Dyea. Good-by."

And that which Mrs. Sayther then did, caused Pierre to marvel greatly. For she threw her arms around the Indian girl, kissed her, and burst into tears.

"Be good to him," she cried. "Be good to him."

Then she slipped half down the face of the bank, called back "Good-by," and dropped into the boat amidships. Pierre followed her and cast off. He shoved the steering oar into place and gave the signal. Le Goire lifted an old French *chanson*; the men, like a row of ghosts in the dim starlight, bent their backs to the tow line; the steering oar cut the black current sharply, and the boat swept out into the night.

WHICH MAKE MEN REMEMBER

FORTUNE LA PEARLE crushed his way through the snow, sobbing, straining, cursing his luck, Alaska, Nome, the cards, and the man who had felt his knife. The hot blood was freezing on his hands, and the scene yet bright in his eyes,—the man, clutching the table and sinking slowly to the floor; the rolling counters and the scattered deck; the swift shiver throughout the room, and the pause; the game-keepers no longer calling, and the clatter of the chips dying away, the startled faces, the infinite instant of silence, and then the great blood-roar and the tide of vengeance which lapped his heels and turned the town mad behind him.

"All hell's broke loose," he sneered, turning aside in the darkness and heading for the beach. Lights were flashing from open doors, and tent, cabin, and dance-hall let slip their denizens upon the chase. The clamor of men and howling of dogs smote his ears and quickened his feet. He ran on and on. The sounds grew dim, and the pursuit dissipated itself in vain rage and aimless groping. But a flitting shadow clung to him. Head thrust over shoulder, he caught glimpses of it, now taking vague shape on an open expanse of snow, now merging into the deeper shadows of some darkened cabin or beach-listed craft.

Fortune La Pearle swore like a woman, weakly, with the hint of tears that comes of exhaustion, and plunged deeper into the maze of heaped ice, tents, and prospect holes. He stumbled over taut hawsers and piles of dunnage, tripped on crazy guy-ropes and insanely planted pegs, and fell again and again upon frozen dumps and mounds of hoarded drift-wood. At times, when he deemed he had drawn clear, his head dizzy with the painful pounding of his heart and the suffocating intake of his breath, he slackened down; and ever the shadow leaped out of the gloom and forced him on in heart-breaking flight. A swift intuition lashed upon him, leaving in its trail the cold chill of superstition. The persistence of the shadow he invested with his gambler's symbolism. Silent, inexorable, not to be shaken off, he took it as the fate which waited at the last turn when chips were cashed in and gains and losses counted up. Fortune La Pearle believed in those rare, illuminating moments, when the intelligence flung from it time and space, to rise naked through eternity and read the facts of life from the open book of chance. That this was such a moment he had no doubt; and when he turned inland and sped across the snow-covered tundra he was not startled because the shadow took upon it greater definiteness and drew in closer. Oppressed with his own impotence, he halted in the midst of the white waste and whirled about. His right hand slipped from its mitten, and a revolver, at level, glistened in the pale light of the stars.

"Don't shoot. I haven't a gun."

The shadow had assumed tangible shape, and at the sound of its human voice a trepidation affected Fortune La Pearle's knees, and his stomach was stricken with the qualms of sudden relief.

Perhaps things fell out differently because Uri Bram had no gun that night when he sat on the hard benches of the El Dorado and saw murder done. To that fact also might be attributed the trip on the Long Trail which he took subsequently with a most unlikely comrade. But be it as it may, he repeated a second time, "Don't shoot. Can't you see I haven't a gun?"

"Then what the flaming hell did you take after me for?" demanded the gambler, lowering his revolver.

Uri Bram shrugged his shoulders. "It don't matter much, anyhow. I want you to come with me."

"Where?"

"To my shack, over on the edge of the camp."

But Fortune La Pearle drove the heel of his moccasin into the snow and attested by his various deities to the madness of Uri Bram. "Who are you," he perorated, "and what am I, that I should put my neck into the rope at your bidding?"

"I am Uri Bram," the other said simply, "and my shack is over there on the edge of camp. I don't know who you are, but you've thrust the soul from a living man's body,—there's the blood red on your sleeve,—and, like a second Cain, the hand of all mankind is against you, and there is no place you may lay your head. Now, I have a shack—"

"For the love of your mother, hold your say, man," interrupted Fortune La Pearle, "or I'll make you a second Abel for the joy of it. So help me, I will! With a thousand men to lay me by the heels, looking high and low, what do I want with your shack? I want to get out of here—away! away! away! Cursed swine! I've half a mind to go back and run amuck, and settle for a few of them, the pigs! One gorgeous, glorious fight, and end the whole damn business! It's a skin game, that's what life is, and I'm sick of it!"

He stopped, appalled, crushed by his great desolation, and Uri Bram seized the moment. He was not given to speech, this man, and that which followed was the longest in his life, save one long afterward in another place.

"That's why I told you about my shack. I can stow you there so they'll never find you, and I've got grub in plenty. Elsewise you can't get away. No dogs, no nothing, the sea closed, St. Michael the nearest post, runners to carry the news before you, the same over the portage to Anvik—not a chance in the world for you! Now wait with me till it blows over. They'll forget all about you in a month or less, what of stampeding to York and what not, and you can hit the trail under their noses and they won't bother. I've got my own ideas of justice. When I ran after you, out of the El Dorado and along the beach, it wasn't to catch you or give you up. My ideas are my own, and that's not one of them."

He ceased as the murderer drew a prayer-book from his pocket. With the aurora borealis glimmering yellow in the northeast, heads bared to the frost and naked hands grasping the sacred book, Fortune La Pearle swore him to the words he had spoken—an oath which Uri Bram never intended breaking, and never broke.

At the door of the shack the gambler hesitated for an instant, marveling at the strangeness of this man who had befriended him, and doubting. But by the candlelight he found the cabin comfortable and without occupants, and he was quickly rolling a cigarette while the other man made coffee. His muscles relaxed in the warmth and he lay back with half-assumed indolence, intently studying Uri's face through the curling wisps of smoke. It was a powerful face, but its strength was of that peculiar sort which stands girt in and unrelated. The seams were deep-graven, more like scars, while the stern features were in no way soft-ened by hints of sympathy or humor. Under prominent bushy brows the eyes shone cold and gray. The cheekbones, high and forbidding, were undermined by deep hollows. The chin and jaw displayed a steadiness of purpose which the narrow forehead advertised as single, and, if needs be, pitiless. Everything was harsh, the nose, the lips, the voice, the lines about the mouth. It was the face of one who communed much with himself, unused to seeking counsel from the world; the face of one who wrestled oft of nights with angels, and rose to face the day with shut lips that no man might know. He was narrow but deep; and Fortune, his own humanity broad and shallow, could make nothing of him. Did Uri sing when merry and sigh when sad, he could have understood; but as it was, the cryptic features were undecipherable; he could not measure the soul they concealed.

"Lend a hand, Mister Man," Uri ordered when the cups had been emptied. "We've got to fix up for visitors."

Fortune purred his name for the other's benefit, and assisted understandingly. The bunk was built against a side and end of the cabin. It was a rude affair, the bottom being composed of drift-wood logs overlaid with moss. At the foot the rough ends of these timbers projected in an uneven row. From the side next the wall Uri ripped back the moss and removed three of the logs. The jagged ends he sawed off and replaced so that the projecting row remained unbroken. Fortune carried in sacks of flour from the cache and piled them on the floor beneath the aperture. On these Uri laid a pair of long sea-bags, and over all spread several thicknesses of moss and blankets. Upon this Fortune could lie, with the sleeping furs stretching over him from one side of the bunk to the other, and all men could look upon it and declare it empty.

In the weeks which followed, several domiciliary visits were paid, not a shack or tent in Nome escaping, but Fortune lay in his cranny undisturbed. In fact, little attention was given to Uri Bram's cabin; for it was the last place under the sun to expect to find the murderer of John Randolph. Except during such interruptions, Fortune lolled about the cabin, playing long games of solitaire and smoking endless cigarettes. Though his volatile nature loved geniality and play of words and laughter, he quickly accommodated himself to Uri's taciturnity. Beyond the actions and plans of his pursuers, the state of the trails, and the price of dogs, they never talked; and these things were only discussed at rare intervals and briefly. But Fortune fell to working out a system, and hour after hour, and day after day, he shuffled and dealt, shuffled and dealt, noted the combinations of the cards in long columns, and shuffled and dealt again. Toward the end even this absorption failed him, and, head bowed upon the table, he visioned the lively all-night houses of Nome, where the gamekeepers and look-outs worked in shifts and the clattering roulette ball never slept. At such times his loneliness and bankruptcy stunned him till he sat for hours in the same unblinking, unchanging position. At other times, his long-pent bitterness found voice in passionate outbursts; for he had rubbed the world the wrong way and did not like the feel of it.

"Life's a skin-game," he was fond of repeating, and on this one note he rang the changes. "I never had half a chance," he complained. "I was faked in my birth and flimflammed with my mother's milk. The dice were loaded when she tossed the box, and I was born to prove the loss. But that was no reason she should blame me for it, and look on me as a cold deck; but she did—ay, she did. Why didn't she give me a show? Why didn't the world? Why did

I go broke in Seattle? Why did I take the steerage, and live like a hog to Nome? Why did I go to the El Dorado? I was heading for Big Pete's and only went for matches. Why didn't I have matches? Why did I want to smoke? Don't you see? All worked out, every bit of it, all parts fitting snug. Before I was born, like as not. I'll put the sack I never hope to get on it, before I was born. That's why! That's why John Randolph passed the word and his checks in at the same time. Damn him! It served him well right! Why didn't he keep his tongue between his teeth and give me a chance? He knew I was next to broke. Why didn't I hold my hand? Oh, why? Why? Why?"

And Fortune La Pearle would roll upon the floor, vainly interrogating the scheme of things. At such outbreaks Uri said no word, gave no sign, save that his grey eyes seemed to turn dull and muddy, as though from lack of interest. There was nothing in common between these two men, and this fact Fortune grasped sufficiently to wonder sometimes why Uri had stood by him.

But the time of waiting came to an end. Even a community's blood lust cannot stand before its gold lust. The murder of John Randolph had already passed into the annals of the camp, and there it rested. Had the murderer appeared, the men of Nome would certainly have stopped stampeding long enough to see justice done, whereas the whereabouts of Fortune La Pearle was no longer an insistent problem. There was gold in the creek beds and ruby beaches, and when the sea opened, the men with healthy sacks would sail away to where the good things of life were sold absurdly cheap.

So, one night, Fortune helped Uri Bram harness the dogs and lash the sled, and the twain took the winter trail south on the ice. But it was not all south; for they left the sea east from St. Michael's, crossed the divide, and struck the Yukon at Anvik, many hundred miles from its mouth. Then on, into the northeast, past Koyokuk, Tanana, and Minook, till they rounded the Great Curve at Fort Yukon, crossed and recrossed the Arctic Circle, and headed south through the Flats. It was a weary journey, and Fortune would have wondered why the man went with him, had not Uri told him that he owned claims and had men working at Eagle. Eagle lay on the edge of the line; a few miles farther on, the British flag waved over the barracks at Fort Cudahy. Then came Dawson, Pelly, the Five Fingers, Windy Arm, Caribou Crossing, Linderman, the Chilcoot and Dyea.

On the morning after passing Eagle, they rose early. This was their last camp, and they were now to part. Fortune's heart was light. There was a promise of spring in the land, and the days were growing longer. The way was passing into Canadian territory. Liberty was at hand, the sun was returning, and each day saw him nearer to the Great Outside. The world was big, and he could once again paint his future in royal red. He whistled about the break-fast and hummed snatches of light song while Uri put the dogs in harness and packed up. But when all was ready, Fortune's feet itching to be off, Uri pulled an unused back-log to the fire and sat down.

"Ever hear of the Dead Horse Trail?"

He glanced up meditatively and Fortune shook his head, inwardly chafing at the delay.

"Sometimes there are meetings under circumstances which make men remember," Uri continued, speaking in a low voice and very slowly, "and I met a man under such circum-stances on the Dead Horse Trail. Freighting an outfit over the White Pass in '97 broke many a man's heart, for there was a world of reason when they gave that trail its name. The horses died like mosquitoes in the first frost, and from Skaguay to Bennett they rotted in heaps. They died at the Rocks, they were poisoned at the Summit, and they starved at the Lakes; they fell off the trail, what there was of it, or they went through it; in the river they drowned under their loads, or were smashed to pieces against the boulders; they snapped their legs in the crevices and broke their backs falling backwards with their packs; in the sloughs they sank from sight or smothered in the slime, and they were disemboweled in the bogs where the corduroy logs turned end up in the mud; men shot them, worked them to death, and when they were gone, went back to the beach and bought more. Some did not bother to shoot them,—stripping the saddles off and the shoes and leaving them where they fell. Their hearts turned to stone—those which did not break—and they became beasts, the men on Dead Horse Trail.

"It was there I met a man with the heart of a Christ and the patience. And he was honest. When he rested at midday he took the packs from the horses so that they, too, might rest. He paid $50 a hundred-weight for their fodder, and more. He used his own bed to blanket their backs when they rubbed raw. Other men let the saddles eat holes the size of water-buckets. Other men, when the shoes gave out, let them wear their hoofs down to the bleeding stumps. He spent his last dollar for horseshoe nails. I know this because we slept in the one bed and ate from the one pot, and became blood brothers where men lost their grip of things and died blaspheming God. He was never too tired to ease a strap or tighten a cinch, and often there were tears in his eyes when he looked on all that waste of misery. At a passage in the rocks, where the brutes upreared hindlegged and stretched their forelegs upward like cats to clear the wall, the way was piled with carcasses where they had toppled back. And here he stood, in the stench of hell, with a cheery word and a hand on the rump at the right time, till the string passed by. And when one bogged he blocked the trail till it was clear again; nor did the man live who crowded him at such time.

"At the end of the trail a man who had killed fifty horses wanted to buy, but we looked at him and at our own,—mountain cayuses from eastern Oregon. Five thousand he offered, and we were broke, but we remembered the poison grass of the Summit and the passage in the Rocks, and the man who was my brother spoke no word, but divided the cayuses into two bunches,—his in the one and mine in the other, and he looked at me and we understood each other. So he drove mine to the one side and I drove his to the other, and we took with us our rifles and shot them to the last one, while the man who had killed fifty horses cursed us till his throat cracked. But that man, with whom I welded blood-brothership on the Dead Horse Trail—"

"Why, that man was John Randolph," Fortune, sneering the while, completed the climax for him.

Uri nodded, and said, "I am glad you understand."

"I am ready," Fortune answered, the old weary bitterness strong in his face again. "Go ahead, but hurry."

Uri Bram rose to his feet.

"I have had faith in God all the days of my life. I believe He loves justice. I believe He is looking down upon us now, choosing between us. I believe He waits to work His will through my own right arm. And such is my belief, that we will take equal chance and let Him speak His own judgment."

Fortune's heart leaped at the words. He did not know much concerning Uri's God, but he believed in Chance, and Chance had been coming his way ever since the night he ran down the beach and across the snow. "But there is only one gun," he objected.

"We will fire turn about," Uri replied, at the same time throwing out the cylinder of the other man's Colt and examining it.

"And the cards to decide! One hand of seven up!"

Fortune's blood was warming to the game, and he drew the deck from his pocket as Uri nodded. Surely Chance would not desert him now! He thought of the returning sun as he cut for deal, and he thrilled when he found the deal was his. He shuffled and dealt, and Uri cut him the Jack of Spades. They laid down their hands. Uri's was bare of trumps, while he held ace, deuce. The outside seemed very near to him as they stepped off the fifty paces.

"If God withholds His hand and you drop me, the dogs and outfit are yours. You'll find a bill of sale, already made out, in my pocket," Uri explained, facing the path of the bullet, straight and broad-breasted.

Fortune shook a vision of the sun shining on the ocean from his eyes and took aim. He was very careful. Twice he lowered as the spring breeze shook the pines. But the third time he dropped on one knee, gripped the revolver steadily in both hands, and fired. Uri whirled half about, threw up his arms, swayed wildly for a moment, and sank into the snow. But Fortune knew he had fired too far to one side, else the man would not have whirled.

When Uri, mastering the flesh and struggling to his feet, beckoned for the weapon, Fortune was minded to fire again. But he thrust the idea from him. Chance had been very good to him already, he felt, and if he tricked now he would have to pay for it afterward. No, he would play fair. Besides Uri was hard hit and could not possibly hold the heavy Colt long enough to draw a bead.

"And where is your God now?" he taunted, as he gave the wounded man the revolver.

And Uri answered: "God has not yet spoken. Prepare that He may speak."

Fortune faced him, but twisted his chest sideways in order to present less surface. Uri tottered about drunkenly, but waited, too, for the moment's calm between the catspaws. The revolver was very heavy, and he doubted, like Fortune, because of its weight. But he held it, arm extended, above his head, and then let it slowly drop forward and down. At the instant Fortune's left breast and the sight flashed into line with his eye, he pulled the trigger. Fortune did not whirl, but gay San Francisco dimmed and faded, and as the sun-bright snow turned black and blacker, he breathed his last malediction on the Chance he had misplayed.

SIWASH

"If I was a man—" Her words were in themselves indecisive, but the withering contempt which flashed from her black eyes was not lost upon the men-folk in the tent.

Tommy, the English sailor, squirmed, but chivalrous old Dick Humphries, Cornish fisherman and erstwhile American salmon capitalist, beamed upon her benevolently as ever. He bore women too large a portion of his rough heart to mind them, as he said, when they were in the doldrums, or when their limited vision would not permit them to see all around a thing. So they said nothing, these two men who had taken the half-frozen woman into their tent three days back, and who had warmed her, and fed her, and rescued her goods from the Indian packers. This latter had necessitated the payment of numerous dollars, to say nothing of a demonstration in force—Dick Humphries squinting along the sights of a Winchester while Tommy apportioned their wages among them at his own appraisement. It had been a little thing in itself, but it meant much to a woman playing a desperate single-hand in the equally desperate Klondike rush of '97. Men were occupied with their own pressing needs, nor did they approve of women playing, single-handed, the odds of the arctic winter. "If I was a man, I know what I would do." Thus reiterated Molly, she of the flashing eyes, and therein spoke the cumulative grit of five American-born generations.

In the succeeding silence, Tommy thrust a pan of biscuits into the Yukon stove and piled on fresh fuel. A reddish flood pounded along under his sun-tanned skin, and as he stooped, the skin of his neck was scarlet. Dick palmed a three-cornered sail needle through a set of broken pack straps, his good nature in nowise disturbed by the feminine cataclysm which was threatening to burst in the storm-beaten tent.

"And if you was a man?" he asked, his voice vibrant with kindness. The three-cornered needle jammed in the damp leather, and he suspended work for the moment.

"I'd be a man. I'd put the straps on my back and light out. I wouldn't lay in camp here, with the Yukon like to freeze most any day, and the goods not half over the portage. And you—you are men, and you sit here, holding your hands, afraid of a little wind and wet. I tell you straight, Yankee-men are made of different stuff. They'd be hitting the trail for Dawson if they had to wade through hell-fire. And you, you—I wish I was a man."

"I'm very glad, my dear, that you're not." Dick Humphries threw the bight of the sail twine over the point of the needle and drew it clear with a couple of deft turns and a jerk.

A snort of the gale dealt the tent a broad-handed slap as it hurtled past, and the sleet rat-tat-tatted with snappy spite against the thin canvas. The smoke, smothered in its exit, drove back through the fire-box door, carrying with it the pungent odor of green spruce.

"Good Gawd! Why can't a woman listen to reason?" Tommy lifted his head from the denser depths and turned upon her a pair of smoke-outraged eyes.

"And why can't a man show his manhood?"

Tommy sprang to his feet with an oath which would have shocked a woman of lesser heart, ripped loose the sturdy reef-knots and flung back the flaps of the tent.

The trio peered out. It was not a heartening spectacle. A few water-soaked tents formed the miserable foreground, from which the streaming ground sloped to a foaming gorge. Down this ramped a mountain torrent. Here and there, dwarf spruce, rooting and groveling in the shallow alluvium, marked the proximity of the timber line. Beyond, on the opposing slope, the vague outlines of a glacier loomed dead-white through the driving rain. Even as they looked, its massive front crumbled into the valley, on the breast of some subterranean vomit, and it lifted its hoarse thunder above the screeching voice of the storm. Involuntarily, Molly shrank back.

"Look, woman! Look with all your eyes! Three miles in the teeth of the gale to Crater Lake, across two glaciers, along the slippery rim-rock, knee-deep in a howling river! Look, I say, you Yankee woman! Look! There's your Yankee-men!" Tommy pointed a passionate hand in the direction of the struggling tents. "Yankees, the last mother's son of them. Are they on trail? Is there one of them with the straps to his back? And you would teach us men our work? Look, I say!"

Another tremendous section of the glacier rumbled earthward. The wind whipped in at the open doorway, bulging out the sides of the tent till it swayed like a huge bladder at its guy ropes. The smoke swirled about them, and the sleet drove sharply into their flesh. Tommy pulled the flaps together hastily, and returned to his tearful task at the fire-box. Dick Humphries threw the mended pack straps into a corner and lighted his pipe. Even Molly was for the moment persuaded.

"There's my clothes," she half-whimpered, the feminine for the moment prevailing. "They're right at the top of the cache, and they'll be ruined! I tell you, ruined!"

"There, there," Dick interposed, when the last quavering syllable had wailed itself out. "Don't let that worry you, little woman. I'm old enough to be your father's brother, and I've a daughter older than you, and I'll tog you out in fripperies when we get to Dawson if it takes my last dollar."

"When we get to Dawson!" The scorn had come back to her throat with a sudden surge. "You'll rot on the way, first. You'll drown in a mudhole. You—you—Britishers!"

The last word, explosive, intensive, had strained the limits of her vituperation. If that would not stir these men, what could? Tommy's neck ran red again, but he kept his tongue between his teeth. Dick's eyes mellowed. He had the advantage over Tommy, for he had once had a white woman for a wife.

The blood of five American-born generations is, under certain circumstances, an uncomfortable heritage; and among these circumstances might be enumerated that of being quartered with next of kin. These men were Britons. On sea and land her ancestry and the generations thereof had thrashed them and theirs. On sea and land they would continue to do so. The traditions of her race clamored for vindication. She was but a woman of the present, but in her bubbled the whole mighty past. It was not alone Molly Travis who pulled on gum boots, mackintosh, and straps; for the phantom hands of ten thousand forbears drew tight the buckles, just so as they squared her jaw and set her eyes with determination. She, Molly Travis, intended to shame these Britishers; they, the innumerable shades, were asserting the dominance of the common race.

The men-folk did not interfere. Once Dick suggested that she take his oilskins, as her mackintosh was worth no more than paper in such a storm. But she sniffed her independence so sharply that he communed with his pipe till she tied the flaps on the outside and slushed away on the flooded trail.

"Think she'll make it?" Dick's face belied the indifference of his voice.

"Make it? If she stands the pressure till she gets to the cache, what of the cold and misery, she'll be stark, raving mad. Stand it? She'll be dumb-crazed. You know it yourself, Dick. You've wind-jammed round the Horn. You know what it is to lay out on a topsail yard in the thick of it, bucking sleet and snow and frozen canvas till you're ready to just let go and cry like a baby. Clothes? She won't be able to tell a bundle of skirts from a gold pan or a tea-kettle."

"Kind of think we were wrong in letting her go, then?"

"Not a bit of it. So help me, Dick, she'd 'a' made this tent a hell for the rest of the trip if we hadn't. Trouble with her she's got too much spirit. This'll tone it down a bit."

"Yes," Dick admitted, "she's too ambitious. But then Molly's all right. A cussed little fool to tackle a trip like this, but a plucky sight better than those pick-me-up-and-carry-me kind of women. She's the stock that carried you and me, Tommy, and you've got to make allowance for the spirit. Takes a woman to breed a man. You can't suck manhood from the dugs of a creature whose only claim to womanhood is her petticoats. Takes a she cat, not a cow, to mother a tiger."

"And when they're unreasonable we've got to put up with it, eh?"

"The proposition. A sharp sheath-knife cuts deeper on a slip than a dull one, but that's no reason for to hack the edge off over a capstan bar."

"All right, if you say so, but when it comes to woman, I guess I'll take mine with a little less edge."

"What do you know about it?" Dick demanded.

"Some." Tommy reached over for a pair of Molly's wet stockings and stretched them across his knees to dry.

Dick, eying him querulously, went fishing in her hand satchel, then hitched up to the front of the stove with divers articles of damp clothing spread likewise to the heat.

"Thought you said you never were married?" he asked.

"Did I? No more was I—that is—yes, by Gawd! I was. And as good a woman as ever cooked grub for a man."

"Slipped her moorings?" Dick symbolized infinity with a wave of his hand.

"Ay."

"Childbirth," he added, after a moment's pause.

The beans bubbled rowdily on the front lid, and he pushed the pot back to a cooler surface. After that he investigated the biscuits, tested them with a splinter of wood, and placed them aside under cover of a damp cloth. Dick, after the manner of his kind, stifled his interest and waited silently. "A different woman to Molly. Siwash."

Dick nodded his understanding.

"Not so proud and willful, but stick by a fellow through thick and thin. Sling a paddle with the next and starve as contentedly as Job. Go for'ard when the sloop's nose was more often under than not, and take in sail like a man. Went prospecting once, up Teslin way, past

Surprise Lake and the Little Yellow-Head. Grub gave out, and we ate the dogs. Dogs gave out, and we ate harnesses, moccasins, and furs. Never a whimper; never a pick-me-up-and-carry-me. Before we went she said look out for grub, but when it happened, never a I-told-you-so. 'Never mind, Tommy,' she'd say, day after day, that weak she could bare lift a snow-shoe and her feet raw with the work. 'Never mind. I'd sooner be flat-bellied of hunger and be your woman, Tommy, than have a *potlach* every day and be Chief George's *klooch.*' George was chief of the Chilcoots, you know, and wanted her bad.

"Great days, those. Was a likely chap myself when I struck the coast. Jumped a whaler, the *Pole Star*, at Unalaska, and worked my way down to Sitka on an otter hunter. Picked up with Happy Jack there—know him?"

"Had charge of my traps for me," Dick answered, "down on the Columbia. Pretty wild, wasn't he, with a warm place in his heart for whiskey and women?"

"The very chap. Went trading with him for a couple of seasons—*hooch*, and blankets, and such stuff. Then got a sloop of my own, and not to cut him out, came down Juneau way. That's where I met Killisnoo; I called her Tilly for short. Met her at a squaw dance down on the beach. Chief George had finished the year's trade with the Sticks over the Passes, and was down from Dyea with half his tribe. No end of Siwashes at the dance, and I the only white. No one knew me, barring a few of the bucks I'd met over Sitka way, but I'd got most of their histories from Happy Jack.

"Everybody talking Chinook, not guessing that I could spit it better than most; and prin-cipally two girls who'd run away from Haine's Mission up the Lynn Canal. They were trim creatures, good to the eye, and I kind of thought of casting that way; but they were fresh as fresh-caught cod. Too much edge, you see. Being a new-comer, they started to twist me, not knowing I gathered in every word of Chinook they uttered.

"I never let on, but set to dancing with Tilly, and the more we danced the more our hearts warmed to each other. 'Looking for a woman,' one of the girls says, and the other tosses her head and answers, 'Small chance he'll get one when the women are looking for men.' And the bucks and squaws standing around began to grin and giggle and repeat what had been said. 'Quite a pretty boy,' says the first one. I'll not deny I was rather smooth-faced and youngish, but I'd been a man amongst men many's the day, and it rankled me. 'Dancing with Chief George's girl,' pipes the second. 'First thing George'll give him the flat of a paddle and send him about his business.' Chief George had been looking pretty black up to now, but at this he laughed and slapped his knees. He was a husky beggar and would have used the paddle too.

"'Who's the girls?' I asked Tilly, as we went ripping down the center in a reel. And as soon as she told me their names I remembered all about them from Happy Jack. Had their pedigree down fine—several things he'd told me that not even their own tribe knew. But I held my hush, and went on courting Tilly, they a-casting sharp remarks and everybody roar-ing. 'Bide a wee, Tommy,' I says to myself; 'bide a wee.'

"And bide I did, till the dance was ripe to break up, and Chief George had brought a paddle all ready for me. Everybody was on the lookout for mischief when we stopped; but I marched, easy as you please, slap into the thick of them. The Mission girls cut me up some-thing clever, and for all I was angry I had to set my teeth to keep from laughing. I turned upon them suddenly.

"'Are you done?' I asked.

"You should have seen them when they heard me spitting Chinook. Then I broke loose. I told them all about themselves, and their people before them; their fathers, mothers, sisters, brothers—everybody, everything. Each mean trick they'd played; every scrape they'd got into; every shame that'd fallen them. And I burned them without fear or favor. All hands crowded round. Never had they heard a white man sling their lingo as I did. Everybody was laughing save the Mission girls. Even Chief George forgot the paddle, or at least he was swallowing too much respect to dare to use it.

"But the girls. 'Oh, don't, Tommy,' they cried, the tears running down their cheeks. 'Please don't. We'll be good. Sure, Tommy, sure.' But I knew them well, and I scorched them on every tender spot. Nor did I slack away till they came down on their knees, begging and pleading with me to keep quiet. Then I shot a glance at Chief George; but he did not know whether to have at me or not, and passed it off by laughing hollowly.

"So be. When I passed the parting with Tilly that night I gave her the word that I was going to be around for a week or so, and that I wanted to see more of her. Not thick-skinned, her kind, when it came to showing like and dislike, and she looked her pleasure for the honest girl she was. Ay, a striking lass, and I didn't wonder that Chief George was taken with her.

"Everything my way. Took the wind from his sails on the first leg. I was for getting her aboard and sailing down Wrangel way till it blew over, leaving him to whistle; but I wasn't to get her that easy. Seems she was living with an uncle of hers—guardian, the way such things go—and seems he was nigh to shuffling off with consumption or some sort of lung trouble. He was good and bad by turns, and she wouldn't leave him till it was over with. Went up to the tepee just before I left, to speculate on how long it'd be; but the old beggar had promised her to Chief George, and when he clapped eyes on me his anger brought on a hemorrhage.

"'Come and take me, Tommy,' she says when we bid good-by on the beach. 'Ay,' I answers; 'when you give the word.' And I kissed her, white-man-fashion and lover-fashion, till she was all of a tremble like a quaking aspen, and I was so beside myself I'd half a mind to go up and give the uncle a lift over the divide.

"So I went down Wrangel way, past St. Mary's and even to the Queen Charlottes, trading, running whiskey, turning the sloop to most anything. Winter was on, stiff and crisp, and I was back to Juneau, when the word came. 'Come,' the beggar says who brought the news. 'Killisnoo say, "Come now."' 'What's the row?' I asks. 'Chief George,' says he. 'Potlach. Killisnoo, makum klooch.'

"Ay, it was bitter—the Taku howling down out of the north, the salt water freezing quick as it struck the deck, and the old sloop and I hammering into the teeth of it for a hundred miles to Dyea. Had a Douglass Islander for crew when I started, but midway up he was washed over from the bows. Jibed all over and crossed the course three times, but never a sign of him."

"Doubled up with the cold most likely," Dick suggested, putting a pause into the narrative while he hung one of Molly's skirts up to dry, "and went down like a pot of lead."

"My idea. So I finished the course alone, half-dead when I made Dyea in the dark of the evening. The tide favored, and I ran the sloop plump to the bank, in the shelter of the river. Couldn't go an inch further, for the fresh water was frozen solid. Halyards and blocks were that iced up I didn't dare lower mainsail or jib. First I broached a pint of the cargo raw, and then, leaving all standing, ready for the start, and with a blanket around me, headed across the flat to the camp. No mistaking, it was a grand layout. The Chilcats had come in a body —dogs, babies, and canoes—to say nothing of the Dog-Ears, the Little Salmons, and the Missions. Full half a thousand of them to celebrate Tilly's wedding, and never a white man in a score of miles.

"Nobody took note of me, the blanket over my head and hiding my face, and I waded knee deep through the dogs and youngsters till I was well up to the front. The show was being pulled off in a big open place among the trees, with great fires burning and the snow moccasin-packed as hard as Portland cement. Next me was Tilly, beaded and scarlet-clothed galore, and against her Chief George and his head men. The shaman was being helped out by the big medicines from the other tribes, and it shivered my spine up and down, the devil-tries they cut. I caught myself wondering if the folks in Liverpool could only see me now; and I thought of yellow-haired Gussie, whose brother I licked after my first voyage, just because he was not for having a sailorman courting his sister. And with Gussie in my eyes I looked at Tilly. A rum old world, thinks I, with man a-stepping in trails the mother little dreamed of when he lay at suck.

"So be. When the noise was loudest, walrus hides booming and priests a-singing, I says, 'Are you ready?' Gawd! Not a start, not a shot of the eyes my way, not the twitch of a muscle. 'I knew,' she answers, slow and steady as a calm spring tide. 'Where?' 'The high bank at the edge of the ice,' I whispers back. 'Jump out when I give the word.'

"Did I say there was no end of huskies? Well, there was no end. Here, there, everywhere, they were scattered about,—tame wolves and nothing less. When the strain runs thin they breed them in the bush with the wild, and they're bitter fighters. Right at the toe of my moccasin lay a big brute, and by the heel another. I doubled the first one's tail, quick, till it snapped in my grip. As his jaws clipped together where my hand should have been, I threw the second one by the scruff straight into his mouth. 'Go!' I cried to Tilly.

"You know how they fight. In the wink of an eye there was a raging hundred of them, top and bottom, ripping and tearing each other, kids and squaws tumbling which way, and the camp gone wild. Tilly'd slipped away, so I followed. But when I looked over my shoulder at the skirt of the crowd, the devil laid me by the heart, and I dropped the blanket and went back.

"By then the dogs'd been knocked apart and the crowd was untangling itself. Nobody was in proper place, so they didn't note that Tilly'd gone. 'Hello,' I says, gripping Chief George by the hand. 'May your potlach-smoke rise often, and the Sticks bring many furs with the spring.'

"Lord love me, Dick, but he was joyed to see me,—him with the upper hand and wedding Tilly. Chance to puff big over me. The tale that I was hot after her had spread through the camps, and my presence did him proud. All hands knew me, without my blanket, and set to grinning and giggling. It was rich, but I made it richer by playing unbeknowing.

"'What's the row?' I asks. 'Who's getting married now?'

"'Chief George,' the shaman says, ducking his reverence to him.

"'Thought he had two *klooches*.'

"'Him takum more,—three,' with another duck.

"'Oh!' And I turned away as though it didn't interest me.

"But this wouldn't do, and everybody begins singing out, 'Killisnoo! Killisnoo!'

"'Killisnoo what?' I asked.

"'Killisnoo, *klooch*, Chief George,' they blathered. 'Killisnoo, *klooch*.'

"I jumped and looked at Chief George. He nodded his head and threw out his chest.

"She'll be no *klooch* of yours,' I says solemnly. 'No *klooch* of yours,' I repeats, while his face went black and his hand began dropping to his hunting-knife.

"'Look!' I cries, striking an attitude. 'Big Medicine. You watch my smoke.'

"I pulled off my mittens, rolled back my sleeves, and made half-a-dozen passes in the air.

"'Killisnoo!' I shouts. 'Killisnoo! Killisnoo!'

"I was making medicine, and they began to scare. Every eye was on me; no time to find out that Tilly wasn't there. Then I called Killisnoo three times again, and waited; and three times more. All for mystery and to make them nervous. Chief George couldn't guess what I was up to, and wanted to put a stop to the foolery; but the shamans said to wait, and that they'd see me and go me one better, or words to that effect. Besides, he was a superstitious cuss, and I fancy a bit afraid of the white man's magic.

"Then I called Killisnoo, long and soft like the howl of a wolf, till the women were all a-tremble and the bucks looking serious.

"'Look!' I sprang for'ard, pointing my finger into a bunch of squaws—easier to deceive women than men, you know. 'Look!' And I raised it aloft as though following the flight of a bird. Up, up, straight overhead, making to follow it with my eyes till it disappeared in the sky.

"'Killisnoo,' I said, looking at Chief George and pointing upward again. 'Killisnoo.'

"So help me, Dick, the gammon worked. Half of them, at least, saw Tilly disappear in the air. They'd drunk my whiskey at Juneau and seen stranger sights, I'll warrant. Why should I not do this thing, I, who sold bad spirits corked in bottles? Some of the women shrieked. Everybody fell to whispering in bunches. I folded my arms and held my head high, and they drew further away from me. The time was ripe to go. 'Grab him,' Chief George cries. Three or four of them came at me, but I whirled, quick, made a couple of passes like to send them after Tilly, and pointed up. Touch me? Not for the kingdoms of the earth. Chief George harangued them, but he couldn't get them to lift a leg. Then he made to take me himself; but I repeated the mummery and his grit went out through his fingers.

"'Let your shamans work wonders the like of which I have done this night,' I says. 'Let them call Killisnoo down out of the sky whither I have sent her.' But the priests knew their limits. 'May your *klooches* bear you sons as the spawn of the salmon,' I says, turning to go; 'and may your totem pole stand long in the land, and the smoke of your camp rise always.'

"But if the beggars could have seen me hitting the high places for the sloop as soon as I was clear of them, they'd thought my own medicine had got after me. Tilly'd kept warm by chopping the ice away, and was all ready to cast off. Gawd! how we ran before it, the Taku howling after us and the freezing seas sweeping over at every clip. With everything battened down, me a-steering and Tilly chopping ice, we held on half the night, till I plumped the sloop ashore on Porcupine Island, and we shivered it out on the beach; blankets wet, and Tilly drying the matches on her breast.

"So I think I know something about it. Seven years, Dick, man and wife, in rough sailing and smooth. And then she died, in the heart of the winter, died in childbirth, up there on the Chilcat Station. She held my hand to the last, the ice creeping up inside the door and spreading thick on the gut of the window. Outside, the lone howl of the wolf and the Silence; inside, death and the Silence. You've never heard the Silence yet, Dick, and Gawd grant you don't ever have to hear it when you sit by the side of death. Hear it? Ay, till the breath whistles like a siren, and the heart booms, booms, booms, like the surf on the shore.

"Siwash, Dick, but a woman. White, Dick, white, clear through. Towards the last she says, 'Keep my feather bed, Tommy, keep it always.' And I agreed. Then she opened her eyes, full with the pain. 'I've been a good woman to you, Tommy, and because of that I want you to promise—to promise'—the words seemed to stick in her throat—'that when you marry, the woman be white. No more Siwash, Tommy. I know. Plenty white women down to Juneau now. I know. Your people call you "squaw-man," your women turn their heads to the one side on the street, and you do not go to their cabins like other men. Why? Your wife

Siwash. Is it not so? And this is not good. Wherefore I die. Promise me. Kiss me in token of your promise.'

"I kissed her, and she dozed off, whispering, 'It is good.' At the end, that near gone my ear was at her lips, she roused for the last time. 'Remember, Tommy; remember my feather bed.' Then she died, in childbirth, up there on the Chilcat Station."

The tent heeled over and half flattened before the gale. Dick refilled his pipe, while Tommy drew the tea and set it aside against Molly's return.

And she of the flashing eyes and Yankee blood? Blinded, falling, crawling on hand and knee, the wind thrust back in her throat by the wind, she was heading for the tent. On her shoulders a bulky pack caught the full fury of the storm. She plucked feebly at the knotted flaps, but it was Tommy and Dick who cast them loose. Then she set her soul for the last effort, staggered in, and fell exhausted on the floor.

Tommy unbuckled the straps and took the pack from her. As he lifted it there was a clanging of pots and pans. Dick, pouring out a mug of whiskey, paused long enough to pass the wink across her body. Tommy winked back. His lips pursed the monosyllable, "clothes," but Dick shook his head reprovingly. "Here, little woman," he said, after she had drunk the whiskey and straightened up a bit.

"Here's some dry togs. Climb into them. We're going out to extra-peg the tent. After that, give us the call, and we'll come in and have dinner. Sing out when you're ready."

"So help me, Dick, that's knocked the edge off her for the rest of this trip," Tommy spluttered as they crouched to the lee of the tent.

"But it's the edge is her saving grace." Dick replied, ducking his head to a volley of sleet that drove around a corner of the canvas. "The edge that you and I've got, Tommy, and the edge of our mothers before us."

THE MAN WITH THE GASH

JACOB KENT HAD SUFFERED from cupidity all the days of his life. This, in turn, had engendered a chronic distrustfulness, and his mind and character had become so warped that he was a very disagreeable man to deal with. He was also a victim to somnambulic propensities, and very set in his ideas. He had been a weaver of cloth from the cradle, until the fever of Klondike had entered his blood and torn him away from his loom. His cabin stood midway between Sixty Mile Post and the Stuart River; and men who made it a custom to travel the trail to Dawson, likened him to a robber baron, perched in his fortress and exacting toll from the caravans that used his ill-kept roads. Since a certain amount of history was required in the construction of this figure, the less cultured wayfarers from Stuart River were prone to describe him after a still more primordial fashion, in which a command of strong adjectives was to be chiefly noted.

This cabin was not his, by the way, having been built several years previously by a couple of miners who had got out a raft of logs at that point for a grub-stake. They had been most hospitable lads, and, after they abandoned it, travelers who knew the route made it an object to arrive there at nightfall. It was very handy, saving them all the time and toil of pitching camp; and it was an unwritten rule that the last man left a neat pile of firewood for the next comer. Rarely a night passed but from half a dozen to a score of men crowded into its shelter. Jacob Kent noted these things, exercised squatter sovereignty, and moved in. Thenceforth, the weary travelers were mulcted a dollar per head for the privilege of sleeping on the floor, Jacob Kent weighing the dust and never failing to steal the down-weight. Besides, he so contrived that his transient guests chopped his wood for him and carried his water. This was rank piracy, but his victims were an easy-going breed, and while they detested him, they yet permitted him to flourish in his sins.

One afternoon in April he sat by his door,—for all the world like a predatory spider,— marveling at the heat of the returning sun, and keeping an eye on the trail for prospective flies. The Yukon lay at his feet, a sea of ice, disappearing around two great bends to the north and south, and stretching an honest two miles from bank to bank. Over its rough breast ran the sled-trail, a slender sunken line, eighteen inches wide and two thousand miles in length, with more curses distributed to the linear foot than any other road in or out of all Christendom.

Jacob Kent was feeling particularly good that afternoon. The record had been broken the previous night, and he had sold his hospitality to no less than twenty-eight visitors. True, it had been quite uncomfortable, and four had snored beneath his bunk all night; but then it had added appreciable weight to the sack in which he kept his gold dust. That sack, with its glittering yellow treasure, was at once the chief delight and the chief bane of his existence. Heaven and hell lay within its slender mouth. In the nature of things, there being no privacy to his one-roomed dwelling, he was tortured by a constant fear of theft. It would be very easy for these bearded, desperate-looking strangers to make away with it. Often he dreamed that such was the case, and awoke in the grip of nightmare. A select number of these robbers haunted him through his dreams, and he came to know them quite well, especially the bronzed leader with the gash on his right cheek. This fellow was the most persistent of the lot, and, because of him, he had, in his waking moments, constructed several score of hiding-places in and about the cabin. After a concealment he would breathe freely again, perhaps for several nights, only to collar the Man with the Gash in the very act of unearthing the sack. Then, on awakening in the midst of the usual struggle, he would at once get up and transfer the bag to a new and more ingenious crypt. It was not that he was the direct victim of these phantasms; but he believed in omens and thought-transference, and he deemed these dream-robbers to be the astral projection of real personages who happened at those particular moments, no matter where they were in the flesh, to be harboring designs, in the spirit, upon his wealth. So he continued to bleed the unfortunates who crossed his threshold, and at the same time to add to his trouble with every ounce that went into the sack.

As he sat sunning himself, a thought came to Jacob Kent that brought him to his feet with a jerk. The pleasures of life had culminated in the continual weighing and reweighing of his dust; but a shadow had been thrown upon this pleasant avocation, which he had hitherto failed to brush aside. His gold-scales were quite small; in fact, their maximum was a pound and a half,—eighteen ounces,—while his hoard mounted up to something like three and a third times that. He had never been able to weigh it all at one operation, and hence considered himself to have been shut out from a new and most edifying coign of contemplation. Being denied this, half the pleasure of possession had been lost; nay, he felt that this miserable obstacle actually minimized the fact, as it did the strength, of possession. It was the solution of this problem flashing across his mind that had just brought him to his feet. He searched the trail carefully in either direction. There was nothing in sight, so he went inside.

In a few seconds he had the table cleared away and the scales set up. On one side he placed the stamped disks to the equivalent of fifteen ounces, and balanced it with dust on the other. Replacing the weights with dust, he then had thirty ounces precisely balanced. These, in turn, he placed together on one side and again balanced with more dust. By this time the gold was exhausted, and he was sweating liberally. He trembled with ecstasy, ravished beyond measure. Nevertheless he dusted the sack thoroughly, to the last least grain, till the balance was overcome and one side of the scales sank to the table. Equilibrium, however, was restored by the addition of a pennyweight and five grains to the opposite side. He stood, head thrown back, transfixed. The sack was empty, but the potentiality of the scales had become immeasurable. Upon them he could weigh any amount, from the tiniest grain to pounds upon pounds. Mammon laid hot fingers on his heart. The sun swung on its westering way till it flashed through the open doorway, full upon the yellow-burdened scales. The precious heaps, like the golden breasts of a bronze Cleopatra, flung back the light in a mellow glow. Time and space were not.

"Gawd blime me! but you 'ave the makin' of several quid there, 'aven't you?"

Jacob Kent wheeled about, at the same time reaching for his double-barreled shotgun, which stood handy. But when his eyes lit on the intruder's face, he staggered back dizzily. *It was the face of the Man with the Gash!*

The man looked at him curiously.

"Oh, that's all right," he said, waving his hand deprecatingly. "You needn't think as I'll 'arm you or your blasted dust.

"You're a rum 'un, you are," he added reflectively, as he watched the sweat pouring from off Kent's face and the quavering of his knees.

"W'y don't you pipe up an' say somethin'?" he went on, as the other struggled for breath. "Wot's gone wrong o' your gaff? Anythink the matter?"

"W—w—where'd you get it?" Kent at last managed to articulate, raising a shaking forefinger to the ghastly scar which seamed the other's cheek.

"Shipmate stove me down with a marlin-spike from the main-royal. An' now as you 'ave your figger'ead in trim, wot I want to know is, wot's it to you? That's wot I want to know—wot's it to you? Gawd blime me! do it 'urt you? Ain't it smug enough for the likes o' you? That's wot I want to know!"

"No, no," Kent answered, sinking upon a stool with a sickly grin. "I was just wondering."

"Did you ever see the like?" the other went on truculently.

"No."

"Ain't it a beute?"

"Yes." Kent nodded his head approvingly, intent on humoring this strange visitor, but wholly unprepared for the outburst which was to follow his effort to be agreeable.

"You blasted, bloomin', burgoo-eatin' son-of-a-sea-swab! Wot do you mean, a sayin' the most onsightly thing Gawd Almighty ever put on the face o' man is a beute? Wot do you mean, you—"

And there at this fiery son of the sea broke off into a string of Oriental profanity, mingling gods and devils, lineages and men, metaphors and monsters, with so savage a virility that Jacob Kent was paralyzed. He shrank back, his arms lifted as though to ward off physical violence. So utterly unnerved was he that the other paused in the mid-swing of a gorgeous peroration and burst into thunderous laughter.

"The sun's knocked the bottom out o' the trail," said the Man with the Gash, between departing paroxysms of mirth. "An' I only 'ope as you'll appreciate the hoppertunity of consortin' with a man o' my mug. Get steam up in that fire-box o' your'n. I'm goin' to unrig the dogs an' grub 'em. An' don't be shy o' the wood, my lad; there's plenty more where that come from, and it's you've got the time to sling an axe. An' tote up a bucket o' water while you're about it. Lively! or I'll run you down, so 'elp me!"

Such a thing was unheard of. Jacob Kent was making the fire, chopping wood, packing water—doing menial tasks for a guest! When Jim Cardegee left Dawson, it was with his head filled with the iniquities of this roadside Shylock; and all along the trail his numerous victims had added to the sum of his crimes. Now, Jim Cardegee, with the sailor's love for a sailor's joke, had determined, when he pulled into the cabin, to bring its inmate down a peg or so. That he had succeeded beyond expectation he could not help but remark, though he was in the dark as to the part the gash on his cheek had played in it. But while he could not understand, he saw the terror it created, and resolved to exploit it as remorselessly as would any modern trader a choice bit of merchandise.

"Strike me blind, but you're a 'ustler," he said admiringly, his head cocked to one side, as his host bustled about. "You never 'ort to 'ave gone Klondiking. It's the keeper of a pub' you was laid out for. An' it's often as I 'ave 'eard the lads up an' down the river speak o' you, but I 'adn't no idea you was so jolly nice."

Jacob Kent experienced a tremendous yearning to try his shotgun on him, but the fascination of the gash was too potent. This was the real Man with the Gash, the man who had so often robbed him in the spirit. This, then, was the embodied entity of the being whose astral form had been projected into his dreams, the man who had so frequently harbored designs against his hoard; hence—there could be no other conclusion—this Man with the Gash had now come in the flesh to dispossess him. And that gash! He could no more keep his eyes from it than stop the beating of his heart. Try as he would, they wandered back to that one point as inevitably as the needle to the pole.

"Do it 'urt you?" Jim Cardegee thundered suddenly, looking up from the spreading of his blankets and encountering the rapt gaze of the other. "It strikes me as 'ow it 'ud be the proper thing for you to draw your jib, douse the glim, an' turn in, seein' as 'ow it worrits you. Jes' lay to that, you swab, or so 'elp me I'll take a pull on your peak-purchases!"

Kent was so nervous that it took three puffs to blow out the slush-lamp, and he crawled into his blankets without even removing his moccasins. The sailor was soon snoring lustily from his hard bed on the floor, but Kent lay staring up into the blackness, one hand on the shotgun, resolved not to close his eyes the whole night. He had not had an opportunity to secrete his five pounds of gold, and it lay in the ammunition box at the head of his bunk. But, try as he would, he at last dozed off with the weight of his dust heavy on his soul. Had he not inadvertently fallen asleep with his mind in such condition, the somnambulic demon would not have been invoked, nor would Jim Cardegee have gone mining next day with a dish-pan.

The fire fought a losing battle, and at last died away, while the frost penetrated the mossy chinks between the logs and chilled the inner atmosphere. The dogs outside ceased their howling, and, curled up in the snow, dreamed of salmon-stocked heavens where dog-drivers and kindred task-masters were not. Within, the sailor lay like a log, while his host tossed restlessly about, the victim of strange fantasies. As midnight drew near he suddenly threw off the blankets and got up. It was remarkable that he could do what he then did without ever striking a light. Perhaps it was because of the darkness that he kept his eyes shut, and perhaps it was for fear he would see the terrible gash on the cheek of his visitor; but, be this as it may, it is a fact that, unseeing, he opened his ammunition box, put a heavy charge into the muzzle of the shotgun without spilling a particle, rammed it down with double wads, and then put everything away and got back into bed.

Just as daylight laid its steel-gray fingers on the parchment window, Jacob Kent awoke. Turning on his elbow, he raised the lid and peered into the ammunition box. Whatever he saw, or whatever he did not see, exercised a very peculiar effect upon him, considering his neurotic temperament. He glanced at the sleeping man on the floor, let the lid down gently, and rolled over on his back. It was an unwonted calm that rested on his face. Not a muscle quivered. There was not the least sign of excitement or perturbation. He lay there a long while, thinking, and when he got up and began to move about, it was in a cool, collected manner, without noise and without hurry.

It happened that a heavy wooden peg had been driven into the ridge-pole just above Jim Cardegee's head. Jacob Kent, working softly, ran a piece of half-inch manila over it, bringing both ends to the ground. One end he tied about his waist, and in the other he rove a running noose. Then he cocked his shotgun and laid it within reach, by the side of numerous moose-hide thongs. By an effort of will he bore the sight of the scar, slipped the noose over the sleeper's head, and drew it taut by throwing back on his weight, at the same time seizing the gun and bringing it to bear.

Jim Cardegee awoke, choking, bewildered, staring down the twin wells of steel.

"Where is it?" Kent asked, at the same time slacking on the rope.

"You blasted—ugh—"

Kent merely threw back his weight, shutting off the other's wind.

"Bloomin'—Bur—ugh—"

"Where is it?" Kent repeated.

"Wot?" Cardegee asked, as soon as he had caught his breath.

"The gold-dust."

"Wot gold-dust?" the perplexed sailor demanded.

"You know well enough,—mine."

"Ain't seen nothink of it. Wot do ye take me for? A safe-deposit? Wot 'ave I got to do with it, any'ow?"

"Mebbe you know, and mebbe you don't know, but anyway, I'm going to stop your breath till you do know. And if you lift a hand, I'll blow your head off!"

"Vast heavin'!" Cardegee roared, as the rope tightened.

Kent eased away a moment, and the sailor, wriggling his neck as though from the pressure, managed to loosen the noose a bit and work it up so the point of contact was just under the chin.

"Well?" Kent questioned, expecting the disclosure.

But Cardegee grinned. "Go ahead with your 'angin', you bloomin' old pot-walloper!"

Then, as the sailor had anticipated, the tragedy became a farce. Cardegee being the heavier of the two, Kent, throwing his body backward and down, could not lift him clear of the ground. Strain and strive to the uttermost, the sailor's feet still stuck to the floor and sustained a part of his weight. The remaining portion was supported by the point of contact just under his chin. Failing to swing him clear, Kent clung on, resolved to slowly throttle him or force him to tell what he had done with the hoard. But the Man with the Gash would not throttle. Five, ten, fifteen minutes passed, and at the end of that time, in despair, Kent let his prisoner down.

"Well," he remarked, wiping away the sweat, "if you won't hang you'll shoot. Some men wasn't born to be hanged, anyway."

"An' it's a pretty mess as you'll make o' this 'ere cabin floor." Cardegee was fighting for time. "Now, look 'ere, I'll tell you wot we do; we'll lay our 'eads 'longside an' reason together. You've lost some dust. You say as 'ow I know, an' I say as 'ow I don't. Let's get a hobservation an' shape a course—"

"Vast heavin'!" Kent dashed in, maliciously imitating the other's enunciation. "I'm going to shape all the courses of this shebang, and you observe; and if you do anything more, I'll bore you as sure as Moses!"

"For the sake of my mother—"

"Whom God have mercy upon if she loves you. Ah! Would you?" He frustrated a hostile move on the part of the other by pressing the cold muzzle against his forehead. "Lay quiet, now! If you lift as much as a hair, you'll get it."

It was rather an awkward task, with the trigger of the gun always within pulling distance of the finger; but Kent was a weaver, and in a few minutes had the sailor tied hand and foot. Then he dragged him without and laid him by the side of the cabin, where he could overlook the river and watch the sun climb to the meridian.

"Now I'll give you till noon, and then—"

"Wot?"

"You'll be hitting the brimstone trail. But if you speak up, I'll keep you till the next bunch of mounted police come by."

"Well, Gawd blime me, if this ain't a go! 'Ere I be, innercent as a lamb, an' 'ere you be, lost all o' your top 'amper an' out o' your reckonin', run me foul an' goin' to rake me into 'ellfire. You bloomin' old pirut! You—"

Jim Cardegee loosed the strings of his profanity and fairly outdid himself. Jacob Kent brought out a stool that he might enjoy it in comfort. Having exhausted all the possible combinations of his vocabulary, the sailor quieted down to hard thinking, his eyes constantly gauging the progress of the sun, which tore up the eastern slope of the heavens with unseemly haste. His dogs, surprised that they had not long since been put to harness, crowded around him. His helplessness appealed to the brutes. They felt that something was wrong, though they knew not what, and they crowded about, howling their mournful sympathy.

"Chook! Mush-on! you Siwashes!" he cried, attempting, in a vermicular way, to kick at them, and discovering himself to be tottering on the edge of a declivity. As soon as the animals had scattered, he devoted himself to the significance of that declivity which he felt to be there but could not see. Nor was he long in arriving at a correct conclusion. In the nature of things, he figured, man is lazy. He does no more than he has to. When he builds a cabin he must put dirt on the roof. From these premises it was logical that he should carry that dirt no further than was absolutely necessary. Therefore, he lay upon the edge of the hole from which the dirt had been taken to roof Jacob Kent's cabin. This knowledge, properly utilized, might prolong things, he thought; and he then turned his attention to the moose-hide thongs which bound him. His hands were tied behind him, and pressing against the snow, they were wet with the contact. This moistening of the raw-hide he knew would tend to make it stretch, and, without apparent effort, he endeavored to stretch it more and more.

He watched the trail hungrily, and when in the direction of Sixty Mile a dark speck appeared for a moment against the white background of an ice-jam, he cast an anxious eye at the sun. It had climbed nearly to the zenith. Now and again he caught the black speck clearing the hills of ice and sinking into the intervening hollows; but he dared not permit himself more than the most cursory glances for fear of rousing his enemy's suspicion. Once, when Jacob Kent rose to his feet and searched the trail with care, Cardegee was frightened, but the dog-sled had struck a piece of trail running parallel with a jam, and remained out of sight till the danger was past.

"I'll see you 'ung for this," Cardegee threatened, attempting to draw the other's attention. "An' you'll rot in 'ell, jes' you see if you don't.

"I say," he cried, after another pause; "d'ye b'lieve in ghosts?" Kent's sudden start made him sure of his ground, and he went on: "Now a ghost 'as the right to 'aunt a man wot don't do wot he says; and you can't shuffle me off till eight bells—wot I mean is twelve o'clock— can you? 'Cos if you do, it'll 'appen as 'ow I'll 'aunt you. D'ye 'ear? A minute, a second too quick, an' I'll 'aunt you, so 'elp me, I will!"

Jacob Kent looked dubious, but declined to talk.

"'Ow's your chronometer? Wot's your longitude? 'Ow do you know as your time's correct?" Cardegee persisted, vainly hoping to beat his executioner out of a few minutes. "Is it Barrack's time you 'ave, or is it the Company time? 'Cos if you do it before the stroke o' the bell, I'll not rest. I give you fair warnin'. I'll come back. An' if you 'aven't the time, 'ow will you know? That's wot I want—'ow will you tell?"

"I'll send you off all right," Kent replied. "Got a sun-dial here."

"No good. Thirty-two degrees variation o' the needle."

"Stakes are all set."

"'Ow did you set 'em? Compass?"

"No; lined them up with the North Star."

"Sure?"

"Sure."

Cardegee groaned, then stole a glance at the trail. The sled was just clearing a rise, barely a mile away, and the dogs were in full lope, running lightly.

"'Ow close is the shadows to the line?"

Kent walked to the primitive timepiece and studied it. "Three inches," he announced, after a careful survey.

"Say, jes' sing out 'eight bells' afore you pull the gun, will you?"

Kent agreed, and they lapsed into silence. The thongs about Cardegee's wrists were slowly stretching, and he had begun to work them over his hands.

"Say, 'ow close is the shadows?"

"One inch."

The sailor wriggled slightly to assure himself that he would topple over at the right moment, and slipped the first turn over his hands.

"'Ow close?"

"Half an inch." Just then Kent heard the jarring churn of the runners and turned his eyes to the trail. The driver was lying flat on the sled and the dogs swinging down the straight stretch to the cabin. Kent whirled back, bringing his rifle to shoulder.

"It ain't eight bells yet!" Cardegee expostulated. "I'll 'aunt you, sure!"

Jacob Kent faltered. He was standing by the sun-dial, perhaps ten paces from his victim. The man on the sled must have seen that something unusual was taking place, for he had risen to his knees, his whip singing viciously among the dogs.

The shadows swept into line. Kent looked along the sights.

"Make ready!" he commanded solemnly. "Eight b—"

But just a fraction of a second too soon, Cardegee rolled backward into the hole. Kent held his fire and ran to the edge. Bang! The gun exploded full in the sailor's face as he rose to his feet. But no smoke came from the muzzle; instead, a sheet of flame burst from the side of the barrel near its butt, and Jacob Kent went down. The dogs dashed up the bank, dragging the sled over his body, and the driver sprang off as Jim Cardegee freed his hands and drew himself from the hole.

"Jim!" The new-comer recognized him. "What's the matter?"

"Wot's the matter? Oh, nothink at all. It jest 'appens as I do little things like this for my 'ealth. Wot's the matter, you bloomin' idjit? Wot's the matter, eh? Cast me loose or I'll show you wot! 'Urry up, or I'll 'olystone the decks with you!"

"Huh!" he added, as the other went to work with his sheath-knife. "Wot's the matter? I want to know. Jes' tell me that, will you, wot's the matter? Hey?"

Kent was quite dead when they rolled him over. The gun, an old-fashioned, heavy-weighted muzzle-loader, lay near him. Steel and wood had parted company. Near the butt of the right-hand barrel, with lips pressed outward, gaped a fissure several inches in length. The sailor picked it up, curiously. A glittering stream of yellow dust ran out through the crack. The facts of the case dawned upon Jim Cardegee.

"Strike me standin'!" he roared; "'ere's a go! 'Ere's 'is bloomin' dust! Gawd blime me, an' you, too, Charley, if you don't run an' get the dish-pan!"

JAN, THE UNREPENTANT

*"For there's never a law of God or man
Runs north of Fifty-three."*

JAN ROLLED OVER, clawing and kicking. He was fighting hand and foot now, and he fought grimly, silently. Two of the three men who hung upon him, shouted directions to each other, and strove to curb the short, hairy devil who would not curb. The third man howled. His finger was between Jan's teeth.

"Quit yer tantrums, Jan, an' ease up!" panted Red Bill, getting a strangle-hold on Jan's neck. "Why on earth can't yeh hang decent and peaceable?"

But Jan kept his grip on the third man's finger, and squirmed over the floor of the tent, into the pots and pans.

"Youah no gentleman, suh," reproved Mr. Taylor, his body following his finger, and endeavoring to accommodate itself to every jerk of Jan's head. "You hev killed Mistah Gordon, as brave and honorable a gentleman as ever hit the trail aftah the dogs. Youah a murderah, suh, and without honah."

"An' yer no comrade," broke in Red Bill. "If you was, you'd hang 'thout rampin' around an' roarin'. Come on, Jan, there's a good fellow. Don't give us no more trouble. Jes' quit, an' we'll hang yeh neat and handy, an' be done with it."

"Steady, all!" Lawson, the sailorman, bawled. "Jam his head into the bean pot and batten down."

"But my fingah, suh," Mr. Taylor protested.

"Leggo with y'r finger, then! Always in the way!"

"But I can't, Mistah Lawson. It's in the critter's gullet, and nigh chewed off as 't is."

"Stand by for stays!" As Lawson gave the warning, Jan half lifted himself, and the struggling quartet floundered across the tent into a muddle of furs and blankets. In its passage it cleared the body of a man, who lay motionless, bleeding from a bullet-wound in the neck.

All this was because of the madness which had come upon Jan—the madness which comes upon a man who has stripped off the raw skin of earth and groveled long in primal

115

nakedness, and before whose eyes rises the fat vales of the homeland, and into whose nostrils steals the whiff of bay, and grass, and flower, and new-turned soil. Through five frigid years Jan had sown the seed. Stuart River, Forty Mile, Circle City, Koyokuk, Kotzebue, had marked his bleak and strenuous agriculture, and now it was Nome that bore the harvest,—not the Nome of golden beaches and ruby sands, but the Nome of '97, before Anvil City was located, or Eldorado District organized. John Gordon was a Yankee, and should have known better. But he passed the sharp word at a time when Jan's blood-shot eyes blazed and his teeth gritted in torment. And because of this, there was a smell of saltpeter in the tent, and one lay quietly, while the other fought like a cornered rat, and refused to hang in the decent and peaceable manner suggested by his comrades.

"If you will allow me, Mistah Lawson, befoah we go further in this rumpus, I would say it wah a good idea to pry this hyer varmint's teeth apart. Neither will he bite off, nor will he let go. He has the wisdom of the sarpint, suh, the wisdom of the sarpint."

"Lemme get the hatchet to him!" vociferated the sailor. "Lemme get the hatchet!" He shoved the steel edge close to Mr. Taylor's finger and used the man's teeth as a fulcrum. Jan held on and breathed through his nose, snorting like a grampus. "Steady, all! Now she takes it!"

"Thank you, suh; it is a powerful relief." And Mr. Taylor proceeded to gather into his arms the victim's wildly waving legs.

But Jan upreared in his Berserker rage; bleeding, frothing, cursing; five frozen years thawing into sudden hell. They swayed backward and forward, panted, sweated, like some cyclopean, many-legged monster rising from the lower deeps. The slush-lamp went over, drowned in its own fat, while the midday twilight scarce percolated through the dirty canvas of the tent.

"For the love of Gawd, Jan, get yer senses back!" pleaded Red Bill. "We ain't goin' to hurt yeh, 'r kill yeh 'r anythin' of that sort Joe' want to hang yeh, that's all, an' you a-messin' round an' rampagin' somethin' terrible. To think of travellin' trail together an' then bein' treated this-a way. Wouldn't 'bleeved it of yeh, Jan!"

"He's got too much steerage-way. Grab holt his legs, Taylor, and heave'm over!"

"Yes, suh, Mistah Lawson. Do you press youah weight above, after I give the word." The Kentuckian groped about him in the murky darkness. "Now, suh, now is the accepted time!"

There was a great surge, and a quarter of a ton of human flesh tottered and crashed to its fall against the side-wall. Pegs drew and guy-ropes parted, and the tent, collapsing, wrapped the battle in its greasy folds.

"Yer only makin' it harder fer yerself," Red Bill continued, at the same time driving both his thumbs into a hairy throat, the possessor of which he had pinned down. "You've made nuisance enough a' ready, an' it'll take half the day to get things straightened when we've strung yeh up."

"I'll thank you to leave go, suh," spluttered Mr. Taylor.

Red Bill grunted and loosed his grip, and the twain crawled out into the open. At the same instant Jan kicked clear of the sailor, and took to his heels across the snow.

"Hi! you lazy devils! Buck! Bright! Sic'm! Pull 'm down!" sang out Lawson, lunging through the snow after the fleeing man. Buck and Bright, followed by the rest of the dogs, outstripped him and rapidly overhauled the murderer.

There was no reason that these men should do this; no reason for Jan to run away; no reason for them to attempt to prevent him. On the one hand stretched the barren snow-land; on the other, the frozen sea. With neither food nor shelter, he could not run far. All they had to do was to wait till he wandered back to the tent, as he inevitably must, when the frost and hunger laid hold of him. But these men did not stop to think. There was a certain taint of madness running in the veins of all of them. Besides, blood had been spilled, and upon them was the blood-lust, thick and hot. "Vengeance is mine," saith the Lord, and He saith it in temperate climes where the warm sun steals away the energies of men. But in the Northland they have discovered that prayer is only efficacious when backed by muscle, and they are accustomed to doing things for themselves. God is everywhere, they have heard, but he flings a shadow over the land for half the year that they may not find him; so they grope in darkness, and it is not to be wondered that they often doubt, and deem the Decalogue out of gear.

Jan ran blindly, reckoning not of the way of his feet, for he was mastered by the verb "to live." To live! To exist! Buck flashed gray through the air, but missed. The man struck madly at him, and stumbled. Then the white teeth of Bright closed on his mackinaw jacket, and he pitched into the snow. *To live! To exist!* He fought wildly as ever, the center of a tossing heap of men and dogs. His left hand gripped a wolf-dog by the scruff of the back, while the arm was passed around the neck of Lawson. Every struggle of the dog helped to throttle the hapless sailor. Jan's right hand was buried deep in the curling tendrils of Red Bill's shaggy head, and beneath all, Mr. Taylor lay pinned and helpless. It was a deadlock, for the strength of his madness was prodigious; but suddenly, without apparent reason, Jan loosed his various grips and rolled over quietly on his back. His adversaries drew away a little, dubious and disconcerted. Jan grinned viciously.

"Mine friends," he said, still grinning, "you haf asked me to be politeful, und now I am politeful. Vot piziness vood you do mit me?"

"That's right, Jan. Be ca'm," soothed Red Bill. "I knowed you'd come to yer senses afore long. Jes' be ca'm now, an' we'll do the trick with neatness and dispatch."

"Vot piziness? Vot trick?"

"The hangin'. An' yeh oughter thank yer lucky stars for havin' a man what knows his business. I've did it afore now, more'n once, down in the States, an' I can do it to a T."

"Hang who? Me?"

"Yep."

"Ha! ha! Shust hear der man speak foolishness! Gif me a hand, Bill, und I vill get up und be hung." He crawled stiffly to his feet and looked about him. "Herr Gott! listen to der man! He vood hang me! Ho! ho! ho! I tank not! Yes, I tank not!"

"And I tank yes, you swab," Lawson spoke up mockingly, at the same time cutting a sled-lashing and coiling it up with ominous care. "Judge Lynch holds court this day."

"Von liddle while." Jan stepped back from the proffered noose. "I haf somedings to ask und to make der great proposition. Kentucky, you know about der Shudge Lynch?"

"Yes, suh. It is an institution of free men and of gentlemen, and it is an ole one and time-honored. Corruption may wear the robe of magistracy, suh, but Judge Lynch can always be relied upon to give justice without court fees. I repeat, suh, without court fees. Law may be bought and sold, but in this enlightened land justice is free as the air we breathe, strong as the licker we drink, prompt as—"

"Cut it short! Find out what the beggar wants," interrupted Lawson, spoiling the peroration.

"Vell, Kentucky, tell me dis: von man kill von odder man, Shudge Lynch hang dot man?"

"If the evidence is strong enough—yes, suh."

"An' the evidence in this here case is strong enough to hang a dozen men, Jan," broke in Red Bill.

"Nefer you mind, Bill. I talk mit you next. Now von anodder ding I ask Kentucky. If Shudge Lynch hang not der man, vot den?"

"If Judge Lynch does not hang the man, then the man goes free, and his hands are washed clean of blood. And further, suh, our great and glorious constitution has said, to wit: that no man may twice be placed in jeopardy of his life for one and the same crime, or words to that effect."

"Unt dey can't shoot him, or hit him mit a club over der head alongside, or do nodings more mit him?"

"No, suh."

"Goot! You hear vot Kentucky speaks, all you noddleheads? Now I talk mit Bill. You know der piziness, Bill, und you hang me up brown, eh? Vot you say?"

"'Betcher life, an', Jan, if yeh don't give no more trouble ye'll be almighty proud of the job. I'm a connesoor."

"You haf der great head, Bill, und know somedings or two. Und you know two und one makes tree—ain't it?"

Bill nodded.

"Und when you haf two dings, you haf not tree dings—ain't it? Now you follow mit me close und I show you. It takes tree dings to hang. First ding, you haf to haf der man. Goot! I am der man. Second ding, you haf to haf der rope. Lawson haf der rope. Goot! Und tird ding, you haf to haf someding to tie der rope to. Sling your eyes over der landscape und find der tird ding to tie der rope to? Eh? Vot you say?"

Mechanically they swept the ice and snow with their eyes. It was a homogeneous scene, devoid of contrasts or bold contours, dreary, desolate, and monotonous,—the ice-packed sea, the slow slope of the beach, the background of low-lying hills, and over all thrown the endless mantle of snow. "No trees, no bluffs, no cabins, no telegraph poles, nothin'," moaned Red Bill; "nothin' respectable enough nor big enough to swing the toes of a five-foot man clear o' the ground. I give it up." He looked yearningly at that portion of Jan's anatomy which joins the head and shoulders. "Give it up," he repeated sadly to Lawson. "Throw the rope down. Gawd never intended this here country for livin' purposes, an' that's a cold frozen fact."

Jan grinned triumphantly. "I tank I go mit der tent und haf a smoke."

"Ostensiblee y'r correct, Bill, me son," spoke up Lawson; "but y'r a dummy, and you can lay to that for another cold frozen fact. Takes a sea farmer to learn you landsmen things. Ever hear of a pair of shears? Then clap y'r eyes to this."

The sailor worked rapidly. From the pile of dunnage where they had pulled up the boat the preceding fall, he unearthed a pair of long oars. These he lashed together, at nearly right angles, close to the ends of the blades. Where the handles rested he kicked holes through the snow to the sand. At the point of intersection he attached two guy-ropes, making the end of one fast to a cake of beach-ice. The other guy he passed over to Red Bill. "Here, me son, lay holt o' that and run it out."

And to his horror, Jan saw his gallows rise in the air. "No! no!" he cried, recoiling and putting up his fists. "It is not goot! I vill not hang! Come, you noddleheads! I vill lick you, all together, von after der odder! I vill blay hell! I vill do eferydings! Und I vill die pefore I hang!"

The sailor permitted the two other men to clinch with the mad creature. They rolled and tossed about furiously, tearing up snow and tundra, their fierce struggle writing a tragedy of human passion on the white sheet spread by nature. And ever and anon a hand or foot of Jan emerged from the tangle, to be gripped by Lawson and lashed fast with rope-yarns.

Pawing, clawing, blaspheming, he was conquered and bound, inch by inch, and drawn to where the inexorable shears lay like a pair of gigantic dividers on the snow. Red Bill adjusted the noose, placing the hangman's knot properly under the left ear. Mr. Taylor and Lawson tailed onto the running-guy, ready at the word to elevate the gallows. Bill lingered, contemplating his work with artistic appreciation.

"Herr Gott! Vood you look at it!"

The horror in Jan's voice caused the rest to desist. The fallen tent had uprisen, and in the gathering twilight it flapped ghostly arms about and titubated toward them drunkenly. But the next instant John Gordon found the opening and crawled forth.

"What the flaming—!" For the moment his voice died away in his throat as his eyes took in the tableau. "Hold on! I'm not dead!" he cried out, coming up to the group with stormy countenance.

"Allow me, Mistah Gordon, to congratulate you upon youah escape," Mr. Taylor ventured. "A close shave, suh, a powahful close shave."

" Congratulate hell! I might have been dead and rotten and no thanks to you, you—!" And thereat John Gordon delivered himself of a vigorous flood of English, terse, intensive, denunciative, and composed solely of expletives and adjectives.

"Simply creased me," he went on when he had eased himself sufficiently. "Ever crease cattle, Taylor?"

"Yes, suh, many a time down in God's country."

"Just so. That's what happened to me. Bullet just grazed the base of my skull at the top of the neck. Stunned me but no harm done." He turned to the bound man. "Get up, Jan. I'm going to lick you to a standstill or you're going to apologize. The rest of you lads stand clear."

"I tank not. Shust tie me loose und you see," replied Jan, the Unrepentant, the devil within him still unconquered. "Und after as I lick you, I take der rest of der noddleheads, von after der odder, altogedder!"

GRIT OF WOMEN

A WOLFISH HEAD, wistful-eyed and frost-rimed, thrust aside the tent-flaps.

"Hi! Chook! Siwash! Chook, you limb of Satan!" chorused the protesting inmates. Bettles rapped the dog sharply with a tin plate, and it withdrew hastily. Louis Savoy refastened the flaps, kicked a frying-pan over against the bottom, and warmed his hands. It was very cold without. Forty-eight hours gone, the spirit thermometer had burst at sixty-eight below, and since that time it had grown steadily and bitterly colder. There was no telling when the snap would end. And it is poor policy, unless the gods will it, to venture far from a stove at such times, or to increase the quantity of cold atmosphere one must breathe. Men sometimes do it, and sometimes they chill their lungs. This leads up to a dry, hacking cough, noticeably irritable when bacon is being fried. After that, somewhere along in the spring or summer, a hole is burned in the frozen muck. Into this a man's carcass is dumped, covered over with moss, and left with the assurance that it will rise on the crack of Doom, wholly and frigidly intact. For those of little faith, skeptical of material integration on that fateful day, no fitter country than the Klondike can be recommended to die in. But it is not to be inferred from this that it is a fit country for living purposes.

It was very cold without, but it was not over-warm within. The only article which might be designated furniture was the stove, and for this the men were frank in displaying their preference. Upon half of the floor pine boughs had been cast; above this were spread the sleeping-furs, beneath lay the winter's snowfall. The remainder of the floor was moccasin-packed snow, littered with pots and pans and the general *impedimenta* of an Arctic camp. The stove was red and roaring hot, but only a bare three feet away lay a block of ice, as sharp-edged and dry as when first quarried from the creek bottom. The pressure of the outside cold forced the inner heat upward. Just above the stove, where the pipe penetrated the roof, was a tiny circle of dry canvas; next, with the pipe always as center, a circle of steaming canvas; next a damp and moisture-exuding ring; and finally, the rest of the tent, sidewalls and top, coated with a half-inch of dry, white, crystal-encrusted frost.

"*Oh!* OH! OH!" A young fellow, lying asleep in the furs, bearded and wan and weary, raised a moan of pain, and without waking increased the pitch and intensity of his anguish.

His body half-lifted from the blankets, and quivered and shrank spasmodically, as though drawing away from a bed of nettles.

"Roll'm over!" ordered Bettles. "He's crampin'."

And thereat, with pitiless good-will, he was pitched upon and rolled and thumped and pounded by half-a-dozen willing comrades.

"Damn the trail," he muttered softly, as he threw off the robes and sat up. "I've run across country, played quarter three seasons hand-running, and hardened myself in all manner of ways; and then I pilgrim it into this God-forsaken land and find myself an effeminate Athenian without the simplest rudiments of manhood!" He hunched up to the fire and rolled a cigarette. "Oh, I'm not whining. I can take my medicine all right, all right; but I'm just decently ashamed of myself, that's all. Here I am, on top of a dirty thirty miles, as knocked up and stiff and sore as a pink-tea degenerate after a five-mile walk on a country turn-pike. Bah! It makes me sick! Got a match?" "Don't git the tantrums, youngster." Bettles passed over the required fire-stick and waxed patriarchal. "Ye've gotter 'low some for the breakin'-in. Sufferin' cracky! don't I recollect the first time I hit the trail! Stiff? I've seen the time it'd take me ten minutes to git my mouth from the water-hole an' come to my feet—every jint crackin' an' kickin' fit to kill. Cramp? In sech knots it'd take the camp half a day to untangle me. You're all right, for a cub, any ye've the true sperrit. Come this day year, you'll walk all us old bucks into the ground any time. An' best in your favor, you hain't got that streak of fat in your make-up which has sent many a husky man to the bosom of Abraham afore his right and proper time."

"Streak of fat?"

"Yep. Comes along of bulk. 'T ain't the big men as is the best when it comes to the trail."

"Never heard of it."

"Never heered of it, eh? Well, it's a dead straight, open-an'-shut fact, an' no gittin' round. Bulk's all well enough for a mighty big effort, but 'thout stayin' powers it ain't worth a continental whoop; an' stayin' powers an' bulk ain't runnin' mates. Takes the small, wiry fellows when it comes to gittin' right down an' hangin' on like a lean-jowled dog to a bone. Why, hell's fire, the big men they ain't in it!"

"By gar!" broke in Louis Savoy, "dat is no, vot you call, josh! I know one mans, so vaire beeg like ze buffalo. Wit him, on ze Sulphur Creek stampede, go one small mans, Lon McFane. You know dat Lon McFane, dat leetle Irisher wit ze red hair and ze grin. An' dey walk an' walk an' walk, all ze day long an' ze night long. And beeg mans, him become vaire tired, an' lay down mooch in ze snow. And leetle mans keek beeg mans, an' him cry like, vot you call—ah! vot you call ze kid. And leetle mans keek an' keek an' keek, an' bime by, long time, long way, keek beeg mans into my cabin. Tree days 'fore him crawl out my blankets. Nevaire I see beeg squaw like him. No nevaire. Him haf vot you call ze streak of fat. You bet."

"But there was Axel Gunderson," Prince spoke up. The great Scandinavian, with the tragic events which shadowed his passing, had made a deep mark on the mining engineer. "He lies up there, somewhere." He swept his hand in the vague direction of the mysterious east.

"Biggest man that ever turned his heels to Salt Water, or run a moose down with sheer grit," supplemented Bettles; "but he's the prove-the-rule exception. Look at his woman, Unga,—tip the scales at a hundred an' ten, clean meat an' nary ounce to spare. She'd bank grit 'gainst his for all there was in him, an' see him, an' go him better if it was possible. Nothing over the earth, or in it, or under it, she wouldn't 'a' done."

"But she loved him," objected the engineer.

"'T ain't that. It—"

"Look you, brothers," broke in Sitka Charley from his seat on the grub-box. "Ye have spoken of the streak of fat that runs in big men's muscles, of the grit of women and the love, and ye have spoken fair; but I have in mind things which happened when the land was young and the fires of men apart as the stars. It was then I had concern with a big man, and a streak of fat, and a woman. And the woman was small; but her heart was greater than the beef-heart of the man, and she had grit. And we traveled a weary trail, even to the Salt Water, and the cold was bitter, the snow deep, the hunger great. And the woman's love was a mighty love—no more can man say than this."

He paused, and with the hatchet broke pieces of ice from the large chunk beside him. These he threw into the gold pan on the stove, where the drinking-water thawed. The men drew up closer, and he of the cramps sought greater comfort vainly for his stiffened body.

"Brothers, my blood is red with Siwash, but my heart is white. To the faults of my fathers I owe the one, to the virtues of my friends the other. A great truth came to me when I was yet a boy. I learned that to your kind and you was given the earth; that the Siwash could not withstand you, and like the caribou and the bear, must perish in the cold. So I came into the warm and sat among you, by your fires, and behold, I became one of you, I have seen much in my time. I have known strange things, and bucked big, on big trails, with men of many breeds. And because of these things, I measure deeds after your manner, and judge men, and think thoughts. Wherefore, when I speak harshly of one of your own kind, I know you will not take it amiss; and when I speak high of one of my father's people, you will not take it upon you to say, 'Sitka Charley is Siwash, and there is a crooked light in his eyes and small honor to his tongue.' Is it not so?"

Deep down in throat, the circle vouchsafed its assent.

"The woman was Passuk. I got her in fair trade from her people, who were of the Coast and whose Chilcat totem stood at the head of a salt arm of the sea. My heart did not go out to the woman, nor did I take stock of her looks. For she scarce took her eyes from the ground, and she was timid and afraid, as girls will be when cast into a stranger's arms whom they have never seen before. As I say, there was no place in my heart for her to creep, for I had a great journey in mind, and stood in need of one to feed my dogs and to lift a paddle with me through the long river days. One blanket would cover the twain; so I chose Passuk.

"Have I not said I was a servant to the Government? If not, it is well that ye know. So I was taken on a warship, sleds and dogs and evaporated foods, and with me came Passuk. And we went north, to the winter ice-rim of Bering Sea, where we were landed,—myself, and Passuk, and the dogs. I was also given moneys of the Government, for I was its servant, and charts of lands which the eyes of man had never dwelt upon, and messages. These messages were sealed, and protected shrewdly from the weather, and I was to deliver them to the whale-ships of the Arctic, ice-bound by the great Mackenzie. Never was there so great a river, forgetting only our own Yukon, the Mother of all Rivers.

"All of which is neither here nor there, for my story deals not with the whale-ships, nor the berg-bound winter I spent by the Mackenzie. Afterward, in the spring, when the days lengthened and there was a crust to the snow, we came south, Passuk and I, to the Country of the Yukon. A weary journey, but the sun pointed out the way of our feet. It was a naked land then, as I have said, and we worked up the current, with pole and paddle, till we came to Forty Mile. Good it was to see white faces once again, so we put into the bank. And that winter was a hard winter. The darkness and the cold drew down upon us, and with them the famine. To each man the agent of the Company gave forty pounds of flour and twenty of bacon. There were no beans. And, the dogs howled always, and there were flat bellies and deep-lined faces, and strong men became weak, and weak men died. There was also much scurvy.

"Then came we together in the store one night, and the empty shelves made us feel our own emptiness the more. We talked low, by the light of the fire, for the candles had been set aside for those who might yet gasp in the spring. Discussion was held, and it was said that a man must go forth to the Salt Water and tell to the world our misery. At this all eyes turned to me, for it was understood that I was a great traveler. 'It is seven hundred miles,' said I, 'to Haines Mission by the sea, and every inch of it snowshoe work. Give me the pick of your dogs and the best of your grub, and I will go. And with me shall go Passuk.'

"To this they were agreed. But there arose one, Long Jeff, a Yankee-man, big-boned and big-muscled. Also his talk was big. He, too, was a mighty traveler, he said, born to the snowshoe and bred up on buffalo milk. He would go with me, in case I fell by the trail, that he might carry the word on to the Mission. I was young, and I knew not Yankee-men. How was I to know that big talk betokened the streak of fat, or that Yankee-men who did great things kept their teeth together? So we took the pick of the dogs and the best of the grub, and struck the trail, we three,—Passuk, Long Jeff, and I.

"Well, ye have broken virgin snow, labored at the gee-pole, and are not unused to the packed river-jams; so I will talk little of the toil, save that on some days we made ten miles, and on others thirty, but more often ten. And the best of the grub was not good, while we went on stint from the start. Likewise the pick of the dogs was poor, and we were hard put to keep them on their legs. At the White River our three sleds became two sleds, and we had only come two hundred miles. But we lost nothing; the dogs that left the traces went into the bellies of those that remained.

"Not a greeting, not a curl of smoke, till we made Pelly. Here I had counted on grub; and here I had counted on leaving Long Jeff, who was whining and trail-sore. But the factor's lungs were wheezing, his eyes bright, his cache nigh empty; and he showed us the empty cache of the missionary, also his grave with the rocks piled high to keep off the dogs. There was a bunch of Indians there, but babies and old men there were none, and it was clear that few would see the spring.

"So we pulled on, light-stomached and heavy-hearted, with half a thousand miles of snow and silence between us and Haines Mission by the sea. The darkness was at its worst, and at midday the sun could not clear the sky-line to the south. But the ice-jams were smaller, the going better; so I pushed the dogs hard and traveled late and early. As I said at Forty Mile, every inch of it was snow-shoe work. And the shoes made great sores on our feet, which cracked and scabbed but would not heal. And every day these sores grew more grievous, till in the morning, when we girded on the shoes, Long Jeff cried like a child. I put him at the fore of the light sled to break trail, but he slipped off the shoes for comfort. Because of this the trail was not packed, his moccasins made great holes, and into these holes the dogs wallowed. The bones of the dogs were ready to break through their hides, and this was not good for them. So I spoke hard words to the man, and he promised, and broke his word. Then I beat him with the dog-whip, and after that the dogs wallowed no more. He was a child, what of the pain and the streak of fat.

"But Passuk. While the man lay by the fire and wept, she cooked, and in the morning helped lash the sleds, and in the evening to unlash them. And she saved the dogs. Ever was she to the fore, lifting the webbed shoes and making the way easy. Passuk—how shall I say? —I took it for granted that she should do these things, and thought no more about it. For my mind was busy with other matters, and besides, I was young in years and knew little of woman. It was only on looking back that I came to understand.

"And the man became worthless. The dogs had little strength in them, but he stole rides on the sled when he lagged behind. Passuk said she would take the one sled, so the man had nothing to do. In the morning I gave him his fair share of grub and started him on the trail alone. Then the woman and I broke camp, packed the sleds, and harnessed the dogs. By midday, when the sun mocked us, we would overtake the man, with the tears frozen on his cheeks, and pass him. In the night we made camp, set aside his fair share of grub, and spread his furs. Also we made a big fire, that he might see. And hours afterward he would come limping in, and eat his grub with moans and groans, and sleep. He was not sick, this man. He was only trail-sore and tired, and weak with hunger. But Passuk and I were trail-sore and tired, and weak with hunger; and we did all the work and he did none. But he had the streak of fat of which our brother Bettles has spoken. Further, we gave the man always his fair share of grub.

"Then one day we met two ghosts journeying through the Silence. They were a man and a boy, and they were white. The ice had opened on Lake Le Barge, and through it had gone their main outfit. One blanket each carried about his shoulders. At night they built a fire and crouched over it till morning. They had a little flour. This they stirred in warm water and drank. The man showed me eight cups of flour—all they had, and Pelly, stricken with famine, two hundred miles away. They said, also, that there was an Indian behind; that they had whacked fair, but that he could not keep up. I did not believe they had whacked fair, else would the Indian have kept up. But I could give them no grub. They strove to steal a dog—the fattest, which was very thin—but I shoved my pistol in their faces and told them begone. And they went away, like drunken men, through the Silence toward Pelly.

"I had three dogs now, and one sled, and the dogs were only bones and hair. When there is little wood, the fire burns low and the cabin grows cold. So with us. With little grub the frost bites sharp, and our faces were black and frozen till our own mothers would not have known us. And our feet were very sore. In the morning, when I hit the trail, I sweated to keep down the cry when the pain of the snowshoes smote me. Passuk never opened her lips, but stepped to the fore to break the way. The man howled.

"The Thirty Mile was swift, and the current ate away the ice from beneath, and there were many air-holes and cracks, and much open water. One day we came upon the man, resting, for he had gone ahead, as was his wont, in the morning. But between us was open water. This he had passed around by taking to the rim-ice where it was too narrow for a sled. So we found an ice-bridge. Passuk weighed little, and went first, with a long pole crosswise in her hands in chance she broke through. But she was light, and her shoes large, and she passed over. Then she called the dogs. But they had neither poles nor shoes, and they broke through and were swept under by the water. I held tight to the sled from behind, till the traces broke and the dogs went on down under the ice. There was little meat to them, but I had counted on them for a week's grub, and they were gone.

"The next morning I divided all the grub, which was little, into three portions. And I told Long Jeff that he could keep up with us, or not, as he saw fit; for we were going to travel light and fast. But he raised his voice and cried over his sore feet and his troubles, and said harsh things against comradeship. Passuk's feet were sore, and my feet were sore—ay, sorer than his, for we had worked with the dogs; also, we looked to see. Long Jeff swore he would die before he hit the trail again; so Passuk took a fur robe, and I a cooking pot and an axe, and we made ready to go. But she looked on the man's portion, and said, 'It is wrong to waste good food on a baby. He is better dead.' I shook my head and said no—that a comrade once was a comrade always. Then she spoke of the men of Forty Mile; that they were many men and good; and that they looked to me for grub in the spring. But when I still said no, she snatched the pistol from my belt, quick, and as our brother Bettles has spoken, Long Jeff went to the bosom of Abraham before his time. I chided Passuk for this; but she showed no sorrow, nor was she sorrowful. And in my heart I knew she was right."

Sitka Charley paused and threw pieces of ice into the gold pan on the stove. The men were silent, and their backs chilled to the sobbing cries of the dogs as they gave tongue to their misery in the outer cold.

"And day by day we passed in the snow the sleeping-places of the two ghosts—Passuk and I—and we knew we would be glad for such ere we made Salt Water. Then we came to the Indian, like another ghost, with his face set toward Pelly. They had not whacked up fair, the man and the boy, he said, and he had had no flour for three days. Each night he boiled pieces of his moccasins in a cup, and ate them. He did not have much moccasins left. And he was a Coast Indian, and told us these things through Passuk, who talked his tongue. He was a stranger in the Yukon, and he knew not the way, but his face was set to Pelly. How far was it? Two sleeps? ten? a hundred—he did not know, but he was going to Pelly. It was too far to turn back; he could only keep on.

"He did not ask for grub, for he could see we, too, were hard put. Passuk looked at the man, and at me, as though she were of two minds, like a mother partridge whose young are in trouble. So I turned to her and said, 'This man has been dealt unfair. Shall I give him of our grub a portion?' I saw her eyes light, as with quick pleasure; but she looked long at the man and at me, and her mouth drew close and hard, and she said, 'No. The Salt Water is afar off, and Death lies in wait. Better it is that he take this stranger man and let my man Charley pass.' So the man went away in the Silence toward Pelly. That night she wept. Never had I seen her weep before. Nor was it the smoke of the fire, for the wood was dry wood. So I marveled at her sorrow, and thought her woman's heart had grown soft at the darkness of the trail and the pain.

"Life is a strange thing. Much have I thought on it, and pondered long, yet daily the strangeness of it grows not less, but more. Why this longing for Life? It is a game which no man wins. To live is to toil hard, and to suffer sore, till Old Age creeps heavily upon us and we throw down our hands on the cold ashes of dead fires. It is hard to live. In pain the babe sucks his first breath, in pain the old man gasps his last, and all his days are full of trouble and sorrow; yet he goes down to the open arms of Death, stumbling, falling, with head turned backward, fighting to the last. And Death is kind. It is only Life, and the things of Life that hurt. Yet we love Life, and we hate Death. It is very strange.

"We spoke little, Passuk and I, in the days which came. In the night we lay in the snow like dead people, and in the morning we went on our way, walking like dead people. And all things were dead. There were no ptarmigan, no squirrels, no snowshoe rabbits,—nothing. The river made no sound beneath its white robes. The sap was frozen in the forest. And it became cold, as now; and in the night the stars drew near and large, and leaped and danced; and in the day the sun-dogs mocked us till we saw many suns, and all the air flashed and sparkled, and the snow was diamond dust. And there was no heat, no sound, only the bitter cold and the Silence. As I say, we walked like dead people, as in a dream, and we kept no count of time. Only our faces were set to Salt Water, our souls strained for Salt Water, and our feet carried us toward Salt Water. We camped by the Tahkeena, and knew it not. Our eyes looked upon the White Horse, but we saw it not. Our feet trod the portage of the Canyon, but they felt it not. We felt nothing. And we fell often by the way, but we fell, always, with our faces toward Salt Water.

"Our last grub went, and we had shared fair, Passuk and I, but she fell more often, and at Caribou Crossing her strength left her. And in the morning we lay beneath the one robe and did not take the trail. It was in my mind to stay there and meet Death hand-in-hand with Passuk; for I had grown old, and had learned the love of woman. Also, it was eighty miles to Haines Mission, and the great Chilcoot, far above the timber-line, reared his storm-swept head between. But Passuk spoke to me, low, with my ear against her lips that I might hear. And now, because she need not fear my anger, she spoke her heart, and told me of her love, and of many things which I did not understand.

"And she said: 'You are my man, Charley, and I have been a good woman to you. And in all the days I have made your fire, and cooked your food, and fed your dogs, and lifted paddle or broken trail, I have not complained. Nor did I say that there was more warmth in the lodge of my father, or that there was more grub on the Chilcat. When you have spoken, I have listened. When you have ordered, I have obeyed. Is it not so, Charley?'

"And I said: 'Ay, it is so.'

"And she said: 'When first you came to the Chilcat, nor looked upon me, but bought me as a man buys a dog, and took me away, my heart was hard against you and filled with bitterness and fear. But that was long ago. For you were kind to me, Charley, as a good man is kind to his dog. Your heart was cold, and there was no room for me; yet you dealt me fair and your ways were just. And I was with you when you did bold deeds and led great ventures, and I measured you against the men of other breeds, and I saw you stood among them full of honor, and your word was wise, your tongue true. And I grew proud of you, till it came that you filled all my heart, and all my thought was of you. You were as the midsummer sun, when its golden trail runs in a circle and never leaves the sky. And whatever way I cast my eyes I beheld the sun. But your heart was ever cold, Charley, and there was no room.'

"And I said: 'It is so. It was cold, and there was no room. But that is past. Now my heart is like the snowfall in the spring, when the sun has come back. There is a great thaw and a bending, a sound of running waters, and a budding and sprouting of green things. And there is drumming of partridges, and songs of robins, and great music, for the winter is broken, Passuk, and I have learned the love of woman.'

"She smiled and moved for me to draw her closer. And she said, 'I am glad.' After that she lay quiet for a long time, breathing softly, her head upon my breast. Then she whispered: 'The trail ends here, and I am tired. But first I would speak of other things. In the long ago, when I was a girl on the Chilcat, I played alone among the skin bales of my father's lodge; for the men were away on the hunt, and the women and boys were dragging in the meat. It was in the spring, and I was alone. A great brown bear, just awake from his winter's sleep, hungry, his fur hanging to the bones in flaps of leanness, shoved his head within the lodge and said, "Oof!" My brother came running back with the first sled of meat. And he fought the bear with burning sticks from the fire, and the dogs in their harnesses, with the sled behind them, fell upon the bear. There was a great battle and much noise. They rolled in the fire, the skin bales were scattered, the lodge overthrown. But in the end the bear lay dead, with the fingers of my brother in his mouth and the marks of his claws upon my brother's face. Did you mark the Indian by the Pelly trail, his mitten which had no thumb, his hand which he warmed by our fire? He was my brother. And I said he should have no grub. And he went away in the Silence without grub.'

"This, my brothers, was the love of Passuk, who died in the snow, by the Caribou Crossing. It was a mighty love, for she denied her brother for the man who led her away on weary trails to a bitter end. And, further, such was this woman's love, she denied herself. Ere her eyes closed for the last time she took my hand and slipped it under her squirrel-skin *parka* to her waist. I felt there a well-filled pouch, and learned the secret of her lost strength. Day by day we had shared fair, to the last least bit; and day by day but half her share had she eaten. The other half had gone into the well-filled pouch.

"And she said: 'This is the end of the trail for Passuk; but your trail, Charley, leads on and on, over the great Chilcoot, down to Haines Mission and the sea. And it leads on and on, by the light of many suns, over unknown lands and strange waters, and it is full of years and honors and great glories. It leads you to the lodges of many women, and good women, but it will never lead you to a greater love than the love of Passuk.'

"And I knew the woman spoke true. But a madness came upon me, and I threw the well-filled pouch from me, and swore that my trail had reached an end, till her tired eyes grew soft with tears, and she said: 'Among men has Sitka Charley walked in honor, and ever has his word been true. Does he forget that honor now, and talk vain words by the Caribou Crossing? Does he remember no more the men of Forty Mile, who gave him of their grub the best, of their dogs the pick? Ever has Passuk been proud of her man. Let him lift himself up, gird on his snowshoes, and begone, that she may still keep her pride.'

"And when she grew cold in my arms I arose, and sought out the well-filled pouch, and girt on my snowshoes, and staggered along the trail; for there was a weakness in my knees, and my head was dizzy, and in my ears there was a roaring, and a flashing of fire upon my eyes. The forgotten trails of boyhood came back to me. I sat by the full pots of the *potlach* feast, and raised my voice in song, and danced to the chanting of the men and maidens and the booming of the walrus drums. And Passuk held my hand and walked by my side. When I laid down to sleep, she waked me. When I stumbled and fell, she raised me. When I wandered in the deep snow, she led me back to the trail. And in this wise, like a man bereft of reason, who sees strange visions and whose thoughts are light with wine, I came to Haines Mission by the sea."

Sitka Charley threw back the tent-flaps. It was midday. To the south, just clearing the bleak Henderson Divide, poised the cold-disked sun. On either hand the sun-dogs blazed. The air was a gossamer of glittering frost. In the foreground, beside the trail, a wolf-dog, bristling with frost, thrust a long snout heavenward and mourned.

WHERE THE TRAIL FORKS

"Must I, then, must I, then, now leave this town —
And you, my love, stay here?"

— SCHWABIAN FOLK-SONG.

THE SINGER, clean-faced and cheery-eyed, bent over and added water to a pot of simmering beans, and then, rising, a stick of firewood in hand, drove back the circling dogs from the grub-box and cooking-gear. He was blue of eye, and his long hair was golden, and it was a pleasure to look upon his lusty freshness. A new moon was thrusting a dim horn above the white line of close-packed snow-capped pines which ringed the camp and segregated it from all the world. Overhead, so clear it was and cold, the stars danced with quick, pulsating movements. To the southeast an evanescent greenish glow heralded the opening revels of the aurora borealis. Two men, in the immediate foreground, lay upon the bearskin which was their bed. Between the skin and naked snow was a six-inch layer of pine boughs. The blankets were rolled back. For shelter, there was a fly at their backs,—a sheet of canvas stretched between two trees and angling at forty-five degrees. This caught the radiating heat from the fire and flung it down upon the skin. Another man sat on a sled, drawn close to the blaze, mending moccasins. To the right, a heap of frozen gravel and a rude windlass denoted where they toiled each day in dismal groping for the pay-streak. To the left, four pairs of snowshoes stood erect, showing the mode of travel which obtained when the stamped snow of the camp was left behind.

That Schwabian folk-song sounded strangely pathetic under the cold northern stars, and did not do the men good who lounged about the fire after the toil of the day. It put a dull ache into their hearts, and a yearning which was akin to belly-hunger, and sent their souls questing southward across the divides to the sun-lands.

"For the love of God, Sigmund, shut up!" expostulated one of the men. His hands were clenched painfully, but he hid them from sight in the folds of the bearskin upon which he lay.

"And what for, Dave Wertz?" Sigmund demanded. "Why shall I not sing when the heart is glad?"

"Because you've got no call to, that's why. Look about you, man, and think of the grub we've been defiling our bodies with for the last twelvemonth, and the way we've lived and worked like beasts!"

Thus abjured, Sigmund, the golden-haired, surveyed it all, and the frost-rimmed wolf-dogs and the vapor breaths of the men. "And why shall not the heart be glad?" he laughed. "It is good; it is all good. As for the grub—" He doubled up his arm and caressed the swelling biceps. "And if we have lived and worked like beasts, have we not been paid like kings? Twenty dollars to the pan the streak is running, and we know it to be eight feet thick. It is another Klondike—and we know it—Jim Hawes there, by your elbow, knows it and complains not. And there's Hitchcock! He sews moccasins like an old woman, and waits against the time. Only you can't wait and work until the wash-up in the spring. Then we shall all be rich, rich as kings, only you cannot wait. You want to go back to the States. So do I, and I was born there, but I can wait, when each day the gold in the pan shows up yellow as butter in the churning. But you want your good time, and, like a child, you cry for it now. Bah! Why shall I not sing:

> "In a year, in a year, when the grapes are ripe,
>   I shall stay no more away.
> Then if you still are true, my love,
>   It will be our wedding day.
> In a year, in a year, when my time is past,
>   Then I'll live in your love for aye.
> Then if you still are true, my love,
>   It will be our wedding day."

The dogs, bristling and growling, drew in closer to the firelight. There was a monotonous crunch-crunch of webbed shoes, and between each crunch the dragging forward of the heel of the shoe like the sound of sifting sugar. Sigmund broke off from his song to hurl oaths and firewood at the animals. Then the light was parted by a fur-clad figure, and an Indian girl slipped out of the webs, threw back the hood of her squirrel-skin *parka*, and stood in their midst. Sigmund and the men on the bearskin greeted her as "Sipsu," with the customary "Hello," but Hitchcock made room on the sled that she might sit beside him.

"And how goes it, Sipsu?" he asked, talking, after her fashion, in broken English and bastard Chinook. "Is the hunger still mighty in the camp? and has the witch doctor yet found the cause wherefore game is scarce and no moose in the land?"

"Yes; even so. There is little game, and we prepare to eat the dogs. Also has the witch doctor found the cause of all this evil, and to-morrow will he make sacrifice and cleanse the camp."

"And what does the sacrifice chance to be?—a new-born babe or some poor devil of a squaw, old and shaky, who is a care to the tribe and better out of the way?"

"It chanced not that wise; for the need was great, and he chose none other than the chief's daughter; none other than I, Sipsu."

"Hell!" The word rose slowly to Hitchcock's lips, and brimmed over full and deep, in a way which bespoke wonder and consideration.

"Wherefore we stand by a forking of the trail, you and I," she went on calmly, "and I have come that we may look once more upon each other, and once more only."

She was born of primitive stock, and primitive had been her traditions and her days; so she regarded life stoically, and human sacrifice as part of the natural order. The powers which ruled the day-light and the dark, the flood and the frost, the bursting of the bud and the withering of the leaf, were angry and in need of propitiation. This they exacted in many ways,—death in the bad water, through the treacherous ice-crust, by the grip of the grizzly, or a wasting sickness which fell upon a man in his own lodge till he coughed, and the life of his lungs went out through his mouth and nostrils. Likewise did the powers receive sacrifice. It was all one. And the witch doctor was versed in the thoughts of the powers and chose unerringly. It was very natural. Death came by many ways, yet was it all one after all, —a manifestation of the all-powerful and inscrutable.

But Hitchcock came of a later world-breed. His traditions were less concrete and without reverence, and he said, "Not so, Sipsu. You are young, and yet in the full joy of life. The witch doctor is a fool, and his choice is evil. This thing shall not be."

She smiled and answered, "Life is not kind, and for many reasons. First, it made of us twain the one white and the other red, which is bad. Then it crossed our trails, and now it parts them again; and we can do nothing. Once before, when the gods were angry, did your brothers come to the camp. They were three, big men and white, and they said the thing shall not be. But they died quickly, and the thing was."

Hitchcock nodded that he heard, half-turned, and lifted his voice. "Look here, you fellows! There's a lot of foolery going on over to the camp, and they're getting ready to murder Sipsu. What d'ye say?"

Wertz looked at Hawes, and Hawes looked back, but neither spoke. Sigmund dropped his head, and petted the shepherd dog between his knees. He had brought Shep in with him from the outside, and thought a great deal of the animal. In fact, a certain girl, who was much in his thoughts, and whose picture in the little locket on his breast often inspired him to sing, had given him the dog and her blessing when they kissed good by and he started on his Northland quest.

"What d'ye say?" Hitchcock repeated.

"Mebbe it's not so serious," Hawes answered with deliberation. "Most likely it's only a girl's story."

"That isn't the point!" Hitchcock felt a hot flush of anger sweep over him at their evident reluctance. "The question is, if it is so, are we going to stand it? What are we going to do?"

"I don't see any call to interfere," spoke up Wertz. "If it is so, it is so, and that's all there is about it. It's a way these people have of doing. It's their religion, and it's no concern of ours. Our concern is to get the dust and then get out of this God-forsaken land. 'T isn't fit for naught else but beasts? And what are these black devils but beasts? Besides, it'd be damn poor policy."

"That's what I say," chimed in Hawes. "Here we are, four of us, three hundred miles from the Yukon or a white face. And what can we do against half-a-hundred Indians? If we quarrel with them, we have to vamose; if we fight, we are wiped out. Further, we've struck pay, and, by God! I, for one, am going to stick by it!"

"Ditto here," supplemented Wertz.

Hitchcock turned impatiently to Sigmund, who was softly singing,—

"In a year, in a year, when the grapes are ripe,
I shall stay no more away."

"Well, it's this way, Hitchcock," he finally said, "I'm in the same boat with the rest. If three-score bucks have made up their mind to kill the girl, why, we can't help it. One rush, and we'd be wiped off the landscape. And what good'd that be? They'd still have the girl. There's no use in going against the customs of a people except you're in force."

"But we are in force!" Hitchcock broke in. "Four whites are a match for a hundred times as many reds. And think of the girl!"

Sigmund stroked the dog meditatively. "But I do think of the girl. And her eyes are blue like summer skies, and laughing like summer seas, and her hair is yellow, like mine, and braided in ropes the size of a big man's arms. She's waiting for me, out there, in a better land. And she's waited long, and now my pile's in sight I'm not going to throw it away."

"And shamed I would be to look into the girl's blue eyes and remember the black ones of the girl whose blood was on my hands," Hitchcock sneered; for he was born to honor and championship, and to do the thing for the thing's sake, nor stop to weigh or measure.

Sigmund shook his head. "You can't make me mad, Hitchcock, nor do mad things because of your madness. It's a cold business proposition and a question of facts. I didn't come to this country for my health, and, further, it's impossible for us to raise a hand. If it is so, it is too bad for the girl, that's all. It's a way of her people, and it just happens we're on the spot this one time. They've done the same for a thousand-thousand years, and they're going to do it now, and they'll go doing it for all time to come. Besides, they're not our kind. Nor's the girl. No, I take my stand with Wertz and Hawes, and—"

But the dogs snarled and drew in, and he broke off, listening to the crunch-crunch of many snowshoes. Indian after Indian stalked into the firelight, tall and grim, fur-clad and silent, their shadows dancing grotesquely on the snow. One, the witch doctor, spoke gutturally to Sipsu. His face was daubed with savage paint blotches, and over his shoulders was drawn a wolfskin, the gleaming teeth and cruel snout surmounting his head. No other word was spoken. The prospectors held the peace. Sipsu arose and slipped into her snowshoes.

"Good-by, O my man," she said to Hitchcock. But the man who had sat beside her on the sled gave no sign, nor lifted his head as they filed away into the white forest.

Unlike many men, his faculty of adaptation, while large, had never suggested the expediency of an alliance with the women of the Northland. His broad cosmopolitanism had never impelled toward covenanting in marriage with the daughters of the soil. If it had, his philosophy of life would not have stood between. But it simply had not. Sipsu? He had pleasured in camp-fire chats with her, not as a man who knew himself to be man and she woman, but as a man might with a child, and as a man of his make certainly would if for no other reason than to vary the tedium of a bleak existence. That was all. But there was a certain chivalric thrill of warm blood in him, despite his Yankee ancestry and New England upbringing, and he was so made that the commercial aspect of life often seemed meaningless and bore contradiction to his deeper impulses.

So he sat silent, with head bowed forward, an organic force, greater than himself, as great as his race, at work within him. Wertz and Hawes looked askance at him from time to time, a faint but perceptible trepidation in their manner. Sigmund also felt this. Hitchcock was strong, and his strength had been impressed upon them in the course of many an event in their precarious life. So they stood in a certain definite awe and curiosity as to what his conduct would be when he moved to action.

But his silence was long, and the fire nigh out, when Wertz stretched his arms and yawned, and thought he'd go to bed. Then Hitchcock stood up his full height.

"May God damn your souls to the deepest hells, you chicken-hearted cowards! I'm done with you!" He said it calmly enough, but his strength spoke in every syllable, and every intonation was advertisement of intention. "Come on," he continued, "whack up, and in whatever way suits you best. I own a quarter-interest in the claims; our contracts show that. There're twenty-five or thirty ounces in the sack from the test pans. Fetch out the scales. We'll divide that now. And you, Sigmund, measure me my quarter-share of the grub and set it apart. Four of the dogs are mine, and I want four more. I'll trade you my share in the camp outfit and mining-gear for the dogs. And I'll throw in my six or seven ounces and the spare 45-90 with the ammunition. What d'ye say?"

The three men drew apart and conferred. When they returned, Sigmund acted as spokesman. "We'll whack up fair with you, Hitchcock. In everything you'll get your quarter-share, neither more nor less; and you can take it or leave it. But we want the dogs as bad as you do, so you get four, and that's all. If you don't want to take your share of the outfit and gear, why, that's your lookout. If you want it, you can have it; if you don't, leave it."

"The letter of the law," Hitchcock sneered. "But go ahead. I'm willing. And hurry up. I can't get out of this camp and away from its vermin any too quick."

The division was effected without further comment. He lashed his meagre belongings upon one of the sleds, rounded in his four dogs, and harnessed up. His portion of outfit and gear he did not touch, though he threw onto the sled half a dozen dog harnesses, and challenged them with his eyes to interfere. But they shrugged their shoulders and watched him disappear in the forest.

A MAN CRAWLED upon his belly through the snow. On every hand loomed the moose-hide lodges of the camp. Here and there a miserable dog howled or snarled abuse upon his neighbor. Once, one of them approached the creeping man, but the man became motionless. The dog came closer and sniffed, and came yet closer, till its nose touched the strange object which had not been there when darkness fell. Then Hitchcock, for it was Hitchcock, upreared suddenly, shooting an unmittened hand out to the brute's shaggy throat. And the dog knew its death in that clutch, and when the man moved on, was left broken-necked under the stars. In this manner Hitchcock made the chief's lodge. For long he lay in the snow without, listening to the voices of the occupants and striving to locate Sipsu. Evidently there were many in the tent, and from the sounds they were in high excitement. At last he heard the girl's voice, and crawled around so that only the moose-hide divided them. Then burrowing in the snow, he slowly wormed his head and shoulders underneath. When the warm inner air smote his face, he stopped and waited, his legs and the greater part of his body still on the outside. He could see nothing, nor did he dare lift his head. On one side of him was a skin bale. He could smell it, though he carefully felt to be certain. On the other side his face barely touched a furry garment which he knew clothed a body. This must be Sipsu. Though he wished she would speak again, he resolved to risk it.

He could hear the chief and the witch doctor talking high, and in a far corner some hungry child whimpering to sleep. Squirming over on his side, he carefully raised his head, still just touching the furry garment. He listened to the breathing. It was a woman's breathing; he would chance it.

He pressed against her side softly but firmly, and felt her start at the contact. Again he waited, till a questioning hand slipped down upon his head and paused among the curls. The next instant the hand turned his face gently upward, and he was gazing into Sipsu's eyes.

She was quite collected. Changing her position casually, she threw an elbow well over on the skin bale, rested her body upon it, and arranged her *parka*. In this way he was completely concealed. Then, and still most casually, she reclined across him, so that he could breathe between her arm and breast, and when she lowered her head her ear pressed lightly against his lips.

"When the time suits, go thou," he whispered, "out of the lodge and across the snow, down the wind to the bunch of jackpine in the curve of the creek. There wilt thou find my dogs and my sled, packed for the trail. This night we go down to the Yukon; and since we go fast, lay thou hands upon what dogs come nigh thee, by the scruff of the neck, and drag them to the sled in the curve of the creek."

Sipsu shook her head in dissent; but her eyes glistened with gladness, and she was proud that this man had shown toward her such favor. But she, like the women of all her race, was born to obey the will masculine, and when Hitchcock repeated "Go!" he did it with authority, and though she made no answer he knew that his will was law.

"And never mind harness for the dogs," he added, preparing to go. "I shall wait. But waste no time. The day chaseth the night alway, nor does it linger for man's pleasure."

Half an hour later, stamping his feet and swinging his arms by the sled, he saw her coming, a surly dog in either hand. At the approach of these his own animals waxed truculent, and he favored them with the butt of his whip till they quieted. He had approached the camp up the wind, and sound was the thing to be most feared in making his presence known.

"Put them into the sled," he ordered when she had got the harness on the two dogs. "I want my leaders to the fore."

But when she had done this, the displaced animals pitched upon the aliens. Though Hitchcock plunged among them with clubbed rifle, a riot of sound went up and across the sleeping camp.

"Now we shall have dogs, and in plenty," he remarked grimly, slipping an axe from the sled lashings. "Do thou harness whichever I fling thee, and betweenwhiles protect the team."

He stepped a space in advance and waited between two pines. The dogs of the camp were disturbing the night with their jangle, and he watched for their coming. A dark spot, growing rapidly, took form upon the dim white expanse of snow. It was a forerunner of the pack, leaping cleanly, and, after the wolf fashion, singing direction to its brothers. Hitchcock stood in the shadow. As it sprang past, he reached out, gripped its forelegs in mid-career, and sent it whirling earthward. Then he struck it a well-judged blow beneath the ear, and flung it to Sipsu. And while she clapped on the harness, he, with his axe, held the passage between the trees, till a shaggy flood of white teeth and glistening eyes surged and crested just beyond reach. Sipsu worked rapidly. When she had finished, he leaped forward, seized and stunned a second, and flung it to her. This he repeated thrice again, and when the sled team stood snarling in a string of ten, he called, "Enough!"

But at this instant a young buck, the forerunner of the tribe, and swift of limb, wading through the dogs and cuffing right and left, attempted the passage. The butt of Hitchcock's rifle drove him to his knees, whence he toppled over sideways. The witch doctor, running lustily, saw the blow fall.

Hitchcock called to Sipsu to pull out. At her shrill "Chook!" the maddened brutes shot straight ahead, and the sled, bounding mightily, just missed unseating her. The powers were evidently angry with the witch doctor, for at this moment they plunged him upon the trail. The lead-dog fouled his snowshoes and tripped him up, and the nine succeeding dogs trod him under foot and the sled bumped over him. But he was quick to his feet, and the night might have turned out differently had not Sipsu struck backward with the long dog-whip and smitten him a blinding blow across the eyes. Hitchcock, hurrying to overtake her, collided against him as he swayed with pain in the middle of the trail. Thus it was, when this primitive theologian got back to the chief's lodge, that his wisdom had been increased in so far as concerns the efficacy of the white man's fist. So, when he orated then and there in the council, he was wroth against all white men.

"Tumble out, you loafers! Tumble out! Grub'll be ready before you get into your footgear!"

Dave Wertz threw off the bearskin, sat up, and yawned.

Hawes stretched, discovered a lame muscle in his arm, and rubbed it sleepily. "Wonder where Hitchcock bunked last night?" he queried, reaching for his moccasins. They were stiff, and he walked gingerly in his socks to the fire to thaw them out. "It's a blessing he's gone," he added, "though he was a mighty good worker."

"Yep. Too masterful. That was his trouble. Too bad for Sipsu. Think he cared for her much?"

"Don't think so. Just principle. That's all. He thought it wasn't right—and, of course, it wasn't,—but that was no reason for us to interfere and get hustled over the divide before our time."

"Principle is principle, and it's good in its place, but it's best left to home when you go to Alaska. Eh?" Wertz had joined his mate, and both were working pliability into their frozen moccasins. "Think we ought to have taken a hand?"

Sigmund shook his head. He was very busy. A scud of chocolate-colored foam was rising in the coffee-pot, and the bacon needed turning. Also, he was thinking about the girl with laughing eyes like summer seas, and he was humming softly.

His mates chuckled to each other and ceased talking. Though it was past seven, daybreak was still three hours distant. The aurora borealis had passed out of the sky, and the camp was an oasis of light in the midst of deep darkness. And in this light the forms of the three men were sharply defined. Emboldened by the silence, Sigmund raised his voice and opened the last stanza of the old song:-

"In a year, in a year, when the grapes are ripe—"

Then the night was split with a rattling volley of rifle-shots. Hawes sighed, made an effort to straighten himself, and collapsed. Wertz went over on an elbow with drooping head. He choked a little, and a dark stream flowed from his mouth. And Sigmund, the Golden-Haired, his throat a-gurgle with the song, threw up his arms and pitched across the fire.

The witch doctor's eyes were well blackened, and his temper none of the best; for he quarreled with the chief over the possession of Wertz's rifle, and took more than his share of the part-sack of beans. Also he appropriated the bearskin, and caused grumbling among the tribesmen. And finally, he tried to kill Sigmund's dog, which the girl had given him, but the dog ran away, while he fell into the shaft and dislocated his shoulder on the bucket. When the camp was well looted they went back to their own lodges, and there was a great rejoicing among the women. Further, a band of moose strayed over the south divide and fell before the hunters, so the witch doctor attained yet greater honor, and the people whispered among themselves that he spoke in council with the gods.

But later, when all were gone, the shepherd dog crept back to the deserted camp, and all the night long and a day it wailed the dead. After that it disappeared, though the years were not many before the Indian hunters noted a change in the breed of timber wolves, and there were dashes of bright color and variegated markings such as no wolf bore before.

A DAUGHTER OF THE AURORA

"You—what you call—lazy mans, you lazy mans would desire me to haf for wife. It is not good. Nevaire, no, nevaire, will lazy mans my hoosband be."

Thus Joy Molineau spoke her mind to Jack Harrington, even as she had spoken it, but more tritely and in his own tongue, to Louis Savoy the previous night.

"Listen, Joy—"

"No, no; why moos' I listen to lazy mans? It is vaire bad, you hang rount, make visitation to my cabin, and do nothing. How you get grub for the famine? Why haf not you the dust? Odder mans haf plentee."

"But I work hard, Joy. Never a day am I not on trail or up creek. Even now have I just come off. My dogs are yet tired. Other men have luck and find plenty of gold; but I—I have no luck."

"Ah! But when this mans with the wife which is Indian, this mans McCormack, when him discovaire the Klondike, you go not. Odder mans go; odder mans now rich."

"You know I was prospecting over on the head-reaches of the Tanana," Harrington protested, "and knew nothing of the Eldorado or Bonanza until it was too late."

"That is deeferent; only you are—what you call way off."

"What?"

"Way off. In the—yes—in the dark. It is nevaire too late. One vaire rich mine is there, on the creek which is Eldorado. The mans drive the stake and him go 'way. No odddr mans know what of him become. The mans, him which drive the stake, is nevaire no more. Sixty days no mans on that claim file the papaire. Then odder mans, plentee odder mans—what you call—jump that claim. Then they race, O so queek, like the wind, to file the papaire. Him be vaire rich. Him get grub for famine."

Harrington hid the major portion of his interest.

"When's the time up?" he asked. "What claim is it?"

"So I speak Louis Savoy last night," she continued, ignoring him. "Him I think the winnaire."

"Hang Louis Savoy!"

"So Louis Savoy speak in my cabin last night. Him say, 'Joy, I am strong mans. I haf good dogs. I haf long wind. I will be winnaire. Then you will haf me for hoosband?' And I say to him, I say—"

"What'd you say?"

"I say, 'If Louis Savoy is winnaire, then will he haf me for wife.'"

"And if he don't win?"

"Then Louis Savoy, him will not be—what you call—the father of my children."

"And if I win?"

"You winnaire? Ha! ha! Nevaire!"

Exasperating as it was, Joy Molineau's laughter was pretty to hear. Harrington did not mind it. He had long since been broken in. Besides, he was no exception. She had forced all her lovers to suffer in kind. And very enticing she was just then, her lips parted, her color heightened by the sharp kiss of the frost, her eyes vibrant with the lure which is the greatest of all lures and which may be seen nowhere save in woman's eyes. Her sled-dogs clustered about her in hirsute masses, and the leader, Wolf Fang, laid his long snout softly in her lap.

"If I do win?" Harrington pressed.

She looked from dog to lover and back again.

"What you say, Wolf Fang? If him strong mans and file the papaire, shall we his wife become? Eh? What you say?"

Wolf Fang picked up his ears and growled at Harrington.

"It is vaire cold," she suddenly added with feminine irrelevance, rising to her feet and straightening out the team.

Her lover looked on stolidly. She had kept him guessing from the first time they met, and patience had been joined unto his virtues.

"Hi! Wolf Fang!" she cried, springing upon the sled as it leaped into sudden motion. "Ai! Ya! Mush-on!"

From the corner of his eye Harrington watched her swinging down the trail to Forty Mile. Where the road forked and crossed the river to Fort Cudahy, she halted the dogs and turned about.

"O Mistaire Lazy Mans!" she called back. "Wolf Fang, him say yes—if you winnaire!"

⬧⬧⬧

BUT SOMEHOW, as such things will, it leaked out, and all Forty Mile, which had hitherto speculated on Joy Molineau's choice between her two latest lovers, now hazarded bets and guesses as to which would win in the forthcoming race. The camp divided itself into two factions, and every effort was put forth in order that their respective favorites might be the first in at the finish. There was a scramble for the best dogs the country could afford, for dogs, and good ones, were essential, above all, to success. And it meant much to the victor. Besides the possession of a wife, the like of which had yet to be created, it stood for a mine worth a million at least.

That fall, when news came down of McCormack's discovery on Bonanza, all the Lower Country, Circle City and Forty Mile included, had stampeded up the Yukon,—at least all save those who, like Jack Harrington and Louis Savoy, were away prospecting in the west. Moose pastures and creeks were staked indiscriminately and promiscuously; and incidentally, one of the unlikeliest of creeks, Eldorado. Olaf Nelson laid claim to five hundred of its linear feet, duly posted his notice, and as duly disappeared. At that time the nearest recording office was in the police barracks at Fort Cudahy, just across the river from Forty

Mile; but when it became bruited abroad that Eldorado Creek was a treasure-house, it was quickly discovered that Olaf Nelson had failed to make the down-Yukon trip to file upon his property. Men cast hungry eyes upon the ownerless claim, where they knew a thousand-thousand dollars waited but shovel and sluice-box. Yet they dared not touch it; for there was a law which permitted sixty days to lapse between the staking and the filing, during which time a claim was immune. The whole country knew of Olaf Nelson's disappearance, and scores of men made preparation for the jumping and for the consequent race to Fort Cudahy.

But competition at Forty Mile was limited. With the camp devoting its energies to the equipping either of Jack Harrington or Louis Savoy, no man was unwise enough to enter the contest single-handed. It was a stretch of a hundred miles to the Recorder's office, and it was planned that the two favorites should have four relays of dogs stationed along the trail. Naturally, the last relay was to be the crucial one, and for these twenty-five miles their respective partisans strove to obtain the strongest possible animals. So bitter did the factions wax, and so high did they bid, that dogs brought stiffer prices than ever before in the annals of the country. And, as it chanced, this scramble for dogs turned the public eye still more searchingly upon Joy Molineau. Not only was she the cause of it all, but she possessed the finest sled-dog from Chilkoot to Bering Sea. As wheel or leader, Wolf Fang had no equal. The man whose sled he led down the last stretch was bound to win. There could be no doubt of it. But the community had an innate sense of the fitness of things, and not once was Joy vexed by overtures for his use. And the factions drew consolation from the fact that if one man did not profit by him, neither should the other.

However, since man, in the individual or in the aggregate, has been so fashioned that he goes through life blissfully obtuse to the deeper subtleties of his womankind, so the men of Forty Mile failed to divine the inner deviltry of Joy Molineau. They confessed, afterward, that they had failed to appreciate this dark-eyed daughter of the aurora, whose father had traded furs in the country before ever they dreamed of invading it, and who had herself first opened eyes on the scintillant northern lights. Nay, accident of birth had not rendered her less the woman, nor had it limited her woman's understanding of men. They knew she played with them, but they did not know the wisdom of her play, its deepness and its deftness. They failed to see more than the exposed card, so that to the very last Forty Mile was in a state of pleasant obfuscation, and it was not until she cast her final trump that it came to reckon up the score.

Early in the week the camp turned out to start Jack Harrington and Louis Savoy on their way. They had taken a shrewd margin of time, for it was their wish to arrive at Olaf Nelson's claim some days previous to the expiration of its immunity, that they might rest themselves, and their dogs be fresh for the first relay. On the way up they found the men of Dawson already stationing spare dog teams along the trail, and it was manifest that little expense had been spared in view of the millions at stake.

A couple of days after the departure of their champions, Forty Mile began sending up their relays,—first to the seventy-five station, then to the fifty, and last to the twenty-five. The teams for the last stretch were magnificent, and so equally matched that the camp discussed their relative merits for a full hour at fifty below, before they were permitted to pull out. At the last moment Joy Molineau dashed in among them on her sled. She drew Lon McFane, who had charge of Harrington's team, to one side, and hardly had the first words left her lips when it was noticed that his lower jaw dropped with a celerity and emphasis suggestive of great things. He unhitched Wolf Fang from her sled, put him at the head of Harrington's team, and mushed the string of animals into the Yukon trail.

"Poor Louis Savoy!" men said; but Joy Molineau flashed her black eyes defiantly and drove back to her father's cabin.

MIDNIGHT DREW near on Olaf Nelson's claim. A few hundred fur-clad men had preferred sixty below and the jumping, to the inducements of warm cabins and comfortable bunks. Several score of them had their notices prepared for posting and their dogs at hand. A bunch of Captain Constantine's mounted police had been ordered on duty that fair play might rule. The command had gone forth that no man should place a stake till the last second of the day had ticked itself into the past. In the northland such commands are equal to Jehovah's in the matter of potency; the dum-dum as rapid and effective as the thunderbolt. It was clear and cold. The aurora borealis painted palpitating color revels on the sky. Rosy waves of cold brilliancy swept across the zenith, while great coruscating bars of greenish white blotted out the stars, or a Titan's hand reared mighty arches above the Pole. And at this mighty display the wolf-dogs howled as had their ancestors of old time.

A bearskin-coated policeman stepped prominently to the fore, watch in hand. Men hurried among the dogs, rousing them to their feet, untangling their traces, straightening them out. The entries came to the mark, firmly gripping stakes and notices. They had gone over the boundaries of the claim so often that they could now have done it blindfolded. The policeman raised his hand. Casting off their superfluous furs and blankets, and with a final cinching of belts, they came to attention.

"Time!"

Sixty pairs of hands unmitted; as many pairs of moccasins gripped hard upon the snow.

"Go!"

They shot across the wide expanse, round the four sides, sticking notices at every corner, and down the middle where the two center stakes were to be planted. Then they sprang for the sleds on the frozen bed of the creek. An anarchy of sound and motion broke out. Sled collided with sled, and dog-team fastened upon dog-team with bristling manes and screaming fangs. The narrow creek was glutted with the struggling mass. Lashes and butts of dog-whips were distributed impartially among men and brutes. And to make it of greater moment, each participant had a bunch of comrades intent on breaking him out of jam. But one by one, and by sheer strength, the sleds crept out and shot from sight in the darkness of the overhanging banks.

Jack Harrington had anticipated this crush and waited by his sled until it untangled. Louis Savoy, aware of his rival's greater wisdom in the matter of dog-driving, had followed his lead and also waited. The rout had passed beyond earshot when they took the trail, and it was not till they had travelled the ten miles or so down to Bonanza that they came upon it, speeding along in single file, but well bunched. There was little noise, and less chance of one passing another at that stage. The sleds, from runner to runner, measured sixteen inches, the trail eighteen; but the trail, packed down fully a foot by the traffic, was like a gutter. On either side spread the blanket of soft snow crystals. If a man turned into this in an endeavor to pass, his dogs would wallow perforce to their bellies and slow down to a snail's pace. So the men lay close to their leaping sleds and waited. No alteration in position occurred down the fifteen miles of Bonanza and Klondike to Dawson, where the Yukon was encountered. Here the first relays waited. But here, intent to kill their first teams, if necessary, Harrington and Savoy had had their fresh teams placed a couple of miles beyond those of the others. In the confusion of changing sleds they passed full half the bunch. Perhaps thirty men were still leading them when they shot on to the broad breast of the Yukon. Here was the tug. When the river froze in the fall, a mile of open water had been left between two mighty jams. This had but recently crusted, the current being swift, and now it was as level, hard, and slippery as a dance floor. The instant they struck this glare ice Harrington came to his knees, holding precariously on with one hand, his whip singing fiercely among his dogs and fearsome abjurations hurtling about their ears. The teams spread out on the smooth surface, each straining to the uttermost. But few men in the North could lift their dogs as did Jack Harrington. At once he began to pull ahead, and Louis Savoy, taking the pace, hung on desperately, his leaders running even with the tail of his rival's sled.

Midway on the glassy stretch their relays shot out from the bank. But Harrington did not slacken. Watching his chance when the new sled swung in close, he leaped across, shouting as he did so and jumping up the pace of his fresh dogs. The other driver fell off somehow. Savoy did likewise with his relay, and the abandoned teams, swerving to right and left, collided with the others and piled the ice with confusion. Harrington cut out the pace; Savoy hung on. As they neared the end of the glare ice, they swept abreast of the leading sled. When they shot into the narrow trail between the soft snowbanks, they led the race; and Dawson, watching by the light of the aurora, swore that it was neatly done.

When the frost grows lusty at sixty below, men cannot long remain without fire or excessive exercise, and live. So Harrington and Savoy now fell to the ancient custom of "ride and run." Leaping from their sleds, tow-thongs in hand, they ran behind till the blood resumed its wonted channels and expelled the frost, then back to the sleds till the heat again ebbed away. Thus, riding and running, they covered the second and third relays. Several times, on smooth ice, Savoy spurted his dogs, and as often failed to gain past. Strung along for five miles in the rear, the remainder of the race strove to overtake them, but vainly, for to Louis Savoy alone was the glory given of keeping Jack Harrington's killing pace.

As they swung into the seventy-five mile station, Lon McFane dashed alongside; Wolf Fang in the lead caught Harrington's eye, and he knew that the race was his. No team in the North could pass him on those last twenty-five miles. And when Savoy saw Wolf Fang heading his rival's team, he knew that he was out of the running, and he cursed softly to himself, in the way woman is most frequently cursed. But he still clung to the other's smoking trail, gambling on chance to the last. And as they churned along, the day breaking in the southeast, they marveled in joy and sorrow at that which Joy Molineau had done.

FORTY MILE HAD EARLY CRAWLED out of its sleeping furs and congregated near the edge of the trail. From this point it could view the up-Yukon course to its first bend several miles away. Here it could also see across the river to the finish at Fort Cudahy, where the Gold Recorder nervously awaited. Joy Molineau had taken her position several rods back from the trail, and under the circumstances, the rest of Forty Mile forbore interposing itself. So the space was clear between her and the slender line of the course. Fires had been built, and around these men wagered dust and dogs, the long odds on Wolf Fang.

"Here they come!" shrilled an Indian boy from the top of a pine.

Up the Yukon a black speck appeared against the snow, closely followed by a second. As these grew larger, more black specks manifested themselves, but at a goodly distance to the rear. Gradually they resolved themselves into dogs and sleds, and men lying flat upon them. "Wolf Fang leads," a lieutenant of police whispered to Joy. She smiled her interest back.

"Ten to one on Harrington!" cried a Birch Creek King, dragging out his sack.

"The Queen, her pay you not mooch?" queried Joy.

The lieutenant shook his head.

"You have some dust, ah, how mooch?" she continued.

He exposed his sack. She gauged it with a rapid eye.

"Mebbe—say—two hundred, eh? Good. Now I give—what you call—the tip. Covaire the bet." Joy smiled inscrutably. The lieutenant pondered. He glanced up the trail. The two men had risen to their knees and were lashing their dogs furiously, Harrington in the lead.

"Ten to one on Harrington!" bawled the Birch Creek King, flourishing his sack in the lieutenant's face.

"Covaire the bet," Joy prompted.

He obeyed, shrugging his shoulders in token that he yielded, not to the dictate of his reason, but to her charm. Joy nodded to reassure him.

All noise ceased. Men paused in the placing of bets.

Yawing and reeling and plunging, like luggers before the wind, the sleds swept wildly upon them. Though he still kept his leader up to the tail of Harrington's sled, Louis Savoy's face was without hope. Harrington's mouth was set. He looked neither to the right nor to the left. His dogs were leaping in perfect rhythm, firm-footed, close to the trail, and Wolf Fang, head low and unseeing, whining softly, was leading his comrades magnificently.

Forty Mile stood breathless. Not a sound, save the roar of the runners and the voice of the whips.

Then the clear voice of Joy Molineau rose on the air. "Ai! Ya! Wolf Fang! Wolf Fang!"

Wolf Fang heard. He left the trail sharply, heading directly for his mistress. The team dashed after him, and the sled poised an instant on a single runner, then shot Harrington into the snow. Savoy was by like a flash. Harrington pulled to his feet and watched him skimming across the river to the Gold Recorder's. He could not help hearing what was said.

"Ah, him do vaire well," Joy Molineau was explaining to the lieutenant. "Him—what you call—set the pace. Yes, him set the pace vaire well."

AT THE RAINBOW'S END

I.

It was for two reasons that Montana Kid discarded his "chaps" and Mexican spurs, and shook the dust of the Idaho ranges from his feet. In the first place, the encroachments of a steady, sober, and sternly moral civilization had destroyed the primeval status of the western cattle ranges, and refined society turned the cold eye of disfavor upon him and his ilk. In the second place, in one of its cyclopean moments the race had arisen and shoved back its frontier several thousand miles. Thus, with unconscious foresight, did mature society make room for its adolescent members. True, the new territory was mostly barren; but its several hundred thousand square miles of frigidity at least gave breathing space to those who else would have suffocated at home.

Montana Kid was such a one. Heading for the sea-coast, with a haste several sheriff's posses might possibly have explained, and with more nerve than coin of the realm, he succeeded in shipping from a Puget Sound port, and managed to survive the contingent miseries of steerage sea-sickness and steerage grub. He was rather sallow and drawn, but still his own indomitable self, when he landed on the Dyea beach one day in the spring of the year. Between the cost of dogs, grub, and outfits, and the customs exactions of the two clashing governments, it speedily penetrated to his understanding that the Northland was anything save a poor man's Mecca. So he cast about him in search of quick harvests. Between the beach and the passes were scattered many thousands of passionate pilgrims. These pilgrims Montana Kid proceeded to farm. At first he dealt faro in a pine-board gambling shack; but disagreeable necessity forced him to drop a sudden period into a man's life, and to move on up trail. Then he effected a corner in horseshoe nails, and they circulated at par with legal tender, four to the dollar, till an unexpected consignment of a hundred barrels or so broke the market and forced him to disgorge his stock at a loss. After that he located at Sheep Camp, organized the professional packers, and jumped the freight ten cents a pound in a single day. In token of their gratitude, the packers patronized his faro and roulette layouts and were mulcted cheerfully of their earnings. But his commercialism was of too lusty a growth to be long endured; so they rushed him one night, burned his shanty, divided the bank, and headed him up the trail with empty pockets.

Ill-luck was his running mate. He engaged with responsible parties to run whisky across the line by way of precarious and unknown trails, lost his Indian guides, and had the very first outfit confiscated by the Mounted Police. Numerous other misfortunes tended to make him bitter of heart and wanton of action, and he celebrated his arrival at Lake Bennett by terrorizing the camp for twenty straight hours. Then a miners' meeting took him in hand, and commanded him to make himself scarce. He had a wholesome respect for such assemblages, and he obeyed in such haste that he inadvertently removed himself at the tail-end of another man's dog team. This was equivalent to horse-stealing in a more mellow clime, so he hit only the high places across Bennett and down Tagish, and made his first camp a full hundred miles to the north.

Now it happened that the break of spring was at hand, and many of the principal citizens of Dawson were travelling south on the last ice. These he met and talked with, noted their names and possessions, and passed on. He had a good memory, also a fair imagination; nor was veracity one of his virtues.

II.

Dawson, always eager for news, beheld Montana Kid's sled heading down the Yukon, and went out on the ice to meet him. No, he hadn't any newspapers; didn't know whether Durrant was hanged yet, nor who had won the Thanksgiving game; hadn't heard whether the United States and Spain had gone to fighting; didn't know who Dreyfus was; but O'Brien? Hadn't they heard? O'Brien, why, he was drowned in the White Horse; Sitka Charley the only one of the party who escaped. Joe Ladue? Both legs frozen and amputated at the Five Fingers. And Jack Dalton? Blown up on the "Sea Lion" with all hands. And Bettles? Wrecked on the "Carthagina," in Seymour Narrows,—twenty survivors out of three hundred. And Swiftwater Bill? Gone through the rotten ice of Lake LeBarge with six female members of the opera troupe he was convoying. Governor Walsh? Lost with all hands and eight sleds on the Thirty Mile. Devereaux? Who was Devereaux? Oh, the courier! Shot by Indians on Lake Marsh.

So it went. The word was passed along. Men shouldered in to ask after friends and partners, and in turn were shouldered out, too stunned for blasphemy. By the time Montana Kid gained the bank he was surrounded by several hundred fur-clad miners. When he passed the Barracks he was the center of a procession. At the Opera House he was the nucleus of an excited mob, each member struggling for a chance to ask after some absent comrade. On every side he was being invited to drink. Never before had the Klondike thus opened its arms to a che-cha-qua. All Dawson was humming. Such a series of catastrophes had never occurred in its history. Every man of note who had gone south in the spring had been wiped out. The cabins vomited forth their occupants. Wild-eyed men hurried down from the creeks and gulches to seek out this man who had told a tale of such disaster. The Russian half-breed wife of Bettles sought the fireplace, inconsolable, and rocked back and forth, and ever and anon flung white wood-ashes upon her raven hair. The flag at the Barracks flopped dismally at half-mast. Dawson mourned its dead.

Why Montana Kid did this thing no man may know. Nor beyond the fact that the truth was not in him, can explanation be hazarded. But for five whole days he plunged the land in wailing and sorrow, and for five whole days he was the only man in the Klondike. The country gave him its best of bed and board. The saloons granted him the freedom of their bars. Men sought him continuously. The high officials bowed down to him for further information, and he was feasted at the Barracks by Constantine and his brother officers. And then, one day, Devereaux, the government courier, halted his tired dogs before the gold commissioner's office. Dead? Who said so? Give him a moose steak and he'd show them how dead he was. Why, Governor Walsh was in camp on the Little Salmon, and O'Brien coming in on the first water. Dead? Give him a moose steak and he'd show them.

And forthwith Dawson hummed. The Barracks' flag rose to the masthead, and Bettles' wife washed herself and put on clean raiment. The community subtly signified its desire that Montana Kid obliterate himself from the landscape. And Montana Kid obliterated; as usual, at the tail-end of someone else's dog team. Dawson rejoiced when he headed down the Yukon, and wished him godspeed to the ultimate destination of the case-hardened sinner. After that the owner of the dogs bestirred himself, made complaint to Constantine, and from him received the loan of a policeman.

III.

With Circle City in prospect and the last ice crumbling under his runners, Montana Kid took advantage of the lengthening days and travelled his dogs late and early. Further, he had but little doubt that the owner of the dogs in question had taken his trail, and he wished to make American territory before the river broke. But by the afternoon of the third day it became evident that he had lost in his race with spring. The Yukon was growling and straining at its fetters. Long détours became necessary, for the trail had begun to fall through into the swift current beneath, while the ice, in constant unrest, was thundering apart in great gaping fissures. Through these and through countless airholes, the water began to sweep across the surface of the ice, and by the time he pulled into a woodchopper's cabin on the point of an island, the dogs were being rushed off their feet and were swimming more often than not. He was greeted sourly by the two residents, but he unharnessed and proceeded to cook up.

Donald and Davy were fair specimens of frontier inefficients. Canadian-born, city-bred Scots, in a foolish moment they had resigned their counting-house desks, drawn upon their savings, and gone Klondiking. And now they were feeling the rough edge of the country. Grubless, spiritless, with a lust for home in their hearts, they had been staked by the P. C. Company to cut wood for its steamers, with the promise at the end of a passage home. Disregarding the possibilities of the ice-run, they had fittingly demonstrated their inefficiency by their choice of the island on which they located. Montana Kid, though possessing little knowledge of the break-up of a great river, looked about him dubiously, and cast yearning glances at the distant bank where the towering bluffs promised immunity from all the ice of the Northland.

After feeding himself and dogs, he lighted his pipe and strolled out to get a better idea of the situation. The island, like all its river brethren, stood higher at the upper end, and it was here that Donald and Davy had built their cabin and piled many cords of wood. The far shore was a full mile away, while between the island and the near shore lay a back-channel perhaps a hundred yards across. At first sight of this, Montana Kid was tempted to take his dogs and escape to the mainland, but on closer inspection he discovered a rapid current flooding on top. Below, the river twisted sharply to the west, and in this turn its breast was studded by a maze of tiny islands.

"That's where she'll jam," he remarked to himself.

Half a dozen sleds, evidently bound up-stream to Dawson, were splashing through the chill water to the tail of the island. Travel on the river was passing from the precarious to the impossible, and it was nip and tuck with them till they gained the island and came up the path of the wood-choppers toward the cabin. One of them, snow-blind, towed helplessly at the rear of a sled. Husky young fellows they were, rough-garmented and trail-worn, yet Montana Kid had met the breed before and knew at once that it was not his kind.

"Hello! How's things up Dawson-way?" queried the foremost, passing his eye over Donald and Davy and settling it upon the Kid.

A first meeting in the wilderness is not characterized by formality. The talk quickly became general, and the news of the Upper and Lower Countries was swapped equitably back and forth. But the little the newcomers had was soon over with, for they had wintered at Minook, a thousand miles below, where nothing was doing. Montana Kid, however, was fresh from Salt Water, and they annexed him while they pitched camp, swamping him with questions concerning the outside, from which they had been cut off for a twelvemonth.

A shrieking split, suddenly lifting itself above the general uproar on the river, drew everybody to the bank. The surface water had increased in depth, and the ice, assailed from above and below, was struggling to tear itself from the grip of the shores. Fissures reverberated into life before their eyes, and the air was filled with multitudinous crackling, crisp and sharp, like the sound that goes up on a clear day from the firing line.

From up the river two men were racing a dog team toward them on an uncovered stretch of ice. But even as they looked, the pair struck the water and began to flounder through. Behind, where their feet had sped the moment before, the ice broke up and turned turtle. Through this opening the river rushed out upon them to their waists, burying the sled and swinging the dogs off at right angles in a drowning tangle. But the men stopped their flight to give the animals a fighting chance, and they groped hurriedly in the cold confusion, slashing at the detaining traces with their sheath-knives. Then they fought their way to the bank through swirling water and grinding ice, where, foremost in leaping to the rescue among the jarring fragments, was the Kid.

"Why, blime me, if it ain't Montana Kid!" exclaimed one of the men whom the Kid was just placing upon his feet at the top of the bank. He wore the scarlet tunic of the Mounted Police and jocularly raised his right hand in salute.

"Got a warrant for you, Kid," he continued, drawing a bedraggled paper from his breast pocket, "an' I 'ope as you'll come along peaceable."

Montana Kid looked at the chaotic river and shrugged his shoulders, and the policeman, following his glance, smiled.

"Where are the dogs?" his companion asked.

"Gentlemen," interrupted the policeman, "this 'ere mate o' mine is Jack Sutherland, owner of Twenty-Two Eldorado—"

"Not Sutherland of '92?" broke in the snow-blinded Minook man, groping feebly toward him.

"The same." Sutherland gripped his hand.

"And you?"

"Oh, I'm after your time, but I remember you in my freshman year,—you were doing P. G. work then. Boys," he called, turning half about, "this is Sutherland, Jack Sutherland, erstwhile full-back on the 'Varsity. Come up, you gold-chasers, and fall upon him! Sutherland, this is Greenwich,—played quarter two seasons back."

"Yes, I read of the game," Sutherland said, shaking hands. "And I remember that big run of yours for the first touchdown."

Greenwich flushed darkly under his tanned skin and awkwardly made room for another.

"And here's Matthews,—Berkeley man. And we've got some Eastern cracks knocking about, too. Come up, you Princeton men! Come up! This is Sutherland, Jack Sutherland!"

Then they fell upon him heavily, carried him into camp, and supplied him with dry clothes and numerous mugs of black tea.

Donald and Davy, overlooked, had retired to their nightly game of crib. Montana Kid followed them with the policeman.

"Here, get into some dry togs," he said, pulling them from out his scanty kit. "Guess you'll have to bunk with me, too."

"Well, I say, you're a good 'un," the policeman remarked as he pulled on the other man's socks. "Sorry I've got to take you back to Dawson, but I only 'ope they won't be 'ard on you."

"Not so fast." The Kid smiled curiously. "We ain't under way yet. When I go I'm going down river, and I guess the chances are you'll go along."

"Not if I know myself—"

"Come on outside, and I'll show you, then. These damn fools," thrusting a thumb over his shoulder at the two Scots, "played smash when they located here. Fill your pipe, first— this is pretty good plug—and enjoy yourself while you can. You haven't many smokes before you."

The policeman went with him wonderingly, while Donald and Davy dropped their cards and followed. The Minook men noticed Montana Kid pointing now up the river, now down, and came over.

"What's up?" Sutherland demanded.

"Nothing much." Nonchalance sat well upon the Kid. "Just a case of raising hell and putting a chunk under. See that bend down there? That's where she'll jam millions of tons of ice. Then she'll jam in the bends up above, millions of tons. Upper jam breaks first, lower jam holds, pouf!" He dramatically swept the island with his hand. "Millions of tons," he added reflectively.

"And what of the woodpiles?" Davy questioned.

The Kid repeated his sweeping gestures and Davy wailed, "The labor of months! It canna be! Na, na, lad, it canna be. I doot not it's a jowk. Ay, say that it is," he appealed.

But when the Kid laughed harshly and turned on his heel, Davy flung himself upon the piles and began frantically to toss the cordwood back from the bank.

"Lend a hand, Donald!" he cried. "Can ye no lend a hand? 'T is the labor of months and the passage home!"

Donald caught him by the arm and shook him, but he tore free. "Did ye no hear, man? Millions of tons, and the island shall be sweepit clean."

"Straighten yersel' up, man," said Donald. "It's a bit fashed ye are."

But Davy fell upon the cordwood. Donald stalked back to the cabin, buckled on his money belt and Davy's, and went out to the point of the island where the ground was highest and where a huge pine towered above its fellows.

The men before the cabin heard the ringing of his axe and smiled. Greenwich returned from across the island with the word that they were penned in. It was impossible to cross the back-channel. The blind Minook man began to sing, and the rest joined in with—

"Wonder if it's true?
Does it seem so to you?
Seems to me he's lying—

Oh, I wonder if it's true?"

"It's ay sinfu'," Davy moaned, lifting his head and watching them dance in the slanting rays of the sun. "And my guid wood a' going to waste."

"Oh, I wonder if it's true,"
was flaunted back.

The noise of the river ceased suddenly. A strange calm wrapped about them. The ice had ripped from the shores and was floating higher on the surface of the river, which was rising. Up it came, swift and silent, for twenty feet, till the huge cakes rubbed softly against the crest of the bank. The tail of the island, being lower, was overrun. Then, without effort, the white flood started down-stream. But the sound increased with the momentum, and soon the whole island was shaking and quivering with the shock of the grinding bergs. Under pressure, the mighty cakes, weighing hundreds of tons, were shot into the air like peas. The frigid anarchy increased its riot, and the men had to shout into one another's ears to be heard. Occasionally the racket from the back channel could be heard above the tumult. The island shuddered with the impact of an enormous cake which drove in squarely upon its point. It ripped a score of pines out by the roots, then swinging around and over, lifted its muddy base from the bottom of the river and bore down upon the cabin, slicing the bank and trees away like a gigantic knife. It seemed barely to graze the corner of the cabin, but the cribbed logs tilted up like matches, and the structure, like a toy house, fell backward in ruin.

"The labor of months! The labor of months, and the passage home!" Davy wailed, while Montana Kid and the policeman dragged him backward from the woodpiles.

"You'll 'ave plenty o' hoppertunity all in good time for yer passage 'ome," the policeman growled, clouting him alongside the head and sending him flying into safety.

Donald, from the top of the pine, saw the devastating berg sweep away the cordwood and disappear down-stream. As though satisfied with this damage, the ice-flood quickly dropped to its old level and began to slacken its pace. The noise likewise eased down, and the others could hear Donald shouting from his eyrie to look down-stream. As forecast, the jam had come among the islands in the bend, and the ice was piling up in a great barrier which stretched from shore to shore. The river came to a standstill, and the water finding no outlet began to rise. It rushed up till the island was awash, the men splashing around up to their knees, and the dogs swimming to the ruins of the cabin. At this stage it abruptly became stationary, with no perceptible rise or fall.

Montana Kid shook his head. "It's jammed above, and no more's coming down."

"And the gamble is, which jam will break first," Sutherland added.

"Exactly," the Kid affirmed. "If the upper jam breaks first, we haven't a chance. Nothing will stand before it."

The Minook men turned away in silence, but soon "Rumsky Ho" floated upon the quiet air, followed by "The Orange and the Black." Room was made in the circle for Montana Kid and the policeman, and they quickly caught the ringing rhythm of the choruses as they drifted on from song to song.

"Oh, Donald, will ye no lend a hand?" Davy sobbed at the foot of the tree into which his comrade had climbed. "Oh, Donald, man, will ye no lend a hand?" he sobbed again, his hands bleeding from vain attempts to scale the slippery trunk.

But Donald had fixed his gaze up river, and now his voice rang out, vibrant with fear:—

"God Almichty, here she comes!"

Standing knee-deep in the icy water, the Minook men, with Montana Kid and the police-

man, gripped hands and raised their voices in the terrible, "Battle Hymn of the Republic."
But the words were drowned in the advancing roar.

And to Donald was vouchsafed a sight such as no man may see and live. A great wall of
white flung itself upon the island. Trees, dogs, men, were blotted out, as though the hand of
God had wiped the face of nature clean. This much he saw, then swayed an instant longer in
his lofty perch and hurtled far out into the frozen hell.

THE SCORN OF WOMEN

I.

ONCE FREDA and Mrs. Eppingwell clashed.

Now Freda was a Greek girl and a dancer. At least she purported to be Greek; but this was doubted by many, for her classic face had overmuch strength in it, and the tides of hell which rose in her eyes made at rare moments her ethnology the more dubious. To a few— men—this sight had been vouchsafed, and though long years may have passed, they have not forgotten, nor will they ever forget. She never talked of herself, so that it were well to let it go down that when in repose, expurgated, Greek she certainly was. Her furs were the most magnificent in all the country from Chilcoot to St. Michael's, and her name was common on the lips of men. But Mrs. Eppingwell was the wife of a captain; also a social constellation of the first magnitude, the path of her orbit marking the most select coterie in Dawson,—a coterie captioned by the profane as the "official clique." Sitka Charley had travelled trail with her once, when famine drew tight and a man's life was less than a cup of flour, and his judgment placed her above all women. Sitka Charley was an Indian; his criteria were primitive; but his word was flat, and his verdict a hall-mark in every camp under the circle.

These two women were man-conquering, man-subduing machines, each in her own way, and their ways were different. Mrs. Eppingwell ruled in her own house, and at the Barracks, where were younger sons galore, to say nothing of the chiefs of the police, the executive, and the judiciary. Freda ruled down in the town; but the men she ruled were the same who functioned socially at the Barracks or were fed tea and canned preserves at the hand of Mrs. Eppingwell in her hillside cabin of rough-hewn logs. Each knew the other existed; but their lives were apart as the Poles, and while they must have heard stray bits of news and were curious, they were never known to ask a question. And there would have been no trouble had not a free lance in the shape of the model-woman come into the land on the first ice, with a spanking dog-team and a cosmopolitan reputation. Loraine Lisznayi—alliterative, dramatic, and Hungarian—precipitated the strife, and because of her Mrs. Eppingwell left her hillside and invaded Freda's domain, and Freda likewise went up from the town to spread confusion and embarrassment at the Governor's ball.

All of which may be ancient history so far as the Klondike is concerned, but very few, even in Dawson, know the inner truth of the matter; nor beyond those few are there any fit to measure the wife of the captain or the Greek dancer. And that all are now permitted to understand, let honor be accorded Sitka Charley. From his lips fell the main facts in the screed herewith presented. It ill befits that Freda herself should have waxed confidential to a mere scribbler of words, or that Mrs. Eppingwell made mention of the things which happened. They may have spoken, but it is unlikely.

II.

Floyd Vanderlip was a strong man, apparently. Hard work and hard grub had no terrors for him, as his early history in the country attested. In danger he was a lion, and when he held in check half a thousand starving men, as he once did, it was remarked that no cooler eye ever took the glint of sunshine on a rifle-sight. He had but one weakness, and even that, rising from out his strength, was of a negative sort. His parts were strong, but they lacked co-ordination. Now it happened that while his center of amativeness was pronounced, it had lain mute and passive during the years he lived on moose and salmon and chased glowing Eldorados over chill divides. But when he finally blazed the corner-post and center-stakes on one of the richest Klondike claims, it began to quicken; and when he took his place in society, a full-fledged Bonanza King, it awoke and took charge of him. He suddenly recollected a girl in the States, and it came to him quite forcibly, not only that she might be waiting for him, but that a wife was a very pleasant acquisition for a man who lived some several degrees north of 53. So he wrote an appropriate note, enclosed a letter of credit generous enough to cover all expenses, including trousseau and chaperon, and addressed it to one Flossie. Flossie? One could imagine the rest. However, after that he built a comfortable cabin on his claim, bought another in Dawson, and broke the news to his friends.

And just here is where the lack of co-ordination came into play. The waiting was tedious, and having been long denied, the amative element could not brook further delay. Flossie was coming; but Loraine Lisznayi was here. And not only was Loraine Lisznayi here, but her cosmopolitan reputation was somewhat the worse for wear, and she was not exactly so young as when she posed in the studios of artist queens and received at her door the cards of cardinals and princes. Also, her finances were unhealthy. Having run the gamut in her time, she was now not averse to trying conclusions with a Bonanza King whose wealth was such that he could not guess it within six figures. Like a wise soldier casting about after years of service for a comfortable billet, she had come into the Northland to be married. So, one day, her eyes flashed up into Floyd Vanderlip's as he was buying table linen for Flossie in the P. C. Company's store, and the thing was settled out of hand.

When a man is free much may go unquestioned, which, should he be rash enough to cumber himself with domestic ties, society will instantly challenge. Thus it was with Floyd Vanderlip. Flossie was coming, and a low buzz went up when Loraine Lisznayi rode down the main street behind his wolf-dogs. She accompanied the lady reporter of the "Kansas City Star" when photographs were taken of his Bonanza properties, and watched the genesis of a six-column article. At that time they were dined royally in Flossie's cabin, on Flossie's table linen. Likewise there were comings and goings, and junketings, all perfectly proper, by the way, which caused the men to say sharp things and the women to be spiteful. Only Mrs.

Eppingwell did not hear. The distant hum of wagging tongues rose faintly, but she was prone to believe good of people and to close her ears to evil; so she paid no heed.

Not so with Freda. She had no cause to love men, but, by some strange alchemy of her nature, her heart went out to women,—to women whom she had less cause to love. And her heart went out to Flossie, even then travelling the Long Trail and facing into the bitter North to meet a man who might not wait for her. A shrinking, clinging sort of a girl, Freda pictured her, with weak mouth and pretty pouting lips, blow-away sun-kissed hair, and eyes full of the merry shallows and the lesser joys of life. But she also pictured Flossie, face nose-strapped and frost-rimed, stumbling wearily behind the dogs. Wherefore she smiled, dancing one night, upon Floyd Vanderlip.

Few men are so constituted that they may receive the smile of Freda unmoved; nor among them can Floyd Vanderlip be accounted. The grace he had found with the model-woman had caused him to re-measure himself, and by the favor in which he now stood with the Greek dancer he felt himself doubly a man. There were unknown qualities and depths in him, evidently, which they perceived. He did not know exactly what those qualities and depths were, but he had a hazy idea that they were there somewhere, and of them was bred a great pride in himself. A man who could force two women such as these to look upon him a second time, was certainly a most remarkable man. Someday, when he had the time, he would sit down and analyze his strength; but now, just now, he would take what the gods had given him. And a thin little thought began to lift itself, and he fell to wondering what-ever under the sun he had seen in Flossie, and to regret exceedingly that he had sent for her. Of course, Freda was out of the running. His dumps were the richest on Bonanza Creek, and they were many, while he was a man of responsibility and position. But Loraine Lisznayi— she was just the woman. Her life had been large; she could do the honors of his establish-ment and give tone to his dollars.

But Freda smiled, and continued to smile, till he came to spend much time with her. When she, too, rode down the street behind his wolf-dogs, the model-woman found food for thought, and the next time they were together dazzled him with her princes and cardinals and personal little anecdotes of courts and kings. She also showed him dainty missives, superscribed, "My dear Loraine," and ended "Most affectionately yours," and signed by the given name of a real live queen on a throne. And he marveled in his heart that the great woman should deign to waste so much as a moment upon him. But she played him cleverly, making flattering contrasts and comparisons between him and the noble phantoms she drew mainly from her fancy, till he went away dizzy with self-delight and sorrowing for the world which had been denied him so long. Freda was a more masterful woman. If she flattered, no one knew it. Should she stoop, the stoop were unobserved. If a man felt she thought well of him, so subtly was the feeling conveyed that he could not for the life of him say why or how. So she tightened her grip upon Floyd Vanderlip and rode daily behind his dogs.

And just here is where the mistake occurred. The buzz rose loudly and more definitely, coupled now with the name of the dancer, and Mrs. Eppingwell heard. She, too, thought of Flossie lifting her moccasined feet through the endless hours, and Floyd Vanderlip was invited up the hillside to tea, and invited often. This quite took his breath away, and he became drunken with appreciation of himself. Never was man so maltreated. His soul had become a thing for which three women struggled, while a fourth was on the way to claim it. And three such women!

But Mrs. Eppingwell and the mistake she made. She spoke of the affair, tentatively, to Sitka Charley, who had sold dogs to the Greek girl. But no names were mentioned. The nearest approach to it was when Mrs. Eppingwell said, "This—er—horrid woman," and

Sitka Charley, with the model-woman strong in his thoughts, had echoed, "—er—horrid woman." And he agreed with her, that it was a wicked thing for a woman to come between a man and the girl he was to marry. "A mere girl, Charley," she said, "I am sure she is. And she is coming into a strange country without a friend when she gets here. We must do something." Sitka Charley promised his help, and went away thinking what a wicked woman this Loraine Lisznayi must be, also what noble women Mrs. Eppingwell and Freda were to interest themselves in the welfare of the unknown Flossie.

Now Mrs. Eppingwell was open as the day. To Sitka Charley, who took her once past the Hills of Silence, belongs the glory of having memorialized her clear-searching eyes, her clear-ringing voice, and her utter downright frankness. Her lips had a way of stiffening to command, and she was used to coming straight to the point. Having taken Floyd Vander-lip's measurement, she did not dare this with him; but she was not afraid to go down into the town to Freda. And down she went, in the bright light of day, to the house of the dancer. She was above silly tongues, as was her husband, the captain. She wished to see this woman and to speak with her, nor was she aware of any reason why she should not. So she stood in the snow at the Greek girl's door, with the frost at sixty below, and parleyed with the waiting-maid for a full five minutes. She had also the pleasure of being turned away from that door, and of going back up the hill, wroth at heart for the indignity which had been put upon her. "Who was this woman that she should refuse to see her?" she asked herself. One would think it the other way around, and she herself but a dancing girl denied at the door of the wife of a captain. As it was, she knew, had Freda come up the hill to her,—no matter what the errand,—she would have made her welcome at her fire, and they would have sat there as two women, and talked, merely as two women. She had overstepped convention and lowered herself, but she had thought it different with the women down in the town. And she was ashamed that she had laid herself open to such dishonor, and her thoughts of Freda were unkind.

Not that Freda deserved this. Mrs. Eppingwell had descended to meet her who was without caste, while she, strong in the traditions of her own earlier status, had not permitted it. She could worship such a woman, and she would have asked no greater joy than to have had her into the cabin and sat with her, just sat with her, for an hour. But her respect for Mrs. Eppingwell, and her respect for herself, who was beyond respect, had prevented her doing that which she most desired. Though not quite recovered from the recent visit of Mrs. McFee, the wife of the minister, who had descended upon her in a whirlwind of exhortation and brimstone, she could not imagine what had prompted the present visit. She was not aware of any particular wrong she had done, and surely this woman who waited at the door was not concerned with the welfare of her soul. Why had she come? For all the curiosity she could not help but feel, she steeled herself in the pride of those who are without pride, and trembled in the inner room like a maid on the first caress of a lover. If Mrs. Eppingwell suffered going up the hill, she too suffered, lying face downward on the bed, dry-eyed, dry-mouthed, dumb.

Mrs. Eppingwell's knowledge of human nature was great. She aimed at universality. She had found it easy to step from the civilized and contemplate things from the barbaric aspect. She could comprehend certain primal and analogous characteristics in a hungry wolf-dog or a starving man, and predicate lines of action to be pursued by either under like conditions. To her, a woman was a woman, whether garbed in purple or the rags of the gutter; Freda was a woman. She would not have been surprised had she been taken into the dancer's cabin and encountered on common ground; nor surprised had she been taken in and flaunted in prideless arrogance. But to be treated as she had been treated, was unexpected and disappointing. Ergo, she had not caught Freda's point of view. And this was good. There are some points of view which cannot be gained save through much travail and personal cruci-fixion, and it were well for the world that its Mrs. Eppingwells should, in certain ways, fall short of universality. One cannot understand defilement without laying hands to pitch, which is very sticky, while there be plenty willing to undertake the experiment. All of which is of small concern, beyond the fact that it gave Mrs. Eppingwell ground for grievance, and bred for her a greater love in the Greek girl's heart.

III.

And in this way things went along for a month,—Mrs. Eppingwell striving to withhold the man from the Greek dancer's blandishments against the time of Flossie's coming; Flossie lessening the miles each day on the dreary trail; Freda pitting her strength against the model-woman; the model-woman straining every nerve to land the prize; and the man moving through it all like a flying shuttle, very proud of himself, whom he believed to be a second Don Juan.

It was nobody's fault except the man's that Loraine Lisznayi at last landed him. The way of a man with a maid may be too wonderful to know, but the way of a woman with a man passeth all conception; whence the prophet were indeed unwise who would dare forecast Floyd Vanderlip's course twenty-four hours in advance. Perhaps the model-woman's attrac-tion lay in that to the eye she was a handsome animal; perhaps she fascinated him with her old-world talk of palaces and princes; leastwise she dazzled him whose life had been worked out in uncultured roughness, and he at last agreed to her suggestion of a run down the river and a marriage at Forty Mile. In token of his intention he bought dogs from Sitka Charley,— more than one sled is necessary when a woman like Loraine Lisznayi takes to the trail, and then went up the creek to give orders for the superintendence of his Bonanza mines during his absence.

He had given it out, rather vaguely, that he needed the animals for sledding lumber from the mill to his sluices, and right here is where Sitka Charley demonstrated his fitness. He agreed to furnish dogs on a given date, but no sooner had Floyd Vanderlip turned his toes up-creek, than Charley hied himself away in perturbation to Loraine Lisznayi. Did she know where Mr. Vanderlip had gone? He had agreed to supply that gentleman with a big string of dogs by a certain time; but that shameless one, the German trader Meyers, had been buying up the brutes and skimped the market. It was very necessary he should see Mr. Vanderlip, because of the shameless one he would be all of a week behindhand in filling the contract. She did know where he had gone? Up-creek? Good! He would strike out after him at once and inform him of the unhappy delay. Did he understand her to say that Mr. Vanderlip needed the dogs on Friday night? that he must have them by that time? It was too bad, but it was the fault of the shameless one who had bid up the prices. They had jumped fifty dollars per head, and should he buy on the rising market he would lose by the contract. He wondered if Mr. Vanderlip would be willing to meet the advance. She knew he would? Being Mr. Vanderlip's friend, she would even meet the difference herself? And he was to say nothing about it? She was kind to so look to his interests. Friday night, did she say? Good! The dogs would be on hand.

An hour later, Freda knew the elopement was to be pulled off on Friday night; also, that Floyd Vanderlip had gone up-creek, and her hands were tied. On Friday morning, Devereaux, the official courier, bearing dispatches from the Governor, arrived over the ice. Besides the dispatches, he brought news of Flossie. He had passed her camp at Sixty Mile;

humans and dogs were in good condition; and she would doubtless be in on the morrow. Mrs. Eppingwell experienced a great relief on hearing this; Floyd Vanderlip was safe up-creek, and ere the Greek girl could again lay hands upon him, his bride would be on the ground. But that afternoon her big St. Bernard, valiantly defending her front stoop, was downed by a foraging party of trail-starved Malemutes. He was buried beneath the hirsute mass for about thirty seconds, when rescued by a couple of axes and as many stout men. Had he remained down two minutes, the chances were large that he would have been roughly apportioned and carried away in the respective bellies of the attacking party; but as it was, it was a mere case of neat and expeditious mangling. Sitka Charley came to repair the damages, especially a right fore-paw which had inadvertently been left a fraction of a second too long in some other dog's mouth. As he put on his mittens to go, the talk turned upon Flossie and in natural sequence passed on to the—"er horrid woman." Sitka Charley remarked incidentally that she intended jumping out down river that night with Floyd Vanderlip, and further ventured the information that accidents were very likely at that time of year.

So Mrs. Eppingwell's thoughts of Freda were unkinder than ever. She wrote a note, addressed it to the man in question, and entrusted it to a messenger who lay in wait at the mouth of Bonanza Creek. Another man, bearing a note from Freda, also waited at that strategic point. So it happened that Floyd Vanderlip, riding his sled merrily down with the last daylight, received the notes together. He tore Freda's across. No, he would not go to see her. There were greater things afoot that night. Besides, she was out of the running. But Mrs. Eppingwell! He would observe her last wish,—or rather, the last wish it would be possible for him to observe, and meet her at the Governor's ball to hear what she had to say. From the tone of the writing it was evidently important; perhaps— He smiled fondly, but failed to shape the thought. Confound it all, what a lucky fellow he was with the women any way! Scattering her letter to the froot, he mushed the dogs into a swinging lope and headed for his cabin. It was to be a masquerade, and he had to dig up the costume used at the Opera House a couple of months before. Also, he had to shave and to eat. Thus it was that he, alone of all interested, was unaware of Flossie's proximity.

"Have them down to the water-hole off the hospital, at midnight, sharp. Don't fail me," he said to Sitka Charley, who dropped in with the advice that only one dog was lacking to fill the bill, and that that one would be forthcoming in an hour or so. "Here's the sack. There's the scales. Weigh out your own dust and don't bother me. I've got to get ready for the ball."

Sitka Charley weighed out his pay and departed, carrying with him a letter to Loraine Lisznayi, the contents of which he correctly imagined to refer to a meeting at the water-hole of the hospital, at midnight, sharp.

IV.

Twice Freda sent messengers up to the Barracks, where the dance was in full swing, and as often they came back without answers. Then she did what only Freda could do—put on her furs, masked her face, and went up herself to the Governor's ball. Now there happened to be a custom—not an original one by any means—to which the official clique had long since become addicted. It was a very wise custom, for it furnished protection to the womankind of the officials and gave greater selectness to their revels. Whenever a masquerade was given, a committee was chosen, the sole function of which was to stand by the door and peep beneath each and every mask. Most men did not clamor to be placed upon this committee, while the very ones who least desired the honor were the ones whose services were most required. The chaplain was not well enough acquainted with the faces and places of the townspeople to know whom to admit and whom to turn away. In like condition were the several other worthy gentlemen who would have asked nothing better than to so serve. To fill the coveted place, Mrs. McFee would have risked her chance of salvation, and did, one night, when a certain trio passed in under her guns and muddled things considerably before their identity was discovered. Thereafter only the fit were chosen, and very ungracefully did they respond.

On this particular night Prince was at the door. Pressure had been brought to bear, and he had not yet recovered from amaze at his having consented to undertake a task which bid fair to lose him half his friends, merely for the sake of pleasing the other half. Three or four of the men he had refused were men whom he had known on creek and trail,—good comrades, but not exactly eligible for so select an affair. He was canvassing the expediency of resigning the post there and then, when a woman tripped in under the light. Freda! He could swear it by the furs, did he not know that poise of head so well. The last one to expect in all the world. He had given her better judgment than to thus venture the ignominy of refusal, or, if she passed, the scorn of women. He shook his head, without scrutiny; he knew her too well to be mistaken. But she pressed closer. She lifted the black silk ribbon and as quickly lowered it again. For one flashing, eternal second he looked upon her face. It was not for nothing, the saying which had arisen in the country, that Freda played with men as a child with bubbles. Not a word was spoken. Prince stepped aside, and a few moments later might have been seen resigning, with warm incoherence, the post to which he had been unfaithful.

A WOMAN, flexible of form, slender, yet rhythmic of strength in every movement, now pausing with this group, now scanning that, urged a restless and devious course among the revelers. Men recognized the furs, and marveled,—men who should have served upon the door committee; but they were not prone to speech. Not so with the women. They had better eyes for the lines of figure and tricks of carriage, and they knew this form to be one with which they were unfamiliar; likewise the furs. Mrs. McFee, emerging from the supper-room where all was in readiness, caught one flash of the blazing, questing eyes through the silken mask-slits, and received a start. She tried to recollect where she had seen the like, and a vivid picture was recalled of a certain proud and rebellious sinner whom she had once encountered on a fruitless errand for the Lord.

So it was that the good woman took the trail in hot and righteous wrath, a trail which brought her ultimately into the company of Mrs. Eppingwell and Floyd Vanderlip. Mrs. Eppingwell had just found the opportunity to talk with the man. She had determined, now that Flossie was so near at hand, to proceed directly to the point, and an incisive little ethical discourse was titillating on the end of her tongue, when the couple became three. She noted, and pleasurably, the faintly foreign accent of the "Beg pardon" with which the furred woman prefaced her immediate appropriation of Floyd Vanderlip; and she courteously bowed her permission for them to draw a little apart.

Then it was that Mrs. McFee's righteous hand descended, and accompanying it in its descent was a black mask torn from a startled woman. A wonderful face and brilliant eyes were exposed to the quiet curiosity of those who looked that way, and they were everybody. Floyd Vanderlip was rather confused. The situation demanded instant action on the part of a man who was not beyond his depth, while *he* hardly knew where he was. He stared helplessly about him. Mrs. Eppingwell was perplexed. She could not comprehend. An explanation was forthcoming, somewhere, and Mrs. McFee was equal to it.

"Mrs. Eppingwell," and her Celtic voice rose shrilly, "it is with great pleasure I make you acquainted with Freda Moloof, *Miss* Freda Moloof, as I understand."

Freda involuntarily turned. With her own face bared, she felt as in a dream, naked, upon her turned the clothed features and gleaming eyes of the masked circle. It seemed, almost, as though a hungry wolf-pack girdled her, ready to drag her down. It might chance that some felt pity for her, she thought, and at the thought, hardened. She would by far prefer their scorn. Strong of heart was she, this woman, and though she had hunted the prey into the midst of the pack, Mrs. Eppingwell or no Mrs. Eppingwell, she could not forego the kill.

But here Mrs. Eppingwell did a strange thing. So this, at last, was Freda, she mused, the dancer and the destroyer of men; the woman from whose door she had been turned. And she, too, felt the imperious creature's nakedness as though it were her own. Perhaps it was this, her Saxon disinclination to meet a disadvantaged foe, perhaps, forsooth, that it might give her greater strength in the struggle for the man, and it might have been a little of both; but be that as it may, she did do this strange thing. When Mrs. McFee's thin voice, vibrant with malice, had raised, and Freda turned involuntarily, Mrs. Eppingwell also turned, removed her mask, and inclined her head in acknowledgment.

It was another flashing, eternal second, during which these two women regarded each other. The one, eyes blazing, meteoric; at bay, aggressive; suffering in advance and resenting in advance the scorn and ridicule and insult she had thrown herself open to; a beautiful, burning, bubbling lava cone of flesh and spirit. And the other, calm-eyed, cool-browed, serene; strong in her own integrity, with faith in herself, thoroughly at ease; dispassionate, imperturbable; a figure chiseled from some cold marble quarry. Whatever gulf there might exist, she recognized it not. No bridging, no descending; her attitude was that of perfect equality. She stood tranquilly on the ground of their common womanhood. And this maddened Freda. Not so, had she been of lesser breed; but her soul's plummet knew not the bottomless, and she could follow the other into the deeps of her deepest depths and read her aright. "Why do you not draw back your garment's hem?" she was fain to cry out, all in that flashing, dazzling second. "Spit upon me, revile me, and it were greater mercy than this!" She trembled. Her nostrils distended and quivered. But she drew herself in check, returned the inclination of head, and turned to the man.

"Come with me, Floyd," she said simply. "I want you now."

"What the—" he began explosively, and quit as suddenly, discreet enough to not round it off. Where the deuce had his wits gone, anyway? Was ever a man more foolishly placed? He gurgled deep down in his throat and high up in the roof of his mouth, heaved as one his big shoulders and his indecision, and glared appealingly at the two women.

"I beg pardon, just a moment, but may I speak first with Mr. Vanderlip?" Mrs. Eppingwell's voice, though flute-like and low, predicated will in its every cadence.

The man looked his gratitude. He, at least, was willing enough.

"I'm very sorry," from Freda. "There isn't time. He must come at once." The conventional phrases dropped easily from her lips, but she could not forbear to smile inwardly at their inadequacy and weakness. She would much rather have shrieked.

"But, Miss Moloof, who are you that you may possess yourself of Mr. Vanderlip and command his actions?"

Whereupon relief brightened his face, and the man beamed his approval. Trust Mrs. Eppingwell to drag him clear. Freda had met her match this time.

"I—I—" Freda hesitated, and then her feminine mind putting on its harness—"and who are you to ask this question?"

"I? I am Mrs. Eppingwell, and—"

"There!" the other broke in sharply. "You are the wife of a captain, who is therefore your husband. I am only a dancing girl. What do you with this man?"

"Such unprecedented behavior!" Mrs. McFee ruffled herself and cleared for action, but Mrs. Eppingwell shut her mouth with a look and developed a new attack.

"Since Miss Moloof appears to hold claims upon you, Mr. Vanderlip, and is in too great haste to grant me a few seconds of your time, I am forced to appeal directly to you. May I speak with you, alone, and now?"

Mrs. McFee's jaws brought together with a snap. That settled the disgraceful situation.

"Why, er—that is, certainly," the man stammered. "Of course, of course," growing more effusive at the prospect of deliverance.

Men are only gregarious vertebrates, domesticated and evolved, and the chances are large that it was because the Greek girl had in her time dealt with wilder masculine beasts of the human sort; for she turned upon the man with hell's tides aflood in her blazing eyes, much as a bespangled lady upon a lion which has suddenly imbibed the pernicious theory that he is a free agent. The beast in him fawned to the lash.

"That is to say, ah, afterward. To-morrow, Mrs. Eppingwell; yes, to-morrow. That is what I meant." He solaced himself with the fact, should he remain, that more embarrassment awaited. Also, he had an engagement which he must keep shortly, down by the water-hole off the hospital. Ye gods! he had never given Freda credit! Wasn't she magnificent!

"I'll thank you for my mask, Mrs. McFee."

That lady, for the nonce speechless, turned over the article in question.

"Good-night, Miss Moloof." Mrs. Eppingwell was royal even in defeat.

Freda reciprocated, though barely downing the impulse to clasp the other's knees and beg forgiveness,—no, not forgiveness, but something, she knew not what, but which she none the less greatly desired.

The man was for her taking his arm; but she had made her kill in the midst of the pack, and that which led kings to drag their vanquished at the chariot-tail, led her toward the door alone, Floyd Vanderlip close at heel and striving to re-establish his mental equilibrium.

V.

It was bitter cold. As the trail wound, a quarter of a mile brought them to the dancer's cabin, by which time her moist breath had coated her face frostily, while his had massed his heavy mustache till conversation was painful. By the greenish light of the aurora borealis, the quicksilver showed itself frozen hard in the bulb of the thermometer which hung outside the door. A thousand dogs, in pitiful chorus, wailed their ancient wrongs and claimed mercy from the unheeding stars. Not a breath of air was moving. For them there was no shelter from the cold, no shrewd crawling to leeward in snug nooks. The frost was everywhere, and they lay in the open, ever and anon stretching their trail-stiffened muscles and lifting the long wolf-howl.

They did not talk at first, the man and the woman. While the maid helped Freda off with her wraps, Floyd Vanderlip replenished the fire; and by the time the maid had withdrawn to an inner room, his head over the stove, he was busily thawing out his burdened upper lip. After that he rolled a cigarette and watched her lazily through the fragrant eddies. She stole a glance at the clock. It lacked half an hour of midnight. How was she to hold him? Was he angry for that which she had done? What was his mood? What mood of hers could meet his best? Not that she doubted herself. No, no. Hold him she could, if need be at pistol point, till Sitka Charley's work was done, and Devereaux's too.

There were many ways, and with her knowledge of this her contempt for the man increased. As she leaned her head on her hand, a fleeting vision of her own girlhood, with its mournful climacteric and tragic ebb, was vouchsafed her, and for the moment she was minded to read him a lesson from it. God! it must be less than human brute who could not be held by such a tale, told as she could tell it, but—bah! He was not worth it, nor worth the pain to her. The candle was positioned just right, and even as she thought of these things sacredly shameful to her, he was pleasuring in the transparent pinkiness of her ear. She noted his eye, took the cue, and turned her head till the clean profile of the face was presented. Not the least was that profile among her virtues. She could not help the lines upon which she had been builded, and they were very good; but she had long since learned those lines, and though little they needed, was not above advantaging them to the best of her ability. The candle began to flicker. She could not do anything ungracefully, but that did not prevent her improving upon nature a bit, when she reached forth and deftly snuffed the red wick from the midst of the yellow flame. Again she rested head on hand, this time regarding the man thoughtfully, and any man is pleased when thus regarded by a pretty woman.

She was in little haste to begin. If dalliance were to his liking, it was to hers. To him it was very comfortable, soothing his lungs with nicotine and gazing upon her. It was snug and warm here, while down by the water-hole began a trail which he would soon be hitting through the chilly hours. He felt he ought to be angry with Freda for the scene she had created, but somehow he didn't feel a bit wrathful. Like as not there wouldn't have been any scene if it hadn't been for that McFee woman. If he were the Governor, he would put a poll tax of a hundred ounces a quarter upon her and her kind and all gospel sharks and sky pilots. And certainly Freda had behaved very ladylike, held her own with Mrs. Eppingwell besides. Never gave the girl credit for the grit. He looked lingeringly over her, coming back now and again to the eyes, behind the deep earnestness of which he could not guess lay concealed a deeper sneer. And, Jove, wasn't she well put up! Wonder why she looked at him so? Did she want to marry him, too? Like as not; but she wasn't the only one. Her looks were in her favor, weren't they? And young—younger than Loraine Lisznayi. She couldn't be more than twenty-three or four, twenty-five at most. And she'd never get stout. Anybody could guess that the first time. He couldn't say it of Loraine, though. *She* certainly had put on flesh since the day she served as model. Huh! once he got her on trail he'd take it off. Put her on the snowshoes to break ahead of the dogs. Never knew it to fail, yet. But his thought leaped ahead to the palace under the lazy Mediterranean sky—and how would it be with Loraine then? No frost, no trail, no famine now and again to cheer the monotony, and she getting older and piling it on with every sunrise. While this girl Freda—he sighed his unconscious regret that he had missed being born under the flag of the Turk, and came back to Alaska.

"Well?" Both hands of the clock pointed perpendicularly to midnight, and it was high time he was getting down to the water-hole.

"Oh!" Freda started, and she did it prettily, delighting him as his fellows have ever been delighted by their womankind. When a man is made to believe that a woman, looking upon him thoughtfully, has lost herself in meditation over him, that man needs be an extremely cold-blooded individual in order to trim his sheets, set a lookout, and steer clear.

"I was just wondering what you wanted to see me about," he explained, drawing his chair up to hers by the table.

"Floyd," she looked him steadily in the eyes, "I am tired of the whole business. I want to go away. I can't live it out here till the river breaks. If I try, I'll die. I am sure of it. I want to quit it all and go away, and I want to do it at once."

She laid her hand in mute appeal upon the back of his, which turned over and became a prison. Another one, he thought, just throwing herself at him. Guess it wouldn't hurt Loraine to cool her feet by the water-hole a little longer.

"Well?" This time from Freda, but softly and anxiously.

"I don't know what to say," he hastened to answer, adding to himself that it was coming along quicker than he had expected. "Nothing I'd like better, Freda. You know that well enough." He pressed her hand, palm to palm. She nodded. Could she wonder that she despised the breed?

"But you see, I—I'm engaged. Of course you know that. And the girl's coming into the country to marry me. Don't know what was up with me when I asked her, but it was a long while back, and I was all-fired young—"

"I want to go away, out of the land, anywhere," she went on, disregarding the obstacle he had reared up and apologized for. "I have been running over the men I know and reached the conclusion that—that—"

"I was the likeliest of the lot?"

She smiled her gratitude for his having saved her the embarrassment of confession. He drew her head against his shoulder with the free hand, and somehow the scent of her hair got into his nostrils. Then he discovered that a common pulse throbbed, throbbed, throbbed, where their palms were in contact. This phenomenon is easily comprehensible from a physiological standpoint, but to the man who makes the discovery for the first time, it is a most wonderful thing. Floyd Vanderlip had caressed more shovel-handles than women's hands in his time, so this was an experience quite new and delightfully strange. And when Freda turned her head against his shoulder, her hair brushing his cheek till his eyes met hers, full and at close range, luminously soft, ay, and tender—why, whose fault was it that he lost his grip utterly? False to Flossie, why not to Loraine? Even if the women did keep bothering him, that was no reason he should make up his mind in a hurry. Why, he had slathers of money, and Freda was just the girl to grace it. A wife she'd make him for other men to envy. But go slow. He must be cautious.

"You don't happen to care for palaces, do you?" he asked.

She shook her head.

"Well, I had a hankering after them myself, till I got to thinking, a while back, and I've about sized it up that one'd get fat living in palaces, and soft and lazy."

"Yes, it's nice for a time, but you soon grow tired of it, I imagine," she hastened to reassure him. "The world is good, but life should be many-sided. Rough and knock about for a while, and then rest up somewhere. Off to the South Seas on a yacht, then a nibble of Paris; a winter in South America and a summer in Norway; a few months in England—"

"Good society?"

"Most certainly—the best; and then, heigho! for the dogs and sleds and the Hudson Bay Country. Change, you know. A strong man like you, full of vitality and go, could not possibly stand a palace for a year. It is all very well for effeminate men, but you weren't made for such a life. You are masculine, intensely masculine."

"Think so?"

"It does not require thinking. I know. Have you ever noticed that it was easy to make women care for you?"

His dubious innocence was superb.

"It is very easy. And why? Because you are masculine. You strike the deepest chords of a woman's heart. You are something to cling to,—big-muscled, strong, and brave. In short, because you *are* a man."

She shot a glance at the clock. It was half after the hour. She had given a margin of thirty minutes to Sitka Charley; and it did not matter, now, when Devereaux arrived. Her work was done. She lifted her head, laughed her genuine mirth, slipped her hand clear, and rising to her feet called the maid.

"Alice, help Mr. Vanderlip on with his *parka*. His mittens are on the sill by the stove."

The man could not understand.

"Let me thank you for your kindness, Floyd. Your time was invaluable to me, and it was indeed good of you. The turning to the left, as you leave the cabin, leads the quickest to the water-hole. Good-night. I am going to bed."

Floyd Vanderlip employed strong words to express his perplexity and disappointment. Alice did not like to hear men swear, so dropped his *parka* on the floor and tossed his mittens on top of it. Then he made a break for Freda, and she ruined her retreat to the inner room by tripping over the *parka*. He brought her up standing with a rude grip on the wrist. But she only laughed. She was not afraid of men. Had they not wrought their worst with her, and did she not still endure?

"Don't be rough," she said finally. "On second thought," here she looked at his detaining hand, "I've decided not to go to bed yet a while. Do sit down and be comfortable instead of ridiculous. Any questions?"

"Yes, my lady, and reckoning, too." He still kept his hold. "What do you know about the water-hole? What did you mean by—no, never mind. One question at a time."

"Oh, nothing much. Sitka Charley had an appointment there with somebody you may know, and not being anxious for a man of your known charm to be present, fell back upon me to kindly help him. That's all. They're off now, and a good half hour ago."

"Where? Down river and without me? And he an Indian!"

"There's no accounting for taste, you know, especially in a woman."

"But how do I stand in this deal? I've lost four thousand dollars' worth of dogs and a tidy bit of a woman, and nothing to show for it. Except you," he added as an afterthought, "and cheap you are at the price."

Freda shrugged her shoulders.

"You might as well get ready. I'm going out to borrow a couple of teams of dogs, and we'll start in as many hours."

"I am very sorry, but I'm going to bed."

"You'll pack if you know what's good for you. Go to bed, or not, when I get my dogs outside, so help me, onto the sled you go. Mebbe you fooled with me, but I'll just see your bluff and take you in earnest. Hear me?"

He closed on her wrist till it hurt, but on her lips a smile was growing, and she seemed to listen intently to some outside sound. There was a jingle of dog bells, and a man's voice crying "Haw!" as a sled took the turning and drew up at the cabin.

"*Now* will you let me go to bed?"

As Freda spoke she threw open the door. Into the warm room rushed the frost, and on the threshold, garbed in trail-worn furs, knee-deep in the swirling vapor, against a background of flaming borealis, a woman hesitated. She removed her nose-trap and stood blinking blindly in the white candlelight. Floyd Vanderlip stumbled forward.

"Floyd!" she cried, relieved and glad, and met him with a tired bound.

What could he but kiss the armful of furs? And a pretty armful it was, nestling against him wearily, but happy.

"It was good of you," spoke the armful, "to send Mr. Devereaux with fresh dogs after me, else I would not have been in till to-morrow."

The man looked blankly across at Freda, then the light breaking in upon him, "And wasn't it good of Devereaux to go?"

"Couldn't wait a bit longer, could you, dear?" Flossie snuggled closer.

"Well, I was getting sort of impatient," he confessed glibly, at the same time drawing her up till her feet left the floor, and getting outside the door.

That same night an inexplicable thing happened to the Reverend James Brown, missionary, who lived among the natives several miles down the Yukon and saw to it that the trails they trod led to the white man's paradise. He was roused from his sleep by a strange Indian, who gave into his charge not only the soul but the body of a woman, and having done this drove quickly away. This woman was heavy, and handsome, and angry, and in her wrath unclean words fell from her mouth. This shocked the worthy man, but he was yet young and her presence would have been pernicious (in the simple eyes of his flock), had she not struck out on foot for Dawson with the first gray of dawn.

The shock to Dawson came many days later, when the summer had come and the population honored a certain royal lady at Windsor by lining the Yukon's bank and watching Sitka Charley rise up with flashing paddle and drive the first canoe across the line. On this day of the races, Mrs. Eppingwell, who had learned and unlearned numerous things, saw Freda for the first time since the night of the ball. "Publicly, mind you," as Mrs. McFee expressed it, "without regard or respect for the morals of the community," she went up to the dancer and held out her hand. At first, it is remembered by those who saw, the girl shrank back, then words passed between the two, and Freda, great Freda, broke down and wept on the shoulder of the captain's wife. It was not given to Dawson to know why Mrs. Eppingwell should crave forgiveness of a Greek dancing girl, but she did it publicly, and it was unseemly.

It were well not to forget Mrs. McFee. She took a cabin passage on the first steamer going out. She also took with her a theory which she had achieved in the silent watches of the long dark nights; and it is her conviction that the Northland is unregenerate because it is so cold there. Fear of hell-fire cannot be bred in an ice-box. This may appear dogmatic, but it is Mrs. McFee's theory.

IN THE FORESTS OF THE NORTH

A WEARY JOURNEY beyond the last scrub timber and straggling copses, into the heart of the Barrens where the niggard North is supposed to deny the Earth, are to be found great sweeps of forests and stretches of smiling land. But this the world is just beginning to know. The world's explorers have known it, from time to time, but hitherto they have never returned to tell the world.

The Barrens — well, they are the Barrens, the bad lands of the Arctic, the deserts of the Circle, the bleak and bitter home of the musk-ox and the lean plains wolf. So Avery Van Brunt found them, treeless and cheerless, sparsely clothed with moss and lichens, and altogether uninviting. At least so he found them till he penetrated to the white blank spaces on the map, and came upon undreamed-of rich spruce forests and unrecorded Eskimo tribes. It had been his intention, (and his bid for fame), to break up these white blank spaces and diversify them with the black markings of mountain-chains, sinks and basins, and sinuous river courses; and it was with added delight that he came to speculate upon the possibilities of timber belts and native villages.

Avery Van Brunt, or, in full distinction, Professor A. Van Brunt of the Geological Survey, was second in command of the expedition, and first in command of the sub-expedition which he had led on a side tour of some half a thousand miles up one of the branches of the Thelon and which he was now leading into one of his unrecorded villages. At his back plodded eight men, two of them French-Canadian *voyageurs*, and the remainder strapping Crees from Manitoba-way. He, alone, was full-blooded Saxon, and his blood was pounding fiercely through his veins to the traditions of his race. Clive and Hastings, Drake and Raleigh, Hengest and Horsa, walked with him. First of all men of his breed was he to enter this lone Northland village, and at the thought an exultancy came upon him, an exaltation, and his followers noted that his leg-weariness fell from him and that he insensibly quickened the pace.

The village emptied itself, and a motley crowd trooped out to meet him, men in the forefront, with bows and spears clutched menacingly, and women and children faltering timidly in the rear. Van Brunt lifted his right arm and made the universal peace sign, a sign which all peoples know, and the villagers answered in peace. But to his chagrin, a skin-clad man ran forward and thrust out his hand with a familiar "Hello." He was a bearded man, with cheeks and brow bronzed to copper-brown, and in him Van Brunt knew his kind.

"Who are you?" he asked, gripping the extended hand. "Andrée?"

"Who's Andrée?" the man asked back.

Van Brunt looked at him more sharply. "By George, you've been here some time."

"Five years," the man answered, a dim flicker of pride in his eyes. "But come on, let's talk."

"Let them camp alongside of me," he answered Van Brunt's glance at his party. "Old Tantlatch will take care of them. Come on."

He swung off in a long stride, Van Brunt following at his heels through the village. In irregular fashion, wherever the ground favored, the lodges of moose hide were pitched. Van Brunt ran his practised eye over them and calculated.

"Two hundred, not counting the young ones," he summed up.

The man nodded. "Pretty close to it. But here's where I live, out of the thick of it, you know—more privacy and all that. Sit down. I'll eat with you when your men get something cooked up. I've forgotten what tea tastes like.... Five years and never a taste or smell.... Any tobacco?... Ah, thanks, and a pipe? Good. Now for a fire-stick and we'll see if the weed has lost its cunning."

He scratched the match with the painstaking care of the woodsman, cherished its young flame as though there were never another in all the world, and drew in the first mouthful of smoke. This he retained meditatively for a time, and blew out through his pursed lips slowly and caressingly. Then his face seemed to soften as he leaned back, and a soft blur to film his eyes. He sighed heavily, happily, with immeasurable content, and then said suddenly:

"God! But that tastes good!"

Van Brunt nodded sympathetically. "Five years, you say?"

"Five years." The man sighed again. "And you, I presume, wish to know about it, being naturally curious, and this a sufficiently strange situation, and all that. But it's not much. I came in from Edmonton after musk-ox, and like Pike and the rest of them, had my mischances, only I lost my party and outfit. Starvation, hardship, the regular tale, you know, sole survivor and all that, till I crawled into Tantlatch's, here, on hand and knee."

"Five years," Van Brunt murmured retrospectively, as though turning things over in his mind.

"Five years on February last. I crossed the Great Slave early in May—"

"And you are ... Fairfax?" Van Brunt interjected.

The man nodded.

"Let me see ... John, I think it is, John Fairfax."

"How did you know?" Fairfax queried lazily, half-absorbed in curling smoke-spirals upward in the quiet air.

"The papers were full of it at the time. Prevanche—"

"Prevanche!" Fairfax sat up, suddenly alert. "He was lost in the Smoke Mountains."

"Yes, but he pulled through and came out."

Fairfax settled back again and resumed his smoke-spirals. "I am glad to hear it," he remarked reflectively. "Prevanche was a bully fellow if he *did* have ideas about head-straps, the beggar. And he pulled through? Well, I'm glad."

Five years ... the phrase drifted recurrently through Van Brunt's thought, and somehow the face of Emily Southwaithe seemed to rise up and take form before him. Five years ... A wedge of wild-fowl honked low overhead and at sight of the encampment veered swiftly to the north into the smouldering sun. Van Brunt could not follow them. He pulled out his watch. It was an hour past midnight. The northward clouds flushed bloodily, and rays of sombre-red shot southward, firing the gloomy woods with a lurid radiance. The air was in breathless calm, not a needle quivered, and the least sounds of the camp were distinct and clear as trumpet calls. The Crees and *voyageurs* felt the spirit of it and mumbled in dreamy undertones, and the cook unconsciously subdued the clatter of pot and pan. Somewhere a child was crying, and from the depths of the forest, like a silver thread, rose a woman's voice in mournful chant: "O-o-o-o-o-o-a-haa-ha-a-ha-aa-a-a, O-o-o-o-o-o-a-ha-a-ha-a."

Van Brunt shivered and rubbed the backs of his hands briskly.

"And they gave me up for dead?" his companion asked slowly.

"Well, you never came back, so your friends—"

"Promptly forgot." Fairfax laughed harshly, defiantly.

"Why didn't you come out?"

"Partly disinclination, I suppose, and partly because of circumstances over which I had no control. You see, Tantlatch, here, was down with a broken leg when I made his acquaintance,—a nasty fracture,—and I set it for him and got him into shape. I stayed some time, getting my strength back. I was the first white man he had seen, and of course I seemed very wise and showed his people no end of things. Coached them up in military tactics, among other things, so that they conquered the four other tribal villages, (which you have not yet seen), and came to rule the land. And they naturally grew to think a good deal of me, so much so that when I was ready to go they wouldn't hear of it. Were most hospitable, in fact. Put a couple of guards over me and watched me day and night. And then Tantlatch offered me inducements,—in a sense, inducements,—so to say, and as it didn't matter much one way or the other, I reconciled myself to remaining."

"I knew your brother at Freiburg. I am Van Brunt."

Fairfax reached forward impulsively and shook his hand. "You were Billy's friend, eh? Poor Billy! He spoke of you often."

"Rum meeting place, though," he added, casting an embracing glance over the primordial landscape and listening for a moment to the woman's mournful notes. "Her man was clawed by a bear, and she's taking it hard."

"Beastly life!" Van Brunt grimaced his disgust. "I suppose, after five years of it, civilization will be sweet? What do you say?"

Fairfax's face took on a stolid expression. "Oh, I don't know. At least they're honest folk and live according to their lights. And then they are amazingly simple. No complexity about them, no thousand and one subtle ramifications to every single emotion they experience. They love, fear, hate, are angered, or made happy, in common, ordinary, and unmistakable terms. It may be a beastly life, but at least it is easy to live. No philandering, no dallying. If a woman likes you, she'll not be backward in telling you so. If she hates you, she'll tell you so, and then, if you feel inclined, you can beat her, but the thing is, she knows precisely what you mean, and you know precisely what she means. No mistakes, no misunderstandings. It has its charm, after civilization's fitful fever. Comprehend?"

"No, it's a pretty good life," he continued, after a pause; "good enough for me, and I intend to stay with it."

Van Brunt lowered his head in a musing manner, and an imperceptible smile played on his mouth. No philandering, no dallying, no misunderstanding. Fairfax also was taking it hard, he thought, just because Emily Southwaithe had been mistakenly clawed by a bear. And not a bad sort of a bear, either, was Carlton Southwaithe.

"But you are coming along with me," Van Brunt said deliberately.

"No, I'm not."

"Yes, you are."

"Life's too easy here, I tell you." Fairfax spoke with decision. "I understand everything, and I am understood. Summer and winter alternate like the sun flashing through the palings of a fence, the seasons are a blur of light and shade, and time slips by, and life slips by, and then ... a wailing in the forest, and the dark. Listen!"

He held up his hand, and the silver thread of the woman's sorrow rose through the silence and the calm. Fairfax joined in softly.

"O-o-o-o-o-o-a-haa-ha-a-ha-aa-a-a, O-o-o-o-o-o-a-ha-a-ha-a," he sang. "Can't you hear it? Can't you see it? The women mourning? the funeral chant? my hair white-locked and patri-archal? my skins wrapped in rude splendor about me? my hunting-spear by my side? And who shall say it is not well?"

Van Brunt looked at him coolly. "Fairfax, you are a damned fool. Five years of this is enough to knock any man, and you are in an unhealthy, morbid condition. Further, Carlton Southwaithe is dead."

Van Brunt filled his pipe and lighted it, the while watching slyly and with almost profes-sional interest. Fairfax's eyes flashed on the instant, his fists clenched, he half rose up, then his muscles relaxed and he seemed to brood. Michael, the cook, signaled that the meal was ready, but Van Brunt motioned back to delay. The silence hung heavy, and he fell to analyzing the forest scents, the odors of mould and rotting vegetation, the resiny smells of pine cones and needles, the aromatic savors of many camp-smokes. Twice Fairfax looked up, but said nothing, and then:

"And ... Emily ...?"

"Three years a widow; still a widow."

Another long silence settled down, to be broken by Fairfax finally with a naïve smile. "I guess you're right, Van Brunt. I'll go along."

"I knew you would." Van Brunt laid his hand on Fairfax's shoulder. "Of course, one cannot know, but I imagine—for one in her position—she has had offers—"

"When do you start?" Fairfax interrupted.

"After the men have had some sleep. Which reminds me, Michael is getting angry, so come and eat."

After supper, when the Crees and *voyageurs* had rolled into their blankets, snoring, the two men lingered by the dying fire. There was much to talk about,—wars and politics and explorations, the doings of men and the happening of things, mutual friends, marriages, deaths,—five years of history for which Fairfax clamored.

"So the Spanish fleet was bottled up in Santiago," Van Brunt was saying, when a young woman stepped lightly before him and stood by Fairfax's side. She looked swiftly into his face, then turned a troubled gaze upon Van Brunt.

"Chief Tantlatch's daughter, sort of princess," Fairfax explained, with an honest flush. "One of the inducements, in short, to make me stay. Thom, this is Van Brunt, friend of mine."

Van Brunt held out his hand, but the woman maintained a rigid repose quite in keeping with her general appearance. Not a line of her face softened, not a feature unbent. She looked him straight in the eyes, her own piercing, questioning, searching.

"Precious lot she understands," Fairfax laughed. "Her first introduction, you know. But as you were saying, with the Spanish fleet bottled up in Santiago?"

Thom crouched down by her husband's side, motionless as a bronze statue, only her eyes flashing from face to face in ceaseless search. And Avery Van Brunt, as he talked on and on, felt a nervousness under the dumb gaze. In the midst of his most graphic battle descriptions, he would become suddenly conscious of the black eyes burning into him, and would stumble and flounder till he could catch the gait and go again. Fairfax, hands clasped round knees, pipe out, absorbed, spurred him on when he lagged, and repictured the world he thought he had forgotten.

One hour passed, and two, and Fairfax rose reluctantly to his feet. "And Cronje was cornered, eh? Well, just wait a moment till I run over to Tantlatch. He'll be expecting you, and I'll arrange for you to see him after breakfast. That will be all right, won't it?"

He went off between the pines, and Van Brunt found himself staring into Thom's warm eyes. Five years, he mused, and she can't be more than twenty now. A most remarkable creature. Being Eskimo, she should have a little flat excuse for a nose, and lo, it is neither broad nor flat, but aquiline, with nostrils delicately and sensitively formed as any fine lady's of a whiter breed—the Indian strain somewhere, be assured, Avery Van Brunt. And, Avery Van Brunt, don't be nervous, she won't eat you; she's only a woman, and not a bad-looking one at that. Oriental rather than aborigine. Eyes large and fairly wide apart, with just the faintest hint of Mongol obliquity. Thom, you're an anomaly. You're out of place here among these Eskimos, even if your father is one. Where did your mother come from? or your grand-mother? And Thom, my dear, you're a beauty, a frigid, frozen little beauty with Alaskan lava in your blood, and please don't look at me that way.

He laughed and stood up. Her insistent stare disconcerted him. A dog was prowling among the grub-sacks. He would drive it away and place them into safety against Fairfax's return. But Thom stretched out a detaining hand and stood up, facing him.

"You?" she said, in the Arctic tongue which differs little from Greenland to Point Barrow. "You?"

And the swift expression of her face demanded all for which "you" stood, his reason for existence, his presence there, his relation to her husband—everything.

"Brother," he answered in the same tongue, with a sweeping gesture to the south. "Brothers we be, your man and I."

She shook her head. "It is not good that you be here."

"After one sleep I go."

"And my man?" she demanded, with tremulous eagerness.

Van Brunt shrugged his shoulders. He was aware of a certain secret shame, of an impersonal sort of shame, and an anger against Fairfax. And he felt the warm blood in his face as he regarded the young savage. She was just a woman. That was all—a woman. The whole sordid story over again, over and over again, as old as Eve and young as the last new love-light.

"My man! My man! My man!" she was reiterating vehemently, her face passionately dark, and the ruthless tenderness of the Eternal Woman, the Mate-Woman, looking out at him from her eyes.

"Thom," he said gravely, in English, "you were born in the Northland forest, and you have eaten fish and meat, and fought with frost and famine, and lived simply all the days of your life. And there are many things, indeed not simple, which you do not know and cannot come to understand. You do not know what it is to long for the fleshpots afar, you cannot understand what it is to yearn for a fair woman's face. And the woman is fair, Thom, the woman is nobly fair. You have been woman to this man, and you have been your all, but your all is very little, very simple. Too little and too simple, and he is an alien man. Him you have never known, you can never know. It is so ordained. You held him in your arms, but you never held his heart, this man with his blurring seasons and his dreams of a barbaric end. Dreams and dream-dust, that is what he has been to you. You clutched at form and gripped shadow, gave yourself to a man and bedded with the wraith of a man. In such manner, of old, did the daughters of men whom the gods found fair. And, Thom, Thom, I should not like to be John Fairfax in the night-watches of the years to come, in the night-watches, when his eyes shall see, not the sun-gloried hair of the woman by his side, but the dark tresses of a mate forsaken in the forests of the North."

Though she did not understand, she had listened with intense attention, as though life hung on his speech. But she caught at her husband's name and cried out in Eskimo:—

"Yes! Yes! Fairfax! My man!"

"Poor little fool, how could he be your man?"

But she could not understand his English tongue, and deemed that she was being trifled with. The dumb, insensate anger of the Mate-Woman flamed in her face, and it almost seemed to the man as though she crouched panther-like for the spring.

He cursed softly to himself and watched the fire fade from her face and the soft luminous glow of the appealing woman spring up, of the appealing woman who foregoes strength and panoplies herself wisely in her weakness.

"He is my man," she said gently. "Never have I known other. It cannot be that I should ever know other. Nor can it be that he should go from me."

"Who has said he shall go from thee?" he demanded sharply, half in exasperation, half in impotence.

"It is for thee to say he shall not go from me," she answered softly, a half-sob in her throat.

Van Brunt kicked the embers of the fire savagely and sat down.

"It is for thee to say. He is my man. Before all women he is my man. Thou art big, thou art strong, and behold, I am very weak. See, I am at thy feet. It is for thee to deal with me. It is for thee."

"Get up!" He jerked her roughly erect and stood up himself. "Thou art a woman. Wherefore the dirt is no place for thee, nor the feet of any man."

"He is my man."

"Then Jesus forgive all men!" Van Brunt cried out passionately.

"He is my man," she repeated monotonously, beseechingly.

"He is my brother," he answered.

"My father is Chief Tantlatch. He is a power over five villages. I will see that the five villages be searched for thy choice of all maidens, that thou mayest stay here by thy brother, and dwell in comfort."

"After one sleep I go."

"And my man?"

"Thy man comes now. Behold!"

From among the gloomy spruces came the light caroling of Fairfax's voice.

As the day is quenched by a sea of fog, so his song smote the light out of her face. "It is the tongue of his own people," she said; "the tongue of his own people."

She turned, with the free movement of a lithe young animal, and made off into the forest.

"It's all fixed," Fairfax called as he came up. "His regal highness will receive you after breakfast."

"Have you told him?" Van Brunt asked.

"No. Nor shall I tell him till we're ready to pull out."

Van Brunt looked with moody affection over the sleeping forms of his men.

"I shall be glad when we are a hundred leagues upon our way," he said.

. . .

THOM RAISED the skin-flap of her father's lodge. Two men sat with him, and the three looked at her with swift interest. But her face betokened nothing as she entered and took seat quietly, without speech. Tantlatch drummed with his knuckles on a spear-heft across his knees, and gazed idly along the path of a sun-ray which pierced a lacing-hole and flung a glittering track across the murky atmosphere of the lodge. To his right, at his shoulder, crouched Chugungatte, the shaman. Both were old men, and the weariness of many years brooded in their eyes. But opposite them sat Keen, a young man and chief favorite in the tribe. He was quick and alert of movement, and his black eyes flashed from face to face in ceaseless scrutiny and challenge.

Silence reigned in the place. Now and again camp noises penetrated, and from the distance, faint and far, like the shadows of voices, came the wrangling of boys in thin shrill tones. A dog thrust his head into the entrance and blinked wolfishly at them for a space, the slaver dripping from his ivory-white fangs. After a time he growled tentatively, and then, awed by the immobility of the human figures, lowered his head and groveled away backward. Tantlatch glanced apathetically at his daughter.

"And thy man, how is it with him and thee?"

"He sings strange songs," Thom made answer, "and there is a new look on his face."

"So? He hath spoken?"

"Nay, but there is a new look on his face, a new light in his eyes, and with the New-Comer he sits by the fire, and they talk and talk, and the talk is without end."

Chugungatte whispered in his master's ear, and Keen leaned forward from his hips.

"There be something calling him from afar," she went on, "and he seems to sit and listen, and to answer, singing, in his own people's tongue."

Again Chugungatte whispered and Keen leaned forward, and Thom held her speech till her father nodded his head that she might proceed.

"It be known to thee, O Tantlatch, that the wild goose and the swan and the little ringed duck be born here in the low-lying lands. It be known that they go away before the face of the frost to unknown places. And it be known, likewise, that always do they return when the sun is in the land and the waterways are free. Always do they return to where they were born, that new life may go forth. The land calls to them and they come. And now there is another land that calls, and it is calling to my man,—the land where he was born,—and he hath it in mind to answer the call. Yet is he my man. Before all women is he my man."

"Is it well, Tantlatch? Is it well?" Chugungatte demanded, with the hint of menace in his voice.

"Ay, it is well!" Keen cried boldly. "The land calls to its children, and all lands call their children home again. As the wild goose and the swan and the little ringed duck are called, so is called this Stranger Man who has lingered with us and who now must go. Also there be the call of kind. The goose mates with the goose, nor does the swan mate with the little ringed duck. It is not well that the swan should mate with the little ringed duck. Nor is it well that stranger men should mate with the women of our villages. Wherefore I say the man should go, to his own kind, in his own land."

"He is my own man," Thom answered, "and he is a great man."

"Ay, he is a great man." Chugungatte lifted his head with a faint recrudescence of youthful vigor. "He is a great man, and he put strength in thy arm, O Tantlatch, and gave thee power, and made thy name to be feared in the land, to be feared and to be respected. He is very wise, and there be much profit in his wisdom. To him are we beholden for many things,—for the cunning in war and the secrets of the defence of a village and a rush in the forest, for the discussion in council and the undoing of enemies by word of mouth and the hard-sworn promise, for the gathering of game and the making of traps and the preserving of food, for the curing of sickness and mending of hurts of trail and fight. Thou, Tantlatch, wert a lame old man this day, were it not that the Stranger Man came into our midst and attended on thee. And ever, when in doubt on strange questions, have we gone to him, that out of his wisdom he might make things clear, and ever has he made things clear. And there be questions yet to arise, and needs upon his wisdom yet to come, and we cannot bear to let him go. It is not well that we should let him go."

Tantlatch continued to drum on the spear-haft, and gave no sign that he had heard. Thom studied his face in vain, and Chugungatte seemed to shrink together and droop down as the weight of years descended upon him again.

"No man makes my kill." Keen smote his breast a valorous blow. "I make my own kill. I am glad to live when I make my own kill. When I creep through the snow upon the great moose, I am glad. And when I draw the bow, so, with my full strength, and drive the arrow fierce and swift and to the heart, I am glad. And the meat of no man's kill tastes as sweet as the meat of my kill. I am glad to live, glad in my own cunning and strength, glad that I am a doer of things, a doer of things for myself. Of what other reason to live than that? Why should I live if I delight not in myself and the things I do? And it is because I delight and am glad that I go forth to hunt and fish, and it is because I go forth to hunt and fish that I grow cunning and strong. The man who stays in the lodge by the fire grows not cunning and strong. He is not made happy in the eating of my kill, nor is living to him a delight. He does not live. And so I say it is well this Stranger Man should go. His wisdom does not make us wise. If he be cunning, there is no need that we be cunning. If need arise, we go to him for his cunning. We eat the meat of his kill, and it tastes unsweet. We merit by his strength, and in it there is no delight. We do not live when he does our living for us. We grow fat and like women, and we are afraid to work, and we forget how to do things for ourselves. Let the man go, O Tantlatch, that we may be men! I am Keen, a man, and I make my own kill!"

Tantlatch turned a gaze upon him in which seemed the vacancy of eternity. Keen waited the decision expectantly; but the lips did not move, and the old chief turned toward his daughter.

"That which be given cannot be taken away," she burst forth. "I was but a girl when this Stranger Man, who is my man, came among us. And I knew not men, or the ways of men, and my heart was in the play of girls, when thou, Tantlatch, thou and none other, didst call me to thee and press me into the arms of the Stranger Man. Thou and none other, Tantlatch; and as thou didst give me to the man, so didst thou give the man to me. He is my man. In my arms has he slept, and from my arms he cannot be taken."

"It were well, O Tantlatch," Keen followed quickly, with a significant glance at Thom, "it were well to remember that that which be given cannot be taken away."

Chugungatte straightened up. "Out of thy youth, Keen, come the words of thy mouth. As for ourselves, O Tantlatch, we be old men and we understand. We, too, have looked into the eyes of women and felt our blood go hot with strange desires. But the years have chilled us, and we have learned the wisdom of the council, the shrewdness of the cool head and hand, and we know that the warm heart be over-warm and prone to rashness. We know that Keen found favor in thy eyes. We know that Thom was promised him in the old days when she was yet a child. And we know that the new days came, and the Stranger Man, and that out of our wisdom and desire for welfare was Thom lost to Keen and the promise broken."

The old shaman paused, and looked directly at the young man.

"And be it known that I, Chugungatte, did advise that the promise be broken."

"Nor have I taken other woman to my bed," Keen broke in. "And I have builded my own fire, and cooked my own food, and ground my teeth in my loneliness."

Chugungatte waved his hand that he had not finished. "I am an old man and I speak from understanding. It be good to be strong and grasp for power. It be better to forego power that good come out of it. In the old days I sat at thy shoulder, Tantlatch, and my voice was heard over all in the council, and my advice taken in affairs of moment. And I was strong and held power. Under Tantlatch I was the greatest man. Then came the Stranger Man, and I saw that he was cunning and wise and great. And in that he was wiser and greater than I, it was plain that greater profit should arise from him than from me. And I had thy ear, Tantlatch, and thou didst listen to my words, and the Stranger Man was given power and place and thy daughter, Thom. And the tribe prospered under the new laws in the new days, and so shall it continue to prosper with the Stranger Man in our midst. We be old men, we two, O Tantlatch, thou and I, and this be an affair of head, not heart. Hear my words, Tantlatch! Hear my words! The man remains!"

There was a long silence. The old chief pondered with the massive certitude of God, and Chugungatte seemed to wrap himself in the mists of a great antiquity. Keen looked with yearning upon the woman, and she, unnoting, held her eyes steadfastly upon her father's face. The wolf-dog shoved the flap aside again, and plucking courage at the quiet, wormed forward on his belly. He sniffed curiously at Thom's listless hand, cocked ears challengingly at Chugungatte, and hunched down upon his haunches before Tantlatch. The spear rattled to the ground, and the dog, with a frightened yell, sprang sideways, snapping in mid-air, and on the second leap cleared the entrance.

Tantlatch looked from face to face, pondering each one long and carefully. Then he raised his head, with rude royalty, and gave judgment in cold and even tones: "The man remains. Let the hunters be called together. Send a runner to the next village with word to bring on the fighting men. I shall not see the New Comer. Do thou, Chugungatte, have talk with him. Tell him he may go at once, if he would go in peace. And if fight there be, kill, kill, kill, to the last man; but let my word go forth that no harm befall our man,—the man whom my daughter hath wedded. It is well."

Chugungatte rose and tottered out; Thom followed; but as Keen stooped to the entrance the voice of Tantlatch stopped him.

"Keen, it were well to hearken to my word. The man remains. Let no harm befall him."

Because of Fairfax's instructions in the art of war, the tribesmen did not hurl themselves forward boldly and with clamor. Instead, there was great restraint and self-control, and they were content to advance silently, creeping and crawling from shelter to shelter. By the river bank, and partly protected by a narrow open space, crouched the Crees and *voyageurs*. Their eyes could see nothing, and only in vague ways did their ears hear, but they felt the thrill of life which ran through the forest, the indistinct, indefinable movement of an advancing host.

"Damn them," Fairfax muttered. "They've never faced powder, but I taught them the trick."

Avery Van Brunt laughed, knocked the ashes out of his pipe, and put it carefully away with the pouch, and loosened the hunting-knife in its sheath at his hip.

"Wait," he said. "We'll wither the face of the charge and break their hearts."

"They'll rush scattered if they remember my teaching."

"Let them. Magazine rifles were made to pump. We'll—good! First blood! Extra tobacco, Loon!"

Loon, a Cree, had spotted an exposed shoulder and with a stinging bullet apprised its owner of his discovery.

"If we can tease them into breaking forward," Fairfax muttered,—"if we can only tease them into breaking forward."

Van Brunt saw a head peer from behind a distant tree, and with a quick shot sent the man sprawling to the ground in a death struggle. Michael potted a third, and Fairfax and the rest took a hand, firing at every exposure and into each clump of agitated brush. In crossing one little swale out of cover, five of the tribesmen remained on their faces, and to the left, where the covering was sparse, a dozen men were struck. But they took the punishment with sullen steadiness, coming on cautiously, deliberately, without haste and without lagging.

Ten minutes later, when they were quite close, all movement was suspended, the advance ceased abruptly, and the quietness that followed was portentous, threatening. Only could be seen the green and gold of the woods, and undergrowth, shivering and trembling to the first faint puffs of the day-wind. The wan white morning sun mottled the earth with long shadows and streaks of light. A wounded man lifted his head and crawled painfully out of the swale, Michael following him with his rifle but forbearing to shoot. A whistle ran along the invisible line from left to right, and a flight of arrows arched through the air.

"Get ready," Van Brunt commanded, a new metallic note in his voice. "Now!"

They broke cover simultaneously. The forest heaved into sudden life. A great yell went up, and the rifles barked back sharp defiance. Tribesmen knew their deaths in mid-leap, and as they fell, their brothers surged over them in a roaring, irresistible wave. In the forefront of the rush, hair flying and arms swinging free, flashing past the tree-trunks, and leaping the obstructing logs, came Thom. Fairfax sighted on her and almost pulled trigger ere he knew her.

"The woman! Don't shoot!" he cried. "See! She is unarmed!"

The Crees never heard, nor Michael and his brother *voyageur*, nor Van Brunt, who was keeping one shell continuously in the air. But Thom bore straight on, unharmed, at the heels of a skin-clad hunter who had veered in before her from the side. Fairfax emptied his magazine into the men to right and left of her, and swung his rifle to meet the big hunter. But the man, seeming to recognize him, swerved suddenly aside and plunged his spear into the body of Michael. On the moment Thom had one arm passed around her husband's neck, and twisting half about, with voice and gesture was splitting the mass of charging warriors. A score of men hurled past on either side, and Fairfax, for a brief instant's space, stood looking upon her and her bronze beauty, thrilling, exulting, stirred to unknown deeps, visioning strange things, dreaming, immortally dreaming. Snatches and scraps of old-world philosophies and new-world ethics floated through his mind, and things wonderfully concrete and woefully incongruous—hunting scenes, stretches of sombre forest, vastnesses of silent snow, the glittering of ballroom lights, great galleries and lecture halls, a fleeting shimmer of glistening test-tubes, long rows of book-lined shelves, the throb of machinery and the roar of traffic, a fragment of forgotten song, faces of dear women and old chums, a lonely watercourse amid upstanding peaks, a shattered boat on a pebbly strand, quiet moonlit fields, fat vales, the smell of hay....

A hunter, struck between the eyes with a rifle-ball, pitched forward lifeless, and with the momentum of his charge slid along the ground. Fairfax came back to himself. His comrades, those that lived, had been swept far back among the trees beyond. He could hear the fierce "Hia! Hia!" of the hunters as they closed in and cut and thrust with their weapons of bone and ivory. The cries of the stricken men smote him like blows. He knew the fight was over, the cause was lost, but all his race traditions and race loyalty impelled him into the welter that he might die at least with his kind.

"My man! My man!" Thom cried. "Thou art safe!"

He tried to struggle on, but her dead weight clogged his steps.

"There is no need! They are dead, and life be good!"

She held him close around the neck and twined her limbs about his till he tripped and stumbled, reeled violently to recover footing, tripped again, and fell backward to the ground. His head struck a jutting root, and he was half-stunned and could struggle but feebly. In the fall she had heard the feathered swish of an arrow darting past, and she covered his body with hers, as with a shield, her arms holding him tightly, her face and lips pressed upon his neck.

Then it was that Keen rose up from a tangled thicket a score of feet away. He looked about him with care. The fight had swept on and the cry of the last man was dying away. There was no one to see. He fitted an arrow to the string and glanced at the man and woman. Between her breast and arm the flesh of the man's side showed white. Keen bent the bow and drew back the arrow to its head. Twice he did so, calmly and for certainty, and then drove the bone-barbed missile straight home to the white flesh, gleaming yet more white in the dark-armed, dark-breasted embrace.

THE LAW OF LIFE

OLD KOSKOOSH LISTENED GREEDILY. Though his sight had long since faded, his hearing was still acute, and the slightest sound penetrated to the glimmering intelligence which yet abode behind the withered forehead, but which no longer gazed forth upon the things of the world. Ah! that was Sit-cum-to-ha, shrilly anathematizing the dogs as she cuffed and beat them into the harnesses. Sit-cum-to-ha was his daughter's daughter, but she was too busy to waste a thought upon her broken grandfather, sitting alone there in the snow, forlorn and helpless. Camp must be broken. The long trail waited while the short day refused to linger. Life called her, and the duties of life, not death. And he was very close to death now.

The thought made the old man panicky for the moment, and he stretched forth a palsied hand which wandered tremblingly over the small heap of dry wood beside him. Reassured that it was indeed there, his hand returned to the shelter of his mangy furs, and he again fell to listening. The sulky crackling of half-frozen hides told him that the chief's moose-skin lodge had been struck, and even then was being rammed and jammed into portable compass. The chief was his son, stalwart and strong, head man of the tribesmen, and a mighty hunter. As the women toiled with the camp luggage, his voice rose, chiding them for their slowness. Old Koskoosh strained his ears. It was the last time he would hear that voice. There went Geehow's lodge! And Tusken's! Seven, eight, nine; only the shaman's could be still standing. There! They were at work upon it now. He could hear the shaman grunt as he piled it on the sled. A child whimpered, and a woman soothed it with soft, crooning gutturals. Little Koo-tee, the old man thought, a fretful child, and not overstrong. It would die soon, perhaps, and they would burn a hole through the frozen tundra and pile rocks above to keep the wolver-ines away. Well, what did it matter? A few years at best, and as many an empty belly as a full one. And in the end, Death waited, ever-hungry and hungriest of them all.

What was that? Oh, the men lashing the sleds and drawing tight the thongs. He listened, who would listen no more. The whip-lashes snarled and bit among the dogs. Hear them whine! How they hated the work and the trail! They were off! Sled after sled churned slowly away into the silence. They were gone. They had passed out of his life, and he faced the last bitter hour alone. No. The snow crunched beneath a moccasin; a man stood beside him; upon his head a hand rested gently. His son was good to do this thing. He remembered other old men whose sons had not waited after the tribe. But his son had. He wandered away into the past, till the young man's voice brought him back.

"Is it well with you?" he asked.

And the old man answered, "It is well."

"There be wood beside you," the younger man continued, "and the fire burns bright. The morning is gray, and the cold has broken. It will snow presently. Even now is it snowing."

"Ay, even now is it snowing."

"The tribesmen hurry. Their bales are heavy, and their bellies flat with lack of feasting. The trail is long and they travel fast. I go now. It is well?"

"It is well. I am as a last year's leaf, clinging lightly to the stem. The first breath that blows, and I fall. My voice is become like an old woman's. My eyes no longer show me the way of my feet, and my feet are heavy, and I am tired. It is well."

He bowed his head in content till the last noise of the complaining snow had died away, and he knew his son was beyond recall. Then his hand crept out in haste to the wood. It alone stood between him and the eternity that yawned in upon him. At last the measure of his life was a handful of fagots. One by one they would go to feed the fire, and just so, step by step, death would creep upon him. When the last stick had surrendered up its heat, the frost would begin to gather strength. First his feet would yield, then his hands; and the numbness would travel, slowly, from the extremities to the body. His head would fall forward upon his knees, and he would rest. It was easy. All men must die.

He did not complain. It was the way of life, and it was just. He had been born close to the earth, close to the earth had he lived, and the law thereof was not new to him. It was the law of all flesh. Nature was not kindly to the flesh. She had no concern for that concrete thing called the individual. Her interest lay in the species, the race. This was the deepest abstraction old Koskoosh's barbaric mind was capable of, but he grasped it firmly. He saw it exemplified in all life. The rise of the sap, the bursting greenness of the willow bud, the fall of the yellow leaf—in this alone was told the whole history. But one task did Nature set the individual. Did he not perform it, he died. Did he perform it, it was all the same, he died. Nature did not care; there were plenty who were obedient, and it was only the obedience in this matter, not the obedient, which lived and lived always. The tribe of Koskoosh was very old. The old men he had known when a boy, had known old men before them. Therefore it was true that the tribe lived, that it stood for the obedience of all its members, way down into the forgotten past, whose very resting-places were unremembered. They did not count; they were episodes. They had passed away like clouds from a summer sky. He also was an episode, and would pass away. Nature did not care. To life she set one task, gave one law. To perpetuate was the task of life, its law was death. A maiden was a good creature to look upon, full-breasted and strong, with spring to her step and light in her eyes. But her task was yet before her. The light in her eyes brightened, her step quickened, she was now bold with the young men, now timid, and she gave them of her own unrest. And ever she grew fairer and yet fairer to look upon, till some hunter, able no longer to withhold himself, took her to his lodge to cook and toil for him and to become the mother of his children. And with the coming of her offspring her looks left her. Her limbs dragged and shuffled, her eyes dimmed and bleared, and only the little children found joy against the withered cheek of the old squaw by the fire. Her task was done. But a little while, on the first pinch of famine or the first long trail, and she would be left, even as he had been left, in the snow, with a little pile of wood. Such was the law.

He placed a stick carefully upon the fire and resumed his meditations. It was the same everywhere, with all things. The mosquitoes vanished with the first frost. The little tree-squirrel crawled away to die. When age settled upon the rabbit it became slow and heavy, and could no longer outfoot its enemies. Even the big bald-face grew clumsy and blind and quarrelsome, in the end to be dragged down by a handful of yelping huskies. He remembered how he had abandoned his own father on an upper reach of the Klondike one winter, the winter before the missionary came with his talk-books and his box of medicines. Many a time had Koskoosh smacked his lips over the recollection of that box, though now his mouth refused to moisten. The "painkiller" had been especially good. But the missionary was a bother after all, for he brought no meat into the camp, and he ate heartily, and the hunters grumbled. But he chilled his lungs on the divide by the Mayo, and the dogs afterwards nosed the stones away and fought over his bones.

Koskoosh placed another stick on the fire and harked back deeper into the past. There was the time of the Great Famine, when the old men crouched empty-bellied to the fire, and let fall from their lips dim traditions of the ancient day when the Yukon ran wide open for three winters, and then lay frozen for three summers. He had lost his mother in that famine. In the summer the salmon run had failed, and the tribe looked forward to the winter and the coming of the caribou. Then the winter came, but with it there were no caribou. Never had the like been known, not even in the lives of the old men. But the caribou did not come, and it was the seventh year, and the rabbits had not replenished, and the dogs were naught but bundles of bones. And through the long darkness the children wailed and died, and the women, and the old men; and not one in ten of the tribe lived to meet the sun when it came back in the spring. That *was* a famine!

But he had seen times of plenty, too, when the meat spoiled on their hands, and the dogs were fat and worthless with overeating—times when they let the game go unkilled, and the women were fertile, and the lodges were cluttered with sprawling men-children and women-children. Then it was the men became high-stomached, and revived ancient quarrels, and crossed the divides to the south to kill the Pellys, and to the west that they might sit by the dead fires of the Tananas. He remembered, when a boy, during a time of plenty, when he saw a moose pulled down by the wolves. Zing-ha lay with him in the snow and watched—Zing-ha, who later became the craftiest of hunters, and who, in the end, fell through an air-hole on the Yukon. They found him, a month afterward, just as he had crawled halfway out and frozen stiff to the ice.

But the moose. Zing-ha and he had gone out that day to play at hunting after the manner of their fathers. On the bed of the creek they struck the fresh track of a moose, and with it the tracks of many wolves. "An old one," Zing-ha, who was quicker at reading the sign, said —"an old one who cannot keep up with the herd. The wolves have cut him out from his brothers, and they will never leave him." And it was so. It was their way. By day and by night, never resting, snarling on his heels, snapping at his nose, they would stay by him to the end. How Zing-ha and he felt the blood-lust quicken! The finish would be a sight to see!

Eager-footed, they took the trail, and even he, Koskoosh, slow of sight and an unversed tracker, could have followed it blind, it was so wide. Hot were they on the heels of the chase, reading the grim tragedy, fresh-written, at every step. Now they came to where the moose had made a stand. Thrice the length of a grown man's body, in every direction, had the snow been stamped about and uptossed. In the midst were the deep impressions of the splay-hoofed game, and all about, everywhere, were the lighter footmarks of the wolves. Some, while their brothers harried the kill, had lain to one side and rested. The full-stretched impress of their bodies in the snow was as perfect as though made the moment before. One wolf had been caught in a wild lunge of the maddened victim and trampled to death. A few bones, well picked, bore witness.

Again, they ceased the uplift of their snowshoes at a second stand. Here the great animal had fought desperately. Twice had he been dragged down, as the snow attested, and twice had he shaken his assailants clear and gained footing once more. He had done his task long since, but none the less was life dear to him. Zing-ha said it was a strange thing, a moose once down to get free again; but this one certainly had. The shaman would see signs and wonders in this when they told him.

And yet again, they come to where the moose had made to mount the bank and gain the timber. But his foes had laid on from behind, till he reared and fell back upon them, crushing two deep into the snow. It was plain the kill was at hand, for their brothers had left them untouched. Two more stands were hurried past, brief in time-length and very close together. The trail was red now, and the clean stride of the great beast had grown short and slovenly. Then they heard the first sounds of the battle—not the full-throated chorus of the chase, but the short, snappy bark which spoke of close quarters and teeth to flesh. Crawling up the wind, Zing-ha bellied it through the snow, and with him crept he, Koskoosh, who was to be chief of the tribesmen in the years to come. Together they shoved aside the under branches of a young spruce and peered forth. It was the end they saw.

The picture, like all of youth's impressions, was still strong with him, and his dim eyes watched the end played out as vividly as in that far-off time. Koskoosh marveled at this, for in the days which followed, when he was a leader of men and a head of councilors, he had done great deeds and made his name a curse in the mouths of the Pellys, to say naught of the strange white man he had killed, knife to knife, in open fight.

For long he pondered on the days of his youth, till the fire died down and the frost bit deeper. He replenished it with two sticks this time, and gauged his grip on life by what remained. If Sit-cum-to-ha had only remembered her grandfather, and gathered a larger armful, his hours would have been longer. It would have been easy. But she was ever a careless child, and honored not her ancestors from the time the Beaver, son of the son of Zing-ha, first cast eyes upon her. Well, what mattered it? Had he not done likewise in his own quick youth? For a while he listened to the silence. Perhaps the heart of his son might soften, and he would come back with the dogs to take his old father on with the tribe to where the caribou ran thick and the fat hung heavy upon them.

He strained his ears, his restless brain for the moment stilled. Not a stir, nothing. He alone took breath in the midst of the great silence. It was very lonely. Hark! What was that? A chill passed over his body. The familiar, long-drawn howl broke the void, and it was close at hand. Then on his darkened eyes was projected the vision of the moose—the old bull moose—the torn flanks and bloody sides, the riddled mane, and the great branching horns, down low and tossing to the last. He saw the flashing forms of gray, the gleaming eyes, the lolling tongues, the slavered fangs. And he saw the inexorable circle close in till it became a dark point in the midst of the stamped snow.

A cold muzzle thrust against his cheek, and at its touch his soul leaped back to the present. His hand shot into the fire and dragged out a burning faggot. Overcome for the nonce by his hereditary fear of man, the brute retreated, raising a prolonged call to his brothers; and greedily they answered, till a ring of crouching, jaw-slobbered gray was stretched round about. The old man listened to the drawing in of this circle. He waved his brand wildly, and sniffs turned to snarls; but the panting brutes refused to scatter. Now one wormed his chest forward, dragging his haunches after, now a second, now a third; but never a one drew back. Why should he cling to life? he asked, and dropped the blazing stick into the snow. It sizzled and went out. The circle grunted uneasily, but held its own. Again he saw the last stand of the old bull moose, and Koskoosh dropped his head wearily upon his knees. What did it matter after all? Was it not the law of life?

NAM-BOK THE UNVERACIOUS

"A BIDARKA, is it not so? Look! a bidarka, and one man who drives clumsily with a paddle!"

Old Bask-Wah-Wan rose to her knees, trembling with weakness and eagerness, and gazed out over the sea.

"Nam-Bok was ever clumsy at the paddle," she maundered reminiscently, shading the sun from her eyes and staring across the silver-spilled water. "Nam-Bok was ever clumsy. I remember...."

But the women and children laughed loudly, and there was a gentle mockery in their laughter, and her voice dwindled till her lips moved without sound.

Koogah lifted his grizzled head from his bone-carving and followed the path of her eyes. Except when wide yaws took it off its course, a bidarka was heading in for the beach. Its occupant was paddling with more strength than dexterity, and made his approach along the zigzag line of most resistance. Koogah's head dropped to his work again, and on the ivory tusk between his knees he scratched the dorsal fin of a fish the like of which never swam in the sea.

"It is doubtless the man from the next village," he said finally, "come to consult with me about the marking of things on bone. And the man is a clumsy man. He will never know how."

"It is Nam-Bok," old Bask-Wah-Wan repeated. "Should I not know my son?" she demanded shrilly. "I say, and I say again, it is Nam-Bok."

"And so thou hast said these many summers," one of the women chided softly. "Ever when the ice passed out of the sea hast thou sat and watched through the long day, saying at each chance canoe, 'This is Nam-Bok.' Nam-Bok is dead, O Bask-Wah-Wan, and the dead do not come back. It cannot be that the dead come back."

"Nam-Bok!" the old woman cried, so loud and clear that the whole village was startled and looked at her.

She struggled to her feet and tottered down the sand. She stumbled over a baby lying in the sun, and the mother hushed its crying and hurled harsh words after the old woman, who took no notice. The children ran down the beach in advance of her, and as the man in the

178

bidarka drew closer, nearly capsizing with one of his ill-directed strokes, the women followed. Koogah dropped his walrus tusk and went also, leaning heavily upon his staff, and after him loitered the men in twos and threes.

The bidarka turned broadside and the ripple of surf threatened to swamp it, only a naked boy ran into the water and pulled the bow high up on the sand. The man stood up and sent a questing glance along the line of villagers. A rainbow sweater, dirty and the worse for wear, clung loosely to his broad shoulders, and a red cotton handkerchief was knotted in sailor fashion about his throat. A fisherman's tam-o'-shanter on his close-clipped head, and dungaree trousers and heavy brogans, completed his outfit.

But he was none the less a striking personage to these simple fisherfolk of the great Yukon Delta, who, all their lives, had stared out on Bering Sea and in that time seen but two white men,—the census enumerator and a lost Jesuit priest. They were a poor people, with neither gold in the ground nor valuable furs in hand, so the whites had passed them afar. Also, the Yukon, through the thousands of years, had shoaled that portion of the sea with the detritus of Alaska till vessels grounded out of sight of land. So the sodden coast, with its long inside reaches and huge mud-land archipelagoes, was avoided by the ships of men, and the fisherfolk knew not that such things were.

Koogah, the Bone-Scratcher, retreated backward in sudden haste, tripping over his staff and falling to the ground. "Nam-Bok!" he cried, as he scrambled wildly for footing. "Nam-Bok, who was blown off to sea, come back!"

The men and women shrank away, and the children scuttled off between their legs. Only Opee-Kwan was brave, as befitted the head man of the village. He strode forward and gazed long and earnestly at the new-comer.

"It *is* Nam-Bok," he said at last, and at the conviction in his voice the women wailed apprehensively and drew farther away.

The lips of the stranger moved indecisively, and his brown throat writhed and wrestled with unspoken words.

"La la, it is Nam-Bok," Bask-Wah-Wan croaked, peering up into his face. "Ever did I say Nam-Bok would come back."

"Ay, it is Nam-Bok come back." This time it was Nam-Bok himself who spoke, putting a leg over the side of the bidarka and standing with one foot afloat and one ashore. Again his throat writhed and wrestled as he grappled after forgotten words. And when the words came forth they were strange of sound and a spluttering of the lips accompanied the gutturals. "Greeting, O brothers," he said, "brothers of old time before I went away with the off-shore wind."

He stepped out with both feet on the sand, and Opee-Kwan waved him back.

"Thou art dead, Nam-Bok," he said.

Nam-Bok laughed. "I am fat."

"Dead men are not fat," Opee-Kwan confessed. "Thou hast fared well, but it is strange. No man may mate with the off-shore wind and come back on the heels of the years."

"I have come back," Nam-Bok answered simply.

"Mayhap thou art a shadow, then, a passing shadow of the Nam-Bok that was. Shadows come back."

"I am hungry. Shadows do not eat."

But Opee-Kwan doubted, and brushed his hand across his brow in sore puzzlement. Nam-Bok was likewise puzzled, and as he looked up and down the line found no welcome in the eyes of the fisherfolk. The men and women whispered together. The children stole timidly back among their elders, and bristling dogs fawned up to him and sniffed suspiciously.

"I bore thee, Nam-Bok, and I gave thee suck when thou wast little," Bask-Wah-Wan whimpered, drawing closer; "and shadow though thou be, or no shadow, I will give thee to eat now."

Nam-Bok made to come to her, but a growl of fear and menace warned him back. He said something in a strange tongue which sounded like "Goddam," and added, "No shadow am I, but a man."

"Who may know concerning the things of mystery?" Opee-Kwan demanded, half of himself and half of his tribespeople. "We are, and in a breath we are not. If the man may become shadow, may not the shadow become man? Nam-Bok was, but is not. This we know, but we do not know if this be Nam-Bok or the shadow of Nam-Bok."

Nam-Bok cleared his throat and made answer. "In the old time long ago, thy father's father, Opee-Kwan, went away and came back on the heels of the years. Nor was a place by the fire denied him. It is said ..." He paused significantly, and they hung on his utterance. "It is said," he repeated, driving his point home with deliberation, "that Sipsip, his *klooch*, bore him two sons after he came back."

"But he had no doings with the off-shore wind," Opee-Kwan retorted. "He went away into the heart of the land, and it is in the nature of things that a man may go on and on into the land."

"And likewise the sea. But that is neither here nor there. It is said ... that thy father's father told strange tales of the things he saw."

"Ay, strange tales he told."

"I, too, have strange tales to tell," Nam-Bok stated insidiously. And, as they wavered, "And presents likewise."

He pulled from the bidarka a shawl, marvelous of texture and color, and flung it about his mother's shoulders. The women voiced a collective sigh of admiration, and old Bask-Wah-Wan ruffled the gay material and patted it and crooned in childish joy.

"He has tales to tell," Koogah muttered. "And presents," a woman seconded.

And Opee-Kwan knew that his people were eager, and further, he was aware himself of an itching curiosity concerning those untold tales. "The fishing has been good," he said judiciously, "and we have oil in plenty. So come, Nam-Bok, let us feast."

Two of the men hoisted the bidarka on their shoulders and carried it up to the fire. Nam-Bok walked by the side of Opee-Kwan, and the villagers followed after, save those of the women who lingered a moment to lay caressing fingers on the shawl.

There was little talk while the feast went on, though many and curious were the glances stolen at the son of Bask-Wah-Wan. This embarrassed him—not because he was modest of spirit, however, but for the fact that the stench of the seal-oil had robbed him of his appetite, and that he keenly desired to conceal his feelings on the subject.

"Eat; thou art hungry," Opee-Kwan commanded, and Nam-Bok shut both his eyes and shoved his fist into the big pot of putrid fish.

"La la, be not ashamed. The seal were many this year, and strong men are ever hungry." And Bask-Wah-Wan sopped a particularly offensive chunk of salmon into the oil and passed it fondly and dripping to her son.

In despair, when premonitory symptoms warned him that his stomach was not so strong as of old, he filled his pipe and struck up a smoke. The people fed on noisily and watched. Few of them could boast of intimate acquaintance with the precious weed, though now and again small quantities and abominable qualities were obtained in trade from the

Eskimos to the northward. Koogah, sitting next to him, indicated that he was not averse to taking a draw, and between two mouthfuls, with the oil thick on his lips, sucked away at the amber stem. And thereupon Nam-Bok held his stomach with a shaky hand and declined the proffered return. Koogah could keep the pipe, he said, for he had intended so to honor him from the first. And the people licked their fingers and approved of his liberality.

Opee-Kwan rose to his feet "And now, O Nam-Bok, the feast is ended, and we would listen concerning the strange things you have seen."

The fisherfolk applauded with their hands, and gathering about them their work, prepared to listen. The men were busy fashioning spears and carving on ivory, while the women scraped the fat from the hides of the hair seal and made them pliable or sewed muclucs with threads of sinew. Nam-Bok's eyes roved over the scene, but there was not the charm about it that his recollection had warranted him to expect. During the years of his wandering he had looked forward to just this scene, and now that it had come he was disappointed. It was a bare and meagre life, he deemed, and not to be compared to the one to which he had become used. Still, he would open their eyes a bit, and his own eyes sparkled at the thought.

"Brothers," he began, with the smug complacency of a man about to relate the big things he has done, "it was late summer of many summers back, with much such weather as this promises to be, when I went away. You all remember the day, when the gulls flew low, and the wind blew strong from the land, and I could not hold my bidarka against it. I tied the covering of the bidarka about me so that no water could get in, and all of the night I fought with the storm. And in the morning there was no land,—only the sea,—and the off-shore wind held me close in its arms and bore me along. Three such nights whitened into dawn and showed me no land, and the off-shore wind would not let me go.

"And when the fourth day came, I was as a madman. I could not dip my paddle for want of food; and my head went round and round, what of the thirst that was upon me. But the sea was no longer angry, and the soft south wind was blowing, and as I looked about me I saw a sight that made me think I was indeed mad."

Nam-Bok paused to pick away a sliver of salmon lodged between his teeth, and the men and women, with idle hands and heads craned forward, waited.

"It was a canoe, a big canoe. If all the canoes I have ever seen were made into one canoe, it would not be so large."

There were exclamations of doubt, and Koogah, whose years were many, shook his head.

"If each bidarka were as a grain of sand," Nam-Bok defiantly continued, "and if there were as many bidarkas as there be grains of sand in this beach, still would they not make so big a canoe as this I saw on the morning of the fourth day. It was a very big canoe, and it was called a *schooner*. I saw this thing of wonder, this great schooner, coming after me, and on it I saw men—"

"Hold, O Nam-Bok!" Opee-Kwan broke in. "What manner of men were they?—big men?"

"Nay, mere men like you and me."

"Did the big canoe come fast?"

"Ay."

"The sides were tall, the men short." Opee-Kwan stated the premises with conviction. "And did these men dip with long paddles?"

Nam-Bok grinned. "There were no paddles," he said.

Mouths remained open, and a long silence dropped down. Opee-Kwan borrowed

Koogah's pipe for a couple of contemplative sucks. One of the younger women giggled nervously and drew upon herself angry eyes.

"There were no paddles?" Opee-Kwan asked softly, returning the pipe.

"The south wind was behind," Nam-Bok explained.

"But the wind-drift is slow."

"The schooner had wings—thus." He sketched a diagram of masts and sails in the sand, and the men crowded around and studied it. The wind was blowing briskly, and for more graphic elucidation he seized the corners of his mother's shawl and spread them out till it bellied like a sail. Bask-Wah-Wan scolded and struggled, but was blown down the beach for a score of feet and left breathless and stranded in a heap of driftwood. The men uttered sage grunts of comprehension, but Koogah suddenly tossed back his hoary head.

"Ho! Ho!" he laughed. "A foolish thing, this big canoe! A most foolish thing! The plaything of the wind! Wheresoever the wind goes, it goes too. No man who journeys therein may name the landing beach, for always he goes with the wind, and the wind goes everywhere, but no man knows where."

"It is so," Opee-Kwan supplemented gravely. "With the wind the going is easy, but against the wind a man striveth hard; and for that they had no paddles these men on the big canoe did not strive at all."

"Small need to strive," Nam-Bok cried angrily. "The schooner went likewise against the wind."

"And what said you made the sch—sch—schooner go?" Koogah asked, tripping craftily over the strange word.

"The wind," was the impatient response.

"Then the wind made the sch—sch—schooner go against the wind." Old Koogah dropped an open leer to Opee-Kwan, and, the laughter growing around him, continued: "The wind blows from the south and blows the schooner south. The wind blows against the wind. The wind blows one way and the other at the same time. It is very simple. We understand, Nam-Bok. We clearly understand."

"Thou art a fool!"

"Truth falls from thy lips," Koogah answered meekly. "I was over-long in understanding, and the thing was simple."

But Nam-Bok's face was dark, and he said rapid words which they had never heard before. Bone-scratching and skin-scraping were resumed, but he shut his lips tightly on the tongue that could not be believed.

"This sch—sch—schooner," Koogah imperturbably asked; "it was made of a big tree?"

"It was made of many trees," Nam-Bok snapped shortly. "It was very big."

He lapsed into sullen silence again, and Opee-Kwan nudged Koogah, who shook his head with slow amazement and murmured, "It is very strange."

Nam-bok took the bait. "That is nothing," he said airily; "you should see the *steamer*. As the grain of sand is to the bidarka, as the bidarka is to the schooner, so the schooner is to the steamer. Further, the steamer is made of iron. It is all iron."

"Nay, nay, Nam-Bok," cried the head man; "how can that be? Always iron goes to the bottom. For behold, I received an iron knife in trade from the head man of the next village, and yesterday the iron knife slipped from my fingers and went down, down, into the sea. To all things there be law. Never was there one thing outside the law. This we know. And, moreover, we know that things of a kind have the one law, and that all iron has the one law. So unsay thy words, Nam-Bok, that we may yet honor thee."

"It is so," Nam-Bok persisted. "The steamer is all iron and does not sink."

"Nay, nay; this cannot be."

"With my own eyes I saw it."

"It is not in the nature of things."

"But tell me, Nam-Bok," Koogah interrupted, for fear the tale would go no farther, "tell me the manner of these men in finding their way across the sea when there is no land by which to steer."

"The sun points out the path."

"But how?"

"At midday the head man of the schooner takes a thing through which his eye looks at the sun, and then he makes the sun climb down out of the sky to the edge of the earth."

"Now this be evil medicine!" cried Opee-Kwan, aghast at the sacrilege. The men held up their hands in horror, and the women moaned. "This be evil medicine. It is not good to misdirect the great sun which drives away the night and gives us the seal, the salmon, and warm weather."

"What if it be evil medicine?" Nam-Bok demanded truculently. "I, too, have looked through the thing at the sun and made the sun climb down out of the sky."

Those who were nearest drew away from him hurriedly, and a woman covered the face of a child at her breast so that his eye might not fall upon it.

"But on the morning of the fourth day, O Nam-Bok," Koogah suggested; "on the morning of the fourth day when the sch—sch—schooner came after thee?"

"I had little strength left in me and could not run away. So I was taken on board and water was poured down my throat and good food given me. Twice, my brothers, you have seen a white man. These men were all white and as many as have I fingers and toes. And when I saw they were full of kindness, I took heart, and I resolved to bring away with me report of all that I saw. And they taught me the work they did, and gave me good food and a place to sleep.

"And day after day we went over the sea, and each day the head man drew the sun down out of the sky and made it tell where we were. And when the waves were kind, we hunted the fur seal and I marveled much, for always did they fling the meat and the fat away and save only the skin."

Opee-Kwan's mouth was twitching violently, and he was about to make denunciation of such waste when Koogah kicked him to be still.

"After a weary time, when the sun was gone and the bite of the frost come into the air, the head man pointed the nose of the schooner south. South and east we travelled for days upon days, with never the land in sight, and we were near to the village from which hailed the men—"

"How did they know they were near?" Opee-Kwan, unable to contain himself longer, demanded. "There was no land to see."

Nam-Bok glowered on him wrathfully. "Did I not say the head man brought the sun down out of the sky?"

Koogah interposed, and Nam-Bok went on.

"As I say, when we were near to that village a great storm blew up, and in the night we were helpless and knew not where we were—"

"Thou hast just said the head man knew—"

"Oh, peace, Opee-Kwan! Thou art a fool and cannot understand. As I say, we were helpless in the night, when I heard, above the roar of the storm, the sound of the sea on the beach. And next we struck with a mighty crash and I was in the water, swimming. It was a rock-bound coast, with one patch of beach in many miles, and the law was that I should dig my hands into the sand and draw myself clear of the surf. The other men must have pounded against the rocks, for none of them came ashore but the head man, and him I knew only by the ring on his finger.

"When day came, there being nothing of the schooner, I turned my face to the land and journeyed into it that I might get food and look upon the faces of the people. And when I came to a house I was taken in and given to eat, for I had learned their speech, and the white men are ever kindly. And it was a house bigger than all the houses built by us and our fathers before us."

"It was a mighty house," Koogah said, masking his unbelief with wonder.

"And many trees went into the making of such a house," Opee-Kwan added, taking the cue.

"That is nothing." Nam-Bok shrugged his shoulders in belittling fashion. "As our houses are to that house, so that house was to the houses I was yet to see."

"And they are not big men?"

"Nay; mere men like you and me," Nam-Bok answered. "I had cut a stick that I might walk in comfort, and remembering that I was to bring report to you, my brothers, I cut a notch in the stick for each person who lived in that house. And I stayed there many days, and worked, for which they gave me *money*—a thing of which you know nothing, but which is very good.

"And one day I departed from that place to go farther into the land. And as I walked I met many people, and I cut smaller notches in the stick, that there might be room for all. Then I came upon a strange thing. On the ground before me was a bar of iron, as big in thickness as my arm, and a long step away was another bar of iron—"

"Then wert thou a rich man," Opee-Kwan asserted; "for iron be worth more than anything else in the world. It would have made many knives."

"Nay, it was not mine."

"It was a find, and a find be lawful."

"Not so; the white men had placed it there And further, these bars were so long that no man could carry them away—so long that as far as I could see there was no end to them."

"Nam-Bok, that is very much iron," Opee-Kwan cautioned.

"Ay, it was hard to believe with my own eyes upon it; but I could not gainsay my eyes. And as I looked I heard...." He turned abruptly upon the head man. "Opee-Kwan, thou hast heard the sea-lion bellow in his anger. Make it plain in thy mind of as many sea-lions as there be waves to the sea, and make it plain that all these sea-lions be made into one sea-lion, and as that one sea-lion would bellow so bellowed the thing I heard."

The fisherfolk cried aloud in astonishment, and Opee-Kwan's jaw lowered and remained lowered.

"And in the distance I saw a monster like unto a thousand whales. It was one-eyed, and vomited smoke, and it snorted with exceeding loudness. I was afraid and ran with shaking legs along the path between the bars. But it came with the speed of the wind, this monster, and I leaped the iron bars with its breath hot on my face...."

Opee-Kwan gained control of his jaw again. "And—and then, O Nam-Bok?"

"Then it came by on the bars, and harmed me not; and when my legs could hold me up again it was gone from sight. And it is a very common thing in that country. Even the women and children are not afraid. Men make them to do work, these monsters."

"As we make our dogs do work?" Koogah asked, with sceptic twinkle in his eye.

"Ay, as we make our dogs do work."

"And how do they breed these—these things?" Opee-Kwan questioned.

"They breed not at all. Men fashion them cunningly of iron, and feed them with stone, and give them water to drink. The stone becomes fire, and the water becomes steam, and the steam of the water is the breath of their nostrils, and—"

"There, there, O Nam-Bok," Opee-Kwan interrupted. "Tell us of other wonders. We grow tired of this which we may not understand."

"You do not understand?" Nam-Bok asked despairingly.

"Nay, we do not understand," the men and women wailed back. "We cannot understand."

Nam-Bok thought of a combined harvester, and of the machines wherein visions of living men were to be seen, and of the machines from which came the voices of men, and he knew his people could never understand.

"Dare I say I rode this iron monster through the land?" he asked bitterly.

Opee-Kwan threw up his hands, palms outward, in open incredulity. "Say on; say anything. We listen."

"Then did I ride the iron monster, for which I gave money—"

"Thou saidst it was fed with stone."

"And likewise, thou fool, I said money was a thing of which you know nothing. As I say, I rode the monster through the land, and through many villages, until I came to a big village on a salt arm of the sea. And the houses shoved their roofs among the stars in the sky, and the clouds drifted by them, and everywhere was much smoke. And the roar of that village was like the roar of the sea in storm, and the people were so many that I flung away my stick and no longer remembered the notches upon it."

"Hadst thou made small notches," Koogah reproved, "thou mightst have brought report."

Nam-Bok whirled upon him in anger. "Had I made small notches! Listen, Koogah, thou scratcher of bone! If I had made small notches, neither the stick, nor twenty sticks, could have borne them—nay, not all the driftwood of all the beaches between this village and the next. And if all of you, the women and children as well, were twenty times as many, and if you had twenty hands each, and in each hand a stick and a knife, still the notches could not be cut for the people I saw, so many were they and so fast did they come and go."

"There cannot be so many people in all the world," Opee-Kwan objected, for he was stunned and his mind could not grasp such magnitude of numbers.

"What dost thou know of all the world and how large it is?" Nam-Bok demanded.

"But there cannot be so many people in one place."

"Who art thou to say what can be and what cannot be?"

"It stands to reason there cannot be so many people in one place. Their canoes would clutter the sea till there was no room. And they could empty the sea each day of its fish, and they would not all be fed."

"So it would seem," Nam-Bok made final answer; "yet it was so. With my own eyes I saw, and flung my stick away." He yawned heavily and rose to his feet. "I have paddled far. The day has been long, and I am tired. Now I will sleep, and to-morrow we will have further talk upon the things I have seen."

Bask-Wah-Wan, hobbling fearfully in advance, proud indeed, yet awed by her wonderful son, led him to her igloo and stowed him away among the greasy, ill-smelling furs. But the men lingered by the fire, and a council was held wherein was there much whispering and low-voiced discussion.

An hour passed, and a second, and Nam-Bok slept, and the talk went on. The evening sun dipped toward the northwest, and at eleven at night was nearly due north. Then it was that the head man and the bone-scratcher separated themselves from the council and aroused Nam-Bok. He blinked up into their faces and turned on his side to sleep again. Opee-Kwan gripped him by the arm and kindly but firmly shook his senses back into him.

"Come, Nam-Bok, arise!" he commanded. "It be time."

"Another feast?" Nam-Bok cried. "Nay, I am not hungry. Go on with the eating and let me sleep."

"Time to be gone!" Koogah thundered.

But Opee-Kwan spoke more softly. "Thou wast bidarka-mate with me when we were boys," he said. "Together we first chased the seal and drew the salmon from the traps. And thou didst drag me back to life, Nam-Bok, when the sea closed over me and I was sucked down to the black rocks. Together we hungered and bore the chill of the frost, and together we crawled beneath the one fur and lay close to each other. And because of these things, and the kindness in which I stood to thee, it grieves me sore that thou shouldst return such a remarkable liar. We cannot understand, and our heads be dizzy with the things thou hast spoken. It is not good, and there has been much talk in the council. Wherefore we send thee away, that our heads may remain clear and strong and be not troubled by the unaccountable things."

"These things thou speakest of be shadows," Koogah took up the strain. "From the shadow-world thou hast brought them, and to the shadow-world thou must return them. Thy bidarka be ready, and the tribespeople wait. They may not sleep until thou art gone."

Nam-Bok was perplexed, but hearkened to the voice of the head man.

"If thou art Nam-Bok," Opee-Kwan was saying, "thou art a fearful and most wonderful liar; if thou art the shadow of Nam-Bok, then thou speakest of shadows, concerning which it is not good that living men have knowledge. This great village thou hast spoken of we deem the village of shadows. Therein flutter the souls of the dead; for the dead be many and the living few. The dead do not come back. Never have the dead come back—save thou with thy wonder-tales. It is not meet that the dead come back, and should we permit it, great trouble may be our portion."

Nam-Bok knew his people well and was aware that the voice of the council was supreme. So he allowed himself to be led down to the water's edge, where he was put aboard his bidarka and a paddle thrust into his hand. A stray wild-fowl honked somewhere to seaward, and the surf broke limply and hollowly on the sand. A dim twilight brooded over land and water, and in the north the sun smouldered, vague and troubled, and draped about with blood-red mists. The gulls were flying low. The off-shore wind blew keen and chill, and the black-massed clouds behind it gave promise of bitter weather.

"Out of the sea thou earnest," Opee-Kwan chanted oracularly, "and back into the sea thou goest. Thus is balance achieved and all things brought to law."

Bask-Wah-Wan limped to the froth-mark and cried, "I bless thee, Nam-Bok, for that thou remembered me."

But Koogah, shoving Nam-Bok clear of the beach, tore the shawl from her shoulders and flung it into the bidarka.

"It is cold in the long nights," she wailed; "and the frost is prone to nip old bones."

"The thing is a shadow," the bone-scratcher answered, "and shadows cannot keep thee warm."

Nam-Bok stood up that his voice might carry. "O Bask-Wah-Wan, mother that bore me!" he called. "Listen to the words of Nam-Bok, thy son. There be room in his bidarka for two, and he would that thou camest with him. For his journey is to where there are fish and oil in plenty. There the frost comes not, and life is easy, and the things of iron do the work of men. Wilt thou come, O Bask-Wah-Wan?"

She debated a moment, while the bidarka drifted swiftly from her, then raised her voice to a quavering treble. "I am old, Nam-Bok, and soon I shall pass down among the shadows. But I have no wish to go before my time. I am old, Nam-Bok, and I am afraid."

A shaft of light shot across the dim-lit sea and wrapped boat and man in a splendor of red and gold. Then a hush fell upon the fisherfolk, and only was heard the moan of the off-shore wind and the cries of the gulls flying low in the air.

THE MASTER OF MYSTERY

THERE WAS complaint in the village. The women chattered together with shrill, high-pitched voices. The men were glum and doubtful of aspect, and the very dogs wandered dubiously about, alarmed in vague ways by the unrest of the camp, and ready to take to the woods on the first outbreak of trouble. The air was filled with suspicion. No man was sure of his neighbor, and each was conscious that he stood in like unsureness with his fellows. Even the children were oppressed and solemn, and little Di Ya, the cause of it all, had been soundly thrashed, first by Hooniah, his mother, and then by his father, Bawn, and was now whimpering and looking pessimistically out upon the world from the shelter of the big overturned canoe on the beach.

And to make the matter worse, Scundoo, the shaman, was in disgrace, and his known magic could not be called upon to seek out the evil-doer. Forsooth, a month gone, he had promised a fair south wind so that the tribe might journey to the *potlatch* at Tonkin, where Taku Jim was giving away the savings of twenty years; and when the day came, lo, a grievous north wind blew, and of the first three canoes to venture forth, one was swamped in the big seas, and two were pounded to pieces on the rocks, and a child was drowned. He had pulled the string of the wrong bag, he explained,—a mistake. But the people refused to listen; the offerings of meat and fish and fur ceased to come to his door; and he sulked within—so they thought, fasting in bitter penance; in reality, eating generously from his well-stored cache and meditating upon the fickleness of the mob.

The blankets of Hooniah were missing. They were good blankets, of most marvelous thickness and warmth, and her pride in them was greatened in that they had been come by so cheaply. Ty-Kwan, of the next village but one, was a fool to have so easily parted with them. But then, she did not know they were the blankets of the murdered Englishman, because of whose take-off the United States cutter nosed along the coast for a time, while its launches puffed and snorted among the secret inlets. And not knowing that Ty-Kwan had disposed of them in haste so that his own people might not have to render account to the Government, Hooniah's pride was unshaken. And because the women envied her, her pride was without end and boundless, till it filled the village and spilled over along the Alaskan

188

shore from Dutch Harbor to St. Mary's. Her totem had become justly celebrated, and her name known on the lips of men wherever men fished and feasted, what of the blankets and their marvelous thickness and warmth. It was a most mysterious happening, the manner of their going.

"I but stretched them up in the sun by the side-wall of the house," Hooniah disclaimed for the thousandth time to her Thlinget sisters. "I but stretched them up and turned my back; for Di Ya, dough-thief and eater of raw flour that he is, with head into the big iron pot, over-turned and stuck there, his legs waving like the branches of a forest tree in the wind. And I did but drag him out and twice knock his head against the door for riper understanding, and behold, the blankets were not!"

"The blankets were not!" the women repeated in awed whispers.

"A great loss," one added. A second, "Never were there such blankets." And a third, "We be sorry, Hooniah, for thy loss." Yet each woman of them was glad in her heart that the odious, dissension-breeding blankets were gone. "I but stretched them up in the sun," Hooniah began for the thousand and first time.

"Yea, yea," Bawn spoke up, wearied. "But there were no gossips in the village from other places. Wherefore it be plain that some of our own tribespeople have laid unlawful hand upon the blankets."

"How can that be, O Bawn?" the women chorussed indignantly. "Who should there be?"

"Then has there been witchcraft," Bawn continued stolidly enough, though he stole a sly glance at their faces.

"*Witchcraft!*" And at the dread word their voices hushed and each looked fearfully at each.

"Ay," Hooniah affirmed, the latent malignancy of her nature flashing into a moment's exultation. "And word has been sent to Klok-No-Ton, and strong paddles. Truly shall he be here with the afternoon tide."

The little groups broke up, and fear descended upon the village. Of all misfortune, witch-craft was the most appalling. With the intangible and unseen things only the shamans could cope, and neither man, woman, nor child could know, until the moment of ordeal, whether devils possessed their souls or not. And of all shamans, Klok-No-Ton, who dwelt in the next village, was the most terrible. None found more evil spirits than he, none visited his victims with more frightful tortures. Even had he found, once, a devil residing within the body of a three-months babe—a most obstinate devil which could only be driven out when the babe had lain for a week on thorns and briers. The body was thrown into the sea after that, but the waves tossed it back again and again as a curse upon the village, nor did it finally go away till two strong men were staked out at low tide and drowned.

And Hooniah had sent for this Klok-No-Ton. Better had it been if Scundoo, their own shaman, were undisgraced. For he had ever a gentler way, and he had been known to drive forth two devils from a man who afterward begat seven healthy children. But Klok-No-Ton! They shuddered with dire foreboding at thought of him, and each one felt himself the centre of accusing eyes, and looked accusingly upon his fellows—each one and all, save Sime, and Sime was a scoffer whose evil end was destined with a certitude his successes could not shake.

"Hoh! Hoh!" he laughed. "Devils and Klok-No-Ton!—than whom no greater devil can be found in Thlinket Land."

"Thou fool! Even now he cometh with witcheries and sorceries; so beware thy tongue, lest evil befall thee and thy days be short in the land!"

So spoke La-lah, otherwise the Cheater, and Sime laughed scornfully.

"I am Sime, unused to fear, unafraid of the dark. I am a strong man, as my father before me, and my head is clear. Nor you nor I have seen with our eyes the unseen evil things—"

"But Scundoo hath," La-lah made answer. "And likewise Klok-No-Ton. This we know."

"How dost thou know, son of a fool?" Sime thundered, the choleric blood darkening his thick bull neck.

"By the word of their mouths—even so."

Sime snorted. "A shaman is only a man. May not his words be crooked, even as thine and mine? Bah! Bah! And once more, bah! And this for thy shamans and thy shamans' devils! and this! and this!"

And snapping his fingers to right and left, Sime strode through the on-lookers, who made over-zealous and fearsome way for him.

"A good fisher and strong hunter, but an evil man," said one.

"Yet does he flourish," speculated another.

"Wherefore be thou evil and flourish," Sime retorted over his shoulder. "And were all evil, there would be no need for shamans. Bah! You children-afraid-of-the-dark!"

And when Klok-No-Ton arrived on the afternoon tide, Sime's defiant laugh was unabated; nor did he forbear to make a joke when the shaman tripped on the sand in the landing. Klok-No-Ton looked at him sourly, and without greeting stalked straight through their midst to the house of Scundoo.

Of the meeting with Scundoo none of the tribespeople might know, for they clustered reverently in the distance and spoke in whispers while the masters of mystery were together.

"Greeting, O Scundoo!" Klok-No-Ton rumbled, wavering perceptibly from doubt of his reception.

He was a giant in stature, and towered massively above little Scundoo, whose thin voice floated upward like the faint far rasping of a cricket.

"Greeting, Klok-No-Ton," he returned. "The day is fair with thy coming."

"Yet it would seem ..." Klok-No-Ton hesitated.

"Yea, yea," the little shaman put in impatiently, "that I have fallen on ill days, else would I not stand in gratitude to you in that you do my work."

"It grieves me, friend Scundoo ..."

"Nay, I am made glad, Klok-No-Ton."

"But will I give thee half of that which be given me."

"Not so, good Klok-No-Ton," murmured Scundoo, with a deprecatory wave of the hand. "It is I who am thy slave, and my days shall be filled with desire to befriend thee."

"As I—"

"As thou now befriendest me."

"That being so, it is then a bad business, these blankets of the woman Hooniah?"

The big shaman blundered tentatively in his quest, and Scundoo smiled a wan, gray smile, for he was used to reading men, and all men seemed very small to him.

"Ever hast thou dealt in strong medicine," he said. "Doubtless the evil-doer will be briefly known to thee."

"Ay, briefly known when I set eyes upon him." Again Klok-No-Ton hesitated. "Have there been gossips from other places?" he asked.

Scundoo shook his head. "Behold! Is this not a most excellent mucluc?"

He held up the foot-covering of sealskin and walrus hide, and his visitor examined it with secret interest.

"It did come to me by a close-driven bargain."

Klok-No-Ton nodded attentively.

"I got it from the man La-lah. He is a remarkable man, and often have I thought ..."

"So?" Klok-No-Ton ventured impatiently.

"Often have I thought," Scundoo concluded, his voice falling as he came to a full pause. "It is a fair day, and thy medicine be strong, Klok-No-Ton."

Klok-No-Ton's face brightened. "Thou art a great man, Scundoo, a shaman of shamans. I go now. I shall remember thee always. And the man La-lah, as you say, is a remarkable man."

Scundoo smiled yet more wan and gray, closed the door on the heels of his departing visitor, and barred and double-barred it.

Sime was mending his canoe when Klok-No-Ton came down the beach, and he broke off from his work only long enough to ostentatiously load his rifle and place it near him.

The shaman noted the action and called out: "Let all the people come together on this spot! It is the word of Klok-No-Ton, devil-seeker and driver of devils!"

He had been minded to assemble them at Hooniah's house, but it was necessary that all should be present, and he was doubtful of Sime's obedience and did not wish trouble. Sime was a good man to let alone, his judgment ran, and withal, a bad one for the health of any shaman.

"Let the woman Hooniah be brought," Klok-No-Ton commanded, glaring ferociously about the circle and sending chills up and down the spines of those he looked upon.

Hooniah waddled forward, head bent and gaze averted.

"Where be thy blankets?"

"I but stretched them up in the sun, and behold, they were not!" she whined.

"So?"

"It was because of Di Ya."

"So?"

"Him have I beaten sore, and he shall yet be beaten, for that he brought trouble upon us who be poor people."

"The blankets!" Klok-No-Ton bellowed hoarsely, foreseeing her desire to lower the price to be paid. "The blankets, woman! Thy wealth is known."

"I but stretched them up in the sun," she sniffled, "and we be poor people and have nothing."

He stiffened suddenly, with a hideous distortion of the face, and Hooniah shrank back. But so swiftly did he spring forward, with in-turned eyeballs and loosened jaw, that she stumbled and fell down groveling at his feet. He waved his arms about, wildly flagellating the air, his body writhing and twisting in torment. An epilepsy seemed to come upon him. A white froth flecked his lips, and his body was convulsed with shiverings and tremblings.

The women broke into a wailing chant, swaying backward and forward in abandonment, while one by one the men succumbed to the excitement till only Sime remained. He, perched upon his canoe, looked on in mockery; yet the ancestors whose seed he bore pressed heavily upon him, and he swore his strongest oaths that his courage might be cheered. Klok-No-Ton was horrible to behold. He had cast off his blanket and torn his clothes from him, so that he was quite naked, save for a girdle of eagle-claws about his thighs. Shrieking and yelling, his long black hair flying like a blot of night, he leaped frantically about the circle. A certain rude rhythm characterized his frenzy, and when all were under its sway, swinging their bodies in accord with his and venting their cries in unison, he sat bolt upright, with arm outstretched and long, talon-like finger extended. A low moaning, as of the dead, greeted this, and the people cowered with shaking knees as the dread finger passed them slowly by. For death went with it, and life remained with those who watched it go; and being rejected, they watched with eager intentness.

Finally, with a tremendous cry, the fateful finger rested upon La-lah. He shook like an aspen, seeing himself already dead, his household goods divided, and his widow married to his brother. He strove to speak, to deny, but his tongue clove to his mouth and his throat was sanded with an intolerable thirst. Klok-No-Ton seemed to half swoon away, now that his work was done; but he waited, with closed eyes, listening for the great blood-cry to go up— the great blood-cry, familiar to his ear from a thousand conjurations, when the tribespeople flung themselves like wolves upon the trembling victim. But only was there silence, then a low tittering, from nowhere in particular, which spread and spread until a vast laughter welled up to the sky.

"Wherefore?" he cried.

"Na! Na!" the people laughed. "Thy medicine be ill, O Klok-No-Ton!"

"It be known to all," La-lah stuttered. "For eight weary months have I been gone afar with the Siwash sealers, and but this day am I come back to find the blankets of Hooniah gone ere I came!"

"It be true!" they cried with one accord. "The blankets of Hooniah were gone ere he came!"

"And thou shalt be paid nothing for thy medicine which is of no avail," announced Hooniah, on her feet once more and smarting from a sense of ridiculousness.

But Klok-No-Ton saw only the face of Scundoo and its wan, gray smile, heard only the faint far cricket's rasping. "I got it from the man La-lah, and often have I thought," and, "It is a fair day and thy medicine be strong."

He brushed by Hooniah, and the circle instinctively gave way for him to pass. Sime flung a jeer from the top of the canoe, the women snickered in his face, cries of derision rose in his wake, but he took no notice, pressing onward to the house of Scundoo. He hammered on the door, beat it with his fists, and howled vile imprecations. Yet there was no response, save that in the lulls Scundoo's voice rose eerily in incantation. Klok-No-Ton raged about like a madman, but when he attempted to break in the door with a huge stone, murmurs arose from the men and women. And he, Klok-No-Ton, knew that he stood shorn of his strength and authority before an alien people. He saw a man stoop for a stone, and a second, and a bodily fear ran through him.

"Harm not Scundoo, who is a master!" a woman cried out.

"Better you return to your own village," a man advised menacingly.

Klok-No-Ton turned on his heel and went down among them to the beach, a bitter rage at his heart, and in his head a just apprehension for his defenseless back. But no stones were cast. The children swarmed mockingly about his feet, and the air was wild with laughter and derision, but that was all. Yet he did not breathe freely until the canoe was well out upon the water, when he rose up and laid a futile curse upon the village and its people, not forgetting to particularly specify Scundoo who had made a mock of him.

Ashore there was a clamor for Scundoo, and the whole population crowded his door, entreating and imploring in confused babel till he came forth and raised his hand.

"In that ye are my children I pardon freely," he said. "But never again. For the last time thy foolishness goes unpunished. That which ye wish shall be granted, and it be already known to me. This night, when the moon has gone behind the world to look upon the mighty dead, let all the people gather in the blackness before the house of Hooniah. Then shall the evil-doer stand forth and take his merited reward. I have spoken."

"It shall be death!" Bawn vociferated, "for that it hath brought worry upon us, and shame."

"So be it," Scundoo replied, and shut his door.

"Now shall all be made clear and plain, and content rest upon us once again," La-lah declaimed oracularly.

"Because of Scundoo, the little man," Sime sneered.

"Because of the medicine of Scundoo, the little man," La-lah corrected.

"Children of foolishness, these Thlinket people!" Sime smote his thigh a resounding blow. "It passeth understanding that grown women and strong men should get down in the dirt to dream-things and wonder tales."

"I am a travelled man," La-lah answered. "I have journeyed on the deep seas and seen signs and wonders, and I know that these things be so. I am La-lah—"

"The Cheater—"

"So called, but the Far-Journeyer right-named."

"I am not so great a traveler—" Sime began.

"Then hold thy tongue," Bawn cut in, and they separated in anger.

When the last silver moonlight had vanished beyond the world, Scundoo came among the people huddled about the house of Hooniah. He walked with a quick, alert step, and those who saw him in the light of Hooniah's slush-lamp noticed that he came empty-handed, without rattles, masks, or shaman's paraphernalia, save for a great sleepy raven carried under one arm.

"Is there wood gathered for a fire, so that all may see when the work be done?" he demanded.

"Yea," Bawn answered. "There be wood in plenty."

"Then let all listen, for my words be few. With me have I brought Jelchs, the Raven, diviner of mystery and seer of things. Him, in his blackness, shall I place under the big black pot of Hooniah, in the blackest corner of her house. The slush-lamp shall cease to burn, and all remain in outer darkness. It is very simple. One by one shall ye go into the house, lay hand upon the pot for the space of one long intake of the breath, and withdraw again. Doubtless Jelchs will make outcry when the hand of the evil-doer is nigh him. Or who knows but otherwise he may manifest his wisdom. Are ye ready?"

"We be ready," came the multi-voiced response.

"Then will I call the name aloud, each in his turn and hers, till all are called."

Thereat La-lah was first chosen, and he passed in at once. Every ear strained, and through the silence they could hear his footsteps creaking across the rickety floor. But that was all. Jelchs made no outcry, gave no sign. Bawn was next chosen, for it well might be that a man should steal his own blankets with intent to cast shame upon his neighbors. Hooniah followed, and other women and children, but without result.

"Sime!" Scundoo called out.

"Sime!" he repeated.

But Sime did not stir.

"Art thou afraid of the dark?" La-lah, his own integrity being proved, demanded fiercely.

Sime chuckled. "I laugh at it all, for it is a great foolishness. Yet will I go in, not in belief in wonders, but in token that I am unafraid."

And he passed in boldly, and came out still mocking.

"Someday shalt thou die with great suddenness," La-lah whispered, righteously indignant.

"I doubt not," the scoffer answered airily. "Few men of us die in our beds, what of the shamans and the deep sea."

When half the villagers had safely undergone the ordeal, the excitement, because of its repression, was painfully intense. When two-thirds had gone through, a young woman, close on her first child-bed, broke down and in nervous shrieks and laughter gave form to her terror.

Finally the turn came for the last of all to go in, and nothing had happened. And Di Ya was the last of all. It must surely be he. Hooniah let out a lament to the stars, while the rest drew back from the luckless lad. He was half-dead from fright, and his legs gave under him so that he staggered on the threshold and nearly fell. Scundoo shoved him inside and closed the door. A long time went by, during which could be heard only the boy's weeping. Then, very slowly, came the creak of his steps to the far corner, a pause, and the creaking of his return. The door opened and he came forth. Nothing had happened, and he was the last.

"Let the fire be lighted," Scundoo commanded.

The bright flames rushed upward, revealing faces yet marked with vanishing fear, but also clouded with doubt.

"Surely the thing has failed," Hooniah whispered hoarsely.

"Yea," Bawn answered complacently. "Scundoo groweth old, and we stand in need of a new shaman."

"Where now is the wisdom of Jelchs?" Sime snickered in La-lah's ear.

La-lah brushed his brow in a puzzled manner and said nothing.

Sime threw his chest out arrogantly and strutted up to the little shaman. "Hoh! Hoh! As I said, nothing has come of it!"

"So it would seem, so it would seem," Scundoo answered meekly. "And it would seem strange to those unskilled in the affairs of mystery."

"As thou?" Sime queried audaciously.

"Mayhap even as I." Scundoo spoke quite softly, his eyelids drooping, slowly drooping, down, down, till his eyes were all but hidden. "So I am minded of another test. Let every man, woman, and child, now and at once, hold their hands well up above their heads!"

So unexpected was the order, and so imperatively was it given, that it was obeyed without question. Every hand was in the air.

"Let each look on the other's hands, and let all look," Scundoo commanded, "so that—"

But a noise of laughter, which was more of wrath, drowned his voice. All eyes had come to rest upon Sime. Every hand but his was black with soot, and his was guiltless of the smirch of Hooniah's pot.

A stone hurtled through the air and struck him on the cheek.

"It is a lie!" he yelled. "A lie! I know naught of Hooniah's blankets!"

A second stone gashed his brow, a third whistled past his head, the great blood-cry went up, and everywhere were people groping on the ground for missiles. He staggered and half sank down.

"It was a joke! Only a joke!" he shrieked. "I but took them for a joke!"

"Where hast thou hidden them?" Scundoo's shrill, sharp voice cut through the tumult like a knife.

"In the large skin-bale in my house, the one slung by the ridge-pole," came the answer. "But it was a joke, I say, only—"

Scundoo nodded his head, and the air went thick with flying stones. Sime's wife was crying silently, her head upon her knees; but his little boy, with shrieks and laughter, was flinging stones with the rest.

Hooniah came waddling back with the precious blankets. Scundoo stopped her.

"We be poor people and have little," she whimpered. "So be not hard upon us, O Scundoo."

The people ceased from the quivering stone-pile they had builded, and looked on.

"Nay, it was never my way, good Hooniah," Scundoo made answer, reaching for the blankets. "In token that I am not hard, these only shall I take."

"Am I not wise, my children?" he demanded.

"Thou art indeed wise, O Scundoo!" they cried in one voice.

And he went away into the darkness, the blankets around him, and Jelchs nodding sleepily under his arm.

THE SUNLANDERS

MANDELL IS an obscure village on the rim of the polar sea. It is not large, and the people are peaceable, more peaceable even than those of the adjacent tribes. There are few men in Mandell, and many women; wherefore a wholesome and necessary polygamy is in practice; the women bear children with ardor, and the birth of a man-child is hailed with acclamation. Then there is Aab-Waak, whose head rests always on one shoulder, as though at some time the neck had become very tired and refused forevermore its wonted duty.

The cause of all these things,—the peaceableness, and the polygamy, and the tired neck of Aab-Waak,—goes back among the years to the time when the schooner *Search* dropped anchor in Mandell Bay, and when Tyee, chief man of the tribe, conceived a scheme of sudden wealth. To this day the story of things that happened is remembered and spoken of with bated breath by the people of Mandell, who are cousins to the Hungry Folk who live in the west. Children draw closer when the tale is told, and marvel sagely to themselves at the madness of those who might have been their forebears had they not provoked the Sunlanders and come to bitter ends.

It began to happen when six men came ashore from the *Search*, with heavy outfits, as though they had come to stay, and quartered themselves in Neegah's igloo. Not but that they paid well in flour and sugar for the lodging, but Neegah was aggrieved because Mesahchie, his daughter, elected to cast her fortunes and seek food and blanket with Bill-Man, who was leader of the party of white men.

"She is worth a price," Neegah complained to the gathering by the council-fire, when the six white men were asleep. "She is worth a price, for we have more men than women, and the men be bidding high. The hunter Ounenk offered me a kayak, new-made, and a gun which he got in trade from the Hungry Folk. This was I offered, and behold, now she is gone and I have nothing!"

"I, too, did bid for Mesahchie," grumbled a voice, in tones not altogether joyless, and Peelo shoved his broad-cheeked, jovial face for a moment into the light.

"Thou, too," Neegah affirmed. "And there were others. Why is there such a restlessness upon the Sunlanders?" he demanded petulantly. "Why do they not stay at home? The Snow People do not wander to the lands of the Sunlanders."

"Better were it to ask why they come," cried a voice from the darkness, and Aab-Waak pushed his way to the front.

"Ay! Why they come!" clamored many voices, and Aab-Waak waved his hand for silence.

"Men do not dig in the ground for nothing," he began. "And I have it in mind of the Whale People, who are likewise Sunlanders, and who lost their ship in the ice. You all remember the Whale People, who came to us in their broken boats, and who went away into the south with dogs and sleds when the frost arrived and snow covered the land. And you remember, while they waited for the frost, that one man of them dug in the ground, and then two men and three, and then all men of them, with great excitement and much disturbance. What they dug out of the ground we do not know, for they drove us away so we could not see. But afterward, when they were gone, we looked and found nothing. Yet there be much ground and they did not dig it all."

"Ay, Aab-Waak! Ay!" cried the people in admiration.

"Wherefore I have it in mind," he concluded, "that one Sunlander tells another, and that these Sunlanders have been so told and are come to dig in the ground."

"But how can it be that Bill-Man speaks our tongue?" demanded a little weazened old hunter,—"Bill-Man, upon whom never before our eyes have rested?"

"Bill-Man has been other times in the Snow Lands," Aab-Waak answered, "else would he not speak the speech of the Bear People, which is like the speech of the Hungry Folk, which is very like the speech of the Mandells. For there have been many Sunlanders among the Bear People, few among the Hungry Folk, and none at all among the Mandells, save the Whale People and those who sleep now in the igloo of Neegah."

"Their sugar is very good," Neegah commented, "and their flour."

"They have great wealth," Ounenk added. "Yesterday I was to their ship, and beheld most cunning tools of iron, and knives, and guns, and flour, and sugar, and strange foods without end."

"It is so, brothers!" Tyee stood up and exulted inwardly at the respect and silence his people accorded him. "They be very rich, these Sunlanders. Also, they be fools. For behold! They come among us boldly, blindly, and without thought for all of their great wealth. Even now they snore, and we are many and unafraid."

"Mayhap they, too, are unafraid, being great fighters," the weazened little old hunter objected.

But Tyee scowled upon him. "Nay, it would not seem so. They live to the south, under the path of the sun, and are soft as their dogs are soft. You remember the dog of the Whale People? Our dogs ate him the second day, for he was soft and could not fight. The sun is warm and life easy in the Sun Lands, and the men are as women, and the women as children."

Heads nodded in approval, and the women craned their necks to listen.

"It is said they are good to their women, who do little work," tittered Likeeta, a broad-hipped, healthy young woman, daughter to Tyee himself.

"Thou wouldst follow the feet of Mesahchie, eh?" he cried angrily. Then he turned swiftly to the tribesmen. "Look you, brothers, this is the way of the Sunlanders! They have eyes for our women, and take them one by one. As Mesahchie has gone, cheating Neegah of her price, so will Likeeta go, so will they all go, and we be cheated. I have talked with a hunter from the Bear People, and I know. There be Hungry Folk among us; let them speak if my words be true."

The six hunters of the Hungry Folk attested the truth and fell each to telling his neighbor of the Sunlanders and their ways. There were mutterings from the younger men, who had wives to seek, and from the older men, who had daughters to fetch prices, and a low hum of rage rose higher and clearer.

"They are very rich, and have cunning tools of iron, and knives, and guns without end," Tyee suggested craftily, his dream of sudden wealth beginning to take shape.

"I shall take the gun of Bill-Man for myself," Aab-Waak suddenly proclaimed.

"Nay, it shall be mine!" shouted Neegah; "for there is the price of Mesahchie to be reckoned."

"Peace! O brothers!" Tyee swept the assembly with his hands. "Let the women and children go to their igloos. This is the talk of men; let it be for the ears of men."

"There be guns in plenty for all," he said when the women had unwillingly withdrawn. "I doubt not there will be two guns for each man, without thought of the flour and sugar and other things. And it is easy. The six Sunlanders in Neegah's igloo will we kill to-night while they sleep. To-morrow will we go in peace to the ship to trade, and there, when the time favors, kill all their brothers. And to-morrow night there shall be feasting and merriment and division of wealth. And the least man shall possess more than did ever the greatest before. Is it wise, that which I have spoken, brothers?"

A low growl of approval answered him, and preparation for the attack was begun. The six Hungry Folk, as became members of a wealthier tribe, were armed with rifles and plenteously supplied with ammunition. But it was only here and there that a Mandell possessed a gun, many of which were broken, and there was a general slackness of powder and shells. This poverty of war weapons, however, was relieved by myriads of bone-headed arrows and casting-spears for work at a distance, and for close quarters steel knives of Russian and Yankee make.

"Let there be no noise," Tyee finally instructed; "but be there many on every side of the igloo, and close, so that the Sunlanders may not break through. Then do you, Neegah, with six of the young men behind, crawl in to where they sleep. Take no guns, which be prone to go off at unexpected times, but put the strength of your arms into the knives."

"And be it understood that no harm befall Mesahchie, who is worth a price," Neegah whispered hoarsely.

Flat upon the ground, the small army concentred on the igloo, and behind, deliciously expectant, crouched many women and children, come out to witness the murder. The brief August night was passing, and in the gray of dawn could be dimly discerned the creeping forms of Neegah and the young men. Without pause, on hands and knees, they entered the long passageway and disappeared. Tyee rose up and rubbed his hands. All was going well. Head after head in the big circle lifted and waited. Each man pictured the scene according to his nature—the sleeping men, the plunge of the knives, and the sudden death in the dark.

A loud hail, in the voice of a Sunlander, rent the silence, and a shot rang out. Then an uproar broke loose inside the igloo. Without premeditation, the circle swept forward into the passageway. On the inside, half a dozen repeating rifles began to chatter, and the Mandells, jammed in the confined space, were powerless. Those at the front strove madly to retreat from the fire-spitting guns in their very faces, and those in the rear pressed as madly forward to the attack. The bullets from the big 45:90's drove through half a dozen men at a shot, and the passageway, gorged with surging, helpless men, became a shambles. The rifles, pumped without aim into the mass, withered it away like a machine gun, and against that steady stream of death no man could advance.

"Never was there the like!" panted one of the Hungry Folk. "I did but look in, and the dead were piled like seals on the ice after a killing!"

"Did I not say, mayhap, they were fighters?" cackled the weazened old hunter.

"It was to be expected," Aab-Waak answered stoutly. "We fought in a trap of our making."

"O ye fools!" Tyee chided. "Ye sons of fools! It was not planned, this thing ye have done. To Neegah and the six young men only was it given to go inside. My cunning is superior to the cunning of the Sunlanders, but ye take away its edge, and rob me of its strength, and make it worse than no cunning at all!"

No one made reply, and all eyes centred on the igloo, which loomed vague and monstrous against the clear northeast sky. Through a hole in the roof the smoke from the rifles curled slowly upward in the pulseless air, and now and again a wounded man crawled painfully through the gray.

"Let each ask of his neighbor for Neegah and the six young men," Tyee commanded.

And after a time the answer came back, "Neegah and the six young men are not."

"And many more are not!" wailed a woman to the rear.

"The more wealth for those who are left," Tyee grimly consoled. Then, turning to Aab-Waak, he said: "Go thou, and gather together many sealskins filled with oil. Let the hunters empty them on the outside wood of the igloo and of the passage. And let them put fire to it ere the Sunlanders make holes in the igloo for their guns."

Even as he spoke a hole appeared in the dirt plastered between the logs, a rifle muzzle protruded, and one of the Hungry Folk clapped hand to his side and leaped in the air. A second shot, through the lungs, brought him to the ground. Tyee and the rest scattered to either side, out of direct range, and Aab-Waak hastened the men forward with the skins of oil. Avoiding the loopholes, which were making on every side of the igloo, they emptied the skins on the dry drift-logs brought down by the Mandell River from the tree-lands to the south. Ounenk ran forward with a blazing brand, and the flames leaped upward. Many minutes passed, without sign, and they held their weapons ready as the fire gained headway.

Tyee rubbed his hands gleefully as the dry structure burned and crackled. "Now we have them, brothers! In the trap!"

"And no one may gainsay me the gun of Bill-Man," Aab-Waak announced.

"Save Bill-Man," squeaked the old hunter. "For behold, he cometh now!"

Covered with a singed and blackened blanket, the big white man leaped out of the blazing entrance, and on his heels, likewise shielded, came Mesahchie, and the five other Sunlanders. The Hungry Folk tried to check the rush with an ill-directed volley, while the Mandells hurled in a cloud of spears and arrows. But the Sunlanders cast their flaming blankets from them as they ran, and it was seen that each bore on his shoulders a small pack of ammunition. Of all their possessions, they had chosen to save that. Running swiftly and with purpose, they broke the circle and headed directly for the great cliff, which towered blackly in the brightening day a half-mile to the rear of the village.

But Tyee knelt on one knee and lined the sights of his rifle on the rearmost Sunlander. A great shout went up when he pulled the trigger and the man fell forward, struggled partly up, and fell again. Without regard for the rain of arrows, another Sunlander ran back, bent over him, and lifted him across his shoulders. But the Mandell spearmen were crowding up into closer range, and a strong cast transfixed the wounded man. He cried out and became swiftly limp as his comrade lowered him to the ground. In the meanwhile, Bill-Man and the three others had made a stand and were driving a leaden hail into the advancing spearmen.

The fifth Sunlander bent over his stricken fellow, felt the heart, and then coolly cut the straps of the pack and stood up with the ammunition and extra gun.

"Now is he a fool!" cried Tyee, leaping high, as he ran forward, to clear the squirming body of one of the Hungry Folk.

His own rifle was clogged so that he could not use it, and he called out for someone to spear the Sunlander, who had turned and was running for safety under the protecting fire. The little old hunter poised his spear on the throwing-stick, swept his arm back as he ran, and delivered the cast.

"By the body of the Wolf, say I, it was a good throw!" Tyee praised, as the fleeing man pitched forward, the spear standing upright between his shoulders and swaying slowly forward and back.

The little weazened old man coughed and sat down. A streak of red showed on his lips and welled into a thick stream. He coughed again, and a strange whistling came and went with his breath.

"They, too, are unafraid, being great fighters," he wheezed, pawing aimlessly with his hands. "And behold! Bill-Man comes now!"

Tyee glanced up. Four Mandells and one of the Hungry Folk had rushed upon the fallen man and were spearing him from his knees back to the earth. In the twinkling of an eye, Tyee saw four of them cut down by the bullets of the Sunlanders. The fifth, as yet unhurt, seized the two rifles, but as he stood up to make off he was whirled almost completely around by the impact of a bullet in the arm, steadied by a second, and overthrown by the shock of a third. A moment later and Bill-Man was on the spot, cutting the pack-straps and picking up the guns.

This Tyee saw, and his own people falling as they straggled forward, and he was aware of a quick doubt, and resolved to lie where he was and see more. For some unaccountable reason, Mesahchie was running back to Bill-Man; but before she could reach him, Tyee saw Peelo run out and throw arms about her. He essayed to sling her across his shoulder, but she grappled with him, tearing and scratching at his face. Then she tripped him, and the pair fell heavily. When they regained their feet, Peelo had shifted his grip so that one arm was passed under her chin, the wrist pressing into her throat and strangling her. He buried his face in her breast, taking the blows of her hands on his thick mat of hair, and began slowly to force her off the field. Then it was, retreating with the weapons of his fallen comrades, that Bill-Man came upon them. As Mesahchie saw him, she twirled the victim around and held him steady. Bill-Man swung the rifle in his right hand, and hardly easing his stride, delivered the blow. Tyee saw Peelo drive to the earth as smote by a falling star, and the Sunlander and Neegah's daughter fleeing side by side.

A bunch of Mandells, led by one of the Hungry Folk, made a futile rush which melted away into the earth before the scorching fire.

Tyee caught his breath and murmured, "Like the young frost in the morning sun."

"As I say, they are great fighters," the old hunter whispered weakly, far gone in hemorrhage. "I know. I have heard. They be sea-robbers and hunters of seals; and they shoot quick and true, for it is their way of life and the work of their hands."

"Like the young frost in the morning sun," Tyee repeated, crouching for shelter behind the dying man and peering at intervals about him.

It was no longer a fight, for no Mandell man dared venture forward, and as it was, they were too close to the Sunlanders to go back. Three tried it, scattering and scurrying like rabbits; but one came down with a broken leg, another was shot through the body, and the third, twisting and dodging, fell on the edge of the village. So the tribesmen crouched in the hollow places and burrowed into the dirt in the open, while the Sunlanders' bullets searched the plain.

"Move not," Tyee pleaded, as Aab-Waak came worming over the ground to him. "Move not, good Aab-Waak, else you bring death upon us."

"Death sits upon many," Aab-Waak laughed; "wherefore, as you say, there will be much wealth in division. My father breathes fast and short behind the big rock yon, and beyond, twisted like in a knot, lieth my brother. But their share shall be my share, and it is well."

"As you say, good Aab-Waak, and as I have said; but before division must come that which we may divide, and the Sunlanders be not yet dead."

A bullet glanced from a rock before them, and singing shrilly, rose low over their heads on its second flight. Tyee ducked and shivered, but Aab-Waak grinned and sought vainly to follow it with his eyes.

"So swiftly they go, one may not see them," he observed.

"But many be dead of us," Tyee went on.

"And many be left," was the reply. "And they hug close to the earth, for they have become wise in the fashion of righting. Further, they are angered. Moreover, when we have killed the Sunlanders on the ship, there will remain but four on the land. These may take long to kill, but in the end it will happen."

"How may we go down to the ship when we cannot go this way or that?" Tyee questioned.

"It is a bad place where lie Bill-Man and his brothers," Aab-Waak explained. "We may come upon them from every side, which is not good. So they aim to get their backs against the cliff and wait until their brothers of the ship come to give them aid."

"Never shall they come from the ship, their brothers! I have said it."

Tyee was gathering courage again, and when the Sunlanders verified the prediction by retreating to the cliff, he was light-hearted as ever.

"There be only three of us!" complained one of the Hungry Folk as they came together for council.

"Therefore, instead of two, shall you have four guns each," was Tyee's rejoinder.

"We did good fighting."

"Ay; and if it should happen that two of you be left, then will you have six guns each. Therefore, fight well."

"And if there be none of them left?" Aab-Waak whispered slyly.

"Then will *we* have the guns, you and I," Tyee whispered back.

However, to propitiate the Hungry Folk, he made one of them leader of the ship expedition. This party comprised fully two-thirds of the tribesmen, and departed for the coast, a dozen miles away, laden with skins and things to trade. The remaining men were disposed in a large half-circle about the breastwork which Bill-Man and his Sunlanders had begun to throw up. Tyee was quick to note the virtues of things, and at once set his men to digging shallow trenches.

"The time will go before they are aware," he explained to Aab-Waak; "and their minds being busy, they will not think overmuch of the dead that are, nor gather trouble to themselves. And in the dark of night they may creep closer, so that when the Sunlanders look forth in the morning light they will find us very near."

In the midday heat the men ceased from their work and made a meal of dried fish and seal oil which the women brought up. There was some clamor for the food of the Sunlanders in the igloo of Neegah, but Tyee refused to divide it until the return of the ship party. Speculations upon the outcome became rife, but in the midst of it a dull boom drifted up over the land from the sea. The keen-eyed ones made out a dense cloud of smoke, which quickly disappeared, and which they averred was directly over the ship of the Sunlanders. Tyee was of the opinion that it was a big gun. Aab-Waak did not know, but thought it might be a signal of some sort. Anyway, he said, it was time something happened.

Five or six hours afterward a solitary man was descried coming across the wide flat from the sea, and the women and children poured out upon him in a body. It was Ounenk, naked, winded, and wounded. The blood still trickled down his face from a gash on the forehead. His left arm, frightfully mangled, hung helpless at his side. But most significant of all, there was a wild gleam in his eyes which betokened the women knew not what.

"Where be Peshack?" an old squaw queried sharply.

"And Olitlie?" "And Polak?" "And Mah-Kook?" the voices took up the cry.

But he said nothing, brushing his way through the clamorous mass and directing his staggering steps toward Tyee. The old squaw raised the wail, and one by one the women joined her as they swung in behind. The men crawled out of their trenches and ran back to gather about Tyee, and it was noticed that the Sunlanders climbed upon their barricade to see.

Ounenk halted, swept the blood from his eyes, and looked about. He strove to speak, but his dry lips were glued together. Likeeta fetched him water, and he grunted and drank again.

"Was it a fight?" Tyee demanded finally,—"a good fight?"

"Ho! ho! ho!" So suddenly and so fiercely did Ounenk laugh that every voice hushed. "Never was there such a fight! So I say, I, Ounenk, fighter beforetime of beasts and men. And ere I forget, let me speak fat words and wise. By fighting will the Sunlanders teach us Mandell Folk how to fight. And if we fight long enough, we shall be great fighters, even as the Sunlanders, or else we shall be—dead. Ho! ho! ho! It was a fight!"

"Where be thy brothers?" Tyee shook him till he shrieked from the pain of his hurts.

Ounenk sobered. "My brothers? They are not."

"And Pome-Lee?" cried one of the two Hungry Folk; "Pome-Lee, the son of my mother?"

"Pome-Lee is not," Ounenk answered in a monotonous voice.

"And the Sunlanders?" from Aab-Waak.

"The Sunlanders are not."

"Then the ship of the Sunlanders, and the wealth and guns and things?" Tyee demanded.

"Neither the ship of the Sunlanders, nor the wealth and guns and things," was the unvarying response. "All are not. Nothing is. I only am."

"And thou art a fool."

"It may be so," Ounenk answered, unruffled. "I have seen that which would well make me a fool."

Tyee held his tongue, and all waited till it should please Ounenk to tell the story in his own way.

"We took no guns, O Tyee," he at last began; "no guns, my brothers—only knives and hunting bows and spears. And in twos and threes, in our kayaks, we came to the ship. They were glad to see us, the Sunlanders, and we spread our skins and they brought out their articles of trade, and everything was well. And Pome-Lee waited—waited till the sun was well overhead and they sat at meat, when he gave the cry and we fell upon them. Never was there such a fight, and never such fighters. Half did we kill in the quickness of surprise, but the half that was left became as devils, and they multiplied themselves, and everywhere they fought like devils. Three put their backs against the mast of the ship, and we ringed them with our dead before they died. And some got guns and shot with both eyes wide open, and very quick and sure. And one got a big gun, from which at one time he shot many small bullets. And so, behold!"

Ounenk pointed to his ear, neatly pierced by a buckshot.

"But I, Ounenk, drove my spear through his back from behind. And in such fashion, one way and another, did we kill them all—all save the head man. And him we were about, many of us, and he was alone, when he made a great cry and broke through us, five or six dragging upon him, and ran down inside the ship. And then, when the wealth of the ship was ours, and only the head man down below whom we would kill presently, why then there was a sound as of all the guns in the world—a mighty sound! And like a bird I rose up in the air, and the living Mandell Folk, and the dead Sunlanders, the little kayaks, the big ship, the guns, the wealth—everything rose up in the air. So I say, I, Ounenk, who tell the tale, am the only one left."

A great silence fell upon the assemblage. Tyee looked at Aab-Waak with awe-struck eyes, but forbore to speak. Even the women were too stunned to wail the dead.

Ounenk looked about him with pride. "I, only, am left," he repeated.

But at that instant a rifle cracked from Bill-Man's barricade, and there was a sharp spat and thud on the chest of Ounenk. He swayed backward and came forward again, a look of startled surprise on his face. He gasped, and his lips writhed in a grim smile. There was a shrinking together of the shoulders and a bending of the knees. He shook himself, as might a drowsing man, and straightened up. But the shrinking and bending began again, and he sank down slowly, quite slowly, to the ground.

It was a clean mile from the pit of the Sunlanders, and death had spanned it. A great cry of rage went up, and in it there was much of blood-vengeance, much of the unreasoned ferocity of the brute. Tyee and Aab-Waak tried to hold the Mandell Folk back, were thrust aside, and could only turn and watch the mad charge. But no shots came from the Sunlanders, and ere half the distance was covered, many, affrighted by the mysterious silence of the pit, halted and waited. The wilder spirits bore on, and when they had cut the remaining distance in half, the pit still showed no sign of life. At two hundred yards they slowed down and bunched; at one hundred, they stopped, a score of them, suspicious, and conferred together.

Then a wreath of smoke crowned the barricade, and they scattered like a handful of pebbles thrown at random. Four went down, and four more, and they continued swiftly to fall, one and two at a time, till but one remained, and he in full flight with death singing about his ears. It was Nok, a young hunter, long-legged and tall, and he ran as never before. He skimmed across the naked open like a bird, and soared and sailed and curved from side to side. The rifles in the pit rang out in solid volley; they flut-flut-flut-flutted in ragged sequence; and still Nok rose and dipped and rose again unharmed. There was a lull in the firing, as though the Sunlanders had given over, and Nok curved less and less in his flight till he darted straight forward at every leap. And then, as he leaped cleanly and well, one lone rifle barked from the pit, and he doubled up in mid-air, struck the ground in a ball, and like a ball bounced from the impact, and came down in a broken heap.

"Who so swift as the swift-winged lead?" Aab-Waak pondered.

Tyee grunted and turned away. The incident was closed and there was more pressing matter at hand. One Hungry Man and forty fighters, some of them hurt, remained; and there were four Sunlanders yet to reckon with.

"We will keep them in their hole by the cliff," he said, "and when famine has gripped them hard we will slay them like children."

"But of what matter to fight?" queried Oloof, one of the younger men. "The wealth of the Sunlanders is not; only remains that in the igloo of Neegah, a paltry quantity—"

He broke off hastily as the air by his ear split sharply to the passage of a bullet.

Tyee laughed scornfully. "Let that be thy answer. What else may we do with this mad breed of Sunlanders which will not die?"

"What a thing is foolishness!" Oloof protested, his ears furtively alert for the coming of other bullets. "It is not right that they should fight so, these Sunlanders. Why will they not die easily? They are fools not to know that they are dead men, and they give us much trouble."

"We fought before for great wealth; we fight now that we may live," Aab-Waak summed up succinctly.

That night there was a clash in the trenches, and shots exchanged. And in the morning the igloo of Neegah was found empty of the Sunlanders' possessions. These they themselves had taken, for the signs of their trail were visible to the sun. Oloof climbed to the brow of the cliff to hurl great stones down into the pit, but the cliff overhung, and he hurled down abuse and insult instead, and promised bitter torture to them in the end. Bill-Man mocked him back in the tongue of the Bear Folk, and Tyee, lifting his head from a trench to see, had his shoulder scratched deeply by a bullet.

And in the dreary days that followed, and in the wild nights when they pushed the trenches closer, there was much discussion as to the wisdom of letting the Sunlanders go. But of this they were afraid, and the women raised a cry always at the thought This much they had seen of the Sunlanders; they cared to see no more. All the time the whistle and blub-blub of bullets filled the air, and all the time the death-list grew. In the golden sunrise came the faint, far crack of a rifle, and a stricken woman would throw up her hands on the distant edge of the village; in the noonday heat, men in the trenches heard the shrill sing-song and knew their deaths; or in the gray afterglow of evening, the dirt kicked up in puffs by the winking fires. And through the nights the long "Wah-hoo-ha-a wah-hoo-ha-a!" of mourning women held dolorous sway.

As Tyee had promised, in the end famine gripped the Sunlanders. And once, when an early fall gale blew, one of them crawled through the darkness past the trenches and stole many dried fish.

But he could not get back with them, and the sun found him vainly hiding in the village. So he fought the great fight by himself, and in a narrow ring of Mandell Folk shot four with his revolver, and ere they could lay hands on him for the torture, turned it on himself and died.

This threw a gloom upon the people. Oloof put the question, "If one man die so hard, how hard will die the three who yet are left?"

Then Mesahchie stood up on the barricade and called in by name three dogs which had wandered close,—meat and life,—which set back the day of reckoning and put despair in the hearts of the Mandell Folk. And on the head of Mesahchie were showered the curses of a generation.

The days dragged by. The sun hurried south, the nights grew long and longer, and there was a touch of frost in the air. And still the Sunlanders held the pit. Hearts were breaking under the unending strain, and Tyee thought hard and deep. Then he sent forth word that all the skins and hides of all the tribe be collected. These he had made into huge cylindrical bales, and behind each bale he placed a man.

When the word was given the brief day was almost spent, and it was slow work and tedious, rolling the big bales forward foot by foot The bullets of the Sunlanders blub-blubbed and thudded against them, but could not go through, and the men howled their delight But the dark was at hand, and Tyee, secure of success, called the bales back to the trenches.

In the morning, in the face of an unearthly silence from the pit, the real advance began. At first with large intervals between, the bales slowly converged as the circle drew in. At a hundred yards they were quite close together, so that Tyee's order to halt was passed along in whispers. The pit showed no sign of life. They watched long and sharply, but nothing stirred. The advance was taken up and the manoeuvre repeated at fifty yards. Still no sign nor sound. Tyee shook his head, and even Aab-Waak was dubious. But the order was given to go on, and go on they did, till bale touched bale and a solid rampart of skin and hide bowed out from the cliff about the pit and back to the cliff again.

Tyee looked back and saw the women and children clustering blackly in the deserted trenches. He looked ahead at the silent pit. The men were wriggling nervously, and he ordered every second bale forward. This double line advanced till bale touched bale as before. Then Aab-Waak, of his own will, pushed one bale forward alone. When it touched the barricade, he waited a long while. After that he tossed unresponsive rocks over into the pit, and finally, with great care, stood up and peered in. A carpet of empty cartridges, a few white-picked dog bones, and a soggy place where water dripped from a crevice, met his eyes. That was all. The Sunlanders were gone.

There were murmurings of witchcraft, vague complaints, dark looks which foreshadowed to Tyee dread things which yet might come to pass, and he breathed easier when Aab-Waak took up the trail along the base of the cliff.

"The cave!" Tyee cried. "They foresaw my wisdom of the skin-bales and fled away into the cave!"

The cliff was honey-combed with a labyrinth of subterranean passages which found vent in an opening midway between the pit and where the trench tapped the wall. Thither, and with many exclamations, the tribesmen followed Aab-Waak, and, arrived, they saw plainly where the Sunlanders had climbed to the mouth, twenty and odd feet above.

"Now the thing is done," Tyee said, rubbing his hands. "Let word go forth that rejoicing be made, for they are in the trap now, these Sunlanders, in the trap. The young men shall climb up, and the mouth of the cave be filled with stones, so that Bill-Man and his brothers and Mesahchie shall by famine be pinched to shadows and die cursing in the silence and dark."

Cries of delight and relief greeted this, and Howgah, the last of the Hungry Folk, swarmed up the steep slant and drew himself, crouching, upon the lip of the opening. But as he crouched, a muffled report rushed forth, and as he clung desperately to the slippery edge, a second. His grip loosed with reluctant weakness, and he pitched down at the feet of Tyee, quivered for a moment like some monstrous jelly, and was still.

"How should I know they were great fighters and unafraid?" Tyee demanded, spurred to defence by recollection of the dark looks and vague complaints.

"We were many and happy," one of the men stated baldly. Another fingered his spear with a prurient hand.

But Oloof cried them cease. "Give ear, my brothers! There be another way! As a boy I chanced upon it playing along the steep. It is hidden by the rocks, and there is no reason that a man should go there; wherefore it is secret, and no man knows. It is very small, and you crawl on your belly a long way, and then you are in the cave. To-night we will so crawl, without noise, on our bellies, and come upon the Sunlanders from behind. And to-morrow we will be at peace, and never again will we quarrel with the Sunlanders in the years to come."

"Never again!" chorussed the weary men. "Never again!" And Tyee joined with them.

That night, with the memory of their dead in their hearts, and in their hands stones and spears and knives, the horde of women and children collected about the known mouth of the cave. Down the twenty and odd precarious feet to the ground no Sunlander could hope to pass and live. In the village remained only the wounded men, while every able man—and there were thirty of them—followed Oloof to the secret opening. A hundred feet of broken ledges and insecurely heaped rocks were between it and the earth, and because of the rocks, which might be displaced by the touch of hand or foot, but one man climbed at a time. Oloof went up first, called softly for the next to come on, and disappeared inside. A man followed, a second, and a third, and so on, till only Tyee remained. He received the call of the last man, but a quick doubt assailed him and he stayed to ponder. Half an hour later he swung up to the opening and peered in. He could feel the narrowness of the passage, and the darkness before him took on solidity. The fear of the walled-in earth chilled him and he could not venture. All the men who had died, from Neegah the first of the Mandells, to Howgah the last of the Hungry Folk, came and sat with him, but he chose the terror of their company rather than face the horror which he felt to lurk in the thick blackness. He had been sitting long when something soft and cold fluttered lightly on his cheek, and he knew the first winter's snow was falling. The dim dawn came, and after that the bright day, when he heard a low guttural sobbing, which came and went at intervals along the passage and which drew closer each time and more distinct He slipped over the edge, dropped his feet to the first ledge, and waited.

That which sobbed made slow progress, but at last, after many halts, it reached him, and he was sure no Sunlander made the noise. So he reached a hand inside, and where there should have been a head felt the shoulders of a man uplifted on bent arms. The head he found later, not erect, but hanging straight down so that the crown rested on the floor of the passage.

"Is it you, Tyee?" the head said. "For it is I, Aab-Waak, who am helpless and broken as a rough-flung spear. My head is in the dirt, and I may not climb down unaided."

Tyee clambered in, dragged him up with his back against the wall, but the head hung down on the chest and sobbed and wailed.

"Ai-oo-o, ai-oo-o!" it went "Oloof forgot, for Mesahchie likewise knew the secret and showed the Sunlanders, else they would not have waited at the end of the narrow way. Wherefore, I am a broken man, and helpless—ai-oo-o, ai-oo-o!"

"And did they die, the cursed Sunlanders, at the end of the narrow way?" Tyee demanded.

"How should I know they waited?" Aab-Waak gurgled. "For my brothers had gone before, many of them, and there was no sound of struggle. How should I know why there should be no sound of struggle? And ere I knew, two hands were about my neck so that I could not cry out and warn my brothers yet to come. And then there were two hands more on my head, and two more on my feet. In this fashion the three Sunlanders had me. And while the hands held my head in the one place, the hands on my feet swung my body around, and as we wring the neck of a duck in the marsh, so my week was wrung.

"But it was not given that I should die," he went on, a remnant of pride yet glimmering. "I, only, am left. Oloof and the rest lie on their backs in a row, and their faces turn this way and that, and the faces of some be underneath where the backs of their heads should be. It is not good to look upon; for when life returned to me I saw them all by the light of a torch which the Sunlanders left, and I had been laid with them in the row."

"So? So?" Tyee mused, too stunned for speech.

He started suddenly, and shivered, for the voice of Bill-Man shot out at him from the passage.

"It is well," it said. "I look for the man who crawls with the broken neck, and lo, do I find Tyee. Throw down thy gun, Tyee, so that I may hear it strike among the rocks."

Tyee obeyed passively, and Bill-Man crawled forward into the light. Tyee looked at him curiously. He was gaunt and worn and dirty, and his eyes burned like twin coals in their cavernous sockets.

"I am hungry, Tyee," he said. "Very hungry."

"And I am dirt at thy feet," Tyee responded.

"Thy word is my law. Further, I commanded my people not to withstand thee. I counselled—"

But Bill-Man had turned and was calling back into the passage. "Hey! Charley! Jim! Fetch the woman along and come on!"

"We go now to eat," he said, when his comrades and Mesahchie had joined him.

Tyee rubbed his hands deprecatingly. "We have little, but it is thine."

"After that we go south on the snow," Bill-Man continued.

"May you go without hardship and the trail be easy."

"It is a long way. We will need dogs and food—much!"

"Thine the pick of our dogs and the food they may carry."

Bill-Man slipped over the edge of the opening and prepared to descend. "But we come again, Tyee. We come again, and our days shall be long in the land."

And so they departed into the trackless south, Bill-Man, his brothers, and Mesahchie. And when the next year came, the *Search Number Two* rode at anchor in Mandell Bay. The few Mandell men, who survived because their wounds had prevented their crawling into the cave, went to work at the best of the Sunlanders and dug in the ground. They hunt and fish no more, but receive a daily wage, with which they buy flour, sugar, calico, and such things which the *Search Number Two* brings on her yearly trip from the Sunlands.

And this mine is worked in secret, as many Northland mines have been worked; and no white man outside the Company, which is Bill-Man, Jim, and Charley, knows the whereabouts of Mandell on the rim of the polar sea. Aab-Waak still carries his head on one shoulder, is become an oracle, and preaches peace to the younger generation, for which he receives a pension from the Company. Tyee is foreman of the mine. But he has achieved a new theory concerning the Sunlanders.

"They that live under the path of the sun are not soft," he says, smoking his pipe and watching the day-shift take itself off and the night-shift go on. "For the sun enters into their blood and burns them with a great fire till they are filled with lusts and passions. They burn always, so that they may not know when they are beaten. Further, there is an unrest in them, which is a devil, and they are flung out over the earth to toil and suffer and fight without end. I know. I am Tyee."

THE SICKNESS OF LONE CHIEF

This is a tale that was told to me by two old men. We sat in the smoke of a mosquito-smudge, in the cool of the day, which was midnight; and ever and anon, throughout the telling, we smote lustily and with purpose at such of the winged pests as braved the smoke for a snack at our hides. To the right, beneath us, twenty feet down the crumbling bank, the Yukon gurgled lazily. To the left, on the rose-leaf rim of the low-lying hills, smouldered the sleepy sun, which saw no sleep that night nor was destined to see sleep for many nights to come.

The old men who sat with me and valorously slew mosquitoes were Lone Chief and Mutsak, erstwhile comrades in arms, and now withered repositories of tradition and ancient happening. They were the last of their generation and without honor among the younger set which had grown up on the farthest fringe of a mining civilization. Who cared for tradition in these days, when spirits could be evoked from black bottles, and black bottles could be evoked from the complaisant white men for a few hours' sweat or a mangy fur? Of what potency the fearful rites and masked mysteries of shamanism, when daily that living wonder, the steamboat, coughed and spluttered up and down the Yukon in defiance of all law, a veritable fire-breathing monster? And of what value was hereditary prestige, when he who now chopped the most wood, or best conned a stern-wheeler through the island mazes, attained the chiefest consideration of his fellows?

Of a truth, having lived too long, they had fallen on evil days, these two old men, Lone Chief and Mutsak, and in the new order they were without honor or place. So they waited drearily for death, and the while their hearts warmed to the strange white man who shared with them the torments of the mosquito-smudge and lent ready ear to their tales of old time before the steamboat came.

"So a girl was chosen for me," Lone Chief was saying. His voice, shrill and piping, ever and again dropped plummet-like into a hoarse and rattling bass, and, just as one became accustomed to it, soaring upward into the thin treble—alternate cricket chirpings and bull-frog croakings, as it were.

"So a girl was chosen for me," he was saying. "For my father, who was Kask-ta-ka, the Otter, was angered because I looked not with a needful eye upon women. He was an old

208

man, and chief of his tribe. I was the last of his sons to be alive, and through me, only, could he look to see his blood go down among those to come after and as yet unborn. But know, O White Man, that I was very sick; and when neither the hunting nor the fishing delighted me, and by meat my belly was not made warm, how should I look with favor upon women? or prepare for the feast of marriage? or look forward to the prattle and troubles of little children?"

"Ay," Mutsak interrupted. "For had not Lone Chief fought in the arms of a great bear till his head was cracked and blood ran from out his ears?"

Lone Chief nodded vigorously. "Mutsak speaks true. In the time that followed, my head was well, and it was not well. For though the flesh healed and the sore went away, yet was I sick inside. When I walked, my legs shook under me, and when I looked at the light, my eyes became filled with tears. And when I opened my eyes, the world outside went around and around, and when I closed my eyes, my head inside went around and around, and all the things I had ever seen went around and around inside my head. And above my eyes there was a great pain, as though something heavy rested always upon me, or like a band that is drawn tight and gives much hurt. And speech was slow to me, and I waited long for each right word to come to my tongue. And when I waited not long, all manner of words crowded in, and my tongue spoke foolishness. I was very sick, and when my father, the Otter, brought the girl Kasaan before me—"

"Who was a young girl, and strong, my sister's child," Mutsak broke in. "Strong-hipped for children was Kasaan, and straight-legged and quick of foot. She made better moccasins than any of all the young girls, and the bark-rope she braided was the stoutest. And she had a smile in her eyes, and a laugh on her lips; and her temper was not hasty, nor was she unmindful that men give the law and women ever obey."

"As I say, I was very sick," Lone Chief went on. "And when my father, the Otter, brought the girl Kasaan before me, I said rather should they make me ready for burial than for marriage. Whereat the face of my father went black with anger, and he said that I should be served according to my wish, and that I who was yet alive should be made ready for death as one already dead—"

"Which be not the way of our people, O White Man," spoke up Mutsak. "For know that these things that were done to Lone Chief it was our custom to do only to dead men. But the Otter was very angry."

"Ay," said Lone Chief. "My father, the Otter, was a man short of speech and swift of deed. And he commanded the people to gather before the lodge wherein I lay. And when they were gathered, he commanded them to mourn for his son who was dead—"

"And before the lodge they sang the death-song—O-o-o-o-o-o-a-haa-ha-a-ich-klu-kuk-ich-klu-kuk," wailed Mutsak, in so excellent an imitation that all the tendrils of my spine crawled and curved in sympathy.

"And inside the lodge," continued Lone Chief, "my mother blackened her face with soot, and flung ashes upon her head, and mourned for me as one already dead; for so had my father commanded. So Okiakuta, my mother, mourned with much noise, and beat her breasts and tore her hair; and likewise Hooniak, my sister, and Seenatah, my mother's sister; and the noise they made caused a great ache in my head, and I felt that I would surely and immediately die.

"And the elders of the tribe gathered about me where I lay and discussed the journey my soul must take. One spoke of the thick and endless forests where lost souls wandered crying, and where I, too, might chance to wander and never see the end. And another spoke of the big rivers, rapid with bad water, where evil spirits shrieked and lifted up their formless arms to drag one down by the hair. For these rivers, all said together, a canoe must be provided me. And yet another spoke of the storms, such as no live man ever saw, when the stars rained down out of the sky, and the earth gaped wide in many cracks, and all the rivers in the heart of the earth rushed out and in. Whereupon they that sat by me flung up their arms and wailed loudly; and those outside heard, and wailed more loudly. And as to them I was as dead, so was I to my own mind dead. I did not know when, or how, yet did I know that I had surely died.

"And Okiakuta, my mother, laid beside me my squirrel-skin parka. Also she laid beside me my parka of caribou hide, and my rain coat of seal gut, and my wet-weather muclucs, that my soul should be warm and dry on its long journey. Further, there was mention made of a steep hill, thick with briers and devil's-club, and she fetched heavy moccasins to make the way easy for my feet.

"And when the elders spoke of the great beasts I should have to slay, the young men laid beside me my strongest bow and straightest arrows, my throwing-stick, my spear and knife. And when the elders spoke of the darkness and silence of the great spaces my soul must wander through, my mother wailed yet more loudly and flung yet more ashes upon her head.

"And the girl, Kasaan, crept in, very timid and quiet, and dropped a little bag upon the things for my journey. And in the little bag, I knew, were the flint and steel and the well-dried tinder for the fires my soul must build. And the blankets were chosen which were to be wrapped around me. Also were the slaves selected that were to be killed that my soul might have company. There were seven of these slaves, for my father was rich and powerful, and it was fit that I, his son, should have proper burial. These slaves we had got in war from the Mukumuks, who live down the Yukon. On the morrow, Skolka, the shaman, would kill them, one by one, so that their souls should go questing with mine through the Unknown. Among other things, they would carry my canoe till we came to the big river, rapid with bad water. And there being no room, and their work being done, they would come no farther, but remain and howl forever in the dark and endless forest.

"And as I looked on my fine warm clothes, and my blankets and weapons of war, and as I thought of the seven slaves to be slain, I felt proud of my burial and knew that I must be the envy of many men. And all the while my father, the Otter, sat silent and black. And all that day and night the people sang my death-song and beat the drums, till it seemed that I had surely died a thousand times.

"But in the morning my father arose and made talk. He had been a fighting man all his days, he said, as the people knew. Also the people knew that it were a greater honor to die fighting in battle than on the soft skins by the fire. And since I was to die anyway, it were well that I should go against the Mukumuks and be slain. Thus would I attain honor and chieftainship in the final abode of the dead, and thus would honor remain to my father, who was the Otter. Wherefore he gave command that a war party be made ready to go down the river. And that when we came upon the Mukumuks I was to go forth alone from my party, giving semblance of battle, and so be slain."

"Nay, but hear, O White Man!" cried Mutsak, unable longer to contain himself. "Skolka, the shaman, whispered long that night in the ear of the Otter, and it was his doing that Lone Chief should be sent forth to die. For the Otter being old, and Lone Chief the last of his sons, Skolka had it in mind to become chief himself over the people. And when the people had made great noise for a day and a night and Lone Chief was yet alive, Skolka was become afraid that he would not die. So it was the counsel of Skolka, with fine words of honor and deeds, that spoke through the mouth of the Otter.

"Ay," replied Lone Chief. "Well did I know it was the doing of Skolka, but I was unmind-ful, being very sick. I had no heart for anger, nor belly for stout words, and I cared little, one way or the other, only I cared to die and have done with it all. So, O White Man, the war party was made ready. No tried fighters were there, nor elders, crafty and wise—naught but five score of young men who had seen little fighting. And all the village gathered together above the bank of the river to see us depart. And we departed amid great rejoicing and the singing of my praises. Even thou, O White Man, wouldst rejoice at sight of a young man going forth to battle, even though doomed to die.

"So we went forth, the five score young men, and Mutsak came also, for he was likewise young and untried. And by command of my father, the Otter, my canoe was lashed on either side to the canoe of Mutsak and the canoe of Kannakut. Thus was my strength saved me from the work of the paddles, so that, for all of my sickness, I might make a brave show at the end. And thus we went down the river.

"Nor will I weary thee with the tale of the journey, which was not long. And not far above the village of the Mukumuks we came upon two of their fighting men in canoes, that fled at the sight of us. And then, according to the command of my father, my canoe was cast loose and I was left to drift down all alone. Also, according to his command, were the young men to see me die, so that they might return and tell the manner of my death. Upon this, my father, the Otter, and Skolka, the shaman, had been very clear, with stern promises of punish-ment in case they were not obeyed.

"I dipped my paddle and shouted words of scorn after the fleeing warriors. And the vile things I shouted made them turn their heads in anger, when they beheld that the young men held back, and that I came on alone. Whereupon, when they had made a safe distance, the two warriors drew their canoes somewhat apart and waited side by side for me to come between. And I came between, spear in hand, and singing the war-song of my people. Each flung a spear, but I bent my body, and the spears whistled over me, and I was unhurt. Then, and we were all together, we three, I cast my spear at the one to the right, and it drove into his throat and he pitched backward into the water.

"Great was my surprise thereat, for I had killed a man. I turned to the one on the left and drove strong with my paddle, to meet Death face to face; but the man's second spear, which was his last, but bit into the flesh of my shoulder. Then was I upon him, making no cast, but pressing the point into his breast and working it through him with both my hands. And while I worked, pressing with all my strength, he smote me upon my head, once and twice, with the broad of his paddle.

"Even as the point of the spear sprang out beyond his back, he smote me upon the head. There was a flash, as of bright light, and inside my head I felt something give, with a snap— just like that, with a snap. And the weight that pressed above my eyes so long was lifted, and the band that bound my brows so tight was broken. And a great gladness came upon me, and my heart sang with joy.

"This be death, I thought; wherefore I thought that death was very good. And then I saw the two empty canoes, and I knew that I was not dead, but well again. The blows of the man upon my head had made me well. I knew that I had killed, and the taste of the blood made me fierce, and I drove my paddle into the breast of the Yukon and urged my canoe toward the village of the Mukumuks. The young men behind me gave a great cry. I looked over my shoulder and saw the water foaming white from their paddles—"

"Ay, it foamed white from our paddles," said Mutsak. "For we remembered the command of the Otter, and of Skolka, that we behold with our own eyes the manner of Lone Chief's death. A young man of the Mukumuks, on his way to a salmon trap, beheld the coming of

Lone Chief, and of the five score men behind him. And the young man fled in his canoe, straight for the village, that alarm might be given and preparation made. But Lone Chief hurried after him, and we hurried after Lone Chief to behold the manner of his death. Only, in the face of the village, as the young man leaped to the shore, Lone Chief rose up in his canoe and made a mighty cast. And the spear entered the body of the young man above the hips, and the young man fell upon his face.

"Whereupon Lone Chief leaped up the bank war-club in hand and a great war-cry on his lips, and dashed into the village. The first man he met was Itwilie, chief over the Mukumuks, and him Lone Chief smote upon the head with his war-club, so that he fell dead upon the ground. And for fear we might not behold the manner of his death, we too, the five score young men, leaped to the shore and followed Lone Chief into the village. Only the Mukumuks did not understand, and thought we had come to fight; so their bow-thongs sang and their arrows whistled among us. Whereat we forgot our errand, and fell upon them with our spears and clubs; and they being unprepared, there was great slaughter—"

"With my own hands I slew their shaman," proclaimed Lone Chief, his withered face a-work with memory of that old-time day. "With my own hands I slew him, who was a greater shaman than Skolka, our own shaman. And each time I faced a man, I thought, 'Now cometh Death; and each time I slew the man, and Death came not. It seemed the breath of life was strong in my nostrils and I could not die—"

"And we followed Lone Chief the length of the village and back again," continued Mutsak. "Like a pack of wolves we followed him, back and forth, and here and there, till there were no more Mukumuks left to fight. Then we gathered together five score men-slaves, and double as many women, and countless children, and we set fire and burned all the houses and lodges, and departed. And that was the last of the Mukumuks."

"And that was the last of the Mukumuks," Lone Chief repeated exultantly. "And when we came to our own village, the people were amazed at our burden of wealth and slaves, and in that I was still alive they were more amazed. And my father, the Otter, came trembling with gladness at the things I had done. For he was an old man, and I the last of his sons. And all the tried fighting men came, and the crafty and wise, till all the people were gathered together. And then I arose, and with a voice like thunder, commanded Skolka, the shaman, to stand forth—"

"Ay, O White Man," exclaimed Mutsak. "With a voice like thunder, that made the people shake at the knees and become afraid."

"And when Skolka had stood forth," Lone Chief went on, "I said that I was not minded to die. Also, I said it were not well that disappointment come to the evil spirits that wait beyond the grave. Wherefore I deemed it fit that the soul of Skolka fare forth into the Unknown, where doubtless it would howl forever in the dark and endless forest. And then I slew him, as he stood there, in the face of all the people. Even I, Lone Chief, with my own hands, slew Skolka, the shaman, in the face of all the people. And when a murmuring arose, I cried aloud—"

"With a voice like thunder," prompted Mutsak.

"Ay, with a voice like thunder I cried aloud: 'Behold, O ye people! I am Lone Chief, slayer of Skolka, the false shaman! Alone among men, have I passed down through the gateway of Death and returned again. Mine eyes have looked upon the unseen things. Mine ears have heard the unspoken words. Greater am I than Skolka, the shaman. Greater than all shamans am I. Likewise am I a greater chief than my father, the Otter. All his days did he fight with the Mukumuks, and lo, in one day have I destroyed them all. As with the breathing of a breath have I destroyed them. Wherefore, my father, the Otter, being old, and Skolka, the shaman, being dead, I shall be both chief and shaman. Henceforth shall I be both chief and shaman to you, O my people. And if any man dispute my word, let that man stand forth!'

"I waited, but no man stood forth. Then I cried: 'Hoh! I have tasted blood! Now bring meat, for I am hungry. Break open the caches, tear down the fish-racks, and let the feast be big. Let there be merriment, and songs, not of burial, but marriage. And last of all, let the girl Kasaan be brought. The girl Kasaan, who is to be the mother of the children of Lone Chief!'

"And at my words, and because that he was very old, my father, the Otter, wept like a woman, and put his arms about my knees. And from that day I was both chief and shaman. And great honor was mine, and all men yielded me obedience."

"Until the steamboat came," Mutsak prompted.

"Ay," said Lone Chief. "Until the steamboat came."

KEESH, THE SON OF KEESH

"THUS WILL I give six blankets, warm and double; six files, large and hard; six Hudson Bay knives, keen-edged and long; two canoes, the work of Mogum, The Maker of Things; ten dogs, heavy-shouldered and strong in the harness, and three guns—the trigger of one be broken, but it is a good gun and can doubtless be mended."

Keesh paused and swept his eyes over the circle of intent faces. It was the time of the Great Fishing, and he was bidding to Gnob for Su-Su his daughter. The place was the St. George Mission by the Yukon, and the tribes had gathered for many a hundred miles. From north, south, east, and west they had come, even from Tozikakat and far Tana-naw.

"And further, O Gnob, thou art chief of the Tana-naw; and I, Keesh, the son of Keesh, am chief of the Thlunget. Wherefore, when my seed springs from the loins of thy daughter, there shall be a friendship between the tribes, a great friendship, and Tana-naw and Thlunget shall be brothers of the blood in the time to come. What I have said I will do, that will I do. And how is it with you, O Gnob, in this matter?"

Gnob nodded his head gravely, his gnarled and age-twisted face inscrutably masking the soul that dwelt behind. His narrow eyes burned like twin coals through their narrow slits, as he piped in a high-cracked voice, "But that is not all."

"What more?" Keesh demanded. "Have I not offered full measure? Was there ever yet a Tana-naw maiden who fetched so great a price? Then name her!"

An open snicker passed round the circle, and Keesh knew that he stood in shame before these people.

"Nay, nay, good Keesh, thou dost not understand." Gnob made a soft, stroking gesture. "The price is fair. It is a good price. Nor do I question the broken trigger. But that is not all. What of the man?"

"Ay, what of the man?" the circle snarled.

"It is said," Gnob's shrill voice piped, "it is said that Keesh does not walk in the way of his fathers. It is said that he has wandered into the dark, after strange gods, and that he is become afraid."

The face of Keesh went dark. "It is a lie!" he thundered. "Keesh is afraid of no man!"

"It is said," old Gnob piped on, "that he has harkened to the speech of the white man up at the Big House, and that he bends head to the white man's god, and, moreover, that blood is displeasing to the white man's god."

Keesh dropped his eyes, and his hands clenched passionately. The savage circle laughed derisively, and in the ear of Gnob whispered Madwan, the shaman, high-priest of the tribe and maker of medicine.

The shaman poked among the shadows on the rim of the firelight and roused up a slender young boy, whom he brought face to face with Keesh; and in the hand of Keesh he thrust a knife.

Gnob leaned forward. "Keesh! O Keesh! Darest thou to kill a man? Behold! This be Kitz-noo, a slave. Strike, O Keesh, strike with the strength of thy arm!"

The boy trembled and waited the stroke. Keesh looked at him, and thoughts of Mr. Brown's higher morality floated through his mind, and strong upon him was a vision of the leaping flames of Mr. Brown's particular brand of hell-fire. The knife fell to the ground, and the boy sighed and went out beyond the firelight with shaking knees. At the feet of Gnob sprawled a wolf-dog, which bared its gleaming teeth and prepared to spring after the boy. But the shaman ground his foot into the brute's body, and so doing, gave Gnob an idea.

"And then, O Keesh, what wouldst thou do, should a man do this thing to you?"—as he spoke, Gnob held a ribbon of salmon to White Fang, and when the animal attempted to take it, smote him sharply on the nose with a stick. "And afterward, O Keesh, wouldst thou do thus?"—White Fang was cringing back on his belly and fawning to the hand of Gnob.

"Listen!"—leaning on the arm of Madwan, Gnob had risen to his feet. "I am very old, and because I am very old I will tell thee things. Thy father, Keesh, was a mighty man. And he did love the song of the bowstring in battle, and these eyes have beheld him cast a spear till the head stood out beyond a man's body. But thou art unlike. Since thou left the Raven to worship the Wolf, thou art become afraid of blood, and thou makest thy people afraid. This is not good. For behold, when I was a boy, even as Kitz-noo there, there was no white man in all the land. But they came, one by one, these white men, till now they are many. And they are a restless breed, never content to rest by the fire with a full belly and let the morrow bring its own meat. A curse was laid upon them, it would seem, and they must work it out in toil and hardship."

Keesh was startled. A recollection of a hazy story told by Mr. Brown of one Adam, of old time, came to him, and it seemed that Mr. Brown had spoken true.

"So they lay hands upon all they behold, these white men, and they go everywhere and behold all things. And ever do more follow in their steps, so that if nothing be done they will come to possess all the land and there will be no room for the tribes of the Raven. Wherefore it is meet that we fight with them till none are left. Then will we hold the passes and the land, and perhaps our children and our children's children shall flourish and grow fat. There is a great struggle to come, when Wolf and Raven shall grapple; but Keesh will not fight, nor will he let his people fight. So it is not well that he should take to him my daughter. Thus have I spoken, I, Gnob, chief of the Tana-naw."

"But the white men are good and great," Keesh made answer. "The white men have taught us many things. The white men have given us blankets and knives and guns, such as we have never made and never could make. I remember in what manner we lived before they came. I was unborn then, but I have it from my father. When we went on the hunt we must creep so close to the moose that a spear-cast would cover the distance. To-day we use the white man's rifle, and farther away than can a child's cry be heard. We ate fish and meat and berries—there was nothing else to eat—and we ate without salt. How many be there among you who care to go back to the fish and meat without salt?"

It would have sunk home, had not Madwan leaped to his feet ere silence could come. "And first a question to thee, Keesh. The white man up at the Big House tells you that it is wrong to kill. Yet do we not know that the white men kill? Have we forgotten the great fight on the Koyokuk? or the great fight at Nuklukyeto, where three white men killed twenty of the Tozikakats? Do you think we no longer remember the three men of the Tana-naw that the white man Macklewrath killed? Tell me, O Keesh, why does the Shaman Brown teach you that it is wrong to fight, when all his brothers fight?"

"Nay, nay, there is no need to answer," Gnob piped, while Keesh struggled with the paradox. "It is very simple. The Good Man Brown would hold the Raven tight whilst his brothers pluck the feathers." He raised his voice. "But so long as there is one Tana-naw to strike a blow, or one maiden to bear a man-child, the Raven shall not be plucked!"

Gnob turned to a husky young man across the fire. "And what sayest thou, Makamuk, who art brother to Su-Su?"

Makamuk came to his feet. A long face-scar lifted his upper lip into a perpetual grin which belied the glowing ferocity of his eyes. "This day," he began with cunning irrelevance, "I came by the Trader Macklewrath's cabin. And in the door I saw a child laughing at the sun. And the child looked at me with the Trader Macklewrath's eyes, and it was frightened. The mother ran to it and quieted it. The mother was Ziska, the Thlunget woman."

A snarl of rage rose up and drowned his voice, which he stilled by turning dramatically upon Keesh with outstretched arm and accusing finger.

"So? You give your women away, you Thlunget, and come to the Tana-naw for more? But we have need of our women, Keesh; for we must breed men, many men, against the day when the Raven grapples with the Wolf."

Through the storm of applause, Gnob's voice shrilled clear. "And thou, Nossabok, who art her favorite brother?"

The young fellow was slender and graceful, with the strong aquiline nose and high brows of his type; but from some nervous affliction the lid of one eye drooped at odd times in a suggestive wink. Even as he arose it so drooped and rested a moment against his cheek. But it was not greeted with the accustomed laughter. Every face was grave. "I, too, passed by the Trader Macklewrath's cabin," he rippled in soft, girlish tones, wherein there was much of youth and much of his sister. "And I saw Indians with the sweat running into their eyes and their knees shaking with weariness—I say, I saw Indians groaning under the logs for the store which the Trader Macklewrath is to build. And with my eyes I saw them chopping wood to keep the Shaman Brown's Big House warm through the frost of the long nights. This be squaw work. Never shall the Tana-naw do the like. We shall be blood brothers to men, not squaws; and the Thlunget be squaws."

A deep silence fell, and all eyes centred on Keesh. He looked about him carefully, deliberately, full into the face of each grown man. "So," he said passionlessly. And "So," he repeated. Then turned on his heel without further word and passed out into the darkness.

Wading among sprawling babies and bristling wolf-dogs, he threaded the great camp, and on its outskirts came upon a woman at work by the light of a fire. With strings of bark stripped from the long roots of creeping vines, she was braiding rope for the Fishing. For some time, without speech, he watched her deft hands bringing law and order out of the unruly mass of curling fibres. She was good to look upon, swaying there to her task, strong-limbed, deep-chested, and with hips made for motherhood. And the bronze of her face was golden in the flickering light, her hair blue-black, her eyes jet.

"O Su-Su," he spoke finally, "thou hast looked upon me kindly in the days that have gone and in the days yet young—"

"I looked kindly upon thee for that thou wert chief of the Thlunget," she answered quickly, "and because thou wert big and strong."

"Ay—"

"But that was in the old days of the Fishing," she hastened to add, "before the Shaman Brown came and taught thee ill things and led thy feet on strange trails."

"But I would tell thee the—"

She held up one hand in a gesture which reminded him of her father. "Nay, I know already the speech that stirs in thy throat, O Keesh, and I make answer now. It so happeneth that the fish of the water and the beasts of the forest bring forth after their kind. And this is good. Likewise it happeneth to women. It is for them to bring forth their kind, and even the maiden, while she is yet a maiden, feels the pang of the birth, and the pain of the breast, and the small hands at the neck. And when such feeling is strong, then does each maiden look about her with secret eyes for the man—for the man who shall be fit to father her kind. So have I felt. So did I feel when I looked upon thee and found thee big and strong, a hunter and fighter of beasts and men, well able to win meat when I should eat for two, well able to keep danger afar off when my helplessness drew nigh. But that was before the day the Shaman Brown came into the land and taught thee—"

"But it is not right, Su-Su. I have it on good word—"

"It is not right to kill. I know what thou wouldst say. Then breed thou after thy kind, the kind that does not kill; but come not on such quest among the Tana-naw. For it is said in the time to come, that the Raven shall grapple with the Wolf. I do not know, for this be the affair of men; but I do know that it is for me to bring forth men against that time."

"Su-Su," Keesh broke in, "thou must hear me—"

"A *man* would beat me with a stick and make me hear," she sneered. "But thou ... here!" She thrust a bunch of bark into his hand. "I cannot give thee myself, but this, yes. It looks fittest in thy hands. It is squaw work, so braid away."

He flung it from him, the angry blood pounding a muddy path under his bronze.

"One thing more," she went on. "There be an old custom which thy father and mine were not strangers to. When a man falls in battle, his scalp is carried away in token. Very good. But thou, who have forsworn the Raven, must do more. Thou must bring me, not scalps, but heads, two heads, and then will I give thee, not bark, but a brave-beaded belt, and sheath, and long Russian knife. Then will I look kindly upon thee once again, and all will be well."

"So," the man pondered. "So." Then he turned and passed out through the light.

"Nay, O Keesh!" she called after him. "Not two heads, but three at least!"

BUT KEESH REMAINED true to his conversion, lived uprightly, and made his tribespeople obey the gospel as propounded by the Rev. Jackson Brown. Through all the time of the Fishing he gave no heed to the Tana-naw, nor took notice of the sly things which were said, nor of the laughter of the women of the many tribes. After the Fishing, Gnob and his people, with great store of salmon, sun-dried and smoke-cured, departed for the Hunting on the head reaches of the Tana-naw. Keesh watched them go, but did not fail in his attendance at Mission service, where he prayed regularly and led the singing with his deep bass voice.

The Rev. Jackson Brown delighted in that deep bass voice, and because of his sterling qualities deemed him the most promising convert. Macklewrath doubted this. He did not believe in the efficacy of the conversion of the heathen, and he was not slow in speaking his mind. But Mr. Brown was a large man, in his way, and he argued it out with such convincingness, all of one long fall night, that the trader, driven from position after position, finally announced in desperation, "Knock out my brains with apples, Brown, if I don't become a convert myself, if Keesh holds fast, true blue, for two years!" Mr. Brown never lost an opportunity, so he clinched the matter on the spot with a virile hand-grip, and thenceforth the conduct of Keesh was to determine the ultimate abiding-place of Macklewrath's soul.

But there came news one day, after the winter's rime had settled down over the land sufficiently for travel. A Tana-naw man arrived at the St. George Mission in quest of ammunition and bringing information that Su-Su had set eyes on Nee-Koo, a nervy young hunter who had bid brilliantly for her by old Gnob's fire. It was at about this time that the Rev. Jackson Brown came upon Keesh by the wood-trail which leads down to the river. Keesh had his best dogs in the harness, and shoved under the sled-lashings was his largest and finest pair of snow-shoes.

"Where goest thou, O Keesh? Hunting?" Mr. Brown asked, falling into the Indian manner.

Keesh looked him steadily in the eyes for a full minute, then started up his dogs. Then again, turning his deliberate gaze upon the missionary, he answered, "No; I go to hell."

IN AN OPEN SPACE, striving to burrow into the snow as though for shelter from the appalling desolateness, huddled three dreary lodges. Ringed all about, a dozen paces away, was the sombre forest. Overhead there was no keen, blue sky of naked space, but a vague, misty curtain, pregnant with snow, which had drawn between. There was no wind, no sound, nothing but the snow and silence. Nor was there even the general stir of life about the camp; for the hunting party had run upon the flank of the caribou herd and the kill had been large. Thus, after the period of fasting had come the plenitude of feasting, and thus, in broad daylight, they slept heavily under their roofs of moosehide.

By a fire, before one of the lodges, five pairs of snow-shoes stood on end in their element, and by the fire sat Su-Su. The hood of her squirrel-skin parka was about her hair, and well-drawn up around her throat; but her hands were unmittened and nimbly at work with needle and sinew, completing the last fantastic design on a belt of leather faced with bright scarlet cloth. A dog, somewhere at the rear of one of the lodges, raised a short, sharp bark, then ceased as abruptly as it had begun. Once, her father, in the lodge at her back, gurgled and grunted in his sleep. "Bad dreams," she smiled to herself. "He grows old, and that last joint was too much."

She placed the last bead, knotted the sinew, and replenished the fire. Then, after gazing long into the flames, she lifted her head to the harsh *crunch-crunch* of a moccasined foot against the flinty snow granules. Keesh was at her side, bending slightly forward to a load which he bore upon his back. This was wrapped loosely in a soft-tanned moosehide, and he dropped it carelessly into the snow and sat down. They looked at each other long and without speech.

"It is a far fetch, O Keesh," she said at last, "a far fetch from St. George Mission by the Yukon."

"Ay," he made answer, absently, his eyes fixed keenly upon the belt and taking note of its girth. "But where is the knife?" he demanded.

"Here." She drew it from inside her parka and flashed its naked length in the firelight. "It is a good knife."

"Give it me!" he commanded.

"Nay, O Keesh," she laughed. "It may be that thou wast not born to wear it."

"Give it me!" he reiterated, without change of tone. "I was so born."

But her eyes, glancing coquettishly past him to the moosehide, saw the snow about it slowly reddening. "It is blood, Keesh?" she asked.

"Ay, it is blood. But give me the belt and the long Russian knife."

She felt suddenly afraid, but thrilled when he took the belt roughly from her, thrilled to the roughness. She looked at him softly, and was aware of a pain at the breast and of small hands clutching her throat.

"It was made for a smaller man," he remarked grimly, drawing in his abdomen and clasping the buckle at the first hole.

Su-Su smiled, and her eyes were yet softer. Again she felt the soft hands at her throat. He was good to look upon, and the belt was indeed small, made for a smaller man; but what did it matter? She could make many belts.

"But the blood?" she asked, urged on by a hope new-born and growing. "The blood, Keesh? Is it ... are they ... heads?"

"Ay."

"They must be very fresh, else would the blood be frozen."

"Ay, it is not cold, and they be fresh, quite fresh."

"Oh, Keesh!" Her face was warm and bright. "And for me?"

"Ay; for thee."

He took hold of a corner of the hide, flirted it open, and rolled the heads out before her.

"Three," he whispered savagely; "nay, four at least."

But she sat transfixed. There they lay—the soft-featured Nee-Koo; the gnarled old face of Gnob; Makamuk, grinning at her with his lifted upper lip; and lastly, Nossabok, his eyelid, up to its old trick, drooped on his girlish cheek in a suggestive wink. There they lay, the fire-light flashing upon and playing over them, and from each of them a widening circle dyed the snow to scarlet.

Thawed by the fire, the white crust gave way beneath the head of Gnob, which rolled over like a thing alive, spun around, and came to rest at her feet. But she did not move. Keesh, too, sat motionless, his eyes unblinking, centred steadfastly upon her.

Once, in the forest, an overburdened pine dropped its load of snow, and the echoes reverberated hollowly down the gorge; but neither stirred. The short day had been waning fast, and darkness was wrapping round the camp when White Fang trotted up toward the fire. He paused to reconnoitre, but not being driven back, came closer. His nose shot swiftly to the side, nostrils a-tremble and bristles rising along the spine; and straight and true, he followed the sudden scent to his master's head. He sniffed it gingerly at first and licked the forehead with his red lolling tongue. Then he sat abruptly down, pointed his nose up at the first faint star, and raised the long wolf-howl.

This brought Su-Su to herself. She glanced across at Keesh, who had unsheathed the Russian knife and was watching her intently. His face was firm and set, and in it she read the law. Slipping back the hood of her parka, she bared her neck and rose to her feet There she paused and took a long look about her, at the rimming forest, at the faint stars in the sky, at the camp, at the snow-shoes in the snow—a last long comprehensive look at life. A light breeze stirred her hair from the side, and for the space of one deep breath she turned her head and followed it around until she met it full-faced.

Then she thought of her children, ever to be unborn, and she walked over to Keesh and said, "I am ready."

THE DEATH OF LIGOUN

Blood for blood, rank for rank.

THLINKET CODE.

"Hear now the death of Ligoun—"

The speaker ceased, or rather suspended utterance, and gazed upon me with an eye of understanding. I held the bottle between our eyes and the fire, indicated with my thumb the depth of the draught, and shoved it over to him; for was he not Palitlum, the Drinker? Many tales had he told me, and long had I waited for this scriptless scribe to speak of the things concerning Ligoun; for he, of all men living, knew these things best.

He tilted back his head with a grunt that slid swiftly into a gurgle, and the shadow of a man's torso, monstrous beneath a huge inverted bottle, wavered and danced on the frown of the cliff at our backs. Palitlum released his lips from the glass with a caressing suck and glanced regretfully up into the ghostly vault of the sky where played the wan white light of the summer borealis.

"It be strange," he said; "cold like water and hot like fire. To the drinker it giveth strength, and from the drinker it taketh away strength. It maketh old men young, and young men old. To the man who is weary it leadeth him to get up and go onward, and to the man unweary it burdeneth him into sleep. My brother was possessed of the heart of a rabbit, yet did he drink of it, and forthwith slay four of his enemies. My father was like a great wolf, showing his teeth to all men, yet did he drink of it and was shot through the back, running swiftly away. It be most strange."

"It is 'Three Star,' and a better than what they poison their bellies with down there," I answered, sweeping my hand, as it were, over the yawning chasm of blackness and down to where the beach fires glinted far below—tiny jets of flame which gave proportion and reality to the night.

Palitlum sighed and shook his head. "Wherefore I am here with thee."

And here he embraced the bottle and me in a look which told more eloquently than speech of his shameless thirst.

"Nay," I said, snuggling the bottle in between my knees. "Speak now of Ligoun. Of the 'Three Star' we will hold speech hereafter."

"There be plenty, and I am not wearied," he pleaded brazenly. "But the feel of it on my lips, and I will speak great words of Ligoun and his last days."

"From the drinker it taketh away strength," I mocked, "and to the man unweary it burdeneth him into sleep."

"Thou art wise," he rejoined, without anger and pridelessly. "Like all of thy brothers, thou art wise. Waking or sleeping, the 'Three Star' be with thee, yet never have I known thee to drink overlong or overmuch. And the while you gather to you the gold that hides in our mountains and the fish that swim in our seas; and Palitlum, and the brothers of Palitlum, dig the gold for thee and net the fish, and are glad to be made glad when out of thy wisdom thou deemest it fit that the 'Three Star' should wet our lips."

"I was minded to hear of Ligoun," I said impatiently. "The night grows short, and we have a sore journey to-morrow."

I yawned and made as though to rise, but Palitlum betrayed a quick anxiety, and with abruptness began:—

"It was Ligoun's desire, in his old age, that peace should be among the tribes. As a young man he had been first of the fighting men and chief over the war-chiefs of the Islands and the Passes. All his days had been full of fighting. More marks he boasted of bone and lead and iron than any other man. Three wives he had, and for each wife two sons; and the sons, eldest born and last and all died by his side in battle. Restless as the bald-face, he ranged wide and far—north to Unalaska and the Shallow Sea; south to the Queen Charlottes, ay, even did he go with the Kakes, it is told, to far Puget Sound, and slay thy brothers in their sheltered houses.

"But, as I say, in his old age he looked for peace among the tribes. Not that he was become afraid, or overfond of the corner by the fire and the well-filled pot. For he slew with the shrewdness and blood-hunger of the fiercest, drew in his belly to famine with the youngest, and with the stoutest faced the bitter seas and stinging trail. But because of his many deeds, and in punishment, a warship carried him away, even to thy country, O Hair-Face and Boston Man; and the years were many ere he came back, and I was grown to something more than a boy and something less than a young man. And Ligoun, being childless in his old age, made much of me, and grown wise, gave me of his wisdom.

"'It be good to fight, O Palitlum,' said he. Nay, O Hair-Face, for I was unknown as Palitlum in those days, being called Olo, the Ever-Hungry. The drink was to come after. 'It be good to fight,' spoke Ligoun, 'but it be foolish. In the Boston Man Country, as I saw with mine eyes, they are not given to fighting one with another, and they be strong. Wherefore, of their strength, they come against us of the Islands and Passes, and we are as camp smoke and sea mist before them. Wherefore I say it be good to fight, most good, but it be likewise foolish.'

"And because of this, though first always of the fighting men, Ligoun's voice was loudest, ever, for peace. And when he was very old, being greatest of chiefs and richest of men, he gave a potlatch. Never was there such a potlatch. Five hundred canoes were lined against the river bank, and in each canoe there came not less than ten of men and women. Eight tribes were there; from the first and oldest man to the last and youngest babe were they there. And then there were men from far-distant tribes, great travelers and seekers who had heard of the potlatch of Ligoun.

And for the length of seven days they filled their bellies with his meat and drink. Eight thousand blankets did he give to them, as I well know, for who but I kept the tally and apportioned according to degree and rank? And in the end Ligoun was a poor man; but his name was on all men's lips, and other chiefs gritted their teeth in envy that he should be so great.

"And so, because there was weight to his words, he counselled peace; and he journeyed to every potlatch and feast and tribal gathering that he might counsel peace. And so it came that we journeyed together, Ligoun and I, to the great feast given by Niblack, who was chief over the river Indians of the Skoot, which is not far from the Stickeen. This was in the last days, and Ligoun was very old and very close to death. He coughed of cold weather and camp smoke, and often the red blood ran from out his mouth till we looked for him to die.

"'Nay,' he said once at such time; 'it were better that I should die when the blood leaps to the knife, and there is a clash of steel and smell of powder, and men crying aloud what of the cold iron and quick lead.' So, it be plain, O Hair-Face, that his heart was yet strong for battle.

"It is very far from the Chilcat to the Skoot, and we were many days in the canoes. And the while the men bent to the paddles, I sat at the feet of Ligoun and received the Law. Of small need for me to say the Law, O Hair-Face, for it be known to me that in this thou art well skilled. Yet do I speak of the Law of blood for blood, and rank for rank. Also did Ligoun go deeper into the matter, saying:—

"'But know this, O Olo, that there be little honor in the killing of a man less than thee. Kill always the man who is greater, and thy honor shall be according to his greatness. But if, of two men, thou killest the lesser, then is shame thine, for which the very squaws will lift their lips at thee. As I say, peace be good; but remember, O Olo, if kill thou must, that thou killest by the Law.'

"It is a way of the Thlinket-folk," Palitlum vouchsafed half apologetically.

And I remembered the gun-fighters and bad men of my own Western land, and was not perplexed at the way of the Thlinket folk.

"In time," Palitlum continued, "we came to Chief Niblack and the Skoots. It was a feast great almost as the potlatch of Ligoun. There were we of the Chilcat, and the Sitkas, and the Stickeens who are neighbors to the Skoots, and the Wrangels and the Hoonahs. There were Sundowns and Tahkos from Port Houghton, and their neighbors the Awks from Douglass Channel; the Naass River people, and the Tongas from north of Dixon, and the Kakes who come from the island called Kupreanoff. Then there were Siwashes from Vancouver, Cassiars from the Gold Mountains, Teslin men, and even Sticks from the Yukon Country.

"It was a mighty gathering. But first of all, there was to be a meeting of the chiefs with Niblack, and a drowning of all enmities in quass. The Russians it was who showed us the way of making quass, for so my father told me,—my father, who got it from his father before him. But to this quass had Niblack added many things, such as sugar, flour, dried apples, and hops, so that it was a man's drink, strong and good. Not so good as 'Three Star,' O Hair-Face, yet good.

"This quass-feast was for the chiefs, and the chiefs only, and there was a score of them. But Ligoun being very old and very great, it was given that I walk with him that he might lean upon my shoulder and that I might ease him down when he took his seat and raise him up when he arose. At the door of Niblack's house, which was of logs and very big, each chief, as was the custom, laid down his spear or rifle and his knife. For as thou knowest, O Hair-Face, strong drink quickens, and old hates flame up, and head and hand are swift to act. But I noted that Ligoun had brought two knives, the one he left outside the door, the other slipped under his blanket, snug to the grip. The other chiefs did likewise, and I was troubled for what was to come.

"The chiefs were ranged, sitting, in a big circle about the room. I stood at Ligoun's elbow. In the middle was the barrel of quass, and by it a slave to serve the drink. First, Niblack made oration, with much show of friendship and many fine words. Then he gave a sign, and the slave dipped a gourd full of quass and passed it to Ligoun, as was fit, for his was the highest rank.

"Ligoun drank it, to the last drop, and I gave him my strength to get on his feet so that he, too, might make oration. He had kind speech for the many tribes, noted the greatness of Niblack to give such a feast, counselled for peace as was his custom, and at the end said that the quass was very good.

"Then Niblack drank, being next of rank to Ligoun, and after him one chief and another in degree and order. And each spoke friendly words and said that the quass was good, till all had drunk. Did I say all? Nay, not all, O Hair-Face. For last of them was one, a lean and catlike man, young of face, with a quick and daring eye, who drank darkly, and spat forth upon the ground, and spoke no word.

"To not say that the quass was good were insult; to spit forth upon the ground were worse than insult. And this very thing did he do. He was known for a chief over the Sticks of the Yukon, and further naught was known of him.

"As I say, it was an insult. But mark this, O Hair-Face: it was an insult, not to Niblack the feast-giver, but to the man chiefest of rank who sat among those of the circle. And that man was Ligoun. There was no sound. All eyes were upon him to see what he might do. He made no movement. His withered lips trembled not into speech; nor did a nostril quiver, nor an eyelid droop. But I saw that he looked wan and gray, as I have seen old men look of bitter mornings when famine pressed, and the women wailed and the children whimpered, and there was no meat nor sign of meat. And as the old men looked, so looked Ligoun.

"There was no sound. It were as a circle of the dead, but that each chief felt beneath his blanket to make sure, and that each chief glanced to his neighbor, right and left, with a measuring eye. I was a stripling; the things I had seen were few; yet I knew it to be the moment one meets but once in all a lifetime.

"The Stick rose up, with every eye upon him, and crossed the room till he stood before Ligoun.

"'I am Opitsah, the Knife,' he said.

"But Ligoun said naught, nor looked at him, but gazed unblinking at the ground.

"'You are Ligoun,' Opitsah said. 'You have killed many men. I am still alive.'

"And still Ligoun said naught, though he made the sign to me and with my strength arose and stood upright on his two feet. He was as an old pine, naked and gray, but still a-shoulder to the frost and storm. His eyes were unblinking, and as he had not heard Opitsah, so it seemed he did not see him.

"And Opitsah was mad with anger, and danced stiff-legged before him, as men do when they wish to give another shame. And Opitsah sang a song of his own greatness and the greatness of his people, filled with bad words for the Chilcats and for Ligoun. And as he danced and sang, Opitsah threw off his blanket and with his knife drew bright circles before the face of Ligoun. And the song he sang was the Song of the Knife.

"And there was no other sound, only the singing of Opitsah, and the circle of chiefs that were as dead, save that the flash of the knife seemed to draw smouldering fire from their eyes. And Ligoun, also, was very still. Yet did he know his death, and was unafraid. And the knife sang closer and yet closer to his face, but his eyes were unblinking and he swayed not to right or left, or this way or that.

"And Opitsah drove in the knife, so, twice on the forehead of Ligoun, and the red blood leaped after it. And then it was that Ligoun gave me the sign to bear up under him with my youth that he might walk. And he laughed with a great scorn, full in the face of Opitsah, the Knife. And he brushed Opitsah to the side, as one brushes to the side a low-hanging branch on the trail and passes on.

"And I knew and understood, for there was but shame in the killing of Opitsah before the faces of a score of greater chiefs. I remembered the Law, and knew Ligoun had it in mind to kill by the Law. And who, chiefest of rank but himself, was there but Niblack? And toward Niblack, leaning on my arm, he walked. And to his other arm, clinging and striking, was Opitsah, too small to soil with his blood the hands of so great a man. And though the knife of Opitsah bit in again and again, Ligoun noted it not, nor winced. And in this fashion we three went our way across the room, Niblack sitting in his blanket and fearful of our coming.

"And now old hates flamed up and forgotten grudges were remembered. Lamuk, a Kake, had had a brother drowned in the bad water of the Stickeen, and the Stickeens had not paid in blankets for their bad water, as was the custom to pay. So Lamuk drove straight with his long knife to the heart of Klok-Kutz the Stickeen. And Katchahook remembered a quarrel of the Naass River people with the Tongas of north of Dixon, and the chief of the Tongas he slew with a pistol which made much noise. And the blood-hunger gripped all the men who sat in the circle, and chief slew chief, or was slain, as chance might be. Also did they stab and shoot at Ligoun, for whoso killed him won great honor and would be unforgotten for the deed. And they were about him like wolves about a moose, only they were so many they were in their own way, and they slew one another to make room. And there was great confusion.

"But Ligoun went slowly, without haste, as though many years were yet before him. It seemed that he was certain he would make his kill, in his own way, ere they could slay him. And as I say, he went slowly, and knives bit into him, and he was red with blood. And though none sought after me, who was a mere stripling, yet did the knives find me, and the hot bullets burn me. And still Ligoun leaned his weight on my youth, and Opitsah struck at him, and we three went forward. And when we stood by Niblack, he was afraid, and covered his head with his blanket. The Skoots were ever cowards.

"And Goolzug and Kadishan, the one a fish-eater and the other a meat-killer, closed together for the honor of their tribes. And they raged madly about, and in their battling swung against the knees of Opitsah, who was overthrown and trampled upon. And a knife, singing through the air, smote Skulpin, of the Sitkas, in the throat, and he flung his arms out blindly, reeling, and dragged me down in his fall.

"And from the ground I beheld Ligoun bend over Niblack, and uncover the blanket from his head, and turn up his face to the light. And Ligoun was in no haste. Being blinded with his own blood, he swept it out of his eyes with the back of his hand, so he might see and be sure. And when he was sure that the upturned face was the face of Niblack, he drew the knife across his throat as one draws a knife across the throat of a trembling deer. And then Ligoun stood erect, singing his death-song and swaying gently to and fro. And Skulpin, who had dragged me down, shot with a pistol from where he lay, and Ligoun toppled and fell, as an old pine topples and falls in the teeth of the wind."

Palitlum ceased. His eyes, smouldering moodily, were bent upon the fire, and his cheek was dark with blood.

"And thou, Palitlum?" I demanded. "And thou?"

"I? I did remember the Law, and I slew Opitsah the Knife, which was well. And I drew Ligoun's own knife from the throat of Niblack, and slew Skulpin, who had dragged me down. For I was a stripling, and I could slay any man and it were honor. And further, Ligoun being dead, there was no need for my youth, and I laid about me with his knife, choosing the chiefest of rank that yet remained."

Palitlum fumbled under his shirt and drew forth a beaded sheath, and from the sheath, a knife. It was a knife home-wrought and crudely fashioned from a whip-saw file; a knife such as one may find possessed by old men in a hundred Alaskan villages.

"The knife of Ligoun?" I said, and Palitlum nodded.

"And for the knife of Ligoun," I said, "will I give thee ten bottles of 'Three Star.'"

But Palitlum looked at me slowly. "Hair-Face, I am weak as water, and easy as a woman. I have soiled my belly with quass, and hooch, and 'Three Star.' My eyes are blunted, my ears have lost their keenness, and my strength has gone into fat. And I am without honor in these days, and am called Palitlum, the Drinker. Yet honor was mine at the potlatch of Niblack, on the Skoot, and the memory of it, and the memory of Ligoun, be dear to me. Nay, didst thou turn the sea itself into 'Three Star' and say that it were all mine for the knife, yet would I keep the knife. I am Palitlum, the Drinker, but I was once Olo, the Ever-Hungry, who bore up Ligoun with his youth!"

"Thou art a great man, Palitlum," I said, "and I honor thee."

Palitlum reached out his hand.

"The 'Three Star' between thy knees be mine for the tale I have told," he said.

And as I looked on the frown of the cliff at our backs, I saw the shadow of a man's torso, monstrous beneath a huge inverted bottle.

LI WAN, THE FAIR

"The sun sinks, Canim, and the heat of the day is gone!"

So called Li Wan to the man whose head was hidden beneath the squirrel-skin robe, but she called softly, as though divided between the duty of waking him and the fear of him awake. For she was afraid of this big husband of hers, who was like unto none of the men she had known. The moose-meat sizzled uneasily, and she moved the frying-pan to one side of the red embers. As she did so she glanced warily at the two Hudson Bay dogs dripping eager slaver from their scarlet tongues and following her every movement. They were huge, hairy fellows, crouched to leeward in the thin smoke-wake of the fire to escape the swarming myriads of mosquitoes. As Li Wan gazed down the steep to where the Klondike flung its swollen flood between the hills, one of the dogs bellied its way forward like a worm, and with a deft, catlike stroke of the paw dipped a chunk of hot meat out of the pan to the ground. But Li Wan caught him from out the tail of her eye, and he sprang back with a snap and a snarl as she rapped him over the nose with a stick of firewood.

"Nay, Olo," she laughed, recovering the meat without removing her eye from him. "Thou art ever hungry, and for that thy nose leads thee into endless troubles."

But the mate of Olo joined him, and together they defied the woman. The hair on their backs and shoulders bristled in recurrent waves of anger, and the thin lips writhed and lifted into ugly wrinkles, exposing the flesh-tearing fangs, cruel and menacing. Their very noses serrulated and shook in brute passion, and they snarled as the wolves snarl, with all the hatred and malignity of the breed impelling them to spring upon the woman and drag her down.

"And thou, too, Bash, fierce as thy master and never at peace with the hand that feeds thee! This is not thy quarrel, so that be thine! and that!"

As she cried, she drove at them with the firewood, but they avoided the blows and refused to retreat. They separated and approached her from either side, crouching low and snarling. Li Wan had struggled with the wolf-dog for mastery from the time she toddled among the skin-bales of the teepee, and she knew a crisis was at hand. Bash had halted, his muscles stiff and tense for the spring; Olo was yet creeping into striking distance.

226

Grasping two blazing sticks by the charred ends, she faced the brutes. The one held back, but Bash sprang, and she met him in mid-air with the flaming weapon. There were sharp yelps of pain and swift odors of burning hair and flesh as he rolled in the dirt and the woman ground the fiery embers into his mouth. Snapping wildly, he flung himself sidewise out of her reach and in a frenzy of fear scrambled for safety. Olo, on the other side, had begun his retreat, when Li Wan reminded him of her primacy by hurling a heavy stick of wood into his ribs. Then the pair retreated under a rain of firewood, and on the edge of the camp fell to licking their wounds and whimpering by turns and snarling.

Li Wan blew the ashes off the meat and sat down again. Her heart had not gone up a beat, and the incident was already old, for this was the routine of life. Canim had not stirred during the disorder, but instead had set up a lusty snoring.

"Come, Canim!" she called. "The heat of the day is gone, and the trail waits for our feet."

The squirrel-skin robe was agitated and cast aside by a brown arm. Then the man's eyelids fluttered and drooped again.

"His pack is heavy," she thought, "and he is tired with the work of the morning."

A mosquito stung her on the neck, and she daubed the unprotected spot with wet clay from a ball she had convenient to hand. All morning, toiling up the divide and enveloped in a cloud of the pests, the man and woman had plastered themselves with the sticky mud, which, drying in the sun, covered their faces with masks of clay. These masks, broken in divers places by the movement of the facial muscles, had constantly to be renewed, so that the deposit was irregular of depth and peculiar of aspect.

Li Wan shook Canim gently but with persistence till he roused and sat up. His first glance was to the sun, and after consulting the celestial timepiece he hunched over to the fire and fell-to ravenously on the meat. He was a large Indian fully six feet in height, deep-chested and heavy-muscled, and his eyes were keener and vested with greater mental vigor than the average of his kind. The lines of will had marked his face deeply, and this, coupled with a sternness and primitiveness, advertised a native indomitability, unswerving of purpose, and prone, when thwarted, to sullen cruelty.

"To-morrow, Li Wan, we shall feast." He sucked a marrow-bone clean and threw it to the dogs. "We shall have *flapjacks* fried in *bacon grease*, and *sugar*, which is more toothsome—"

"*Flapjacks*?" she questioned, mouthing the word curiously.

"Ay," Canim answered with superiority; "and I shall teach you new ways of cookery. Of these things I speak you are ignorant, and of many more things besides. You have lived your days in a little corner of the earth and know nothing. But I,"—he straightened himself and looked at her pridefully,—"I am a great traveler, and have been all places, even among the white people, and I am versed in their ways, and in the ways of many peoples. I am not a tree, born to stand in one place always and know not what there be over the next hill; for I am Canim, the Canoe, made to go here and there and to journey and quest up and down the length and breadth of the world."

She bowed her head humbly. "It is true. I have eaten fish and meat and berries all my days and lived in a little corner of the earth. Nor did I dream the world was so large until you stole me from my people and I cooked and carried for you on the endless trails." She looked up at him suddenly. "Tell me, Canim, does this trail ever end?"

"Nay," he answered. "My trail is like the world; it never ends. My trail *is* the world, and I have travelled it since the time my legs could carry me, and I shall travel it until I die. My father and my mother may be dead, but it is long since I looked upon them, and I do not care. My tribe is like your tribe. It stays in the one place—which is far from here,—but I care naught for my tribe, for I am Canim, the Canoe!"

"And must I, Li Wan, who am weary, travel always your trail until I die?"

"You, Li Wan, are my wife, and the wife travels the husband's trail wheresoever it goes. It is the law. And were it not the law, yet would it be the law of Canim, who is lawgiver unto himself and his."

She bowed her head again, for she knew no other law than that man was the master of woman.

"Be not in haste," Canim cautioned her, as she began to strap the meagre camp outfit to her pack. "The sun is yet hot, and the trail leads down and the footing is good."

She dropped her work obediently and resumed her seat.

Canim regarded her with speculative interest. "You do not squat on your hams like other women," he remarked.

"No," she answered. "It never came easy. It tires me, and I cannot take my rest that way."

"And why is it your feet point not straight before you?"

"I do not know, save that they are unlike the feet of other women."

A satisfied light crept into his eyes, but otherwise he gave no sign.

"Like other women, your hair is black; but have you ever noticed that it is soft and fine, softer and finer than the hair of other women?"

"I have noticed," she answered shortly, for she was not pleased at such cold analysis of her sex-deficiencies.

"It is a year, now, since I took you from your people," he went on, "and you are nigh as shy and afraid of me as when first I looked upon you. How does this thing be?"

Li Wan shook her head. "I am afraid of you, Canim, you are so big and strange. And further, before you looked upon me even, I was afraid of all the young men. I do not know ... I cannot say ... only it seemed, somehow, as though I should not be for them, as though ..."

"Ay," he encouraged, impatient at her faltering.

"As though they were not my kind."

"Not your kind?" he demanded slowly. "Then what is your kind?"

"I do not know, I ..." She shook her head in a bewildered manner. "I cannot put into words the way I felt. It was strangeness in me. I was unlike other maidens, who sought the young men slyly. I could not care for the young men that way. It would have been a great wrong, it seemed, and an ill deed."

"What is the first thing you remember?" Canim asked with abrupt irrelevance.

"Pow-Wah-Kaan, my mother."

"And naught else before Pow-Wah-Kaan?"

"Naught else."

But Canim, holding her eyes with his, searched her secret soul and saw it waver.

"Think, and think hard, Li Wan!" he threatened.

She stammered, and her eyes were piteous and pleading, but his will dominated her and wrung from her lips the reluctant speech.

"But it was only dreams, Canim, ill dreams of childhood, shadows of things not real, visions such as the dogs, sleeping in the sun-warmth, behold and whine out against."

"Tell me," he commanded, "of the things before Pow-Wah-Kaan, your mother."

"They are forgotten memories," she protested. "As a child I dreamed awake, with my eyes open to the day, and when I spoke of the strange things I saw I was laughed at, and the other children were afraid and drew away from me. And when I spoke of the things I saw to Pow-Wah-Kaan, she chided me and said they were evil; also she beat me. It was a sickness, I believe, like the falling-sickness that comes to old men; and in time I grew better and dreamed no more. And now ... I cannot remember"—she brought her hand in a confused manner to her forehead—"they are there, somewhere, but I cannot find them, only ..."

"Only," Canim repeated, holding her.

"Only one thing. But you will laugh at its foolishness, it is so unreal."

"Nay, Li Wan. Dreams are dreams. They may be memories of other lives we have lived. I was once a moose. I firmly believe I was once a moose, what of the things I have seen in dreams, and heard."

Strive as he would to hide it, a growing anxiety was manifest, but Li Wan, groping after the words with which to paint the picture, took no heed.

"I see a snow-tramped space among the trees," she began, "and across the snow the sign of a man where he has dragged himself heavily on hand and knee. And I see, too, the man in the snow, and it seems I am very close to him when I look. He is unlike real men, for he has hair on his face, much hair, and the hair of his face and head is yellow like the summer coat of the weasel. His eyes are closed, but they open and search about. They are blue like the sky, and look into mine and search no more. And his hand moves, slow, as from weakness, and I feel ..."

"Ay," Canim whispered hoarsely. "You feel—?"

"No! no!" she cried in haste. "I feel nothing. Did I say 'feel'? I did not mean it. It could not be that I should mean it. I see, and I see only, and that is all I see—a man in the snow, with eyes like the sky, and hair like the weasel. I have seen it many times, and always it is the same—a man in the snow—"

"And do you see yourself?" he asked, leaning forward and regarding her intently. "Do you ever see yourself and the man in the snow?"

"Why should I see myself? Am I not real?"

His muscles relaxed and he sank back, an exultant satisfaction in his eyes which he turned from her so that she might not see.

"I will tell you, Li Wan," he spoke decisively; "you were a little bird in some life before, a little moose-bird, when you saw this thing, and the memory of it is with you yet. It is not strange. I was once a moose, and my father's father afterward became a bear—so said the shaman, and the shaman cannot lie. Thus, on the Trail of the Gods we pass from life to life, and the gods know only and understand. Dreams and the shadows of dreams be memories, nothing more, and the dog, whining asleep in the sun-warmth, doubtless sees and remembers things gone before. Bash, there, was a warrior once. I do firmly believe he was once a warrior."

Canim tossed a bone to the brute and got upon his feet. "Come, let us begone. The sun is yet hot, but it will get no cooler."

"And these white people, what are they like?" Li Wan made bold to ask.

"Like you and me," he answered, "only they are less dark of skin. You will be among them ere the day is dead."

Canim lashed the sleeping-robe to his one-hundred-and-fifty-pound pack, smeared his face with wet clay, and sat down to rest till Li Wan had finished loading the dogs. Olo cringed at sight of the club in her hand, and gave no trouble when the bundle of forty pounds and odd was strapped upon him. But Bash was aggrieved and truculent, and could not forbear to whimper and snarl as he was forced to receive the burden. He bristled his back and bared his teeth as she drew the straps tight, the while throwing all the malignancy of his nature into the glances shot at her sideways and backward. And Canim chuckled and said, "Did I not say he was once a very great warrior?"

"These furs will bring a price," he remarked as he adjusted his head-strap and lifted his pack clear of the ground. "A big price. The white men pay well for such goods, for they have no time to hunt and are soft to the cold. Soon shall we feast, Li Wan, as you have feasted never in all the lives you have lived before."

She grunted acknowledgment and gratitude for her lord's condescension, slipped into the harness, and bent forward to the load.

"The next time I am born, I would be born a white man," he added, and swung off down the trail which dived into the gorge at his feet.

The dogs followed close at his heels, and Li Wan brought up the rear. But her thoughts were far away, across the Ice Mountains to the east, to the little corner of the earth where her childhood had been lived. Ever as a child, she remembered, she had been looked upon as strange, as one with an affliction. Truly she had dreamed awake and been scolded and beaten for the remarkable visions she saw, till, after a time, she had outgrown them. But not utterly. Though they troubled her no more waking, they came to her in her sleep, grown woman that she was, and many a night of nightmare was hers, filled with fluttering shapes, vague and meaningless. The talk with Canim had excited her, and down all the twisted slant of the divide she harked back to the mocking fantasies of her dreams.

"Let us take breath," Canim said, when they had tapped midway the bed of the main creek.

He rested his pack on a jutting rock, slipped the head-strap, and sat down. Li Wan joined him, and the dogs sprawled panting on the ground beside them. At their feet rippled the glacial drip of the hills, but it was muddy and discolored, as if soiled by some commotion of the earth.

"Why is this?" Li Wan asked.

"Because of the white men who work in the ground. Listen!" He held up his hand, and they heard the ring of pick and shovel, and the sound of men's voices. "They are made mad by gold, and work without ceasing that they may find it. Gold? It is yellow and comes from the ground, and is considered of great value. It is also a measure of price."

But Li Wan's roving eyes had called her attention from him. A few yards below and partly screened by a clump of young spruce, the tiered logs of a cabin rose to meet its overhanging roof of dirt. A thrill ran through her, and all her dream-phantoms roused up and stirred about uneasily.

"Canim," she whispered in an agony of apprehension. "Canim, what is that?"

"The white man's teepee, in which he eats and sleeps."

She eyed it wistfully, grasping its virtues at a glance and thrilling again at the unaccountable sensations it aroused. "It must be very warm in time of frost," she said aloud, though she felt that she must make strange sounds with her lips.

She felt impelled to utter them, but did not, and the next instant Canim said, "It is called a *cabin*."

Her heart gave a great leap. The sounds! the very sounds! She looked about her in sudden awe. How should she know that strange word before ever she heard it? What could be the matter? And then with a shock, half of fear and half of delight, she realized that for the first time in her life there had been sanity and significance in the promptings of her dreams.

"*Cabin*" she repeated to herself. "*Cabin*." An incoherent flood of dream-stuff welled up and up till her head was dizzy and her heart seemed bursting. Shadows, and looming bulks of things, and unintelligible associations fluttered and whirled about, and she strove vainly with her consciousness to grasp and hold them. For she felt that there, in that welter of memories, was the key of the mystery; could she but grasp and hold it, all would be clear and plain—

O Canim! O Pow-Wah-Kaan! O shades and shadows, what was that?

She turned to Canim, speechless and trembling, the dream-stuff in mad, overwhelming riot. She was sick and fainting, and could only listen to the ravishing sounds which proceeded from the cabin in a wonderful rhythm.

"Hum, *fiddle*," Canim vouchsafed.

But she did not hear him, for in the ecstasy she was experiencing, it seemed at last that all things were coming clear. Now! now! she thought. A sudden moisture swept into her eyes, and the tears trickled down her cheeks. The mystery was unlocking, but the faintness was overpowering her. If only she could hold herself long enough! If only—but the landscape bent and crumpled up, and the hills swayed back and forth across the sky as she sprang upright and screamed, "*Daddy! Daddy!*" Then the sun reeled, and darkness smote her, and she pitched forward limp and headlong among the rocks.

Canim looked to see if her neck had been broken by the heavy pack, grunted his satisfaction, and threw water upon her from the creek. She came to slowly, with choking sobs, and sat up.

"It is not good, the hot sun on the head," he ventured.

And she answered, "No, it is not good, and the pack bore upon me hard."

"We shall camp early, so that you may sleep long and win strength," he said gently. "And if we go now, we shall be the quicker to bed."

Li Wan said nothing, but tottered to her feet in obedience and stirred up the dogs. She took the swing of his pace mechanically, and followed him past the cabin, scarce daring to breathe. But no sounds issued forth, though the door was open and smoke curling upward from the sheet-iron stovepipe.

They came upon a man in the bend of the creek, white of skin and blue of eye, and for a moment Li Wan saw the other man in the snow. But she saw dimly, for she was weak and tired from what she had undergone. Still, she looked at him curiously, and stopped with Canim to watch him at his work. He was washing gravel in a large pan, with a circular, tilting movement; and as they looked, giving a deft flirt, he flashed up the yellow gold in a broad streak across the bottom of the pan.

"Very rich, this creek," Canim told her, as they went on. "Sometime I will find such a creek, and then I shall be a big man."

Cabins and men grew more plentiful, till they came to where the main portion of the creek was spread out before them. It was the scene of a vast devastation. Everywhere the earth was torn and rent as though by a Titan's struggles. Where there were no upthrown mounds of gravel, great holes and trenches yawned, and chasms where the thick rime of the earth had been peeled to bed-rock. There was no worn channel for the creek, and its waters, dammed up, diverted, flying through the air on giddy flumes, trickling into sinks and low places, and raised by huge water-wheels, were used and used again a thousand times. The hills had been stripped of their trees, and their raw sides gored and perforated by great timber-slides and prospect holes. And over all, like a monstrous race of ants, was flung an army of men—mud-covered, dirty, disheveled men, who crawled in and out of the holes of their digging, crept like big bugs along the flumes, and toiled and sweated at the gravel-heaps which they kept in constant unrest—men, as far as the eye could see, even to the rims of the hilltops, digging, tearing, and scouring the face of nature.

Li Wan was appalled at the tremendous upheaval. "Truly, these men are mad," she said to Canim.

"Small wonder. The gold they dig after is a great thing," he replied. "It is the greatest thing in the world."

For hours they threaded the chaos of greed, Canim eagerly intent, Li Wan weak and list-less. She knew she had been on the verge of disclosure, and she felt that she was still on the verge of disclosure, but the nervous strain she had undergone had tired her, and she passively waited for the thing, she knew not what, to happen. From every hand her senses snatched up and conveyed to her innumerable impressions, each of which became a dull excitation to her jaded imagination. Somewhere within her, responsive notes were answering to the things without, forgotten and undreamed-of correspondences were being renewed; and she was aware of it in an incurious way, and her soul was troubled, but she was not equal to the mental exultation necessary to transmute and understand. So she plodded wearily on at the heels of her lord, content to wait for that which she knew, somewhere, somehow, must happen.

After undergoing the mad bondage of man, the creek finally returned to its ancient ways, all soiled and smirched from its toil, and coiled lazily among the broad flats and timbered spaces where the valley widened to its mouth. Here the "pay" ran out, and men were loth to loiter with the lure yet beyond. And here, as Li Wan paused to prod Olo with her staff, she heard the mellow silver of a woman's laughter.

Before a cabin sat a woman, fair of skin and rosy as a child, dimpling with glee at the words of another woman in the doorway. But the woman who sat shook about her great masses of dark, wet hair which yielded up its dampness to the warm caresses of the sun.

For an instant Li Wan stood transfixed. Then she was aware of a blinding flash, and a snap, as though something gave way; and the woman before the cabin vanished, and the cabin and the tall spruce timber, and the jagged sky-line, and Li Wan saw another woman, in the shine of another sun, brushing great masses of black hair, and singing as she brushed. And Li Wan heard the words of the song, and understood, and was a child again. She was smitten with a vision, wherein all the troublesome dreams merged and became one, and shapes and shadows took up their accustomed round, and all was clear and plain and real. Many pictures jostled past, strange scenes, and trees, and flowers, and people; and she saw them and knew them all.

"When you were a little bird, a little moose-bird," Canim said, his eyes upon her and burning into her.

"When I was a little moose-bird," she whispered, so faint and low he scarcely heard. And she knew she lied, as she bent her head to the strap and took the swing of the trail.

And such was the strangeness of it, the real now became unreal. The mile tramp and the pitching of camp by the edge of the stream seemed like a passage in a nightmare. She cooked the meat, fed the dogs, and unlashed the packs as in a dream, and it was not until Canim began to sketch his next wandering that she became herself again.

"The Klondike runs into the Yukon," he was saying; "a mighty river, mightier than the Mackenzie, of which you know. So we go, you and I, down to Fort o' Yukon. With dogs, in time of winter, it is twenty sleeps. Then we follow the Yukon away into the west—one hundred sleeps, two hundred—I have never heard. It is very far. And then we come to the sea. You know nothing of the sea, so let me tell you. As the lake is to the island, so the sea is to the land; all the rivers run to it, and it is without end. I have seen it at Hudson Bay; I have yet to see it in Alaska. And then we may take a great canoe upon the sea, you and I, Li Wan, or we may follow the land into the south many a hundred sleeps. And after that I do not know, save that I am Canim, the Canoe, wanderer and far-journeyer over the earth!"

She sat and listened, and fear ate into her heart as she pondered over this plunge into the illimitable wilderness. "It is a weary way," was all she said, head bowed on knee in resignation.

Then it was a splendid thought came to her, and at the wonder of it she was all aglow. She went down to the stream and washed the dried clay from her face. When the ripples died away, she stared long at her mirrored features; but sun and weather-beat had done their work, and, what of roughness and bronze, her skin was not soft and dimpled as a child's. But the thought was still splendid and the glow unabated as she crept in beside her husband under the sleeping-robe.

She lay awake, staring up at the blue of the sky and waiting for Canim to sink into the first deep sleep. When this came about, she wormed slowly and carefully away, tucked the robe around him, and stood up. At her second step, Bash growled savagely. She whispered persuasively to him and glanced at the man. Canim was snoring profoundly. Then she turned, and with swift, noiseless feet sped up the back trail.

Mrs. Evelyn Van Wyck was just preparing for bed. Bored by the duties put upon her by society, her wealth, and widowed blessedness, she had journeyed into the Northland and gone to housekeeping in a cosey cabin on the edge of the diggings. Here, aided and abetted by her friend and companion, Myrtle Giddings, she played at living close to the soil, and cultivated the primitive with refined abandon.

She strove to get away from the generations of culture and parlor selection, and sought the earth-grip her ancestors had forfeited. Likewise she induced mental states which she fondly believed to approximate those of the stone-folk, and just now, as she put up her hair for the pillow, she was indulging her fancy with a palaeolithic wooing. The details consisted principally of cave-dwellings and cracked marrow-bones, intersprinkled with fierce carnivora, hairy mammoths, and combats with rude flaked knives of flint; but the sensations were delicious. And as Evelyn Van Wyck fled through the sombre forest aisles before the too arduous advances of her slant-browed, skin-clad wooer, the door of the cabin opened, without the courtesy of a knock, and a skin-clad woman, savage and primitive, came in.

"Mercy!"

With a leap that would have done credit to a cave-woman, Miss Giddings landed in safety behind the table. But Mrs. Van Wyck held her ground. She noticed that the intruder was laboring under a strong excitement, and cast a swift glance backward to assure herself that the way was clear to the bunk, where the big Colt's revolver lay beneath a pillow.

"Greeting, O Woman of the Wondrous Hair," said Li Wan.

But she said it in her own tongue, the tongue spoken in but a little corner of the earth, and the women did not understand.

"Shall I go for help?" Miss Giddings quavered.

"The poor creature is harmless, I think," Mrs. Van Wyck replied. "And just look at her skin-clothes, ragged and trail-worn and all that. They are certainly unique. I shall buy them for my collection. Get my sack, Myrtle, please, and set up the scales."

Li Wan followed the shaping of the lips, but the words were unintelligible, and then, and for the first time, she realized, in a moment of suspense and indecision, that there was no medium of communication between them.

And at the passion of her dumbness she cried out, with arms stretched wide apart, "O Woman, thou art sister of mine!"

The tears coursed down her cheeks as she yearned toward them, and the break in her voice carried the sorrow she could not utter. But Miss Giddings was trembling, and even Mrs. Van Wyck was disturbed.

"I would live as you live. Thy ways are my ways, and our ways be one. My husband is Canim, the Canoe, and he is big and strange, and I am afraid. His trail is all the world and never ends, and I am weary. My mother was like you, and her hair was as thine, and her eyes. And life was soft to me then, and the sun warm."

She knelt humbly, and bent her head at Mrs. Van Wyck's feet. But Mrs. Van Wyck drew away, frightened at her vehemence.

Li Wan stood up, panting for speech. Her dumb lips could not articulate her overmastering consciousness of kind.

"Trade? you trade?" Mrs. Van Wyck questioned, slipping, after the fashion of the superior peoples, into pigeon tongue.

She touched Li Wan's ragged skins to indicate her choice, and poured several hundreds of gold into the blower. She stirred the dust about and trickled its yellow lustre temptingly through her fingers. But Li Wan saw only the fingers, milk-white and shapely, tapering daintily to the rosy, jewel-like nails. She placed her own hand alongside, all work-worn and calloused, and wept.

Mrs. Van Wyck misunderstood. "Gold," she encouraged. "Good gold! You trade? You changee for changee?" And she laid her hand again on Li Wan's skin garments.

"How much? You sell? How much?" she persisted, running her hand against the way of the hair so that she might make sure of the sinew-thread seam.

But Li Wan was deaf as well, and the woman's speech was without significance. Dismay at her failure sat upon her. How could she identify herself with these women? For she knew they were of the one breed, blood-sisters among men and the women of men. Her eyes roved wildly about the interior, taking in the soft draperies hanging around, the feminine garments, the oval mirror, and the dainty toilet accessories beneath. And the things haunted her, for she had seen like things before, and as she looked at them her lips involuntarily formed sounds which her throat trembled to utter. Then a thought flashed upon her, and she steadied herself. She must be calm. She must control herself, for there must be no misunderstanding this time, or else,—and she shook with a storm of suppressed tears and steadied herself again.

She put her hand on the table. "*Table*," she clearly and distinctly enunciated. "*Table*," she repeated.

She looked at Mrs. Van Wyck, who nodded approbation. Li Wan exulted, but brought her will to bear and held herself steady. "*Stove*" she went on. "*Stove*."

And at every nod of Mrs. Van Wyck, Li Wan's excitement mounted. Now stumbling and halting, and again in feverish haste, as the recrudescence of forgotten words was fast or slow, she moved about the cabin, naming article after article. And when she paused finally, it was in triumph, with body erect and head thrown back, expectant, waiting.

"Cat," Mrs. Van Wyck, laughing, spelled out in kindergarten fashion. "I—see—the—cat—catch—the—rat."

Li Wan nodded her head seriously. They were beginning to understand her at last, these women. The blood flushed darkly under her bronze at the thought, and she smiled and nodded her head still more vigorously.

Mrs. Van Wyck turned to her companion. "Received a smattering of mission education somewhere, I fancy, and has come to show it off."

"Of course," Miss Giddings tittered. "Little fool! We shall lose our sleep with her vanity."

"All the same I want that jacket. If it *is* old, the workmanship is good—a most excellent specimen." She returned to her visitor. "Changee for changee? You! Changee for changee? How much? Eh? How much, you?"

"Perhaps she'd prefer a dress or something," Miss Giddings suggested.

Mrs. Van Wyck went up to Li Wan and made signs that she would exchange her wrapper for the jacket. And to further the transaction, she took Li Wan's hand and placed it amid the lace and ribbons of the flowing bosom, and rubbed the fingers back and forth so they might feel the texture. But the jeweled butterfly which loosely held the fold in place was insecurely fastened, and the front of the gown slipped to the side, exposing a firm white breast, which had never known the lip-clasp of a child.

Mrs. Van Wyck coolly repaired the mischief; but Li Wan uttered a loud cry, and ripped and tore at her skin-shirt till her own breast showed firm and white as Evelyn Van Wyck's. Murmuring inarticulately and making swift signs, she strove to establish the kinship.

"A half-breed," Mrs. Van Wyck commented. "I thought so from her hair."

Miss Giddings made a fastidious gesture. "Proud of her father's white skin. It's beastly! Do give her something, Evelyn, and make her go."

But the other woman sighed. "Poor creature, I wish I could do something for her."

A heavy foot crunched the gravel without. Then the cabin door swung wide, and Canim stalked in. Miss Giddings saw a vision of sudden death, and screamed; but Mrs. Van Wyck faced him composedly.

"What do you want?" she demanded.

"How do?" Canim answered suavely and directly, pointing at the same time to Li Wan. "Um my wife."

He reached out for her, but she waved him back.

"Speak, Canim! Tell them that I am—"

"Daughter of Pow-Wah-Kaan? Nay, of what is it to them that they should care? Better should I tell them thou art an ill wife, given to creeping from thy husband's bed when sleep is heavy in his eyes."

Again he reached out for her, but she fled away from him to Mrs. Van Wyck, at whose feet she made frenzied appeal, and whose knees she tried to clasp. But the lady stepped back and gave permission with her eyes to Canim. He gripped Li Wan under the shoulders and raised her to her feet. She fought with him, in a madness of despair, till his chest was heaving with the exertion, and they had reeled about over half the room.

"Let me go, Canim," she sobbed.

But he twisted her wrist till she ceased to struggle. "The memories of the little moose-bird are overstrong and make trouble," he began.

"I know! I know!" she broke in. "I see the man in the snow, and as never before I see him crawl on hand and knee. And I, who am a little child, am carried on his back. And this is before Pow-Wah-Kaan and the time I came to live in a little corner of the earth."

"You know," he answered, forcing her toward the door; "but you will go with me down the Yukon and forget."

"Never shall I forget! So long as my skin is white shall I remember!" She clutched frantically at the door-post and looked a last appeal to Mrs. Evelyn Van Wyck.

"Then will I teach thee to forget, I, Canim, the Canoe!"

As he spoke he pulled her fingers clear and passed out with her upon the trail.

THE LEAGUE OF THE OLD MEN

AT THE BARRACKS a man was being tried for his life. He was an old man, a native from the Whitefish River, which empties into the Yukon below Lake Le Barge. All Dawson was wrought up over the affair, and likewise the Yukon dwellers for a thousand miles up and down. It has been the custom of the land-robbing and sea-robbing Anglo-Saxon to give the law to conquered peoples, and ofttimes this law is harsh. But in the case of Imber the law for once seemed inadequate and weak. In the mathematical nature of things, equity did not reside in the punishment to be accorded him. The punishment was a foregone conclusion, there could be no doubt of that; and though it was capital, Imber had but one life, while the tale against him was one of scores.

In fact, the blood of so many was upon his hands that the killings attributed to him did not permit of precise enumeration. Smoking a pipe by the trail-side or lounging around the stove, men made rough estimates of the numbers that had perished at his hand. They had been whites, all of them, these poor murdered people, and they had been slain singly, in pairs, and in parties. And so purposeless and wanton had been these killings, that they had long been a mystery to the mounted police, even in the time of the captains, and later, when the creeks realized, and a governor came from the Dominion to make the land pay for its prosperity.

But more mysterious still was the coming of Imber to Dawson to give himself up. It was in the late spring, when the Yukon was growling and writhing under its ice, that the old Indian climbed painfully up the bank from the river trail and stood blinking on the main street. Men who had witnessed his advent, noted that he was weak and tottery, and that he staggered over to a heap of cabin-logs and sat down. He sat there a full day, staring straight before him at the unceasing tide of white men that flooded past. Many a head jerked curiously to the side to meet his stare, and more than one remark was dropped anent the old Siwash with so strange a look upon his face. No end of men remembered afterward that they had been struck by his extraordinary figure, and forever afterward prided themselves upon their swift discernment of the unusual.

But it remained for Dickensen, Little Dickensen, to be the hero of the occasion. Little Dickensen had come into the land with great dreams and a pocketful of cash; but with the cash the dreams vanished, and to earn his passage back to the States he had accepted a clerical position with the brokerage firm of Holbrook and Mason. Across the street from the office of Holbrook and Mason was the heap of cabin-logs upon which Imber sat. Dickensen looked out of the window at him before he went to lunch; and when he came back from lunch he looked out of the window, and the old Siwash was still there.

Dickensen continued to look out of the window, and he, too, forever afterward prided himself upon his swiftness of discernment. He was a romantic little chap, and he likened the immobile old heathen to the genius of the Siwash race, gazing calm-eyed upon the hosts of the invading Saxon. The hours swept along, but Imber did not vary his posture, did not by a hair's-breadth move a muscle; and Dickensen remembered the man who once sat upright on a sled in the main street where men passed to and fro. They thought the man was resting, but later, when they touched him, they found him stiff and cold, frozen to death in the midst of the busy street. To undouble him, that he might fit into a coffin, they had been forced to lug him to a fire and thaw him out a bit. Dickensen shivered at the recollection.

Later on, Dickensen went out on the sidewalk to smoke a cigar and cool off; and a little later Emily Travis happened along. Emily Travis was dainty and delicate and rare, and whether in London or Klondike she gowned herself as befitted the daughter of a millionaire mining engineer. Little Dickensen deposited his cigar on an outside window ledge where he could find it again, and lifted his hat.

They chatted for ten minutes or so, when Emily Travis, glancing past Dickensen's shoulder, gave a startled little scream. Dickensen turned about to see, and was startled, too. Imber had crossed the street and was standing there, a gaunt and hungry-looking shadow, his gaze riveted upon the girl.

"What do you want?" Little Dickensen demanded, tremulously plucky.

Imber grunted and stalked up to Emily Travis. He looked her over, keenly and carefully, every square inch of her. Especially did he appear interested in her silky brown hair, and in the color of her cheek, faintly sprayed and soft, like the downy bloom of a butterfly wing. He walked around her, surveying her with the calculating eye of a man who studies the lines upon which a horse or a boat is builded. In the course of his circuit the pink shell of her ear came between his eye and the westering sun, and he stopped to contemplate its rosy transparency. Then he returned to her face and looked long and intently into her blue eyes. He grunted and laid a hand on her arm midway between the shoulder and elbow. With his other hand he lifted her forearm and doubled it back. Disgust and wonder showed in his face, and he dropped her arm with a contemptuous grunt. Then he muttered a few guttural syllables, turned his back upon her, and addressed himself to Dickensen.

Dickensen could not understand his speech, and Emily Travis laughed. Imber turned from one to the other, frowning, but both shook their heads. He was about to go away, when she called out:

"Oh, Jimmy! Come here!"

Jimmy came from the other side of the street. He was a big, hulking Indian clad in approved white-man style, with an Eldorado king's sombrero on his head. He talked with Imber, haltingly, with throaty spasms. Jimmy was a Sitkan, possessed of no more than a passing knowledge of the interior dialects.

"Him Whitefish man," he said to Emily Travis. "Me savve um talk no very much. Him want to look see chief white man."

"The Governor," suggested Dickensen.

Jimmy talked some more with the Whitefish man, and his face went grave and puzzled.

"I t'ink um want Cap'n Alexander," he explained. "Him say um kill white man, white woman, white boy, plenty kill um white people. Him want to die."

"Insane, I guess," said Dickensen.

"What you call dat?" queried Jimmy.

Dickensen thrust a finger figuratively inside his head and imparted a rotary motion thereto.

"Mebbe so, mebbe so," said Jimmy, returning to Imber, who still demanded the chief man of the white men.

A mounted policeman (unmounted for Klondike service) joined the group and heard Imber's wish repeated. He was a stalwart young fellow, broad-shouldered, deep-chested, legs cleanly built and stretched wide apart, and tall though Imber was, he towered above him by half a head. His eyes were cool, and gray, and steady, and he carried himself with the peculiar confidence of power that is bred of blood and tradition. His splendid masculinity was emphasized by his excessive boyishness,—he was a mere lad,—and his smooth cheek promised a blush as willingly as the cheek of a maid.

Imber was drawn to him at once. The fire leaped into his eyes at sight of a sabre slash that scarred his cheek. He ran a withered hand down the young fellow's leg and caressed the swelling thew. He smote the broad chest with his knuckles, and pressed and prodded the thick muscle-pads that covered the shoulders like a cuirass. The group had been added to by curious passers-by—husky miners, mountaineers, and frontiersmen, sons of the long-legged and broad-shouldered generations. Imber glanced from one to another, then he spoke aloud in the Whitefish tongue.

"What did he say?" asked Dickensen.

"Him say um all the same one man, dat p'liceman," Jimmy interpreted.

Little Dickensen was little, and what of Miss Travis, he felt sorry for having asked the question.

The policeman was sorry for him and stepped into the breach. "I fancy there may be something in his story. I'll take him up to the captain for examination. Tell him to come along with me, Jimmy."

Jimmy indulged in more throaty spasms, and Imber grunted and looked satisfied.

"But ask him what he said, Jimmy, and what he meant when he took hold of my arm."

So spoke Emily Travis, and Jimmy put the question and received the answer.

"Him say you no afraid," said Jimmy.

Emily Travis looked pleased.

"Him say you no *skookum*, no strong, all the same very soft like little baby. Him break you, in um two hands, to little pieces. Him t'ink much funny, very strange, how you can be mother of men so big, so strong, like dat p'liceman."

Emily Travers kept her eyes up and unfaltering, but her cheeks were sprayed with scarlet. Little Dickensen blushed and was quite embarrassed. The policeman's face blazed with his boy's blood.

"Come along, you," he said gruffly, setting his shoulder to the crowd and forcing a way.

Thus it was that Imber found his way to the Barracks, where he made full and voluntary confession, and from the precincts of which he never emerged.

Imber looked very tired. The fatigue of hopelessness and age was in his face. His shoulders drooped depressingly, and his eyes were lack-lustre. His mop of hair should have been white, but sun and weatherbeat had burned and bitten it so that it hung limp and lifeless and colorless. He took no interest in what went on around him. The courtroom was jammed with the men of the creeks and trails, and there was an ominous note in the rumble and grumble of their low-pitched voices, which came to his ears like the growl of the sea from deep caverns.

He sat close by a window, and his apathetic eyes rested now and again on the dreary scene without. The sky was overcast, and a gray drizzle was falling. It was flood-time on the Yukon. The ice was gone, and the river was up in the town. Back and forth on the main street, in canoes and poling-boats, passed the people that never rested. Often he saw these boats turn aside from the street and enter the flooded square that marked the Barracks' parade-ground. Sometimes they disappeared beneath him, and he heard them jar against the house-logs and their occupants scramble in through the window. After that came the slush of water against men's legs as they waded across the lower room and mounted the stairs. Then they appeared in the doorway, with doffed hats and dripping sea-boots, and added themselves to the waiting crowd.

And while they centred their looks on him, and in grim anticipation enjoyed the penalty he was to pay, Imber looked at them, and mused on their ways, and on their Law that never slept, but went on unceasing, in good times and bad, in flood and famine, through trouble and terror and death, and which would go on unceasing, it seemed to him, to the end of time.

A man rapped sharply on a table, and the conversation droned away into silence. Imber looked at the man. He seemed one in authority, yet Imber divined the square-browed man who sat by a desk farther back to be the one chief over them all and over the man who had rapped. Another man by the same table uprose and began to read aloud from many fine sheets of paper. At the top of each sheet he cleared his throat, at the bottom moistened his fingers. Imber did not understand his speech, but the others did, and he knew that it made them angry. Sometimes it made them very angry, and once a man cursed him, in single syllables, stinging and tense, till a man at the table rapped him to silence.

For an interminable period the man read. His monotonous, sing-song utterance lured Imber to dreaming, and he was dreaming deeply when the man ceased. A voice spoke to him in his own Whitefish tongue, and he roused up, without surprise, to look upon the face of his sister's son, a young man who had wandered away years agone to make his dwelling with the whites.

"Thou dost not remember me," he said by way of greeting.

"Nay," Imber answered. "Thou art Howkan who went away. Thy mother be dead."

"She was an old woman," said Howkan.

But Imber did not hear, and Howkan, with hand upon his shoulder, roused him again.

"I shall speak to thee what the man has spoken, which is the tale of the troubles thou hast done and which thou hast told, O fool, to the Captain Alexander. And thou shalt understand and say if it be true talk or talk not true. It is so commanded."

Howkan had fallen among the mission folk and been taught by them to read and write. In his hands he held the many fine sheets from which the man had read aloud, and which had been taken down by a clerk when Imber first made confession, through the mouth of Jimmy, to Captain Alexander. Howkan began to read. Imber listened for a space, when a wonderment rose up in his face and he broke in abruptly.

"That be my talk, Howkan. Yet from thy lips it comes when thy ears have not heard."

Howkan smirked with self-appreciation. His hair was parted in the middle. "Nay, from the paper it comes, O Imber. Never have my ears heard. From the paper it comes, through my eyes, into my head, and out of my mouth to thee. Thus it comes."

"Thus it comes? It be there in the paper?" Imber's voice sank in whisperful awe as he crackled the sheets 'twixt thumb and finger and stared at the charactery scrawled thereon. "It be a great medicine, Howkan, and thou art a worker of wonders."

"It be nothing, it be nothing," the young man responded carelessly and pridefully. He read at hazard from the document: "*In that year, before the break of the ice, came an old man, and a boy who was lame of one foot. These also did I kill, and the old man made much noise —*"

"It be true," Imber interrupted breathlessly. "He made much noise and would not die for a long time. But how dost thou know, Howkan? The chief man of the white men told thee, mayhap? No one beheld me, and him alone have I told."

Howkan shook his head with impatience. "Have I not told thee it be there in the paper, O fool?"

Imber stared hard at the ink-scrawled surface. "As the hunter looks upon the snow and says, Here but yesterday there passed a rabbit; and here by the willow scrub it stood and listened, and heard, and was afraid; and here it turned upon its trail; and here it went with great swiftness, leaping wide; and here, with greater swiftness and wider leapings, came a lynx; and here, where the claws cut deep into the snow, the lynx made a very great leap; and here it struck, with the rabbit under and rolling belly up; and here leads off the trail of the lynx alone, and there is no more rabbit,—as the hunter looks upon the markings of the snow and says thus and so and here, dost thou, too, look upon the paper and say thus and so and here be the things old Imber hath done?"

"Even so," said Howkan. "And now do thou listen, and keep thy woman's tongue between thy teeth till thou art called upon for speech."

Thereafter, and for a long time, Howkan read to him the confession, and Imber remained musing and silent At the end, he said:

"It be my talk, and true talk, but I am grown old, Howkan, and forgotten things come back to me which were well for the head man there to know. First, there was the man who came over the Ice Mountains, with cunning traps made of iron, who sought the beaver of the Whitefish. Him I slew. And there were three men seeking gold on the Whitefish long ago. Them also I slew, and left them to the wolverines. And at the Five Fingers there was a man with a raft and much meat."

At the moments when Imber paused to remember, Howkan translated and a clerk reduced to writing. The courtroom listened stolidly to each unadorned little tragedy, till Imber told of a red-haired man whose eyes were crossed and whom he had killed with a remarkably long shot.

"Hell," said a man in the forefront of the onlookers. He said it soulfully and sorrowfully. He was red-haired. "Hell," he repeated. "That was my brother Bill." And at regular intervals throughout the session, his solemn "Hell" was heard in the courtroom; nor did his comrades check him, nor did the man at the table rap him to order.

Imber's head drooped once more, and his eyes went dull, as though a film rose up and covered them from the world. And he dreamed as only age can dream upon the colossal futility of youth.

Later, Howkan roused him again, saying: "Stand up, O Imber. It be commanded that thou tellest why you did these troubles, and slew these people, and at the end journeyed here seeking the Law."

Imber rose feebly to his feet and swayed back and forth. He began to speak in a low and faintly rumbling voice, but Howkan interrupted him.

"This old man, he is damn crazy," he said in English to the square-browed man. "His talk is foolish and like that of a child."

"We will hear his talk which is like that of a child," said the square-browed man. "And we will hear it, word for word, as he speaks it. Do you understand?"

Howkan understood, and Imber's eyes flashed, for he had witnessed the play between his sister's son and the man in authority. And then began the story, the epic of a bronze patriot which might well itself be wrought into bronze for the generations unborn. The crowd fell strangely silent, and the square-browed judge leaned head on hand and pondered his soul and the soul of his race. Only was heard the deep tones of Imber, rhythmically alternating with the shrill voice of the interpreter, and now and again, like the bell of the Lord, the wondering and meditative "Hell" of the red-haired man.

"I am Imber of the Whitefish people." So ran the interpretation of Howkan, whose inherent barbarism gripped hold of him, and who lost his mission culture and veneered civilization as he caught the savage ring and rhythm of old Imber's tale. "My father was Otsbaok, a strong man. The land was warm with sunshine and gladness when I was a boy. The people did not hunger after strange things, nor hearken to new voices, and the ways of their fathers were their ways. The women found favor in the eyes of the young men, and the young men looked upon them with content. Babes hung at the breasts of the women, and they were heavy-hipped with increase of the tribe. Men were men in those days. In peace and plenty, and in war and famine, they were men.

"At that time there was more fish in the water than now, and more meat in the forest. Our dogs were wolves, warm with thick hides and hard to the frost and storm. And as with our dogs so with us, for we were likewise hard to the frost and storm. And when the Pellys came into our land we slew them and were slain. For we were men, we Whitefish, and our fathers and our fathers' fathers had fought against the Pellys and determined the bounds of the land.

"As I say, with our dogs, so with us. And one day came the first white man. He dragged himself, so, on hand and knee, in the snow. And his skin was stretched tight, and his bones were sharp beneath. Never was such a man, we thought, and we wondered of what strange tribe he was, and of its land. And he was weak, most weak, like a little child, so that we gave him a place by the fire, and warm furs to lie upon, and we gave him food as little children are given food.

"And with him was a dog, large as three of our dogs, and very weak. The hair of this dog was short, and not warm, and the tail was frozen so that the end fell off. And this strange dog we fed, and bedded by the fire, and fought from it our dogs, which else would have killed him. And what of the moose meat and the sun-dried salmon, the man and dog took strength to themselves; and what of the strength they became big and unafraid. And the man spoke loud words and laughed at the old men and young men, and looked boldly upon the maidens. And the dog fought with our dogs, and for all of his short hair and softness slew three of them in one day.

"When we asked the man concerning his people, he said, 'I have many brothers,' and laughed in a way that was not good. And when he was in his full strength he went away, and with him went Noda, daughter to the chief. First, after that, was one of our bitches brought to pup. And never was there such a breed of dogs,—big-headed, thick-jawed, and short-haired, and helpless. Well do I remember my father, Otsbaok, a strong man. His face was black with anger at such helplessness, and he took a stone, so, and so, and there was no more helplessness. And two summers after that came Noda back to us with a man-child in the hollow of her arm.

"And that was the beginning. Came a second white man, with short-haired dogs, which he left behind him when he went. And with him went six of our strongest dogs, for which, in trade, he had given Koo-So-Tee, my mother's brother, a wonderful pistol that fired with great swiftness six times. And Koo-So-Tee was very big, what of the pistol, and laughed at our bows and arrows. 'Woman's things,' he called them, and went forth against the bald-face grizzly, with the pistol in his hand. Now it be known that it is not good to hunt the bald-face with a pistol, but how were we to know? and how was Koo-So-Tee to know? So he went against the bald-face, very brave, and fired the pistol with great swiftness six times; and the bald-face but grunted and broke in his breast like it were an egg, and like honey from a bee's nest dripped the brains of Koo-So-Tee upon the ground. He was a good hunter, and there was no one to bring meat to his squaw and children. And we were bitter, and we said, 'That which for the white men is well, is for us not well.' And this be true. There be many white men and fat, but their ways have made us few and lean.

"Came the third white man, with great wealth of all manner of wonderful foods and things. And twenty of our strongest dogs he took from us in trade. Also, what of presents and great promises, ten of our young hunters did he take with him on a journey which fared no man knew where. It is said they died in the snow of the Ice Mountains where man has never been, or in the Hills of Silence which are beyond the edge of the earth. Be that as it may, dogs and young hunters were seen never again by the Whitefish people.

"And more white men came with the years, and ever, with pay and presents, they led the young men away with them. And sometimes the young men came back with strange tales of dangers and toils in the lands beyond the Pellys, and sometimes they did not come back. And we said: 'If they be unafraid of life, these white men, it is because they have many lives; but we be few by the Whitefish, and the young men shall go away no more.' But the young men did go away; and the young women went also; and we were very wroth.

"It be true, we ate flour, and salt pork, and drank tea which was a great delight; only, when we could not get tea, it was very bad and we became short of speech and quick of anger. So we grew to hunger for the things the white men brought in trade. Trade! trade! all the time was it trade! One winter we sold our meat for clocks that would not go, and watches with broken guts, and files worn smooth, and pistols without cartridges and worthless. And then came famine, and we were without meat, and two score died ere the break of spring.

"'Now are we grown weak,' we said; 'and the Pellys will fall upon us, and our bounds be overthrown.' But as it fared with us, so had it fared with the Pellys, and they were too weak to come against us.

"My father, Otsbaok, a strong man, was now old and very wise. And he spoke to the chief, saying: 'Behold, our dogs be worthless. No longer are they thick-furred and strong, and they die in the frost and harness. Let us go into the village and kill them, saving only the wolf ones, and these let us tie out in the night that they may mate with the wild wolves of the forest. Thus shall we have dogs warm and strong again.'

"And his word was harkened to, and we Whitefish became known for our dogs, which were the best in the land. But known we were not for ourselves. The best of our young men and women had gone away with the white men to wander on trail and river to far places. And the young women came back old and broken, as Noda had come, or they came not at all. And the young men came back to sit by our fires for a time, full of ill speech and rough ways, drinking evil drinks and gambling through long nights and days, with a great unrest always in their hearts, till the call of the white men came to them and they went away again to the unknown places. And they were without honor and respect, jeering the old-time customs and laughing in the faces of chief and shamans.

"As I say, we were become a weak breed, we Whitefish. We sold our warm skins and furs for tobacco and whiskey and thin cotton things that left us shivering in the cold. And the coughing sickness came upon us, and men and women coughed and sweated through the long nights, and the hunters on trail spat blood upon the snow. And now one, and now another, bled swiftly from the mouth and died. And the women bore few children, and those they bore were weak and given to sickness. And other sicknesses came to us from the white men, the like of which we had never known and could not understand. Smallpox, likewise measles, have I heard these sicknesses named, and we died of them as die the salmon in the still eddies when in the fall their eggs are spawned and there is no longer need for them to live.

"And yet, and here be the strangeness of it, the white men come as the breath of death; all their ways lead to death, their nostrils are filled with it; and yet they do not die. Theirs the whiskey, and tobacco, and short-haired dogs; theirs the many sicknesses, the smallpox and measles, the coughing and mouth-bleeding; theirs the white skin, and softness to the frost and storm; and theirs the pistols that shoot six times very swift and are worthless. And yet they grow fat on their many ills, and prosper, and lay a heavy hand over all the world and tread mightily upon its peoples. And their women, too, are soft as little babes, most breakable and never broken, the mothers of men. And out of all this softness, and sickness, and weakness, come strength, and power, and authority. They be gods, or devils, as the case may be. I do not know. What do I know, I, old Imber of the Whitefish? Only do I know that they are past understanding, these white men, far-wanderers and fighters over the earth that they be.

"As I say, the meat in the forest became less and less. It be true, the white man's gun is most excellent and kills a long way off; but of what worth the gun, when there is no meat to kill? When I was a boy on the Whitefish there was moose on every hill, and each year came the caribou uncountable. But now the hunter may take the trail ten days and not one moose gladden his eyes, while the caribou uncountable come no more at all. Small worth the gun, I say, killing a long way off, when there be nothing to kill.

"And I, Imber, pondered upon these things, watching the while the Whitefish, and the Pellys, and all the tribes of the land, perishing as perished the meat of the forest. Long I pondered. I talked with the shamans and the old men who were wise. I went apart that the sounds of the village might not disturb me, and I ate no meat so that my belly should not press upon me and make me slow of eye and ear. I sat long and sleepless in the forest, wide-eyed for the sign, my ears patient and keen for the word that was to come. And I wandered alone in the blackness of night to the river bank, where was wind-moaning and sobbing of water, and where I sought wisdom from the ghosts of old shamans in the trees and dead and gone.

"And in the end, as in a vision, came to me the short-haired and detestable dogs, and the way seemed plain. By the wisdom of Otsbaok, my father and a strong man, had the blood of our own wolf-dogs been kept clean, wherefore had they remained warm of hide and strong in the harness. So I returned to my village and made oration to the men. 'This be a tribe, these white men,' I said. 'A very large tribe, and doubtless there is no longer meat in their land, and they are come among us to make a new land for themselves. But they weaken us, and we die. They are a very hungry folk. Already has our meat gone from us, and it were well, if we would live, that we deal by them as we have dealt by their dogs.'

"And further oration I made, counselling fight. And the men of the Whitefish listened, and some said one thing, and some another, and some spoke of other and worthless things, and no man made brave talk of deeds and war. But while the young men were weak as water and afraid, I watched that the old men sat silent, and that in their eyes fires came and went. And later, when the village slept and no one knew, I drew the old men away into the forest and made more talk. And now we were agreed, and we remembered the good young days, and the free land, and the times of plenty, and the gladness and sunshine; and we called ourselves brothers, and swore great secrecy, and a mighty oath to cleanse the land of the evil breed that had come upon it. It be plain we were fools, but how were we to know, we old men of the Whitefish?

"And to hearten the others, I did the first deed. I kept guard upon the Yukon till the first canoe came down. In it were two white men, and when I stood upright upon the bank and raised my hand they changed their course and drove in to me. And as the man in the bow lifted his head, so, that he might know wherefore I wanted him, my arrow sang through the air straight to his throat, and he knew. The second man, who held paddle in the stern, had his rifle half to his shoulder when the first of my three spear-casts smote him.

"'These be the first,' I said, when the old men had gathered to me. 'Later we will bind together all the old men of all the tribes, and after that the young men who remain strong, and the work will become easy.'

"And then the two dead white men we cast into the river. And of the canoe, which was a very good canoe, we made a fire, and a fire, also, of the things within the canoe. But first we looked at the things, and they were pouches of leather which we cut open with our knives. And inside these pouches were many papers, like that from which thou hast read, O Howkan, with markings on them which we marveled at and could not understand. Now, I am become wise, and I know them for the speech of men as thou hast told me."

A whisper and buzz went around the courtroom when Howkan finished interpreting the affair of the canoe, and one man's voice spoke up: "That was the lost '91 mail, Peter James and Delaney bringing it in and last spoken at Le Barge by Matthews going out." The clerk scratched steadily away, and another paragraph was added to the history of the North.

"There be little more," Imber went on slowly. "It be there on the paper, the things we did. We were old men, and we did not understand. Even I, Imber, do not now understand. Secretly we slew, and continued to slay, for with our years we were crafty and we had learned the swiftness of going without haste. When white men came among us with black looks and rough words, and took away six of the young men with irons binding them helpless, we knew we must slay wider and farther. And one by one we old men departed up river and down to the unknown lands. It was a brave thing. Old we were, and unafraid, but the fear of far places is a terrible fear to men who are old.

"So we slew, without haste and craftily. On the Chilcoot and in the Delta we slew, from the passes to the sea, wherever the white men camped or broke their trails. It be true, they died, but it was without worth. Ever did they come over the mountains, ever did they grow and grow, while we, being old, became less and less. I remember, by the Caribou Crossing, the camp of a white man. He was a very little white man, and three of the old men came upon him in his sleep. And the next day I came upon the four of them. The white man alone still breathed, and there was breath in him to curse me once and well before he died.

"And so it went, now one old man, and now another. Sometimes the word reached us long after of how they died, and sometimes it did not reach us. And the old men of the other tribes were weak and afraid, and would not join with us. As I say, one by one, till I alone was left. I am Imber, of the Whitefish people. My father was Otsbaok, a strong man. There are no Whitefish now. Of the old men I am the last. The young men and young women are gone away, some to live with the Pellys, some with the Salmons, and more with the white men. I am very old, and very tired, and it being vain fighting the Law, as thou sayest, Howkan, I am come seeking the Law."

"O Imber, thou art indeed a fool," said Howkan.

But Imber was dreaming. The square-browed judge likewise dreamed, and all his race rose up before him in a mighty phantasmagoria—his steel-shod, mail-clad race, the lawgiver and world-maker among the families of men. He saw it dawn red-flickering across the dark forests and sullen seas; he saw it blaze, bloody and red, to full and triumphant noon; and down the shaded slope he saw the blood-red sands dropping into night. And through it all he observed the Law, pitiless and potent, ever unswerving and ever ordaining, greater than the motes of men who fulfilled it or were crushed by it, even as it was greater than he, his heart speaking for softness.

LOVE OF LIFE

"This out of all will remain —
They have lived and have tossed:
So much of the game will be gain,
Though the gold of the dice has been lost."

THEY LIMPED PAINFULLY DOWN the bank, and once the foremost of the two men staggered among the rough-strewn rocks. They were tired and weak, and their faces had the drawn expression of patience which comes of hardship long endured. They were heavily burdened with blanket packs which were strapped to their shoulders. Head-straps, passing across the forehead, helped support these packs. Each man carried a rifle. They walked in a stooped posture, the shoulders well forward, the head still farther forward, the eyes bent upon the ground.

"I wish we had just about two of them cartridges that's layin' in that cache of ourn," said the second man.

His voice was utterly and drearily expressionless. He spoke without enthusiasm; and the first man, limping into the milky stream that foamed over the rocks, vouchsafed no reply.

The other man followed at his heels. They did not remove their foot-gear, though the water was icy cold—so cold that their ankles ached and their feet went numb. In places the water dashed against their knees, and both men staggered for footing.

The man who followed slipped on a smooth boulder, nearly fell, but recovered himself with a violent effort, at the same time uttering a sharp exclamation of pain. He seemed faint and dizzy and put out his free hand while he reeled, as though seeking support against the air. When he had steadied himself he stepped forward, but reeled again and nearly fell. Then he stood still and looked at the other man, who had never turned his head.

The man stood still for fully a minute, as though debating with himself. Then he called out:

"I say, Bill, I've sprained my ankle."

Bill staggered on through the milky water. He did not look around. The man watched

246

him go, and though his face was expressionless as ever, his eyes were like the eyes of a wounded deer.

The other man limped up the farther bank and continued straight on without looking back. The man in the stream watched him. His lips trembled a little, so that the rough thatch of brown hair which covered them was visibly agitated. His tongue even strayed out to moisten them.

"Bill!" he cried out.

It was the pleading cry of a strong man in distress, but Bill's head did not turn. The man watched him go, limping grotesquely and lurching forward with stammering gait up the slow slope toward the soft sky-line of the low-lying hill. He watched him go till he passed over the crest and disappeared. Then he turned his gaze and slowly took in the circle of the world that remained to him now that Bill was gone.

Near the horizon the sun was smouldering dimly, almost obscured by formless mists and vapors, which gave an impression of mass and density without outline or tangibility. The man pulled out his watch, the while resting his weight on one leg. It was four o'clock, and as the season was near the last of July or first of August,—he did not know the precise date within a week or two,—he knew that the sun roughly marked the northwest. He looked to the south and knew that somewhere beyond those bleak hills lay the Great Bear Lake; also, he knew that in that direction the Arctic Circle cut its forbidding way across the Canadian Barrens. This stream in which he stood was a feeder to the Coppermine River, which in turn flowed north and emptied into Coronation Gulf and the Arctic Ocean. He had never been there, but he had seen it, once, on a Hudson Bay Company chart.

Again his gaze completed the circle of the world about him. It was not a heartening spectacle. Everywhere was soft sky-line. The hills were all low-lying. There were no trees, no shrubs, no grasses—naught but a tremendous and terrible desolation that sent fear swiftly dawning into his eyes.

"Bill!" he whispered, once and twice; "Bill!"

He cowered in the midst of the milky water, as though the vastness were pressing in upon him with overwhelming force, brutally crushing him with its complacent awfulness. He began to shake as with an ague-fit, till the gun fell from his hand with a splash. This served to rouse him. He fought with his fear and pulled himself together, groping in the water and recovering the weapon. He hitched his pack farther over on his left shoulder, so as to take a portion of its weight from off the injured ankle. Then he proceeded, slowly and carefully, wincing with pain, to the bank.

He did not stop. With a desperation that was madness, unmindful of the pain, he hurried up the slope to the crest of the hill over which his comrade had disappeared—more grotesque and comical by far than that limping, jerking comrade. But at the crest he saw a shallow valley, empty of life. He fought with his fear again, overcame it, hitched the pack still farther over on his left shoulder, and lurched on down the slope.

The bottom of the valley was soggy with water, which the thick moss held, spongelike, close to the surface. This water squirted out from under his feet at every step, and each time he lifted a foot the action culminated in a sucking sound as the wet moss reluctantly released its grip. He picked his way from muskeg to muskeg, and followed the other man's footsteps along and across the rocky ledges which thrust like islets through the sea of moss.

Though alone, he was not lost. Farther on he knew he would come to where dead spruce and fir, very small and weazened, bordered the shore of a little lake, the *titchin-nichilie*, in the tongue of the country, the "land of little sticks." And into that lake flowed a small stream, the water of which was not milky. There was rush-grass on that stream—this he remembered well—but no timber, and he would follow it till its first trickle ceased at a divide. He would cross this divide to the first trickle of another stream, flowing to the west, which he would follow until it emptied into the river Dease, and here he would find a cache under an upturned canoe and piled over with many rocks. And in this cache would be ammunition for his empty gun, fish-hooks and lines, a small net—all the utilities for the killing and snaring of food. Also, he would find flour,—not much,—a piece of bacon, and some beans.

Bill would be waiting for him there, and they would paddle away south down the Dease to the Great Bear Lake. And south across the lake they would go, ever south, till they gained the Mackenzie. And south, still south, they would go, while the winter raced vainly after them, and the ice formed in the eddies, and the days grew chill and crisp, south to some warm Hudson Bay Company post, where timber grew tall and generous and there was grub without end.

These were the thoughts of the man as he strove onward. But hard as he strove with his body, he strove equally hard with his mind, trying to think that Bill had not deserted him, that Bill would surely wait for him at the cache. He was compelled to think this thought, or else there would not be any use to strive, and he would have lain down and died. And as the dim ball of the sun sank slowly into the northwest he covered every inch—and many times— of his and Bill's flight south before the downcoming winter. And he conned the grub of the cache and the grub of the Hudson Bay Company post over and over again. He had not eaten for two days; for a far longer time he had not had all he wanted to eat. Often he stooped and picked pale muskeg berries, put them into his mouth, and chewed and swallowed them. A muskeg berry is a bit of seed enclosed in a bit of water. In the mouth the water melts away and the seed chews sharp and bitter. The man knew there was no nourishment in the berries, but he chewed them patiently with a hope greater than knowledge and defying experience.

At nine o'clock he stubbed his toe on a rocky ledge, and from sheer weariness and weakness staggered and fell. He lay for some time, without movement, on his side. Then he slipped out of the pack-straps and clumsily dragged himself into a sitting posture. It was not yet dark, and in the lingering twilight he groped about among the rocks for shreds of dry moss. When he had gathered a heap he built a fire,—a smouldering, smudgy fire,—and put a tin pot of water on to boil.

He unwrapped his pack and the first thing he did was to count his matches. There were sixty-seven. He counted them three times to make sure. He divided them into several portions, wrapping them in oil paper, disposing of one bunch in his empty tobacco pouch, of another bunch in the inside band of his battered hat, of a third bunch under his shirt on the chest. This accomplished, a panic came upon him, and he unwrapped them all and counted them again. There were still sixty-seven.

He dried his wet foot-gear by the fire. The moccasins were in soggy shreds. The blanket socks were worn through in places, and his feet were raw and bleeding. His ankle was throbbing, and he gave it an examination. It had swollen to the size of his knee. He tore a long strip from one of his two blankets and bound the ankle tightly. He tore other strips and bound them about his feet to serve for both moccasins and socks. Then he drank the pot of water, steaming hot, wound his watch, and crawled between his blankets.

He slept like a dead man. The brief darkness around midnight came and went. The sun arose in the northeast—at least the day dawned in that quarter, for the sun was hidden by gray clouds.

At six o'clock he awoke, quietly lying on his back. He gazed straight up into the gray sky and knew that he was hungry. As he rolled over on his elbow he was startled by a loud snort, and saw a bull caribou regarding him with alert curiosity. The animal was not mere than fifty feet away, and instantly into the man's mind leaped the vision and the savor of a caribou steak sizzling and frying over a fire. Mechanically he reached for the empty gun, drew a bead, and pulled the trigger. The bull snorted and leaped away, his hoofs rattling and clattering as he fled across the ledges.

The man cursed and flung the empty gun from him. He groaned aloud as he started to drag himself to his feet. It was a slow and arduous task.

His joints were like rusty hinges. They worked harshly in their sockets, with much friction, and each bending or unbending was accomplished only through a sheer exertion of will. When he finally gained his feet, another minute or so was consumed in straightening up, so that he could stand erect as a man should stand.

He crawled up a small knoll and surveyed the prospect. There were no trees, no bushes, nothing but a gray sea of moss scarcely diversified by gray rocks, gray lakelets, and gray streamlets. The sky was gray. There was no sun nor hint of sun. He had no idea of north, and he had forgotten the way he had come to this spot the night before. But he was not lost. He knew that. Soon he would come to the land of the little sticks. He felt that it lay off to the left somewhere, not far—possibly just over the next low hill.

He went back to put his pack into shape for travelling. He assured himself of the existence of his three separate parcels of matches, though he did not stop to count them. But he did linger, debating, over a squat moose-hide sack. It was not large. He could hide it under his two hands. He knew that it weighed fifteen pounds,—as much as all the rest of the pack, —and it worried him. He finally set it to one side and proceeded to roll the pack. He paused to gaze at the squat moose-hide sack. He picked it up hastily with a defiant glance about him, as though the desolation were trying to rob him of it; and when he rose to his feet to stagger on into the day, it was included in the pack on his back.

He bore away to the left, stopping now and again to eat muskeg berries. His ankle had stiffened, his limp was more pronounced, but the pain of it was as nothing compared with the pain of his stomach. The hunger pangs were sharp. They gnawed and gnawed until he could not keep his mind steady on the course he must pursue to gain the land of little sticks. The muskeg berries did not allay this gnawing, while they made his tongue and the roof of his mouth sore with their irritating bite.

He came upon a valley where rock ptarmigan rose on whirring wings from the ledges and muskegs. Ker—ker—ker was the cry they made. He threw stones at them, but could not hit them. He placed his pack on the ground and stalked them as a cat stalks a sparrow. The sharp rocks cut through his pants' legs till his knees left a trail of blood; but the hurt was lost in the hurt of his hunger. He squirmed over the wet moss, saturating his clothes and chilling his body; but he was not aware of it, so great was his fever for food. And always the ptarmigan rose, whirring, before him, till their ker—ker—ker became a mock to him, and he cursed them and cried aloud at them with their own cry.

Once he crawled upon one that must have been asleep. He did not see it till it shot up in his face from its rocky nook. He made a clutch as startled as was the rise of the ptarmigan, and there remained in his hand three tail-feathers. As he watched its flight he hated it, as though it had done him some terrible wrong. Then he returned and shouldered his pack.

As the day wore along he came into valleys or swales where game was more plentiful. A band of caribou passed by, twenty and odd animals, tantalizingly within rifle range. He felt a wild desire to run after them, a certitude that he could run them down. A black fox came toward him, carrying a ptarmigan in his mouth. The man shouted. It was a fearful cry, but the fox, leaping away in fright, did not drop the ptarmigan.

Late in the afternoon he followed a stream, milky with lime, which ran through sparse patches of rush-grass. Grasping these rushes firmly near the root, he pulled up what resembled a young onion-sprout no larger than a shingle-nail. It was tender, and his teeth sank into it with a crunch that promised deliciously of food. But its fibers were tough. It was composed of stringy filaments saturated with water, like the berries, and devoid of nourishment. He threw off his pack and went into the rush-grass on hands and knees, crunching and munching, like some bovine creature.

He was very weary and often wished to rest—to lie down and sleep; but he was continually driven on—not so much by his desire to gain the land of little sticks as by his hunger. He searched little ponds for frogs and dug up the earth with his nails for worms, though he knew in spite that neither frogs nor worms existed so far north.

He looked into every pool of water vainly, until, as the long twilight came on, he discovered a solitary fish, the size of a minnow, in such a pool. He plunged his arm in up to the shoulder, but it eluded him. He reached for it with both hands and stirred up the milky mud at the bottom. In his excitement he fell in, wetting himself to the waist. Then the water was too muddy to admit of his seeing the fish, and he was compelled to wait until the sediment had settled.

The pursuit was renewed, till the water was again muddied. But he could not wait. He unstrapped the tin bucket and began to bale the pool. He baled wildly at first, splashing himself and flinging the water so short a distance that it ran back into the pool. He worked more carefully, striving to be cool, though his heart was pounding against his chest and his hands were trembling. At the end of half an hour the pool was nearly dry. Not a cupful of water remained. And there was no fish. He found a hidden crevice among the stones through which it had escaped to the adjoining and larger pool—a pool which he could not empty in a night and a day. Had he known of the crevice, he could have closed it with a rock at the beginning and the fish would have been his.

Thus he thought, and crumpled up and sank down upon the wet earth. At first he cried softly to himself, then he cried loudly to the pitiless desolation that ringed him around; and for a long time after he was shaken by great dry sobs.

He built a fire and warmed himself by drinking quarts of hot water, and made camp on a rocky ledge in the same fashion he had the night before. The last thing he did was to see that his matches were dry and to wind his watch. The blankets were wet and clammy. His ankle pulsed with pain. But he knew only that he was hungry, and through his restless sleep he dreamed of feasts and banquets and of food served and spread in all imaginable ways.

He awoke chilled and sick. There was no sun. The gray of earth and sky had become deeper, more profound. A raw wind was blowing, and the first flurries of snow were whitening the hilltops. The air about him thickened and grew white while he made a fire and boiled more water. It was wet snow, half rain, and the flakes were large and soggy. At first they melted as soon as they came in contact with the earth, but ever more fell, covering the ground, putting out the fire, spoiling his supply of moss-fuel.

This was a signal for him to strap on his pack and stumble onward, he knew not where. He was not concerned with the land of little sticks, nor with Bill and the cache under the upturned canoe by the river Dease. He was mastered by the verb "to eat." He was hunger-mad. He took no heed of the course he pursued, so long as that course led him through the swale bottoms. He felt his way through the wet snow to the watery muskeg berries, and went by feel as he pulled up the rush-grass by the roots. But it was tasteless stuff and did not satisfy. He found a weed that tasted sour and he ate all he could find of it, which was not much, for it was a creeping growth, easily hidden under the several inches of snow.

He had no fire that night, nor hot water, and crawled under his blanket to sleep the broken hunger-sleep. The snow turned into a cold rain. He awakened many times to feel it falling on his upturned face. Day came—a gray day and no sun. It had ceased raining. The keenness of his hunger had departed. Sensibility, as far as concerned the yearning for food, had been exhausted. There was a dull, heavy ache in his stomach, but it did not bother him so much. He was more rational, and once more he was chiefly interested in the land of little sticks and the cache by the river Dease.

He ripped the remnant of one of his blankets into strips and bound his bleeding feet. Also, he recinched the injured ankle and prepared himself for a day of travel. When he came to his pack, he paused long over the squat moose-hide sack, but in the end it went with him.

The snow had melted under the rain, and only the hilltops showed white. The sun came out, and he succeeded in locating the points of the compass, though he knew now that he was lost. Perhaps, in his previous days' wanderings, he had edged away too far to the left. He now bore off to the right to counteract the possible deviation from his true course.

Though the hunger pangs were no longer so exquisite, he realized that he was weak. He was compelled to pause for frequent rests, when he attacked the muskeg berries and rush-grass patches. His tongue felt dry and large, as though covered with a fine hairy growth, and it tasted bitter in his mouth. His heart gave him a great deal of trouble. When he had travelled a few minutes it would begin a remorseless thump, thump, thump, and then leap up and away in a painful flutter of beats that choked him and made him go faint and dizzy.

In the middle of the day he found two minnows in a large pool. It was impossible to bale it, but he was calmer now and managed to catch them in his tin bucket. They were no longer than his little finger, but he was not particularly hungry. The dull ache in his stomach had been growing duller and fainter. It seemed almost that his stomach was dozing. He ate the fish raw, masticating with painstaking care, for the eating was an act of pure reason. While he had no desire to eat, he knew that he must eat to live.

In the evening he caught three more minnows, eating two and saving the third for breakfast. The sun had dried stray shreds of moss, and he was able to warm himself with hot water. He had not covered more than ten miles that day; and the next day, travelling whenever his heart permitted him, he covered no more than five miles. But his stomach did not give him the slightest uneasiness. It had gone to sleep. He was in a strange country, too, and the caribou were growing more plentiful, also the wolves. Often their yelps drifted across the desolation, and once he saw three of them slinking away before his path.

Another night; and in the morning, being more rational, he untied the leather string that fastened the squat moose-hide sack. From its open mouth poured a yellow stream of coarse gold-dust and nuggets. He roughly divided the gold in halves, caching one half on a prominent ledge, wrapped in a piece of blanket, and returning the other half to the sack. He also began to use strips of the one remaining blanket for his feet. He still clung to his gun, for there were cartridges in that cache by the river Dease.

This was a day of fog, and this day hunger awoke in him again. He was very weak and was afflicted with a giddiness which at times blinded him. It was no uncommon thing now for him to stumble and fall; and stumbling once, he fell squarely into a ptarmigan nest. There were four newly hatched chicks, a day old—little specks of pulsating life no more than a mouthful; and he ate them ravenously, thrusting them alive into his mouth and crunching them like egg-shells between his teeth. The mother ptarmigan beat about him with great outcry. He used his gun as a club with which to knock her over, but she dodged out of reach. He threw stones at her and with one chance shot broke a wing. Then she fluttered away, running, trailing the broken wing, with him in pursuit.

The little chicks had no more than whetted his appetite. He hopped and bobbed clumsily along on his injured ankle, throwing stones and screaming hoarsely at times; at other times hopping and bobbing silently along, picking himself up grimly and patiently when he fell, or rubbing his eyes with his hand when the giddiness threatened to overpower him.

The chase led him across swampy ground in the bottom of the valley, and he came upon footprints in the soggy moss. They were not his own—he could see that. They must be Bill's. But he could not stop, for the mother ptarmigan was running on. He would catch her first, then he would return and investigate.

He exhausted the mother ptarmigan; but he exhausted himself. She lay panting on her side. He lay panting on his side, a dozen feet away, unable to crawl to her. And as he recovered she recovered, fluttering out of reach as his hungry hand went out to her. The chase was resumed. Night settled down and she escaped. He stumbled from weakness and pitched head foremost on his face, cutting his cheek, his pack upon his back. He did not move for a long while; then he rolled over on his side, wound his watch, and lay there until morning.

Another day of fog. Half of his last blanket had gone into foot-wrappings. He failed to pick up Bill's trail. It did not matter. His hunger was driving him too compellingly—only—only he wondered if Bill, too, were lost. By midday the irk of his pack became too oppressive. Again he divided the gold, this time merely spilling half of it on the ground. In the afternoon he threw the rest of it away, there remaining to him only the half-blanket, the tin bucket, and the rifle.

An hallucination began to trouble him. He felt confident that one cartridge remained to him. It was in the chamber of the rifle and he had overlooked it. On the other hand, he knew all the time that the chamber was empty. But the hallucination persisted. He fought it off for hours, then threw his rifle open and was confronted with emptiness. The disappointment was as bitter as though he had really expected to find the cartridge.

He plodded on for half an hour, when the hallucination arose again. Again he fought it, and still it persisted, till for very relief he opened his rifle to unconvince himself. At times his mind wandered farther afield, and he plodded on, a mere automaton, strange conceits and whimsicalities gnawing at his brain like worms. But these excursions out of the real were of brief duration, for ever the pangs of the hunger-bite called him back. He was jerked back abruptly once from such an excursion by a sight that caused him nearly to faint. He reeled and swayed, doddering like a drunken man to keep from falling. Before him stood a horse. A horse! He could not believe his eyes. A thick mist was in them, intershot with sparkling points of light. He rubbed his eyes savagely to clear his vision, and beheld, not a horse, but a great brown bear. The animal was studying him with bellicose curiosity.

The man had brought his gun halfway to his shoulder before he realized. He lowered it and drew his hunting-knife from its beaded sheath at his hip. Before him was meat and life. He ran his thumb along the edge of his knife. It was sharp. The point was sharp. He would fling himself upon the bear and kill it. But his heart began its warning thump, thump, thump. Then followed the wild upward leap and tattoo of flutters, the pressing as of an iron band about his forehead, the creeping of the dizziness into his brain.

His desperate courage was evicted by a great surge of fear. In his weakness, what if the animal attacked him? He drew himself up to his most imposing stature, gripping the knife and staring hard at the bear. The bear advanced clumsily a couple of steps, reared up, and gave vent to a tentative growl. If the man ran, he would run after him; but the man did not run. He was animated now with the courage of fear. He, too, growled, savagely, terribly, voicing the fear that is to life germane and that lies twisted about life's deepest roots.

The bear edged away to one side, growling menacingly, himself appalled by this mysterious creature that appeared upright and unafraid. But the man did not move. He stood like a statue till the danger was past, when he yielded to a fit of trembling and sank down into the wet moss.

He pulled himself together and went on, afraid now in a new way. It was not the fear that he should die passively from lack of food, but that he should be destroyed violently before starvation had exhausted the last particle of the endeavor in him that made toward surviving. There were the wolves. Back and forth across the desolation drifted their howls, weaving the very air into a fabric of menace that was so tangible that he found himself, arms in the air, pressing it back from him as it might be the walls of a wind-blown tent.

Now and again the wolves, in packs of two and three, crossed his path. But they sheered clear of him. They were not in sufficient numbers, and besides they were hunting the caribou, which did not battle, while this strange creature that walked erect might scratch and bite.

In the late afternoon he came upon scattered bones where the wolves had made a kill. The debris had been a caribou calf an hour before, squawking and running and very much alive. He contemplated the bones, clean-picked and polished, pink with the cell-life in them which had not yet died. Could it possibly be that he might be that ere the day was done! Such was life, eh? A vain and fleeting thing. It was only life that pained. There was no hurt in death. To die was to sleep. It meant cessation, rest. Then why was he not content to die?

But he did not moralize long. He was squatting in the moss, a bone in his mouth, sucking at the shreds of life that still dyed it faintly pink. The sweet meaty taste, thin and elusive almost as a memory, maddened him. He closed his jaws on the bones and crunched. Sometimes it was the bone that broke, sometimes his teeth. Then he crushed the bones between rocks, pounded them to a pulp, and swallowed them. He pounded his fingers, too, in his haste, and yet found a moment in which to feel surprise at the fact that his fingers did not hurt much when caught under the descending rock.

Came frightful days of snow and rain. He did not know when he made camp, when he broke camp. He travelled in the night as much as in the day. He rested wherever he fell, crawled on whenever the dying life in him flickered up and burned less dimly. He, as a man, no longer strove. It was the life in him, unwilling to die, that drove him on. He did not suffer. His nerves had become blunted, numb, while his mind was filled with weird visions and delicious dreams.

But ever he sucked and chewed on the crushed bones of the caribou calf, the least remnants of which he had gathered up and carried with him. He crossed no more hills or divides, but automatically followed a large stream which flowed through a wide and shallow valley. He did not see this stream nor this valley. He saw nothing save visions. Soul and body walked or crawled side by side, yet apart, so slender was the thread that bound them.

He awoke in his right mind, lying on his back on a rocky ledge. The sun was shining bright and warm. Afar off he heard the squawking of caribou calves. He was aware of vague memories of rain and wind and snow, but whether he had been beaten by the storm for two days or two weeks he did not know.

For some time he lay without movement, the genial sunshine pouring upon him and saturating his miserable body with its warmth. A fine day, he thought. Perhaps he could manage to locate himself. By a painful effort he rolled over on his side. Below him flowed a wide and sluggish river. Its unfamiliarity puzzled him. Slowly he followed it with his eyes, winding in wide sweeps among the bleak, bare hills, bleaker and barer and lower-lying than any hills he had yet encountered. Slowly, deliberately, without excitement or more than the most casual interest, he followed the course of the strange stream toward the sky-line and saw it emptying into a bright and shining sea. He was still unexcited. Most unusual, he thought, a vision or a mirage—more likely a vision, a trick of his disordered mind. He was confirmed in this by sight of a ship lying at anchor in the midst of the shining sea. He closed his eyes for a while, then opened them. Strange how the vision persisted! Yet not strange. He knew there were no seas or ships in the heart of the barren lands, just as he had known there was no cartridge in the empty rifle.

He heard a snuffle behind him—a half-choking gasp or cough. Very slowly, because of his exceeding weakness and stiffness, he rolled over on his other side. He could see nothing near at hand, but he waited patiently. Again came the snuffle and cough, and outlined between two jagged rocks not a score of feet away he made out the gray head of a wolf. The sharp ears were not pricked so sharply as he had seen them on other wolves; the eyes were bleared and bloodshot, the head seemed to droop limply and forlornly. The animal blinked continually in the sunshine. It seemed sick. As he looked it snuffled and coughed again.

This, at least, was real, he thought, and turned on the other side so that he might see the reality of the world which had been veiled from him before by the vision. But the sea still shone in the distance and the ship was plainly discernible. Was it reality, after all? He closed his eyes for a long while and thought, and then it came to him. He had been making north by east, away from the Dease Divide and into the Coppermine Valley. This wide and sluggish river was the Coppermine. That shining sea was the Arctic Ocean. That ship was a whaler, strayed east, far east, from the mouth of the Mackenzie, and it was lying at anchor in Coronation Gulf. He remembered the Hudson Bay Company chart he had seen long ago, and it was all clear and reasonable to him.

He sat up and turned his attention to immediate affairs. He had worn through the blanket wrappings, and his feet were shapeless lumps of raw meat. His last blanket was gone. Rifle and knife were both missing. He had lost his hat somewhere, with the bunch of matches in the band, but the matches against his chest were safe and dry inside the tobacco pouch and oil paper. He looked at his watch. It marked eleven o'clock and was still running. Evidently he had kept it wound.

He was calm and collected. Though extremely weak, he had no sensation of pain. He was not hungry. The thought of food was not even pleasant to him, and whatever he did was done by his reason alone. He ripped off his pants' legs to the knees and bound them about his feet. Somehow he had succeeded in retaining the tin bucket. He would have some hot water before he began what he foresaw was to be a terrible journey to the ship.

His movements were slow. He shook as with a palsy. When he started to collect dry moss, he found he could not rise to his feet. He tried again and again, then contented himself with crawling about on hands and knees. Once he crawled near to the sick wolf. The animal dragged itself reluctantly out of his way, licking its chops with a tongue which seemed hardly to have the strength to curl. The man noticed that the tongue was not the customary healthy red. It was a yellowish brown and seemed coated with a rough and half-dry mucus.

After he had drunk a quart of hot water the man found he was able to stand, and even to walk as well as a dying man might be supposed to walk. Every minute or so he was compelled to rest. His steps were feeble and uncertain, just as the wolf's that trailed him were feeble and uncertain; and that night, when the shining sea was blotted out by blackness, he knew he was nearer to it by no more than four miles.

Throughout the night he heard the cough of the sick wolf, and now and then the squawking of the caribou calves. There was life all around him, but it was strong life, very much alive and well, and he knew the sick wolf clung to the sick man's trail in the hope that the man would die first. In the morning, on opening his eyes, he beheld it regarding him with a wistful and hungry stare. It stood crouched, with tail between its legs, like a miserable and woe-begone dog. It shivered in the chill morning wind, and grinned dispiritedly when the man spoke to it in a voice that achieved no more than a hoarse whisper.

The sun rose brightly, and all morning the man tottered and fell toward the ship on the shining sea. The weather was perfect. It was the brief Indian Summer of the high latitudes. It might last a week. To-morrow or next day it might be gone.

In the afternoon the man came upon a trail. It was of another man, who did not walk, but who dragged himself on all fours. The man thought it might be Bill, but he thought in a dull, uninterested way. He had no curiosity. In fact, sensation and emotion had left him. He was no longer susceptible to pain. Stomach and nerves had gone to sleep. Yet the life that was in him drove him on. He was very weary, but it refused to die. It was because it refused to die that he still ate muskeg berries and minnows, drank his hot water, and kept a wary eye on the sick wolf.

He followed the trail of the other man who dragged himself along, and soon came to the end of it—a few fresh-picked bones where the soggy moss was marked by the foot-pads of many wolves. He saw a squat moose-hide sack, mate to his own, which had been torn by sharp teeth. He picked it up, though its weight was almost too much for his feeble fingers. Bill had carried it to the last. Ha! ha! He would have the laugh on Bill. He would survive and carry it to the ship in the shining sea. His mirth was hoarse and ghastly, like a raven's croak, and the sick wolf joined him, howling lugubriously. The man ceased suddenly. How could he have the laugh on Bill if that were Bill; if those bones, so pinky-white and clean, were Bill?

He turned away. Well, Bill had deserted him; but he would not take the gold, nor would he suck Bill's bones. Bill would have, though, had it been the other way around, he mused as he staggered on.

He came to a pool of water. Stooping over in quest of minnows, he jerked his head back as though he had been stung. He had caught sight of his reflected face. So horrible was it that sensibility awoke long enough to be shocked. There were three minnows in the pool, which was too large to drain; and after several ineffectual attempts to catch them in the tin bucket he forbore. He was afraid, because of his great weakness, that he might fall in and drown. It was for this reason that he did not trust himself to the river astride one of the many drift-logs which lined its sand-spits.

That day he decreased the distance between him and the ship by three miles; the next day by two—for he was crawling now as Bill had crawled; and the end of the fifth day found the ship still seven miles away and him unable to make even a mile a day. Still the Indian Summer held on, and he continued to crawl and faint, turn and turn about; and ever the sick wolf coughed and wheezed at his heels. His knees had become raw meat like his feet, and though he padded them with the shirt from his back it was a red track he left behind him on the moss and stones. Once, glancing back, he saw the wolf licking hungrily his bleeding trail, and he saw sharply what his own end might be—unless—unless he could get the wolf. Then began as grim a tragedy of existence as was ever played—a sick man that crawled, a sick wolf that limped, two creatures dragging their dying carcasses across the desolation and hunting each other's lives.

Had it been a well wolf, it would not have mattered so much to the man; but the thought of going to feed the maw of that loathsome and all but dead thing was repugnant to him. He was finicky. His mind had begun to wander again, and to be perplexed by hallucinations, while his lucid intervals grew rarer and shorter.

He was awakened once from a faint by a wheeze close in his ear. The wolf leaped lamely back, losing its footing and falling in its weakness. It was ludicrous, but he was not amused.

Nor was he even afraid. He was too far gone for that. But his mind was for the moment clear, and he lay and considered. The ship was no more than four miles away. He could see it quite distinctly when he rubbed the mists out of his eyes, and he could see the white sail of a small boat cutting the water of the shining sea. But he could never crawl those four miles. He knew that, and was very calm in the knowledge. He knew that he could not crawl half a mile. And yet he wanted to live. It was unreasonable that he should die after all he had undergone. Fate asked too much of him. And, dying, he declined to die. It was stark madness, perhaps, but in the very grip of Death he defied Death and refused to die.

He closed his eyes and composed himself with infinite precaution. He steeled himself to keep above the suffocating languor that lapped like a rising tide through all the wells of his being. It was very like a sea, this deadly languor, that rose and rose and drowned his consciousness bit by bit. Sometimes he was all but submerged, swimming through oblivion with a faltering stroke; and again, by some strange alchemy of soul, he would find another shred of will and strike out more strongly.

Without movement he lay on his back, and he could hear, slowly drawing near and nearer, the wheezing intake and output of the sick wolf's breath. It drew closer, ever closer, through an infinitude of time, and he did not move. It was at his ear. The harsh dry tongue grated like sandpaper against his cheek. His hands shot out—or at least he willed them to shoot out. The fingers were curved like talons, but they closed on empty air. Swiftness and certitude require strength, and the man had not this strength.

The patience of the wolf was terrible. The man's patience was no less terrible. For half a day he lay motionless, fighting off unconsciousness and waiting for the thing that was to feed upon him and upon which he wished to feed. Sometimes the languid sea rose over him and he dreamed long dreams; but ever through it all, waking and dreaming, he waited for the wheezing breath and the harsh caress of the tongue.

He did not hear the breath, and he slipped slowly from some dream to the feel of the tongue along his hand. He waited. The fangs pressed softly; the pressure increased; the wolf was exerting its last strength in an effort to sink teeth in the food for which it had waited so long. But the man had waited long, and the lacerated hand closed on the jaw. Slowly, while the wolf struggled feebly and the hand clutched feebly, the other hand crept across to a grip. Five minutes later the whole weight of the man's body was on top of the wolf. The hands had not sufficient strength to choke the wolf, but the face of the man was pressed close to the throat of the wolf and the mouth of the man was full of hair. At the end of half an hour the man was aware of a warm trickle in his throat. It was not pleasant. It was like molten lead being forced into his stomach, and it was forced by his will alone. Later the man rolled over on his back and slept.

There were some members of a scientific expedition on the whale-ship *Bedford*. From the deck they remarked a strange object on the shore. It was moving down the beach toward the water. They were unable to classify it, and, being scientific men, they climbed into the whale-boat alongside and went ashore to see. And they saw something that was alive but which could hardly be called a man. It was blind, unconscious. It squirmed along the ground like some monstrous worm. Most of its efforts were ineffectual, but it was persistent, and it writhed and twisted and went ahead perhaps a score of feet an hour.

THREE WEEKS afterward the man lay in a bunk on the whale-ship *Bedford*, and with tears streaming down his wasted cheeks told who he was and what he had undergone. He also babbled incoherently of his mother, of sunny Southern California, and a home among the orange groves and flowers.

The days were not many after that when he sat at table with the scientific men and ship's officers. He gloated over the spectacle of so much food, watching it anxiously as it went into the mouths of others. With the disappearance of each mouthful an expression of deep regret came into his eyes. He was quite sane, yet he hated those men at mealtime. He was haunted by a fear that the food would not last. He inquired of the cook, the cabin-boy, the captain, concerning the food stores. They reassured him countless times; but he could not believe them, and pried cunningly about the lazarette to see with his own eyes.

It was noticed that the man was getting fat. He grew stouter with each day. The scientific men shook their heads and theorized. They limited the man at his meals, but still his girth increased and he swelled prodigiously under his shirt.

The sailors grinned. They knew. And when the scientific men set a watch on the man, they knew too. They saw him slouch for'ard after breakfast, and, like a mendicant, with outstretched palm, accost a sailor. The sailor grinned and passed him a fragment of sea biscuit. He clutched it avariciously, looked at it as a miser looks at gold, and thrust it into his shirt bosom. Similar were the donations from other grinning sailors.

The scientific men were discreet. They let him alone. But they privily examined his bunk. It was lined with hardtack; the mattress was stuffed with hardtack; every nook and cranny was filled with hardtack. Yet he was sane. He was taking precautions against another possible famine—that was all. He would recover from it, the scientific men said; and he did, ere the *Bedford's* anchor rumbled down in San Francisco Bay.

A DAY'S LODGING

It was the gosh-dangdest stampede I ever seen. A thousand dog-teams hittin' the ice. You couldn't see 'm fer smoke. Two white men an' a Swede froze to death that night, an' there was a dozen busted their lungs. But didn't I see with my own eyes the bottom of the water-hole? It was yellow with gold like a mustard-plaster. That's why I staked the Yukon for a minin' claim. That's what made the stampede. An' then there was nothin' to it. That's what I said—NOTHIN' to it. An' I ain't got over guessin' yet.

— NARRATIVE OF SHORTY.

JOHN MESSNER CLUNG with mittened hand to the bucking gee-pole and held the sled in the trail. With the other mittened hand he rubbed his cheeks and nose. He rubbed his cheeks and nose every little while. In point of fact, he rarely ceased from rubbing them, and sometimes, as their numbness increased, he rubbed fiercely. His forehead was covered by the visor of his fur cap, the flaps of which went over his ears. The rest of his face was protected by a thick beard, golden-brown under its coating of frost.

Behind him churned a heavily loaded Yukon sled, and before him toiled a string of five dogs. The rope by which they dragged the sled rubbed against the side of Messner's leg. When the dogs swung on a bend in the trail, he stepped over the rope. There were many bends, and he was compelled to step over it often. Sometimes he tripped on the rope, or stumbled, and at all times he was awkward, betraying a weariness so great that the sled now and again ran upon his heels.

When he came to a straight piece of trail, where the sled could get along for a moment without guidance, he let go the gee-pole and batted his right hand sharply upon the hard wood. He found it difficult to keep up the circulation in that hand. But while he pounded the one hand, he never ceased from rubbing his nose and cheeks with the other.

"It's too cold to travel, anyway," he said. He spoke aloud, after the manner of men who are much by themselves. "Only a fool would travel at such a temperature. If it isn't eighty below, it's because it's seventy-nine."

258

He pulled out his watch, and after some fumbling got it back into the breast pocket of his thick woollen jacket. Then he surveyed the heavens and ran his eye along the white sky-line to the south.

"Twelve o'clock," he mumbled, "A clear sky, and no sun."

He plodded on silently for ten minutes, and then, as though there had been no lapse in his speech, he added:

"And no ground covered, and it's too cold to travel."

Suddenly he yelled "Whoa!" at the dogs, and stopped. He seemed in a wild panic over his right hand, and proceeded to hammer it furiously against the gee-pole.

"You—poor—devils!" he addressed the dogs, which had dropped down heavily on the ice to rest. His was a broken, jerky utterance, caused by the violence with which he hammered his numb hand upon the wood. "What have you done anyway that a two-legged other animal should come along, break you to harness, curb all your natural proclivities, and make slave-beasts out of you?"

He rubbed his nose, not reflectively, but savagely, in order to drive the blood into it, and urged the dogs to their work again. He travelled on the frozen surface of a great river. Behind him it stretched away in a mighty curve of many miles, losing itself in a fantastic jumble of mountains, snow-covered and silent. Ahead of him the river split into many channels to accommodate the freight of islands it carried on its breast. These islands were silent and white. No animals nor humming insects broke the silence. No birds flew in the chill air. There was no sound of man, no mark of the handiwork of man. The world slept, and it was like the sleep of death.

John Messner seemed succumbing to the apathy of it all. The frost was benumbing his spirit. He plodded on with bowed head, unobservant, mechanically rubbing nose and cheeks, and batting his steering hand against the gee-pole in the straight trail-stretches.

But the dogs were observant, and suddenly they stopped, turning their heads and looking back at their master out of eyes that were wistful and questioning. Their eyelashes were frosted white, as were their muzzles, and they had all the seeming of decrepit old age, what of the frost-rime and exhaustion.

The man was about to urge them on, when he checked himself, roused up with an effort, and looked around. The dogs had stopped beside a water-hole, not a fissure, but a hole man-made, chopped laboriously with an axe through three and a half feet of ice. A thick skin of new ice showed that it had not been used for some time. Messner glanced about him. The dogs were already pointing the way, each wistful and hoary muzzle turned toward the dim snow-path that left the main river trail and climbed the bank of the island.

"All right, you sore-footed brutes," he said. "I'll investigate. You're not a bit more anxious to quit than I am."

He climbed the bank and disappeared. The dogs did not lie down, but on their feet eagerly waited his return. He came back to them, took a hauling-rope from the front of the sled, and put it around his shoulders. Then he gee'd the dogs to the right and put them at the bank on the run. It was a stiff pull, but their weariness fell from them as they crouched low to the snow, whining with eagerness and gladness as they struggled upward to the last ounce of effort in their bodies. When a dog slipped or faltered, the one behind nipped his hind quarters. The man shouted encouragement and threats, and threw all his weight on the haul-ing-rope.

They cleared the bank with a rush, swung to the left, and dashed up to a small log cabin. It was a deserted cabin of a single room, eight feet by ten on the inside. Messner unhar-nessed the animals, unloaded his sled and took possession. The last chance wayfarer had left a supply of firewood. Messner set up his light sheet-iron stove and starred a fire. He put five sun-cured salmon into the oven to thaw out for the dogs, and from the water-hole filled his coffee-pot and cooking-pail.

While waiting for the water to boil, he held his face over the stove. The moisture from his breath had collected on his beard and frozen into a great mass of ice, and this he proceeded to thaw out. As it melted and dropped upon the stove it sizzled and rose about him in steam. He helped the process with his fingers, working loose small ice-chunks that fell rattling to the floor.

A wild outcry from the dogs without did not take him from his task. He heard the wolfish snarling and yelping of strange dogs and the sound of voices. A knock came on the door.

"Come in," Messner called, in a voice muffled because at the moment he was sucking loose a fragment of ice from its anchorage on his upper lip.

The door opened, and, gazing out of his cloud of steam, he saw a man and a woman pausing on the threshold.

"Come in," he said peremptorily, "and shut the door!"

Peering through the steam, he could make out but little of their personal appearance. The nose and cheek strap worn by the woman and the trail-wrappings about her head allowed only a pair of black eyes to be seen. The man was dark-eyed and smooth-shaven all except his mustache, which was so iced up as to hide his mouth.

"We just wanted to know if there is any other cabin around here," he said, at the same time glancing over the unfurnished state of the room. "We thought this cabin was empty."

"It isn't my cabin," Messner answered. "I just found it a few minutes ago. Come right in and camp. Plenty of room, and you won't need your stove. There's room for all."

At the sound of his voice the woman peered at him with quick curiousness.

"Get your things off," her companion said to her. "I'll unhitch and get the water so we can start cooking."

Messner took the thawed salmon outside and fed his dogs. He had to guard them against the second team of dogs, and when he had reëntered the cabin the other man had unpacked the sled and fetched water. Messner's pot was boiling. He threw in the coffee, settled it with half a cup of cold water, and took the pot from the stove. He thawed some sour-dough biscuits in the oven, at the same time heating a pot of beans he had boiled the night before and that had ridden frozen on the sled all morning.

Removing his utensils from the stove, so as to give the newcomers a chance to cook, he proceeded to take his meal from the top of his grub-box, himself sitting on his bed-roll. Between mouthfuls he talked trail and dogs with the man, who, with head over the stove, was thawing the ice from his mustache. There were two bunks in the cabin, and into one of them, when he had cleared his lip, the stranger tossed his bed-roll.

"We'll sleep here," he said, "unless you prefer this bunk. You're the first comer and you have first choice, you know."

"That's all right," Messner answered. "One bunk's just as good as the other."

He spread his own bedding in the second bunk, and sat down on the edge. The stranger thrust a physician's small travelling case under his blankets at one end to serve for a pillow.

"Doctor?" Messner asked.

"Yes," came the answer, "but I assure you I didn't come into the Klondike to practise."

The woman busied herself with cooking, while the man sliced bacon and fired the stove. The light in the cabin was dim, filtering through in a small window made of onion-skin writing paper and oiled with bacon grease, so that John Messner could not make out very well what the woman looked like. Not that he tried. He seemed to have no interest in her. But she glanced curiously from time to time into the dark corner where he sat.

"Oh, it's a great life," the doctor proclaimed enthusiastically, pausing from sharpening his knife on the stovepipe. "What I like about it is the struggle, the endeavor with one's own hands, the primitiveness of it, the realness."

"The temperature is real enough," Messner laughed.

"Do you know how cold it actually is?" the doctor demanded.

The other shook his head.

"Well, I'll tell you. Seventy-four below zero by spirit thermometer on the sled."

"That's one hundred and six below freezing point—too cold for travelling, eh?"

"Practically suicide," was the doctor's verdict. "One exerts himself. He breathes heavily, taking into his lungs the frost itself. It chills his lungs, freezes the edges of the tissues. He gets a dry, hacking cough as the dead tissue sloughs away, and dies the following summer of pneumonia, wondering what it's all about. I'll stay in this cabin for a week, unless the thermometer rises at least to fifty below."

"I say, Tess," he said, the next moment, "don't you think that coffee's boiled long enough!"

At the sound of the woman's name, John Messner became suddenly alert. He looked at her quickly, while across his face shot a haunting expression, the ghost of some buried misery achieving swift resurrection. But the next moment, and by an effort of will, the ghost was laid again. His face was as placid as before, though he was still alert, dissatisfied with what the feeble light had shown him of the woman's face.

Automatically, her first act had been to set the coffee-pot back. It was not until she had done this that she glanced at Messner. But already he had composed himself. She saw only a man sitting on the edge of the bunk and incuriously studying the toes of his moccasins. But, as she turned casually to go about her cooking, he shot another swift look at her, and she, glancing as swiftly back, caught his look. He shifted on past her to the doctor, though the slightest smile curled his lip in appreciation of the way she had trapped him.

She drew a candle from the grub-box and lighted it. One look at her illuminated face was enough for Messner. In the small cabin the widest limit was only a matter of several steps, and the next moment she was alongside of him. She deliberately held the candle close to his face and stared at him out of eyes wide with fear and recognition. He smiled quietly back at her.

"What are you looking for, Tess?" the doctor called.

"Hairpins," she replied, passing on and rummaging in a clothes-bag on the bunk.

They served their meal on their grub-box, sitting on Messner's grub-box and facing him. He had stretched out on his bunk to rest, lying on his side, his head on his arm. In the close quarters it was as though the three were together at table.

"What part of the States do you come from?" Messner asked.

"San Francisco," answered the doctor. "I've been in here two years, though."

"I hail from California myself," was Messner's announcement.

The woman looked at him appealingly, but he smiled and went on:

"Berkeley, you know."

The other man was becoming interested.

"U. C.?" he asked.

"Yes, Class of '86."

"I meant faculty," the doctor explained. "You remind me of the type."

"Sorry to hear you say so," Messner smiled back. "I'd prefer being taken for a prospector or a dog-musher."

"I don't think he looks any more like a professor than you do a doctor," the woman broke in.

"Thank you," said Messner. Then, turning to her companion, "By the way, Doctor, what is your name, if I may ask?"

"Haythorne, if you'll take my word for it. I gave up cards with civilization."

"And Mrs. Haythorne," Messner smiled and bowed.

She flashed a look at him that was more anger than appeal.

Haythorne was about to ask the other's name. His mouth had opened to form the question when Messner cut him off.

"Come to think of it, Doctor, you may possibly be able to satisfy my curiosity. There was a sort of scandal in faculty circles some two or three years ago. The wife of one of the English professors—er, if you will pardon me, Mrs. Haythorne—disappeared with some San Francisco doctor, I understood, though his name does not just now come to my lips. Do you remember the incident?"

Haythorne nodded his head. "Made quite a stir at the time. His name was Womble—Graham Womble. He had a magnificent practice. I knew him somewhat."

"Well, what I was trying to get at was what had become of them. I was wondering if you had heard. They left no trace, hide nor hair."

"He covered his tracks cunningly." Haythorne cleared his throat. "There was rumor that they went to the South Seas—were lost on a trading schooner in a typhoon, or something like that."

"I never heard that," Messner said. "You remember the case, Mrs. Haythorne?"

"Perfectly," she answered, in a voice the control of which was in amazing contrast to the anger that blazed in the face she turned aside so that Haythorne might not see.

The latter was again on the verge of asking his name, when Messner remarked:

"This Dr. Womble, I've heard he was very handsome, and—er—quite a success, so to say, with the ladies."

"Well, if he was, he finished himself off by that affair," Haythorne grumbled.

"And the woman was a termagant—at least so I've been told. It was generally accepted in Berkeley that she made life—er—not exactly paradise for her husband."

"I never heard that," Haythorne rejoined. "In San Francisco the talk was all the other way."

"Woman sort of a martyr, eh?—crucified on the cross of matrimony?"

The doctor nodded. Messner's gray eyes were mildly curious as he went on:

"That was to be expected—two sides to the shield. Living in Berkeley I only got the one side. She was a great deal in San Francisco, it seems."

"Some coffee, please," Haythorne said.

The woman refilled his mug, at the same time breaking into light laughter.

"You're gossiping like a pair of beldames," she chided them.

"It's so interesting," Messner smiled at her, then returned to the doctor. "The husband seems then to have had a not very savory reputation in San Francisco?"

"On the contrary, he was a moral prig," Haythorne blurted out, with apparently undue warmth. "He was a little scholastic shrimp without a drop of red blood in his body."

"Did you know him?"

"Never laid eyes on him. I never knocked about in university circles."

"One side of the shield again," Messner said, with an air of weighing the matter judicially. "While he did not amount to much, it is true—that is, physically—I'd hardly say he was as bad as all that. He did take an active interest in student athletics. And he had some talent. He once wrote a Nativity play that brought him quite a bit of local appreciation. I have heard, also, that he was slated for the head of the English department, only the affair happened and he resigned and went away. It quite broke his career, or so it seemed. At any rate, on our side the shield, it was considered a knock-out blow to him. It was thought he cared a great deal for his wife."

Haythorne, finishing his mug of coffee, grunted uninterestedly and lighted his pipe.

"It was fortunate they had no children," Messner continued.

But Haythorne, with a glance at the stove, pulled on his cap and mittens.

"I'm going out to get some wood," he said. "Then I can take off my moccasins and he comfortable."

The door slammed behind him. For a long minute there was silence. The man continued in the same position on the bed. The woman sat on the grub-box, facing him.

"What are you going to do?" she asked abruptly.

Messner looked at her with lazy indecision. "What do you think I ought to do? Nothing scenic, I hope. You see I am stiff and trail-sore, and this bunk is so restful."

She gnawed her lower lip and fumed dumbly.

"But—" she began vehemently, then clenched her hands and stopped.

"I hope you don't want me to kill Mr.—er—Haythorne," he said gently, almost pleadingly. "It would be most distressing, and, I assure you, really it is unnecessary."

"But you must do something," she cried.

"On the contrary, it is quite conceivable that I do not have to do anything."

"You would stay here?"

He nodded.

She glanced desperately around the cabin and at the bed unrolled on the other bunk. "Night is coming on. You can't stop here. You can't! I tell you, you simply can't!"

"Of course I can. I might remind you that I found this cabin first and that you are my guests."

Again her eyes travelled around the room, and the terror in them leaped up at sight of the other bunk.

"Then we'll have to go," she announced decisively.

"Impossible. You have a dry, hacking cough—the sort Mr.—er—Haythorne so aptly described. You've already slightly chilled your lungs. Besides, he is a physician and knows. He would never permit it."

"Then what are you going to do?" she demanded again, with a tense, quiet utterance that boded an outbreak.

Messner regarded her in a way that was almost paternal, what of the profundity of pity and patience with which he contrived to suffuse it.

"My dear Theresa, as I told you before, I don't know. I really haven't thought about it."

"Oh! You drive me mad!" She sprang to her feet, wringing her hands in impotent wrath. "You never used to be this way."

"I used to be all softness and gentleness," he nodded concurrence. "Was that why you left me?"

"You are so different, so dreadfully calm. You frighten me. I feel you have something terrible planned all the while. But whatever you do, don't do anything rash. Don't get excited—"

"I don't get excited any more," he interrupted. "Not since you went away."

"You have improved—remarkably," she retorted.

He smiled acknowledgment. "While I am thinking about what I shall do, I'll tell you what you will have to do—tell Mr.—er—Haythorne who I am. It may make our stay in this cabin more—may I say, sociable?"

"Why have you followed me into this frightful country?" she asked irrelevantly.

"Don't think I came here looking for you, Theresa. Your vanity shall not be tickled by any such misapprehension. Our meeting is wholly fortuitous. I broke with the life academic and I had to go somewhere. To be honest, I came into the Klondike because I thought it the place you were least liable to be in."

There was a fumbling at the latch, then the door swung in and Haythorne entered with an armful of firewood. At the first warning, Theresa began casually to clear away the dishes. Haythorne went out again after more wood.

"Why didn't you introduce us?" Messner queried.

"I'll tell him," she replied, with a toss of her head. "Don't think I'm afraid."

"I never knew you to be afraid, very much, of anything."

"And I'm not afraid of confession, either," she said, with softening face and voice.

"In your case, I fear, confession is exploitation by indirection, profit-making by ruse, self-aggrandizement at the expense of God."

"Don't be literary," she pouted, with growing tenderness. "I never did like epigrammatic discussion. Besides, I'm not afraid to ask you to forgive me."

"There is nothing to forgive, Theresa. I really should thank you. True, at first I suffered; and then, with all the graciousness of spring, it dawned upon me that I was happy, very happy. It was a most amazing discovery."

"But what if I should return to you?" she asked.

"I should" (he looked at her whimsically), "be greatly perturbed."

"I am your wife. You know you have never got a divorce."

"I see," he meditated. "I have been careless. It will be one of the first things I attend to."

She came over to his side, resting her hand on his arm. "You don't want me, John?" Her voice was soft and caressing, her hand rested like a lure. "If I told you I had made a mistake? If I told you that I was very unhappy?—and I am. And I did make a mistake."

Fear began to grow on Messner. He felt himself wilting under the lightly laid hand. The situation was slipping away from him, all his beautiful calmness was going. She looked at him with melting eyes, and he, too, seemed all dew and melting. He felt himself on the edge of an abyss, powerless to withstand the force that was drawing him over.

"I am coming back to you, John. I am coming back to-day . . . now."

As in a nightmare, he strove under the hand. While she talked, he seemed to hear, rippling softly, the song of the Lorelei. It was as though, somewhere, a piano were playing and the actual notes were impinging on his ear-drums.

Suddenly he sprang to his feet, thrust her from him as her arms attempted to clasp him, and retreated backward to the door. He was in a panic.

"I'll do something desperate!" he cried.

"I warned you not to get excited." She laughed mockingly, and went about washing the dishes. "Nobody wants you. I was just playing with you. I am happier where I am."

But Messner did not believe. He remembered her facility in changing front. She had changed front now. It was exploitation by indirection. She was not happy with the other man. She had discovered her mistake. The flame of his ego flared up at the thought. She wanted to come back to him, which was the one thing he did not want. Unwittingly, his hand rattled the door-latch.

"Don't run away," she laughed. "I won't bite you."

"I am not running away," he replied with child-like defiance, at the same time pulling on his mittens. "I'm only going to get some water."

He gathered the empty pails and cooking pots together and opened the door. He looked back at her.

"Don't forget you're to tell Mr.—er—Haythorne who I am."

Messner broke the skin that had formed on the water-hole within the hour, and filled his pails. But he did not return immediately to the cabin. Leaving the pails standing in the trail, he walked up and down, rapidly, to keep from freezing, for the frost bit into the flesh like fire. His beard was white with his frozen breath when the perplexed and frowning brows relaxed and decision came into his face. He had made up his mind to his course of action, and his frigid lips and cheeks crackled into a chuckle over it. The pails were already skinned over with young ice when he picked them up and made for the cabin.

When he entered he found the other man waiting, standing near the stove, a certain stiff awkwardness and indecision in his manner. Messner set down his water-pails.

"Glad to meet you, Graham Womble," he said in conventional tones, as though acknowledging an introduction.

Messner did not offer his hand. Womble stirred uneasily, feeling for the other the hatred one is prone to feel for one he has wronged.

"And so you're the chap," Messner said in marvelling accents. "Well, well. You see, I really am glad to meet you. I have been—er—curious to know what Theresa found in you—where, I may say, the attraction lay. Well, well."

And he looked the other up and down as a man would look a horse up and down.

"I know how you must feel about me," Womble began.

"Don't mention it," Messner broke in with exaggerated cordiality of voice and manner. "Never mind that. What I want to know is how do you find her? Up to expectations? Has she worn well? Life been all a happy dream ever since?"

"Don't be silly," Theresa interjected.

"I can't help being natural," Messner complained.

"You can be expedient at the same time, and practical," Womble said sharply. "What we want to know is what are you going to do?"

Messner made a well-feigned gesture of helplessness. "I really don't know. It is one of those impossible situations against which there can be no provision."

"All three of us cannot remain the night in this cabin."

Messner nodded affirmation.

"Then somebody must get out."

"That also is incontrovertible," Messner agreed. "When three bodies cannot occupy the same space at the same time, one must get out."

"And you're that one," Womble announced grimly. "It's a ten-mile pull to the next camp, but you can make it all right."

"And that's the first flaw in your reasoning," the other objected. "Why, necessarily, should I be the one to get out? I found this cabin first."

"But Tess can't get out," Womble explained. "Her lungs are already slightly chilled."

"I agree with you. She can't venture ten miles of frost. By all means she must remain."

"Then it is as I said," Womble announced with finality.

Messner cleared his throat. "Your lungs are all right, aren't they?"

"Yes, but what of it?"

Again the other cleared his throat and spoke with painstaking and judicial slowness.

"Why, I may say, nothing of it, except, ah, according to your own reasoning, there is nothing to prevent your getting out, hitting the frost, so to speak, for a matter of ten miles. You can make it all right."

Womble looked with quick suspicion at Theresa and caught in her eyes a glint of pleased surprise.

"Well?" he demanded of her.

She hesitated, and a surge of anger darkened his face. He turned upon Messner.

"Enough of this. You can't stop here."

"Yes, I can."

"I won't let you." Womble squared his shoulders. "I'm running things."

"I'll stay anyway," the other persisted.

"I'll put you out."

"I'll come back."

Womble stopped a moment to steady his voice and control himself. Then he spoke slowly, in a low, tense voice.

"Look here, Messner, if you refuse to get out, I'll thrash you. This isn't California. I'll beat you to a jelly with my two fists."

Messner shrugged his shoulders. "If you do, I'll call a miners' meeting and see you strung up to the nearest tree. As you said, this is not California. They're a simple folk, these miners, and all I'll have to do will be to show them the marks of the beating, tell them the truth about you, and present my claim for my wife."

The woman attempted to speak, but Womble turned upon her fiercely.

"You keep out of this," he cried.

In marked contrast was Messner's "Please don't intrude, Theresa."

What of her anger and pent feelings, her lungs were irritated into the dry, hacking cough, and with blood-suffused face and one hand clenched against her chest, she waited for the paroxysm to pass.

Womble looked gloomily at her, noting her cough.

"Something must be done," he said. "Yet her lungs can't stand the exposure. She can't travel till the temperature rises. And I'm not going to give her up."

Messner hemmed, cleared his throat, and hemmed again, semi-apologetically, and said, "I need some money."

Contempt showed instantly in Womble's face. At last, beneath him in vileness, had the other sunk himself.

"You've got a fat sack of dust," Messner went on. "I saw you unload it from the sled."

"How much do you want?" Womble demanded, with a contempt in his voice equal to that in his face.

"I made an estimate of the sack, and I—ah—should say it weighed about twenty pounds. What do you say we call it four thousand?"

"But it's all I've got, man!" Womble cried out.

"You've got her," the other said soothingly. "She must be worth it. Think what I'm giving up. Surely it is a reasonable price."

"All right." Womble rushed across the floor to the gold-sack. "Can't put this deal through too quick for me, you—you little worm!"

"Now, there you err," was the smiling rejoinder. "As a matter of ethics isn't the man who gives a bribe as bad as the man who takes a bribe? The receiver is as bad as the thief, you know; and you needn't console yourself with any fictitious moral superiority concerning this little deal."

"To hell with your ethics!" the other burst out. "Come here and watch the weighing of this dust. I might cheat you."

And the woman, leaning against the bunk, raging and impotent, watched herself weighed out in yellow dust and nuggets in the scales erected on the grub-box. The scales were small, making necessary many weighings, and Messner with precise care verified each weighing.

"There's too much silver in it," he remarked as he tied up the gold-sack. "I don't think it will run quite sixteen to the ounce. You got a trifle the better of me, Womble."

He handled the sack lovingly, and with due appreciation of its preciousness carried it out to his sled.

Returning, he gathered his pots and pans together, packed his grub-box, and rolled up his bed. When the sled was lashed and the complaining dogs harnessed, he returned into the cabin for his mittens.

"Good-by, Tess," he said, standing at the open door.

She turned on him, struggling for speech but too frantic to word the passion that burned in her.

"Good-by, Tess," he repeated gently.

"Beast!" she managed to articulate.

She turned and tottered to the bunk, flinging herself face down upon it, sobbing: "You beasts! You beasts!"

John Messner closed the door softly behind him, and, as he started the dogs, looked back at the cabin with a great relief in his face. At the bottom of the bank, beside the water-hole, he halted the sled. He worked the sack of gold out between the lashings and carried it to the water-hole. Already a new skin of ice had formed. This he broke with his fist. Untying the knotted mouth with his teeth, he emptied the contents of the sack into the water. The river was shallow at that point, and two feet beneath the surface he could see the bottom dull-yellow in the fading light. At the sight of it, he spat into the hole.

He started the dogs along the Yukon trail. Whining spiritlessly, they were reluctant to work. Clinging to the gee-pole with his right band and with his left rubbing cheeks and nose, he stumbled over the rope as the dogs swung on a bend.

"Mush-on, you poor, sore-footed brutes!" he cried. "That's it, mush-on!"

THE WHITE MAN'S WAY

"To cook by your fire and to sleep under your roof for the night," I had announced on entering old Ebbits's cabin; and he had looked at me blear-eyed and vacuous, while Zilla had favored me with a sour face and a contemptuous grunt. Zilla was his wife, and no more bitter-tongued, implacable old squaw dwelt on the Yukon. Nor would I have stopped there had my dogs been less tired or had the rest of the village been inhabited. But this cabin alone had I found occupied, and in this cabin, perforce, I took my shelter.

Old Ebbits now and again pulled his tangled wits together, and hints and sparkles of intelligence came and went in his eyes. Several times during the preparation of my supper he even essayed hospitable inquiries about my health, the condition and number of my dogs, and the distance I had travelled that day. And each time Zilla had looked sourer than ever and grunted more contemptuously.

Yet I confess that there was no particular call for cheerfulness on their part. There they crouched by the fire, the pair of them, at the end of their days, old and withered and helpless, racked by rheumatism, bitten by hunger, and tantalized by the frying-odors of my abundance of meat. They rocked back and forth in a slow and hopeless way, and regularly, once every five minutes, Ebbits emitted a low groan. It was not so much a groan of pain, as of pain-weariness. He was oppressed by the weight and the torment of this thing called life, and still more was he oppressed by the fear of death. His was that eternal tragedy of the aged, with whom the joy of life has departed and the instinct for death has not come.

When my moose-meat spluttered rowdily in the frying-pan, I noticed old Ebbits's nostrils twitch and distend as he caught the food-scent. He ceased rocking for a space and forgot to groan, while a look of intelligence seemed to come into his face.

Zilla, on the other hand, rocked more rapidly, and for the first time, in sharp little yelps, voiced her pain. It came to me that their behavior was like that of hungry dogs, and in the fitness of things I should not have been astonished had Zilla suddenly developed a tail and thumped it on the floor in right doggish fashion. Ebbits drooled a little and stopped his rocking very frequently to lean forward and thrust his tremulous nose nearer to the source of gustatory excitement.

When I passed them each a plate of the fried meat, they ate greedily, making loud mouth-noises—champings of worn teeth and sucking intakes of the breath, accompanied by a continuous spluttering and mumbling. After that, when I gave them each a mug of scalding tea, the noises ceased. Easement and content came into their faces. Zilla relaxed her sour mouth long enough to sigh her satisfaction. Neither rocked any more, and they seemed to have fallen into placid meditation. Then a dampness came into Ebbits's eyes, and I knew that the sorrow of self-pity was his. The search required to find their pipes told plainly that they had been without tobacco a long time, and the old man's eagerness for the narcotic rendered him helpless, so that I was compelled to light his pipe for him.

"Why are you all alone in the village?" I asked. "Is everybody dead? Has there been a great sickness? Are you alone left of the living?"

Old Ebbits shook his head, saying: "Nay, there has been no great sickness. The village has gone away to hunt meat. We be too old, our legs are not strong, nor can our backs carry the burdens of camp and trail. Wherefore we remain here and wonder when the young men will return with meat."

"What if the young men do return with meat?" Zilla demanded harshly.

"They may return with much meat," he quavered hopefully.

"Even so, with much meat," she continued, more harshly than before. "But of what worth to you and me? A few bones to gnaw in our toothless old age. But the back-fat, the kidneys, and the tongues—these shall go into other mouths than thine and mine, old man."

Ebbits nodded his head and wept silently.

"There be no one to hunt meat for us," she cried, turning fiercely upon me.

There was accusation in her manner, and I shrugged my shoulders in token that I was not guilty of the unknown crime imputed to me.

"Know, O White Man, that it is because of thy kind, because of all white men, that my man and I have no meat in our old age and sit without tobacco in the cold."

"Nay," Ebbits said gravely, with a stricter sense of justice. "Wrong has been done us, it be true; but the white men did not mean the wrong."

"Where be Moklan?" she demanded. "Where be thy strong son, Moklan, and the fish he was ever willing to bring that you might eat?"

The old man shook his head.

"And where be Bidarshik, thy strong son? Ever was he a mighty hunter, and ever did he bring thee the good back-fat and the sweet dried tongues of the moose and the caribou. I see no back-fat and no sweet dried tongues. Your stomach is full with emptiness through the days, and it is for a man of a very miserable and lying people to give you to eat."

"Nay," old Ebbits interposed in kindliness, "the white man's is not a lying people. The white man speaks true. Always does the white man speak true." He paused, casting about him for words wherewith to temper the severity of what he was about to say. "But the white man speaks true in different ways. To-day he speaks true one way, to-morrow he speaks true another way, and there is no understanding him nor his way."

"To-day speak true one way, to-morrow speak true another way, which is to lie," was Zilla's dictum.

"There is no understanding the white man," Ebbits went on doggedly.

The meat, and the tea, and the tobacco seemed to have brought him back to life, and he gripped tighter hold of the idea behind his age-bleared eyes. He straightened up somewhat. His voice lost its querulous and whimpering note, and became strong and positive. He turned upon me with dignity, and addressed me as equal addresses equal.

"The white man's eyes are not shut," he began. "The white man sees all things, and thinks greatly, and is very wise. But the white man of one day is not the white man of next day, and there is no understanding him. He does not do things always in the same way. And what way his next way is to be, one cannot know. Always does the Indian do the one thing in the one way. Always does the moose come down from the high mountains when the winter is here. Always does the salmon come in the spring when the ice has gone out of the river. Always does everything do all things in the same way, and the Indian knows and understands. But the white man does not do all things in the same way, and the Indian does not know nor understand.

"Tobacco be very good. It be food to the hungry man. It makes the strong man stronger, and the angry man to forget that he is angry. Also is tobacco of value. It is of very great value. The Indian gives one large salmon for one leaf of tobacco, and he chews the tobacco for a long time. It is the juice of the tobacco that is good. When it runs down his throat it makes him feel good inside. But the white man! When his mouth is full with the juice, what does he do? That juice, that juice of great value, he spits it out in the snow and it is lost. Does the white man like tobacco? I do not know. But if he likes tobacco, why does he spit out its value and lose it in the snow? It is a great foolishness and without understanding."

He ceased, puffed at the pipe, found that it was out, and passed it over to Zilla, who took the sneer at the white man off her lips in order to pucker them about the pipe-stem. Ebbits seemed sinking back into his senility with the tale untold, and I demanded:

"What of thy sons, Moklan and Bidarshik? And why is it that you and your old woman are without meat at the end of your years?"

He roused himself as from sleep, and straightened up with an effort.

"It is not good to steal," he said. "When the dog takes your meat you beat the dog with a club. Such is the law. It is the law the man gave to the dog, and the dog must live to the law, else will it suffer the pain of the club. When man takes your meat, or your canoe, or your wife, you kill that man. That is the law, and it is a good law. It is not good to steal, wherefore it is the law that the man who steals must die. Whoso breaks the law must suffer hurt. It is a great hurt to die."

"But if you kill the man, why do you not kill the dog?" I asked.

Old Ebbits looked at me in childlike wonder, while Zilla sneered openly at the absurdity of my question.

"It is the way of the white man," Ebbits mumbled with an air of resignation.

"It is the foolishness of the white man," snapped Zilla.

"Then let old Ebbits teach the white man wisdom," I said softly.

"The dog is not killed, because it must pull the sled of the man. No man pulls another man's sled, wherefore the man is killed."

"Oh," I murmured.

"That is the law," old Ebbits went on. "Now listen, O White Man, and I will tell you of a great foolishness. There is an Indian. His name is Mobits. From white man he steals two pounds of flour. What does the white man do? Does he beat Mobits? No. Does he kill Mobits? No. What does he do to Mobits? I will tell you, O White Man. He has a house. He puts Mobits in that house. The roof is good. The walls are thick. He makes a fire that Mobits may be warm. He gives Mobits plenty grub to eat. It is good grub. Never in his all days does Mobits eat so good grub. There is bacon, and bread, and beans without end. Mobits have very good time.

"There is a big lock on door so that Mobits does not run away. This also is a great foolishness. Mobits will not run away. All the time is there plenty grub in that place, and warm blankets, and a big fire. Very foolish to run away. Mobits is not foolish. Three months

Mobits stop in that place. He steal two pounds of flour. For that, white man take plenty good care of him. Mobits eat many pounds of flour, many pounds of sugar, of bacon, of beans without end. Also, Mobits drink much tea. After three months white man open door and tell Mobits he must go. Mobits does not want to go. He is like dog that is fed long time in one place. He want to stay in that place, and the white man must drive Mobits away. So Mobits come back to this village, and he is very fat. That is the white man's way, and there is no understanding it. It is a foolishness, a great foolishness."

"But thy sons?" I insisted. "Thy very strong sons and thine old-age hunger?"

"There was Moklan," Ebbits began.

"A strong man," interrupted the mother. "He could dip paddle all of a day and night and never stop for the need of rest. He was wise in the way of the salmon and in the way of the water. He was very wise."

"There was Moklan," Ebbits repeated, ignoring the interruption. "In the spring, he went down the Yukon with the young men to trade at Cambell Fort. There is a post there, filled with the goods of the white man, and a trader whose name is Jones. Likewise is there a white man's medicine man, what you call missionary. Also is there bad water at Cambell Fort, where the Yukon goes slim like a maiden, and the water is fast, and the currents rush this way and come together, and there are whirls and sucks, and always are the currents changing and the face of the water changing, so at any two times it is never the same. Moklan is my son, wherefore he is brave man—"

"Was not my father brave man?" Zilla demanded.

"Thy father was brave man," Ebbits acknowledged, with the air of one who will keep peace in the house at any cost. "Moklan is thy son and mine, wherefore he is brave. Mayhap, because of thy very brave father, Moklan is too brave. It is like when too much water is put in the pot it spills over. So too much bravery is put into Moklan, and the bravery spills over.

"The young men are much afraid of the bad water at Cambell Fort. But Moklan is not afraid. He laughs strong, Ho! ho! and he goes forth into the bad water. But where the currents come together the canoe is turned over. A whirl takes Moklan by the legs, and he goes around and around, and down and down, and is seen no more."

"Ai! ai!" wailed Zilla. "Crafty and wise was he, and my first-born!"

"I am the father of Moklan," Ebbits said, having patiently given the woman space for her noise. "I get into canoe and journey down to Cambell Fort to collect the debt!"

"Debt!" interrupted. "What debt?"

"The debt of Jones, who is chief trader," came the answer. "Such is the law of travel in a strange country."

I shook my head in token of my ignorance, and Ebbits looked compassion at me, while Zilla snorted her customary contempt.

"Look you, O White Man," he said. "In thy camp is a dog that bites. When the dog bites a man, you give that man a present because you are sorry and because it is thy dog. You make payment. Is it not so? Also, if you have in thy country bad hunting, or bad water, you must make payment. It is just. It is the law. Did not my father's brother go over into the Tanana Country and get killed by a bear? And did not the Tanana tribe pay my father many blankets and fine furs? It was just. It was bad hunting, and the Tanana people made payment for the bad hunting.

"So I, Ebbits, journeyed down to Cambell Fort to collect the debt. Jones, who is chief trader, looked at me, and he laughed. He made great laughter, and would not give payment. I went to the medicine-man, what you call missionary, and had large talk about the bad water and the payment that should be mine. And the missionary made talk about other things. He talk about where Moklan has gone, now he is dead. There be large fires in that place, and if missionary make true talk, I know that Moklan will be cold no more. Also the missionary talk about where I shall go when I am dead. And he say bad things. He say that I am blind. Which is a lie. He say that I am in great darkness. Which is a lie. And I say that the day come and the night come for everybody just the same, and that in my village it is no more dark than at Cambell Fort. Also, I say that darkness and light and where we go when we die be different things from the matter of payment of just debt for bad water. Then the missionary make large anger, and call me bad names of darkness, and tell me to go away. And so I come back from Cambell Fort, and no payment has been made, and Moklan is dead, and in my old age I am without fish and meat."

"Because of the white man," said Zilla.

"Because of the white man," Ebbits concurred. "And other things because of the white man. There was Bidarshik. One way did the white man deal with him; and yet another way for the same thing did the white man deal with Yamikan. And first must I tell you of Yamikan, who was a young man of this village and who chanced to kill a white man. It is not good to kill a man of another people. Always is there great trouble. It was not the fault of Yamikan that he killed the white man. Yamikan spoke always soft words and ran away from wrath as a dog from a stick. But this white man drank much whiskey, and in the night-time came to Yamikan's house and made much fight. Yamikan cannot run away, and the white man tries to kill him. Yamikan does not like to die, so he kills the white man.

"Then is all the village in great trouble. We are much afraid that we must make large payment to the white man's people, and we hide our blankets, and our furs, and all our wealth, so that it will seem that we are poor people and can make only small payment. After long time white men come. They are soldier white men, and they take Yamikan away with them. His mother make great noise and throw ashes in her hair, for she knows Yamikan is dead. And all the village knows that Yamikan is dead, and is glad that no payment is asked.

"That is in the spring when the ice has gone out of the river. One year go by, two years go by. It is spring-time again, and the ice has gone out of the river. And then Yamikan, who is dead, comes back to us, and he is not dead, but very fat, and we know that he has slept warm and had plenty grub to eat. He has much fine clothes and is all the same white man, and he has gathered large wisdom so that he is very quick head man in the village.

"And he has strange things to tell of the way of the white man, for he has seen much of the white man and done a great travel into the white man's country. First place, soldier white men take him down the river long way. All the way do they take him down the river to the end, where it runs into a lake which is larger than all the land and large as the sky. I do not know the Yukon is so big river, but Yamikan has seen with his own eyes. I do not think there is a lake larger than all the land and large as the sky, but Yamikan has seen. Also, he has told me that the waters of this lake be salt, which is a strange thing and beyond understanding.

"But the White Man knows all these marvels for himself, so I shall not weary him with the telling of them. Only will I tell him what happened to Yamikan. The white man give Yamikan much fine grub. All the time does Yamikan eat, and all the time is there plenty more grub. The white man lives under the sun, so said Yamikan, where there be much warmth, and animals have only hair and no fur, and the green things grow large and strong and become flour, and beans, and potatoes. And under the sun there is never famine. Always is there plenty grub. I do not know. Yamikan has said.

"And here is a strange thing that befell Yamikan. Never did the white man hurt him.

Only did they give him warm bed at night and plenty fine grub. They take him across the salt lake which is big as the sky. He is on white man's fire-boat, what you call steamboat, only he is on boat maybe twenty times bigger than steamboat on Yukon. Also, it is made of iron, this boat, and yet does it not sink. This I do not understand, but Yamikan has said, 'I have journeyed far on the iron boat; behold! I am still alive.' It is a white man's soldier-boat with many soldier men upon it.

"After many sleeps of travel, a long, long time, Yamikan comes to a land where there is no snow. I cannot believe this. It is not in the nature of things that when winter comes there shall be no snow. But Yamikan has seen. Also have I asked the white men, and they have said yes, there is no snow in that country. But I cannot believe, and now I ask you if snow never come in that country. Also, I would hear the name of that country. I have heard the name before, but I would hear it again, if it be the same—thus will I know if I have heard lies or true talk."

Old Ebbits regarded me with a wistful face. He would have the truth at any cost, though it was his desire to retain his faith in the marvel he had never seen.

"Yes," I answered, "it is true talk that you have heard. There is no snow in that country, and its name is California."

"Cal-ee-forn-ee-yeh," he mumbled twice and thrice, listening intently to the sound of the syllables as they fell from his lips. He nodded his head in confirmation. "Yes, it is the same country of which Yamikan made talk."

I recognized the adventure of Yamikan as one likely to occur in the early days when Alaska first passed into the possession of the United States. Such a murder case, occurring before the instalment of territorial law and officials, might well have been taken down to the United States for trial before a Federal court.

"When Yamikan is in this country where there is no snow," old Ebbits continued, "he is taken to large house where many men make much talk. Long time men talk. Also many questions do they ask Yamikan. By and by they tell Yamikan he have no more trouble. Yamikan does not understand, for never has he had any trouble. All the time have they given him warm place to sleep and plenty grub.

"But after that they give him much better grub, and they give him money, and they take him many places in white man's country, and he see many strange things which are beyond the understanding of Ebbits, who is an old man and has not journeyed far. After two years, Yamikan comes back to this village, and he is head man, and very wise until he dies.

"But before he dies, many times does he sit by my fire and make talk of the strange things he has seen. And Bidarshik, who is my son, sits by the fire and listens; and his eyes are very wide and large because of the things he hears. One night, after Yamikan has gone home, Bidarshik stands up, so, very tall, and he strikes his chest with his fist, and says, 'When I am a man, I shall journey in far places, even to the land where there is no snow, and see things for myself.'"

"Always did Bidarshik journey in far places," Zilla interrupted proudly.

"It be true," Ebbits assented gravely. "And always did he return to sit by the fire and hunger for yet other and unknown far places."

"And always did he remember the salt lake as big as the sky and the country under the sun where there is no snow," quoth Zilla.

"And always did he say, 'When I have the full strength of a man, I will go and see for myself if the talk of Yamikan be true talk,'" said Ebbits.

"But there was no way to go to the white man's country," said Zilla.

"Did he not go down to the salt lake that is big as the sky?" Ebbits demanded.

"And there was no way for him across the salt lake," said Zilla.

"Save in the white man's fire-boat which is of iron and is bigger than twenty steamboats on the Yukon," said Ebbits. He scowled at Zilla, whose withered lips were again writhing into speech, and compelled her to silence. "But the white man would not let him cross the salt lake in the fire-boat, and he returned to sit by the fire and hunger for the country under the sun where there is no snow.'"

"Yet on the salt lake had he seen the fire-boat of iron that did not sink," cried out Zilla the irrepressible.

"Ay," said Ebbits, "and he saw that Yamikan had made true talk of the things he had seen. But there was no way for Bidarshik to journey to the white man's land under the sun, and he grew sick and weary like an old man and moved not away from the fire. No longer did he go forth to kill meat—"

"And no longer did he eat the meat placed before him," Zilla broke in. "He would shake his head and say, 'Only do I care to eat the grub of the white man and grow fat after the manner of Yamikan.'"

"And he did not eat the meat," Ebbits went on. "And the sickness of Bidarshik grew into a great sickness until I thought he would die. It was not a sickness of the body, but of the head. It was a sickness of desire. I, Ebbits, who am his father, make a great think. I have no more sons and I do not want Bidarshik to die. It is a head-sickness, and there is but one way to make it well. Bidarshik must journey across the lake as large as the sky to the land where there is no snow, else will he die. I make a very great think, and then I see the way for Bidarshik to go.

"So, one night when he sits by the fire, very sick, his head hanging down, I say, 'My son, I have learned the way for you to go to the white man's land.' He looks at me, and his face is glad. 'Go,' I say, 'even as Yamikan went.' But Bidarshik is sick and does not understand. 'Go forth,' I say, 'and find a white man, and, even as Yamikan, do you kill that white man.' Then will the soldier white men come and get you, and even as they took Yamikan will they take you across the salt lake to the white man's land. And then, even as Yamikan, will you return very fat, your eyes full of the things you have seen, your head filled with wisdom.'

"And Bidarshik stands up very quick, and his hand is reaching out for his gun. 'Where do you go?' I ask. 'To kill the white man,' he says. And I see that my words have been good in the ears of Bidarshik and that he will grow well again. Also do I know that my words have been wise.

"There is a white man come to this village. He does not seek after gold in the ground, nor after furs in the forest. All the time does he seek after bugs and flies. He does not eat the bugs and flies, then why does he seek after them? I do not know. Only do I know that he is a funny white man. Also does he seek after the eggs of birds. He does not eat the eggs. All that is inside he takes out, and only does he keep the shell. Eggshell is not good to eat. Nor does he eat the eggshells, but puts them away in soft boxes where they will not break. He catch many small birds. But he does not eat the birds. He takes only the skins and puts them away in boxes. Also does he like bones. Bones are not good to eat. And this strange white man likes best the bones of long time ago which he digs out of the ground.

"But he is not a fierce white man, and I know he will die very easy; so I say to Bidarshik, 'My son, there is the white man for you to kill.' And Bidarshik says that my words be wise. So he goes to a place he knows where are many bones in the ground. He digs up very many of these bones and brings them to the strange white man's camp. The white man is made very glad. His face shines like the sun, and he smiles with much gladness as he looks at the bones. He bends his head over, so, to look well at the bones, and then Bidarshik strikes him hard on the head, with axe, once, so, and the strange white man kicks and is dead.

"'Now,' I say to Bidarshik, 'will the white soldier men come and take you away to the land under the sun, where you will eat much and grow fat.' Bidarshik is happy. Already has his sickness gone from him, and he sits by the fire and waits for the coming of the white soldier men.

"How was I to know the way of the white man is never twice the same?" the old man demanded, whirling upon me fiercely. "How was I to know that what the white man does yesterday he will not do to-day, and that what he does to-day he will not do to-morrow?" Ebbits shook his head sadly. "There is no understanding the white man. Yesterday he takes Yamikan to the land under the sun and makes him fat with much grub. To-day he takes Bidarshik and—what does he do with Bidarshik? Let me tell you what he does with Bidarshik.

"I, Ebbits, his father, will tell you. He takes Bidarshik to Cambell Fort, and he ties a rope around his neck, so, and, when his feet are no more on the ground, he dies."

"Ai! ai!" wailed Zilla. "And never does he cross the lake large as the sky, nor see the land under the sun where there is no snow."

"Wherefore," old Ebbits said with grave dignity, "there be no one to hunt meat for me in my old age, and I sit hungry by my fire and tell my story to the White Man who has given me grub, and strong tea, and tobacco for my pipe."

"Because of the lying and very miserable white people," Zilla proclaimed shrilly.

"Nay," answered the old man with gentle positiveness. "Because of the way of the white man, which is without understanding and never twice the same."

THE STORY OF KEESH

Keesh lived long ago on the rim of the polar sea, was head man of his village through many and prosperous years, and died full of honors with his name on the lips of men. So long ago did he live that only the old men remember his name, his name and the tale, which they got from the old men before them, and which the old men to come will tell to their children and their children's children down to the end of time. And the winter darkness, when the north gales make their long sweep across the ice-pack, and the air is filled with flying white, and no man may venture forth, is the chosen time for the telling of how Keesh, from the poorest *igloo* in the village, rose to power and place over them all.

He was a bright boy, so the tale runs, healthy and strong, and he had seen thirteen suns, in their way of reckoning time. For each winter the sun leaves the land in darkness, and the next year a new sun returns so that they may be warm again and look upon one another's faces. The father of Keesh had been a very brave man, but he had met his death in a time of famine, when he sought to save the lives of his people by taking the life of a great polar bear. In his eagerness he came to close grapples with the bear, and his bones were crushed; but the bear had much meat on him and the people were saved. Keesh was his only son, and after that Keesh lived alone with his mother. But the people are prone to forget, and they forgot the deed of his father; and he being but a boy, and his mother only a woman, they, too, were swiftly forgotten, and ere long came to live in the meanest of all the *igloos*.

It was at a council, one night, in the big *igloo* of Klosh-Kwan, the chief, that Keesh showed the blood that ran in his veins and the manhood that stiffened his back. With the dignity of an elder, he rose to his feet, and waited for silence amid the babble of voices.

"It is true that meat be apportioned me and mine," he said. "But it is ofttimes old and tough, this meat, and, moreover, it has an unusual quantity of bones."

The hunters, grizzled and gray, and lusty and young, were aghast. The like had never been known before. A child, that talked like a grown man, and said harsh things to their very faces!

But steadily and with seriousness, Keesh went on. "For that I know my father, Bok, was a great hunter, I speak these words. It is said that Bok brought home more meat than any of

276

the two best hunters, that with his own hands he attended to the division of it, that with his own eyes he saw to it that the least old woman and the last old man received fair share."

"Na! Na!" the men cried. "Put the child out!" "Send him off to bed!" "He is no man that he should talk to men and graybeards!"

He waited calmly till the uproar died down.

"Thou hast a wife, Ugh-Gluk," he said, "and for her dost thou speak. And thou, too, Massuk, a mother also, and for them dost thou speak. My mother has no one, save me; wherefore I speak. As I say, though Bok be dead because he hunted over-keenly, it is just that I, who am his son, and that Ikeega, who is my mother and was his wife, should have meat in plenty so long as there be meat in plenty in the tribe. I, Keesh, the son of Bok, have spoken."

He sat down, his ears keenly alert to the flood of protest and indignation his words had created.

"That a boy should speak in council!" old Ugh-Gluk was mumbling.

"Shall the babes in arms tell us men the things we shall do?" Massuk demanded in a loud voice. "Am I a man that I should be made a mock by every child that cries for meat?"

The anger boiled a white heat. They ordered him to bed, threatened that he should have no meat at all, and promised him sore beatings for his presumption. Keesh's eyes began to flash, and the blood to pound darkly under his skin. In the midst of the abuse he sprang to his feet.

"Hear me, ye men!" he cried. "Never shall I speak in the council again, never again till the men come to me and say, 'It is well, Keesh, that thou shouldst speak, it is well and it is our wish.' Take this now, ye men, for my last word. Bok, my father, was a great hunter. I, too, his son, shall go and hunt the meat that I eat. And be it known, now, that the division of that which I kill shall be fair. And no widow nor weak one shall cry in the night because there is no meat, when the strong men are groaning in great pain for that they have eaten overmuch. And in the days to come there shall be shame upon the strong men who have eaten overmuch. I, Keesh, have said it!"

Jeers and scornful laughter followed him out of the *igloo*, but his jaw was set and he went his way, looking neither to right nor left.

The next day he went forth along the shore-line where the ice and the land met together. Those who saw him go noted that he carried his bow, with a goodly supply of bone-barbed arrows, and that across his shoulder was his father's big hunting-spear. And there was laughter, and much talk, at the event. It was an unprecedented occurrence. Never did boys of his tender age go forth to hunt, much less to hunt alone. Also were there shaking of heads and prophetic mutterings, and the women looked pityingly at Ikeega, and her face was grave and sad.

"He will be back ere long," they said cheeringly.

"Let him go; it will teach him a lesson," the hunters said. "And he will come back shortly, and he will be meek and soft of speech in the days to follow."

But a day passed, and a second, and on the third a wild gale blew, and there was no Keesh. Ikeega tore her hair and put soot of the seal-oil on her face in token of her grief; and the women assailed the men with bitter words in that they had mistreated the boy and sent him to his death; and the men made no answer, preparing to go in search of the body when the storm abated.

Early next morning, however, Keesh strode into the village. But he came not shamefaced-ly. Across his shoulders he bore a burden of fresh-killed meat. And there was importance in his step and arrogance in his speech.

"Go, ye men, with the dogs and sledges, and take my trail for the better part of a day's travel," he said. "There is much meat on the ice—a she-bear and two half-grown cubs."

Ikeega was overcome with joy, but he received her demonstrations in manlike fashion, saying: "Come, Ikeega, let us eat. And after that I shall sleep, for I am weary."

And he passed into their *igloo* and ate profoundly, and after that slept for twenty running hours.

There was much doubt at first, much doubt and discussion. The killing of a polar bear is very dangerous, but thrice dangerous is it, and three times thrice, to kill a mother bear with her cubs. The men could not bring themselves to believe that the boy Keesh, single-handed, had accomplished so great a marvel. But the women spoke of the fresh-killed meat he had brought on his back, and this was an overwhelming argument against their unbelief. So they finally departed, grumbling greatly that in all probability, if the thing were so, he had neglected to cut up the carcasses. Now in the north it is very necessary that this should be done as soon as a kill is made. If not, the meat freezes so solidly as to turn the edge of the sharpest knife, and a three-hundred-pound bear, frozen stiff, is no easy thing to put upon a sled and haul over the rough ice. But arrived at the spot, they found not only the kill, which they had doubted, but that Keesh had quartered the beasts in true hunter fashion, and removed the entrails.

Thus began the mystery of Keesh, a mystery that deepened and deepened with the passing of the days. His very next trip he killed a young bear, nearly full-grown, and on the trip following, a large male bear and his mate. He was ordinarily gone from three to four days, though it was nothing unusual for him to stay away a week at a time on the ice-field. Always he declined company on these expeditions, and the people marvelled. "How does he do it?" they demanded of one another. "Never does he take a dog with him, and dogs are of such great help, too."

"Why dost thou hunt only bear?" Klosh-Kwan once ventured to ask him.

And Keesh made fitting answer. "It is well known that there is more meat on the bear," he said.

But there was also talk of witchcraft in the village. "He hunts with evil spirits," some of the people contended, "wherefore his hunting is rewarded. How else can it be, save that he hunts with evil spirits?"

"Mayhap they be not evil, but good, these spirits," others said. "It is known that his father was a mighty hunter. May not his father hunt with him so that he may attain excellence and patience and understanding? Who knows?"

None the less, his success continued, and the less skilful hunters were often kept busy hauling in his meat. And in the division of it he was just. As his father had done before him, he saw to it that the least old woman and the last old man received a fair portion, keeping no more for himself than his needs required. And because of this, and of his merit as a hunter, he was looked upon with respect, and even awe; and there was talk of making him chief after old Klosh-Kwan. Because of the things he had done, they looked for him to appear again in the council, but he never came, and they were ashamed to ask.

"I am minded to build me an *igloo*," he said one day to Klosh-Kwan and a number of the hunters. "It shall be a large *igloo*, wherein Ikeega and I can dwell in comfort."

"Ay," they nodded gravely.

"But I have no time. My business is hunting, and it takes all my time. So it is but just that the men and women of the village who eat my meat should build me my *igloo*."

And the *igloo* was built accordingly, on a generous scale which exceeded even the dwelling of Klosh-Kwan. Keesh and his mother moved into it, and it was the first prosperity she had enjoyed since the death of Bok. Nor was material prosperity alone hers, for, because of her wonderful son and the position he had given her, she came to be looked upon as the first woman in all the village; and the women were given to visiting her, to asking her advice, and to quoting her wisdom when arguments arose among themselves or with the men.

But it was the mystery of Keesh's marvellous hunting that took chief place in all their minds. And one day Ugh-Gluk taxed him with witchcraft to his face.

"It is charged," Ugh-Gluk said ominously, "that thou dealest with evil spirits, wherefore thy hunting is rewarded."

"Is not the meat good?" Keesh made answer. "Has one in the village yet to fall sick from the eating of it? How dost thou know that witchcraft be concerned? Or dost thou guess, in the dark, merely because of the envy that consumes thee?"

And Ugh-Gluk withdrew discomfited, the women laughing at him as he walked away. But in the council one night, after long deliberation, it was determined to put spies on his track when he went forth to hunt, so that his methods might be learned. So, on his next trip, Bim and Bawn, two young men, and of hunters the craftiest, followed after him, taking care not to be seen. After five days they returned, their eyes bulging and their tongues a-tremble to tell what they had seen. The council was hastily called in Klosh-Kwan's dwelling, and Bim took up the tale.

"Brothers! As commanded, we journeyed on the trail of Keesh, and cunningly we journeyed, so that he might not know. And midway of the first day he picked up with a great he-bear. It was a very great bear."

"None greater," Bawn corroborated, and went on himself. "Yet was the bear not inclined to fight, for he turned away and made off slowly over the ice. This we saw from the rocks of the shore, and the bear came toward us, and after him came Keesh, very much unafraid. And he shouted harsh words after the bear, and waved his arms about, and made much noise. Then did the bear grow angry, and rise up on his hind legs, and growl. But Keesh walked right up to the bear."

"Ay," Bim continued the story. "Right up to the bear Keesh walked. And the bear took after him, and Keesh ran away. But as he ran he dropped a little round ball on the ice. And the bear stopped and smelled of it, then swallowed it up. And Keesh continued to run away and drop little round balls, and the bear continued to swallow them up."

Exclamations and cries of doubt were being made, and Ugh-Gluk expressed open unbelief.

"With our own eyes we saw it," Bim affirmed.

And Bawn—"Ay, with our own eyes. And this continued until the bear stood suddenly upright and cried aloud in pain, and thrashed his fore paws madly about. And Keesh continued to make off over the ice to a safe distance. But the bear gave him no notice, being occupied with the misfortune the little round balls had wrought within him."

"Ay, within him," Bim interrupted. "For he did claw at himself, and leap about over the ice like a playful puppy, save from the way he growled and squealed it was plain it was not play but pain. Never did I see such a sight!"

"Nay, never was such a sight seen," Bawn took up the strain. "And furthermore, it was such a large bear."

"Witchcraft," Ugh-Gluk suggested.

"I know not," Bawn replied. "I tell only of what my eyes beheld. And after a while the bear grew weak and tired, for he was very heavy and he had jumped about with exceeding violence, and he went off along the shore-ice, shaking his head slowly from side to side and sitting down ever and again to squeal and cry. And Keesh followed after the bear, and we followed after Keesh, and for that day and three days more we followed. The bear grew weak, and never ceased crying from his pain."

"It was a charm!" Ugh-Gluk exclaimed. "Surely it was a charm!"

"It may well be."

And Bim relieved Bawn. "The bear wandered, now this way and now that, doubling back and forth and crossing his trail in circles, so that at the end he was near where Keesh had first come upon him. By this time he was quite sick, the bear, and could crawl no farther, so Keesh came up close and speared him to death."

"And then?" Klosh-Kwan demanded.

"Then we left Keesh skinning the bear, and came running that the news of the killing might be told."

And in the afternoon of that day the women hauled in the meat of the bear while the men sat in council assembled. When Keesh arrived a messenger was sent to him, bidding him come to the council. But he sent reply, saying that he was hungry and tired; also that his *igloo* was large and comfortable and could hold many men.

And curiosity was so strong on the men that the whole council, Klosh-Kwan to the fore, rose up and went to the *igloo* of Keesh. He was eating, but he received them with respect and seated them according to their rank. Ikeega was proud and embarrassed by turns, but Keesh was quite composed.

Klosh-Kwan recited the information brought by Bim and Bawn, and at its close said in a stern voice: "So explanation is wanted, O Keesh, of thy manner of hunting. Is there witch-craft in it?"

Keesh looked up and smiled. "Nay, O Klosh-Kwan. It is not for a boy to know aught of witches, and of witches I know nothing. I have but devised a means whereby I may kill the ice-bear with ease, that is all. It be headcraft, not witchcraft."

"And may any man?"

"Any man."

There was a long silence. The men looked in one another's faces, and Keesh went on eating.

"And . . . and . . . and wilt thou tell us, O Keesh?" Klosh-Kwan finally asked in a tremulous voice.

"Yea, I will tell thee." Keesh finished sucking a marrow-bone and rose to his feet. "It is quite simple. Behold!"

He picked up a thin strip of whalebone and showed it to them. The ends were sharp as needle-points. The strip he coiled carefully, till it disappeared in his hand. Then, suddenly releasing it, it sprang straight again. He picked up a piece of blubber.

"So," he said, "one takes a small chunk of blubber, thus, and thus makes it hollow. Then into the hollow goes the whalebone, so, tightly coiled, and another piece of blubber is fitted over the whale-bone. After that it is put outside where it freezes into a little round ball. The bear swallows the little round ball, the blubber melts, the whalebone with its sharp ends stands out straight, the bear gets sick, and when the bear is very sick, why, you kill him with a spear. It is quite simple."

And Ugh-Gluk said "Oh!" and Klosh-Kwan said "Ah!" And each said something after his own manner, and all understood.

And this is the story of Keesh, who lived long ago on the rim of the polar sea. Because he exercised headcraft and not witchcraft, he rose from the meanest *igloo* to be head man of his village, and through all the years that he lived, it is related, his tribe was prosperous, and neither widow nor weak one cried aloud in the night because there was no meat.

THE UNEXPECTED

It is a simple matter to see the obvious, to do the expected. The tendency of the individual life is to be static rather than dynamic, and this tendency is made into a propulsion by civilization, where the obvious only is seen, and the unexpected rarely happens. When the unexpected does happen, however, and when it is of sufficiently grave import, the unfit perish. They do not see what is not obvious, are unable to do the unexpected, are incapable of adjusting their well-grooved lives to other and strange grooves. In short, when they come to the end of their own groove, they die.

On the other hand, there are those that make toward survival, the fit individuals who escape from the rule of the obvious and the expected and adjust their lives to no matter what strange grooves they may stray into, or into which they may be forced. Such an individual was Edith Whittlesey. She was born in a rural district of England, where life proceeds by rule of thumb and the unexpected is so very unexpected that when it happens it is looked upon as an immorality. She went into service early, and while yet a young woman, by rule-of-thumb progression, she became a lady's maid.

The effect of civilization is to impose human law upon environment until it becomes machine-like in its regularity. The objectionable is eliminated, the inevitable is foreseen. One is not even made wet by the rain nor cold by the frost; while death, instead of stalking about grewsome and accidental, becomes a prearranged pageant, moving along a well-oiled groove to the family vault, where the hinges are kept from rusting and the dust from the air is swept continually away.

Such was the environment of Edith Whittlesey. Nothing happened. It could scarcely be called a happening, when, at the age of twenty-five, she accompanied her mistress on a bit of travel to the United States. The groove merely changed its direction. It was still the same groove and well oiled. It was a groove that bridged the Atlantic with uneventfulness, so that the ship was not a ship in the midst of the sea, but a capacious, many-corridored hotel that moved swiftly and placidly, crushing the waves into submission with its colossal bulk until the sea was a mill-pond, monotonous with quietude. And at the other side the groove continued on over the land—a well-disposed, respectable groove that supplied hotels at every stopping-place, and hotels on wheels between the stopping-places.

In Chicago, while her mistress saw one side of social life, Edith Whittlesey saw another side; and when she left her lady's service and became Edith Nelson, she betrayed, perhaps faintly, her ability to grapple with the unexpected and to master it. Hans Nelson, immigrant, Swede by birth and carpenter by occupation, had in him that Teutonic unrest that drives the race ever westward on its great adventure. He was a large-muscled, stolid sort of a man, in whom little imagination was coupled with immense initiative, and who possessed, withal, loyalty and affection as sturdy as his own strength.

"When I have worked hard and saved me some money, I will go to Colorado," he had told Edith on the day after their wedding. A year later they were in Colorado, where Hans Nelson saw his first mining and caught the mining-fever himself. His prospecting led him through the Dakotas, Idaho, and eastern Oregon, and on into the mountains of British Columbia. In camp and on trail, Edith Nelson was always with him, sharing his luck, his hardship, and his toil. The short step of the house-reared woman she exchanged for the long stride of the mountaineer. She learned to look upon danger clear-eyed and with understanding, losing forever that panic fear which is bred of ignorance and which afflicts the city-reared, making them as silly as silly horses, so that they await fate in frozen horror instead of grappling with it, or stampede in blind self-destroying terror which clutters the way with their crushed carcasses.

Edith Nelson met the unexpected at every turn of the trail, and she trained her vision so that she saw in the landscape, not the obvious, but the concealed. She, who had never cooked in her life, learned to make bread without the mediation of hops, yeast, or baking-powder, and to bake bread, top and bottom, in a frying-pan before an open fire. And when the last cup of flour was gone and the last rind of bacon, she was able to rise to the occasion, and of moccasins and the softer-tanned bits of leather in the outfit to make a grub-stake substitute that somehow held a man's soul in his body and enabled him to stagger on. She learned to pack a horse as well as a man,—a task to break the heart and the pride of any city-dweller, and she knew how to throw the hitch best suited for any particular kind of pack. Also, she could build a fire of wet wood in a downpour of rain and not lose her temper. In short, in all its guises she mastered the unexpected. But the Great Unexpected was yet to come into her life and put its test upon her.

The gold-seeking tide was flooding northward into Alaska, and it was inevitable that Hans Nelson and his wife should be caught up by the stream and swept toward the Klondike. The fall of 1897 found them at Dyea, but without the money to carry an outfit across Chilcoot Pass and float it down to Dawson. So Hans Nelson worked at his trade that winter and helped rear the mushroom outfitting-town of Skaguay.

He was on the edge of things, and throughout the winter he heard all Alaska calling to him. Latuya Bay called loudest, so that the summer of 1898 found him and his wife threading the mazes of the broken coast-line in seventy-foot Siwash canoes. With them were Indians, also three other men. The Indians landed them and their supplies in a lonely bight of land a hundred miles or so beyond Latuya Bay, and returned to Skaguay; but the three other men remained, for they were members of the organized party. Each had put an equal share of capital into the outfitting, and the profits were to be divided equally. In that Edith Nelson undertook to cook for the outfit, a man's share was to be her portion.

First, spruce trees were cut down and a three-room cabin constructed. To keep this cabin was Edith Nelson's task. The task of the men was to search for gold, which they did; and to find gold, which they likewise did. It was not a startling find, merely a low-pay placer where long hours of severe toil earned each man between fifteen and twenty dollars a day. The brief Alaskan summer protracted itself beyond its usual length, and they took advantage of the opportunity, delaying their return to Skaguay to the last moment. And then it was too late. Arrangements had been made to accompany the several dozen local Indians on their fall trading trip down the coast. The Siwashes had waited on the white people until the eleventh hour, and then departed. There was no course left the party but to wait for chance transportation. In the meantime the claim was cleaned up and firewood stocked in.

The Indian summer had dreamed on and on, and then, suddenly, with the sharpness of bugles, winter came. It came in a single night, and the miners awoke to howling wind, driving snow, and freezing water. Storm followed storm, and between the storms there was the silence, broken only by the boom of the surf on the desolate shore, where the salt spray rimmed the beach with frozen white.

All went well in the cabin. Their gold-dust had weighed up something like eight thousand dollars, and they could not but be contented. The men made snowshoes, hunted fresh meat for the larder, and in the long evenings played endless games of whist and pedro. Now that the mining had ceased, Edith Nelson turned over the fire-building and the dish-washing to the men, while she darned their socks and mended their clothes.

There was no grumbling, no bickering, nor petty quarrelling in the little cabin, and they often congratulated one another on the general happiness of the party. Hans Nelson was stolid and easy-going, while Edith had long before won his unbounded admiration by her capacity for getting on with people. Harkey, a long, lank Texan, was unusually friendly for one with a saturnine disposition, and, as long as his theory that gold grew was not challenged, was quite companionable. The fourth member of the party, Michael Dennin, contributed his Irish wit to the gayety of the cabin. He was a large, powerful man, prone to sudden rushes of anger over little things, and of unfailing good-humor under the stress and strain of big things. The fifth and last member, Dutchy, was the willing butt of the party. He even went out of his way to raise a laugh at his own expense in order to keep things cheerful. His deliberate aim in life seemed to be that of a maker of laughter. No serious quarrel had ever vexed the serenity of the party; and, now that each had sixteen hundred dollars to show for a short summer's work, there reigned the well-fed, contented spirit of prosperity.

And then the unexpected happened. They had just sat down to the breakfast table. Though it was already eight o'clock (late breakfasts had followed naturally upon cessation of the steady work at mining) a candle in the neck of a bottle lighted the meal. Edith and Hans sat at each end of the table. On one side, with their backs to the door, sat Harkey and Dutchy. The place on the other side was vacant. Dennin had not yet come in.

Hans Nelson looked at the empty chair, shook his head slowly, and, with a ponderous attempt at humor, said: "Always is he first at the grub. It is very strange. Maybe he is sick."

"Where is Michael?" Edith asked.

"Got up a little ahead of us and went outside," Harkey answered.

Dutchy's face beamed mischievously. He pretended knowledge of Dennin's absence, and affected a mysterious air, while they clamored for information. Edith, after a peep into the men's bunk-room, returned to the table. Hans looked at her, and she shook her head.

"He was never late at meal-time before," she remarked.

"I cannot understand," said Hans. "Always has he the great appetite like the horse."

"It is too bad," Dutchy said, with a sad shake of his head.

They were beginning to make merry over their comrade's absence.

"It is a great pity!" Dutchy volunteered.

"What?" they demanded in chorus.

"Poor Michael," was the mournful reply.

"Well, what's wrong with Michael?" Harkey asked.

"He is not hungry no more," wailed Dutchy. "He has lost der appetite. He do not like der grub."

"Not from the way he pitches into it up to his ears," remarked Harkey.

"He does dot shust to be politeful to Mrs. Nelson," was Dutchy's quick retort. "I know, I know, and it is too pad. Why is he not here? Pecause he haf gone out. Why haf he gone out? For der defelopment of der appetite. How does he defelop der appetite? He walks barefoots in der snow. Ach! don't I know? It is der way der rich peoples chases after der appetite when it is no more and is running away. Michael haf sixteen hundred dollars. He is rich peoples. He haf no appetite. Derefore, pecause, he is chasing der appetite. Shust you open der door und you will see his barefoots in der snow. No, you will not see der appetite. Dot is shust his trouble. When he sees der appetite he will catch it und come to preak-fast."

They burst into loud laughter at Dutchy's nonsense. The sound had scarcely died away when the door opened and Dennin came in. All turned to look at him. He was carrying a shot-gun. Even as they looked, he lifted it to his shoulder and fired twice. At the first shot Dutchy sank upon the table, overturning his mug of coffee, his yellow mop of hair dabbling in his plate of mush. His forehead, which pressed upon the near edge of the plate, tilted the plate up against his hair at an angle of forty-five degrees. Harkey was in the air, in his spring to his feet, at the second shot, and he pitched face down upon the floor, his "My God!" gurgling and dying in his throat.

It was the unexpected. Hans and Edith were stunned. They sat at the table with bodies tense, their eyes fixed in a fascinated gaze upon the murderer. Dimly they saw him through the smoke of the powder, and in the silence nothing was to be heard save the drip-drip of Dutchy's spilled coffee on the floor. Dennin threw open the breech of the shot-gun, ejecting the empty shells. Holding the gun with one hand, he reached with the other into his pocket for fresh shells.

He was thrusting the shells into the gun when Edith Nelson was aroused to action. It was patent that he intended to kill Hans and her. For a space of possibly three seconds of time she had been dazed and paralysed by the horrible and inconceivable form in which the unexpected had made its appearance. Then she rose to it and grappled with it. She grappled with it concretely, making a cat-like leap for the murderer and gripping his neck-cloth with both her hands. The impact of her body sent him stumbling backward several steps. He tried to shake her loose and still retain his hold on the gun. This was awkward, for her firm-fleshed body had become a cat's. She threw herself to one side, and with her grip at his throat nearly jerked him to the floor. He straightened himself and whirled swiftly. Still faithful to her hold, her body followed the circle of his whirl so that her feet left the floor, and she swung through the air fastened to his throat by her hands. The whirl culminated in a collision with a chair, and the man and woman crashed to the floor in a wild struggling fall that extended itself across half the length of the room.

Hans Nelson was half a second behind his wife in rising to the unexpected. His nerve processed and mental processes were slower than hers. His was the grosser organism, and it had taken him half a second longer to perceive, and determine, and proceed to do. She had already flown at Dennin and gripped his throat, when Hans sprang to his feet. But her coolness was not his. He was in a blind fury, a Berserker rage. At the instant he sprang from his chair his mouth opened and there issued forth a sound that was half roar, half bellow. The whirl of the two bodies had already started, and still roaring, or bellowing, he pursued this whirl down the room, overtaking it when it fell to the floor.

Hans hurled himself upon the prostrate man, striking madly with his fists. They were sledge-like blows, and when Edith felt Dennin's body relax she loosed her grip and rolled clear. She lay on the floor, panting and watching. The fury of blows continued to rain down. Dennin did not seem to mind the blows. He did not even move. Then it dawned upon her that he was unconscious. She cried out to Hans to stop. She cried out again. But he paid no heed to her voice. She caught him by the arm, but her clinging to it merely impeded his effort.

It was no reasoned impulse that stirred her to do what she then did. Nor was it a sense of pity, nor obedience to the "Thou shalt not" of religion. Rather was it some sense of law, an ethic of her race and early environment, that compelled her to interpose her body between her husband and the helpless murderer. It was not until Hans knew he was striking his wife that he ceased. He allowed himself to be shoved away by her in much the same way that a ferocious but obedient dog allows itself to be shoved away by its master. The analogy went even farther. Deep in his throat, in an animal-like way, Hans's rage still rumbled, and several times he made as though to spring back upon his prey and was only prevented by the woman's swiftly interposed body.

Back and farther back Edith shoved her husband. She had never seen him in such a condition, and she was more frightened of him than she had been of Dennin in the thick of the struggle. She could not believe that this raging beast was her Hans, and with a shock she became suddenly aware of a shrinking, instinctive fear that he might snap her hand in his teeth like any wild animal. For some seconds, unwilling to hurt her, yet dogged in his desire to return to the attack, Hans dodged back and forth. But she resolutely dodged with him, until the first glimmerings of reason returned and he gave over.

Both crawled to their feet. Hans staggered back against the wall, where he leaned, his face working, in his throat the deep and continuous rumble that died away with the seconds and at last ceased. The time for the reaction had come. Edith stood in the middle of the floor, wringing her hands, panting and gasping, her whole body trembling violently.

Hans looked at nothing, but Edith's eyes wandered wildly from detail to detail of what had taken place. Dennin lay without movement. The overturned chair, hurled onward in the mad whirl, lay near him. Partly under him lay the shot-gun, still broken open at the breech. Spilling out of his right hand were the two cartridges which he had failed to put into the gun and which he had clutched until consciousness left him. Harkey lay on the floor, face downward, where he had fallen; while Dutchy rested forward on the table, his yellow mop of hair buried in his mush-plate, the plate itself still tilted at an angle of forty-five degrees. This tilted plate fascinated her. Why did it not fall down? It was ridiculous. It was not in the nature of things for a mush-plate to up-end itself on the table, even if a man or so had been killed.

She glanced back at Dennin, but her eyes returned to the tilted plate. It was so ridiculous! She felt a hysterical impulse to laugh. Then she noticed the silence, and forgot the plate in a desire for something to happen. The monotonous drip of the coffee from the table to the floor merely emphasized the silence. Why did not Hans do something? say something? She looked at him and was about to speak, when she discovered that her tongue refused its wonted duty. There was a peculiar ache in her throat, and her mouth was dry and furry. She could only look at Hans, who, in turn, looked at her.

Suddenly the silence was broken by a sharp, metallic clang. She screamed, jerking her eyes back to the table. The plate had fallen down. Hans sighed as though awakening from sleep. The clang of the plate had aroused them to life in a new world. The cabin epitomized the new world in which they must thenceforth live and move. The old cabin was gone forever. The horizon of life was totally new and unfamiliar. The unexpected had swept its wizardry over the face of things, changing the perspective, juggling values, and shuffling the real and the unreal into perplexing confusion.

"My God, Hans!" was Edith's first speech.

He did not answer, but stared at her with horror. Slowly his eyes wandered over the room, for the first time taking in its details. Then he put on his cap and started for the door.

"Where are you going?" Edith demanded, in an agony of apprehension.

His hand was on the door-knob, and he half turned as he answered, "To dig some graves."

"Don't leave me, Hans, with—" her eyes swept the room—"with this."

"The graves must be dug sometime," he said.

"But you do not know how many," she objected desperately. She noted his indecision, and added, "Besides, I'll go with you and help."

Hans stepped back to the table and mechanically snuffed the candle. Then between them they made the examination. Both Harkey and Dutchy were dead—frightfully dead, because of the close range of the shot-gun. Hans refused to go near Dennin, and Edith was forced to conduct this portion of the investigation by herself.

"He isn't dead," she called to Hans.

He walked over and looked down at the murderer.

"What did you say?" Edith demanded, having caught the rumble of inarticulate speech in her husband's throat.

"I said it was a damn shame that he isn't dead," came the reply.

Edith was bending over the body.

"Leave him alone," Hans commanded harshly, in a strange voice.

She looked at him in sudden alarm. He had picked up the shot-gun dropped by Dennin and was thrusting in the shells.

"What are you going to do?" she cried, rising swiftly from her bending position.

Hans did not answer, but she saw the shot-gun going to his shoulder. She grasped the muzzle with her hand and threw it up.

"Leave me alone!" he cried hoarsely.

He tried to jerk the weapon away from her, but she came in closer and clung to him.

"Hans! Hans! Wake up!" she cried. "Don't be crazy!"

"He killed Dutchy and Harkey!" was her husband's reply; "and I am going to kill him."

"But that is wrong," she objected. "There is the law."

He sneered his incredulity of the law's potency in such a region, but he merely iterated, dispassionately, doggedly, "He killed Dutchy and Harkey."

Long she argued it with him, but the argument was one-sided, for he contented himself with repeating again and again, "He killed Dutchy and Harkey." But she could not escape from her childhood training nor from the blood that was in her. The heritage of law was hers, and right conduct, to her, was the fulfilment of the law. She could see no other righteous course to pursue. Hans's taking the law in his own hands was no more justifiable than Dennin's deed. Two wrongs did not make a right, she contended, and there was only one way to punish Dennin, and that was the legal way arranged by society. At last Hans gave in to her.

"All right," he said. "Have it your own way. And to-morrow or next day look to see him kill you and me."

She shook her head and held out her hand for the shot-gun. He started to hand it to her, then hesitated.

"Better let me shoot him," he pleaded.

Again she shook her head, and again he started to pass her the gun, when the door opened, and an Indian, without knocking, came in. A blast of wind and flurry of snow came in with him. They turned and faced him, Hans still holding the shot-gun. The intruder took in the scene without a quiver. His eyes embraced the dead and wounded in a sweeping glance. No surprise showed in his face, not even curiosity. Harkey lay at his feet, but he took no notice of him. So far as he was concerned, Harkey's body did not exist.

"Much wind," the Indian remarked by way of salutation. "All well? Very well?"

Hans, still grasping the gun, felt sure that the Indian attributed to him the mangled corpses. He glanced appealingly at his wife.

"Good morning, Negook," she said, her voice betraying her effort. "No, not very well. Much trouble."

"Good-by, I go now, much hurry," the Indian said, and without semblance of haste, with great deliberation stepping clear of a red pool on the floor, he opened the door and went out.

The man and woman looked at each other.

"He thinks we did it," Hans gasped, "that I did it."

Edith was silent for a space. Then she said, briefly, in a businesslike way:

"Never mind what he thinks. That will come after. At present we have two graves to dig. But first of all, we've got to tie up Dennin so he can't escape."

Hans refused to touch Dennin, but Edith lashed him securely, hand and foot. Then she and Hans went out into the snow. The ground was frozen. It was impervious to a blow of the pick. They first gathered wood, then scraped the snow away and on the frozen surface built a fire. When the fire had burned for an hour, several inches of dirt had thawed. This they shovelled out, and then built a fresh fire. Their descent into the earth progressed at the rate of two or three inches an hour.

It was hard and bitter work. The flurrying snow did not permit the fire to burn any too well, while the wind cut through their clothes and chilled their bodies. They held but little conversation. The wind interfered with speech. Beyond wondering at what could have been Dennin's motive, they remained silent, oppressed by the horror of the tragedy. At one o'clock, looking toward the cabin, Hans announced that he was hungry.

"No, not now, Hans," Edith answered. "I couldn't go back alone into that cabin the way it is, and cook a meal."

At two o'clock Hans volunteered to go with her; but she held him to his work, and four o'clock found the two graves completed. They were shallow, not more than two feet deep, but they would serve the purpose. Night had fallen. Hans got the sled, and the two dead men were dragged through the darkness and storm to their frozen sepulchre. The funeral procession was anything but a pageant. The sled sank deep into the drifted snow and pulled hard. The man and the woman had eaten nothing since the previous day, and were weak from hunger and exhaustion. They had not the strength to resist the wind, and at times its buffets hurled them off their feet. On several occasions the sled was overturned, and they were compelled to reload it with its sombre freight. The last hundred feet to the graves was up a steep slope, and this they took on all fours, like sled-dogs, making legs of their arms and thrusting their hands into the snow. Even so, they were twice dragged backward by the weight of the sled, and slid and fell down the hill, the living and the dead, the haul-ropes and the sled, in ghastly entanglement.

"To-morrow I will put up head-boards with their names," Hans said, when the graves were filled in.

Edith was sobbing. A few broken sentences had been all she was capable of in the way of a funeral service, and now her husband was compelled to half-carry her back to the cabin.

Dennin was conscious. He had rolled over and over on the floor in vain efforts to free himself. He watched Hans and Edith with glittering eyes, but made no attempt to speak. Hans still refused to touch the murderer, and sullenly watched Edith drag him across the floor to the men's bunk-room. But try as she would, she could not lift him from the floor into his bunk.

"Better let me shoot him, and we'll have no more trouble," Hans said in final appeal.

Edith shook her head and bent again to her task. To her surprise the body rose easily, and she knew Hans had relented and was helping her. Then came the cleansing of the kitchen. But the floor still shrieked the tragedy, until Hans planed the surface of the stained wood away and with the shavings made a fire in the stove.

The days came and went. There was much of darkness and silence, broken only by the storms and the thunder on the beach of the freezing surf. Hans was obedient to Edith's slightest order. All his splendid initiative had vanished. She had elected to deal with Dennin in her way, and so he left the whole matter in her hands.

The murderer was a constant menace. At all times there was the chance that he might free himself from his bonds, and they were compelled to guard him day and night. The man or the woman sat always beside him, holding the loaded shot-gun. At first, Edith tried eight-hour watches, but the continuous strain was too great, and afterwards she and Hans relieved each other every four hours. As they had to sleep, and as the watches extended through the night, their whole waking time was expended in guarding Dennin. They had barely time left over for the preparation of meals and the getting of firewood.

Since Negook's inopportune visit, the Indians had avoided the cabin. Edith sent Hans to their cabins to get them to take Dennin down the coast in a canoe to the nearest white settlement or trading post, but the errand was fruitless. Then Edith went herself and interviewed Negook. He was head man of the little village, keenly aware of his responsibility, and he elucidated his policy thoroughly in few words.

"It is white man's trouble," he said, "not Siwash trouble. My people help you, then will it be Siwash trouble too. When white man's trouble and Siwash trouble come together and make a trouble, it is a great trouble, beyond understanding and without end. Trouble no good. My people do no wrong. What for they help you and have trouble?"

So Edith Nelson went back to the terrible cabin with its endless alternating four-hour watches. Sometimes, when it was her turn and she sat by the prisoner, the loaded shot-gun in her lap, her eyes would close and she would doze. Always she aroused with a start, snatching up the gun and swiftly looking at him. These were distinct nervous shocks, and their effect was not good on her. Such was her fear of the man, that even though she were wide awake, if he moved under the bedclothes she could not repress the start and the quick reach for the gun.

She was preparing herself for a nervous break-down, and she knew it. First came a fluttering of the eyeballs, so that she was compelled to close her eyes for relief. A little later the eyelids were afflicted by a nervous twitching that she could not control. To add to the strain, she could not forget the tragedy. She remained as close to the horror as on the first morning when the unexpected stalked into the cabin and took possession. In her daily ministrations upon the prisoner she was forced to grit her teeth and steel herself, body and spirit.

Hans was affected differently. He became obsessed by the idea that it was his duty to kill Dennin; and whenever he waited upon the bound man or watched by him, Edith was troubled by the fear that Hans would add another red entry to the cabin's record. Always he cursed Dennin savagely and handled him roughly. Hans tried to conceal his homicidal mania, and he would say to his wife: "By and by you will want me to kill him, and then I will not kill him. It would make me sick." But more than once, stealing into the room, when it was her watch off, she would catch the two men glaring ferociously at each other, wild animals the pair of them, in Hans's face the lust to kill, in Dennin's the fierceness and savagery of the cornered rat. "Hans!" she would cry, "wake up!" and he would come to a recollection of himself, startled and shamefaced and unrepentant.

So Hans became another factor in the problem the unexpected had given Edith Nelson to solve. At first it had been merely a question of right conduct in dealing with Dennin, and right conduct, as she conceived it, lay in keeping him a prisoner until he could be turned over for trial before a proper tribunal. But now entered Hans, and she saw that his sanity and his salvation were involved. Nor was she long in discovering that her own strength and endurance had become part of the problem. She was breaking down under the strain. Her left arm had developed involuntary jerkings and twitchings. She spilled her food from her spoon, and could place no reliance in her afflicted arm. She judged it to be a form of St. Vitus's dance, and she feared the extent to which its ravages might go. What if she broke down? And the vision she had of the possible future, when the cabin might contain only Dennin and Hans, was an added horror.

After the third day, Dennin had begun to talk. His first question had been, "What are you going to do with me?" And this question he repeated daily and many times a day. And always Edith replied that he would assuredly be dealt with according to law. In turn, she put a daily question to him,—"Why did you do it?" To this he never replied. Also, he received the question with out-bursts of anger, raging and straining at the rawhide that bound him and threatening her with what he would do when he got loose, which he said he was sure to do sooner or later. At such times she cocked both triggers of the gun, prepared to meet him with leaden death if he should burst loose, herself trembling and palpitating and dizzy from the tension and shock.

But in time Dennin grew more tractable. It seemed to her that he was growing weary of his unchanging recumbent position. He began to beg and plead to be released. He made wild promises. He would do them no harm. He would himself go down the coast and give himself up to the officers of the law. He would give them his share of the gold. He would go away into the heart of the wilderness, and never again appear in civilization. He would take his own life if she would only free him. His pleadings usually culminated in involuntary raving, until it seemed to her that he was passing into a fit; but always she shook her head and denied him the freedom for which he worked himself into a passion.

But the weeks went by, and he continued to grow more tractable. And through it all the weariness was asserting itself more and more. "I am so tired, so tired," he would murmur, rolling his head back and forth on the pillow like a peevish child. At a little later period he began to make impassioned pleas for death, to beg her to kill him, to beg Hans to put him our of his misery so that he might at least rest comfortably.

The situation was fast becoming impossible. Edith's nervousness was increasing, and she knew her break-down might come any time. She could not even get her proper rest, for she was haunted by the fear that Hans would yield to his mania and kill Dennin while she slept.

Though January had already come, months would have to elapse before any trading schooner was even likely to put into the bay. Also, they had not expected to winter in the cabin, and the food was running low; nor could Hans add to the supply by hunting. They were chained to the cabin by the necessity of guarding their prisoner.

Something must be done, and she knew it. She forced herself to go back into a reconsideration of the problem. She could not shake off the legacy of her race, the law that was of her blood and that had been trained into her. She knew that whatever she did she must do according to the law, and in the long hours of watching, the shot-gun on her knees, the murderer restless beside her and the storms thundering without, she made original sociological researches and worked out for herself the evolution of the law. It came to her that the law was nothing more than the judgment and the will of any group of people. It mattered not how large was the group of people. There were little groups, she reasoned, like Switzerland, and there were big groups like the United States. Also, she reasoned, it did not matter how small was the group of people. There might be only ten thousand people in a country, yet their collective judgment and will would be the law of that country. Why, then, could not one thousand people constitute such a group? she asked herself. And if one thousand, why not one hundred? Why not fifty? Why not five? Why not—two?

She was frightened at her own conclusion, and she talked it over with Hans. At first he could not comprehend, and then, when he did, he added convincing evidence. He spoke of miners' meetings, where all the men of a locality came together and made the law and executed the law. There might be only ten or fifteen men altogether, he said, but the will of the majority became the law for the whole ten or fifteen, and whoever violated that will was punished.

Edith saw her way clear at last. Dennin must hang. Hans agreed with her. Between them they constituted the majority of this particular group. It was the group-will that Dennin should be hanged. In the execution of this will Edith strove earnestly to observe the customary forms, but the group was so small that Hans and she had to serve as witnesses, as jury, and as judges—also as executioners. She formally charged Michael Dennin with the murder of Dutchy and Harkey, and the prisoner lay in his bunk and listened to the testimony, first of Hans, and then of Edith. He refused to plead guilty or not guilty, and remained silent when she asked him if he had anything to say in his own defence. She and Hans, without leaving their seats, brought in the jury's verdict of guilty. Then, as judge, she imposed the sentence. Her voice shook, her eyelids twitched, her left arm jerked, but she carried it out.

"Michael Dennin, in three days' time you are to be hanged by the neck until you are dead."

Such was the sentence. The man breathed an unconscious sigh of relief, then laughed defiantly, and said, "Thin I'm thinkin' the damn bunk won't be achin' me back anny more, an' that's a consolation."

With the passing of the sentence a feeling of relief seemed to communicate itself to all of them. Especially was it noticeable in Dennin. All sullenness and defiance disappeared, and he talked sociably with his captors, and even with flashes of his old-time wit. Also, he found great satisfaction in Edith's reading to him from the Bible. She read from the New Testament, and he took keen interest in the prodigal son and the thief on the cross.

On the day preceding that set for the execution, when Edith asked her usual question, "Why did you do it?" Dennin answered, "'Tis very simple. I was thinkin'—"

But she hushed him abruptly, asked him to wait, and hurried to Hans's bedside. It was his watch off, and he came out of his sleep, rubbing his eyes and grumbling.

"Go," she told him, "and bring up Negook and one other Indian. Michael's going to confess. Make them come. Take the rifle along and bring them up at the point of it if you have to."

Half an hour later Negook and his uncle, Hadikwan, were ushered into the death chamber. They came unwillingly, Hans with his rifle herding them along.

"Negook," Edith said, "there is to be no trouble for you and your people. Only is it for you to sit and do nothing but listen and understand."

Thus did Michael Dennin, under sentence of death, make public confession of his crime. As he talked, Edith wrote his story down, while the Indians listened, and Hans guarded the door for fear the witnesses might bolt.

He had not been home to the old country for fifteen years, Dennin explained, and it had always been his intention to return with plenty of money and make his old mother comfortable for the rest of her days.

"An' how was I to be doin' it on sixteen hundred?" he demanded. "What I was after wantin' was all the goold, the whole eight thousan'. Thin I cud go back in style. What ud be aisier, thinks I to myself, than to kill all iv yez, report it at Skaguay for an Indian-killin', an' thin pull out for Ireland? An' so I started in to kill all iv yez, but, as Harkey was fond of sayin', I cut out too large a chunk an' fell down on the swallowin' iv it. An' that's me confession. I did me duty to the devil, an' now, God willin', I'll do me duty to God."

"Negook and Hadikwan, you have heard the white man's words," Edith said to the Indians. "His words are here on this paper, and it is for you to make a sign, thus, on the paper, so that white men to come after will know that you have heard."

The two Siwashes put crosses opposite their signatures, received a summons to appear on the morrow with all their tribe for a further witnessing of things, and were allowed to go.

Dennin's hands were released long enough for him to sign the document. Then a silence fell in the room. Hans was restless, and Edith felt uncomfortable. Dennin lay on his back, staring straight up at the moss-chinked roof.

"An' now I'll do me duty to God," he murmured. He turned his head toward Edith. "Read to me," he said, "from the book;" then added, with a glint of playfulness, "Mayhap 'twill help me to forget the bunk."

The day of the execution broke clear and cold. The thermometer was down to twenty-five below zero, and a chill wind was blowing which drove the frost through clothes and flesh to the bones. For the first time in many weeks Dennin stood upon his feet. His muscles had remained inactive so long, and he was so out of practice in maintaining an erect position, that he could scarcely stand.

He reeled back and forth, staggered, and clutched hold of Edith with his bound hands for support.

"Sure, an' it's dizzy I am," he laughed weakly.

A moment later he said, "An' it's glad I am that it's over with. That damn bunk would iv been the death iv me, I know."

When Edith put his fur cap on his head and proceeded to pull the flaps down over his ears, he laughed and said:

"What are you doin' that for?"

"It's freezing cold outside," she answered.

"An' in tin minutes' time what'll matter a frozen ear or so to poor Michael Dennin?" he asked.

She had nerved herself for the last culminating ordeal, and his remark was like a blow to her self-possession. So far, everything had seemed phantom-like, as in a dream, but the brutal truth of what he had said shocked her eyes wide open to the reality of what was taking place. Nor was her distress unnoticed by the Irishman.

"I'm sorry to be troublin' you with me foolish spache," he said regretfully. "I mint nothin' by it. 'Tis a great day for Michael Dennin, an' he's as gay as a lark."

He broke out in a merry whistle, which quickly became lugubrious and ceased.

"I'm wishin' there was a priest," he said wistfully; then added swiftly, "But Michael Dennin's too old a campaigner to miss the luxuries when he hits the trail."

He was so very weak and unused to walking that when the door opened and he passed outside, the wind nearly carried him off his feet. Edith and Hans walked on either side of him and supported him, the while he cracked jokes and tried to keep them cheerful, breaking off, once, long enough to arrange the forwarding of his share of the gold to his mother in Ireland.

They climbed a slight hill and came out into an open space among the trees. Here, circled solemnly about a barrel that stood on end in the snow, were Negook and Hadikwan, and all the Siwashes down to the babies and the dogs, come to see the way of the white man's law. Near by was an open grave which Hans had burned into the frozen earth.

Dennin cast a practical eye over the preparations, noting the grave, the barrel, the thickness of the rope, and the diameter of the limb over which the rope was passed.

"Sure, an' I couldn't iv done better meself, Hans, if it'd been for you."

He laughed loudly at his own sally, but Hans's face was frozen into a sullen ghastliness that nothing less than the trump of doom could have broken. Also, Hans was feeling very sick. He had not realized the enormousness of the task of putting a fellow-man out of the world. Edith, on the other hand, had realized; but the realization did not make the task any easier. She was filled with doubt as to whether she could hold herself together long enough to finish it. She felt incessant impulses to scream, to shriek, to collapse into the snow, to put her hands over her eyes and turn and run blindly away, into the forest, anywhere, away. It was only by a supreme effort of soul that she was able to keep upright and go on and do what she had to do. And in the midst of it all she was grateful to Dennin for the way he helped her.

"Lind me a hand," he said to Hans, with whose assistance he managed to mount the barrel.

He bent over so that Edith could adjust the rope about his neck. Then he stood upright while Hans drew the rope taut across the overhead branch.

"Michael Dennin, have you anything to say?" Edith asked in a clear voice that shook in spite of her.

Dennin shuffled his feet on the barrel, looked down bashfully like a man making his maiden speech, and cleared his throat.

"I'm glad it's over with," he said. "You've treated me like a Christian, an' I'm thankin' you hearty for your kindness."

"Then may God receive you, a repentant sinner," she said.

"Ay," he answered, his deep voice as a response to her thin one, "may God receive me, a repentant sinner."

"Good-by, Michael," she cried, and her voice sounded desperate.

She threw her weight against the barrel, but it did not overturn.

"Hans! Quick! Help me!" she cried faintly.

She could feel her last strength going, and the barrel resisted her. Hans hurried to her, and the barrel went out from under Michael Dennin.

She turned her back, thrusting her fingers into her ears. Then she began to laugh, harshly, sharply, metallically; and Hans was shocked as he had not been shocked through the whole tragedy. Edith Nelson's break-down had come. Even in her hysteria she knew it, and she was glad that she had been able to hold up under the strain until everything had been accomplished. She reeled toward Hans.

"Take me to the cabin, Hans," she managed to articulate.

"And let me rest," she added. "Just let me rest, and rest, and rest."

With Hans's arm around her, supporting her weight and directing her helpless steps, she went off across the snow. But the Indians remained solemnly to watch the working of the white man's law that compelled a man to dance upon the air.

BROWN WOLF

SHE HAD DELAYED, because of the dew-wet grass, in order to put on her overshoes, and when she emerged from the house found her waiting husband absorbed in the wonder of a bursting almond-bud. She sent a questing glance across the tall grass and in and out among the orchard trees.

"Where's Wolf?" she asked.

"He was here a moment ago." Walt Irvine drew himself away with a jerk from the meta physics and poetry of the organic miracle of blossom, and surveyed the landscape. "He was running a rabbit the last I saw of him."

"Wolf! Wolf! Here Wolf!" she called, as they left the clearing and took the trail that led down through the waxen-belled manzanita jungle to the county road.

Irvine thrust between his lips the little finger of each hand and lent to her efforts a shrill whistling.

She covered her ears hastily and made a wry grimace.

"My! for a poet, delicately attuned and all the rest of it, you can make unlovely noises. My ear-drums are pierced. You outwhistle—"

"Orpheus."

"I was about to say a street-arab," she concluded severely.

"Poesy does not prevent one from being practical—at least it doesn't prevent *me*. Mine is no futility of genius that can't sell gems to the magazines."

He assumed a mock extravagance, and went on:

"I am no attic singer, no ballroom warbler. And why? Because I am practical. Mine is no squalor of song that cannot transmute itself, with proper exchange value, into a flower-crowned cottage, a sweet mountain-meadow, a grove of redwoods, an orchard of thirty-seven trees, one long row of blackberries and two short rows of strawberries, to say nothing of a quarter of a mile of gurgling brook. I am a beauty-merchant, a trader in song, and I pursue utility, dear Madge. I sing a song, and thanks to the magazine editors I transmute my song into a waft of the west wind sighing through our redwoods, into a murmur of waters over mossy stones that sings back to me another song than the one I sang and yet the same song wonderfully—er—transmuted."

"O that all your song-transmutations were as successful!" she laughed.

"Name one that wasn't."

"Those two beautiful sonnets that you transmuted into the cow that was accounted the worst milker in the township."

"She was beautiful—" he began,

"But she didn't give milk," Madge interrupted.

"But she *was* beautiful, now, wasn't she?" he insisted.

"And here's where beauty and utility fall out," was her reply. "And there's the Wolf!"

From the thicket-covered hillside came a crashing of underbrush, and then, forty feet above them, on the edge of the sheer wall of rock, appeared a wolf's head and shoulders. His braced fore paws dislodged a pebble, and with sharp-pricked ears and peering eyes he watched the fall of the pebble till it struck at their feet. Then he transferred his gaze and with open mouth laughed down at them.

"You Wolf, you!" and "You blessed Wolf!" the man and woman called out to him.

The ears flattened back and down at the sound, and the head seemed to snuggle under the caress of an invisible hand.

They watched him scramble backward into the thicket, then proceeded on their way. Several minutes later, rounding a turn in the trail where the descent was less precipitous, he joined them in the midst of a miniature avalanche of pebbles and loose soil. He was not demonstrative. A pat and a rub around the ears from the man, and a more prolonged caressing from the woman, and he was away down the trail in front of them, gliding effortlessly over the ground in true wolf fashion.

In build and coat and brush he was a huge timber-wolf; but the lie was given to his wolf-hood by his color and marking. There the dog unmistakably advertised itself. No wolf was ever colored like him. He was brown, deep brown, red-brown, an orgy of browns. Back and shoulders were a warm brown that paled on the sides and underneath to a yellow that was dingy because of the brown that lingered in it. The white of the throat and paws and the spots over the eyes was dirty because of the persistent and ineradicable brown, while the eyes themselves were twin topazes, golden and brown.

The man and woman loved the dog very much; perhaps this was because it had been such a task to win his love. It had been no easy matter when he first drifted in mysteriously out of nowhere to their little mountain cottage. Footsore and famished, he had killed a rabbit under their very noses and under their very windows, and then crawled away and slept by the spring at the foot of the blackberry bushes. When Walt Irvine went down to inspect the intruder, he was snarled at for his pains, and Madge likewise was snarled at when she went down to present, as a peace-offering, a large pan of bread and milk.

A most unsociable dog he proved to be, resenting all their advances, refusing to let them lay hands on him, menacing them with bared fangs and bristling hair. Nevertheless he remained, sleeping and resting by the spring, and eating the food they gave him after they set it down at a safe distance and retreated. His wretched physical condition explained why he lingered; and when he had recuperated, after several days' sojourn, he disappeared.

And this would have been the end of him, so far as Irvine and his wife were concerned, had not Irvine at that particular time been called away into the northern part of the state. Riding along on the train, near to the line between California and Oregon, he chanced to look out of the window and saw his unsociable guest sliding along the wagon road, brown and wolfish, tired yet tireless, dust-covered and soiled with two hundred miles of travel.

Now Irvine was a man of impulse, a poet. He got off the train at the next station, bought a piece of meat at a butcher shop, and captured the vagrant on the outskirts of the town. The return trip was made in the baggage car, and so Wolf came a second time to the mountain cottage. Here he was tied up for a week and made love to by the man and woman. But it was very circumspect love-making. Remote and alien as a traveller from another planet, he snarled down their soft-spoken love-words. He never barked. In all the time they had him he was never known to bark.

To win him became a problem. Irvine liked problems. He had a metal plate made, on which was stamped: Return to Walt Irvine, Glen Ellen, Sonoma County, California. This was riveted to a collar and strapped about the dog's neck. Then he was turned loose, and promptly he disappeared. A day later came a telegram from Mendocino County. In twenty hours he had made over a hundred miles to the north, and was still going when captured.

He came back by Wells Fargo Express, was tied up three days, and was loosed on the fourth and lost. This time he gained southern Oregon before he was caught and returned. Always, as soon as he received his liberty, he fled away, and always he fled north. He was possessed of an obsession that drove him north. The homing instinct, Irvine called it, after he had expended the selling price of a sonnet in getting the animal back from northern Oregon.

Another time the brown wanderer succeeded in traversing half the length of California, all of Oregon, and most of Washington, before he was picked up and returned "Collect." A remarkable thing was the speed with which he travelled. Fed up and rested, as soon as he was loosed he devoted all his energy to getting over the ground. On the first day's run he was known to cover as high as a hundred and fifty miles, and after that he would average a hundred miles a day until caught. He always arrived back lean and hungry and savage, and always departed fresh and vigorous, cleaving his way northward in response to some prompting of his being that no one could understand.

But at last, after a futile year of flight, he accepted the inevitable and elected to remain at the cottage where first he had killed the rabbit and slept by the spring. Even after that, a long time elapsed before the man and woman succeeded in patting him. It was a great victory, for they alone were allowed to put hands on him. He was fastidiously exclusive, and no guest at the cottage ever succeeded in making up to him. A low growl greeted such approach; if any one had the hardihood to come nearer, the lips lifted, the naked fangs appeared, and the growl became a snarl—a snarl so terrible and malignant that it awed the stoutest of them, as it likewise awed the farmers' dogs that knew ordinary dog-snarling, but had never seen wolf-snarling before.

He was without antecedents. His history began with Walt and Madge. He had come up from the south, but never a clew did they get of the owner from whom he had evidently fled. Mrs. Johnson, their nearest neighbor and the one who supplied them with milk, proclaimed him a Klondike dog. Her brother was burrowing for frozen pay-streaks in that far country, and so she constituted herself an authority on the subject.

But they did not dispute her. There were the tips of Wolf's ears, obviously so severely frozen at some time that they would never quite heal again. Besides, he looked like the photographs of the Alaskan dogs they saw published in magazines and newspapers. They often speculated over his past, and tried to conjure up (from what they had read and heard) what his northland life had been. That the northland still drew him, they knew; for at night they sometimes heard him crying softly; and when the north wind blew and the bite of frost was in the air, a great restlessness would come upon him and he would lift a mournful lament which they knew to be the long wolf-howl. Yet he never barked. No provocation was great enough to draw from him that canine cry.

Long discussion they had, during the time of winning him, as to whose dog he was. Each claimed him, and each proclaimed loudly any expression of affection made by him. But the man had the better of it at first, chiefly because he was a man. It was patent that Wolf had had no experience with women. He did not understand women. Madge's skirts were something he never quite accepted. The swish of them was enough to set him a-bristle with suspicion, and on a windy day she could not approach him at all.

On the other hand, it was Madge who fed him; also it was she who ruled the kitchen, and it was by her favor, and her favor alone, that he was permitted to come within that sacred precinct. It was because of these things that she bade fair to overcome the handicap of her garments. Then it was that Walt put forth special effort, making it a practice to have Wolf lie at his feet while he wrote, and, between petting and talking, losing much time from his work. Walt won in the end, and his victory was most probably due to the fact that he was a man, though Madge averred that they would have had another quarter of a mile of gurgling brook, and at least two west winds sighing through their redwoods, had Wait properly devoted his energies to song-transmutation and left Wolf alone to exercise a natural taste and an unbiassed judgment.

"It's about time I heard from those triolets," Walt said, after a silence of five minutes, during which they had swung steadily down the trail. "There'll be a check at the post-office, I know, and we'll transmute it into beautiful buckwheat flour, a gallon of maple syrup, and a new pair of overshoes for you."

"And into beautiful milk from Mrs. Johnson's beautiful cow," Madge added. "To-morrow's the first of the month, you know."

Walt scowled unconsciously; then his face brightened, and he clapped his hand to his breast pocket.

"Never mind. I have here a nice beautiful new cow, the best milker in California."

"When did you write it?" she demanded eagerly. Then, reproachfully, "And you never showed it to me."

"I saved it to read to you on the way to the post-office, in a spot remarkably like this one," he answered, indicating, with a wave of his hand, a dry log on which to sit.

A tiny stream flowed out of a dense fern-brake, slipped down a mossy-lipped stone, and ran across the path at their feet. From the valley arose the mellow song of meadow-larks, while about them, in and out, through sunshine and shadow, fluttered great yellow butterflies.

Up from below came another sound that broke in upon Walt reading softly from his manuscript. It was a crunching of heavy feet, punctuated now and again by the clattering of a displaced stone. As Walt finished and looked to his wife for approval, a man came into view around the turn of the trail. He was bare-headed and sweaty. With a handkerchief in one hand he mopped his face, while in the other hand he carried a new hat and a wilted starched collar which he had removed from his neck. He was a well-built man, and his muscles seemed on the point of bursting out of the painfully new and ready-made black clothes he wore.

"Warm day," Walt greeted him. Walt believed in country democracy, and never missed an opportunity to practise it.

The man paused and nodded.

"I guess I ain't used much to the warm," he vouchsafed half apologetically. "I'm more accustomed to zero weather."

"You don't find any of that in this country," Walt laughed.

"Should say not," the man answered. "An' I ain't here a-lookin' for it neither. I'm tryin' to find my sister. Mebbe you know where she lives. Her name's Johnson, Mrs. William Johnson."

"You're not her Klondike brother!" Madge cried, her eyes bright with interest, "about whom we've heard so much?"

"Yes'm, that's me," he answered modestly. "My name's Miller, Skiff Miller. I just thought I'd s'prise her."

"You are on the right track then. Only you've come by the foot-path." Madge stood up to direct him, pointing up the canyon a quarter of a mile. "You see that blasted redwood? Take the little trail turning off to the right. It's the short cut to her house. You can't miss it."

"Yes'm, thank you, ma'am," he said. He made tentative efforts to go, but seemed awkwardly rooted to the spot. He was gazing at her with an open admiration of which he was quite unconscious, and which was drowning, along with him, in the rising sea of embarrassment in which he floundered.

"We'd like to hear you tell about the Klondike," Madge said. "Mayn't we come over some day while you are at your sister's? Or, better yet, won't you come over and have dinner with us?"

"Yes'm, thank you, ma'am," he mumbled mechanically. Then he caught himself up and added: "I ain't stoppin' long. I got to be pullin' north again. I go out on to-night's train. You see, I've got a mail contract with the government."

When Madge had said that it was too bad, he made another futile effort to go. But he could not take his eyes from her face. He forgot his embarrassment in his admiration, and it was her turn to flush and feel uncomfortable.

It was at this juncture, when Walt had just decided it was time for him to be saying something to relieve the strain, that Wolf, who had been away nosing through the brush, trotted wolf-like into view.

Skiff Miller's abstraction disappeared. The pretty woman before him passed out of his field of vision. He had eyes only for the dog, and a great wonder came into his face.

"Well, I'll be damned!" he enunciated slowly and solemnly.

He sat down ponderingly on the log, leaving Madge standing. At the sound of his voice, Wolf's ears had flattened down, then his mouth had opened in a laugh. He trotted slowly up to the stranger and first smelled his hands, then licked them with his tongue.

Skiff Miller patted the dog's head, and slowly and solemnly repeated, "Well, I'll be damned!"

"Excuse me, ma'am," he said the next moment "I was just s'prised some, that was all."

"We're surprised, too," she answered lightly. "We never saw Wolf make up to a stranger before."

"Is that what you call him—Wolf?" the man asked.

Madge nodded. "But I can't understand his friendliness toward you—unless it's because you're from the Klondike. He's a Klondike dog, you know."

"Yes'm," Miller said absently. He lifted one of Wolf's fore legs and examined the foot-pads, pressing them and denting them with his thumb. "Kind of soft," he remarked. "He ain't been on trail for a long time."

"I say," Walt broke in, "it is remarkable the way he lets you handle him."

Skiff Miller arose, no longer awkward with admiration of Madge, and in a sharp, businesslike manner asked, "How long have you had him?"

But just then the dog, squirming and rubbing against the newcomer's legs, opened his mouth and barked. It was an explosive bark, brief and joyous, but a bark.

"That's a new one on me," Skiff Miller remarked.

Walt and Madge stared at each other. The miracle had happened. Wolf had barked.

"It's the first time he ever barked," Madge said.

"First time I ever heard him, too," Miller volunteered.

Madge smiled at him. The man was evidently a humorist.

"Of course," she said, "since you have only seen him for five minutes."

Skiff Miller looked at her sharply, seeking in her face the guile her words had led him to suspect.

"I thought you understood," he said slowly. "I thought you'd tumbled to it from his makin' up to me. He's my dog. His name ain't Wolf. It's Brown."

"Oh, Walt!" was Madge's instinctive cry to her husband.

Walt was on the defensive at once.

"How do you know he's your dog?" he demanded.

"Because he is," was the reply.

"Mere assertion," Walt said sharply.

In his slow and pondering way, Skiff Miller looked at him, then asked, with a nod of his head toward Madge:

"How d'you know she's your wife? You just say, 'Because she is,' and I'll say it's mere assertion. The dog's mine. I bred 'm an' raised 'm, an' I guess I ought to know. Look here. I'll prove it to you."

Skiff Miller turned to the dog. "Brown!" His voice rang out sharply, and at the sound the dog's ears flattened down as to a caress. "Gee!" The dog made a swinging turn to the right. "Now mush-on!" And the dog ceased his swing abruptly and started straight ahead, halting obediently at command.

"I can do it with whistles," Skiff Miller said proudly. "He was my lead dog."

"But you are not going to take him away with you?" Madge asked tremulously.

The man nodded.

"Back into that awful Klondike world of suffering?"

He nodded and added: "Oh, it ain't so bad as all that. Look at me. Pretty healthy specimen, ain't I?"

"But the dogs! The terrible hardship, the heart-breaking toil, the starvation, the frost! Oh, I've read about it and I know."

"I nearly ate him once, over on Little Fish River," Miller volunteered grimly. "If I hadn't got a moose that day was all that saved 'm."

"I'd have died first!" Madge cried.

"Things is different down here," Miller explained. "You don't have to eat dogs. You think different just about the time you're all in. You've never ben all in, so you don't know anything about it."

"That's the very point," she argued warmly. "Dogs are not eaten in California. Why not leave him here? He is happy. He'll never want for food—you know that. He'll never suffer from cold and hardship. Here all is softness and gentleness. Neither the human nor nature is savage. He will never know a whip-lash again. And as for the weather—why, it never snows here."

"But it's all-fired hot in summer, beggin' your pardon," Skiff Miller laughed.

"But you do not answer," Madge continued passionately. "What have you to offer him in that northland life?"

"Grub, when I've got it, and that's most of the time," came the answer.

"And the rest of the time?"

"No grub."

"And the work?"

"Yes, plenty of work," Miller blurted out impatiently. "Work without end, an' famine, an' frost, an all the rest of the miseries—that's what he'll get when he comes with me. But he likes it. He is used to it. He knows that life. He was born to it an' brought up to it. An' you don't know anything about it. You don't know what you're talking about. That's where the dog belongs, and that's where he'll be happiest."

"The dog doesn't go," Walt announced in a determined voice. "So there is no need of further discussion."

"What's that?" Skiff Miller demanded, his brows lowering and an obstinate flush of blood reddening his forehead.

"I said the dog doesn't go, and that settles it. I don't believe he's your dog. You may have seen him sometime. You may even sometime have driven him for his owner. But his obeying the ordinary driving commands of the Alaskan trail is no demonstration that he is yours. Any dog in Alaska would obey you as he obeyed. Besides, he is undoubtedly a valuable dog, as dogs go in Alaska, and that is sufficient explanation of your desire to get possession of him. Anyway, you've got to prove property."

Skiff Miller, cool and collected, the obstinate flush a trifle deeper on his forehead, his huge muscles bulging under the black cloth of his coat, carefully looked the poet up and down as though measuring the strength of his slenderness.

The Klondiker's face took on a contemptuous expression as he said finally, "I reckon there's nothin' in sight to prevent me takin' the dog right here an' now."

Walt's face reddened, and the striking-muscles of his arms and shoulders seemed to stiffen and grow tense. His wife fluttered apprehensively into the breach.

"Maybe Mr. Miller is right," she said. "I am afraid that he is. Wolf does seem to know him, and certainly he answers to the name of 'Brown.' He made friends with him instantly, and you know that's something he never did with anybody before. Besides, look at the way he barked. He was just bursting with joy. Joy over what? Without doubt at finding Mr. Miller."

Walt's striking-muscles relaxed, and his shoulders seemed to droop with hopelessness.

"I guess you're right, Madge," he said. "Wolf isn't Wolf, but Brown, and he must belong to Mr. Miller."

"Perhaps Mr. Miller will sell him," she suggested. "We can buy him."

Skiff Miller shook his head, no longer belligerent, but kindly, quick to be generous in response to generousness.

"I had five dogs," he said, casting about for the easiest way to temper his refusal. "He was the leader. They was the crack team of Alaska. Nothin' could touch 'em. In 1898 I refused five thousand dollars for the bunch. Dogs was high, then, anyway; but that wasn't what made the fancy price. It was the team itself. Brown was the best in the team. That winter I refused twelve hundred for 'm. I didn't sell 'm then, an' I ain't a-sellin' 'm now. Besides, I think a mighty lot of that dog. I've ben lookin' for 'm for three years. It made me fair sick when I found he'd ben stole—not the value of him, but the—well, I liked 'm like hell, that's all, beggin' your pardon. I couldn't believe my eyes when I seen 'm just now. I thought I was dreamin'. It was too good to be true. Why, I was his wet-nurse. I put 'm to bed, snug every night. His mother died, and I brought 'm up on condensed milk at two dollars a can when I couldn't afford it in my own coffee. He never knew any mother but me. He used to suck my finger regular, the darn little cuss—that finger right there!"

And Skiff Miller, too overwrought for speech, held up a fore finger for them to see.

"That very finger," he managed to articulate, as though it somehow clinched the proof of ownership and the bond of affection.

He was still gazing at his extended finger when Madge began to speak.

"But the dog," she said. "You haven't considered the dog."

Skiff Miller looked puzzled.

"Have you thought about him?" she asked.

"Don't know what you're drivin' at," was the response.

"Maybe the dog has some choice in the matter," Madge went on. "Maybe he has his likes and desires. You have not considered him. You give him no choice. It has never entered your mind that possibly he might prefer California to Alaska. You consider only what you like. You do with him as you would with a sack of potatoes or a bale of hay."

This was a new way of looking at it, and Miller was visibly impressed as he debated it in his mind. Madge took advantage of his indecision.

"If you really love him, what would be happiness to him would be your happiness also," she urged.

Skiff Miller continued to debate with himself, and Madge stole a glance of exultation to her husband, who looked back warm approval.

"What do you think?" the Klondiker suddenly demanded.

It was her turn to be puzzled. "What do you mean?" she asked.

"D'ye think he'd sooner stay in California?"

She nodded her head with positiveness. "I am sure of it."

Skiff Miller again debated with himself, though this time aloud, at the same time running his gaze in a judicial way over the mooted animal.

"He was a good worker. He's done a heap of work for me. He never loafed on me, an' he was a joe-dandy at hammerin' a raw team into shape. He's got a head on him. He can do everything but talk. He knows what you say to him. Look at 'm now. He knows we're talkin' about him."

The dog was lying at Skiff Miller's feet, head close down on paws, ears erect and listening, and eyes that were quick and eager to follow the sound of speech as it fell from the lips of first one and then the other.

"An' there's a lot of work in 'm yet. He's good for years to come. An' I do like him. I like him like hell."

Once or twice after that Skiff Miller opened his mouth and closed it again without speaking. Finally he said:

"I'll tell you what I'll do. Your remarks, ma'am, has some weight in them. The dog's worked hard, and maybe he's earned a soft berth an' has got a right to choose. Anyway, we'll leave it up to him. Whatever he says, goes. You people stay right here settin' down. I'll say good-by and walk off casual-like. If he wants to stay, he can stay. If he wants to come with me, let 'm come. I won't call 'm to come an' don't you call 'm to come back."

He looked with sudden suspicion at Madge, and added, "Only you must play fair. No persuadin' after my back is turned."

"We'll play fair," Madge began, but Skiff Miller broke in on her assurances.

"I know the ways of women," he announced. "Their hearts is soft. When their hearts is touched they're likely to stack the cards, look at the bottom of the deck, an' lie like the devil —beggin' your pardon, ma'am. I'm only discoursin' about women in general."

"I don't know how to thank you," Madge quavered.

"I don't see as you've got any call to thank me," he replied. "Brown ain't decided yet. Now you won't mind if I go away slow? It's no more'n fair, seein' I'll be out of sight inside a hundred yards."—Madge agreed, and added, "And I promise you faithfully that we won't do anything to influence him."

"Well, then, I might as well be gettin' along," Skiff Miller said in the ordinary tones of one departing.

At this change in his voice, Wolf lifted his head quickly, and still more quickly got to his feet when the man and woman shook hands. He sprang up on his hind legs, resting his fore paws on her hip and at the same time licking Skiff Miller's hand. When the latter shook hands with Walt, Wolf repeated his act, resting his weight on Walt and licking both men's hands.

"It ain't no picnic, I can tell you that," were the Klondiker's last words, as he turned and went slowly up the trail.

For the distance of twenty feet Wolf watched him go, himself all eagerness and expectancy, as though waiting for the man to turn and retrace his steps. Then, with a quick low whine, Wolf sprang after him, overtook him, caught his hand between his teeth with reluctant tenderness, and strove gently to make him pause.

Failing in this, Wolf raced back to where Walt Irvine sat, catching his coat-sleeve in his teeth and trying vainly to drag him after the retreating man.

Wolf's perturbation began to wax. He desired ubiquity. He wanted to be in two places at the same time, with the old master and the new, and steadily the distance between them was increasing. He sprang about excitedly, making short nervous leaps and twists, now toward one, now toward the other, in painful indecision, not knowing his own mind, desiring both and unable to choose, uttering quick sharp whines and beginning to pant.

He sat down abruptly on his haunches, thrusting his nose upward, the mouth opening and closing with jerking movements, each time opening wider. These jerking movements were in unison with the recurrent spasms that attacked the throat, each spasm severer and more intense than the preceding one. And in accord with jerks and spasms the larynx began to vibrate, at first silently, accompanied by the rush of air expelled from the lungs, then sounding a low, deep note, the lowest in the register of the human ear. All this was the nervous and muscular preliminary to howling.

But just as the howl was on the verge of bursting from the full throat, the wide-opened mouth was closed, the paroxysms ceased, and he looked long and steadily at the retreating man. Suddenly Wolf turned his head, and over his shoulder just as steadily regarded Walt. The appeal was unanswered. Not a word nor a sign did the dog receive, no suggestion and no clew as to what his conduct should be.

A glance ahead to where the old master was nearing the curve of the trail excited him again. He sprang to his feet with a whine, and then, struck by a new idea, turned his attention to Madge. Hitherto he had ignored her, but now, both masters failing him, she alone was left. He went over to her and snuggled his head in her lap, nudging her arm with his nose—an old trick of his when begging for favors. He backed away from her and began writhing and twisting playfully, curvetting and prancing, half rearing and striking his fore paws to the earth, struggling with all his body, from the wheedling eyes and flattening ears to the wagging tail, to express the thought that was in him and that was denied him utterance.

This, too, he soon abandoned. He was depressed by the coldness of these humans who had never been cold before. No response could he draw from them, no help could he get. They did not consider him. They were as dead.

He turned and silently gazed after the old master. Skiff Miller was rounding the curve. In a moment he would be gone from view. Yet he never turned his head, plodding straight onward, slowly and methodically, as though possessed of no interest in what was occurring behind his back.

And in this fashion he went out of view. Wolf waited for him to reappear. He waited a long minute, silently, quietly, without movement, as though turned to stone—withal stone quick with eagerness and desire. He barked once, and waited. Then he turned and trotted back to Walt Irvine. He sniffed his hand and dropped down heavily at his feet, watching the trail where it curved emptily from view.

The tiny stream slipping down the mossy-lipped stone seemed suddenly to increase the volume of its gurgling noise. Save for the meadow-larks, there was no other sound. The great yellow butterflies drifted silently through the sunshine and lost themselves in the drowsy shadows. Madge gazed triumphantly at her husband.

A few minutes later Wolf got upon his feet. Decision and deliberation marked his movements. He did not glance at the man and woman. His eyes were fixed up the trail. He had made up his mind. They knew it. And they knew, so far as they were concerned, that the ordeal had just begun.

He broke into a trot, and Madge's lips pursed, forming an avenue for the caressing sound that it was the will of her to send forth. But the caressing sound was not made. She was impelled to look at her husband, and she saw the sternness with which he watched her. The pursed lips relaxed, and she sighed inaudibly.

Wolf's trot broke into a run. Wider and wider were the leaps he made. Not once did he turn his head, his wolf's brush standing out straight behind him. He cut sharply across the curve of the trail and was gone.

THE SUN-DOG TRAIL

Sitka Charley smoked his pipe and gazed thoughtfully at the *Police Gazette* illustration on the wall. For half an hour he had been steadily regarding it, and for half an hour I had been slyly watching him. Something was going on in that mind of his, and, whatever it was, I knew it was well worth knowing. He had lived life, and seen things, and performed that prodigy of prodigies, namely, the turning of his back upon his own people, and, in so far as it was possible for an Indian, becoming a white man even in his mental processes. As he phrased it himself, he had come into the warm, sat among us, by our fires, and become one of us. He had never learned to read nor write, but his vocabulary was remarkable, and more remarkable still was the completeness with which he had assumed the white man's point of view, the white man's attitude toward things.

We had struck this deserted cabin after a hard day on trail. The dogs had been fed, the supper dishes washed, the beds made, and we were now enjoying that most delicious hour that comes each day, and but once each day, on the Alaskan trail, the hour when nothing intervenes between the tired body and bed save the smoking of the evening pipe. Some former denizen of the cabin had decorated its walls with illustrations torn from magazines and newspapers, and it was these illustrations that had held Sitka Charley's attention from the moment of our arrival two hours before. He had studied them intently, ranging from one to another and back again, and I could see that there was uncertainty in his mind, and bepuzzlement.

"Well?" I finally broke the silence.

He took the pipe from his mouth and said simply, "I do not understand."

He smoked on again, and again removed the pipe, using it to point at the *Police Gazette* illustration.

"That picture—what does it mean? I do not understand."

I looked at the picture. A man, with a preposterously wicked face, his right hand pressed dramatically to his heart, was falling backward to the floor. Confronting him, with a face that was a composite of destroying angel and Adonis, was a man holding a smoking revolver.

304

"One man is killing the other man," I said, aware of a distinct bepuzzlement of my own and of failure to explain.

"Why?" asked Sitka Charley.

"I do not know," I confessed.

"That picture is all end," he said. "It has no beginning."

"It is life," I said.

"Life has beginning," he objected.

I was silenced for the moment, while his eyes wandered on to an adjoining decoration, a photographic reproduction of somebody's "Leda and the Swan."

"That picture," he said, "has no beginning. It has no end. I do not understand pictures."

"Look at that picture," I commanded, pointing to a third decoration. "It means something. Tell me what it means to you."

He studied it for several minutes.

"The little girl is sick," he said finally. "That is the doctor looking at her. They have been up all night—see, the oil is low in the lamp, the first morning light is coming in at the window. It is a great sickness; maybe she will die, that is why the doctor looks so hard. That is the mother. It is a great sickness, because the mother's head is on the table and she is crying."

"How do you know she is crying?" I interrupted. "You cannot see her face. Perhaps she is asleep."

Sitka Charley looked at me in swift surprise, then back at the picture. It was evident that he had not reasoned the impression.

"Perhaps she is asleep," he repeated. He studied it closely. "No, she is not asleep. The shoulders show that she is not asleep. I have seen the shoulders of a woman who cried. The mother is crying. It is a very great sickness."

"And now you understand the picture," I cried.

He shook his head, and asked, "The little girl—does it die?"

It was my turn for silence.

"Does it die?" he reiterated. "You are a painter-man. Maybe you know."

"No, I do not know," I confessed.

"It is not life," he delivered himself dogmatically. "In life little girl die or get well. Something happen in life. In picture nothing happen. No, I do not understand pictures."

His disappointment was patent. It was his desire to understand all things that white men understand, and here, in this matter, he failed. I felt, also, that there was challenge in his attitude. He was bent upon compelling me to show him the wisdom of pictures. Besides, he had remarkable powers of visualization. I had long since learned this. He visualized everything. He saw life in pictures, felt life in pictures, generalized life in pictures; and yet he did not understand pictures when seen through other men's eyes and expressed by those men with color and line upon canvas.

"Pictures are bits of life," I said. "We paint life as we see it. For instance, Charley, you are coming along the trail. It is night. You see a cabin. The window is lighted. You look through the window for one second, or for two seconds, you see something, and you go on your way. You saw maybe a man writing a letter. You saw something without beginning or end. Nothing happened. Yet it was a bit of life you saw. You remember it afterward. It is like a picture in your memory. The window is the frame of the picture."

I could see that he was interested, and I knew that as I spoke he had looked through the window and seen the man writing the letter.

"There is a picture you have painted that I understand," he said. "It is a true picture. It has much meaning. It is in your cabin at Dawson. It is a faro table. There are men playing. It is a large game. The limit is off."

"How do you know the limit is off?" I broke in excitedly, for here was where my work could be tried out on an unbiassed judge who knew life only, and not art, and who was a sheer master of reality. Also, I was very proud of that particular piece of work. I had named it "The Last Turn," and I believed it to be one of the best things I had ever done.

"There are no chips on the table," Sitka Charley explained. "The men are playing with markers. That means the roof is the limit. One man play yellow markers—maybe one yellow marker worth one thousand dollars, maybe two thousand dollars. One man play red markers. Maybe they are worth five hundred dollars, maybe one thousand dollars. It is a very big game. Everybody play very high, up to the roof. How do I know? You make the dealer with blood little bit warm in face." (I was delighted.) "The lookout, you make him lean forward in his chair. Why he lean forward? Why his face very much quiet? Why his eyes very much bright? Why dealer warm with blood a little bit in the face? Why all men very quiet?—the man with yellow markers? the man with white markers? the man with red markers? Why nobody talk? Because very much money. Because last turn."

"How do you know it is the last turn?" I asked.

"The king is coppered, the seven is played open," he answered. "Nobody bet on other cards. Other cards all gone. Everybody one mind. Everybody play king to lose, seven to win. Maybe bank lose twenty thousand dollars, maybe bank win. Yes, that picture I understand."

"Yet you do not know the end!" I cried triumphantly. "It is the last turn, but the cards are not yet turned. In the picture they will never be turned. Nobody will ever know who wins nor who loses."

"And the men will sit there and never talk," he said, wonder and awe growing in his face. "And the lookout will lean forward, and the blood will be warm in the face of the dealer. It is a strange thing. Always will they sit there, always; and the cards will never be turned."

"It is a picture," I said. "It is life. You have seen things like it yourself."

He looked at me and pondered, then said, very slowly: "No, as you say, there is no end to it. Nobody will ever know the end. Yet is it a true thing. I have seen it. It is life."

For a long time he smoked on in silence, weighing the pictorial wisdom of the white man and verifying it by the facts of life. He nodded his head several times, and grunted once or twice. Then he knocked the ashes from his pipe, carefully refilled it, and after a thoughtful pause, lighted it again.

"Then have I, too, seen many pictures of life," he began; "pictures not painted, but seen with the eyes. I have looked at them like through the window at the man writing the letter. I have seen many pieces of life, without beginning, without end, without understanding."

With a sudden change of position he turned his eyes full upon me and regarded me thoughtfully.

"Look you," he said; "you are a painter-man. How would you paint this which I saw, a picture without beginning, the ending of which I do not understand, a piece of life with the northern lights for a candle and Alaska for a frame."

"It is a large canvas," I murmured.

But he ignored me, for the picture he had in mind was before his eyes and he was seeing it.

"There are many names for this picture," he said. "But in the picture there are many sun-dogs, and it comes into my mind to call it 'The Sun-Dog Trail.' It was a long time ago, seven years ago, the fall of '97, when I saw the woman first time. At Lake Linderman I had one canoe, very good Peterborough canoe. I came over Chilcoot Pass with two thousand letters for Dawson. I was letter carrier. Everybody rush to Klondike at that time. Many people on trail. Many people chop down trees and make boats. Last water, snow in the air, snow on the ground, ice on the lake, on the river ice in the eddies. Every day more snow, more ice. Maybe one day, maybe three days, maybe six days, any day maybe freeze-up come, then no more water, all ice, everybody walk, Dawson six hundred miles, long time walk. Boat go very quick. Everybody want to go boat. Everybody say, 'Charley, two hundred dollars you take me in canoe,' 'Charley, three hundred dollars,' 'Charley, four hundred dollars.' I say no, all the time I say no. I am letter carrier.

"In morning I get to Lake Linderman. I walk all night and am much tired. I cook breakfast, I eat, then I sleep on the beach three hours. I wake up. It is ten o'clock. Snow is falling. There is wind, much wind that blows fair. Also, there is a woman who sits in the snow alongside. She is white woman, she is young, very pretty, maybe she is twenty years old, maybe twenty-five years old. She look at me. I look at her. She is very tired. She is no dance-woman. I see that right away. She is good woman, and she is very tired.

"'You are Sitka Charley,' she says. I get up quick and roll blankets so snow does not get inside. 'I go to Dawson,' she says. 'I go in your canoe—how much?'

"I do not want anybody in my canoe. I do not like to say no. So I say, 'One thousand dollars.' Just for fun I say it, so woman cannot come with me, much better than say no. She look at me very hard, then she says, 'When you start?' I say right away. Then she says all right, she will give me one thousand dollars.

"What can I say? I do not want the woman, yet have I given my word that for one thousand dollars she can come. I am surprised. Maybe she make fun, too, so I say, 'Let me see thousand dollars.' And that woman, that young woman, all alone on the trail, there in the snow, she take out one thousand dollars, in greenbacks, and she put them in my hand. I look at money, I look at her. What can I say? I say, 'No, my canoe very small. There is no room for outfit.' She laugh. She says, 'I am great traveller. This is my outfit.' She kick one small pack in the snow. It is two fur robes, canvas outside, some woman's clothes inside. I pick it up. Maybe thirty-five pounds. I am surprised. She take it away from me. She says, 'Come, let us start.' She carries pack into canoe. What can I say? I put my blankets into canoe. We start.

"And that is the way I saw the woman first time. The wind was fair. I put up small sail. The canoe went very fast, it flew like a bird over the high waves. The woman was much afraid. 'What for you come Klondike much afraid?' I ask. She laugh at me, a hard laugh, but she is still much afraid. Also is she very tired. I run canoe through rapids to Lake Bennett. Water very bad, and woman cry out because she is afraid. We go down Lake Bennett, snow, ice, wind like a gale, but woman is very tired and go to sleep.

"That night we make camp at Windy Arm. Woman sit by fire and eat supper. I look at her. She is pretty. She fix hair. There is much hair, and it is brown, also sometimes it is like gold in the firelight, when she turn her head, so, and flashes come from it like golden fire. The eyes are large and brown, sometimes warm like a candle behind a curtain, sometimes very hard and bright like broken ice when sun shines upon it. When she smile—how can I say?—when she smile I know white man like to kiss her, just like that, when she smile. She never do hard work. Her hands are soft, like baby's hand. She is soft all over, like baby. She is not thin, but round like baby; her arm, her leg, her muscles, all soft and round like baby. Her waist is small, and when she stand up, when she walk, or move her head or arm, it is—I do not know the word—but it is nice to look at, like—maybe I say she is built on lines like the lines of a good canoe, just like that, and when she move she is like the movement of the good canoe sliding through still water or leaping through water when it is white and fast and angry. It is very good to see.

"Why does she come into Klondike, all alone, with plenty of money? I do not know. Next day I ask her. She laugh and says: 'Sitka Charley, that is none of your business. I give you one thousand dollars take me to Dawson. That only is your business.' Next day after that I ask her what is her name. She laugh, then she says, 'Mary Jones, that is my name.' I do not know her name, but I know all the time that Mary Jones is not her name.

"It is very cold in canoe, and because of cold sometimes she not feel good. Sometimes she feel good and she sing. Her voice is like a silver bell, and I feel good all over like when I go into church at Holy Cross Mission, and when she sing I feel strong and paddle like hell. Then she laugh and says, 'You think we get to Dawson before freeze-up, Charley?' Sometimes she sit in canoe and is thinking far away, her eyes like that, all empty. She does not see Sitka Charley, nor the ice, nor the snow. She is far away. Very often she is like that, thinking far away. Sometimes, when she is thinking far away, her face is not good to see. It looks like a face that is angry, like the face of one man when he want to kill another man.

"Last day to Dawson very bad. Shore-ice in all the eddies, mush-ice in the stream. I cannot paddle. The canoe freeze to ice. I cannot get to shore. There is much danger. All the time we go down Yukon in the ice. That night there is much noise of ice. Then ice stop, canoe stop, everything stop. 'Let us go to shore,' the woman says. I say no, better wait. By and by, everything start down-stream again. There is much snow. I cannot see. At eleven o'clock at night, everything stop. At one o'clock everything start again. At three o'clock everything stop. Canoe is smashed like eggshell, but is on top of ice and cannot sink. I hear dogs howling. We wait. We sleep. By and by morning come. There is no more snow. It is the freeze-up, and there is Dawson. Canoe smash and stop right at Dawson. Sitka Charley has come in with two thousand letters on very last water.

"The woman rent a cabin on the hill, and for one week I see her no more. Then, one day, she come to me. 'Charley,' she says, 'how do you like to work for me? You drive dogs, make camp, travel with me.' I say that I make too much money carrying letters. She says, 'Charley, I will pay you more money.' I tell her that pick-and-shovel man get fifteen dollars a day in the mines. She says, 'That is four hundred and fifty dollars a month.' And I say, 'Sitka Charley is no pick-and-shovel man.' Then she says, 'I understand, Charley. I will give you seven hundred and fifty dollars each month.' It is a good price, and I go to work for her. I buy for her dogs and sled. We travel up Klondike, up Bonanza and Eldorado, over to Indian River, to Sulphur Creek, to Dominion, back across divide to Gold Bottom and to Too Much Gold, and back to Dawson. All the time she look for something, I do not know what. I am puzzled. 'What thing you look for?' I ask. She laugh. 'You look for gold?' I ask. She laugh. Then she says, 'That is none of your business, Charley.' And after that I never ask any more.

"She has a small revolver which she carries in her belt. Sometimes, on trail, she makes practice with revolver. I laugh. 'What for you laugh, Charley?' she ask. 'What for you play with that?' I say. 'It is no good. It is too small. It is for a child, a little plaything.' When we get back to Dawson she ask me to buy good revolver for her. I buy a Colt's 44. It is very heavy, but she carry it in her belt all the time.

"At Dawson comes the man. Which way he come I do not know. Only do I know he is *checha-quo*—what you call tenderfoot. His hands are soft, just like hers. He never do hard work. He is soft all over. At first I think maybe he is her husband. But he is too young. Also, they make two beds at night. He is maybe twenty years old. His eyes blue, his hair yellow, he has a little mustache which is yellow. His name is John Jones. Maybe he is her brother. I do not know. I ask questions no more. Only I think his name not John Jones. Other people call him Mr. Girvan. I do not think that is his name. I do not think her name is Miss Girvan, which other people call her. I think nobody know their names.

"One night I am asleep at Dawson. He wake me up. He says, 'Get the dogs ready; we start.' No more do I ask questions, so I get the dogs ready and we start. We go down the Yukon. It is night-time, it is November, and it is very cold—sixty-five below. She is soft. He is soft. The cold bites. They get tired. They cry under their breaths to themselves. By and by I say better we stop and make camp. But they say that they will go on. Three times I say better to make camp and rest, but each time they say they will go on. After that I say nothing. All the time, day after day, is it that way. They are very soft. They get stiff and sore. They do not understand moccasins, and their feet hurt very much. They limp, they stagger like drunken people, they cry under their breaths; and all the time they say, 'On! on! We will go on!'

"They are like crazy people. All the time do they go on, and on. Why do they go on? I do not know. Only do they go on. What are they after? I do not know. They are not after gold. There is no stampede. Besides, they spend plenty of money. But I ask questions no more. I, too, go on and on, because I am strong on the trail and because I am greatly paid.

"We make Circle City. That for which they look is not there. I think now that we will rest, and rest the dogs. But we do not rest, not for one day do we rest. 'Come,' says the woman to the man, 'let us go on.' And we go on. We leave the Yukon. We cross the divide to the west and swing down into the Tanana Country. There are new diggings there. But that for which they look is not there, and we take the back trail to Circle City.

"It is a hard journey. December is most gone. The days are short. It is very cold. One morning it is seventy below zero. 'Better that we don't travel to-day,' I say, 'else will the frost be unwarmed in the breathing and bite all the edges of our lungs. After that we will have bad cough, and maybe next spring will come pneumonia.' But they are *checha-quo*. They do not understand the trail. They are like dead people they are so tired, but they say, 'Let us go on.' We go on. The frost bites their lungs, and they get the dry cough. They cough till the tears run down their cheeks. When bacon is frying they must run away from the fire and cough half an hour in the snow. They freeze their cheeks a little bit, so that the skin turns black and is very sore. Also, the man freezes his thumb till the end is like to come off, and he must wear a large thumb on his mitten to keep it warm. And sometimes, when the frost bites hard and the thumb is very cold, he must take off the mitten and put the hand between his legs next to the skin, so that the thumb may get warm again.

"We limp into Circle City, and even I, Sitka Charley, am tired. It is Christmas Eve. I dance, drink, make a good time, for to-morrow is Christmas Day and we will rest. But no. It is five o'clock in the morning—Christmas morning. I am two hours asleep. The man stand by my bed. 'Come, Charley,' he says, 'harness the dogs. We start.'

"Have I not said that I ask questions no more? They pay me seven hundred and fifty dollars each month. They are my masters. I am their man. If they say, 'Charley, come, let us start for hell,' I will harness the dogs, and snap the whip, and start for hell. So I harness the dogs, and we start down the Yukon. Where do we go? They do not say. Only do they say, 'On! on! We will go on!'

"They are very weary. They have travelled many hundreds of miles, and they do not understand the way of the trail. Besides, their cough is very bad—the dry cough that makes strong men swear and weak men cry. But they go on. Every day they go on. Never do they rest the dogs. Always do they buy new dogs. At every camp, at every post, at every Indian village, do they cut out the tired dogs and put in fresh dogs. They have much money, money without end, and like water they spend it. They are crazy? Sometimes I think so, for there is a devil in them that drives them on and on, always on. What is it that they try to find? It is not gold. Never do they dig in the ground. I think a long time. Then I think it is a man they try to find. But what man? Never do we see the man. Yet are they like wolves on the trail of the kill. But they are funny wolves, soft wolves, baby wolves who do not understand the way of the trail. They cry aloud in their sleep at night. In their sleep they moan and groan with the pain of their weariness. And in the day, as they stagger along the trail, they cry under their breaths. They are funny wolves.

"We pass Fort Yukon. We pass Fort Hamilton. We pass Minook. January has come and nearly gone. The days are very short. At nine o'clock comes daylight. At three o'clock comes night. And it is cold. And even I, Sitka Charley, am tired. Will we go on forever this way without end? I do not know. But always do I look along the trail for that which they try to find. There are few people on the trail. Sometimes we travel one hundred miles and never see a sign of life. It is very quiet. There is no sound. Sometimes it snows, and we are like wandering ghosts. Sometimes it is clear, and at midday the sun looks at us for a moment over the hills to the south. The northern lights flame in the sky, and the sun-dogs dance, and the air is filled with frost-dust.

"I am Sitka Charley, a strong man. I was born on the trail, and all my days have I lived on the trail. And yet have these two baby wolves made me very tired. I am lean, like a starved cat, and I am glad of my bed at night, and in the morning am I greatly weary. Yet ever are we hitting the trail in the dark before daylight, and still on the trail does the dark after nightfall find us. These two baby wolves! If I am lean like a starved cat, they are lean like cats that have never eaten and have died. Their eyes are sunk deep in their heads, bright sometimes as with fever, dim and cloudy sometimes like the eyes of the dead. Their cheeks are hollow like caves in a cliff. Also are their cheeks black and raw from many freezings. Sometimes it is the woman in the morning who says, 'I cannot get up. I cannot move. Let me die.' And it is the man who stands beside her and says, 'Come, let us go on.' And they go on. And sometimes it is the man who cannot get up, and the woman says, 'Come, let us go on.' But the one thing they do, and always do, is to go on. Always do they go on.

"Sometimes, at the trading posts, the man and woman get letters. I do not know what is in the letters. But it is the scent that they follow, these letters themselves are the scent. One time an Indian gives them a letter. I talk with him privately. He says it is a man with one eye who gives him the letter, a man who travels fast down the Yukon. That is all. But I know that the baby wolves are after the man with the one eye.

"It is February, and we have travelled fifteen hundred miles. We are getting near Bering Sea, and there are storms and blizzards. The going is hard. We come to Anvig. I do not know, but I think sure they get a letter at Anvig, for they are much excited, and they say, 'Come, hurry, let us go on.' But I say we must buy grub, and they say we must travel light and fast. Also, they say that we can get grub at Charley McKeon's cabin. Then do I know that they take the big cut-off, for it is there that Charley McKeon lives where the Black Rock stands by the trail.

"Before we start, I talk maybe two minutes with the priest at Anvig. Yes, there is a man with one eye who has gone by and who travels fast. And I know that for which they look is the man with the one eye. We leave Anvig with little grub, and travel light and fast. There are three fresh dogs bought in Anvig, and we travel very fast. The man and woman are like mad. We start earlier in the morning, we travel later at night. I look sometimes to see them die, these two baby wolves, but they will not die. They go on and on. When the dry cough take hold of them hard, they hold their hands against their stomach and double up in the snow, and cough, and cough, and cough. They cannot walk, they cannot talk. Maybe for ten minutes they cough, maybe for half an hour, and then they straighten up, the tears from the coughing frozen on their faces, and the words they say are, 'Come, let us go on.'

"Even I, Sitka Charley, am greatly weary, and I think seven hundred and fifty dollars is a cheap price for the labor I do. We take the big cut-off, and the trail is fresh. The baby wolves have their noses down to the trail, and they say, 'Hurry!' All the time do they say, 'Hurry! Faster! Faster!' It is hard on the dogs. We have not much food and we cannot give them enough to eat, and they grow weak. Also, they must work hard. The woman has true sorrow for them, and often, because of them, the tears are in her eyes. But the devil in her that drives her on will not let her stop and rest the dogs.

"And then we come upon the man with the one eye. He is in the snow by the trail, and his leg is broken. Because of the leg he has made a poor camp, and has been lying on his blankets for three days and keeping a fire going. When we find him he is swearing. He swears like hell. Never have I heard a man swear like that man. I am glad. Now that they have found that for which they look, we will have rest. But the woman says, 'Let us start. Hurry!'

"I am surprised. But the man with the one eye says, 'Never mind me. Give me your grub. You will get more grub at McKeon's cabin to-morrow. Send McKeon back for me. But do you go on.' Here is another wolf, an old wolf, and he, too, thinks but the one thought, to go on. So we give him our grub, which is not much, and we chop wood for his fire, and we take his strongest dogs and go on. We left the man with one eye there in the snow, and he died there in the snow, for McKeon never went back for him. And who that man was, and why he came to be there, I do not know. But I think he was greatly paid by the man and the woman, like me, to do their work for them.

"That day and that night we had nothing to eat, and all next day we travelled fast, and we were weak with hunger. Then we came to the Black Rock, which rose five hundred feet above the trail. It was at the end of the day. Darkness was coming, and we could not find the cabin of McKeon. We slept hungry, and in the morning looked for the cabin. It was not there, which was a strange thing, for everybody knew that McKeon lived in a cabin at Black Rock. We were near to the coast, where the wind blows hard and there is much snow. Everywhere there were small hills of snow where the wind had piled it up. I have a thought, and I dig in one and another of the hills of snow. Soon I find the walls of the cabin, and I dig down to the door. I go inside. McKeon is dead. Maybe two or three weeks he is dead. A sickness had come upon him so that he could not leave the cabin. The wind and the snow had covered the cabin. He had eaten his grub and died. I looked for his cache, but there was no grub in it.

"'Let us go on,' said the woman. Her eyes were hungry, and her hand was upon her heart, as with the hurt of something inside. She bent back and forth like a tree in the wind as she stood there. 'Yes, let us go on,' said the man. His voice was hollow, like the *klonk* of an old raven, and he was hunger-mad. His eyes were like live coals of fire, and as his body rocked to and fro, so rocked his soul inside. And I, too, said, 'Let us go on.' For that one thought, laid upon me like a lash for every mile of fifteen hundred miles, had burned itself into my soul, and I think that I, too, was mad. Besides, we could only go on, for there was no grub. And we went on, giving no thought to the man with the one eye in the snow.

"There is little travel on the big cut-off. Sometimes two or three months and nobody goes by. The snow had covered the trail, and there was no sign that men had ever come or gone that way. All day the wind blew and the snow fell, and all day we travelled, while our stomachs gnawed their desire and our bodies grew weaker with every step they took. Then the woman began to fall. Then the man. I did not fall, but my feet were heavy and I caught my toes and stumbled many times.

"That night is the end of February. I kill three ptarmigan with the woman's revolver, and we are made somewhat strong again. But the dogs have nothing to eat. They try to eat their harness, which is of leather and walrus-hide, and I must fight them off with a club and hang all the harness in a tree. And all night they howl and fight around that tree. But we do not mind. We sleep like dead people, and in the morning get up like dead people out of their graves and go on along the trail.

"That morning is the 1st of March, and on that morning I see the first sign of that after which the baby wolves are in search. It is clear weather, and cold. The sun stay longer in the sky, and there are sun-dogs flashing on either side, and the air is bright with frost-dust. The snow falls no more upon the trail, and I see the fresh sign of dogs and sled. There is one man with that outfit, and I see in the snow that he is not strong. He, too, has not enough to eat. The young wolves see the fresh sign, too, and they are much excited. 'Hurry!' they say. All the time they say, 'Hurry! Faster, Charley, faster!'

"We make hurry very slow. All the time the man and the woman fall down. When they try to ride on sled the dogs are too weak, and the dogs fall down. Besides, it is so cold that if they ride on the sled they will freeze. It is very easy for a hungry man to freeze. When the woman fall down, the man help her up. Sometimes the woman help the man up. By and by both fall down and cannot get up, and I must help them up all the time, else they will not get up and will die there in the snow. This is very hard work, for I am greatly weary, and as well I must drive the dogs, and the man and woman are very heavy with no strength in their bodies. So, by and by, I, too, fall down in the snow, and there is no one to help me up. I must get up by myself. And always do I get up by myself, and help them up, and make the dogs go on.

"That night I get one ptarmigan, and we are very hungry. And that night the man says to me, 'What time start to-morrow, Charley?' It is like the voice of a ghost. I say, 'All the time you make start at five o'clock.' 'To-morrow,' he says, 'we will start at three o'clock.' I laugh in great bitterness, and I say, 'You are dead man.' And he says, 'To-morrow we will start at three o'clock.'

"And we start at three o'clock, for I am their man, and that which they say is to be done, I do. It is clear and cold, and there is no wind. When daylight comes we can see a long way off. And it is very quiet. We can hear no sound but the beat of our hearts, and in the silence that is a very loud sound. We are like sleep-walkers, and we walk in dreams until we fall down; and then we know we must get up, and we see the trail once more and bear the beating of our hearts. Sometimes, when I am walking in dreams this way, I have strange thoughts. Why does Sitka Charley live? I ask myself. Why does Sitka Charley work hard, and go hungry, and have all this pain? For seven hundred and fifty dollars a month, I make the answer, and I know it is a foolish answer. Also is it a true answer. And after that never again do I care for money. For that day a large wisdom came to me. There was a great light, and I saw clear, and I knew that it was not for money that a man must live, but for a happiness that no man can give, or buy, or sell, and that is beyond all value of all money in the world.

"In the morning we come upon the last-night camp of the man who is before us. It is a poor camp, the kind a man makes who is hungry and without strength. On the snow there are pieces of blanket and of canvas, and I know what has happened. His dogs have eaten their harness, and he has made new harness out of his blankets. The man and woman stare hard at what is to be seen, and as I look at them my back feels the chill as of a cold wind against the skin. Their eyes are toil-mad and hunger-mad, and burn like fire deep in their heads. Their faces are like the faces of people who have died of hunger, and their cheeks are black with the dead flesh of many freezings. 'Let us go on,' says the man. But the woman coughs and falls in the snow. It is the dry cough where the frost has bitten the lungs. For a long time she coughs, then like a woman crawling out of her grave she crawls to her feet. The tears are ice upon her cheeks, and her breath makes a noise as it comes and goes, and she says, 'Let us go on.'

"We go on. And we walk in dreams through the silence. And every time we walk is a dream and we are without pain; and every time we fall down is an awakening, and we see the snow and the mountains and the fresh trail of the man who is before us, and we know all our pain again. We come to where we can see a long way over the snow, and that for which they look is before them. A mile away there are black spots upon the snow. The black spots move. My eyes are dim, and I must stiffen my soul to see. And I see one man with dogs and a sled. The baby wolves see, too. They can no longer talk, but they whisper, 'On, on. Let us hurry!'

"And they fall down, but they go on. The man who is before us, his blanket harness breaks often, and he must stop and mend it. Our harness is good, for I have hung it in trees each night. At eleven o'clock the man is half a mile away. At one o'clock he is a quarter of a mile away. He is very weak. We see him fall down many times in the snow. One of his dogs can no longer travel, and he cuts it out of the harness. But he does not kill it. I kill it with the axe as I go by, as I kill one of my dogs which loses its legs and can travel no more.

"Now we are three hundred yards away. We go very slow. Maybe in two, three hours we go one mile. We do not walk. All the time we fall down. We stand up and stagger two steps, maybe three steps, then we fall down again. And all the time I must help up the man and woman. Sometimes they rise to their knees and fall forward, maybe four or five times before they can get to their feet again and stagger two or three steps and fall. But always do they fall forward. Standing or kneeling, always do they fall forward, gaining on the trail each time by the length of their bodies.

"Sometimes they crawl on hands and knees like animals that live in the forest. We go like snails, like snails that are dying we go so slow. And yet we go faster than the man who is before us. For he, too, falls all the time, and there is no Sitka Charley to lift him up. Now he is two hundred yards away. After a long time he is one hundred yards away.

"It is a funny sight. I want to laugh out loud, Ha! ha! just like that, it is so funny. It is a race of dead men and dead dogs. It is like in a dream when you have a nightmare and run away very fast for your life and go very slow. The man who is with me is mad. The woman is mad. I am mad. All the world is mad, and I want to laugh, it is so funny.

"The stranger-man who is before us leaves his dogs behind and goes on alone across the snow. After a long time we come to the dogs. They lie helpless in the snow, their harness of blanket and canvas on them, the sled behind them, and as we pass them they whine to us and cry like babies that are hungry.

"Then we, too, leave our dogs and go on alone across the snow. The man and the woman are nearly gone, and they moan and groan and sob, but they go on. I, too, go on. I have but one thought. It is to come up to the stranger-man. Then it is that I shall rest, and not until then shall I rest, and it seems that I must lie down and sleep for a thousand years, I am so tired.

"The stranger-man is fifty yards away, all alone in the white snow. He falls and crawls, staggers, and falls and crawls again. He is like an animal that is sore wounded and trying to run from the hunter. By and by he crawls on hands and knees. He no longer stands up. And the man and woman no longer stand up. They, too, crawl after him on hands and knees. But I stand up. Sometimes I fall, but always do I stand up again.

"It is a strange thing to see. All about is the snow and the silence, and through it crawl the man and the woman, and the stranger-man who goes before. On either side the sun are sun-dogs, so that there are three suns in the sky. The frost-dust is like the dust of diamonds, and all the air is filled with it. Now the woman coughs, and lies still in the snow until the fit has passed, when she crawls on again. Now the man looks ahead, and he is blear-eyed as with old age and must rub his eyes so that he can see the stranger-man. And now the stranger-man looks back over his shoulder. And Sitka Charley, standing upright, maybe falls down and stands upright again.

"After a long time the stranger-man crawls no more. He stands slowly upon his feet and rocks back and forth. Also does he take off one mitten and wait with revolver in his hand, rocking back and forth as he waits. His face is skin and bones and frozen black. It is a hungry face. The eyes are deep-sunk in his head, and the lips are snarling. The man and woman, too, get upon their feet and they go toward him very slowly. And all about is the snow and the silence. And in the sky are three suns, and all the air is flashing with the dust of diamonds.

"And thus it was that I, Sitka Charley, saw the baby wolves make their kill. No word is spoken. Only does the stranger-man snarl with his hungry face. Also does he rock to and fro, his shoulders drooping, his knees bent, and his legs wide apart so that he does not fall down. The man and the woman stop maybe fifty feet away. Their legs, too, are wide apart so that they do not fall down, and their bodies rock to and fro. The stranger-man is very weak. His arm shakes, so that when he shoots at the man his bullet strikes in the snow. The man cannot take off his mitten. The stranger-man shoots at him again, and this time the bullet goes by in the air. Then the man takes the mitten in his teeth and pulls it off. But his hand is frozen and he cannot hold the revolver, and it falls in the snow. I look at the woman. Her mitten is off, and the big Colt's revolver is in her hand. Three times she shoot, quick, just like that. The hungry face of the stranger-man is still snarling as he falls forward into the snow.

"They do not look at the dead man. 'Let us go on,' they say. And we go on. But now that they have found that for which they look, they are like dead. The last strength has gone out of them. They can stand no more upon their feet. They will not crawl, but desire only to close their eyes and sleep. I see not far away a place for camp. I kick them. I have my dog-whip, and I give them the lash of it. They cry aloud, but they must crawl. And they do crawl to the place for camp. I build fire so that they will not freeze. Then I go back for sled. Also, I kill the dogs of the stranger-man so that we may have food and not die. I put the man and woman in blankets and they sleep. Sometimes I wake them and give them little bit of food. They are not awake, but they take the food. The woman sleep one day and a half. Then she wake up and go to sleep again. The man sleep two days and wake up and go to sleep again. After that we go down to the coast at St. Michaels. And when the ice goes out of Bering Sea, the man and woman go away on a steamship. But first they pay me my seven hundred and fifty dollars a month. Also, they make me a present of one thousand dollars. And that was the year that Sitka Charley gave much money to the Mission at Holy Cross."

"But why did they kill the man?" I asked.

Sitka Charley delayed reply until he had lighted his pipe. He glanced at the *Police Gazette* illustration and nodded his head at it familiarly. Then he said, speaking slowly and ponderingly:

"I have thought much. I do not know. It is something that happened. It is a picture I remember. It is like looking in at the window and seeing the man writing a letter. They came into my life and they went out of my life, and the picture is as I have said, without beginning, the end without understanding."

"You have painted many pictures in the telling," I said.

"Ay," he nodded his head. "But they were without beginning and without end."

"The last picture of all had an end," I said.

"Ay," he answered. "But what end?"

"It was a piece of life," I said.

"Ay," he answered. "It was a piece of life."

NEGORE, THE COWARD

HE HAD FOLLOWED the trail of his fleeing people for eleven days, and his pursuit had been in itself a flight; for behind him he knew full well were the dreaded Russians, toiling through the swampy lowlands and over the steep divides, bent on no less than the extermination of all his people. He was travelling light. A rabbit-skin sleeping-robe, a muzzle-loading rifle, and a few pounds of sun-dried salmon constituted his outfit. He would have marvelled that a whole people—women and children and aged—could travel so swiftly, had he not known the terror that drove them on.

It was in the old days of the Russian occupancy of Alaska, when the nineteenth century had run but half its course, that Negore fled after his fleeing tribe and came upon it this summer night by the head waters of the Pee-lat. Though near the midnight hour, it was bright day as he passed through the weary camp. Many saw him, all knew him, but few and cold were the greetings he received.

"Negore, the Coward," he heard Illiha, a young woman, laugh, and Sun-ne, his sister's daughter, laughed with her.

Black anger ate at his heart; but he gave no sign, threading his way among the camp-fires until he came to one where sat an old man. A young woman was kneading with skilful fingers the tired muscles of his legs. He raised a sightless face and listened intently as Negore's foot crackled a dead twig.

"Who comes?" he queried in a thin, tremulous voice.

"Negore," said the young woman, scarcely looking up from her task.

Negore's face was expressionless. For many minutes he stood and waited. The old man's head had sunk back upon his chest. The young woman pressed and prodded the wasted muscles, resting her body on her knees, her bowed head hidden as in a cloud by her black wealth of hair. Negore watched the supple body, bending at the hips as a lynx's body might bend, pliant as a young willow stalk, and, withal, strong as only youth is strong. He looked, and was aware of a great yearning, akin in sensation to physical hunger. At last he spoke, saying:

"Is there no greeting for Negore, who has been long gone and has but now come back?"

She looked up at him with cold eyes. The old man chuckled to himself after the manner of the old.

"Thou art my woman, Oona," Negore said, his tones dominant and conveying a hint of menace.

She arose with catlike ease and suddenness to her full height, her eyes flashing, her nostrils quivering like a deer's.

"I was thy woman to be, Negore, but thou art a coward; the daughter of Old Kinoos mates not with a coward!"

She silenced him with an imperious gesture as he strove to speak.

"Old Kinoos and I came among you from a strange land. Thy people took us in by their fires and made us warm, nor asked whence or why we wandered. It was their thought that Old Kinoos had lost the sight of his eyes from age; nor did Old Kinoos say otherwise, nor did I, his daughter. Old Kinoos is a brave man, but Old Kinoos was never a boaster. And now, when I tell thee of how his blindness came to be, thou wilt know, beyond question, that the daughter of Kinoos cannot mother the children of a coward such as thou art, Negore."

Again she silenced the speech that rushed up to his tongue.

"Know, Negore, if journey be added unto journey of all thy journeyings through this land, thou wouldst not come to the unknown Sitka on the Great Salt Sea. In that place there be many Russian folk, and their rule is harsh. And from Sitka, Old Kinoos, who was Young Kinoos in those days, fled away with me, a babe in his arms, along the islands in the midst of the sea. My mother dead tells the tale of his wrong; a Russian, dead with a spear through breast and back, tells the tale of the vengeance of Kinoos.

"But wherever we fled, and however far we fled, always did we find the hated Russian folk. Kinoos was unafraid, but the sight of them was a hurt to his eyes; so we fled on and on, through the seas and years, till we came to the Great Fog Sea, Negore, of which thou hast heard, but which thou hast never seen. We lived among many peoples, and I grew to be a woman; but Kinoos, growing old, took to him no other woman, nor did I take a man.

"At last we came to Pastolik, which is where the Yukon drowns itself in the Great Fog Sea. Here we lived long, on the rim of the sea, among a people by whom the Russians were well hated. But sometimes they came, these Russians, in great ships, and made the people of Pastolik show them the way through the islands uncountable of the many-mouthed Yukon. And sometimes the men they took to show them the way never came back, till the people became angry and planned a great plan.

"So, when there came a ship, Old Kinoos stepped forward and said he would show the way. He was an old man then, and his hair was white; but he was unafraid. And he was cunning, for he took the ship to where the sea sucks in to the land and the waves beat white on the mountain called Romanoff. The sea sucked the ship in to where the waves beat white, and it ground upon the rocks and broke open its sides. Then came all the people of Pastolik, (for this was the plan), with their war-spears, and arrows, and some few guns. But first the Russians put out the eyes of Old Kinoos that he might never show the way again, and then they fought, where the waves beat white, with the people of Pastolik.

"Now the head-man of these Russians was Ivan. He it was, with his two thumbs, who drove out the eyes of Kinoos. He it was who fought his way through the white water, with two men left of all his men, and went away along the rim of the Great Fog Sea into the north. Kinoos was wise. He could see no more and was helpless as a child. So he fled away from the sea, up the great, strange Yukon, even to Nulato, and I fled with him.

"This was the deed my father did, Kinoos, an old man. But how did the young man, Negore?"

Once again she silenced him.

"With my own eyes I saw, at Nulato, before the gates of the great fort, and but few days gone. I saw the Russian, Ivan, who thrust out my father's eyes, lay the lash of his dog-whip upon thee and beat thee like a dog. This I saw, and knew thee for a coward. But I saw thee not, that night, when all thy people—yea, even the boys not yet hunters—fell upon the Russians and slew them all."

"Not Ivan," said Negore, quietly. "Even now is he on our heels, and with him many Russians fresh up from the sea."

Oona made no effort to hide her surprise and chagrin that Ivan was not dead, but went on:

"In the day I saw thee a coward; in the night, when all men fought, even the boys not yet hunters, I saw thee not and knew thee doubly a coward."

"Thou art done? All done?" Negore asked.

She nodded her head and looked at him askance, as though astonished that he should have aught to say.

"Know then that Negore is no coward," he said; and his speech was very low and quiet. "Know that when I was yet a boy I journeyed alone down to the place where the Yukon drowns itself in the Great Fog Sea. Even to Pastolik I journeyed, and even beyond, into the north, along the rim of the sea. This I did when I was a boy, and I was no coward. Nor was I coward when I journeyed, a young man and alone, up the Yukon farther than man had ever been, so far that I came to another folk, with white faces, who live in a great fort and talk speech other than that the Russians talk. Also have I killed the great bear of the Tanana country, where no one of my people hath ever been. And I have fought with the Nuklukyets, and the Kaltags, and the Sticks in far regions, even I, and alone. These deeds, whereof no man knows, I speak for myself. Let my people speak for me of things I have done which they know. They will not say Negore is a coward."

He finished proudly, and proudly waited.

"These be things which happened before I came into the land," she said, "and I know not of them. Only do I know what I know, and I know I saw thee lashed like a dog in the day; and in the night, when the great fort flamed red and the men killed and were killed, I saw thee not. Also, thy people do call thee Negore, the Coward. It is thy name now, Negore, the Coward."

"It is not a good name," Old Kinoos chuckled.

"Thou dost not understand, Kinoos," Negore said gently. "But I shall make thee understand. Know that I was away on the hunt of the bear, with Kamo-tah, my mother's son. And Kamo-tah fought with a great bear. We had no meat for three days, and Kamo-tah was not strong of arm nor swift of foot. And the great bear crushed him, so, till his bones cracked like dry sticks. Thus I found him, very sick and groaning upon the ground. And there was no meat, nor could I kill aught that the sick man might eat.

"So I said, 'I will go to Nulato and bring thee food, also strong men to carry thee to camp.' And Kamo-tah said, 'Go thou to Nulato and get food, but say no word of what has befallen me. And when I have eaten, and am grown well and strong, I will kill this bear. Then will I return in honor to Nulato, and no man may laugh and say Kamo-tah was undone by a bear.'

"So I gave heed to my brother's words; and when I was come to Nulato, and the Russian, Ivan, laid the lash of his dog-whip upon me, I knew I must not fight. For no man knew of Kamo-tah, sick and groaning and hungry; and did I fight with Ivan, and die, then would my brother die, too. So it was, Oona, that thou sawest me beaten like a dog.

"Then I heard the talk of the shamans and chiefs that the Russians had brought strange sicknesses upon the people, and killed our men, and stolen our women, and that the land must be made clean. As I say, I heard the talk, and I knew it for good talk, and I knew that in the night the Russians were to be killed. But there was my brother, Kamo-tah, sick and groaning and with no meat; so I could not stay and fight with the men and the boys not yet hunters.

"And I took with me meat and fish, and the lash-marks of Ivan, and I found Kamo-tah no longer groaning, but dead. Then I went back to Nulato, and, behold, there was no Nulato— only ashes where the great fort had stood, and the bodies of many men. And I saw the Russians come up the Yukon in boats, fresh from the sea, many Russians; and I saw Ivan creep forth from where he lay hid and make talk with them. And the next day I saw Ivan lead them upon the trail of the tribe. Even now are they upon the trail, and I am here, Negore, but no coward."

"This is a tale I hear," said Oona, though her voice was gentler than before. "Kamo-tah is dead and cannot speak for thee, and I know only what I know, and I must know thee of my own eyes for no coward."

Negore made an impatient gesture.

"There be ways and ways," she added. "Art thou willing to do no less than what Old Kinoos hath done?"

He nodded his head, and waited.

"As thou hast said, they seek for us even now, these Russians. Show them the way, Negore, even as Old Kinoos showed them the way, so that they come, unprepared, to where we wait for them, in a passage up the rocks. Thou knowest the place, where the wall is broken and high. Then will we destroy them, even Ivan. When they cling like flies to the wall, and top is no less near than bottom, our men shall fall upon them from above and either side, with spears, and arrows, and guns. And the women and children, from above, shall loosen the great rocks and hurl them down upon them. It will be a great day, for the Russians will be killed, the land will be made clean, and Ivan, even Ivan who thrust out my father's eyes and laid the lash of his dog-whip upon thee, will be killed. Like a dog gone mad will he die, his breath crushed out of him beneath the rocks. And when the fighting begins, it is for thee, Negore, to crawl secretly away so that thou be not slain."

"Even so," he answered. "Negore will show them the way. And then?"

"And then I shall be thy woman, Negore's woman, the brave man's woman. And thou shalt hunt meat for me and Old Kinoos, and I shall cook thy food, and sew thee warm parkas and strong, and make thee moccasins after the way of my people, which is a better way than thy people's way. And as I say, I shall be thy woman, Negore, always thy woman. And I shall make thy life glad for thee, so that all thy days will be a song and laughter, and thou wilt know the woman Oona as unlike all other women, for she has journeyed far, and lived in strange places, and is wise in the ways of men and in the ways they may be made glad. And in thine old age will she still make thee glad, and thy memory of her in the days of thy strength will be sweet, for thou wilt know always that she was ease to thee, and peace, and rest, and that beyond all women to other men has she been woman to thee."

"Even so," said Negore, and the hunger for her ate at his heart, and his arms went out for her as a hungry man's arms might go out for food.

"When thou hast shown the way, Negore," she chided him; but her eyes were soft, and warm, and he knew she looked upon him as woman had never looked before.

"It is well," he said, turning resolutely on his heel. "I go now to make talk with the chiefs, so that they may know I am gone to show the Russians the way."

"Oh, Negore, my man! my man!" she said to herself, as she watched him go, but she said it so softly that even Old Kinoos did not hear, and his ears were over keen, what of his blindness.

THREE DAYS LATER, having with craft ill-concealed his hiding-place, Negore was dragged forth like a rat and brought before Ivan—"Ivan the Terrible" he was known by the men who marched at his back. Negore was armed with a miserable bone-barbed spear, and he kept his rabbit-skin robe wrapped closely about him, and though the day was warm he shivered as with an ague. He shook his head that he did not understand the speech Ivan put at him, and made that he was very weary and sick, and wished only to sit down and rest, pointing the while to his stomach in sign of his sickness, and shivering fiercely. But Ivan had with him a man from Pastolik who talked the speech of Negore, and many and vain were the questions they asked him concerning his tribe, till the man from Pastolik, who was called Karduk, said:

"It is the word of Ivan that thou shalt be lashed till thou diest if thou dost not speak. And know, strange brother, when I tell thee the word of Ivan is the law, that I am thy friend and no friend of Ivan. For I come not willingly from my country by the sea, and I desire greatly to live; wherefore I obey the will of my master—as thou wilt obey, strange brother, if thou art wise, and wouldst live."

"Nay, strange brother," Negore answered, "I know not the way my people are gone, for I was sick, and they fled so fast my legs gave out from under me, and I fell behind."

Negore waited while Karduk talked with Ivan. Then Negore saw the Russian's face go dark, and he saw the men step to either side of him, snapping the lashes of their whips. Whereupon he betrayed a great fright, and cried aloud that he was a sick man and knew nothing, but would tell what he knew. And to such purpose did he tell, that Ivan gave the word to his men to march, and on either side of Negore marched the men with the whips, that he might not run away. And when he made that he was weak of his sickness, and stumbled and walked not so fast as they walked, they laid their lashes upon him till he screamed with pain and discovered new strength. And when Karduk told him all would be well with him when they had overtaken his tribe, he asked, "And then may I rest and move not?"

Continually he asked, "And then may I rest and move not?"

And while he appeared very sick and looked about him with dull eyes, he noted the fighting strength of Ivan's men, and noted with satisfaction that Ivan did not recognize him as the man he had beaten before the gates of the fort. It was a strange following his dull eyes saw. There were Slavonian hunters, fair-skinned and mighty-muscled; short, squat Finns, with flat noses and round faces; Siberian half-breeds, whose noses were more like eagle-beaks; and lean, slant-eyed men, who bore in their veins the Mongol and Tartar blood as well as the blood of the Slav. Wild adventurers they were, forayers and destroyers from the far lands beyond the Sea of Bering, who blasted the new and unknown world with fire and sword and clutched greedily for its wealth of fur and hide. Negore looked upon them with satisfaction, and in his mind's eye he saw them crushed and lifeless at the passage up the rocks. And ever he saw, waiting for him at the passage up the rocks, the face and the form of Oona, and ever he heard her voice in his ears and felt the soft, warm glow of her eyes. But never did he forget to shiver, nor to stumble where the footing was rough, nor to cry aloud at the bite of the lash. Also, he was afraid of Karduk, for he knew him for no true man. His was a false eye, and an easy tongue—a tongue too easy, he judged, for the awkwardness of honest speech.

All that day they marched. And on the next, when Karduk asked him at command of Ivan, he said he doubted they would meet with his tribe till the morrow. But Ivan, who had once been shown the way by Old Kinoos, and had found that way to lead through the white water and a deadly fight, believed no more in anything. So when they came to a passage up the rocks, he halted his forty men, and through Karduk demanded if the way were clear.

Negore looked at it shortly and carelessly. It was a vast slide that broke the straight wall of a cliff, and was overrun with brush and creeping plants, where a score of tribes could have lain well hidden.

He shook his head. "Nay, there be nothing there," he said. "The way is clear."

Again Ivan spoke to Karduk, and Karduk said:

"Know, strange brother, if thy talk be not straight, and if thy people block the way and fall upon Ivan and his men, that thou shalt die, and at once."

"My talk is straight," Negore said. "The way is clear."

Still Ivan doubted, and ordered two of his Slavonian hunters to go up alone. Two other men he ordered to the side of Negore. They placed their guns against his breast and waited. All waited. And Negore knew, should one arrow fly, or one spear be flung, that his death would come upon him. The two Slavonian hunters toiled upward till they grew small and smaller, and when they reached the top and waved their hats that all was well, they were like black specks against the sky.

The guns were lowered from Negore's breast and Ivan gave the order for his men to go forward. Ivan was silent, lost in thought. For an hour he marched, as though puzzled, and then, through Karduk's mouth, he said to Negore:

"How didst thou know the way was clear when thou didst look so briefly upon it?"

Negore thought of the little birds he had seen perched among the rocks and upon the bushes, and smiled, it was so simple; but he shrugged his shoulders and made no answer. For he was thinking, likewise, of another passage up the rocks, to which they would soon come, and where the little birds would all be gone. And he was glad that Karduk came from the Great Fog Sea, where there were no trees or bushes, and where men learned water-craft instead of land-craft and wood-craft.

Three hours later, when the sun rode overhead, they came to another passage up the rocks, and Karduk said:

"Look with all thine eyes, strange brother, and see if the way be clear, for Ivan is not minded this time to wait while men go up before."

Negore looked, and he looked with two men by his side, their guns resting against his breast. He saw that the little birds were all gone, and once he saw the glint of sunlight on a rifle-barrel. And he thought of Oona, and of her words: "And when the fighting begins, it is for thee, Negore, to crawl secretly away so that thou be not slain."

He felt the two guns pressing on his breast. This was not the way she had planned. There would be no crawling secretly away. He would be the first to die when the fighting began. But he said, and his voice was steady, and he still feigned to see with dull eyes and to shiver from his sickness:

"The way is clear."

And they started up, Ivan and his forty men from the far lands beyond the Sea of Bering. And there was Karduk, the man from Pastolik, and Negore, with the two guns always upon him. It was a long climb, and they could not go fast; but very fast to Negore they seemed to approach the midway point where top was no less near than bottom.

A gun cracked among the rocks to the right, and Negore heard the war-yell of all his tribe, and for an instant saw the rocks and bushes bristle alive with his kinfolk. Then he felt torn asunder by a burst of flame hot through his being, and as he fell he knew the sharp pangs of life as it wrenches at the flesh to be free.

But he gripped his life with a miser's clutch and would not let it go. He still breathed the air, which bit his lungs with a painful sweetness; and dimly he saw and heard, with passing spells of blindness and deafness, the flashes of sight and sound again wherein he saw the hunters of Ivan falling to their deaths, and his own brothers fringing the carnage and filling the air with the tumult of their cries and weapons, and, far above, the women and children loosing the great rocks that leaped like things alive and thundered down.

The sun danced above him in the sky, the huge walls reeled and swung, and still he heard and saw dimly. And when the great Ivan fell across his legs, hurled there lifeless and crushed by a down-rushing rock, he remembered the blind eyes of Old Kinoos and was glad.

Then the sounds died down, and the rocks no longer thundered past, and he saw his tribespeople creeping close and closer, spearing the wounded as they came. And near to him he heard the scuffle of a mighty Slavonian hunter, loath to die, and, half uprisen, borne back and down by the thirsty spears.

Then he saw above him the face of Oona, and felt about him the arms of Oona; and for a moment the sun steadied and stood still, and the great walls were upright and moved not.

"Thou art a brave man, Negore," he heard her say in his ear; "thou art my man, Negore."

And in that moment he lived all the life of gladness of which she had told him, and the laughter and the song, and as the sun went out of the sky above him, as in his old age, he knew the memory of her was sweet. And as even the memories dimmed and died in the darkness that fell upon him, he knew in her arms the fulfilment of all the ease and rest she had promised him. And as black night wrapped around him, his head upon her breast, he felt a great peace steal about him, and he was aware of the hush of many twilights and the mystery of silence.

LOST FACE

IT WAS THE END. Subienkow had travelled a long trail of bitterness and horror, homing like a dove for the capitals of Europe, and here, farther away than ever, in Russian America, the trail ceased. He sat in the snow, arms tied behind him, waiting the torture. He stared curiously before him at a huge Cossack, prone in the snow, moaning in his pain. The men had finished handling the giant and turned him over to the women. That they exceeded the fiendishness of the men, the man's cries attested.

Subienkow looked on, and shuddered. He was not afraid to die. He had carried his life too long in his hands, on that weary trail from Warsaw to Nulato, to shudder at mere dying. But he objected to the torture. It offended his soul. And this offence, in turn, was not due to the mere pain he must endure, but to the sorry spectacle the pain would make of him. He knew that he would pray, and beg, and entreat, even as Big Ivan and the others that had gone before. This would not be nice. To pass out bravely and cleanly, with a smile and a jest—ah! that would have been the way. But to lose control, to have his soul upset by the pangs of the flesh, to screech and gibber like an ape, to become the veriest beast—ah, that was what was so terrible.

There had been no chance to escape. From the beginning, when he dreamed the fiery dream of Poland's independence, he had become a puppet in the hands of Fate. From the beginning, at Warsaw, at St. Petersburg, in the Siberian mines, in Kamtchatka, on the crazy boats of the fur-thieves, Fate had been driving him to this end. Without doubt, in the foundations of the world was graved this end for him—for him, who was so fine and sensitive, whose nerves scarcely sheltered under his skin, who was a dreamer, and a poet, and an artist. Before he was dreamed of, it had been determined that the quivering bundle of sensitiveness that constituted him should be doomed to live in raw and howling savagery, and to die in this far land of night, in this dark place beyond the last boundaries of the world.

He sighed. So that thing before him was Big Ivan—Big Ivan the giant, the man without nerves, the man of iron, the Cossack turned freebooter of the seas, who was as phlegmatic as an ox, with a nervous system so low that what was pain to ordinary men was scarcely a tickle to him. Well, well, trust these Nulato Indians to find Big Ivan's nerves and trace them to the roots of his quivering soul. They were certainly doing it. It was inconceivable that a man could suffer so much and yet live. Big Ivan was paying for his low order of nerves. Already he had lasted twice as long as any of the others.

Subienkow felt that he could not stand the Cossack's sufferings much longer. Why didn't Ivan die? He would go mad if that screaming did not cease. But when it did cease, his turn would come. And there was Yakaga awaiting him, too, grinning at him even now in anticipation—Yakaga, whom only last week he had kicked out of the fort, and upon whose face he had laid the lash of his dog-whip. Yakaga would attend to him. Doubtlessly Yakaga was saving for him more refined tortures, more exquisite nerve-racking. Ah! that must have been a good one, from the way Ivan screamed. The squaws bending over him stepped back with laughter and clapping of hands. Subienkow saw the monstrous thing that had been perpetrated, and began to laugh hysterically. The Indians looked at him in wonderment that he should laugh. But Subienkow could not stop.

This would never do. He controlled himself, the spasmodic twitchings slowly dying away. He strove to think of other things, and began reading back in his own life. He remembered his mother and his father, and the little spotted pony, and the French tutor who had taught him dancing and sneaked him an old worn copy of Voltaire. Once more he saw Paris, and dreary London, and gay Vienna, and Rome. And once more he saw that wild group of youths who had dreamed, even as he, the dream of an independent Poland with a king of Poland on the throne at Warsaw. Ah, there it was that the long trail began. Well, he had lasted longest. One by one, beginning with the two executed at St. Petersburg, he took up the count of the passing of those brave spirits. Here one had been beaten to death by a jailer, and there, on that bloodstained highway of the exiles, where they had marched for endless months, beaten and maltreated by their Cossack guards, another had dropped by the way. Always it had been savagery—brutal, bestial savagery. They had died—of fever, in the mines, under the knout. The last two had died after the escape, in the battle with the Cossacks, and he alone had won to Kamtchatka with the stolen papers and the money of a traveler he had left lying in the snow.

It had been nothing but savagery. All the years, with his heart in studios, and theatres, and courts, he had been hemmed in by savagery. He had purchased his life with blood. Everybody had killed. He had killed that traveler for his passports. He had proved that he was a man of parts by dueling with two Russian officers on a single day. He had had to prove himself in order to win to a place among the fur-thieves. He had had to win to that place. Behind him lay the thousand-years-long road across all Siberia and Russia. He could not escape that way. The only way was ahead, across the dark and icy sea of Bering to Alaska. The way had led from savagery to deeper savagery. On the scurvy-rotten ships of the fur-thieves, out of food and out of water, buffeted by the interminable storms of that stormy sea, men had become animals. Thrice he had sailed east from Kamtchatka. And thrice, after all manner of hardship and suffering, the survivors had come back to Kamtchatka. There had been no outlet for escape, and he could not go back the way he had come, for the mines and the knout awaited him.

Again, the fourth and last time, he had sailed east. He had been with those who first found the fabled Seal Islands; but he had not returned with them to share the wealth of furs in the mad orgies of Kamtchatka. He had sworn never to go back. He knew that to win to those dear capitals of Europe he must go on. So he had changed ships and remained in the dark new land. His comrades were Slavonian hunters and Russian adventurers, Mongols and Tartars and Siberian aborigines; and through the savages of the new world they had cut a path of blood. They had massacred whole villages that refused to furnish the fur-tribute;

and they, in turn, had been massacred by ships' companies. He, with one Finn, had been the sole survivor of such a company. They had spent a winter of solitude and starvation on a lonely Aleutian isle, and their rescue in the spring by another fur-ship had been one chance in a thousand.

But always the terrible savagery had hemmed him in. Passing from ship to ship, and ever refusing to return, he had come to the ship that explored south. All down the Alaska coast they had encountered nothing but hosts of savages. Every anchorage among the beetling islands or under the frowning cliffs of the mainland had meant a battle or a storm. Either the gales blew, threatening destruction, or the war canoes came off, manned by howling natives with the war-paint on their faces, who came to learn the bloody virtues of the sea-rovers' gunpowder. South, south they had coasted, clear to the myth-land of California. Here, it was said, were Spanish adventurers who had fought their way up from Mexico. He had had hopes of those Spanish adventurers. Escaping to them, the rest would have been easy—a year or two, what did it matter more or less—and he would win to Mexico, then a ship, and Europe would be his. But they had met no Spaniards. Only had they encountered the same impregnable wall of savagery. The denizens of the confines of the world, painted for war, had driven them back from the shores. At last, when one boat was cut off and every man killed, the commander had abandoned the quest and sailed back to the north.

The years had passed. He had served under Tebenkoff when Michaelovski Redoubt was built. He had spent two years in the Kuskokwim country. Two summers, in the month of June, he had managed to be at the head of Kotzebue Sound. Here, at this time, the tribes assembled for barter; here were to be found spotted deerskins from Siberia, ivory from the Diomedes, walrus skins from the shores of the Arctic, strange stone lamps, passing in trade from tribe to tribe, no one knew whence, and, once, a hunting-knife of English make; and here, Subienkow knew, was the school in which to learn geography. For he met Eskimos from Norton Sound, from King Island and St. Lawrence Island, from Cape Prince of Wales, and Point Barrow. Such places had other names, and their distances were measured in days.

It was a vast region these trading savages came from, and a vaster region from which, by repeated trade, their stone lamps and that steel knife had come. Subienkow bullied, and cajoled, and bribed. Every far-journeyer or strange tribesman was brought before him. Perils unaccountable and unthinkable were mentioned, as well as wild beasts, hostile tribes, impenetrable forests, and mighty mountain ranges; but always from beyond came the rumour and the tale of white-skinned men, blue of eye and fair of hair, who fought like devils and who sought always for furs. They were to the east—far, far to the east. No one had seen them. It was the word that had been passed along.

It was a hard school. One could not learn geography very well through the medium of strange dialects, from dark minds that mingled fact and fable and that measured distances by "sleeps" that varied according to the difficulty of the going. But at last came the whisper that gave Subienkow courage. In the east lay a great river where were these blue-eyed men. The river was called the Yukon. South of Michaelovski Redoubt emptied another great river which the Russians knew as the Kwikpak. These two rivers were one, ran the whisper.

Subienkow returned to Michaelovski. For a year he urged an expedition up the Kwikpak. Then arose Malakoff, the Russian half-breed, to lead the wildest and most ferocious of the hell's broth of mongrel adventurers who had crossed from Kamtchatka. Subienkow was his lieutenant. They threaded the mazes of the great delta of the Kwikpak, picked up the first low hills on the northern bank, and for half a thousand miles, in skin canoes loaded to the gunwales with trade-goods and ammunition, fought their way against the five-knot current of a river that ran from two to ten miles wide in a channel many fathoms deep. Malakoff decided to build the fort at Nulato. Subienkow urged to go farther. But he quickly reconciled himself to Nulato. The long winter was coming on. It would be better to wait. Early the following summer, when the ice was gone, he would disappear up the Kwikpak and work his way to the Hudson Bay Company's posts. Malakoff had never heard the whisper that the Kwikpak was the Yukon, and Subienkow did not tell him.

Came the building of the fort. It was enforced labour. The tiered walls of logs arose to the sighs and groans of the Nulato Indians. The lash was laid upon their backs, and it was the iron hand of the freebooters of the sea that laid on the lash. There were Indians that ran away, and when they were caught they were brought back and spread-eagled before the fort, where they and their tribe learned the efficacy of the knout. Two died under it; others were injured for life; and the rest took the lesson to heart and ran away no more. The snow was flying ere the fort was finished, and then it was the time for furs. A heavy tribute was laid upon the tribe. Blows and lashings continued, and that the tribute should be paid, the women and children were held as hostages and treated with the barbarity that only the fur-thieves knew.

Well, it had been a sowing of blood, and now was come the harvest. The fort was gone. In the light of its burning, half the fur-thieves had been cut down. The other half had passed under the torture. Only Subienkow remained, or Subienkow and Big Ivan, if that whimpering, moaning thing in the snow could be called Big Ivan. Subienkow caught Yakaga grinning at him. There was no gainsaying Yakaga. The mark of the lash was still on his face. After all, Subienkow could not blame him, but he disliked the thought of what Yakaga would do to him. He thought of appealing to Makamuk, the head-chief, but his judgment told him that such appeal was useless. Then, too, he thought of bursting his bonds and dying fighting. Such an end would be quick. But he could not break his bonds. Caribou thongs were stronger than he. Still devising, another thought came to him. He signed for Makamuk, and that an interpreter who knew the coast dialect should be brought.

"Oh, Makamuk," he said, "I am not minded to die. I am a great man, and it were foolishness for me to die. In truth, I shall not die. I am not like these other carrion."

He looked at the moaning thing that had once been Big Ivan, and stirred it contemptuously with his toe.

"I am too wise to die. Behold, I have a great medicine. I alone know this medicine. Since I am not going to die, I shall exchange this medicine with you."

"What is this medicine?" Makamuk demanded.

"It is a strange medicine."

Subienkow debated with himself for a moment, as if loth to part with the secret.

"I will tell you. A little bit of this medicine rubbed on the skin makes the skin hard like a rock, hard like iron, so that no cutting weapon can cut it. The strongest blow of a cutting weapon is a vain thing against it. A bone knife becomes like a piece of mud; and it will turn the edge of the iron knives we have brought among you. What will you give me for the secret of the medicine?"

"I will give you your life," Makamuk made answer through the interpreter.

Subienkow laughed scornfully.

"And you shall be a slave in my house until you die."

The Pole laughed more scornfully.

"Untie my hands and feet and let us talk," he said.

The chief made the sign; and when he was loosed Subienkow rolled a cigarette and lighted it.

"This is foolish talk," said Makamuk. "There is no such medicine. It cannot be. A cutting edge is stronger than any medicine."

The chief was incredulous, and yet he wavered. He had seen too many deviltries of fur-thieves that worked. He could not wholly doubt.

"I will give you your life; but you shall not be a slave," he announced.

"More than that."

Subienkow played his game as coolly as if he were bartering for a foxskin.

"It is a very great medicine. It has saved my life many times. I want a sled and dogs, and six of your hunters to travel with me down the river and give me safety to one day's sleep from Michaelovski Redoubt."

"You must live here, and teach us all of your deviltries," was the reply.

Subienkow shrugged his shoulders and remained silent. He blew cigarette smoke out on the icy air, and curiously regarded what remained of the big Cossack.

"That scar!" Makamuk said suddenly, pointing to the Pole's neck, where a livid mark advertised the slash of a knife in a Kamtchatkan brawl. "The medicine is not good. The cutting edge was stronger than the medicine."

"It was a strong man that drove the stroke." (Subienkow considered.) "Stronger than you, stronger than your strongest hunter, stronger than he."

Again, with the toe of his moccasin, he touched the Cossack—a grisly spectacle, no longer conscious—yet in whose dismembered body the pain-racked life clung and was loth to go.

"Also, the medicine was weak. For at that place there were no berries of a certain kind, of which I see you have plenty in this country. The medicine here will be strong."

"I will let you go down river," said Makamuk; "and the sled and the dogs and the six hunters to give you safety shall be yours."

"You are slow," was the cool rejoinder. "You have committed an offence against my medicine in that you did not at once accept my terms. Behold, I now demand more. I want one hundred beaver skins." (Makamuk sneered.)

"I want one hundred pounds of dried fish." (Makamuk nodded, for fish were plentiful and cheap.) "I want two sleds—one for me and one for my furs and fish. And my rifle must be returned to me. If you do not like the price, in a little while the price will grow."

Yakaga whispered to the chief.

"But how can I know your medicine is true medicine?" Makamuk asked.

"It is very easy. First, I shall go into the woods—"

Again Yakaga whispered to Makamuk, who made a suspicious dissent.

"You can send twenty hunters with me," Subienkow went on. "You see, I must get the berries and the roots with which to make the medicine. Then, when you have brought the two sleds and loaded on them the fish and the beaver skins and the rifle, and when you have told off the six hunters who will go with me—then, when all is ready, I will rub the medicine on my neck, so, and lay my neck there on that log. Then can your strongest hunter take the axe and strike three times on my neck. You yourself can strike the three times."

Makamuk stood with gaping mouth, drinking in this latest and most wonderful magic of the fur-thieves.

"But first," the Pole added hastily, "between each blow I must put on fresh medicine. The axe is heavy and sharp, and I want no mistakes."

"All that you have asked shall be yours," Makamuk cried in a rush of acceptance. "Proceed to make your medicine."

Subienkow concealed his elation. He was playing a desperate game, and there must be no slips. He spoke arrogantly.

"You have been slow. My medicine is offended. To make the offence clean you must give me your daughter."

He pointed to the girl, an unwholesome creature, with a cast in one eye and a bristling wolf-tooth. Makamuk was angry, but the Pole remained imperturbable, rolling and lighting another cigarette.

"Make haste," he threatened. "If you are not quick, I shall demand yet more."

In the silence that followed, the dreary northland scene faded before him, and he saw once more his native land, and France, and, once, as he glanced at the wolf-toothed girl, he remembered another girl, a singer and a dancer, whom he had known when first as a youth he came to Paris.

"What do you want with the girl?" Makamuk asked.

"To go down the river with me." Subienkow glanced over her critically. "She will make a good wife, and it is an honour worthy of my medicine to be married to your blood."

Again he remembered the singer and dancer and hummed aloud a song she had taught him. He lived the old life over, but in a detached, impersonal sort of way, looking at the memory-pictures of his own life as if they were pictures in a book of anybody's life. The chief's voice, abruptly breaking the silence, startled him

"It shall be done," said Makamuk. "The girl shall go down the river with you. But be it understood that I myself strike the three blows with the axe on your neck."

"But each time I shall put on the medicine," Subienkow answered, with a show of ill-concealed anxiety.

"You shall put the medicine on between each blow. Here are the hunters who shall see you do not escape. Go into the forest and gather your medicine."

Makamuk had been convinced of the worth of the medicine by the Pole's rapacity. Surely nothing less than the greatest of medicines could enable a man in the shadow of death to stand up and drive an old-woman's bargain.

"Besides," whispered Yakaga, when the Pole, with his guard, had disappeared among the spruce trees, "when you have learned the medicine you can easily destroy him."

"But how can I destroy him?" Makamuk argued. "His medicine will not let me destroy him."

"There will be some part where he has not rubbed the medicine," was Yakaga's reply. "We will destroy him through that part. It may be his ears. Very well; we will thrust a spear in one ear and out the other. Or it may be his eyes. Surely the medicine will be much too strong to rub on his eyes."

The chief nodded. "You are wise, Yakaga. If he possesses no other devil-things, we will then destroy him."

Subienkow did not waste time in gathering the ingredients for his medicine, he selected whatsoever came to hand such as spruce needles, the inner bark of the willow, a strip of birch bark, and a quantity of moss-berries, which he made the hunters dig up for him from beneath the snow. A few frozen roots completed his supply, and he led the way back to camp.

Makamuk and Yakaga crouched beside him, noting the quantities and kinds of the ingredients he dropped into the pot of boiling water.

"You must be careful that the moss-berries go in first," he explained.

"And—oh, yes, one other thing—the finger of a man. Here, Yakaga, let me cut off your finger."

But Yakaga put his hands behind him and scowled.

"Just a small finger," Subienkow pleaded.

"Yakaga, give him your finger," Makamuk commanded.

"There be plenty of fingers lying around," Yakaga grunted, indicating the human wreckage in the snow of the score of persons who had been tortured to death.

"It must be the finger of a live man," the Pole objected.

"Then shall you have the finger of a live man." Yakaga strode over to the Cossack and sliced off a finger.

"He is not yet dead," he announced, flinging the bloody trophy in the snow at the Pole's feet. "Also, it is a good finger, because it is large."

Subienkow dropped it into the fire under the pot and began to sing. It was a French love-song that with great solemnity he sang into the brew.

"Without these words I utter into it, the medicine is worthless," he explained. "The words are the chiefest strength of it. Behold, it is ready."

"Name the words slowly, that I may know them," Makamuk commanded.

"Not until after the test. When the axe flies back three times from my neck, then will I give you the secret of the words."

"But if the medicine is not good medicine?" Makamuk queried anxiously.

Subienkow turned upon him wrathfully.

"My medicine is always good. However, if it is not good, then do by me as you have done to the others. Cut me up a bit at a time, even as you have cut him up." He pointed to the Cossack. "The medicine is now cool. Thus, I rub it on my neck, saying this further medicine."

With great gravity he slowly intoned a line of the "Marseillaise," at the same time rubbing the villainous brew thoroughly into his neck.

An outcry interrupted his play-acting. The giant Cossack, with a last resurgence of his tremendous vitality, had arisen to his knees. Laughter and cries of surprise and applause arose from the Nulatos, as Big Ivan began flinging himself about in the snow with mighty spasms.

Subienkow was made sick by the sight, but he mastered his qualms and made believe to be angry.

"This will not do," he said. "Finish him, and then we will make the test. Here, you, Yakaga, see that his noise ceases."

While this was being done, Subienkow turned to Makamuk.

"And remember, you are to strike hard. This is not baby-work. Here, take the axe and strike the log, so that I can see you strike like a man."

Makamuk obeyed, striking twice, precisely and with vigour, cutting out a large chip.

"It is well." Subienkow looked about him at the circle of savage faces that somehow seemed to symbolize the wall of savagery that had hemmed him about ever since the Czar's police had first arrested him in Warsaw. "Take your axe, Makamuk, and stand so. I shall lie down. When I raise my hand, strike, and strike with all your might. And be careful that no one stands behind you. The medicine is good, and the axe may bounce from off my neck and right out of your hands."

He looked at the two sleds, with the dogs in harness, loaded with furs and fish. His rifle lay on top of the beaver skins. The six hunters who were to act as his guard stood by the sleds.

"Where is the girl?" the Pole demanded. "Bring her up to the sleds before the test goes on."

When this had been carried out, Subienkow lay down in the snow, resting his head on the log like a tired child about to sleep. He had lived so many dreary years that he was indeed tired.

"I laugh at you and your strength, O Makamuk," he said. "Strike, and strike hard."

He lifted his hand. Makamuk swung the axe, a broadaxe for the squaring of logs. The bright steel flashed through the frosty air, poised for a perceptible instant above Makamuk's head, then descended upon Subienkow's bare neck. Clear through flesh and bone it cut its way, biting deeply into the log beneath. The amazed savages saw the head bounce a yard away from the blood-spouting trunk.

There was a great bewilderment and silence, while slowly it began to dawn in their minds that there had been no medicine. The fur-thief had outwitted them. Alone, of all their prisoners, he had escaped the torture. That had been the stake for which he played. A great roar of laughter went up. Makamuk bowed his head in shame. The fur-thief had fooled him. He had lost face before all his people. Still they continued to roar out their laughter. Makamuk turned, and with bowed head stalked away. He knew that thenceforth he would be no longer known as Makamuk. He would be Lost Face; the record of his shame would be with him until he died; and whenever the tribes gathered in the spring for the salmon, or in the summer for the trading, the story would pass back and forth across the camp-fires of how the fur-thief died peaceably, at a single stroke, by the hand of Lost Face.

"Who was Lost Face?" he could hear, in anticipation, some insolent young buck demand, "Oh, Lost Face," would be the answer, "he who once was Makamuk in the days before he cut off the fur-thief's head."

TRUST

ALL LINES HAD BEEN CAST off, and the *Seattle No.* 4 was pulling slowly out from the shore. Her decks were piled high with freight and baggage, and swarmed with a heterogeneous company of Indians, dogs, and dog-mushers, prospectors, traders, and homeward-bound gold-seekers. A goodly portion of Dawson was lined up on the bank, saying good-bye. As the gang-plank came in and the steamer nosed into the stream, the clamour of farewell became deafening. Also, in that eleventh moment, everybody began to remember final farewell messages and to shout them back and forth across the widening stretch of water. Louis Bondell, curling his yellow moustache with one hand and languidly waving the other hand to his friends on shore, suddenly remembered something and sprang to the rail.

"Oh, Fred!" he bawled. "Oh, Fred!"

The "Fred" desired thrust a strapping pair of shoulders through the forefront of the crowd on the bank and tried to catch Louis Bondell's message. The latter grew red in the face with vain vociferation. Still the water widened between steamboat and shore.

"Hey, you, Captain Scott!" he yelled at the pilot-house. "Stop the boat!"

The gongs clanged, and the big stern wheel reversed, then stopped. All hands on steam-boat and on bank took advantage of this respite to exchange final, new, and imperative farewells. More futile than ever was Louis Bondell's effort to make himself heard. The *Seattle No.* 4 lost way and drifted down-stream, and Captain Scott had to go ahead and reverse a second time. His head disappeared inside the pilot-house, coming into view a moment later behind a big megaphone.

Now Captain Scott had a remarkable voice, and the "Shut up!" he launched at the crowd on deck and on shore could have been heard at the top of Moosehide Mountain and as far as Klondike City. This official remonstrance from the pilot-house spread a film of silence over the tumult.

"Now, what do you want to say?" Captain Scott demanded.

"Tell Fred Churchill—he's on the bank there—tell him to go to Macdonald. It's in his safe —a small gripsack of mine. Tell him to get it and bring it out when he comes."

In the silence Captain Scott bellowed the message ashore through the megaphone:—

"You, Fred Churchill, go to Macdonald—in his safe—small gripsack—belongs to Louis Bondell—important! Bring it out when you come! Got it!"

Churchill waved his hand in token that he had got it. In truth, had Macdonald, half a mile away, opened his window, he'd have got it, too. The tumult of farewell rose again, the gongs clanged, and the *Seattle No.* 4 went ahead, swung out into the stream, turned on her heel, and headed down the Yukon, Bondell and Churchill waving farewell and mutual affection to the last.

That was in midsummer. In the fall of the year, the *W. H. Willis* started up the Yukon with two hundred homeward-bound pilgrims on board. Among them was Churchill. In his state-room, in the middle of a clothes-bag, was Louis Bondell's grip. It was a small, stout leather affair, and its weight of forty pounds always made Churchill nervous when he wandered too far from it. The man in the adjoining state-room had a treasure of gold-dust hidden similarly in a clothes-bag, and the pair of them ultimately arranged to stand watch and watch. While one went down to eat, the other kept an eye on the two state-room doors. When Churchill wanted to take a hand at whist, the other man mounted guard, and when the other man wanted to relax his soul, Churchill read four-months' old newspapers on a camp stool between the two doors.

There were signs of an early winter, and the question that was discussed from dawn till dark, and far into the dark, was whether they would get out before the freeze-up or be compelled to abandon the steamboat and tramp out over the ice. There were irritating delays. Twice the engines broke down and had to be tinkered up, and each time there were snow flurries to warn them of the imminence of winter. Nine times the *W. H. Willis* essayed to ascend the Five Finger Rapids with her impaired machinery, and when she succeeded, she was four days behind her very liberal schedule. The question that then arose was whether or not the steamboat *Flora* would wait for her above the Box Cañon. The stretch of water between the head of the Box Cañon and the foot of the White Horse Rapids was unnavigable for steamboats, and passengers were transshipped at that point, walking around the rapids from one steamboat to the other. There were no telephones in the country, hence no way of informing the waiting *Flora* that the *Willis* was four days late, but coming.

When the *W. H. Willis* pulled into White Horse, it was learned that the *Flora* had waited three days over the limit, and had departed only a few hours before. Also, it was learned that she would tie up at Tagish Post till nine o'clock, Sunday morning. It was then four o'clock, Saturday afternoon. The pilgrims called a meeting. On board was a large Peterborough canoe, consigned to the police post at the head of Lake Bennett. They agreed to be responsible for it and to deliver it. Next, they called for volunteers. Two men were needed to make a race for the *Flora*. A score of men volunteered on the instant. Among them was Churchill, such being his nature that he volunteered before he thought of Bondell's gripsack. When this thought came to him, he began to hope that he would not be selected; but a man who had made a name as captain of a college football eleven, as a president of an athletic club, as a dog-musher and a stampeder in the Yukon, and, moreover, who possessed such shoulders as he, had no right to avoid the honour. It was thrust upon him and upon a gigantic German, Nick Antonsen.

While a crowd of the pilgrims, the canoe on their shoulders, started on a trot over the portage, Churchill ran to his state-room. He turned the contents of the clothes-bag on the floor and caught up the grip, with the intention of entrusting it to the man next door. Then the thought smote him that it was not his grip, and that he had no right to let it out of his possession. So he dashed ashore with it and ran up the portage changing it often from one hand to the other, and wondering if it really did not weigh more than forty pounds.

It was half-past four in the afternoon when the two men started. The current of the Thirty Mile River was so strong that rarely could they use the paddles. It was out on one bank with a tow-line over the shoulders, stumbling over the rocks, forcing a way through the under-brush, slipping at times and falling into the water, wading often up to the knees and waist; and then, when an insurmountable bluff was encountered, it was into the canoe, out paddles, and a wild and losing dash across the current to the other bank, in paddles, over the side, and out tow-line again. It was exhausting work. Antonsen toiled like the giant he was, uncomplaining, persistent, but driven to his utmost by the powerful body and indomitable brain of Churchill. They never paused for rest. It was go, go, and keep on going. A crisp wind blew down the river, freezing their hands and making it imperative, from time to time, to beat the blood back into the numbed fingers.

As night came on, they were compelled to trust to luck. They fell repeatedly on the untraveled banks and tore their clothing to shreds in the underbrush they could not see. Both men were badly scratched and bleeding. A dozen times, in their wild dashes from bank to bank, they struck snags and were capsized. The first time this happened, Churchill dived and groped in three feet of water for the gripsack. He lost half an hour in recovering it, and after that it was carried securely lashed to the canoe. As long as the canoe floated it was safe. Antonsen jeered at the grip, and toward morning began to curse it; but Churchill vouchsafed no explanations.

Their delays and mischances were endless. On one swift bend, around which poured a healthy young rapid, they lost two hours, making a score of attempts and capsizing twice. At this point, on both banks, were precipitous bluffs, rising out of deep water, and along which they could neither tow nor pole, while they could not gain with the paddles against the current. At each attempt they strained to the utmost with the paddles, and each time, with heads nigh to bursting from the effort, they were played out and swept back. They succeeded finally by an accident. In the swiftest current, near the end of another failure, a freak of the current sheered the canoe out of Churchill's control and flung it against the bluff. Churchill made a blind leap at the bluff and landed in a crevice. Holding on with one hand, he held the swamped canoe with the other till Antonsen dragged himself out of the water. Then they pulled the canoe out and rested. A fresh start at this crucial point took them by. They landed on the bank above and plunged immediately ashore and into the brush with the tow-line.

Daylight found them far below Tagish Post. At nine o'clock Sunday morning they could hear the *Flora* whistling her departure. And when, at ten o'clock, they dragged themselves in to the Post, they could barely see the *Flora's* smoke far to the southward. It was a pair of worn-out tatterdemalions that Captain Jones of the Mounted Police welcomed and fed, and he afterward averred that they possessed two of the most tremendous appetites he had ever observed. They lay down and slept in their wet rags by the stove. At the end of two hours Churchill got up, carried Bondell's grip, which he had used for a pillow, down to the canoe, kicked Antonsen awake, and started in pursuit of the *Flora*.

"There's no telling what might happen—machinery break down, or something," was his reply to Captain Jones's expostulations. "I'm going to catch that steamer and send her back for the boys."

Tagish Lake was white with a fall gale that blew in their teeth. Big, swinging seas rushed upon the canoe, compelling one man to bale and leaving one man to paddle. Headway could not be made. They ran along the shallow shore and went overboard, one man ahead on the tow-line, the other shoving on the canoe. They fought the gale up to their waists in the icy water, often up to their necks, often over their heads and buried by the big, crested waves. There was no rest, never a moment's pause from the cheerless, heart-breaking battle. That night, at the head of Tagish Lake, in the thick of a driving snow-squall, they overhauled the *Flora*. Antonsen fell on board, lay where he had fallen, and snored. Churchill looked like a wild man. His clothes barely clung to him. His face was iced up and swollen from the protracted effort of twenty-four hours, while his hands were so swollen that he could not close the fingers. As for his feet, it was an agony to stand upon them.

The captain of the *Flora* was loth to go back to White Horse. Churchill was persistent and imperative; the captain was stubborn. He pointed out finally that nothing was to be gained by going back, because the only ocean steamer at Dyea, the *Athenian*, was to sail on Tuesday morning, and that he could not make the back trip to White Horse and bring up the stranded pilgrims in time to make the connection.

"What time does the *Athenian* sail?" Churchill demanded.

"Seven o'clock, Tuesday morning."

"All right," Churchill said, at the same time kicking a tattoo on the ribs of the snoring Antonsen. "You go back to White Home. We'll go ahead and hold the *Athenian*."

Antonsen, stupid with sleep, not yet clothed in his waking mind, was bundled into the canoe, and did not realize what had happened till he was drenched with the icy spray of a big sea, and heard Churchill snarling at him through the darkness:—

"Paddle, can't you! Do you want to be swamped?"

Daylight found them at Caribou Crossing, the wind dying down, and Antonsen too far gone to dip a paddle. Churchill grounded the canoe on a quiet beach, where they slept. He took the precaution of twisting his arm under the weight of his head. Every few minutes the pain of the pent circulation aroused him, whereupon he would look at his watch and twist the other arm under his head. At the end of two hours he fought with Antonsen to rouse him. Then they started. Lake Bennett, thirty miles in length, was like a millpond; but, half way across, a gale from the south smote them and turned the water white. Hour after hour they repeated the struggle on Tagish, over the side, pulling and shoving on the canoe, up to their waists and necks, and over their heads, in the icy water; toward the last the good-natured giant played completely out. Churchill drove him mercilessly; but when he pitched forward and bade fair to drown in three feet of water, the other dragged him into the canoe. After that, Churchill fought on alone, arriving at the police post at the head of Bennett in the early afternoon. He tried to help Antonsen out of the canoe, but failed. He listened to the exhausted man's heavy breathing, and envied him when he thought of what he himself had yet to undergo. Antonsen could lie there and sleep; but he, behind time, must go on over mighty Chilcoot and down to the sea. The real struggle lay before him, and he almost regretted the strength that resided in his frame because of the torment it could inflict upon that frame.

Churchill pulled the canoe up on the beach, seized Bondell's grip, and started on a limping dog-trot for the police post.

"There's a canoe down there, consigned to you from Dawson," he hurled at the officer who answered his knock. "And there's a man in it pretty near dead. Nothing serious; only played out. Take care of him. I've got to rush. Good-bye. Want to catch the *Athenian*."

A mile portage connected Lake Bennett and Lake Linderman, and his last words he flung back after him as he resumed the trot. It was a very painful trot, but he clenched his teeth and kept on, forgetting his pain most of the time in the fervent heat with which he regarded the gripsack. It was a severe handicap. He swung it from one hand to the other, and back again. He tucked it under his arm. He threw one hand over the opposite shoulder, and the bag bumped and pounded on his back as he ran along. He could scarcely hold it in his bruised and swollen fingers, and several times he dropped it. Once, in changing from one hand to the other, it escaped his clutch and fell in front of him, tripped him up, and threw him violently to the ground.

At the far end of the portage he bought an old set of pack-straps for a dollar, and in them he swung the grip. Also, he chartered a launch to run him the six miles to the upper end of Lake Linderman, where he arrived at four in the afternoon. The *Athenian* was to sail from Dyea next morning at seven. Dyea was twenty-eight miles away, and between towered Chilcoot. He sat down to adjust his foot-gear for the long climb, and woke up. He had dozed the instant he sat down, though he had not slept thirty seconds. He was afraid his next doze might be longer, so he finished fixing his foot-gear standing up. Even then he was overpowered for a fleeting moment. He experienced the flash of unconsciousness; becoming aware of it, in mid-air, as his relaxed body was sinking to the ground and as he caught himself together, he stiffened his muscles with a spasmodic wrench, and escaped the fall. The sudden jerk back to consciousness left him sick and trembling. He beat his head with the heel of his hand, knocking wakefulness into the numbed brain.

Jack Burns's pack-train was starting back light for Crater Lake, and Churchill was invited to a mule. Burns wanted to put the gripsack on another animal, but Churchill held on to it, carrying it on his saddle-pommel. But he dozed, and the grip persisted in dropping off the pommel, one side or the other, each time wakening him with a sickening start. Then, in the early darkness, Churchill's mule brushed him against a projecting branch that laid his cheek open. To cap it, the mule blundered off the trail and fell, throwing rider and gripsack out upon the rocks. After that, Churchill walked, or stumbled rather, over the apology for a trail, leading the mule. Stray and awful odours, drifting from each side of the trail, told of the horses that had died in the rush for gold. But he did not mind. He was too sleepy. By the time Long Lake was reached, however, he had recovered from his sleepiness; and at Deep Lake he resigned the gripsack to Burns. But thereafter, by the light of the dim stars, he kept his eyes on Burns. There were not going to be any accidents with that bag.

At Crater Lake, the pack-train went into camp, and Churchill, slinging the grip on his back, started the steep climb for the summit. For the first time, on that precipitous wall, he realized how tired he was. He crept and crawled like a crab, burdened by the weight of his limbs. A distinct and painful effort of will was required each time he lifted a foot. An hallucination came to him that he was shod with lead, like a deep-sea diver, and it was all he could do to resist the desire to reach down and feel the lead. As for Bondell's gripsack, it was inconceivable that forty pounds could weigh so much. It pressed him down like a mountain, and he looked back with unbelief to the year before, when he had climbed that same pass with a hundred and fifty pounds on his back. If those loads had weighed a hundred and fifty pounds, then Bondell's grip weighed five hundred.

The first rise of the divide from Crater Lake was across a small glacier. Here was a well-defined trail. But above the glacier, which was also above timber-line, was naught but a chaos of naked rock and enormous boulders. There was no way of seeing the trail in the darkness, and he blundered on, paying thrice the ordinary exertion for all that he accomplished. He won the summit in the thick of howling wind and driving snow, providentially stumbling upon a small, deserted tent, into which he crawled. There he found and bolted some ancient fried potatoes and half a dozen raw eggs.

When the snow ceased and the wind eased down, he began the almost impossible descent. There was no trail, and he stumbled and blundered, often finding himself, at the last moment, on the edge of rocky walls and steep slopes the depth of which he had no way of judging. Part way down, the stars clouded over again, and in the consequent obscurity he slipped and rolled and slid for a hundred feet, landing bruised and bleeding on the bottom of a large shallow hole. From all about him arose the stench of dead horses. The hole was handy to the trail, and the packers had made a practice of tumbling into it their broken and dying animals. The stench overpowered him, making him deadly sick, and as in a nightmare he scrambled out. Half-way up, he recollected Bondell's gripsack. It had fallen into the hole with him; the pack-strap had evidently broken, and he had forgotten it. Back he went into the pestilential charnel-pit, where he crawled around on hands and knees and groped for half an hour. Altogether he encountered and counted seventeen dead horses (and one horse still alive that he shot with his revolver) before he found Bondell's grip. Looking back upon a life that had not been without valour and achievement, he unhesitatingly declared to himself that this return after the grip was the most heroic act he had ever performed. So heroic was it that he was twice on the verge of fainting before he crawled out of the hole.

By the time he had descended to the Scales, the steep pitch of Chilcoot was past, and the way became easier. Not that it was an easy way, however, in the best of places; but it became a really possible trail, along which he could have made good time if he had not been worn out, if he had had light with which to pick his steps, and if it had not been for Bondell's grip-sack. To him, in his exhausted condition, it was the last straw. Having barely strength to carry himself along, the additional weight of the grip was sufficient to throw him nearly every time he tripped or stumbled. And when he escaped tripping, branches reached out in the darkness, hooked the grip between his shoulders, and held him back.

His mind was made up that if he missed the *Athenian* it would be the fault of the gripsack. In fact, only two things remained in his consciousness—Bondell's grip and the steamer. He knew only those two things, and they became identified, in a way, with some stern mission upon which he had journeyed and toiled for centuries. He walked and struggled on as in a dream. As part of the dream was his arrival at Sheep Camp. He stumbled into a saloon, slid his shoulders out of the straps, and started to deposit the grip at his feet. But it slipped from his fingers and struck the floor with a heavy thud that was not unnoticed by two men who were just leaving. Churchill drank a glass of whisky, told the barkeeper to call him in ten minutes, and sat down, his feet on the grip, his head on his knees.

So badly did his misused body stiffen, that when he was called it required another ten minutes and a second glass of whisky to unbend his joints and limber up the muscles.

"Hey not that way!" the barkeeper shouted, and then went after him and started him through the darkness toward Canyon City. Some little husk of inner consciousness told Churchill that the direction was right, and, still as in a dream, he took the cañon trail. He did not know what warned him, but after what seemed several centuries of travelling, he sensed danger and drew his revolver. Still in the dream, he saw two men step out and heard them halt him. His revolver went off four times, and he saw the flashes and heard the explosions of their revolvers. Also, he was aware that he had been hit in the thigh. He saw one man go down, and, as the other came for him, he smashed him a straight blow with the heavy revolver full in the face. Then he turned and ran. He came from the dream shortly afterward, to find himself plunging down the trail at a limping lope. His first thought was for the gripsack. It was still on his back. He was convinced that what had happened was a dream till he felt for his revolver and found it gone. Next he became aware of a sharp stinging of his thigh, and after investigating, he found his hand warm with blood. It was a superficial wound, but it was incontestable. He became wider awake, and kept up the lumbering run to Canyon City.

He found a man, with a team of horses and a wagon, who got out of bed and harnessed up for twenty dollars. Churchill crawled in on the wagon-bed and slept, the gripsack still on his back. It was a rough ride, over water-washed boulders down the Dyea Valley; but he roused only when the wagon hit the highest places. Any altitude of his body above the wagon-bed of less than a foot did not faze him. The last mile was smooth going, and he slept soundly.

He came to in the grey dawn, the driver shaking him savagely and howling into his ear that the *Athenian* was gone. Churchill looked blankly at the deserted harbour.

"There's a smoke over at Skaguay," the man said.

Churchill's eyes were too swollen to see that far, but he said: "It's she. Get me a boat."

The driver was obliging and found a skiff, and a man to row it for ten dollars, payment in advance. Churchill paid, and was helped into the skiff. It was beyond him to get in by himself. It was six miles to Skaguay, and he had a blissful thought of sleeping those six miles. But the man did not know how to row, and Churchill took the oars and toiled for a few more centuries. He never knew six longer and more excruciating miles. A snappy little breeze blew up the inlet and held him back. He had a gone feeling at the pit of the stomach, and suffered from faintness and numbness. At his command, the man took the baler and threw salt water into his face.

The *Athenian's* anchor was up-and-down when they came alongside, and Churchill was at the end of his last remnant of strength.

"Stop her! Stop her!" he shouted hoarsely.

"Important message! Stop her!"

Then he dropped his chin on his chest and slept. When half a dozen men started to carry him up the gang-plank, he awoke, reached for the grip, and clung to it like a drowning man.

On deck he became a center of horror and curiosity. The clothing in which he had left White Horse was represented by a few rags, and he was as frayed as his clothing. He had travelled for fifty-five hours at the top notch of endurance. He had slept six hours in that time, and he was twenty pounds lighter than when he started. Face and hands and body were scratched and bruised, and he could scarcely see. He tried to stand up, but failed, sprawling out on the deck, hanging on to the gripsack, and delivering his message.

"Now, put me to bed," he finished; "I'll eat when I wake up."

They did him honour, carrying him down in his rags and dirt and depositing him and Bondell's grip in the bridal chamber, which was the biggest and most luxurious state-room in the ship. Twice he slept the clock around, and he had bathed and shaved and eaten and was leaning over the rail smoking a cigar when the two hundred pilgrims from White Horse came alongside.

By the time the *Athenian* arrived in Seattle, Churchill had fully recuperated, and he went ashore with Bondell's grip in his hand. He felt proud of that grip. To him it stood for achievement and integrity and trust. "I've delivered the goods," was the way he expressed these various high terms to himself. It was early in the evening, and he went straight to Bondell's home. Louis Bondell was glad to see him, shaking hands with both hands at the same time and dragging him into the house.

"Oh, thanks, old man; it was good of you to bring it out," Bondell said when he received the gripsack.

He tossed it carelessly upon a couch, and Churchill noted with an appreciative eye the rebound of its weight from the springs. Bondell was volleying him with questions.

"How did you make out? How're the boys? What became of Bill Smithers? Is Del Bishop still with Pierce? Did he sell my dogs? How did Sulphur Bottom show up? You're looking fine. What steamer did you come out on?"

To all of which Churchill gave answer, till half an hour had gone by and the first lull in the conversation had arrived.

"Hadn't you better take a look at it?" he suggested, nodding his head at the gripsack.

"Oh, it's all right," Bondell answered. "Did Mitchell's dump turn out as much as he expected?"

"I think you'd better look at it," Churchill insisted. "When I deliver a thing, I want to be satisfied that it's all right. There's always the chance that somebody might have got into it when I was asleep, or something."

"It's nothing important, old man," Bondell answered, with a laugh.

"Nothing important," Churchill echoed in a faint, small voice. Then he spoke with decision: "Louis, what's in that bag? I want to know."

Louis looked at him curiously, then left the room and returned with a bunch of keys. He inserted his hand and drew out a heavy Colt's revolver. Next came out a few boxes of ammunition for the revolver and several boxes of Winchester cartridges.

Churchill took the gripsack and looked into it. Then he turned it upside down and shook it gently.

"The gun's all rusted," Bondell said. "Must have been out in the rain."

"Yes," Churchill answered. "Too bad it got wet. I guess I was a bit careless."

He got up and went outside. Ten minutes later Louis Bondell went out and found him on the steps, sitting down, elbows on knees and chin on hands, gazing steadfastly out into the darkness.

TO BUILD A FIRE

DAY HAD BROKEN cold and grey, exceedingly cold and grey, when the man turned aside from the main Yukon trail and climbed the high earth-bank, where a dim and little-travelled trail led eastward through the fat spruce timberland. It was a steep bank, and he paused for breath at the top, excusing the act to himself by looking at his watch. It was nine o'clock. There was no sun nor hint of sun, though there was not a cloud in the sky. It was a clear day, and yet there seemed an intangible pall over the face of things, a subtle gloom that made the day dark, and that was due to the absence of sun. This fact did not worry the man. He was used to the lack of sun. It had been days since he had seen the sun, and he knew that a few more days must pass before that cheerful orb, due south, would just peep above the sky-line and dip immediately from view.

The man flung a look back along the way he had come. The Yukon lay a mile wide and hidden under three feet of ice. On top of this ice were as many feet of snow. It was all pure white, rolling in gentle undulations where the ice-jams of the freeze-up had formed. North and south, as far as his eye could see, it was unbroken white, save for a dark hair-line that curved and twisted from around the spruce-covered island to the south, and that curved and twisted away into the north, where it disappeared behind another spruce-covered island. This dark hair-line was the trail—the main trail—that led south five hundred miles to the Chilcoot Pass, Dyea, and salt water; and that led north seventy miles to Dawson, and still on to the north a thousand miles to Nulato, and finally to St. Michael on Bering Sea, a thousand miles and half a thousand more.

But all this—the mysterious, far-reaching hairline trail, the absence of sun from the sky, the tremendous cold, and the strangeness and weirdness of it all—made no impression on the man. It was not because he was long used to it. He was a new-comer in the land, a *chechaquo*, and this was his first winter. The trouble with him was that he was without imagination. He was quick and alert in the things of life, but only in the things, and not in the significances. Fifty degrees below zero meant eighty odd degrees of frost. Such fact impressed him as being cold and uncomfortable, and that was all. It did not lead him to meditate upon his frailty as a creature of temperature, and upon man's frailty in general, able only to live within certain narrow limits of heat and cold; and from there on it did not lead him to the conjectural field of immortality and man's place in the universe. Fifty degrees below zero stood for a bite of frost that hurt and that must be guarded against by the use of mittens, ear-flaps, warm moccasins, and thick socks. Fifty degrees below zero was to him just precisely fifty degrees below zero. That there should be anything more to it than that was a thought that never entered his head.

As he turned to go on, he spat speculatively. There was a sharp, explosive crackle that startled him. He spat again. And again, in the air, before it could fall to the snow, the spittle crackled. He knew that at fifty below spittle crackled on the snow, but this spittle had crackled in the air. Undoubtedly it was colder than fifty below—how much colder he did not know. But the temperature did not matter. He was bound for the old claim on the left fork of Henderson Creek, where the boys were already. They had come over across the divide from the Indian Creek country, while he had come the roundabout way to take a look at the possibilities of getting out logs in the spring from the islands in the Yukon. He would be in to camp by six o'clock; a bit after dark, it was true, but the boys would be there, a fire would be going, and a hot supper would be ready. As for lunch, he pressed his hand against the protruding bundle under his jacket. It was also under his shirt, wrapped up in a handkerchief and lying against the naked skin. It was the only way to keep the biscuits from freezing. He smiled agreeably to himself as he thought of those biscuits, each cut open and sopped in bacon grease, and each enclosing a generous slice of fried bacon.

He plunged in among the big spruce trees. The trail was faint. A foot of snow had fallen since the last sled had passed over, and he was glad he was without a sled, travelling light. In fact, he carried nothing but the lunch wrapped in the handkerchief. He was surprised, however, at the cold. It certainly was cold, he concluded, as he rubbed his numbed nose and cheek-bones with his mittened hand. He was a warm-whiskered man, but the hair on his face did not protect the high cheek-bones and the eager nose that thrust itself aggressively into the frosty air.

At the man's heels trotted a dog, a big native husky, the proper wolf-dog, grey-coated and without any visible or temperamental difference from its brother, the wild wolf. The animal was depressed by the tremendous cold. It knew that it was no time for travelling. Its instinct told it a truer tale than was told to the man by the man's judgment. In reality, it was not merely colder than fifty below zero; it was colder than sixty below, than seventy below. It was seventy-five below zero. Since the freezing-point is thirty-two above zero, it meant that one hundred and seven degrees of frost obtained. The dog did not know anything about thermometers. Possibly in its brain there was no sharp consciousness of a condition of very cold such as was in the man's brain. But the brute had its instinct. It experienced a vague but menacing apprehension that subdued it and made it slink along at the man's heels, and that made it question eagerly every unwonted movement of the man as if expecting him to go into camp or to seek shelter somewhere and build a fire. The dog had learned fire, and it wanted fire, or else to burrow under the snow and cuddle its warmth away from the air.

The frozen moisture of its breathing had settled on its fur in a fine powder of frost, and especially were its jowls, muzzle, and eyelashes whitened by its crystalled breath. The man's red beard and moustache were likewise frosted, but more solidly, the deposit taking the form of ice and increasing with every warm, moist breath he exhaled. Also, the man was chewing tobacco, and the muzzle of ice held his lips so rigidly that he was unable to clear his chin when he expelled the juice. The result was that a crystal beard of the colour and solidity of amber was increasing its length on his chin. If he fell down it would shatter itself, like glass, into brittle fragments. But he did not mind the appendage. It was the penalty all tobacco-chewers paid in that country, and he had been out before in two cold snaps. They had not been so cold as this, he knew, but by the spirit thermometer at Sixty Mile he knew they had been registered at fifty below and at fifty-five.

He held on through the level stretch of woods for several miles, crossed a wide flat of nigger-heads, and dropped down a bank to the frozen bed of a small stream. This was Henderson Creek, and he knew he was ten miles from the forks. He looked at his watch. It was ten o'clock. He was making four miles an hour, and he calculated that he would arrive at the forks at half-past twelve. He decided to celebrate that event by eating his lunch there.

The dog dropped in again at his heels, with a tail drooping discouragement, as the man swung along the creek-bed. The furrow of the old sled-trail was plainly visible, but a dozen inches of snow covered the marks of the last runners. In a month no man had come up or down that silent creek. The man held steadily on. He was not much given to thinking, and just then particularly he had nothing to think about save that he would eat lunch at the forks and that at six o'clock he would be in camp with the boys. There was nobody to talk to and, had there been, speech would have been impossible because of the ice-muzzle on his mouth. So he continued monotonously to chew tobacco and to increase the length of his amber beard.

Once in a while the thought reiterated itself that it was very cold and that he had never experienced such cold. As he walked along he rubbed his cheek-bones and nose with the back of his mittened hand. He did this automatically, now and again changing hands. But rub as he would, the instant he stopped his cheek-bones went numb, and the following instant the end of his nose went numb. He was sure to frost his cheeks; he knew that, and experienced a pang of regret that he had not devised a nose-strap of the sort Bud wore in cold snaps. Such a strap passed across the cheeks, as well, and saved them. But it didn't matter much, after all. What were frosted cheeks? A bit painful, that was all; they were never serious.

Empty as the man's mind was of thoughts, he was keenly observant, and he noticed the changes in the creek, the curves and bends and timber-jams, and always he sharply noted where he placed his feet. Once, coming around a bend, he shied abruptly, like a startled horse, curved away from the place where he had been walking, and retreated several paces back along the trail. The creek he knew was frozen clear to the bottom—no creek could contain water in that arctic winter—but he knew also that there were springs that bubbled out from the hillsides and ran along under the snow and on top the ice of the creek. He knew that the coldest snaps never froze these springs, and he knew likewise their danger. They were traps. They hid pools of water under the snow that might be three inches deep, or three feet. Sometimes a skin of ice half an inch thick covered them, and in turn was covered by the snow. Sometimes there were alternate layers of water and ice-skin, so that when one broke through he kept on breaking through for a while, sometimes wetting himself to the waist.

That was why he had shied in such panic. He had felt the give under his feet and heard the crackle of a snow-hidden ice-skin. And to get his feet wet in such a temperature meant trouble and danger. At the very least it meant delay, for he would be forced to stop and build a fire, and under its protection to bare his feet while he dried his socks and moccasins. He stood and studied the creek-bed and its banks, and decided that the flow of water came from the right. He reflected awhile, rubbing his nose and cheeks, then skirted to the left, stepping gingerly and testing the footing for each step. Once clear of the danger, he took a fresh chew of tobacco and swung along at his four-mile gait.

In the course of the next two hours he came upon several similar traps. Usually the snow above the hidden pools had a sunken, candied appearance that advertised the danger. Once again, however, he had a close call; and once, suspecting danger, he compelled the dog to go on in front. The dog did not want to go. It hung back until the man shoved it forward, and then it went quickly across the white, unbroken surface. Suddenly it broke through, floundered to one side, and got away to firmer footing. It had wet its forefeet and legs, and almost immediately the water that clung to it turned to ice. It made quick efforts to lick the ice off its legs, then dropped down in the snow and began to bite out the ice that had formed between the toes. This was a matter of instinct. To permit the ice to remain would mean sore feet. It did not know this. It merely obeyed the mysterious prompting that arose from the deep crypts of its being. But the man knew, having achieved a judgment on the subject, and he removed the mitten from his right hand and helped tear out the ice-particles. He did not expose his fingers more than a minute, and was astonished at the swift numbness that smote them. It certainly was cold. He pulled on the mitten hastily, and beat the hand savagely across his chest.

At twelve o'clock the day was at its brightest. Yet the sun was too far south on its winter journey to clear the horizon. The bulge of the earth intervened between it and Henderson Creek, where the man walked under a clear sky at noon and cast no shadow. At half-past twelve, to the minute, he arrived at the forks of the creek. He was pleased at the speed he had made. If he kept it up, he would certainly be with the boys by six. He unbuttoned his jacket and shirt and drew forth his lunch. The action consumed no more than a quarter of a minute, yet in that brief moment the numbness laid hold of the exposed fingers. He did not put the mitten on, but, instead, struck the fingers a dozen sharp smashes against his leg. Then he sat down on a snow-covered log to eat. The sting that followed upon the striking of his fingers against his leg ceased so quickly that he was startled, he had had no chance to take a bite of biscuit. He struck the fingers repeatedly and returned them to the mitten, baring the other hand for the purpose of eating. He tried to take a mouthful, but the ice-muzzle prevented. He had forgotten to build a fire and thaw out. He chuckled at his foolishness, and as he chuckled he noted the numbness creeping into the exposed fingers. Also, he noted that the stinging which had first come to his toes when he sat down was already passing away. He wondered whether the toes were warm or numbed. He moved them inside the moccasins and decided that they were numbed.

He pulled the mitten on hurriedly and stood up. He was a bit frightened. He stamped up and down until the stinging returned into the feet. It certainly was cold, was his thought. That man from Sulphur Creek had spoken the truth when telling how cold it sometimes got in the country. And he had laughed at him at the time! That showed one must not be too sure of things. There was no mistake about it, it was cold. He strode up and down, stamping his feet and threshing his arms, until reassured by the returning warmth. Then he got out matches and proceeded to make a fire. From the undergrowth, where high water of the previous spring had lodged a supply of seasoned twigs, he got his firewood. Working carefully from a small beginning, he soon had a roaring fire, over which he thawed the ice from his face and in the protection of which he ate his biscuits. For the moment the cold of space was outwitted. The dog took satisfaction in the fire, stretching out close enough for warmth and far enough away to escape being singed.

When the man had finished, he filled his pipe and took his comfortable time over a smoke. Then he pulled on his mittens, settled the ear-flaps of his cap firmly about his ears, and took the creek trail up the left fork. The dog was disappointed and yearned back toward the fire. This man did not know cold. Possibly all the generations of his ancestry had been ignorant of cold, of real cold, of cold one hundred and seven degrees below freezing-point. But the dog knew; all its ancestry knew, and it had inherited the knowledge. And it knew that it was not good to walk abroad in such fearful cold. It was the time to lie snug in a hole in the snow and wait for a curtain of cloud to be drawn across the face of outer space whence this cold came. On the other hand, there was keen intimacy between the dog and the man. The one was the toil-slave of the other, and the only caresses it had ever received were the caresses of the whip-lash and of harsh and menacing throat-sounds that threatened the whip-lash. So the dog made no effort to communicate its apprehension to the man. It was not concerned in the welfare of the man; it was for its own sake that it yearned back toward the fire. But the man whistled, and spoke to it with the sound of whip-lashes, and the dog swung in at the man's heels and followed after.

The man took a chew of tobacco and proceeded to start a new amber beard. Also, his moist breath quickly powdered with white his moustache, eyebrows, and lashes. There did not seem to be so many springs on the left fork of the Henderson, and for half an hour the man saw no signs of any. And then it happened. At a place where there were no signs, where the soft, unbroken snow seemed to advertise solidity beneath, the man broke through. It was not deep. He wetted himself half-way to the knees before he floundered out to the firm crust.

He was angry, and cursed his luck aloud. He had hoped to get into camp with the boys at six o'clock, and this would delay him an hour, for he would have to build a fire and dry out his foot-gear. This was imperative at that low temperature—he knew that much; and he turned aside to the bank, which he climbed. On top, tangled in the underbrush about the trunks of several small spruce trees, was a high-water deposit of dry firewood—sticks and twigs principally, but also larger portions of seasoned branches and fine, dry, last-year's grasses. He threw down several large pieces on top of the snow. This served for a foundation and prevented the young flame from drowning itself in the snow it otherwise would melt. The flame he got by touching a match to a small shred of birch-bark that he took from his pocket. This burned even more readily than paper. Placing it on the foundation, he fed the young flame with wisps of dry grass and with the tiniest dry twigs.

He worked slowly and carefully, keenly aware of his danger. Gradually, as the flame grew stronger, he increased the size of the twigs with which he fed it. He squatted in the snow, pulling the twigs out from their entanglement in the brush and feeding directly to the flame. He knew there must be no failure. When it is seventy-five below zero, a man must not fail in his first attempt to build a fire—that is, if his feet are wet. If his feet are dry, and he fails, he can run along the trail for half a mile and restore his circulation. But the circulation of wet and freezing feet cannot be restored by running when it is seventy-five below. No matter how fast he runs, the wet feet will freeze the harder.

All this the man knew. The old-timer on Sulphur Creek had told him about it the previous fall, and now he was appreciating the advice. Already all sensation had gone out of his feet. To build the fire he had been forced to remove his mittens, and the fingers had quickly gone numb. His pace of four miles an hour had kept his heart pumping blood to the surface of his body and to all the extremities. But the instant he stopped, the action of the pump eased down. The cold of space smote the unprotected tip of the planet, and he, being on that unprotected tip, received the full force of the blow. The blood of his body recoiled before it. The blood was alive, like the dog, and like the dog it wanted to hide away and cover itself up from the fearful cold. So long as he walked four miles an hour, he pumped that blood, willy-nilly, to the surface; but now it ebbed away and sank down into the recesses of his body. The extremities were the first to feel its absence. His wet feet froze the faster, and his exposed fingers numbed the faster, though they had not yet begun to freeze. Nose and cheeks were already freezing, while the skin of all his body chilled as it lost its blood.

But he was safe. Toes and nose and cheeks would be only touched by the frost, for the fire was beginning to burn with strength. He was feeding it with twigs the size of his finger. In another minute he would be able to feed it with branches the size of his wrist, and then he could remove his wet foot-gear, and, while it dried, he could keep his naked feet warm by the fire, rubbing them at first, of course, with snow. The fire was a success. He was safe. He remembered the advice of the old-timer on Sulphur Creek, and smiled. The old-timer had been very serious in laying down the law that no man must travel alone in the Klondike after fifty below. Well, here he was; he had had the accident; he was alone; and he had saved himself. Those old-timers were rather womanish, some of them, he thought. All a man had to do was to keep his head, and he was all right. Any man who was a man could travel alone. But it was surprising, the rapidity with which his cheeks and nose were freezing. And he had not thought his fingers could go lifeless in so short a time. Lifeless they were, for he could scarcely make them move together to grip a twig, and they seemed remote from his body and from him. When he touched a twig, he had to look and see whether or not he had hold of it. The wires were pretty well down between him and his finger-ends.

All of which counted for little. There was the fire, snapping and crackling and promising life with every dancing flame. He started to untie his moccasins. They were coated with ice; the thick German socks were like sheaths of iron half-way to the knees; and the moccasin strings were like rods of steel all twisted and knotted as by some conflagration. For a moment he tugged with his numbed fingers, then, realizing the folly of it, he drew his sheath-knife.

But before he could cut the strings, it happened. It was his own fault or, rather, his mistake. He should not have built the fire under the spruce tree. He should have built it in the open. But it had been easier to pull the twigs from the brush and drop them directly on the fire. Now the tree under which he had done this carried a weight of snow on its boughs. No wind had blown for weeks, and each bough was fully freighted. Each time he had pulled a twig he had communicated a slight agitation to the tree—an imperceptible agitation, so far as he was concerned, but an agitation sufficient to bring about the disaster. High up in the tree one bough capsized its load of snow. This fell on the boughs beneath, capsizing them. This process continued, spreading out and involving the whole tree. It grew like an avalanche, and it descended without warning upon the man and the fire, and the fire was blotted out! Where it had burned was a mantle of fresh and disordered snow.

The man was shocked. It was as though he had just heard his own sentence of death. For a moment he sat and stared at the spot where the fire had been. Then he grew very calm. Perhaps the old-timer on Sulphur Creek was right. If he had only had a trail-mate he would have been in no danger now. The trail-mate could have built the fire. Well, it was up to him to build the fire over again, and this second time there must be no failure. Even if he succeeded, he would most likely lose some toes. His feet must be badly frozen by now, and there would be some time before the second fire was ready.

Such were his thoughts, but he did not sit and think them. He was busy all the time they were passing through his mind, he made a new foundation for a fire, this time in the open; where no treacherous tree could blot it out. Next, he gathered dry grasses and tiny twigs from the high-water flotsam. He could not bring his fingers together to pull them out, but he was able to gather them by the handful. In this way he got many rotten twigs and bits of green moss that were undesirable, but it was the best he could do. He worked methodically, even collecting an armful of the larger branches to be used later when the fire gathered strength. And all the while the dog sat and watched him, a certain yearning wistfulness in its eyes, for it looked upon him as the fire-provider, and the fire was slow in coming.

When all was ready, the man reached in his pocket for a second piece of birch-bark. He knew the bark was there, and, though he could not feel it with his fingers, he could hear its crisp rustling as he fumbled for it. Try as he would, he could not clutch hold of it. And all the time, in his consciousness, was the knowledge that each instant his feet were freezing. This thought tended to put him in a panic, but he fought against it and kept calm. He pulled on his mittens with his teeth, and threshed his arms back and forth, beating his hands with all his might against his sides. He did this sitting down, and he stood up to do it; and all the while the dog sat in the snow, its wolf-brush of a tail curled around warmly over its forefeet, its sharp wolf-ears pricked forward intently as it watched the man. And the man as he beat and threshed with his arms and hands, felt a great surge of envy as he regarded the creature that was warm and secure in its natural covering.

After a time he was aware of the first far-away signals of sensation in his beaten fingers. The faint tingling grew stronger till it evolved into a stinging ache that was excruciating, but which the man hailed with satisfaction. He stripped the mitten from his right hand and fetched forth the birch-bark. The exposed fingers were quickly going numb again. Next he brought out his bunch of sulphur matches. But the tremendous cold had already driven the life out of his fingers. In his effort to separate one match from the others, the whole bunch fell in the snow. He tried to pick it out of the snow, but failed. The dead fingers could neither touch nor clutch. He was very careful. He drove the thought of his freezing feet; and nose, and cheeks, out of his mind, devoting his whole soul to the matches. He watched, using the sense of vision in place of that of touch, and when he saw his fingers on each side the bunch, he closed them—that is, he willed to close them, for the wires were drawn, and the fingers did not obey. He pulled the mitten on the right hand, and beat it fiercely against his knee. Then, with both mittened hands, he scooped the bunch of matches, along with much snow, into his lap. Yet he was no better off.

After some manipulation he managed to get the bunch between the heels of his mittened hands. In this fashion he carried it to his mouth. The ice crackled and snapped when by a violent effort he opened his mouth. He drew the lower jaw in, curled the upper lip out of the way, and scraped the bunch with his upper teeth in order to separate a match. He succeeded in getting one, which he dropped on his lap. He was no better off. He could not pick it up. Then he devised a way. He picked it up in his teeth and scratched it on his leg. Twenty times he scratched before he succeeded in lighting it. As it flamed he held it with his teeth to the birch-bark. But the burning brimstone went up his nostrils and into his lungs, causing him to cough spasmodically. The match fell into the snow and went out.

The old-timer on Sulphur Creek was right, he thought in the moment of controlled despair that ensued: after fifty below, a man should travel with a partner. He beat his hands, but failed in exciting any sensation. Suddenly he bared both hands, removing the mittens with his teeth. He caught the whole bunch between the heels of his hands. His arm-muscles not being frozen enabled him to press the hand-heels tightly against the matches. Then he scratched the bunch along his leg. It flared into flame, seventy sulphur matches at once! There was no wind to blow them out. He kept his head to one side to escape the strangling fumes, and held the blazing bunch to the birch-bark. As he so held it, he became aware of sensation in his hand. His flesh was burning. He could smell it. Deep down below the surface he could feel it. The sensation developed into pain that grew acute. And still he endured it, holding the flame of the matches clumsily to the bark that would not light readily because his own burning hands were in the way, absorbing most of the flame.

At last, when he could endure no more, he jerked his hands apart. The blazing matches fell sizzling into the snow, but the birch-bark was alight. He began laying dry grasses and the tiniest twigs on the flame. He could not pick and choose, for he had to lift the fuel between the heels of his hands. Small pieces of rotten wood and green moss clung to the twigs, and he bit them off as well as he could with his teeth. He cherished the flame carefully and awkwardly. It meant life, and it must not perish. The withdrawal of blood from the surface of his body now made him begin to shiver, and he grew more awkward. A large piece of green moss fell squarely on the little fire. He tried to poke it out with his fingers, but his shivering frame made him poke too far, and he disrupted the nucleus of the little fire, the burning grasses and tiny twigs separating and scattering. He tried to poke them together again, but in spite of the tenseness of the effort, his shivering got away with him, and the twigs were hopelessly scattered. Each twig gushed a puff of smoke and went out. The fire-provider had failed. As he looked apathetically about him, his eyes chanced on the dog, sitting across the ruins of the fire from him, in the snow, making restless, hunching movements, slightly lifting one forefoot and then the other, shifting its weight back and forth on them with wistful eagerness.

The sight of the dog put a wild idea into his head. He remembered the tale of the man, caught in a blizzard, who killed a steer and crawled inside the carcass, and so was saved. He would kill the dog and bury his hands in the warm body until the numbness went out of them. Then he could build another fire. He spoke to the dog, calling it to him; but in his voice was a strange note of fear that frightened the animal, who had never known the man to speak in such way before. Something was the matter, and its suspicious nature sensed danger,—it knew not what danger but somewhere, somehow, in its brain arose an apprehension of the man. It flattened its ears down at the sound of the man's voice, and its restless, hunching movements and the liftings and shiftings of its forefeet became more pronounced but it would not come to the man. He got on his hands and knees and crawled toward the dog. This unusual posture again excited suspicion, and the animal sidled mincingly away.

The man sat up in the snow for a moment and struggled for calmness. Then he pulled on his mittens, by means of his teeth, and got upon his feet. He glanced down at first in order to assure himself that he was really standing up, for the absence of sensation in his feet left him unrelated to the earth. His erect position in itself started to drive the webs of suspicion from the dog's mind; and when he spoke peremptorily, with the sound of whip-lashes in his voice, the dog rendered its customary allegiance and came to him. As it came within reaching distance, the man lost his control. His arms flashed out to the dog, and he experienced genuine surprise when he discovered that his hands could not clutch, that there was neither bend nor feeling in the lingers. He had forgotten for the moment that they were frozen and that they were freezing more and more. All this happened quickly, and before the animal could get away, he encircled its body with his arms. He sat down in the snow, and in this fashion held the dog, while it snarled and whined and struggled.

But it was all he could do, hold its body encircled in his arms and sit there. He realized that he could not kill the dog. There was no way to do it. With his helpless hands he could neither draw nor hold his sheath-knife nor throttle the animal. He released it, and it plunged wildly away, with tail between its legs, and still snarling. It halted forty feet away and surveyed him curiously, with ears sharply pricked forward. The man looked down at his hands in order to locate them, and found them hanging on the ends of his arms. It struck him as curious that one should have to use his eyes in order to find out where his hands were. He began threshing his arms back and forth, beating the mittened hands against his sides. He did this for five minutes, violently, and his heart pumped enough blood up to the surface to put a stop to his shivering. But no sensation was aroused in the hands. He had an impression that they hung like weights on the ends of his arms, but when he tried to run the impression down, he could not find it.

A certain fear of death, dull and oppressive, came to him. This fear quickly became poignant as he realized that it was no longer a mere matter of freezing his fingers and toes, or of losing his hands and feet, but that it was a matter of life and death with the chances against him. This threw him into a panic, and he turned and ran up the creek-bed along the old, dim trail. The dog joined in behind and kept up with him. He ran blindly, without intention, in fear such as he had never known in his life. Slowly, as he ploughed and floundered through the snow, he began to see things again—the banks of the creek, the old timber-jams, the leafless aspens, and the sky. The running made him feel better. He did not shiver. Maybe, if he ran on, his feet would thaw out; and, anyway, if he ran far enough, he would reach camp and the boys. Without doubt he would lose some fingers and toes and some of his face; but the boys would take care of him, and save the rest of him when he got there. And at the same time there was another thought in his mind that said he would never get to the camp and the boys; that it was too many miles away, that the freezing had too great a start on him, and that he would soon be stiff and dead. This thought he kept in the background and refused to consider. Sometimes it pushed itself forward and demanded to be heard, but he thrust it back and strove to think of other things.

It struck him as curious that he could run at all on feet so frozen that he could not feel them when they struck the earth and took the weight of his body. He seemed to himself to skim along above the surface and to have no connection with the earth. Somewhere he had once seen a winged Mercury, and he wondered if Mercury felt as he felt when skimming over the earth.

His theory of running until he reached camp and the boys had one flaw in it: he lacked the endurance. Several times he stumbled, and finally he tottered, crumpled up, and fell. When he tried to rise, he failed. He must sit and rest, he decided, and next time he would merely walk and keep on going. As he sat and regained his breath, he noted that he was feeling quite warm and comfortable. He was not shivering, and it even seemed that a warm glow had come to his chest and trunk. And yet, when he touched his nose or cheeks, there was no sensation. Running would not thaw them out. Nor would it thaw out his hands and feet. Then the thought came to him that the frozen portions of his body must be extending. He tried to keep this thought down, to forget it, to think of something else; he was aware of the panicky feeling that it caused, and he was afraid of the panic. But the thought asserted itself, and persisted, until it produced a vision of his body totally frozen. This was too much, and he made another wild run along the trail. Once he slowed down to a walk, but the thought of the freezing extending itself made him run again.

And all the time the dog ran with him, at his heels. When he fell down a second time, it curled its tail over its forefeet and sat in front of him facing him curiously eager and intent. The warmth and security of the animal angered him, and he cursed it till it flattened down its ears appeasingly. This time the shivering came more quickly upon the man. He was losing in his battle with the frost. It was creeping into his body from all sides. The thought of it drove him on, but he ran no more than a hundred feet, when he staggered and pitched head-long. It was his last panic. When he had recovered his breath and control, he sat up and entertained in his mind the conception of meeting death with dignity. However, the conception did not come to him in such terms. His idea of it was that he had been making a fool of himself, running around like a chicken with its head cut off—such was the simile that occurred to him. Well, he was bound to freeze anyway, and he might as well take it decently. With this new-found peace of mind came the first glimmerings of drowsiness. A good idea, he thought, to sleep off to death. It was like taking an anæsthetic. Freezing was not so bad as people thought. There were lots worse ways to die.

He pictured the boys finding his body next day. Suddenly he found himself with them, coming along the trail and looking for himself. And, still with them, he came around a turn in the trail and found himself lying in the snow. He did not belong with himself any more, for even then he was out of himself, standing with the boys and looking at himself in the snow. It certainly was cold, was his thought. When he got back to the States he could tell the folks what real cold was. He drifted on from this to a vision of the old-timer on Sulphur Creek. He could see him quite clearly, warm and comfortable, and smoking a pipe.

"You were right, old hoss; you were right," the man mumbled to the old-timer of Sulphur Creek.

Then the man drowsed off into what seemed to him the most comfortable and satisfying sleep he had ever known. The dog sat facing him and waiting. The brief day drew to a close in a long, slow twilight. There were no signs of a fire to be made, and, besides, never in the dog's experience had it known a man to sit like that in the snow and make no fire. As the twilight drew on, its eager yearning for the fire mastered it, and with a great lifting and shifting of forefeet, it whined softly, then flattened its ears down in anticipation of being chidden by the man. But the man remained silent. Later, the dog whined loudly. And still later it crept close to the man and caught the scent of death. This made the animal bristle and back away. A little longer it delayed, howling under the stars that leaped and danced and shone brightly in the cold sky. Then it turned and trotted up the trail in the direction of the camp it knew, where were the other food-providers and fire-providers.

THAT SPOT

I DON'T THINK MUCH of Stephen Mackaye any more, though I used to swear by him. I know that in those days I loved him more than my own brother. If ever I meet Stephen Mackaye again, I shall not be responsible for my actions. It passes beyond me that a man with whom I shared food and blanket, and with whom I mushed over the Chilcoot Trail, should turn out the way he did. I always sized Steve up as a square man, a kindly comrade, without an iota of anything vindictive or malicious in his nature. I shall never trust my judgment in men again. Why, I nursed that man through typhoid fever; we starved together on the headwaters of the Stewart; and he saved my life on the Little Salmon. And now, after the years we were together, all I can say of Stephen Mackaye is that he is the meanest man I ever knew.

We started for the Klondike in the fall rush of 1897, and we started too late to get over Chilcoot Pass before the freeze-up. We packed our outfit on our backs part way over, when the snow began to fly, and then we had to buy dogs in order to sled it the rest of the way. That was how we came to get that Spot. Dogs were high, and we paid one hundred and ten dollars for him. He looked worth it. I say *looked*, because he was one of the finest-appearing dogs I ever saw. He weighed sixty pounds, and he had all the lines of a good sled animal. We never could make out his breed. He wasn't husky, nor Malemute, nor Hudson Bay; he looked like all of them and he didn't look like any of them; and on top of it all he had some of the white man's dog in him, for on one side, in the thick of the mixed yellow-brown-red-and-dirty-white that was his prevailing colour, there was a spot of coal-black as big as a water-bucket. That was why we called him Spot.

He was a good looker all right. When he was in condition his muscles stood out in bunches all over him. And he was the strongest-looking brute I ever saw in Alaska, also the most intelligent-looking. To run your eyes over him, you'd think he could outpull three dogs of his own weight. Maybe he could, but I never saw it. His intelligence didn't run that way. He could steal and forage to perfection; he had an instinct that was positively gruesome for divining when work was to be done and for making a sneak accordingly; and for getting lost and not staying lost he was nothing short of inspired. But when it came to work, the way

349

that intelligence dribbled out of him and left him a mere clot of wobbling, stupid jelly would make your heart bleed.

There are times when I think it wasn't stupidity. Maybe, like some men I know, he was too wise to work. I shouldn't wonder if he put it all over us with that intelligence of his. Maybe he figured it all out and decided that a licking now and again and no work was a whole lot better than work all the time and no licking. He was intelligent enough for such a computation. I tell you, I've sat and looked into that dog's eyes till the shivers ran up and down my spine and the marrow crawled like yeast, what of the intelligence I saw shining out. I can't express myself about that intelligence. It is beyond mere words. I saw it, that's all. At times it was like gazing into a human soul, to look into his eyes; and what I saw there frightened me and started all sorts of ideas in my own mind of reincarnation and all the rest. I tell you I sensed something big in that brute's eyes; there was a message there, but I wasn't big enough myself to catch it. Whatever it was (I know I'm making a fool of myself)—whatever it was, it baffled me. I can't give an inkling of what I saw in that brute's eyes; it wasn't light, it wasn't colour; it was something that moved, away back, when the eyes themselves weren't moving. And I guess I didn't see it move either; I only sensed that it moved. It was an expression—that's what it was—and I got an impression of it. No; it was different from a mere expression; it was more than that. I don't know what it was, but it gave me a feeling of kinship just the same. Oh, no, not sentimental kinship. It was, rather, a kinship of equality. Those eyes never pleaded like a deer's eyes. They challenged. No, it wasn't defiance. It was just a calm assumption of equality. And I don't think it was deliberate. My belief is that it was unconscious on his part. It was there because it was there, and it couldn't help shining out. No, I don't mean shine. It didn't shine, it moved. I know I'm talking rot, but if you'd looked into that animal's eyes the way I have, you'd understand. Steve was affected the same way I was. Why, I tried to kill that Spot once—he was no good for anything; and I fell down on it. I led him out into the brush, and he came along slow and unwilling. He knew what was going on. I stopped in a likely place, put my foot on the rope, and pulled my big Colt's. And that dog sat down and looked at me. I tell you he didn't plead. He just looked. And I saw all kinds of incomprehensible things moving, yes, *moving*, in those eyes of his. I didn't really see them move; I thought I saw them, for, as I said before, I guess I only sensed them. And I want to tell you right now that it got beyond me. It was like killing a man, a conscious, brave man, who looked calmly into your gun as much as to say, "Who's afraid?"

Then, too, the message seemed so near that, instead of pulling the trigger quick, I stopped to see if I could catch the message. There it was, right before me, glimmering all around in those eyes of his. And then it was too late. I got scared. I was trembly all over, and my stomach generated a nervous palpitation that made me seasick. I just sat down and looked at the dog, and he looked at me, till I thought I was going crazy. Do you want to know what I did? I threw down the gun and ran back to camp with the fear of God in my heart. Steve laughed at me. But I notice that Steve led Spot into the woods, a week later, for the same purpose, and that Steve came back alone, and a little later Spot drifted back, too.

At any rate, Spot wouldn't work. We paid a hundred and ten dollars for him from the bottom of our sack, and he wouldn't work. He wouldn't even tighten the traces. Steve spoke to him the first time we put him in harness, and he sort of shivered, that was all. Not an ounce on the traces. He just stood still and wobbled, like so much jelly. Steve touched him with the whip. He yelped, but not an ounce. Steve touched him again, a bit harder, and he howled—the regular long wolf howl. Then Steve got mad and gave him half a dozen, and I came on the run from the tent.

I told Steve he was brutal with the animal, and we had some words—the first we'd ever had. He threw the whip down in the snow and walked away mad. I picked it up and went to it. That Spot trembled and wobbled and cowered before ever I swung the lash, and with the first bite of it he howled like a lost soul. Next he lay down in the snow. I started the rest of the dogs, and they dragged him along while I threw the whip into him. He rolled over on his back and bumped along, his four legs waving in the air, himself howling as though he was going through a sausage machine. Steve came back and laughed at me, and I apologized for what I'd said.

There was no getting any work out of that Spot; and to make up for it, he was the biggest pig-glutton of a dog I ever saw. On top of that, he was the cleverest thief. There was no circumventing him. Many a breakfast we went without our bacon because Spot had been there first. And it was because of him that we nearly starved to death up the Stewart. He figured out the way to break into our meat-cache, and what he didn't eat, the rest of the team did. But he was impartial. He stole from everybody. He was a restless dog, always very busy snooping around or going somewhere. And there was never a camp within five miles that he didn't raid. The worst of it was that they always came back on us to pay his board bill, which was just, being the law of the land; but it was mighty hard on us, especially that first winter on the Chilcoot, when we were busted, paying for whole hams and sides of bacon that we never ate. He could fight, too, that Spot. He could do everything but work. He never pulled a pound, but he was the boss of the whole team. The way he made those dogs stand around was an education. He bullied them, and there was always one or more of them fresh-marked with his fangs. But he was more than a bully. He wasn't afraid of anything that walked on four legs; and I've seen him march, single-handed into a strange team, without any provocation whatever, and put the *kibosh* on the whole outfit. Did I say he could eat? I caught him eating the whip once. That's straight. He started in at the lash, and when I caught him he was down to the handle, and still going.

But he was a good looker. At the end of the first week we sold him for seventy-five dollars to the Mounted Police. They had experienced dog-drivers, and we knew that by the time he'd covered the six hundred miles to Dawson he'd be a good sled-dog. I say we *knew*, for we were just getting acquainted with that Spot. A little later we were not brash enough to know anything where he was concerned. A week later we woke up in the morning to the dangdest dog-fight we'd ever heard. It was that Spot come back and knocking the team into shape. We ate a pretty depressing breakfast, I can tell you; but cheered up two hours afterward when we sold him to an official courier, bound in to Dawson with government dispatches. That Spot was only three days in coming back, and, as usual, celebrated his arrival with a rough house.

We spent the winter and spring, after our own outfit was across the pass, freighting other people's outfits; and we made a fat stake. Also, we made money out of Spot. If we sold him once, we sold him twenty times. He always came back, and no one asked for their money. We didn't want the money. We'd have paid handsomely for anyone to take him off our hands for keeps'. We had to get rid of him, and we couldn't give him away, for that would have been suspicious. But he was such a fine looker that we never had any difficulty in selling him. "Unbroke," we'd say, and they'd pay any old price for him. We sold him as low as twenty-five dollars, and once we got a hundred and fifty for him. That particular party returned him in person, refused to take his money back, and the way he abused us was something awful. He said it was cheap at the price to tell us what he thought of us; and we felt he was so justified that we never talked back. But to this day I've never quite regained all the old self-respect that was mine before that man talked to me.

When the ice cleared out of the lakes and river, we put our outfit in a Lake Bennett boat and started for Dawson. We had a good team of dogs, and of course we piled them on top the outfit. That Spot was along—there was no losing him; and a dozen times, the first day, he knocked one or another of the dogs overboard in the course of fighting with them. It was close quarters, and he didn't like being crowded.

"What that dog needs is space," Steve said the second day. "Let's maroon him."

We did, running the boat in at Caribou Crossing for him to jump ashore. Two of the other dogs, good dogs, followed him; and we lost two whole days trying to find them. We never saw those two dogs again; but the quietness and relief we enjoyed made us decide, like the man who refused his hundred and fifty, that it was cheap at the price. For the first time in months Steve and I laughed and whistled and sang. We were as happy as clams. The dark days were over. The nightmare had been lifted. That Spot was gone.

Three weeks later, one morning, Steve and I were standing on the river-bank at Dawson. A small boat was just arriving from Lake Bennett. I saw Steve give a start, and heard him say something that was not nice and that was not under his breath. Then I looked; and there, in the bow of the boat, with ears pricked up, sat Spot. Steve and I sneaked immediately, like beaten curs, like cowards, like absconders from justice. It was this last that the lieutenant of police thought when he saw us sneaking. He surmised that there were law-officers in the boat who were after us. He didn't wait to find out, but kept us in sight, and in the M. & M. saloon got us in a corner. We had a merry time explaining, for we refused to go back to the boat and meet Spot; and finally he held us under guard of another policeman while he went to the boat. After we got clear of him, we started for the cabin, and when we arrived, there was that Spot sitting on the stoop waiting for us. Now how did he know we lived there? There were forty thousand people in Dawson that summer, and how did he *savve* our cabin out of all the cabins? How did he know we were in Dawson, anyway? I leave it to you. But don't forget what I said about his intelligence and that immortal something I have seen glimmering in his eyes.

There was no getting rid of him anymore. There were too many people in Dawson who had bought him up on Chilcoot, and the story got around. Half a dozen times we put him on board steamboats going down the Yukon; but he merely went ashore at the first landing and trotted back up the bank. We couldn't sell him, we couldn't kill him (both Steve and I had tried), and nobody else was able to kill him. He bore a charmed life. I've seen him go down in a dogfight on the main street with fifty dogs on top of him, and when they were separated, he'd appear on all his four legs, unharmed, while two of the dogs that had been on top of him would be lying dead.

I saw him steal a chunk of moose-meat from Major Dinwiddie's cache so heavy that he could just keep one jump ahead of Mrs. Dinwiddie's squaw cook, who was after him with an axe. As he went up the hill, after the squaw gave up, Major Dinwiddie himself came out and pumped his Winchester into the landscape. He emptied his magazine twice, and never touched that Spot. Then a policeman came along and arrested him for discharging firearms inside the city limits. Major Dinwiddie paid his fine, and Steve and I paid him for the moose-meat at the rate of a dollar a pound, bones and all. That was what he paid for it. Meat was high that year.

I am only telling what I saw with my own eyes. And now I'll tell you something also. I saw that Spot fall through a water-hole. The ice was three and a half feet thick, and the current sucked him under like a straw. Three hundred yards below was the big water-hole used by the hospital. Spot crawled out of the hospital water-hole, licked off the water, bit out the ice that had formed between his toes, trotted up the bank, and whipped a big Newfoundland belonging to the Gold Commissioner.

In the fall of 1898, Steve and I poled up the Yukon on the last water, bound for Stewart River. We took the dogs along, all except Spot. We figured we'd been feeding him long enough. He'd cost us more time and trouble and money and grub than we'd got by selling him on the Chilcoot—especially grub. So Steve and I tied him down in the cabin and pulled our freight. We camped that night at the mouth of Indian River, and Steve and I were pretty facetious over having shaken him. Steve was a funny cuss, and I was just sitting up in the blankets and laughing when a tornado hit camp. The way that Spot walked into those dogs and gave them what-for was hair-raising. Now how did he get loose? It's up to you. I haven't any theory. And how did he get across the Klondike River? That's another facer. And anyway, how did he know we had gone up the Yukon? You see, we went by water, and he couldn't smell our tracks. Steve and I began to get superstitious about that dog. He got on our nerves, too; and, between you and me, we were just a mite afraid of him.

The freeze-up came on when we were at the mouth of Henderson Creek, and we traded him off for two sacks of flour to an outfit that was bound up White River after copper. Now that whole outfit was lost. Never trace nor hide nor hair of men, dogs, sleds, or anything was ever found. They dropped clean out of sight. It became one of the mysteries of the country. Steve and I plugged away up the Stewart, and six weeks afterward that Spot crawled into camp. He was a perambulating skeleton, and could just drag along; but he got there. And what I want to know is, who told him we were up the Stewart? We could have gone to a thousand other places. How did he know? You tell me, and I'll tell you.

No losing him. At the Mayo he started a row with an Indian dog. The buck who owned the dog took a swing at Spot with an axe, missed him, and killed his own dog. Talk about magic and turning bullets aside—I, for one, consider it a blamed sight harder to turn an axe aside with a big buck at the other end of it. And I saw him do it with my own eyes. That buck didn't want to kill his own dog. You've got to show me.

I told you about Spot breaking into our meat cache. It was nearly the death of us. There wasn't any more meat to be killed, and meat was all we had to live on. The moose had gone back several hundred miles and the Indians with them. There we were. Spring was on, and we had to wait for the river to break. We got pretty thin before we decided to eat the dogs, and we decided to eat Spot first. Do you know what that dog did? He sneaked. Now how did he know our minds were made up to eat him? We sat up nights laying for him, but he never came back, and we ate the other dogs. We ate the whole team.

And now for the sequel. You know what it is when a big river breaks up and a few billion tons of ice go out, jamming and milling and grinding. Just in the thick of it, when the Stewart went out, rumbling and roaring, we sighted Spot out in the middle. He'd got caught as he was trying to cross up above somewhere. Steve and I yelled and shouted and ran up and down the bank, tossing our hats in the air. Sometimes we'd stop and hug each other, we were that boisterous, for we saw Spot's finish. He didn't have a chance in a million. He didn't have any chance at all. After the ice-run, we got into a canoe and paddled down to the Yukon, and down the Yukon to Dawson, stopping to feed up for a week at the cabins at the mouth of Henderson Creek. And as we came in to the bank at Dawson, there sat that Spot, waiting for us, his ears pricked up, his tail wagging, his mouth smiling, extending a hearty welcome to us. Now how did he get out of that ice? How did he know we were coming to Dawson, to the very hour and minute, to be out there on the bank waiting for us?

The more I think of that Spot, the more I am convinced that there are things in this world that go beyond science. On no scientific grounds can that Spot be explained. It's psychic phenomena, or mysticism, or something of that sort, I guess, with a lot of Theosophy thrown in. The Klondike is a good country. I might have been there yet, and become a millionaire, if it hadn't been for Spot. He got on my nerves. I stood him for two years altogether, and then I guess my stamina broke. It was the summer of 1899 when I pulled out. I didn't say anything to Steve. I just sneaked. But I fixed it up all right. I wrote Steve a note, and enclosed a package of "rough-on-rats," telling him what to do with it. I was worn down to skin and bone by that Spot, and I was that nervous that I'd jump and look around when there wasn't anybody within hailing distance. But it was astonishing the way I recuperated when I got quit of him. I got back twenty pounds before I arrived in San Francisco, and by the time I'd crossed the ferry to Oakland I was my old self again, so that even my wife looked in vain for any change in me.

Steve wrote to me once, and his letter seemed irritated. He took it kind of hard because I'd left him with Spot. Also, he said he'd used the "rough-on-rats," per directions, and that there was nothing doing. A year went by. I was back in the office and prospering in all ways —even getting a bit fat. And then Steve arrived. He didn't look me up. I read his name in the steamer list, and wondered why. But I didn't wonder long. I got up one morning and found that Spot chained to the gate-post and holding up the milkman. Steve went north to Seattle, I learned, that very morning. I didn't put on any more weight. My wife made me buy him a collar and tag, and within an hour he showed his gratitude by killing her pet Persian cat. There is no getting rid of that Spot. He will be with me until I die, for he'll never die. My appetite is not so good since he arrived, and my wife says I am looking peaked. Last night that Spot got into Mr. Harvey's hen-house (Harvey is my next-door neighbor) and killed nineteen of his fancy-bred chickens. I shall have to pay for them. My neighbors on the other side quarreled with my wife and then moved out. Spot was the cause of it. And that is why I am disappointed in Stephen Mackaye. I had no idea he was so mean a man.

FLUSH OF GOLD

LON MCFANE WAS A BIT GRUMPY, what of losing his tobacco pouch, or else he might have told me, before we got to it, something about the cabin at Surprise Lake. All day, turn and turnabout, we had spelled each other at going to the fore and breaking trail for the dogs. It was heavy snowshoe work, and did not tend to make a man voluble, yet Lon McFane might have found breath enough at noon, when we stopped to boil coffee, with which to tell me. But he didn't. Surprise Lake?—it was Surprise Cabin to me. I had never heard of it before. I confess I was a bit tired. I had been looking for Lon to stop and make camp any time for an hour; but I had too much pride to suggest making camp or to ask him his intentions; and yet he was my man, lured at a handsome wage to mush my dogs for me and to obey my commands. I guess I was a bit grumpy myself. He said nothing, and I was resolved to ask nothing, even if we tramped on all night.

We came upon the cabin abruptly. For a week of trail we had met no one, and, in my mind, there had been little likelihood of meeting any one for a week to come. And yet there it was, right before my eyes, a cabin, with a dim light in the window and smoke curling up from the chimney.

"Why didn't you tell me—" I began, but was interrupted by Lon, who muttered—

"Surprise Lake—it lies up a small feeder half a mile on. It's only a pond."

"Yes, but the cabin—who lives in it?"

"A woman," was the answer, and the next moment Lon had rapped on the door, and a woman's voice bade him enter.

"Have you seen Dave recently?" she asked.

"Nope," Lon answered carelessly. "I've been in the other direction, down Circle City way. Dave's up Dawson way, ain't he?"

The woman nodded, and Lon fell to unharnessing the dogs, while I unlashed the sled and carried the camp outfit into the cabin. The cabin was a large, one-room affair, and the woman was evidently alone in it. She pointed to the stove, where water was already boiling, and Lon set about the preparation of supper, while I opened the fish-bag and fed the dogs. I

355

looked for Lon to introduce us, and was vexed that he did not, for they were evidently old friends.

"You are Lon McFane, aren't you?" I heard her ask him. "Why, I remember you now. The last time I saw you it was on a steamboat, wasn't it? I remember . . . "

Her speech seemed suddenly to be frozen by the spectacle of dread which, I knew, from the tenor I saw mounting in her eyes, must be on her inner vision. To my astonishment, Lon was affected by her words and manner. His face showed desperate, for all his voice sounded hearty and genial, as he said—

"The last time we met was at Dawson, Queen's Jubilee, or Birthday, or something—don't you remember?—the canoe races in the river, and the obstacle races down the main street?"

The terror faded out of her eyes and her whole body relaxed. "Oh, yes, I do remember," she said. "And you won one of the canoe races."

"How's Dave been makin' it lately? Strikin' it as rich as ever, I suppose?" Lon asked, with apparent irrelevance.

She smiled and nodded, and then, noticing that I had unlashed the bed roll, she indicated the end of the cabin where I might spread it. Her own bunk, I noticed, was made up at the opposite end.

"I thought it was Dave coming when I heard your dogs," she said.

After that she said nothing, contenting herself with watching Lon's cooking operations, and listening the while as for the sound of dogs along the trail. I lay back on the blankets and smoked and watched. Here was mystery; I could make that much out, but no more could I make out. Why in the deuce hadn't Lon given me the tip before we arrived? I looked at her face, unnoticed by her, and the longer I looked the harder it was to take my eyes away. It was a wonderfully beautiful face, unearthly, I may say, with a light in it or an expression or something "that was never on land or sea." Fear and terror had completely vanished, and it was a placidly beautiful face—if by "placid" one can characterize that intangible and occult something that I cannot say was a radiance or a light any more than I can say it was an expression.

Abruptly, as if for the first time, she became aware of my presence.

"Have you seen Dave recently?" she asked me. It was on the tip of my tongue to say "Dave who?" when Lon coughed in the smoke that arose from the sizzling bacon. The bacon might have caused that cough, but I took it as a hint and left my question unasked. "No, I haven't," I answered. "I'm new in this part of the country—"

"But you don't mean to say," she interrupted, "that you've never heard of Dave—of Big Dave Walsh?"

"You see," I apologised, "I'm new in the country. I've put in most of my time in the Lower Country, down Nome way."

"Tell him about Dave," she said to Lon.

Lon seemed put out, but he began in that hearty, genial manner that I had noticed before. It seemed a shade too hearty and genial, and it irritated me.

"Oh, Dave is a fine man," he said. "He's a man, every inch of him, and he stands six feet four in his socks. His word is as good as his bond. The man lies who ever says Dave told a lie, and that man will have to fight with me, too, as well—if there's anything left of him when Dave gets done with him. For Dave is a fighter. Oh, yes, he's a scrapper from way back. He got a grizzly with a '38 popgun. He got clawed some, but he knew what he was doin'. He went into the cave on purpose to get that grizzly. 'Fraid of nothing. Free an' easy with his money, or his last shirt an' match when out of money. Why, he drained Surprise Lake here in three weeks an' took out ninety thousand, didn't he?" She flushed and nodded her head proudly. Through his recital she had followed every word with keenest interest. "An' I must say," Lon went on, "that I was disappointed sore on not meeting Dave here to-night."

Lon served supper at one end of the table of whip-sawed spruce, and we fell to eating. A howling of the dogs took the woman to the door. She opened it an inch and listened.

"Where is Dave Walsh?" I asked, in an undertone.

"Dead," Lon answered. "In hell, maybe. I don't know. Shut up."

"But you just said that you expected to meet him here to-night," I challenged.

"Oh, shut up, can't you," was Lon's reply, in the same cautious undertone.

The woman had closed the door and was returning, and I sat and meditated upon the fact that this man who told me to shut up received from me a salary of two hundred and fifty dollars a month and his board.

Lon washed the dishes, while I smoked and watched the woman. She seemed more beautiful than ever—strangely and weirdly beautiful, it is true. After looking at her stead-fastly for five minutes, I was compelled to come back to the real world and to glance at Lon McFane. This enabled me to know, without discussion, that the woman, too, was real. At first I had taken her for the wife of Dave Walsh; but if Dave Walsh were dead, as Lon had said, then she could be only his widow.

It was early to bed, for we faced a long day on the morrow; and as Lon crawled in beside me under the blankets, I ventured a question.

"That woman's crazy, isn't she?"

"Crazy as a loon," he answered.

And before I could formulate my next question, Lon McFane, I swear, was off to sleep. He always went to sleep that way—just crawled into the blankets, closed his eyes, and was off, a demure little heavy breathing rising on the air. Lon never snored.

And in the morning it was quick breakfast, feed the dogs, load the sled, and hit the trail. We said good-bye as we pulled out, and the woman stood in the doorway and watched us off. I carried the vision of her unearthly beauty away with me, just under my eyelids, and all I had to do, any time, was to close them and see her again. The way was unbroken, Surprise Lake being far off the travelled trails, and Lon and I took turnabout at beating down the feathery snow with our big, webbed shoes so that the dogs could travel. "But you said you expected to meet Dave Walsh at the cabin," trembled on the tip of my tongue a score of times. I did not utter it. I could wait until we knocked off in the middle of the day. And when the middle of the day came, we went right on, for, as Lon explained, there was a camp of moose hunters at the forks of the Teelee, and we could make there by dark. But we didn't make there by dark, for Bright, the lead-dog, broke his shoulder-blade, and we lost an hour over him before we shot him. Then, crossing a timber jam on the frozen bed of the Teelee, the sled suffered a wrenching capsize, and it was a case of make camp and repair the runner. I cooked supper and fed the dogs while Lon made the repairs, and together we got in the night's supply of ice and firewood. Then we sat on our blankets, our moccasins steaming on upended sticks before the fire, and had our evening smoke.

"You didn't know her?" Lon queried suddenly. I shook my head.

"You noticed the colour of her hair and eyes and her complexion, well, that's where she got her name—she was like the first warm glow of a golden sunrise. She was called Flush of Gold. Ever heard of her?"

Somewhere I had a confused and misty remembrance of having heard the name, yet it meant nothing to me. "Flush of Gold," I repeated; "sounds like the name of a dance-house girl." Lon shook his head. "No, she was a good woman, at least in that sense, though she sinned greatly just the same."

"But why do you speak always of her in the past tense, as though she were dead?"

"Because of the darkness on her soul that is the same as the darkness of death. The Flush of Gold that I knew, that Dawson knew, and that Forty Mile knew before that, is dead. That dumb, lunatic creature we saw last night was not Flush of Gold."

"And Dave?" I queried.

"He built that cabin," Lon answered, "He built it for her . . . and for himself. He is dead. She is waiting for him there. She half believes he is not dead. But who can know the whim of a crazed mind? Maybe she wholly believes he is not dead. At any rate, she waits for him there in the cabin he built. Who would rouse the dead? Then who would rouse the living that are dead? Not I, and that is why I let on to expect to meet Dave Walsh there last night. I'll bet a stack that I'd a been more surprised than she if I *had* met him there last night."

"I do not understand," I said. "Begin at the beginning, as a white man should, and tell me the whole tale."

And Lon began. "Victor Chauvet was an old Frenchman—born in the south of France. He came to California in the days of gold. He was a pioneer. He found no gold, but, instead, became a maker of bottled sunshine—in short, a grape-grower and wine-maker. Also, he followed gold excitements. That is what brought him to Alaska in the early days, and over the Chilcoot and down the Yukon long before the Carmack strike. The old town site of Ten Mile was Chauvet's. He carried the first mail into Arctic City. He staked those coal-mines on the Porcupine a dozen years ago. He grubstaked Loftus into the Nippennuck Country. Now it happened that Victor Chauvet was a good Catholic, loving two things in this world, wine and woman. Wine of all kinds he loved, but of woman, only one, and she was the mother of Marie Chauvet."

Here I groaned aloud, having meditated beyond self-control over the fact that I paid this man two hundred and fifty dollars a month.

"What's the matter now?" he demanded.

"Matter?" I complained. "I thought you were telling the story of Flush of Gold. I don't want a biography of your old French wine-bibber."

Lon calmly lighted his pipe, took one good puff, then put the pipe aside. "And you asked me to begin at the beginning," he said.

"Yes," said I; "the beginning."

"And the beginning of Flush of Gold is the old French wine-bibber, for he was the father of Marie Chauvet, and Marie Chauvet was the Flush of Gold. What more do you want? Victor Chauvet never had much luck to speak of. He managed to live, and to get along, and to take good care of Marie, who resembled the one woman he had loved. He took very good care of her. Flush of Gold was the pet name he gave her. Flush of Gold Creek was named after her—Flush of Gold town site, too. The old man was great on town sites, only he never landed them.

"Now, honestly," Lon said, with one of his lightning changes, "you've seen her, what do you think of her—of her looks, I mean? How does she strike your beauty sense?"

"She is remarkably beautiful," I said. "I never saw anything like her in my life. In spite of the fact, last night, that I guessed she was mad, I could not keep my eyes off of her. It wasn't curiosity. It was wonder, sheer wonder, she was so strangely beautiful."

"She was more strangely beautiful before the darkness fell upon her," Lon said softly. "She was truly the Flush of Gold. She turned all men's hearts . . . and heads. She recalls, with an effort, that I once won a canoe race at Dawson—I, who once loved her, and was told by her of her love for me. It was her beauty that made all men love her. She'd 'a' got the apple from Paris, on application, and there wouldn't have been any Trojan War, and to top it off she'd have thrown Paris down. And now she lives in darkness, and she who was always fickle, for the first time is constant—and constant to a shade, to a dead man she does not realize is dead.

"And this is the way it was. You remember what I said last night of Dave Walsh—Big Dave Walsh? He was all that I said, and more, many times more. He came into this country in the late eighties—that's a pioneer for you. He was twenty years old then. He was a young bull. When he was twenty-five he could lift clear of the ground thirteen fifty-pound sacks of flour. At first, each fall of the year, famine drove him out. It was a lone land in those days. No river steamboats, no grub, nothing but salmon bellies and rabbit tracks. But after famine chased him out three years, he said he'd had enough of being chased; and the next year he stayed. He lived on straight meat when he was lucky enough to get it; he ate eleven dogs that winter; but he stayed. And the next winter he stayed, and the next. He never did leave the country again. He was a bull, a great bull. He could kill the strongest man in the country with hard work. He could outpack a Chilcat Indian, he could outpaddle a Stick, and he could travel all day with wet feet when the thermometer registered fifty below zero, and that's going some, I tell you, for vitality. You'd freeze your feet at twenty-five below if you wet them and tried to keep on.

"Dave Walsh was a bull for strength. And yet he was soft and easy-natured. Anybody could do him, the latest short-horn in camp could lie his last dollar out of him. 'But it doesn't worry me,' he had a way of laughing off his softness; 'it doesn't keep me awake nights.' Now don't get the idea that he had no backbone. You remember about the bear he went after with the popgun. When it came to fighting Dave was the blamedest ever. He was the limit, if by that I may describe his unlimitedness when he got into action, he was easy and kind with the weak, but the strong had to give trail when he went by. And he was a man that men liked, which is the finest word of all, a man's man.

"Dave never took part in the big stampede to Dawson when Carmack made the Bonanza strike. You see, Dave was just then over on Mammon Creek strikin' it himself. He discovered Mammon Creek. Cleaned eighty-four thousand up that winter, and opened up the claim so that it promised a couple of hundred thousand for the next winter. Then, summer bein' on and the ground sloshy, he took a trip up the Yukon to Dawson to see what Carmack's strike looked like. And there he saw Flush of Gold. I remember the night. I shall always remember. It was something sudden, and it makes one shiver to think of a strong man with all the strength withered out of him by one glance from the soft eyes of a weak, blond, female creature like Flush of Gold. It was at her dad's cabin, old Victor Chauvet's. Some friend had brought Dave along to talk over town sites on Mammon Creek. But little talking did he do, and what he did was mostly gibberish. I tell you the sight of Flush of Gold had sent Dave clean daffy. Old Victor Chauvet insisted after Dave left that he had been drunk. And so he had. He was drunk, but Flush of Gold was the strong drink that made him so.

"That settled it, that first glimpse he caught of her. He did not start back down the Yukon in a week, as he had intended. He lingered on a month, two months, all summer. And we who had suffered understood, and wondered what the outcome would be. Undoubtedly, in our minds, it seemed that Flush of Gold had met her master. And why not? There was romance sprinkled all over Dave Walsh. He was a Mammon King, he had made the Mammon Creek strike; he was an old sour dough, one of the oldest pioneers in the land— men turned to look at him when he went by, and said to one another in awed undertones, 'There goes Dave Walsh.' And why not? He stood six feet four; he had yellow hair himself that curled on his neck; and he was a bull—a yellow-maned bull just turned thirty-one.

"And Flush of Gold loved him, and, having danced him through a whole summer's courtship, at the end their engagement was made known. The fall of the year was at hand, Dave had to be back for the winter's work on Mammon Creek, and Flush of Gold refused to be married right away. Dave put Dusky Burns in charge of the Mammon Creek claim, and himself lingered on in Dawson. Little use. She wanted her freedom a while longer; she must have it, and she would not marry until next year. And so, on the first ice, Dave Walsh went alone down the Yukon behind his dogs, with the understanding that the marriage would take place when he arrived on the first steamboat of the next year.

"Now Dave was as true as the Pole Star, and she was as false as a magnetic needle in a cargo of loadstone. Dave was as steady and solid as she was fickle and fly-away, and in some way Dave, who never doubted anybody, doubted her. It was the jealousy of his love, perhaps, and maybe it was the message ticked off from her soul to his; but at any rate Dave was worried by fear of her inconstancy. He was afraid to trust her till the next year, he had so to trust her, and he was pretty well beside himself. Some of it I got from old Victor Chauvet afterwards, and from all that I have pieced together I conclude that there was something of a scene before Dave pulled north with his dogs. He stood up before the old Frenchman, with Flush of Gold beside him, and announced that they were plighted to each other. He was very dramatic, with fire in his eyes, old Victor said. He talked something about 'until death do us part'; and old Victor especially remembered that at one place Dave took her by the shoulder with his great paw and almost shook her as he said: 'Even unto death are you mine, and I would rise from the grave to claim you.' Old Victor distinctly remembered those words 'Even unto death are you mine, and I would rise from the grave to claim you.' And he told me afterwards that Flush of Gold was pretty badly frightened, and that he afterwards took Dave to one side privately and told him that that wasn't the way to hold Flush of Gold—that he must humour her and gentle her if he wanted to keep her.

"There is no discussion in my mind but that Flush of Gold was frightened. She was a savage herself in her treatment of men, while men had always treated her as a soft and tender and too utterly-utter something that must not be hurt. She didn't know what harshness was . . . until Dave Walsh, standing his six feet four, a big bull, gripped her and pawed her and assured her that she was his until death, and then some. And besides, in Dawson, that winter, was a music-player—one of those macaroni-eating, greasy-tenor-Eye-talian-dago propositions—and Flush of Gold lost her heart to him. Maybe it was only fascination—I don't know. Sometimes it seems to me that she really did love Dave Walsh. Perhaps it was because he had frightened her with that even-unto-death, rise-from-the-grave stunt of his that she in the end inclined to the dago music-player. But it is all guesswork, and the facts are, sufficient. He wasn't a dago; he was a Russian count—this was straight; and he wasn't a professional piano-player or anything of the sort. He played the violin and the piano, and he sang—sang well—but it was for his own pleasure and for the pleasure of those he sang for. He had money, too—and right here let me say that Flush of Gold never cared a rap for money. She was fickle, but she was never sordid.

"But to be getting along. She was plighted to Dave, and Dave was coming up on the first steamboat to get her—that was the summer of '98, and the first steamboat was to be expected the middle of June. And Flush of Gold was afraid to throw Dave down and face him afterwards. It was all planned suddenly. The Russian music-player, the Count, was her obedient slave. She planned it, I know. I learned as much from old Victor afterwards. The Count took his orders from her, and caught that first steamboat down. It was the *Golden Rocket*. And so did Flush of Gold catch it. And so did I. I was going to Circle City, and I was flabbergasted when I found Flush of Gold on board. I didn't see her name down on the passenger list. She was with the Count fellow all the time, happy and smiling, and I noticed that the Count fellow was down on the list as having his wife along. There it was, state-room, number, and all. The first I knew that he was married, only I didn't see anything of the wife . . . unless Flush of Gold was so counted. I wondered if they'd got married ashore before starting. There'd been talk about them in Dawson, you see, and bets had been laid that the Count fellow had cut Dave out.

"I talked with the purser. He didn't know anything more about it than I did; he didn't know Flush of Gold, anyway, and besides, he was almost rushed to death. You know what a Yukon steamboat is, but you can't guess what the *Golden Rocket* was when it left Dawson that June of 1898. She was a hummer. Being the first steamer out, she carried all the scurvy patients and hospital wrecks. Then she must have carried a couple of millions of Klondike dust and nuggets, to say nothing of a packed and jammed passenger list, deck passengers galore, and bucks and squaws and dogs without end. And she was loaded down to the guards with freight and baggage. There was a mountain of the same on the fore-lower-deck, and each little stop along the way added to it. I saw the box come aboard at Teelee Portage, and I knew it for what it was, though I little guessed the joker that was in it. And they piled it on top of everything else on the fore-lower-deck, and they didn't pile it any too securely either. The mate expected to come back to it again, and then forgot about it. I thought at the time that there was something familiar about the big husky dog that climbed over the baggage and freight and lay down next to the box. And then we passed the *Glendale*, bound up for Dawson. As she saluted us, I thought of Dave on board of her and hurrying to Dawson to Flush of Gold. I turned and looked at her where she stood by the rail. Her eyes were bright, but she looked a bit frightened by the sight of the other steamer, and she was leaning closely to the Count fellow as for protection. She needn't have leaned so safely against him, and I needn't have been so sure of a disappointed Dave Walsh arriving at Dawson. For Dave Walsh wasn't on the *Glendale*. There were a lot of things I didn't know, but was soon to know—for instance, that the pair were not yet married. Inside half an hour preparations for the marriage took place. What of the sick men in the main cabin, and of the crowded condition of the *Golden Rocket*, the likeliest place for the ceremony was found forward, on the lower deck, in an open space next to the rail and gang-plank and shaded by the mountain of freight with the big box on top and the sleeping dog beside it. There was a missionary on board, getting off at Eagle City, which was the next step, so they had to use him quick. That's what they'd planned to do, get married on the boat.

"But I've run ahead of the facts. The reason Dave Walsh wasn't on the *Glendale* was because he was on the *Golden Rocket*. It was this way. After loiterin' in Dawson on account of Flush of Gold, he went down to Mammon Creek on the ice. And there he found Dusky Burns doing so well with the claim, there was no need for him to be around. So he put some grub on the sled, harnessed the dogs, took an Indian along, and pulled out for Surprise Lake. He always had a liking for that section. Maybe you don't know how the creek turned out to be a four-flusher; but the prospects were good at the time, and Dave proceeded to build his cabin and hers. That's the cabin we slept in. After he finished it, he went off on a moose hunt to the forks of the Teelee, takin' the Indian along.

"And this is what happened. Came on a cold snap. The juice went down forty, fifty, sixty below zero. I remember that snap—I was at Forty Mile; and I remember the very day. At eleven o'clock in the morning the spirit thermometer at the N. A. T. & T. Company's store went down to seventy-five below zero. And that morning, near the forks of the Teelee, Dave Walsh was out after moose with that blessed Indian of his. I got it all from the Indian afterwards—we made a trip over the ice together to Dyea. That morning Mr. Indian broke through the ice and wet himself to the waist. Of course he began to freeze right away. The proper thing was to build a fire. But Dave Walsh was a bull. It was only half a mile to camp, where a fire was already burning. What was the good of building another? He threw Mr. Indian over his shoulder—and ran with him—half a mile—with the thermometer at seventy-five below. You know what that means. Suicide. There's no other name for it. Why, that buck Indian weighed over two hundred himself, and Dave ran half a mile with him. Of course he froze his lungs. Must have frozen them near solid. It was a tomfool trick for any man to do. And anyway, after lingering horribly for several weeks, Dave Walsh died.

"The Indian didn't know what to do with the corpse. Ordinarily he'd have buried him and let it go at that. But he knew that Dave Walsh was a big man, worth lots of money, a *hi-yu skookum* chief. Likewise he'd seen the bodies of other *hi-yu skookums* carted around the country like they were worth something. So he decided to take Dave's body to Forty Mile, which was Dave's headquarters. You know how the ice is on the grass roots in this country —well, the Indian planted Dave under a foot of soil—in short, he put Dave on ice. Dave could have stayed there a thousand years and still been the same old Dave. You understand —just the same as a refrigerator. Then the Indian brings over a whipsaw from the cabin at Surprise Lake and makes lumber enough for the box. Also, waiting for the thaw, he goes out and shoots about ten thousand pounds of moose. This he keeps on ice, too. Came the thaw. The Teelee broke. He built a raft and loaded it with the meat, the big box with Dave inside, and Dave's team of dogs, and away they went down the Teelee.

"The raft got caught on a timber jam and hung up two days. It was scorching hot weather, and Mr. Indian nearly lost his moose meat. So when he got to Teelee Portage he figured a steamboat would get to Forty Mile quicker than his raft. He transferred his cargo, and there you are, fore-lower deck of the *Golden Rocket*, Flush of Gold being married, and Dave Walsh in his big box casting the shade for her. And there's one thing I clean forgot. No wonder I thought the husky dog that came aboard at Teelee Portage was familiar. It was Pee-lat, Dave Walsh's lead-dog and favourite—a terrible fighter, too. He was lying down beside the box.

"Flush of Gold caught sight of me, called me over, shook hands with me, and introduced me to the Count. She was beautiful. I was as mad for her then as ever. She smiled into my eyes and said I must sign as one of the witnesses. And there was no refusing her. She was ever a child, cruel as children are cruel. Also, she told me she was in possession of the only two bottles of champagne in Dawson—or that had been in Dawson the night before; and before I knew it I was scheduled to drink her and the Count's health. Everybody crowded round, the captain of the steamboat, very prominent, trying to ring in on the wine, I guess. It was a funny wedding. On the upper deck the hospital wrecks, with various feet in the grave, gathered and looked down to see. There were Indians all jammed in the circle, too, big bucks, and their squaws and kids, to say nothing of about twenty-five snarling wolf-dogs. The missionary lined the two of them up and started in with the service. And just then a dog-fight started, high up on the pile of freight—Pee-lat lying beside the big box, and a white-haired brute belonging to one of the Indians. The fight wasn't explosive at all. The brutes just snarled at each other from a distance—tapping at each other long-distance, you know, saying dast and dassent, dast and dassent. The noise was rather disturbing, but you could hear the missionary's voice above it.

"There was no particularly easy way of getting at the two dogs, except from the other side of the pile. But nobody was on that side—everybody watching the ceremony, you see. Even then everything might have been all right if the captain hadn't thrown a club at the dogs. That was what precipitated everything. As I say, if the captain hadn't thrown that club, nothing might have happened.

"The missionary had just reached the point where he was saying 'In sickness and in health,' and 'Till death us do part.' And just then the captain threw the club. I saw the whole thing. It landed on Pee-lat, and at that instant the white brute jumped him. The club caused it. Their two bodies struck the box, and it began to slide, its lower end tilting down. It was a long oblong box, and it slid down slowly until it reached the perpendicular, when it came down on the run. The onlookers on that side the circle had time to get out from under. Flush of Gold and the Count, on the opposite side of the circle, were facing the box; the missionary had his back to it. The box must have fallen ten feet straight up and down, and it hit end on.

"Now mind you, not one of us knew that Dave Walsh was dead. We thought he was on the *Glendale*, bound for Dawson. The missionary had edged off to one side, and so Flush of Gold faced the box when it struck. It was like in a play. It couldn't have been better planned. It struck on end, and on the right end; the whole front of the box came off; and out swept Dave Walsh on his feet, partly wrapped in a blanket, his yellow hair flying and showing bright in the sun. Right out of the box, on his feet, he swept upon Flush of Gold. She didn't know he was dead, but it was unmistakable, after hanging up two days on a timber jam, that he was rising all right from the dead to claim her. Possibly that is what she thought. At any rate, the sight froze her. She couldn't move. She just sort of wilted and watched Dave Walsh coming for her! And he got her. It looked almost as though he threw his arms around her, but whether or not this happened, down to the deck they went together. We had to drag Dave Walsh's body clear before we could get hold of her. She was in a faint, but it would have been just as well if she had never come out of that faint; for when she did, she fell to screaming the way insane people do. She kept it up for hours, till she was exhausted. Oh, yes, she recovered. You saw her last night, and know how much recovered she is. She is not violent, it is true, but she lives in darkness. She believes that she is waiting for Dave Walsh, and so she waits in the cabin he built for her. She is no longer fickle. It is nine years now that she has been faithful to Dave Walsh, and the outlook is that she'll be faithful to him to the end."

Lon McFane pulled down the top of the blankets and prepared to crawl in.

"We have her grub hauled to her each year," he added, "and in general keep an eye on her. Last night was the first time she ever recognized me, though."

"Who are the we?" I asked.

"Oh," was the answer, "the Count and old Victor Chauvet and me. Do you know, I think the Count is the one to be really sorry for. Dave Walsh never did know that she was false to him. And she does not suffer. Her darkness is merciful to her."

I lay silently under the blankets for the space of a minute.

"Is the Count still in the country?" I asked.

But there was a gentle sound of heavy breathing, and I knew Lon McFane was asleep.

THE PASSING OF MARCUS O'BRIEN

"It is the judgment of this court that you vamose the camp . . . in the customary way, sir, in the customary way."

Judge Marcus O'Brien was absent-minded, and Mucluc Charley nudged him in the ribs. Marcus O'Brien cleared his throat and went on—

"Weighing the gravity of the offence, sir, and the extenuating circumstances, it is the opinion of this court, and its verdict, that you be outfitted with three days' grub. That will do, I think."

Arizona Jack cast a bleak glance out over the Yukon. It was a swollen, chocolate flood, running a mile wide and nobody knew how deep. The earth-bank on which he stood was ordinarily a dozen feet above the water, but the river was now growling at the top of the bank, devouring, instant by instant, tiny portions of the top-standing soil. These portions went into the gaping mouths of the endless army of brown swirls and vanished away. Several inches more, and Red Cow would be flooded.

"It won't do," Arizona Jack said bitterly. "Three days' grub ain't enough."

"There was Manchester," Marcus O'Brien replied gravely. "He didn't get any grub."

"And they found his remains grounded on the Lower River an' half eaten by huskies," was Arizona Jack's retort. "And his killin' was without provocation. Joe Deeves never did nothin', never warbled once, an' jes' because his stomach was out of order, Manchester ups an' plugs him. You ain't givin' me a square deal, O'Brien, I tell you that straight. Give me a week's grub, and I play even to win out. Three days' grub, an' I cash in."

"What for did you kill Ferguson?" O'Brien demanded. "I haven't any patience for these unprovoked killings. And they've got to stop. Red Cow's none so populous. It's a good camp, and there never used to be any killings. Now they're epidemic. I'm sorry for you, Jack, but you've got to be made an example of. Ferguson didn't provoke enough for a killing."

"Provoke!" Arizona Jack snorted. "I tell you, O'Brien, you don't savve. You ain't got no artistic sensibilities. What for did I kill Ferguson? What for did Ferguson sing 'Then I wisht I was a little bird'? That's what I want to know. Answer me that. What for did he sing 'little

364

bird, little bird'? One little bird was enough. I could a-stood one little bird. But no, he must sing two little birds. I gave 'm a chanst. I went to him almighty polite and requested him kindly to discard one little bird. I pleaded with him. There was witnesses that testified to that.

"An' Ferguson was no jay-throated songster," some one spoke up from the crowd.

O'Brien betrayed indecision.

"Ain't a man got a right to his artistic feelin's?" Arizona Jack demanded. "I gave Ferguson warnin'. It was violatin' my own nature to go on listening to his little birds. Why, there's music sharps that fine-strung an' keyed-up they'd kill for heaps less'n I did. I'm willin' to pay for havin' artistic feelin's. I can take my medicine an' lick the spoon, but three days' grub is drawin' it a shade fine, that's all, an' I hereby register my kick. Go on with the funeral."

O'Brien was still wavering. He glanced inquiringly at Mucluc Charley.

"I should say, Judge, that three days' grub was a mite severe," the latter suggested; "but you're runnin' the show. When we elected you judge of this here trial court, we agreed to abide by your decisions, an' we've done it, too, b'gosh, an' we're goin' to keep on doin' it."

"Mebbe I've been a trifle harsh, Jack," O'Brien said apologetically—"I'm that worked up over those killings; an' I'm willing to make it a week's grub." He cleared his throat magisterially and looked briskly about him. "And now we might as well get along and finish up the business. The boat's ready. You go and get the grub, Leclaire. We'll settle for it afterward."

Arizona Jack looked grateful, and, muttering something about "damned little birds," stepped aboard the open boat that rubbed restlessly against the bank. It was a large skiff, built of rough pine planks that had been sawed by hand from the standing timber of Lake Linderman, a few hundred miles above, at the foot of Chilcoot. In the boat were a pair of oars and Arizona Jack's blankets. Leclaire brought the grub, tied up in a flour-sack, and put it on board. As he did so, he whispered—"I gave you good measure, Jack. You done it with provocation."

"Cast her off!" Arizona Jack cried.

Somebody untied the painter and threw it in. The current gripped the boat and whirled it away. The murderer did not bother with the oars, contenting himself with sitting in the stern-sheets and rolling a cigarette. Completing it, he struck a match and lighted up. Those that watched on the bank could see the tiny puffs of smoke. They remained on the bank till the boat swung out of sight around the bend half a mile below. Justice had been done.

The denizens of Red Cow imposed the law and executed sentences without the delays that mark the softness of civilization. There was no law on the Yukon save what they made for themselves. They were compelled to make it for themselves. It was in an early day that Red Cow flourished on the Yukon—1887—and the Klondike and its populous stampedes lay in the unguessed future. The men of Red Cow did not even know whether their camp was situated in Alaska or in the North-west Territory, whether they drew breath under the stars and stripes or under the British flag. No surveyor had ever happened along to give them their latitude and longitude. Red Cow was situated somewhere along the Yukon, and that was sufficient for them. So far as flags were concerned, they were beyond all jurisdiction. So far as the law was concerned, they were in No-Man's land.

They made their own law, and it was very simple. The Yukon executed their decrees. Some two thousand miles below Red Cow the Yukon flowed into Bering Sea through a delta a hundred miles wide. Every mile of those two thousand miles was savage wilderness. It was true, where the Porcupine flowed into the Yukon inside the Arctic Circle there was a Hudson Bay Company trading post. But that was many hundreds of miles away. Also, it was rumoured that many hundreds of miles farther on there were missions. This last, however, was merely rumour; the men of Red Cow had never been there. They had entered the lone land by way of Chilcoot and the head-waters of the Yukon.

The men of Red Cow ignored all minor offences. To be drunk and disorderly and to use vulgar language were looked upon as natural and inalienable rights. The men of Red Cow were individualists, and recognized as sacred but two things, property and life. There were no women present to complicate their simple morality. There were only three log-cabins in Red Cow—the majority of the population of forty men living in tents or brush shacks; and there was no jail in which to confine malefactors, while the inhabitants were too busy digging gold or seeking gold to take a day off and build a jail. Besides, the paramount question of grub negatived such a procedure. Wherefore, when a man violated the rights of property or life, he was thrown into an open boat and started down the Yukon. The quantity of grub he received was proportioned to the gravity of the offence. Thus, a common thief might get as much as two weeks' grub; an uncommon thief might get no more than half of that. A murderer got no grub at all. A man found guilty of manslaughter would receive grub for from three days to a week. And Marcus O'Brien had been elected judge, and it was he who apportioned the grub. A man who broke the law took his chances. The Yukon swept him away, and he might or might not win to Bering Sea. A few days' grub gave him a fighting chance. No grub meant practically capital punishment, though there was a slim chance, all depending on the season of the year.

Having disposed of Arizona Jack and watched him out of sight, the population turned from the bank and went to work on its claims—all except Curly Jim, who ran the one faro layout in all the Northland and who speculated in prospect-holes on the sides. Two things happened that day that were momentous. In the late morning Marcus O'Brien struck it. He washed out a dollar, a dollar and a half, and two dollars, from three successive pans. He had found the streak. Curly Jim looked into the hole, washed a few pans himself, and offered O'Brien ten thousand dollars for all rights—five thousand in dust, and, in lieu of the other five thousand, a half interest in his faro layout. O'Brien refused the offer. He was there to make money out of the earth, he declared with heat, and not out of his fellow-men. And anyway, he didn't like faro. Besides, he appraised his strike at a whole lot more than ten thousand.

The second event of moment occurred in the afternoon, when Siskiyou Pearly ran his boat into the bank and tied up. He was fresh from the Outside, and had in his possession a four-months-old newspaper. Furthermore, he had half a dozen barrels of whisky, all consigned to Curly Jim. The men of Red Cow quit work. They sampled the whisky—at a dollar a drink, weighed out on Curly's scales; and they discussed the news. And all would have been well, had not Curly Jim conceived a nefarious scheme, which was, namely, first to get Marcus O'Brien drunk, and next, to buy his mine from him.

The first half of the scheme worked beautifully. It began in the early evening, and by nine o'clock O'Brien had reached the singing stage. He clung with one arm around Curly Jim's neck, and even essayed the late lamented Ferguson's song about the little birds. He considered he was quite safe in this, what of the fact that the only man in camp with artistic feelings was even then speeding down the Yukon on the breast of a five-mile current.

But the second half of the scheme failed to connect. No matter how much whisky was poured down his neck, O'Brien could not be brought to realize that it was his bounden and friendly duty to sell his claim. He hesitated, it is true, and trembled now and again on the verge of giving in. Inside his muddled head, however, he was chuckling to himself. He was up to Curly Jim's game, and liked the hands that were being dealt him. The whisky was good. It came out of one special barrel, and was about a dozen times better than that in the other five barrels.

Siskiyou Pearly was dispensing drinks in the bar-room to the remainder of the population of Red Cow, while O'Brien and Curly had out their business orgy in the kitchen. But there was nothing small about O'Brien. He went into the bar-room and returned with Mucluc Charley and Percy Leclaire.

"Business 'sociates of mine, business 'sociates," he announced, with a broad wink to them and a guileless grin to Curly. "Always trust their judgment, always trust 'em. They're all right. Give 'em some fire-water, Curly, an' le's talk it over."

This was ringing in; but Curly Jim, making a swift revaluation of the claim, and remembering that the last pan he washed had turned out seven dollars, decided that it was worth the extra whisky, even if it was selling in the other room at a dollar a drink.

"I'm not likely to consider," O'Brien was hiccoughing to his two friends in the course of explaining to them the question at issue. "Who? Me?—sell for ten thousand dollars! No indeed. I'll dig the gold myself, an' then I'm goin' down to God's country—Southern California—that's the place for me to end my declinin' days—an' then I'll start . . . as I said before, then I'll start . . . what did I say I was goin' to start?"

"Ostrich farm," Mucluc Charley volunteered.

"Sure, just what I'm goin' to start." O'Brien abruptly steadied himself and looked with awe at Mucluc Charley. "How did you know? Never said so. Jes' thought I said so. You're a min' reader, Charley. Le's have another."

Curly Jim filled the glasses and had the pleasure of seeing four dollars' worth of whisky disappear, one dollar's worth of which he punished himself—O'Brien insisted that he should drink as frequently as his guests.

"Better take the money now," Leclaire argued. "Take you two years to dig it out the hole, an' all that time you might be hatchin' teeny little baby ostriches an' pulling feathers out the big ones."

O'Brien considered the proposition and nodded approval. Curly Jim looked gratefully at Leclaire and refilled the glasses.

"Hold on there!" spluttered Mucluc Charley, whose tongue was beginning to wag loosely and trip over itself. "As your father confessor—there I go—as your brother—O hell!" He paused and collected himself for another start. "As your frien'—business frien', I should say, I would suggest, rather—I would take the liberty, as it was, to mention—I mean, suggest, that there may be more ostriches . . . O hell!" He downed another glass, and went on more carefully. "What I'm drivin' at is . . . what am I drivin' at?" He smote the side of his head sharply half a dozen times with the heel of his palm to shake up his ideas. "I got it!" he cried jubilantly. "Supposen there's slathers more'n ten thousand dollars in that hole!"

O'Brien, who apparently was all ready to close the bargain, switched about.

"Great!" he cried. "Splen'd idea. Never thought of it all by myself." He took Mucluc Charley warmly by the hand. "Good frien'! Good 's'ciate!" He turned belligerently on Curly Jim. "Maybe hundred thousand dollars in that hole. You wouldn't rob your old frien', would you, Curly? Course you wouldn't. I know you—better'n yourself, better'n yourself. Le's have another: We're good frien's, all of us, I say, all of us."

And so it went, and so went the whisky, and so went Curly Jim's hopes up and down. Now Leclaire argued in favour of immediate sale, and almost won the reluctant O'Brien over, only to lose him to the more brilliant counter-argument of Mucluc Charley. And again, it was Mucluc Charley who presented convincing reasons for the sale and Percy Leclaire who held stubbornly back. A little later it was O'Brien himself who insisted on selling, while both friends, with tears and curses, strove to dissuade him. The more whiskey they downed, the more fertile of imagination they became. For one sober pro or con they found a score of drunken ones; and they convinced one another so readily that they were perpetually changing sides in the argument.

The time came when both Mucluc Charley and Leclaire were firmly set upon the sale, and they gleefully obliterated O'Brien's objections as fast as he entered them. O'Brien grew desperate. He exhausted his last argument and sat speechless. He looked pleadingly at the friends who had deserted him. He kicked Mucluc Charley's shins under the table, but that graceless hero immediately unfolded a new and most logical reason for the sale. Curly Jim got pen and ink and paper and wrote out the bill of sale. O'Brien sat with pen poised in hand.

"Le's have one more," he pleaded. "One more before I sign away a hundred thousan' dollars."

Curly Jim filled the glasses triumphantly. O'Brien downed his drink and bent forward with wobbling pen to affix his signature. Before he had made more than a blot, he suddenly started up, impelled by the impact of an idea colliding with his consciousness. He stood upon his feet and swayed back and forth before them, reflecting in his startled eyes the thought process that was taking place behind. Then he reached his conclusion. A benevolent radiance suffused his countenance. He turned to the faro dealer, took his hand, and spoke solemnly.

"Curly, you're my frien'. There's my han'. Shake. Ol' man, I won't do it. Won't sell. Won't rob a frien'. No son-of-a-gun will ever have chance to say Marcus O'Brien robbed frien' cause frien' was drunk. You're drunk, Curly, an' I won't rob you. Jes' had thought—never thought it before—don't know what the matter 'ith me, but never thought it before. Suppose, jes' suppose, Curly, my ol' frien', jes' suppose there ain't ten thousan' in whole damn claim. You'd be robbed. No, sir, won't do it. Marcus O'Brien makes money out of the groun', not out of his frien's."

Percy Leclaire and Mucluc Charley drowned the faro dealer's objections in applause for so noble a sentiment. They fell upon O'Brien from either side, their arms lovingly about his neck, their mouths so full of words they could not hear Curly's offer to insert a clause in the document to the effect that if there weren't ten thousand in the claim he would be given back the difference between yield and purchase price. The longer they talked the more maudlin and the more noble the discussion became. All sordid motives were banished. They were a trio of philanthropists striving to save Curly Jim from himself and his own philanthropy. They insisted that he was a philanthropist. They refused to accept for a moment that there could be found one ignoble thought in all the world. They crawled and climbed and scrambled over high ethical plateaux and ranges, or drowned themselves in metaphysical seas of sentimentality.

Curly Jim sweated and fumed and poured out the whisky. He found himself with a score of arguments on his hands, not one of which had anything to do with the gold-mine he wanted to buy. The longer they talked the farther away they got from that gold-mine, and at two in the morning Curly Jim acknowledged himself beaten. One by one he led his helpless guests across the kitchen floor and thrust them outside. O'Brien came last, and the three, with arms locked for mutual aid, titubated gravely on the stoop.

"Good business man, Curly," O'Brien was saying. "Must say like your style—fine an' generous, free-handed hospital . . . hospital . . . hospitality. Credit to you. Nothin' base 'n graspin' in your make-up. As I was sayin'—"

But just then the faro dealer slammed the door.

The three laughed happily on the stoop. They laughed for a long time. Then Mucluc Charley essayed speech.

"Funny—laughed so hard—ain't what I want to say. My idea is . . . what wash it? Oh, got it! Funny how ideas slip. Elusive idea—chasin' elusive idea—great sport. Ever chase rabbits, Percy, my frien'? I had dog—great rabbit dog. Whash 'is name? Don't know name —never had no name—forget name—elusive name—chasin' elusive name—no, idea— elusive idea, but got it—what I want to say was—O hell!"

Thereafter there was silence for a long time. O'Brien slipped from their arms to a sitting posture on the stoop, where he slept gently. Mucluc Charley chased the elusive idea through all the nooks and crannies of his drowning consciousness. Leclaire hung fascinated upon the delayed utterance. Suddenly the other's hand smote him on the back.

"Got it!" Mucluc Charley cried in stentorian tones.

The shock of the jolt broke the continuity of Leclaire's mental process.

"How much to the pan?" he demanded.

"Pan nothin'!" Mucluc Charley was angry. "Idea—got it—got leg-hold—ran it down."

Leclaire's face took on a rapt, admiring expression, and again he hung upon the other's lips.

" . . . O hell!" said Mucluc Charley.

At this moment the kitchen door opened for an instant, and Curly Jim shouted, "Go home!"

"Funny," said Mucluc Charley. "Shame idea—very shame as mine. Le's go home."

They gathered O'Brien up between them and started. Mucluc Charley began aloud the pursuit of another idea. Leclaire followed the pursuit with enthusiasm. But O'Brien did not follow it. He neither heard, nor saw, nor knew anything. He was a mere wobbling automaton, supported affectionately and precariously by his two business associates.

They took the path down by the bank of the Yukon. Home did not lie that way, but the elusive idea did. Mucluc Charley giggled over the idea that he could not catch for the edification of Leclaire. They came to where Siskiyou Pearly's boat lay moored to the bank. The rope with which it was tied ran across the path to a pine stump. They tripped over it and went down, O'Brien underneath. A faint flash of consciousness lighted his brain. He felt the impact of bodies upon his and struck out madly for a moment with his fists. Then he went to sleep again. His gentle snore arose on the air, and Mucluc Charley began to giggle.

"New idea," he volunteered, "brand new idea. Jes' caught it—no trouble at all. Came right up an' I patted it on the head. It's mine. 'Brien's drunk—beashly drunk. Shame— damn shame—learn'm lesshon. Trash Pearly's boat. Put 'Brien in Pearly's boat. Casht off— let her go down Yukon. 'Brien wake up in mornin'. Current too strong—can't row boat 'gainst current—mush walk back. Come back madder 'n hatter. You an' me headin' for tall timber. Learn 'm lesshon jes' shame, learn 'm lesshon."

Siskiyou Pearly's boat was empty, save for a pair of oars. Its gunwale rubbed against the bank alongside of O'Brien. They rolled him over into it. Mucluc Charley cast off the painter, and Leclaire shoved the boat out into the current. Then, exhausted by their labours, they lay down on the bank and slept.

Next morning all Red Cow knew of the joke that had been played on Marcus O'Brien. There were some tall bets as to what would happen to the two perpetrators when the victim arrived back. In the afternoon a lookout was set, so that they would know when he was sighted. Everybody wanted to see him come in. But he didn't come, though they sat up till midnight. Nor did he come next day, nor the next. Red Cow never saw Marcus O'Brien again, and though many conjectures were entertained, no certain clue was ever gained to dispel the mystery of his passing.

☙❦❧

ONLY MARCUS O'BRIEN KNEW, and he never came back to tell. He awoke next morning in torment. His stomach had been calcined by the inordinate quantity of whisky he had drunk, and was a dry and raging furnace. His head ached all over, inside and out; and, worse than that, was the pain in his face. For six hours countless thousands of mosquitoes had fed upon him, and their ungrateful poison had swollen his face tremendously. It was only by a severe exertion of will that he was able to open narrow slits in his face through which he could peer. He happened to move his hands, and they hurt. He squinted at them, but failed to recognize them, so puffed were they by the mosquito virus. He was lost, or rather, his identity was lost to him. There was nothing familiar about him, which, by association of ideas, would cause to rise in his consciousness the continuity of his existence. He was divorced utterly from his past, for there was nothing about him to resurrect in his consciousness a memory of that past. Besides, he was so sick and miserable that he lacked energy and inclination to seek after who and what he was.

It was not until he discovered a crook in a little finger, caused by an unset breakage of years before, that he knew himself to be Marcus O'Brien. On the instant his past rushed into his consciousness. When he discovered a blood-blister under a thumb-nail, which he had received the previous week, his self-identification became doubly sure, and he knew that those unfamiliar hands belonged to Marcus O'Brien, or, just as much to the point, that Marcus O'Brien belonged to the hands. His first thought was that he was ill—that he had had river fever. It hurt him so much to open his eyes that he kept them closed. A small floating branch struck the boat a sharp rap. He thought it was someone knocking on the cabin door, and said, "Come in." He waited for a while, and then said testily, "Stay out, then, damn you." But just the same he wished they would come in and tell him about his illness.

But as he lay there, the past night began to reconstruct itself in his brain. He hadn't been sick at all, was his thought; he had merely been drunk, and it was time for him to get up and go to work. Work suggested his mine, and he remembered that he had refused ten thousand dollars for it. He sat up abruptly and squeezed open his eyes. He saw himself in a boat, floating on the swollen brown flood of the Yukon. The spruce-covered shores and islands were unfamiliar. He was stunned for a time. He couldn't make it out. He could remember the last night's orgy, but there was no connection between that and his present situation.

He closed his eyes and held his aching head in his hands. What had happened? Slowly the dreadful thought arose in his mind. He fought against it, strove to drive it away, but it persisted: he had killed somebody. That alone could explain why he was in an open boat drifting down the Yukon. The law of Red Cow that he had so long administered had now been administered to him. He had killed someone and been set adrift. But whom? He racked his aching brain for the answer, but all that came was a vague memory of bodies falling upon him and of striking out at them. Who were they? Maybe he had killed more than one. He reached to his belt. The knife was missing from its sheath. He had done it with that undoubtedly. But there must have been some reason for the killing. He opened his eyes and in a panic began to search about the boat. There was no grub, not an ounce of grub. He sat down with a groan. He had killed without provocation. The extreme rigour of the law had been visited upon him.

For half an hour he remained motionless, holding his aching head and trying to think.

Then he cooled his stomach with a drink of water from overside and felt better. He stood up, and alone on the wide-stretching Yukon, with naught but the primeval wilderness to hear, he cursed strong drink. After that he tied up to a huge floating pine that was deeper sunk in the current than the boat and that consequently drifted faster. He washed his face and hands, sat down in the stern-sheets, and did some more thinking. It was late in June. It was two thousand miles to Bering Sea. The boat was averaging five miles an hour. There was no darkness in such high latitudes at that time of the year, and he could run the river every hour of the twenty-four. This would mean, daily, a hundred and twenty miles. Strike out the twenty for accidents, and there remained a hundred miles a day. In twenty days he would reach Bering Sea. And this would involve no expenditure of energy; the river did the work. He could lie down in the bottom of the boat and husband his strength.

For two days he ate nothing. Then, drifting into the Yukon Flats, he went ashore on the low-lying islands and gathered the eggs of wild geese and ducks. He had no matches, and ate the eggs raw. They were strong, but they kept him going. When he crossed the Arctic Circle, he found the Hudson Bay Company's post. The brigade had not yet arrived from the Mackenzie, and the post was completely out of grub. He was offered wild-duck eggs, but he informed them that he had a bushel of the same on the boat. He was also offered a drink of whisky, which he refused with an exhibition of violent repugnance. He got matches, however, and after that he cooked his eggs. Toward the mouth of the river head-winds delayed him, and he was twenty-four days on the egg diet. Unfortunately, while asleep he had drifted by both the missions of St. Paul and Holy Cross. And he could sincerely say, as he afterward did, that talk about missions on the Yukon was all humbug. There weren't any missions, and he was the man to know.

Once on Bering Sea he exchanged the egg diet for seal diet, and he never could make up his mind which he liked least. In the fall of the year he was rescued by a United States revenue cutter, and the following winter he made quite a hit in San Francisco as a temperance lecturer. In this field he found his vocation. "Avoid the bottle" is his slogan and battle-cry. He manages subtly to convey the impression that in his own life a great disaster was wrought by the bottle. He has even mentioned the loss of a fortune that was caused by that hell-bait of the devil, but behind that incident his listeners feel the loom of some terrible and unguessed evil for which the bottle is responsible. He has made a success in his vocation, and has grown grey and respected in the crusade against strong drink. But on the Yukon the passing of Marcus O'Brien remains tradition. It is a mystery that ranks at par with the disappearance of Sir John Franklin.

THE WIT OF PORPORTUK

EL-SOO HAD BEEN A MISSION GIRL. Her mother had died when she was very small, and Sister Alberta had plucked El-Soo as a brand from the burning, one summer day, and carried her away to Holy Cross Mission and dedicated her to God. El-Soo was a full-blooded Indian, yet she exceeded all the half-breed and quarter-breed girls. Never had the good sisters dealt with a girl so adaptable and at the same time so spirited.

El-Soo was quick, and deft, and intelligent; but above all she was fire, the living flame of life, a blaze of personality that was compounded of will, sweetness, and daring. Her father was a chief, and his blood ran in her veins. Obedience, on the part of El-Soo, was a matter of terms and arrangement. She had a passion for equity, and perhaps it was because of this that she excelled in mathematics.

But she excelled in other things. She learned to read and write English as no girl had ever learned in the Mission. She led the girls in singing, and into song she carried her sense of equity. She was an artist, and the fire of her flowed toward creation. Had she from birth enjoyed a more favourable environment, she would have made literature or music.

Instead, she was El-Soo, daughter of Klakee-Nah, a chief, and she lived in the Holy Cross Mission where were no artists, but only pure-souled Sisters who were interested in cleanliness and righteousness and the welfare of the spirit in the land of immortality that lay beyond the skies.

The years passed. She was eight years old when she entered the Mission; she was sixteen, and the Sisters were corresponding with their superiors in the Order concerning the sending of El-Soo to the United States to complete her education, when a man of her own tribe arrived at Holy Cross and had talk with her. El-Soo was somewhat appalled by him. He was dirty. He was a Caliban-like creature, primitively ugly, with a mop of hair that had never been combed. He looked at her disapprovingly and refused to sit down.

"Thy brother is dead," he said shortly.

El-Soo was not particularly shocked. She remembered little of her brother. "Thy father is an old man, and alone," the messenger went on. "His house is large and empty, and he would hear thy voice and look upon thee."

372

Him she remembered—Klakee-Nah, the headman of the village, the friend of the mission-aries and the traders, a large man thewed like a giant, with kindly eyes and masterful ways, and striding with a consciousness of crude royalty in his carriage.

"Tell him that I will come," was El-Soo's answer.

Much to the despair of the Sisters, the brand plucked from the burning went back to the burning. All pleading with El-Soo was vain. There was much argument, expostulation, and weeping. Sister Alberta even revealed to her the project of sending her to the United States. El-Soo stared wide-eyed into the golden vista thus opened up to her, and shook her head. In her eyes persisted another vista. It was the mighty curve of the Yukon at Tana-naw Station. With the St. George Mission on one side, and the trading post on the other, and midway between the Indian village and a certain large log house where lived an old man tended upon by slaves.

All dwellers on the Yukon bank for twice a thousand miles knew the large log house, the old man and the tending slaves; and well did the Sisters know the house, its unending revelry, its feasting and its fun. So there was weeping at Holy Cross when El-Soo departed.

There was a great cleaning up in the large house when El-Soo arrived. Klakee-Nah, himself masterful, protested at this masterful conduct of his young daughter; but in the end, dreaming barbarically of magnificence, he went forth and borrowed a thousand dollars from old Porportuk, than whom there was no richer Indian on the Yukon. Also, Klakee-Nah ran up a heavy bill at the trading post. El-Soo re-created the large house. She invested it with new splendour, while Klakee-Nah maintained its ancient traditions of hospitality and revelry.

All this was unusual for a Yukon Indian, but Klakee-Nah was an unusual Indian. Not alone did he like to render inordinate hospitality, but, what of being a chief and of acquiring much money, he was able to do it. In the primitive trading days he had been a power over his people, and he had dealt profitably with the white trading companies. Later on, with Porportuk, he had made a gold-strike on the Koyokuk River. Klakee-Nah was by training and nature an aristocrat. Porportuk was bourgeois, and Porportuk bought him out of the gold-mine. Porportuk was content to plod and accumulate. Klakee-Nah went back to his large house and proceeded to spend. Porportuk was known as the richest Indian in Alaska. Klakee-Nah was known as the whitest. Porportuk was a money-lender and a usurer. Klakee-Nah was an anachronism—a mediæval ruin, a fighter and a feaster, happy with wine and song.

El-Soo adapted herself to the large house and its ways as readily as she had adapted herself to Holy Cross Mission and its ways. She did not try to reform her father and direct his footsteps toward God. It is true, she reproved him when he drank overmuch and profoundly, but that was for the sake of his health and the direction of his footsteps on solid earth.

The latchstring to the large house was always out. What with the coming and the going, it was never still. The rafters of the great living-room shook with the roar of wassail and of song. At table sat men from all the world and chiefs from distant tribes—Englishmen and Colonials, lean Yankee traders and rotund officials of the great companies, cowboys from the Western ranges, sailors from the sea, hunters and dog-mushers of a score of nationalities.

El-Soo drew breath in a cosmopolitan atmosphere. She could speak English as well as she could her native tongue, and she sang English songs and ballads. The passing Indian cere-monials she knew, and the perishing traditions. The tribal dress of the daughter of a chief she knew how to wear upon occasion. But for the most part she dressed as white women dress. Not for nothing was her needlework at the Mission and her innate artistry. She carried her clothes like a white woman, and she made clothes that could be so carried.

In her way she was as unusual as her father, and the position she occupied was as unique as his. She was the one Indian woman who was the social equal with the several white women at Tana-naw Station. She was the one Indian woman to whom white men honourably made proposals of marriage. And she was the one Indian woman whom no white man ever insulted.

For El-Soo was beautiful—not as white women are beautiful, not as Indian women are beautiful. It was the flame of her, that did not depend upon feature, that was her beauty. So far as mere line and feature went, she was the classic Indian type. The black hair and the fine bronze were hers, and the black eyes, brilliant and bold, keen as sword-light, proud; and hers the delicate eagle nose with the thin, quivering nostrils, the high cheek-bones that were not broad apart, and the thin lips that were not too thin. But over all and through all poured the flame of her—the unanalyzable something that was fire and that was the soul of her, that lay mellow-warm or blazed in her eyes, that sprayed the cheeks of her, that distended the nostrils, that curled the lips, or, when the lip was in repose, that was still there in the lip, the lip palpitant with its presence.

And El-Soo had wit—rarely sharp to hurt, yet quick to search out forgivable weakness. The laughter of her mind played like lambent flame over all about her, and from all about her arose answering laughter. Yet she was never the center of things. This she would not permit. The large house, and all of which it was significant, was her father's; and through it, to the last, moved his heroic figure—host, master of the revels, and giver of the law. It is true, as the strength oozed from him, that she caught up responsibilities from his failing hands. But in appearance he still ruled, dozing, ofttimes at the board, a bacchanalian ruin, yet in all seeming the ruler of the feast.

And through the large house moved the figure of Porportuk, ominous, with shaking head, coldly disapproving, paying for it all. Not that he really paid, for he compounded interest in weird ways, and year by year absorbed the properties of Klakee-Nah. Porportuk once took it upon himself to chide El-Soo upon the wasteful way of life in the large house—it was when he had about absorbed the last of Klakee-Nah's wealth—but he never ventured so to chide again. El-Soo, like her father, was an aristocrat, as disdainful of money as he, and with an equal sense of honour as finely strung.

Porportuk continued grudgingly to advance money, and ever the money flowed in golden foam away. Upon one thing El-Soo was resolved—her father should die as he had lived. There should be for him no passing from high to low, no diminution of the revels, no lessening of the lavish hospitality. When there was famine, as of old, the Indians came groaning to the large house and went away content. When there was famine and no money, money was borrowed from Porportuk, and the Indians still went away content. El-Soo might well have repeated, after the aristocrats of another time and place, that after her came the deluge. In her case the deluge was old Porportuk. With every advance of money, he looked upon her with a more possessive eye, and felt bourgeoning within him ancient fires.

But El-Soo had no eyes for him. Nor had she eyes for the white men who wanted to marry her at the Mission with ring and priest and book. For at Tana-naw Station was a young man, Akoon, of her own blood, and tribe, and village. He was strong and beautiful to her eyes, a great hunter, and, in that he had wandered far and much, very poor; he had been to all the unknown wastes and places; he had journeyed to Sitka and to the United States; he had crossed the continent to Hudson Bay and back again, and as seal-hunter on a ship he had sailed to Siberia and for Japan.

When he returned from the gold-strike in Klondike he came, as was his wont, to the large house to make report to old Klakee-Nah of all the world that he had seen; and there he first saw El-Soo, three years back from the Mission. Thereat, Akoon wandered no more. He refused a wage of twenty dollars a day as pilot on the big steamboats. He hunted some and fished some, but never far from Tana-naw Station, and he was at the large house often and long. And El-Soo measured him against many men and found him good. He sang songs to her, and was ardent and glowed until all Tana-naw Station knew he loved her. And Porportuk but grinned and advanced more money for the upkeep of the large house.

Then came the death table of Klakee-Nah.

He sat at feast, with death in his throat, that he could not drown with wine. And laughter and joke and song went around, and Akoon told a story that made the rafters echo. There were no tears or sighs at that table. It was no more than fit that Klakee-Nah should die as he had lived, and none knew this better than El-Soo, with her artist sympathy. The old roystering crowd was there, and, as of old, three frost-bitten sailors were there, fresh from the long traverse from the Arctic, survivors of a ship's company of seventy-four. At Klakee-Nah's back were four old men, all that were left him of the slaves of his youth. With rheumy eyes they saw to his needs, with palsied hands filling his glass or striking him on the back between the shoulders when death stirred and he coughed and gasped.

It was a wild night, and as the hours passed and the fun laughed and roared along, death stirred more restlessly in Klakee-Nah's throat. Then it was that he sent for Porportuk. And Porportuk came in from the outside frost to look with disapproving eyes upon the meat and wine on the table for which he had paid. But as he looked down the length of flushed faces to the far end and saw the face of El-Soo, the light in his eyes flared up, and for a moment the disapproval vanished.

Place was made for him at Klakee-Nah's side, and a glass placed before him. Klakee-Nah, with his own hands, filled the glass with fervent spirits. "Drink!" he cried. "Is it not good?"

And Porportuk's eyes watered as he nodded his head and smacked his lips.

"When, in your own house, have you had such drink?" Klakee-Nah demanded.

"I will not deny that the drink is good to this old throat of mine," Porportuk made answer, and hesitated for the speech to complete the thought.

"But it costs overmuch," Klakee-Nah roared, completing it for him.

Porportuk winced at the laughter that went down the table. His eyes burned malevolently. "We were boys together, of the same age," he said. "In your throat is death. I am still alive and strong."

An ominous murmur arose from the company. Klakee-Nah coughed and strangled, and the old slaves smote him between the shoulders. He emerged gasping, and waved his hand to still the threatening rumble.

"You have grudged the very fire in your house because the wood cost overmuch!" he cried. "You have grudged life. To live cost overmuch, and you have refused to pay the price. Your life has been like a cabin where the fire is out and there are no blankets on the floor." He signaled to a slave to fill his glass, which he held aloft. "But I have lived. And I have been warm with life as you have never been warm. It is true, you shall live long. But the longest nights are the cold nights when a man shivers and lies awake. My nights have been short, but I have slept warm."

He drained the glass. The shaking hand of a slave failed to catch it as it crashed to the floor. Klakee-Nah sank back, panting, watching the upturned glasses at the lips of the drinkers, his own lips slightly smiling to the applause. At a sign, two slaves attempted to help him sit upright again. But they were weak, his frame was mighty, and the four old men tottered and shook as they helped him forward.

"But manner of life is neither here nor there," he went on. "We have other business, Porportuk, you and I, tonight. Debts are mischances, and I am in mischance with you. What of my debt, and how great is it?"

Porportuk searched in his pouch and brought forth a memorandum. He sipped at his glass and began. "There is the note of August, 1889, for three hundred dollars. The interest has never been paid. And the note of the next year for five hundred dollars. This note was included in the note of two months later for a thousand dollars. Then there is the note—"

"Never mind the many notes!" Klakee-Nah cried out impatiently. "They make my head go around and all the things inside my head. The whole! The round whole! How much is it?"

Porportuk referred to his memorandum. "Fifteen thousand nine hundred and sixty-seven dollars and seventy-five cents," he read with careful precision.

"Make it sixteen thousand, make it sixteen thousand," Klakee-Nah said grandly. "Odd numbers were ever a worry. And now—and it is for this that I have sent for you—make me out a new note for sixteen thousand, which I shall sign. I have no thought of the interest. Make it as large as you will, and make it payable in the next world, when I shall meet you by the fire of the Great Father of all Indians. Then the note will be paid. This I promise you. It is the word of Klakee-Nah."

Porportuk looked perplexed, and loudly the laughter arose and shook the room. Klakee-Nah raised his hands. "Nay," he cried. "It is not a joke. I but speak in fairness. It was for this I sent for you, Porportuk. Make out the note."

"I have no dealings with the next world," Porportuk made answer slowly.

"Have you no thought to meet me before the Great Father!" Klakee-Nah demanded. Then he added, "I shall surely be there."

"I have no dealings with the next world," Porportuk repeated sourly.

The dying man regarded him with frank amazement.

"I know naught of the next world," Porportuk explained. "I do business in this world."

Klakee-Nah's face cleared. "This comes of sleeping cold of nights," he laughed. He pondered for a space, then said, "It is in this world that you must be paid. There remains to me this house. Take it, and burn the debt in the candle there."

"It is an old house and not worth the money," Porportuk made answer.

"There are my mines on the Twisted Salmon."

"They have never paid to work," was the reply.

"There is my share in the steamer *Koyokuk*. I am half owner."

"She is at the bottom of the Yukon."

Klakee-Nah started. "True, I forgot. It was last spring when the ice went out." He mused for a time while the glasses remained untasted, and all the company waited upon his utterance.

"Then it would seem I owe you a sum of money which I cannot pay . . . in this world?" Porportuk nodded and glanced down the table.

"Then it would seem that you, Porportuk, are a poor business man," Klakee-Nah said slyly. And boldly Porportuk made answer, "No; there is security yet untouched."

"What!" cried Klakee-Nah. "Have I still property? Name it, and it is yours, and the debt is no more."

"There it is." Porportuk pointed at El-Soo.

Klakee-Nah could not understand. He peered down the table, brushed his eyes, and peered again.

"Your daughter, El-Soo—her will I take and the debt be no more. I will burn the debt there in the candle."

Klakee-Nah's great chest began to heave. "Ho! ho!—a joke. Ho! ho! ho!" he laughed Homerically. "And with your cold bed and daughters old enough to be the mother of El-Soo! Ho! ho! ho!" He began to cough and strangle, and the old slaves smote him on the back. "Ho! ho!" he began again, and went off into another paroxysm.

Porportuk waited patiently, sipping from his glass and studying the double row of faces down the board. "It is no joke," he said finally. "My speech is well meant."

Klakee-Nah sobered and looked at him, then reached for his glass, but could not touch it. A slave passed it to him, and glass and liquor he flung into the face of Porportuk.

"Turn him out!" Klakee-Nah thundered to the waiting table that strained like a pack of hounds in leash. "And roll him in the snow!"

As the mad riot swept past him and out of doors, he signaled to the slaves, and the four tottering old men supported him on his feet as he met the returning revelers, upright, glass in hand, pledging them a toast to the short night when a man sleeps warm.

It did not take long to settle the estate of Klakee-Nah. Tommy, the little Englishman, clerk at the trading post, was called in by El-Soo to help. There was nothing but debts, notes overdue, mortgaged properties, and properties mortgaged but worthless. Notes and mortgages were held by Porportuk. Tommy called him a robber many times as he pondered the compounding of the interest.

"Is it a debt, Tommy?" El-Soo asked.

"It is a robbery," Tommy answered.

"Nevertheless, it is a debt," she persisted.

The winter wore away, and the early spring, and still the claims of Porportuk remained unpaid. He saw El-Soo often and explained to her at length, as he had explained to her father, the way the debt could be cancelled. Also, he brought with him old medicine-men, who elaborated to her the everlasting damnation of her father if the debt were not paid. One day, after such an elaboration, El-Soo made final announcement to Porportuk.

"I shall tell you two things," she said. "First I shall not be your wife. Will you remember that? Second, you shall be paid the last cent of the sixteen thousand dollars—"

"Fifteen thousand nine hundred and sixty-seven dollars and seventy-five cents," Porportuk corrected.

"My father said sixteen thousand," was her reply. "You shall be paid."

"How?"

"I know not how, but I shall find out how. Now go, and bother me no more. If you do"— she hesitated to find fitting penalty—"if you do, I shall have you rolled in the snow again as soon as the first snow flies."

This was still in the early spring, and a little later El-Soo surprised the country. Word went up and down the Yukon from Chilcoot to the Delta, and was carried from camp to camp to the farthermost camps, that in June, when the first salmon ran, El-Soo, daughter of Klakee-Nah, would sell herself at public auction to satisfy the claims of Porportuk. Vain were the attempts to dissuade her. The missionary at St. George wrestled with her, but she replied—

"Only the debts to God are settled in the next world. The debts of men are of this world, and in this world are they settled."

Akoon wrestled with her, but she replied, "I do love thee, Akoon; but honour is greater than love, and who am I that I should blacken my father?" Sister Alberta journeyed all the way up from Holy Cross on the first steamer, and to no better end.

"My father wanders in the thick and endless forests," said El-Soo. "And there will he wander, with the lost souls crying, till the debt be paid. Then, and not until then, may he go on to the house of the Great Father."

"And you believe this?" Sister Alberta asked.

"I do not know," El-Soo made answer. "It was my father's belief."

Sister Alberta shrugged her shoulders incredulously.

"Who knows but that the things we believe come true?" El-Soo went on. "Why not? The next world to you may be heaven and harps . . . because you have believed heaven and harps; to my father the next world may be a large house where he will sit always at table feasting with God."

"And you?" Sister Alberta asked. "What is your next world?"

El-Soo hesitated but for a moment. "I should like a little of both," she said. "I should like to see your face as well as the face of my father."

The day of the auction came. Tana-naw Station was populous. As was their custom, the tribes had gathered to await the salmon-run, and in the meantime spent the time in dancing and frolicking, trading and gossiping. Then there was the ordinary sprinkling of white adventurers, traders, and prospectors, and, in addition, a large number of white men who had come because of curiosity or interest in the affair.

It had been a backward spring, and the salmon were late in running. This delay but keyed up the interest. Then, on the day of the auction, the situation was made tense by Akoon. He arose and made public and solemn announcement that whosoever bought El-Soo would forthwith and immediately die. He flourished the Winchester in his hand to indicate the manner of the taking-off. El-Soo was angered thereat; but he refused to speak with her, and went to the trading post to lay in extra ammunition.

The first salmon was caught at ten o'clock in the evening, and at midnight the auction began. It took place on top of the high bank alongside the Yukon. The sun was due north just below the horizon, and the sky was lurid red. A great crowd gathered about the table and the two chairs that stood near the edge of the bank. To the fore were many white men and several chiefs. And most prominently to the fore, rifle in hand, stood Akoon. Tommy, at El-Soo's request, served as auctioneer, but she made the opening speech and described the goods about to be sold. She was in native costume, in the dress of a chief's daughter, splendid and barbaric, and she stood on a chair, that she might be seen to advantage.

"Who will buy a wife?" she asked. "Look at me. I am twenty years old and a maid. I will be a good wife to the man who buys me. If he is a white man, I shall dress in the fashion of white women; if he is an Indian, I shall dress as"—she hesitated a moment—"a squaw. I can make my own clothes, and sew, and wash, and mend. I was taught for eight years to do these things at Holy Cross Mission. I can read and write English, and I know how to play the organ. Also I can do arithmetic and some algebra—a little. I shall be sold to the highest bidder, and to him I will make out a bill of sale of myself. I forgot to say that I can sing very well, and that I have never been sick in my life. I weigh one hundred and thirty-two pounds; my father is dead and I have no relatives. Who wants me?"

She looked over the crowd with flaming audacity and stepped down. At Tommy's request she stood upon the chair again, while he mounted the second chair and started the bidding.

Surrounding El-Soo stood the four old slaves of her father. They were age-twisted and palsied, faithful to their meat, a generation out of the past that watched unmoved the antics of younger life. In the front of the crowd were several Eldorado and Bonanza kings from the Upper Yukon, and beside them, on crutches, swollen with scurvy, were two broken prospectors. From the midst of the crowd, thrust out by its own vividness, appeared the face of a wild-eyed squaw from the remote regions of the Upper Tana-naw; a strayed Sitkan from the coast stood side by side with a Stick from Lake Le Barge, and, beyond, a half-dozen French-Canadian voyageurs, grouped by themselves. From afar came the faint cries of myriads of wild-fowl on the nesting-grounds. Swallows were skimming up overhead from the placid surface of the Yukon, and robins were singing. The oblique rays of the hidden sun shot through the smoke, high-dissipated from forest fires a thousand miles away, and turned the heavens to sombre red, while the earth shone red in the reflected glow. This red glow shone in the faces of all, and made everything seem unearthly and unreal.

The bidding began slowly. The Sitkan, who was a stranger in the land and who had arrived only half an hour before, offered one hundred dollars in a confident voice, and was surprised when Akoon turned threateningly upon him with the rifle. The bidding dragged. An Indian from the Tozikakat, a pilot, bid one hundred and fifty, and after some time a gambler, who had been ordered out of the Upper Country, raised the bid to two hundred. El-Soo was saddened; her pride was hurt; but the only effect was that she flamed more audaciously upon the crowd.

There was a disturbance among the onlookers as Porportuk forced his way to the front. "Five hundred dollars!" he bid in a loud voice, then looked about him proudly to note the effect.

He was minded to use his great wealth as a bludgeon with which to stun all competition at the start. But one of the voyageurs, looking on El-Soo with sparkling eyes, raised the bid a hundred.

"Seven hundred!" Porportuk returned promptly.

And with equal promptness came the "Eight hundred" of the voyageur.

Then Porportuk swung his club again.

"Twelve hundred!" he shouted.

With a look of poignant disappointment, the voyageur succumbed. There was no further bidding. Tommy worked hard, but could not elicit a bid.

El-Soo spoke to Porportuk. "It were good, Porportuk, for you to weigh well your bid. Have you forgotten the thing I told you—that I would never marry you!"

"It is a public auction," he retorted. "I shall buy you with a bill of sale. I have offered twelve hundred dollars. You come cheap."

"Too damned cheap!" Tommy cried. "What if I am auctioneer? That does not prevent me from bidding. I'll make it thirteen hundred."

"Fourteen hundred," from Porportuk.

"I'll buy you in to be my—my sister," Tommy whispered to El-Soo, then called aloud, "Fifteen hundred!"

At two thousand one of the Eldorado kings took a hand, and Tommy dropped out.

A third time Porportuk swung the club of his wealth, making a clean raise of five hundred dollars. But the Eldorado king's pride was touched. No man could club him. And he swung back another five hundred.

El-Soo stood at three thousand. Porportuk made it thirty-five hundred, and gasped when the Eldorado king raised it a thousand dollars. Porportuk again raised it five hundred, and again gasped when the king raised a thousand more.

Porportuk became angry. His pride was touched; his strength was challenged, and with him strength took the form of wealth. He would not be ashamed for weakness before the world. El-Soo became incidental. The savings and scrimpings from the cold nights of all his years were ripe to be squandered. El-Soo stood at six thousand. He made it seven thousand. And then, in thousand-dollar bids, as fast as they could be uttered, her price went up. At fourteen thousand the two men stopped for breath.

Then the unexpected happened. A still heavier club was swung. In the pause that ensued, the gambler, who had scented a speculation and formed a syndicate with several of his fellows, bid sixteen thousand dollars.

"Seventeen thousand," Porportuk said weakly.

"Eighteen thousand," said the king.

Porportuk gathered his strength. "Twenty thousand."

The syndicate dropped out. The Eldorado king raised a thousand, and Porportuk raised back; and as they bid, Akoon turned from one to the other, half menacingly, half curiously, as though to see what manner of man it was that he would have to kill. When the king prepared to make his next bid, Akoon having pressed closer, the king first loosed the revolver at his hip, then said:

"Twenty-three thousand."

"Twenty-four thousand," said Porportuk. He grinned viciously, for the certitude of his bidding had at last shaken the king. The latter moved over close to El-Soo. He studied her carefully for a long while.

"And five hundred," he said at last.

"Twenty-five thousand," came Porportuk's raise.

The king looked for a long space, and shook his head. He looked again, and said reluctantly, "And five hundred."

"Twenty-six thousand," Porportuk snapped.

The king shook his head and refused to meet Tommy's pleading eye. In the meantime Akoon had edged close to Porportuk. El-Soo's quick eye noted this, and, while Tommy wrestled with the Eldorado king for another bid, she bent, and spoke in a low voice in the ear of a slave. And while Tommy's "Going—going—going—" dominated the air, the slave went up to Akoon and spoke in a low voice in his ear. Akoon made no sign that he had heard, though El-Soo watched him anxiously.

"Gone!" Tommy's voice rang out. "To Porportuk, for twenty-six thousand dollars."

Porportuk glanced uneasily at Akoon. All eyes were centred upon Akoon, but he did nothing.

"Let the scales be brought," said El-Soo.

"I shall make payment at my house," said Porportuk.

"Let the scales be brought," El-Soo repeated. "Payment shall be made here where all can see."

So the gold scales were brought from the trading post, while Porportuk went away and came back with a man at his heels, on whose shoulders was a weight of gold-dust in moose-hide sacks. Also, at Porportuk's back, walked another man with a rifle, who had eyes only for Akoon.

"Here are the notes and mortgages," said Porportuk, "for fifteen thousand nine hundred and sixty-seven dollars and seventy-five cents."

El-Soo received them into her hands and said to Tommy, "Let them be reckoned as sixteen thousand."

"There remains ten thousand dollars to be paid in gold," Tommy said.

Porportuk nodded, and untied the mouths of the sacks. El-Soo, standing at the edge of the bank, tore the papers to shreds and sent them fluttering out over the Yukon. The weighing began, but halted.

"Of course, at seventeen dollars," Porportuk had said to Tommy, as he adjusted the scales.

"At sixteen dollars," El-Soo said sharply.

"It is the custom of all the land to reckon gold at seventeen dollars for each ounce," Porportuk replied. "And this is a business transaction."

El-Soo laughed. "It is a new custom," she said. "It began this spring. Last year, and the years before, it was sixteen dollars an ounce. When my father's debt was made, it was sixteen dollars. When he spent at the store the money he got from you, for one ounce he was given sixteen dollars' worth of flour, not seventeen. Wherefore, shall you pay for me at sixteen, and not at seventeen." Porportuk grunted and allowed the weighing to proceed.

"Weigh it in three piles, Tommy," she said. "A thousand dollars here, three thousand here, and here six thousand."

It was slow work, and, while the weighing went on, Akoon was closely watched by all.

"He but waits till the money is paid," one said; and the word went around and was accepted, and they waited for what Akoon should do when the money was paid. And Porportuk's man with the rifle waited and watched Akoon.

The weighing was finished, and the gold-dust lay on the table in three dark-yellow heaps. "There is a debt of my father to the Company for three thousand dollars," said El-Soo. "Take it, Tommy, for the Company. And here are four old men, Tommy. You know them. And here is one thousand dollars. Take it, and see that the old men are never hungry and never without tobacco."

Tommy scooped the gold into separate sacks. Six thousand dollars remained on the table. El-Soo thrust the scoop into the heap, and with a sudden turn whirled the contents out and down to the Yukon in a golden shower. Porportuk seized her wrist as she thrust the scoop a second time into the heap.

"It is mine," she said calmly. Porportuk released his grip, but he gritted his teeth and scowled darkly as she continued to scoop the gold into the river till none was left.

The crowd had eyes for naught but Akoon, and the rifle of Porportuk's man lay across the hollow of his arm, the muzzle directed at Akoon a yard away, the man's thumb on the hammer. But Akoon did nothing.

"Make out the bill of sale," Porportuk said grimly.

And Tommy made out the till of sale, wherein all right and title in the woman El-Soo was vested in the man Porportuk. El-Soo signed the document, and Porportuk folded it and put it away in his pouch. Suddenly his eyes flashed, and in sudden speech he addressed El-Soo.

"But it was not your father's debt," he said, "What I paid was the price for you. Your sale is business of to-day and not of last year and the years before. The ounces paid for you will buy at the post to-day seventeen dollars of flour, and not sixteen. I have lost a dollar on each ounce. I have lost six hundred and twenty-five dollars."

El-Soo thought for a moment, and saw the error she had made. She smiled, and then she laughed.

"You are right," she laughed, "I made a mistake. But it is too late. You have paid, and the gold is gone. You did not think quick. It is your loss. Your wit is slow these days, Porportuk. You are getting old."

He did not answer. He glanced uneasily at Akoon, and was reassured. His lips tightened, and a hint of cruelty came into his face. "Come," he said, "we will go to my house."

"Do you remember the two things I told you in the spring?" El-Soo asked, making no movement to accompany him.

"My head would be full with the things women say, did I heed them," he answered.

"I told you that you would be paid," El-Soo went on carefully. "And I told you that I would never be your wife."

"But that was before the bill of sale." Porportuk crackled the paper between his fingers inside the pouch. "I have bought you before all the world. You belong to me. You will not deny that you belong to me."

"I belong to you," El-Soo said steadily.

"I own you."

"You own me."

Porportuk's voice rose slightly and triumphantly. "As a dog, I own you."

"As a dog you own me," El-Soo continued calmly. "But, Porportuk, you forget the thing I told you. Had any other man bought me, I should have been that man's wife. I should have been a good wife to that man. Such was my will. But my will with you was that I should never be your wife. Wherefore, I am your dog."

Porportuk knew that he played with fire, and he resolved to play firmly. "Then I speak to you, not as El-Soo, but as a dog," he said; "and I tell you to come with me." He half reached to grip her arm, but with a gesture she held him back.

"Not so fast, Porportuk. You buy a dog. The dog runs away. It is your loss. I am your dog. What if I run away?"

"As the owner of the dog, I shall beat you—"

"When you catch me?"

"When I catch you."

"Then catch me."

He reached swiftly for her, but she eluded him. She laughed as she circled around the table. "Catch her!" Porportuk commanded the Indian with the rifle, who stood near to her. But as the Indian stretched forth his arm to her, the Eldorado king felled him with a fist blow under the ear. The rifle clattered to the ground. Then was Akoon's chance. His eyes glittered, but he did nothing.

Porportuk was an old man, but his cold nights retained for him his activity. He did not circle the table. He came across suddenly, over the top of the table. El-Soo was taken off her guard. She sprang back with a sharp cry of alarm, and Porportuk would have caught her had it not been for Tommy. Tommy's leg went out, Porportuk tripped and pitched forward on the ground. El-Soo got her start.

"Then catch me," she laughed over her shoulder, as she fled away.

She ran lightly and easily, but Porportuk ran swiftly and savagely. He outran her. In his youth he had been swiftest of all the young men. But El-Soo dodged in a willowy, elusive way. Being in native dress, her feet were not cluttered with skirts, and her pliant body curved a flight that defied the gripping fingers of Porportuk.

With laughter and tumult, the great crowd scattered out to see the chase. It led through the Indian encampment; and ever dodging, circling, and reversing, El-Soo and Porportuk appeared and disappeared among the tents. El-Soo seemed to balance herself against the air with her arms, now one side, now on the other, and sometimes her body, too, leaned out upon the air far from the perpendicular as she achieved her sharpest curves. And Porportuk, always a leap behind, or a leap this side or that, like a lean hound strained after her.

They crossed the open ground beyond the encampment and disappeared in the forest. Tana-naw Station waited their reappearance, and long and vainly it waited.

In the meantime Akoon ate and slept, and lingered much at the steamboat landing, deaf to the rising resentment of Tana-naw Station in that he did nothing. Twenty-four hours later

Porportuk returned. He was tired and savage. He spoke to no one but Akoon, and with him tried to pick a quarrel. But Akoon shrugged his shoulders and walked away. Porportuk did not waste time. He outfitted half a dozen of the young men, selecting the best trackers and travelers, and at their head plunged into the forest.

Next day the steamer *Seattle*, bound up river, pulled in to the shore and wooded up. When the lines were cast off and she churned out from the bank, Akoon was on board in the pilot-house. Not many hours afterward, when it was his turn at the wheel, he saw a small birch-bark canoe put off from the shore. There was only one person in it. He studied it carefully, put the wheel over, and slowed down.

The captain entered the pilot-house. "What's the matter?" he demanded. "The water's good."

Akoon grunted. He saw a larger canoe leaving the bank, and in it were a number of persons. As the *Seattle* lost headway, he put the wheel over some more.

The captain fumed. "It's only a squaw," he protested.

Akoon did not grunt. He was all eyes for the squaw and the pursuing canoe. In the latter six paddles were flashing, while the squaw paddled slowly.

"You'll be aground," the captain protested, seizing the wheel.

But Akoon countered his strength on the wheel and looked him in the eyes. The captain slowly released the spokes.

"Queer beggar," he sniffed to himself.

Akoon held the *Seattle* on the edge of the shoal water and waited till he saw the squaw's fingers clutch the forward rail. Then he signaled for full speed ahead and ground the wheel over. The large canoe was very near, but the gap between it and the steamer was widening.

The squaw laughed and leaned over the rail.

"Then catch me, Porportuk!" she cried.

Akoon left the steamer at Fort Yukon. He outfitted a small poling-boat and went up the Porcupine River. And with him went El-Soo. It was a weary journey, and the way led across the backbone of the world; but Akoon had travelled it before. When they came to the headwaters of the Porcupine, they left the boat and went on foot across the Rocky Mountains.

Akoon greatly liked to walk behind El-Soo and watch the movements of her. There was a music in it that he loved. And especially he loved the well-rounded calves in their sheaths of soft-tanned leather, the slim ankles, and the small moccasined feet that were tireless through the longest days.

"You are light as air," he said, looking up at her. "It is no labour for you to walk. You almost float, so lightly do your feet rise and fall. You are like a deer, El-Soo; you are like a deer, and your eyes are like deer's eyes, sometimes when you look at me, or when you hear a quick sound and wonder if it be danger that stirs. Your eyes are like a deer's eyes now as you look at me."

And El-Soo, luminous and melting, bent and kissed Akoon.

"When we reach the Mackenzie, we will not delay," Akoon said later. "We will go south before the winter catches us. We will go to the sunlands where there is no snow. But we will return. I have seen much of the world, and there is no land like Alaska, no sun like our sun, and the snow is good after the long summer."

"And you will learn to read," said El-Soo.

And Akoon said, "I will surely learn to read." But there was delay when they reached the Mackenzie. They fell in with a band of Mackenzie Indians, and, hunting, Akoon was shot by accident. The rifle was in the hands of a youth. The bullet broke Akoon's right arm and, ranging farther, broke two of his ribs. Akoon knew rough surgery, while El-Soo had learned some refinements at Holy Cross. The bones were finally set, and Akoon lay by the fire for them to knit. Also, he lay by the fire so that the smoke would keep the mosquitoes away.

Then it was that Porportuk, with his six young men, arrived. Akoon groaned in his helplessness and made appeal to the Mackenzies. But Porportuk made demand, and the Mackenzies were perplexed. Porportuk was for seizing upon El-Soo, but this they would not permit. Judgment must be given, and, as it was an affair of man and woman, the council of the old men was called—this that warm judgment might not be given by the young men, who were warm of heart.

The old men sat in a circle about the smudge-fire. Their faces were lean and wrinkled, and they gasped and panted for air. The smoke was not good for them. Occasionally they struck with withered hands at the mosquitoes that braved the smoke. After such exertion they coughed hollowly and painfully. Some spat blood, and one of them sat a bit apart with head bowed forward, and bled slowly and continuously at the mouth; the coughing sickness had gripped them. They were as dead men; their time was short. It was a judgment of the dead.

"And I paid for her a heavy price," Porportuk concluded his complaint. "Such a price you have never seen. Sell all that is yours—sell your spears and arrows and rifles, sell your skins and furs, sell your tents and boats and dogs, sell everything, and you will not have maybe a thousand dollars. Yet did I pay for the woman, El-Soo, twenty-six times the price of all your spears and arrows and rifles, your skins and furs, your tents and boats and dogs. It was a heavy price."

The old men nodded gravely, though their weazened eye-slits widened with wonder that any woman should be worth such a price. The one that bled at the mouth wiped his lips. "Is it true talk?" he asked each of Porportuk's six young men. And each answered that it was true.

"Is it true talk?" he asked El-Soo, and she answered, "It is true."

"But Porportuk has not told that he is an old man," Akoon said, "and that he has daughters older than El-Soo."

"It is true, Porportuk is an old man," said El-Soo.

"It is for Porportuk to measure the strength his age," said he who bled at the mouth. "We be old men. Behold! Age is never so old as youth would measure it."

And the circle of old men champed their gums, and nodded approvingly, and coughed.

"I told him that I would never be his wife," said El-Soo.

"Yet you took from him twenty-six times all that we possess?" asked a one-eyed old man. El-Soo was silent.

"It is true?" And his one eye burned and bored into her like a fiery gimlet.

"It is true," she said.

"But I will run away again," she broke out passionately, a moment later. "Always will I run away."

"That is for Porportuk to consider," said another of the old men. "It is for us to consider the judgment."

"What price did you pay for her?" was demanded of Akoon.

"No price did I pay for her," he answered. "She was above price. I did not measure her in gold-dust, nor in dogs, and tents, and furs."

The old men debated among themselves and mumbled in undertones. "These old men are ice," Akoon said in English. "I will not listen to their judgment, Porportuk. If you take El-Soo, I will surely kill you."

The old men ceased and regarded him suspiciously. "We do not know the speech you make," one said.

"He but said that he would kill me," Porportuk volunteered. "So it were well to take from him his rifle, and to have some of your young men sit by him, that he may not do me hurt. He is a young man, and what are broken bones to youth!"

Akoon, lying helpless, had rifle and knife taken from him, and to either side of his shoulders sat young men of the Mackenzies. The one-eyed old man arose and stood upright. "We marvel at the price paid for one mere woman," he began; "but the wisdom of the price is no concern of ours. We are here to give judgment, and judgment we give. We have no doubt. It is known to all that Porportuk paid a heavy price for the woman El-Soo. Wherefore does the woman El-Soo belong to Porportuk and none other." He sat down heavily, and coughed. The old men nodded and coughed.

"I will kill you," Akoon cried in English.

Porportuk smiled and stood up. "You have given true judgment," he said to the council, "and my young men will give to you much tobacco. Now let the woman be brought to me."

Akoon gritted his teeth. The young men took El-Soo by the arms. She did not resist, and was led, her face a sullen flame, to Porportuk.

"Sit there at my feet till I have made my talk," he commanded. He paused a moment. "It is true," he said, "I am an old man. Yet can I understand the ways of youth. The fire has not all gone out of me. Yet am I no longer young, nor am I minded to run these old legs of mine through all the years that remain to me. El-Soo can run fast and well. She is a deer. This I know, for I have seen and run after her. It is not good that a wife should run so fast. I paid for her a heavy price, yet does she run away from me. Akoon paid no price at all, yet does she run to him.

"When I came among you people of the Mackenzie, I was of one mind. As I listened in the council and thought of the swift legs of El-Soo, I was of many minds. Now am I of one mind again but it is a different mind from the one I brought to the council. Let me tell you my mind. When a dog runs once away from a master, it will run away again. No matter how many times it is brought back, each time it will run away again. When we have such dogs, we sell them. El-Soo is like a dog that runs away. I will sell her. Is there any man of the council that will buy?"

The old men coughed and remained silent

"Akoon would buy," Porportuk went on, "but he has no money. Wherefore I will give El-Soo to him, as he said, without price. Even now will I give her to him."

Reaching down, he took El-Soo by the hand and led her across the space to where Akoon lay on his back.

"She has a bad habit, Akoon," he said, seating her at Akoon's feet. "As she has run away from me in the past, in the days to come she may run away from you. But there is no need to fear that she will ever run away, Akoon. I shall see to that. Never will she run away from you—this is the word of Porportuk. She has great wit. I know, for often has it bitten into me. Yet am I minded myself to give my wit play for once. And by my wit will I secure her to you, Akoon."

Stooping, Porportuk crossed El-Soo's feet, so that the instep of one lay over that of the other; and then, before his purpose could be divined, he discharged his rifle through the two ankles. As Akoon struggled to rise against the weight of the young men, there was heard the crunch of the broken bone rebroken.

"It is just," said the old men, one to another.

El-Soo made no sound. She sat and looked at her shattered ankles, on which she would never walk again.

"My legs are strong, El-Soo," Akoon said. "But never will they bear me away from you."

El-Soo looked at him, and for the first time in all the time he had known her, Akoon saw tears in her eyes.

"Your eyes are like deer's eyes, El-Soo," he said.

"Is it just?" Porportuk asked, and grinned from the edge of the smoke as he prepared to depart.

"It is just," the old men said. And they sat on in the silence.

Made in United States
Orlando, FL
03 December 2023

40067116R00236